Also by JAMES ELLROY

The Underworld U.S.A. Trilogy

American Tabloid

The Cold Six Thousand

Blood's A Rover

The L.A. Quartet

The Black Dahlia

The Big Nowhere

L.A. Confidential

White Jazz

Memoir

My Dark Places

The Hilliker Curse

Short Stories

Hollywood Nocturnes

Journalism/Short Fiction

Crime Wave

Destination: Morgue!

Early Novels

Brown's Requiem

Clandestine

Blood on the Moon

Because the Night

Suicide Hill

Killer on the Road

James Ellroy

Perfidia

WILLIAM HEINEMANN: LONDON

Published by William Heinemann 2014

2 4 6 8 10 9 7 5 3 1

First published in the United States in 2014 by Alfred A. Knopf, a division of Random House LLC, New York, A Penguin Random House company, and in Canada by Random House of Canada Limited, Toronto.

First published in Great Britain in 2014 by
William Heinemann
Random House, 20 Vauxhall Bridge Road,
London SW1V 2SA

www.randomhouse.co.uk

Addresses for companies within The Random House Group Limited can be found at:
www.randomhouse.co.uk/offices.htm

The Random House Group Limited Reg. No. 954009

A CIP catalogue record for this book
is available from the British Library

ISBN 9780434020522 (Hardback)
ISBN 9780434020539 (Trade paperback)

The Random House Group Limited supports the Forest Stewardship Council® (FSC®), the leading international forest-certification organisation. Our books carrying the FSC label are printed on FSC®-certified paper. FSC is the only forest-certification scheme supported by the leading environmental organisations, including Greenpeace.
Our paper procurement policy can be found at:
www.randomhouse.co.uk/environment

Book design by Betty Lew

Printed and bound in Great Britain by

Clays Ltd, St Ives Plc

To **LISA STAFFORD**

Envy thou not the oppressor,
And choose none of his ways.

—Proverbs 3:31

Fifth Column: noun, and a popular colloquialism of 1941 America. The term derived from the recent Spanish Civil War. Four columns of soldiers were sent into battle. The Fifth Column stayed at home and performed industrial sabotage, the dissemination of propaganda, and numerous other forms of less detectable subversion. Fifth Columnists sought to remain anonymous; their ambiguous and/or fully unidentified status made them seem as dangerous or more dangerous than the four columns engaged in day-to-day war.

Perfidia

Reminiscenza.

I wandered off in a prairie blizzard 85 years ago. The cold rendered me spellbound, then to now. I have outlived the decree and find myself afraid to die. I cannot will cloudbursts the way I once did. I must recollect with yet greater fury.

It was a fever then. It remains a fever now. I will not die as long as I live this story. I run to Then to buy myself moments Now.

Twenty-three days.

Blood libel.

A policeman knocks on a young woman's door. Murderers' flags, aswirl.

Twenty-three days.

This storm.

Reminiscenza.

THE THUNDERBOLT BROADCAST

GERALD L. K. SMITH | K-L-A-N RADIO, LOS ANGELES | BOOTLEG TRANSMITTER/TIJUANA, MEXICO | FRIDAY, DECEMBER 5, 1941

The Jew Control Apparatus mandated this war—and now it's ours, whether we want it or not. It has been said that no news is good news, but that maxim predates the wondrous invention of radio, with its power to deliver *all* the news—good *and* bad—at rocket-ship speed. Regrettably, tonight's news is *all bad*, for the Nazis and the Japs are on a ripsnorting rampage—and the war is rapidly heading *our* undeserved and unwanted way.

Item: Adolf Hitler breached his deal with Red Boss Joseph Stalin in the summer and invaded the vast wasteland of repugnant Red Russia. Hammer-and-sickle armies are currently grinding *der Führer's* stalwart soldiers to bratwurst outside Moscow—but the natty Nazis have *already* bombed Britain to smithereens and have placed half of central Europe under Nordic Nationalist rule. Hitler's *still* got the pep to give American ground troops a fair fight—which will assuredly occur at some not-too-far-off point in our great nation's future. Does it make you apoplectically ambivalent, my friends? We don't want this war—but in for a penny, in for a pound.

Item: the illustrious *Il Duce*, Benito Mussolini, is faring poorly in his North African campaign—but don't count him out. Italians are lovers more than fighters, it has been said—grand opera is much more their style. That is certainly true—but those bel canto–belting bambinos *still* represent a strategic threat in the lower-European theater. Yes, storm clouds are forming in the east. Storm clouds are *breaking* to our west, I'm sad to say—in the form of our most presently poised *alleged* enemies: the Japs.

Are you that much more amply ambivalent, my friends? Like me, you've opened your ardent arms to America First. But, Hirohito's heathen hornets are now heading across the high seas—and I don't like it one bit.

Item: the State Department just issued a bulletin. Jap convoys are currently headed for Siam, and an invasion is expected momentarily.

Item: civilians are fleeing Manila, the capital city of the Philippines.

Item: President Franklin "Double-Cross" Rosenfeld has sent a personal message to the Jap Emperor. That message is both entreaty and warning: Desist in your aggressions or run the risk of full-scale American intervention.

Uncle Sam is getting hot. The Hawaiian Islands are *our* possession and the Pacific gateway to mainland America. The lush tropical atolls that beeline in our direction are now targets for Jap gun sights. This undeserved, unwarranted and unwanted war is heading *our* way—whether we want it or not.

Item: President Rosenfeld wants to know why Hirohito's hellions are massing in French Indochina.

Item: Radio Bangkok has issued warnings of a possible Jap sneak attack on Thailand. Jap envoys are conferring with Secretary of State Cordell Hull at this very moment. The Japs are hissing with forked tongues—because they say they want peace, even as Jap Foreign Minister Shigenori Togo lambasts America for our refusal to understand Japanese "ideals" and our continued protests against *alleged* Japanese pogroms in East Asia and the Pacific.

Yes, my friends—it's becoming *Jew*niversally apparent. This Communist-concocted war is heading *our* way—whether we want it or not.

No sane American desires our participation in a Fight-for-the-Kikes foreign war. No sane American wants to send American boys off to certain peril. No sane American denies that *this* war cannot be kept off *our* shores unless we circumvent and interdict it on *foreign* soil. I'm ripsnortingly right about this, my friends—I'm apple-cheeked with apostasy.

We didn't start this war. Adolf Hitler and hotsy-totsy Hirohito didn't start this war, either. The Jew Control apparatchiks cooked up this Red borscht stew and turned friend upon friend, the world over. Are you apoplectically ambivalent, my good friends?

Yes, the war is coming our way, even though we sure as shooting don't want it. And America *never* runs from a fight.

Part One

THE JAPS

(December 6–December 11, 1941)

December 6, 1941

1

HIDEO ASHIDA

LOS ANGELES | SATURDAY, DECEMBER 6, 1941

9:08 a.m.

There—Whalen's Drugstore, 6th and Spring streets. The site of four recent felonies. 211 PC—Armed Robbery.

The store was jinxed. Four heists in one month predicted a fifth heist. It was probably the same bandit. The man worked solo. He covered his face with a bandanna and carried a long-barreled gat. He always stole narcotics and till cash.

The Robbery Squad was shorthanded. A geek wearing a Hitler mask hit three taverns in Silver Lake. It was 211 plus mayhem. The geek pistol-whipped the bartenders and groped female customers. He was gun-happy. He shot up jukeboxes and shelves full of booze.

Robbery was swamped. Ashida built the trip-wire gizmo and chose this test spot. He'd created the prototype in high school. His first test spot was the Belmont High showers. He used it to photograph Bucky after basketball prac—

A car swerved northbound on Spring. The driver saw Ashida. Of course—he yelled, "Goddamn Jap!"

Ray Pinker responded. Of course—he yelled, "Screw you!"

Ashida stared at the ground. The feeder cord ran across the street and stopped at the curb in front of the drugstore. The geek bandit parked in the same spot all four times. The cord led to a trip-action camera encased in hard rubber. The wheel jolts of cars parking activated gears. A shutter and flashbulb clicked and snapped photos of rear license plates. Rolls of film were stashed in rubber-coated tubes. A single load would cover a full day's worth of cars.

Pinker lit a cigarette. "It's a wild-goose chase. We're civilian criminologists, not cops. We know the damn thing works, so why are we here? It's not like we've been tipped to another job."

Ashida smiled. "You know the answer to that."

"If the answer is 'We've got nothing better to do,' or 'We're scientists with no personal lives worth a damn,' then you're right."

A bus passed southbound. A Mexican guy blew smoke rings out his window. He saw Ashida. He yelled, "*Puto* Jap!"

Pinker flipped his cigarette. It fell short of the bus.

"Which one of you was born here? Which one of you did *not* swim the Rio Grande illegally?"

Ashida squared off his necktie. "Say it again. You were exasperated the first time you said it, so I know it was a candid response."

Pinker grinned. "You're my protégé, so you're *my* Jap, which gives me a vested interest in you. You're the only Jap employed by the Los Angeles Police Department, which makes you that much more unique and gives me that much more cachet."

Ashida laughed. A '38 DeSoto pulled up in front of the drugstore. The wheels hit the wire, the lens clicked, the flashbulb popped. A tall man got out. He had Bucky Bleichert's dark hair and small brown eyes. Ashida watched him enter the drugstore.

Pinker ducked across the street and futzed with the bulb slot. Ashida window-peeped the drugstore and tracked the man. The glass distorted his features. Ashida *made* him Bucky. He shut his eyes, he blinked, he opened his eyes and transformed him. The man evinced Bucky's grace now. He *glided.* He smiled and displayed big buck teeth.

The man walked out. Pinker ran back across the street and blocked Ashida's view. The car drove off. Ashida blinked. The world lost its one-minute Bucky Bleichert glow.

They settled back in. Pinker leaned on a lamppost and chain-smoked. Ashida stood still and felt the downtown L.A. whir.

The war was coming. The whir was all about it. He was a native-born Nisei and second son. His father was a gandy dancer. Pops guzzled terpin hydrate and worked himself to death laying railroad track. His mother had an apartment in Little Tokyo. She was pro-Emperor and spoke Japanese just to torque him. The family owned a truck farm in the San Fernando Valley. His brother Akira ran it. It was mostly Nisei acreage out there. Mexican illegals picked their crops. It was a common Nisei practice. It was shameful, it was prudent, it was labor at low cost. The practice bordered on indentured servitude. The practice assured solvency for the Nisei farmer class.

The practice entailed collusion. The family paid bribes to a Mexican State Police captain. The payments saved the wetbacks from deportation. Akira accepted the practice and implemented it sans moral probe. It permitted second son Hideo to ignore the family trade and pursue his criminological passion.

He had advanced degrees in chemistry and biology. He was a Stanford Ph.D. at twenty-two. He knew serology, fingerprinting, ballistics. He went on the Los Angeles Police Department a year ago. He wanted to work with its legendary head chemist. He was a protégé looking for a mentor. Ray Pinker was a pedagogue looking for a pupil. The bond was formed in that manner. The assigned roles blurred very fast.

They became colleagues. Pinker was admirably blind per racial matters. He compared Ashida to Charlie Chan's number-one son. Ashida told Pinker that Charlie Chan was Chinese. Pinker said, "It's all Greek to me."

Spring Street was lined with mock-snow Christmas trees. They were coated with bird dung and soot. A kid hawked *Herald*s outside the drugstore. He shouted the headline: "*FDR in Last-Ditch Talks with Japs!*"

Pinker said, "The damn gizmo works."

"I know."

"You're a goddamn genius."

"I know."

"That rape-o's still operating. The Central Vice guys make him for an MP. He dicked another lady two nights ago."

Ashida nodded. "The first victim resisted and tore off a strip of his armband. He wore his uniform shirt under his civilian coat. I've got fiber samples at my lab in my mother's apartment."

Pinker ogled a big blonde draped around a sailor. The sailor fish-eyed Ashida.

"Bucky Bleichert's fighting at the Olympic tomorrow night. The skinny is he'll fight a few more times and come on the Department."

Ashida flushed. "I knew Bucky in high school."

"I know. That's why I said it."

"Who's he fighting?"

"A stumblebum named Junior Wilkins. Elmer Jackson collared

him for flimflam. He was running a back-to-Africa con with some shine preacher."

A '37 Ford coupe parked upside the drugstore. There—the wheels hit the wire, the lens clicks, the flashbulb pops on cue.

Pinker coughed and turned away from Ashida. A man got out of the car. He wore a fedora and an overcoat with the collar up. Ashida prickled. It was *no-overcoat* warm.

Pinker hacked and coughed. He was almost doubled up. The man pulled a handkerchief over his face.

Ashida tingled.

It was perfect. It was ideal. Pinker didn't see the man. They had the plate number. He could let the crime occur. He could run his forensic study from inception.

The man entered the drugstore.

Ashida checked his watch. It was 9:24 a.m.

Pinker turned around and lit a cigarette. Ashida scanned the drugstore window. The man walked down the toothpaste aisle. Ashida checked his watch on the sly.

The man hunkered out of sight. 9:25, 9:26, 9:27.

Pinker said, "My wife thinks it's dirt in the air, but I say it's just excess phlegm."

The man ran out of the drugstore. He gripped a paper bag and a half-visible pistol. He knocked over the newsboy. He shagged his car and peeled out.

Pinker said, "Holy shit." The cigarette dropped from his mouth.

The newsboy ran into the drugstore. Pinker ran toward a call box. Ashida ran up to the gizmo.

He unlocked it and knelt close. He studied the negative in the feeder. There, faint and blurred: Cal KFE-621.

A car idled by. The driver was a Shriner, replete with fez. He saw Ashida and got all contorted. Ashida stood up and made fists. The car pulled away.

"*FDR in Last-Ditch Talks with Japs!*" The newsboy stared at Ashida and shrieked it.

There—a cop siren at 9:31.

Ashida stood poised. A K-car took the corner and skid-stopped just short of the gizmo. Ashida was eyeball close. He recognized the guys: Buzz Meeks and Lee Blanchard.

They got out. Meeks worked Headquarters Robbery. Blanchard

worked Central Patrol. Meeks wore a fresh-pressed suit. Blanchard wore a slept-in uniform.

Meeks said, "What gives, kid? How come you beat us here?"

Blanchard said, "What gives, Hirohito?"

Meeks jerked Blanchard's necktie and snapped his head. Blanchard blushed.

Ashida pointed to the gizmo. "Mr. Pinker and I were testing this device. The store's a patsy, so we chose it for our test site. Car wheels set off a camera under that tubing. We lucked into the robbery. The suspect's plate number is KFE-621."

Meeks winked and squatted by the gizmo. Blanchard got in the car and sent out the squawk. Meeks was a Dust Bowl vet and ex–cowboy film actor. He came on under James Edgar "Two-Gun" Davis. He was a bagman to Mayor Frank Shaw. The county grand jury sacked Shaw and Chief Davis. Meeks dodged fourteen indictments.

Blanchard was an ex–heavyweight contender. He bought a house above the Sunset Strip with his fight stash. He cracked a big bank job in '39 and cinched his cop reputation. He was shacked up with a woman—Kay something. Shack jobs were verboten under Chief C. B. Horrall. The Chief was soft on Lee and turned a blind eye. Meeks and Blanchard were rumor magnets. The most prevalent: Lee was tight with Ben Siegel and the Jewish syndicate.

The drugstore was all hubbub. Voices bounced off the windows. Ashida looked inside. Pinker had the witnesses huddled.

Meeks picked his teeth and admired the gizmo. Blanchard stepped out of the K-car.

"The car was snatched in front of a pool hall on East Slauson. The 77th Street desk logged it at 8:16. It's got to be a spook. White don't survive from Jefferson south."

Meeks checked his watch. "Call Traffic, tell them to issue a bulletin, and tell them to spice it up. One-man crime wave, armed and dangerous. Make it sound like a meat-and-potatoes job."

Blanchard made the Churchill V sign. Meeks primped in the window reflection. Ashida walked into the drugstore.

He imprinted the floor plan. He memorized the witnesses' faces. He gauged distances geometrically. He moved his eyes, details accrued, he smelled body odors imbued with adrenaline.

Two white-coat pharmacists. A suit-and-tie manager. Two old-lady customers. The fat pharmacist had a boil on his neck. The thin pharmacist had the shakes. One old lady was obese. Her vein pattern indicated arterial sclerosis.

The witnesses were pressed in tight. Meeks walked behind the front counter and stood facing them.

"I'm Sergeant Turner Meeks, and I'm listening."

The manager said, "He walked in and went straight to the pharmacy. He wore a mask and had a gun, but I don't think it was the man who robbed us those other times. This man was taller and thinner."

The pharmacists bobbed their heads—yeah, boss, we agree.

Meeks said, "What happened then?"

The fat pharmacist said, "He lined us up and stole our wallets. He walked us down the first pill aisle, stole a bottle of phenobarbital and fired his gun into the ceiling."

Ashida prickled. There—the uncommon detail.

"Mr. Pinker and I were across the street. We would have heard the shot."

The fat pharmacist went nix. "The gun had a silencer. It stuck off the end of the barrel."

Ashida walked back to the pharmacy. Note the cash register, Hershey bars and Christmas-card display. He rang up a one-dollar sale. The money drawer popped open. The slots were stuffed with ones through twenties.

Instinct.

The bandit wanted dope more than money. The wallet thefts were secondary. They were undertaken to obscure the primary motive.

Anomaly.

Why steal only *one* bottle of phenobarbital? The action rebutted the dope-fiend robber archetype.

Ashida vaulted the counter and walked down the first aisle. There—no ejected shell casing. There—*two* options.

The robber picked it up, or the gun was a revolver.

There—the bullet hole in the ceiling. Metal shards on the floor below—decomposed silencer threads.

He knelt down and studied them. The edges were burned from muzzle heat. The threads dropped off in little swirls.

Ashida walked back to the front counter. Pinker had his evidence kit. Meeks uncorked a bottle of drugstore hooch and passed it around. Blanchard raided the chewing-gum rack. Meeks stuffed his pockets full of rubbers.

The jug made the rounds. Ashida declined it. The pharmacists took healthy pulls. The old ladies giggled and sipped.

Blanchard said, "We got a kickback from Traffic. The car was dumped three blocks from here. We got glove prints on the dashboard so far."

Meeks lit a cigar. "Did he touch anything inside the store? Can you folks help me with that?"

The fat pharmacist coughed. "He brushed the comic-book rack on his way out. I think he might have snagged his coat."

Pinker went *Now*. Ashida caught it and ducked past the witnesses. The rack was stuffed with *Mickey Mouse* and *Tarzan*. Ashida swiveled it twice. Nothing and nothing. Yes—right *there*.

Bright red threads, attached to one prong.

Wool felt, densely woven, *familiar*.

Ashida pulled out a pen and evidence envelope. He plucked the threads and sealed them. He wrote "211 PC/Whalen's Drugstore/10:09 a.m., 12/6/41" on the envelope flap.

More laughs up front—Blanchard and Meeks made like the Ritz Brothers. Ashida sniffed the envelope. He smelled the fabric through the paper. He made the synaptic catch.

The suspected MP rapist. The fibers off his armband. Pinker said he just raped another lady. The fool wore the armband on his rape prowls.

There was no red in the robber's overcoat. The rack prongs were situated at the man's waist level. The overcoat featured open-topped pockets. The fabric threads might have come from something sticking out. He had comparison fibers at his mother's place. He could confirm or exclude the match.

There's the whistle—Pinker's I need you *now*.

Ashida tracked the sound. Pinker was back in the pharmacy. He had his evidence camera out. He shot three exposures of the bullet hole, three exposures of the silencer shards.

"This job intrigues me. He didn't terrorize the witnesses with the gun, he didn't steal till cash, he squeezed a gunshot off for kicks."

Ashida nodded. "It's as if he was testing the silencer. And why did he only steal *one* bottle of the phenobarbital?"

Pinker nodded. "I like the test-fire theory. It's obviously a home-made suppressor, because you've got thread burns from a single firing. Eight or ten shots would render the thing useless."

"You're right, and the manager said it's not the same man who robbed the store on the prior occasions. Whatever his primary and secondary motives, he picked out a patsy."

Pinker scooped shards into an envelope. "There's probably a crawl space between the ceiling and the roof."

The ceiling was made from loose gypsum-board panels. Ashida jumped and popped the one beside the bullet hole. Pinker made hand stirrups. Ashida caught the boost and got up.

The crawl space was all mildewed planks and cobwebs. Ashida hoisted himself in. He smelled stale gunpowder. He stood up and snagged himself on a cobweb. He brushed it off and got out his pocket flashlight. The beam caught insect swarms and a scurrying rat. There—six decomposed bullet chunks.

Be careful. You've been in this from inception. There's your official duty—and there's You.

Stanford, '36. Introductory Forensics: "All true clinicians succumb and hoard evidence. The practice creates a symbiosis of *it* and *you.*"

He checked his watch. He held the flashlight in his teeth and got out another envelope. He wrote "211 PC/Whalen's Drugstore/ 10:16 a.m., 12/6/41" on the front. He scooped four bullet chunks into it. He put the other two in his pocket.

The rat squirmed by him. He brushed himself off and dropped out of the hole. He landed deftly. He saw Buzz Meeks eyeballing the narcotics shelves.

"Look at this, kid."

Ashida looked. Bingo—four bottle rows neatly arrayed. The fifth row—*dis*arrayed. Vials of morphine paregoric—rifled, for sure.

"The pharmacist said he only stole phenobarbital."

Meeks said, "Yeah, and I believe him. But the skinny pharmacy guy's got the heebie-jeebies, and his shirt collar's soaked through. My guess is he's got a habit."

"Yes. He took advantage of the robbery to steal a vial of the paregoric. He only took what the robber could have carried on his person, and what he could hide himself."

Meeks winked. "You are *so* right, Charlie Chan."

"I'm Japanese, Sergeant. I know you can't tell the difference, but I'm not a goddamn Chinaman."

Meeks grinned. "You look like an American to me."

Ashida went swoony. Praise always made him flutter like a—

He glanced up front. Pinker dusted the door. Blanchard scrounged razor blades off the manager. The hophead pharmacist was green at the gills. His hands twitched, his Adam's apple bob-bobbed.

Meeks walked up to him and grabbed his necktie. The tie was a leash. Meeks pulled him back to the pharmacy and shoved him into Ashida. The hophead pissed his pants. Ashida shoved him into the counter and checked himself for stains.

The hophead quaked. The piss stain spread. Meeks pulled the sap off his belt.

"You swipe a jug of the paregoric? That a regular practice of yours?"

"One a week, boss. I'm cutting down. If I'm lyin', I'm flyin'."

"You got thirty seconds to convince me that you didn't finger this here robbery. You got twenty-nine seconds as of right now."

The hophead made prayer hands. "Not me, boss. I went to pharmacy school at Saint John Bosco J.C. I was raised by the Dominican Brothers."

Meeks grabbed a bottle of morph off the shelf. The hophead licked his lips.

"Who are you going to call to snitch off pushers in exchange for confiscated hop? Who's your Oklahoma-born-and-bred papa?"

"S-S-S-Sergeant T-T-Turner M-M-Meeks. He's my daddy—if I'm lyin', I'm flyin'."

Meeks tossed the jug at him. The hophead caught it and vamoosed down the aisle. Meeks said, "You're fastidious, Ashida. I don't know why you got such a fascination for this line of work."

The party up front was adjourning. Blanchard hugged the old ladies. The manager whipped out a camera and took snapshots. He got Pinker with his print brush and Big Lee in a boxer's crouch. Meeks walked over and traded mock blows with him. The old ladies squealed.

They all waved bye-bye on the sidewalk. Ashida smoothed out his suit coat and let the crowd disperse. Pinker, Blanchard and Meeks stood over the gizmo. Blanchard and Meeks had that *Holy shit* look.

Ashida walked outside and over. A prowl car swung north and grazed the curb. Pinker, Blanchard and Meeks snapped to.

Pinker said, "Look sharp now."

Meeks said, "Whiskey Bill."

Blanchard said, "Pious cocksucker."

A uniformed captain got out and inspected the gizmo. He wore glasses. He was dark-haired, midsize and trim. Odds on Captain William H. Parker.

Ashida snapped to. Parker examined the feeder cords. Pinker, Blanchard and Meeks stood at parade rest.

Parker toed the cord. "It's innovative, but the wider practical applications are eluding me. Address this point and describe the creative genesis and full mechanical workings in significant detail, and have your report on my desk by 9:00 a.m. tomorrow."

Ashida and Pinker nodded.

Parker looked at Meeks. "You're offensively overweight. Lose thirty pounds within the next thirty days, or I'll have Chief Horrall put you on the 'Fat Husband's Diet' recently extolled in the *Ladies' Home Journal.*"

Meeks nodded.

Parker looked at Blanchard. "Roll down your sleeves. Your mermaid tattoo is repugnant."

Blanchard rolled down his sleeves.

Parker tapped his watch. "It's now 10:31. I want a stolen-car report, with a synopsis of the robbery, on my desk in fifty-nine minutes."

Pinker nodded. Ashida nodded. Ditto Blanchard and Meeks. Parker got in his car and took off.

Meeks said, "Whiskey Bill."

Blanchard said, "He lost money on my fight with Jimmy Bivens. He can't let it go."

Pinker said, "The fight was fixed. You should have told him."

10:32 a.m.

Army half-tracks rolled down Spring. Trucks hauling howitzers tailed them. The convoy ran for blocks. It was all over the radio. Fortifications for defense plants and Fort MacArthur.

Soldier-drivers waved to the locals. Pedestrians stopped to applaud. Men doffed their hats, kids cheered, women blew kisses.

The traffic rumble was bad. Ashida cut east on 4th Street and north on Broadway. Passersby kept eyeing him.

He felt disembodied. He broke the law to observe lawlessness from a criminal act's inception. He succumbed to criminal pathology. He initiated an experiment. Would early access and distanced empathy allow him to understand criminals more clearly?

Introductory Forensics. He knew he'd succumb in time. He'd know the case as it grabbed him. That symbiosis—*it* and *you*.

He seized a textbook opportunity. He had to determine the pathology of a prosaic heist and report his findings first. His findings might serve the greater cause of forensic criminology. His findings might serve no cause at all. He was compelled to act. He was quintessentially Japanese. Japanese men were born to embody the concept of *Act*.

Ashida turned east and hit Little Tokyo. His pulse decelerated, his breath relaxed. A black-and-white cruised by. The driver recognized him and waved.

His mother had a walk-up at 2nd and San Pedro. The halls always reeked of broiled eel. He had his own apartment, across from Belmont High.

It was brimful of lab gear. The overflow filled his old bedroom at his mother's place. Mariko welcomed his intrusions. They allowed her to torque him at whim.

Ashida entered the building and unlocked the door. The place was quiet. Mariko was off somewhere, probably boozing and fomenting. He walked to his old bedroom and locked himself in.

Shelves packed with textbooks. Chemical vials and vats. Beakers, Bunsen burners, a hot plate. A spectrograph and three microscopes bolted to a table.

Ashida placed the bullet chunks on the table and grabbed his ammo-ID text. He held a magnifying glass over the chunks and studied the creases and dents.

The bullet pierced gypsum. The book was cross-referenced—ammo types to material fired upon. The photos were clear. Page 68—gypsum board. Two pages on—a bullet fragment with near-identical creases and dents.

The classic German firearm. The 9mm Luger.

The Luger had a floating-toggle ejector. The rounds always arced slowly. A deft shooter could catch an ejected shell in the air.

He ID'd the bullet independently. He withheld two fragments.

He gave Ray Pinker the remaining four. Pinker would or would not ID them.

Pinker was not as skilled at bullet identification. He was cultivating *this* evidential lead all by himself.

The fibers next.

Pinker knew he kept the book-rack fibers. Pinker knew he had the armband fibers here. They were sharing this lead. It was hypothetical, thus far.

Ashida got out both fiber sets. They looked naked-eye similar. He placed them under the slides of his comparison microscope.

He swiveled in close. He scanned for texture and color consistency. *Almost, almost, go in closer still.* Yes—the book-rack fibers were cut from the same type of armband cloth.

He could boil out the fabric dye and blotter-dry it. He could run chemical tests. The tests carried their own systematic flaws. The results would prove inconclusive.

A key-in-lock noise jarred him. He walked into the living room. Mariko had 11:00 a.m. booze breath.

He said, "Hello, Mother." She spoke slurred Japanese back. He bowed and tried to take her hand. She pulled away and flashed a magazine.

A "picture bride" rag. Choose a photograph and send for a young woman. She'll be shipped from Japan. Include the five-hundred-dollar steamship fare. All brides guaranteed to be fertile and subservient.

"I've told you, Mother. I'm not going to marry a fifteen-year-old girl out of a brothel."

"You too old to be bachelor. Neighbors get suspicious."

"The neighbors don't concern me. Akira's a bachelor, why don't you pester him?"

Mariko segued to pidgin talk. She learned it in railroad camps, circa 1905. She spoke it to demean his education.

"Speak straight English, Mother. You've been here for thirty-six years."

Mariko plopped on the couch. "Franklin Double-Cross Rosenfeld back down to Minister Togo. 'U.S. surrender to China imminent,' Chiang Kai-shek say."

Ashida laughed. "You've got your geopolitics confused, Mother. I'd ask you where you heard it, but I'm afraid you'll tell me."

Mariko giggled. "Father Coughlin. Christian Front. 'No war for Jew bankers,' Gerald L. K. Smith say. Lucky Lindy *ichiban*. He fly Atlantic solo, land at Hirohito's feet."

Enough.

Ashida walked to the kitchen. The Hiram Walker Ten High stood by the dish rack. Ashida poured a double shot and walked it in to Mariko. She knocked it back and tee-heed. She patted the couch.

He sat down. "Tell me something that isn't crazy. Pretend that I'm Akira and we have business to discuss."

"Farm profits up 16% last quarter. Jew accountant find way to deduct bribes to Captain Madrano. He say 'Care and feeding of wetbacks good deduction.'"

Ashida tapped her arm. "Parts of speech, Mother. Don't drop your articles. You always do it when you've been drinking."

Mariko jabbed his arm. "This better? I read about Bucky Bleichert in the *Herald*. It say he got fight coming up, but it don't say my son's friend a cream puff who only fight bums he can beat. It don't say my son think his mama's Fifth Column, but Bucky's papa Fifth Column, 'cause he in German-American Bund."

Sucker punch. She got drunk, she played dumb, she hit low.

"Don't talk that way about Bucky, Mama. You know it isn't true."

"Bucky scaredy-cat. Afraid to fight Mexican boy. Papa in Bund, Bucky cream puff."

Ashida stood up and knocked over a lamp stand. Mariko put two fingers over her lips and went *Sieg Heil!* Ashida swerved to his room and slammed the door.

The room was too hot now. Heat pressurized his chemicals and caused vapor leak. He turned on the fan and called the Robbery squadroom direct.

He got three rings. He heard "It's Meeks, and I'm listening."

"Hideo Ashida, Sergeant."

"Yeah, and you're Johnny-on-the-spot, given what time it is. Did you call to tell me something I don't know?"

"I did, yes."

Meeks coughed. "Then tell me, 'cause I'm listening."

"The book-rack fiber matched the armband fiber. It *is* the same cloth, so it's quite likely that the fiber came from an Army-issue armband. It may or may not be the *exact* armband worn by the same man, but it *is* the same cloth, and the chronological order of the crimes makes the rapist a suspect for the robbery."

Meeks whistled. "Well, I think I should tell Dudley Smith about this. He'll see what Jack Horrall wants to do."

Ashida said, "What do you mean?"

"Well, you got the rape-to-armed-robbery parlay, and the likelihood of some U.S. armed services fiend on the loose. It sounds like this guy's good for some mother dog shit, and it might notch us some cachet with the Army if we stop this short of a court-martial."

Ashida gulped. "Or a civilian trial?"

"You're getting the picture, son. Mrs. Ashida didn't raise any dumb kids."

Ashida dropped the receiver. Squadroom noise bounced up off the floor.

He chose this male world. He's learning its customs and codes. It's unbearably thrilling.

2

KAY LAKE'S DIARY

[COMPILED AND CHRONOLOGICALLY INSERTED BY THE LOS ANGELES POLICE MUSEUM]

LOS ANGELES | SATURDAY, DECEMBER 6, 1941

11:23 a.m.

I've begun this diary on impulse. An extraordinary scene unfolded as I sat on my separate bedroom terrace. I was sketching the southern view and heard the rumble of engines below me on the Strip. I immediately got up and wrote down the precise time and date. I sensed what the rumble portended, and I was right.

A line of armored vehicles chugged west on Sunset, to fevered scrutiny and applause. It took a full ten minutes for the armada to pass. The noise was loud, the cheers louder. People stopped their cars to get out and salute the young soldiers. It played hell with the flow of traffic—but no one seemed to care. The soldiers were delighted by this display of respect and affection. They waved and blew kisses; a half dozen waitresses from Dave's Blue Room ran out and passed them cases of liquor. Somebody shouted, "*America!*" That's when I knew.

The war is coming. I'm going to enlist.

I always do what I say I'm going to do. I formally state my intent and proceed from that point. I am going to write a diary entry every day, until the present world conflict concludes or the world blows up. I will walk away from my easy existence and seek official postings near the front lines. I live a dilettante's life now. My compulsive sketch artistry is a schoolgirl's attempt to capture confounding realities. My piano studies and emerging proficiency with the easier Chopin nocturnes stall my pursuit of a true cause. This lovely home in no way allays my psychic discomfort; Lee Blanchard's indulgence is disconcerting more than anything else. This diary is a broadside against stasis and unrest.

I have always felt superior to my surroundings. This house states the case most tellingly. I picked out every German Expressionist print and every stick of blond-wood furniture. I'm a prairie girl from Sioux Falls, South Dakota—and a gifted arriviste.

I'm moving into my separate bedroom now. My own work is arrogantly displayed on the walls, interspersed with Klee and Kandinsky. There are a dozen drawings of a light heavyweight named Bucky Bleichert. He has a hungry young man's body and large bucked teeth. I have sketched him many times, from ringside seats at the Olympic. Bucky Bleichert is a local celebrity who understands the ephemeral quality of celebrity and does not view boxing as a true cause. His circumspection in the ring delights me. I have never spoken to Bucky Bleichert, but I am certain that I understand him.

Because I was a local celebrity once. It was February '39. I was nineteen. It all pertained to a bank robbery and its alleged solution.

This house. A refuge a few years ago, a trap now.

The robbery got me this house, not Lee's prudently invested fight winnings. Lee Blanchard is not a savvy investor, as is commonly held. Nor is he my lover, in the common sense. He entered my life to facilitate my destiny—whatever that is. I know it now.

Sioux Falls was an insufficient destiny. The winter cold spells and summer heat waves left people dead. Indians strayed from nearby reservations and stabbed one another in speakeasies. Klansmen broke a Negro man out of the county jail. He was accused of raping a dim-witted white girl. The Klansmen convened a kangaroo court. The girl was slow to condemn or exonerate the man accused. The Klansmen staked him over a red-ant hill in mid-August. The summer sun or the ants killed him. Local lore was divided on this.

Protestants despised the few local Catholics. Nativist groups flourished throughout the Depression. Methodists were at odds with Lutherans and Baptists and vice versa. A range war over prize cattle broke out in '34. Fourteen men were killed near the Iowa state line.

My parents and older brother were sweet-natured and content. Their only sin was lack of imagination. I pretended to be one of them in order to live within myself unobstructed. I lived to read, draw and roam. People talked about me. I dropped racy bons mots in church.

I did not care about my family. The fact mildly horrified me. I wanted to run away to Los Angeles and become someone else there. I got a job at a bookstore and stole a month's worth of cash receipts. I left my parents a perfunctory note of farewell.

It was November '36. I was sixteen. The bus ride west featured dust storms and a flash flood near Albuquerque. Armed goons were stationed at the California border. They were charged to keep indigent Okies out. They were L.A. policemen.

I rented cot space at a career girls' residence in Hollywood and carhopped at Simon's Drive-In on the Miracle Mile. I wore roller skates and twirled flamboyantly to amuse myself and scrounge tips. The other girls hated me and spread the rumor that I was a prostitute. I was fired. I relinquished myself to an aimless bohemianism.

The Depression was winding down; privation and inequity were vividly present still. I roamed L.A. with my sketch pad. I drew polemical pictures of local labor strife. I read Karl Marx, only believed a third of it and went to numerous left-wing soirées. I embraced the Left as a fashion accessory. They lacked the grandeur I had come to see as my birthright.

I loved men and was going mad with suppressed desire. It pushed me into a series of affairs with dubious jazz musicians. Sex was not what I imagined. It was tension, scent and prosaic misalliance. It was sweet and sad revelation, and all expectation dashed.

I lent money to a string of lovers and went through my carhop stash. I was evicted from the career girls' residence and took it with strident good cheer. I ate in soup kitchens and slept bedroll-swaddled in Griffith Park. I cleaned up daily at the YWCA and never appeared unkempt. I was equal parts innocence and lunatic grit. I was impervious to danger and too addled by men to assess them past my own desire.

Bobby De Witt was a jazz drummer. He personified the appellation "lounge lizard." He wore high-waisted flannels and two-tone loafer jackets; he kept up with his pachuco bunk mates from the Preston Reformatory. He caught me sketching him. I convinced myself that he recognized my talent and Norma Shearer–like aplomb. I was mistaken there. All he recognized was my penchant for the outré.

He had a small house out at Venice Beach. I had my own room. I slept away months of taxing outdoor days and too hot and too cold outdoor nights. I ate myself back from the brink of malnutrition and pondered what to do next.

Bobby seduced me then. I thought I was seducing him. I was mistaken. He saw that I was growing wings and set out to clip them.

Bobby was quite sweet to me at first. It started changing shortly after New Year's. His business picked up. He got me hooked on laudanum and made me stay home to answer the phone and book dates with his girls and their "clients." It got worse. He held a dope kick over me and coerced me into his stable. It got much worse.

Jazz drummer is always a synonym for *dope peddler* and *pimp*. I have the knife scars on the back of my thighs to prove it.

It was winter '39 now. My local celebrity was at hand. The newspapers and radio have their version. The Los Angeles Police Department has theirs. Both versions assert *this:* Kay Lake meets Lee Blanchard at Bobby De Witt's trial.

It wasn't true. I met Lee before the Boulevard-Citizens heist.

We met at the Olympic Auditorium. Bobby let me out of the house-brothel on "furlough." I was a full year into my Bucky Bleichert craze and went to all of his fights.

Bucky knocked out his opponent in the sixth round. I dawdled with the crowd as they left the arena. Lee introduced himself. I recognized him as an ex-boxer. I didn't know that he was a cop.

We talked. I liked Lee. I worked to disguise my acute dissolution. I hurried home to laudanum and white slavery. Lee tailed me back to Venice Beach. I did not know it that night.

Two more fight-night furloughs followed. I ran into Lee both times. He had tailed me from the house to the Olympic. I did not know it then.

Lee drew me out gently. He saw through my lies and euphemisms and got very angry. He told me that he had a business opportunity pending. He hinted that he could "work in my situation."

February 11, 1939, arrived. The papers got the physical facts right. The bank was at Yucca and Ivar in Hollywood. Four men hijacked an armored car headed there. A downed motorcycle served as a diversion. The men overpowered and chloroformed three guards. They substituted six cash bags full of phone-book scraps for six bags full of cash.

They huddled in the back of the armored car. They changed into guard uniforms and drove to the bank. The manager saw the scrap bags and opened the vault. They sapped him and added the vault cash to their take. They locked the tellers in the vault and went back out the front door.

A teller had tripped an alarm switch. Four nearby patrol cars roared up. A shoot-out resulted. Two robbers were killed, two robbers escaped. No policemen were wounded or in any way harmed.

The two dead robbers were identified as "out-of-town muscle." The two escaped robbers were not ID'd.

The papers got all that right. The papers got it *all* right for the next two weeks. The *Herald* ran a headline on February 28: TIP FROM EX-BOXER COP CRACKS BLOODY BANK ROBBERY.

The official version:

Officer Lee Blanchard strung together tips. Informants and "fight-game acquaintances" supplied "the lurid lowdown." They fingered Bobby De Witt as the "brains behind the Boulevard-Citizens job."

Of course, it was a lie. Of course, the "fourth man" remained unidentified. I know who he is. The public and the Los Angeles Police Department do not.

The real version:

Lee Blanchard masterminded the Boulevard-Citizens job. I knew it then; I know it now. Lee and I have never discussed it. We simply share the knowledge in the same way that we do not share a bed.

Bobby went to trial in June. Planted evidence convicted him. Lee Blanchard is far more cunning and intelligent than he plays. Bobby drew ten to life. The *Herald* ran a human-interest piece. The tagline was quite perverse: GANG GIRL FALLS IN LOVE—WITH COP! GOING STRAIGHT—TO ALTAR?

I attended the trial and testified against Bobby. I tapered off the laudanum to assure a harrowing witness-stand performance. The DA's Office presented a threadbare case. My recounted degradation was the indictment, the closing argument, the sentence writ as my decree of damnation. I complied with the lie that I met Lee in the courtroom.

We did not go straight to the altar. Lee bought us this house. Bobby De Witt was consigned to San Quentin. Lee fumbled at making love to me a few heartbreaking times and broke off that part of our union. I live off of Lee's police salary and his alleged boxing savings. I'm working toward degrees at UCLA; my piano teacher calls my beginner Chopin bravura. I sleep with men at whim—because I want to and because I need to extinguish the power of Bobby De Witt. I bring men here, to the house Lee Blanchard bought for me. Lee expresses no resentment. He sleeps in the Detective Bureau cot room most nights. He wants a Bureau transfer very badly. He's in the thrall of a suavely brutal cop named Dudley Smith, and wants to join his cadre of goons.

I have my dilettante world and my more compelling world of criminals and policemen. I inhabit the two worlds seamlessly and *do* exhibit Norma Shearer–like aplomb. I revel in my insider status. The genesis was Bobby De Witt. He bid me to enter this world. I owe him for that.

Bobby introduced me to a call-service madam named Brenda Allen. Brenda weaned me through my dope kick. We've stayed in touch. We have coffee, talk and smoke ourselves hoarse. Brenda runs girls through a telephone exchange and services an elite clientele. Her lover is a Vice sergeant named Elmer Jackson. Elmer is funny and droll; he blithely facilitates this exclusive brand of police-sanctioned prostitution. Chief Jack Horrall gets a 7% cut.

I love both my worlds. I'm much more engaged by the cop-criminal world. I paid a very dear price to get in.

Another convoy is crossing Sunset and Doheny. I feel the rumble all through my body.

Paul Robeson is appearing at Philharmonic Hall Monday night. I might go. Some of my old leftist chums might be there. I could lord my local celebrity over them and argue that Stalin is just as bad as Hitler. I might even create a scene.

I'm bored. My life is all busywork. Lee reported a rumor floating around City Hall: Bucky Bleichert has applied to the PD.

I hope he gets on. I'll go to his Academy graduation and sketch him in cop blue. Sunday night marks his farewell fight. I'll be there to capture the last punch he throws. The papers have been running cartoons of Emperor Hirohito. The artists always give him Bucky's big teeth.

The convoy has passed out of range. That rumble has left my body.

Nothing before this moment exists. The war is coming. I'm going to enlist.

3

WILLIAM H. PARKER

LOS ANGELES | SATURDAY, DECEMBER 6, 1941

1:02 p.m.

Another fucking convoy. Stalled traffic at Pico and Crenshaw.

A major intersection. All six lanes blocked. Civilian motorists honking their horns—part fervor, part frustration.

Parker checked his watch. He was now two minutes late. He was meeting Carl Hull at Wilshire Station. Carl kept the Department's Fifth Column files. Carl was half intelligence agent, half cop.

A motorcycle punk jumped a half-track hitch and zoomed off,

westbound. The act broke four traffic-code laws. The heist-hot car call cost him an hour. The Ashida kid's gizmo compensated.

Soldiers applauded the jump. The punk flipped them the finger.

Parker stepped out of his car. The convoy stretched to Olympic north and Washington south. Crisscross traffic, lumbering vehicles, Army fools running red lights.

His siren was useless. Street noise would smother it. The fortifications were pledged to defense plants. Two howitzers were pledged to Douglas Aircraft. His old boss ran the plant police. James Edgar "Two-Gun" Davis would get two more guns.

He was stalled in traffic. He was stalled in *Traffic Division*. He was The Man Who Would Be Chief. He was dead-stalled on all flanks.

He hailed from Deadwood, South Dakota. He was a son of the Holy Church and mining-town justice. He *will* be Chief. He will derail the Protestant line of succession. He will enact rigorous reforms. His brusque-tempered reformer's zeal was divinely bestowed. He *will* be Chief. He's been laying the groundwork for years.

He's William H. Parker III. Bill Parker I was a Union army colonel and U.S. attorney. Bill Parker I closed down Deadwood's whorehouses and dope dens. Bill Parker I was elected to Congress in 1906. Cirrhosis killed him at age sixty-one.

Bill Parker I had The Thirst. Line of succession: Bill Parker II and III inherited it.

His police department moniker is "Whiskey Bill." It's colorful, but incomplete. It fails to denote his comportment within the affliction.

He stayed dry throughout Prohibition. Alcohol was *illegal* then. 1933 brought repeal. He's been drinking at odd intervals since then.

Deadwood. He acquired The Thirst there.

Deadwood *formed* him the way L.A. *made* him. He graduated from high school in '20. He was the brightest kid in his class. His mother divorced Bill Parker II in '22. She uprooted to L.A. then. He helped with the move and stayed on.

L.A. was a hundred times bigger than Deadwood and a hundred times more corrupt. He worked as a movie usher and cabbie. L.A.'s sinfulness enraged him. The scale of the place drew him in.

There was a horrible kid marriage. His bride was a trollop. He did vile things to her. He cannot say the woman's name. He confessed his vile acts to a priest and received absolution.

He got a Church annulment and married again. Helen Schultz was a prudently chosen wife. She was an ex-policewoman. His first wife was a tawdry drunk dream. Helen was probity defined.

He drove taxicabs and attended law school. He joined the Los Angeles Police Department in '27. It was sickeningly corrupt. *Protestant* hoodlums ran the Department. He held his tongue and made rank. He became the hatchet man for Two-Gun Davis. The man was bone-dirty. He acceded to the man's designs. He heard things he shouldn't have heard and did things he shouldn't have done. His brutal ambition was forged from this ghastly descent.

He began his ascent. It started with his law school degree and stunning bar-exam performance. Jim Davis taught him the law from a morally forfeited perspective. He changed the law to vouch his career path.

Jim Davis and Mayor Frank Shaw were ousted. Fletcher Bowron was elected mayor. Bowron was a dimwit and half-assed reformer. Bowron brought in and sacked Chief Art Hohmann. Chief Art squawked when Fletch tapped "Call-Me-Jack" Horrall. Call-Me-Jack was a hear-no-evil/see-no-evil Chief. He maintained a clean façade. He was buffered by hatchet men and bagmen. Captain William H. Parker was frozen in place. The promotion list was an ice floe. He deployed his legal knowledge to thaw himself out.

He crafted legal documents. They fortified civil-service statutes, curtailed political influence and buttressed police autonomy. He had reform-minded jurists introduce the measures. They were straw men and kept his name out of it. The first measures altered the L.A. City Charter and were voted into law. A final measure granted civil service protection to police chiefs. That law now protected Call-Me-Jack Horrall. It would protect him one day.

The Los Angeles Police Department was a snake pit. Rampant factionalism, feudal-warlord cops. City Hall was hot-wired. The Detective Bureau was full of mop-closet listening posts and wire-recording gadgets spackled to ledges and lamps. Cops talked heedlessly, cops kept tabs. Smart cops made their dirty calls from pay phones.

Like Dudley Smith.

They monitored one another. They played at civility. Their

shared Catholicism served them there. They had monthly dinners with Archbishop Cantwell. Call-Me-Jack let Dudley peddle dope to southside Negroes. Call-Me-Jack cosigned Dudley's loathsome theories of racial sedation. Dudley was a Coughlinite and America Firster. He was Irish-born. He hated the English. He smugly relished the Nazi bombing of London.

Parker leaned on his black-and-white. The northbound traffic was stacked down to Adams now. Soldiers whooped at Dorsey High girls. A girl flipped her skirt and displayed her undies. It created an uproar.

Traffic jam. Logjam in Traffic Division.

He ran the Accident Investigation Detail. It was boring work, crucial work, not a career booster. The L.A. boom continued. The automobile boom boomed exponentially. More cars, more car crashes, more injuries and fatalities.

Call-Me-Jack sent him to Northwestern U. last year. He matriculated at a school for ranking traffic cops. His professors predicted an "auto-wreck apocalypse." He kept seeing a young woman on campus. She was tall, red-haired, about twenty-five. He asked a few students about her. They said she was a registered nurse and biology major. Her name was Joan something. She was from the Wisconsin boonies. She liked to drink.

It was 1:14 p.m. The convoy was impregnable. Wait—a northbound half-track stalled out.

Thread the needle. Hit the wiggle spot.

Parker got in the car and tapped his cherry lights and siren. Little kids on the sidewalk squealed. He gunned it and squeaked through the opening. He hit Wilshire Station at 1:16.

He parked and ran upstairs. Young cops gawked at the captain in full sprint.

Carl Hull had an office across from the squadroom. He ran the Red Squad in the '30s and reformed it. The Department hired out cops as strikebreaker thugs. Hull kiboshed the practice and took on his file-keeper job.

Parker stepped into the office. Hull sat at his desk, with his feet up. A war map covered two walls. Blue and red pins denoted troops in Europe. Yellow pins denoted the Japs' Pacific march.

Hull said, "You're seventeen minutes late."

Parker straddled a chair. "An auto theft and a drugstore heist pushed me back."

"I've got scuttlebutt on that."

"Tell me."

Hull packed his pipe. "It's off the Bureau pipeline. That Jap lab kid called Buzz Meeks. He got a fiber match to that rape-o MP."

"Conclusive?"

"No, and the kid told Meeks that."

Parker drummed the chair slats. "Who'd Meeks tell?"

"Dudley Smith."

"And Dudley went to Call-Me-Jack, who said, 'You take care of it, Dud.'"

Hull lit the pipe. "Yes, and in an ideal world, I'd prefer due process."

Parker lit a cigarette. "As much as I despise rapists and heist men, so would I."

A breeze buckled the war map. Parker studied the Russian-front pins. The resisting reds swarmed the advancing blues. It was a near rout.

"We'll be up against Russia after the war, Carl."

"Unless we intercede after Hitler bleeds them dry."

Parker shook his head. "They're our allies now. We need them to win *this* war, which hasn't even started for us yet."

Hull smiled. "Stalin will angle for a property split in eastern Europe. We'll have to forfeit territories and hold on to some strategic possessions."

Parker pointed to the map. "The conflict will be largely ideological then. It's been that way since their goddamn revolution. They hate us, we hate them. We can't let a momentary alliance blunt us to the fact that the world isn't big enough for both of us."

Hull twirled an ashtray. "You're leading me, William."

Parker smiled. "Here's my cross-examination, then. Do you predict a U.S. versus Russia war of territorial chess, the moment that peace is declared?"

Hull said, "Yes, I do."

"Then I'll classify you as a friendly witness and capitalize on that concession. Do you consider our homegrown Fifth Column to be clever and farsighted enough to begin their subversive activities *before* our inevitable engagement in the current world conflict?"

Hull pointed to the map. "Yes. They know that Hitler can't fight a two-front war and win, just like we do. They'll play up the fact that Russian blood paved our way to victory, portray us as panfascists and ingrates, and roll out every cliché in the books from that point on."

Parker pulled out a pocket-size tract. "Here's some quotes from this. 'A draconian policy of U.S. aggression against Russia, our current brave ally, after the war is won.' 'Escalating war hysteria and the racially inspired mass imprisonment of innocent Japanese citizens, a collusive tangle of the Los Angeles Police Department and the FBI.'"

Hull tamped his pipe. "Devil's advocate, William. The Feds *do* have a Jap subversive list, and they *will* use us if any type of detentions are required. You can't fault the bastards' logic here."

Parker said, "Their logic is specious, seditious, disingenuous and criminally defamatory. These shitheels allege to be antifascist, yet they give aid and comfort to our shared fascist enemy with the very writing and publication of this tract. And if you require further verification of the pervertedly circuitous logic of it all, the tract was printed by the same outfit that prints Gerald L. K. Smith's hate tracts."

Hull stared at the wall maps. Parker tossed the tract in his lap. Hull skimmed it.

"I know who wrote this. I've got her prose style and vocabulary memorized."

"Tell me."

"It's a woman. She's a socialite, for want of less kind descriptions, and she runs a Red cell. She lords it over some screenwriters and actors. They show up at rallies, make speeches and cause a ruckus. The Feds have an informant in the cell. He's a Beverly Hills psychiatrist that all the Reds spill their woes to. A pal on the Feds passes me the good doctor's dirt. I'll show you my file, if you quit leading me and come clean."

Parker shook his head. "Give me some names first. Come on, Carl. I outrank you."

Hull laughed. "The doctor's name is Saul Lesnick. His daughter was riding a vehicular-manslaughter term at Tehachapi. The Feds sprung her on the proviso that he turn snitch."

"The others?"

"The woman's name is Claire De Haven. Her chief acolytes are a fairy actor named Reynolds Loftis and his inamorata Chaz Minear."

No bells rang. The Urge hit out of nowhere. Come on—revoke The Pledge. One drink won't kill you.

"These Reds are defaming our police department, Carl. We can't have that."

"You'll be Chief one day, William. I look forward to that day, and I'll serve proudly under you. For now, though, I'd be happy with an explanation."

Parker stood up. "We'll plant someone in the cell. Our own informant. Someone we've got a wedge on."

Hull opened a drawer and pulled out four photographs. Parker leaned over the desk.

Hull laid the photos out. "I was checking my surveillance files a few weeks ago. These jumped out at me. I thought they might be useful at some point, so you might call this serendipitous."

Four sneak snapshots. Group pix. Two indoor meetings, two outdoor rallies. Dates: mid-'37 to fall '38. A young woman's face circled, four times.

She had dark hair. She stared intently at *something*. She looked provocative.

"Who is she?"

"Katherine Ann Lake, age twenty-one. Here's a hint. Her boyfriend was the bluesuit at your heist call a few hours ago."

Bells rang. Provocative—*sure*.

The Boulevard-Citizens job. That persistent rumor: Lee Blanchard bossed the heist and framed a fall guy. Blanchard was allegedly tight with Ben Siegel. "Bugsy" was now in the Hall of Justice jail. He allegedly snuffed a hood named Greenie Greenberg. It was a Jew gang rubout—November '39.

Siegel would be out soon. The prosecution's key witness took a window dive. Last month—Coney Island, New York. Gangland thug Abe Reles falls to his death. NYPD men are guarding him. He fashions a bedsheet rope and attempts to escape. He plummets eight stories.

Katherine Ann Lake. The girl Blanchard met at the robbery trial. The prosecution's stunning star witness.

Parker stared at the photos. "Blanchard's a shitheel. You've heard the rumors."

Hull coughed. "Yes, and I credit them. If you're thinking of the

Boulevard-Citizens caper for a wedge on the girl, you wouldn't be far off."

Parker said, "He wants to link up with Dudley and his boys. You've heard the rumors."

Hull said, "Here's something you haven't heard. The NYPD Intelligence Squad spotted Blanchard in Coney Island, right before that witness in the Siegel trial jumped. The cops recognized him from his fight days."

Parker stared at the photographs. The resolution was sharp. The Lake girl had fierce dark eyes.

4

DUDLEY SMITH

LOS ANGELES | SATURDAY, DECEMBER 6, 1941

2:16 p.m.

Lineup.

Five rape suspects, four rape victims, one-way glass between. A raised stage and height strips marked on the wall.

Chairs for eyeball witnesses. Standing ashtrays. A discomfiting wall poster.

It featured flags and dyspeptic eagles. It was a war-bond pitch. It supported intervention in this Jew-inspired war.

Dudley was America First. He loved Father Coughlin's weekly broadcasts. He enjoyed Gerald L. K. Smith's tirades. He shared a surname and no blood with Pastor Smith. The pastor was vilely antipapist.

Mike Breuning said, "The rape ladies are next door. They all say they could ID the guy, so we're in luck there. The lineup guys are backstage. They're all MPs from the Fort MacArthur battalion, and they all fit the suspect's description."

Dick Carlisle cracked his knuckles. Elmer Jackson flipped through his notebook. He'd worked the rape string from the start.

Dudley watched him read. Yes—the rapes felt consistent with the drugstore heist this a.m. That Jap lab whiz was right—the book-rack fibers do not *assuredly* place the rape-o at the drugstore. The *possible* two-crime parlay was irrelevant. Rape devastated women. The offense equaled murder. He told Call-Me-Jack that. Call-Me-Jack said, "You take care of it, Dud."

Elmer chewed a cigar. Elmer ran whores with Brenda Allen. The Vice Squad phones were tapped. Everyone knew everyone's shit. City Hall was one big listening post.

Carlisle lit a cigarette. Breuning stood poised. Elmer wagged his cigar.

"We've got four incidents. The victims all described the fucker as blond, medium-size and about twenty-five. Our guys fit that bill, and they were all on overnight leave when the incidents occurred. On top of that, they all had battery beefs involving women before they enlisted. For MO, we've got this. All four victims were out walking, alone, in West L.A. The rape-o abducted them, gagged them and drove them to four different vacant lots nearby. Here's the crazy shit. The rape-o hits them twice, rolls on a rubber and cries out like he's in pain when he's giving it to them."

Dudley smiled. Breuning leaned in close. Dudley put an arm around him.

"Call the infirmary at Fort MacArthur, lad. Get the names of all the soldiers treated for syph and the clap within the past six months, both in the MP battalion and the camp at large. Compile separate lists and report back within half an hour."

Breuning vamoosed. Elmer said, "What gives, boss?"

"An instinct and a hypothesis, lad. Let's say the MP's armband was a ruse to foil identification, because wearing such an identifying item on a rape string is tantamount to suicidal. Let's say he's miffed at some long-ago woman for having given him a dose. Let's say he's a smart lad with scientific knowledge. He knows that we can determine blood type from pus or seminal discharge. Let's say that for some fiendishly unfathomable reason, he wants the rapes to cause him pain."

Elmer went *Huh?* Carlisle went *Oh, yeah—I get it.*

Dot Rothstein walked the women in. Dot was a Sheriff's matron and a grand bull dyke. She ran six one, 240. Male cops stood tall around her.

The women had that schoolmarm look that rape-o's found fetching. They wore church frocks to a lineup. Carlisle dispensed cigarettes and lights.

The room smoked up. The women eyeballed the stage and made faces. The Dotstress scrammed.

Dudley said, "You're all grand and brave ladies for submitting to this ordeal, so we will do our best to ensure that it will be brief. Five men will walk in and stand on that stage, under the wall numbers one through five. You can see them, but they cannot see you. If you see the man who so heinously assaulted you, please tell me."

The women gulped en masse. Elmer tripped a wall switch. Five soldiers walked onstage and faced the room. They wore olive drabs and red armbands. They ran to the rape man's type.

Two women squinted. One woman leaked tears. One woman put on her glasses. They studied the stage. The moment built and fizzled. They all shook their heads no.

Elmer tapped the wall switch. The soldiers filed offstage. The women clustered around an ashtray and stubbed out their cigarettes.

One said, "They just weren't him."

One rubbed her eyes. "He was more mean-looking."

One nodded.

One said, "He had mean eyes."

Dudley smiled. Dudley touched their arms. It meant *There, there.*

Breuning returned. He was breathing hard. His shirt was wet. He waved a mug-shot strip.

Dudley walked over. Breuning leaned into the doorway.

"One case. The guy's an MP corporal, and he fits the description. He was on overnight leave on the dates of all four incidents, and he got his dose treated *after* the last rape. The provost captain told me he was a suspect in a rape string in Seattle, but the Army took him anyway. He's on leave now. He's a racetrack fiend, and the Oak Tree Meet's at Santa Anita today. I've got a plate number for him."

Dudley grabbed the strip. *Aaaaaah*—Jerome Joseph Pavlik. Young, blond, *mean.*

Two women hovered. Dudley flashed the strip. The women studied it.

One woman cried. One woman screamed.

Dudley pulled out two shamrock charms. They were fourteen-karat gold. He bought them bulk off a Yid jeweler.

He drew the women to him. He placed the charms in their hands. He said, "I'll take care of it."

2:46 p.m.

The last race ran at 3:30. Santa Anita was off the Arroyo Seco Parkway. It was *très* tight.

They ran through the City Hall garage. Breuning owned a souped-up Ford. They piled in and peeled out.

Breuning drove. Dudley sat up front. Carlisle sat in back, with three sawed-off shotguns.

They were 10-gauge and twin-barreled. They were fitted for bear slugs and triple-aught buck.

They pulled onto Main Street and cut through Chinatown. They made the parkway, fast.

Breuning gunned it. The juice needle jumped to eighty. Dudley smoked and looked out his window. He caught a wreck on the southbound side.

Skid marks, road flares, collision. Impact—a Navy flatbed and shine Cadillac. Traffic grief. It brought to mind Whiskey Bill Parker. He had grand dirt on him.

You should not have indulged that youthful marriage. Did you think your misconduct would escape my scrutiny?

Whiskey Bill had remarried. His second union was plainly humdrum. Dudley had his own Irish-born wife and four daughters. He had a rogue fifth daughter in Boston. She was seventeen now. They exchanged frequent letters and phone calls.

Elizabeth Short. His child with a married woman named Phoebe. A scold with her own daughter brood.

The Short girls all looked like Phoebe. It cloaked Beth's paternal blood. Phoebe was older than him. He was a mere nineteen when they coupled. He was a raw Irish conscript.

Joe Kennedy lived in Boston. Joe was filthy rich and donated money to Irish causes. Joe financed his citizenship. The price was strongarm work.

Beth knew that he was her father. She loved him and cleaved to the notion of her rough policeman dad. He just sent her a plane ticket. She wanted to see Los Angeles at Christmas. Her last letter disturbed him. She hinted at a "horrible thing" last year. Beth had a blind chum named Tommy Gilfoyle. He should call Tommy and inquire about that "horrible thing."

Family.

Bold men required it. The constraints were minimal. The vows were laughable. The joys were rich. Family was a necessary tether. The hellhound within him would go berserk without it. Whiskey Bill was childless. He ran unchecked in his prim lunacy.

The parkway was near dead. Breuning took hairpin turns fast. The juice needle jumped in the straightaways.

Dudley checked his watch. It was 2:54. The next-to-last race ran at 3:00. Most track fiends left before the closer.

Lincoln Heights whizzed by. A cowboy movie was filming up in the hills. A gunfight blurred by. Dudley recognized a man in a loincloth. Some Apache—a skid row bookie and three-time loser out of Big Q.

Dudley smoked. His thoughts drifted.

He moonlighted for Columbia Pictures. He was Harry Cohn's morals watchdog. Film stars ran unruly. The studio führers controlled them with rigid conduct codes. Violations construed breach of contract. He's nailed queer movie stars. He's nailed dipsos and hopheads galore. He's got legions of bellboys and whores bribed to report indiscretions. He's building quite the grand scrapbook of Hollywood at play.

Bette Davis will love his candid photos. She'll be at the Shrine Friday night. The *Examiner* is throwing its newsboys' Christmas bash. He'll be there to provoke a chance meet.

Wetbacks tilled crops above the film site. Carlos Madrano probably supplied them. Carlos. *El Capitán*, Mexican State Police. Close pal of Call-Me-Jack and Two-Gun Davis. Carlos shared his antipathy for the Reds and the Jews. Carlos viewed the Japs as *der Führer*'s pesky kin.

Dudley checked the mug strip. The rape-o looked like a small Lee Blanchard.

Aaaaah, Leland. Are you still troubled by Coney Island, on November 12? You would love to join my cadre, but have you the gumption for the work?

Ben Siegel wanted Abe Reles dead. Lee Blanchard owed Ben, per the Boulevard-Citizens job. Jew syndicate lads bribed two NYPD guards. Hotel-room doors were left open.

They Mickey Finn'd Reles' food. It was a quick two-man job. Blanchard fashioned the escape rope—a euphemism for noose. He did the hoisting himself.

The New York *Daily News* captured the moment. CANARY FALLS TO DEATH! HE CAN SING, BUT HE CAN'T FLY!

The train ride home was vexing. Blanchard waxed weepy and stayed drunk. The lad went back with Ben S. Benny bought out his fight contract and advised Lee to take some prudent dives. Lee refused, Lee owed Benny, Lee behaved rashly with the Boulevard-Citizens job. Benny banked at Boulevard-Citizens and played golf with the prexy. Benny was quite insane and obsessed with respectability. That caper was one large snafu.

Breuning pulled off the parkway. It was 3:01. Carlisle loaded the shotguns. They cut through South Pasadena. They made Arcadia and Santa Anita in two minutes flat.

The San Gabriels loomed behind the racetrack proper. The crest line framed the grandstands and clubhouse. The parking lot was two-thirds empty. Loudspeakers blared. A race ran down the home stretch.

Breuning cruised the parking rows. Dudley and Carlisle scanned plates. Cheers squelched up the speakers. Track fools walked out of the clubhouse and made for their cars.

Carlisle said, "Right there."

Yes—a '36 Olds sedan. Forest green/whip antenna/California ADL-642.

Breuning swung into an empty space and idled. Dudley chained cigarettes. The crowd fanned through the car rows. A man and two women peeled off their way. *Yes*—Jerome Joseph Pavlik and a Chinatown whore duet.

Carlisle said, "Tong chippies."

Breuning said, "Four Families, and protected. The boss Chink plays mah-jongg with Call-Me-Jack."

They looked blotto. The rape-o wore wilted khakis. The chippies wore moth-eaten fur coats.

They piled into the Olds. Dudley said, "Tail them."

They brodied out of the lot. Breuning stuck close. They were stinko. They wouldn't notice. Breuning rode their bumper—hard.

Two-car caravan. Residential streets, Fair Oaks Boulevard. The Parkway, due south.

The Olds fishtailed and weaved. Breuning eased off the gas. A Packard got between them. The whip antenna stayed in sight.

Carlisle blanket-wrapped the shotguns. Breuning said, "Bon voyage, sweetheart."

The Olds pulled off at Alameda, southbound. Chinatown was straight ahead. Kwan's Chinese Pagoda was quite close.

The Olds bumped the curb and stopped. The whores stumbled out. They got their sea legs. They tucked cash rolls into their garter belts and blew the rape-o kisses. They weaved down an alley behind a chop suey pit.

Carlisle passed out the shotguns. Jerome Joseph Pavlik stepped from his car and eyed the world, shit-faced. He gawked a vacant lot, catty-corner. It was full of palm trees and high grass.

He staggered into the lot. He walked up to a palm tree and pulled out his dick. He launched a world's record piss.

Dudley said, "Now, lads."

The street was no-one-out quiet. They beelined to the lot. Soft dirt covered their footsteps. The rape-o swayed and sprayed grass.

They came up behind him. He didn't hear shit.

Dudley said, "Those grand girls won't be the same now. This prevents recurring grief."

He started to turn around. He started to say "Say what?"

Six triggers snapped. The rape-o blew up. Bone shards took down palm fronds. Carlisle's glasses got residual-spritzed.

Big booms overlapped. Note those buckshot-on-wood echoes. 3:30 church bells pealed through all of it.

3:31 p.m.

Bug-eyed dragons flanked the Pagoda. Their tongues lit up and waggled at night. Uncle Ace Kwan ran the Hop Sing tong. His joint catered to white stiffs and Chinks with white taste buds. L.A. cops dined gratis.

Dudley walked through the restaurant. Mayor Bowron and DA McPherson were snout-deep in chow mein. Fletch B. was a peppy civic booster and all-around stupe. McPherson was a narcoleptic rumdum and mud shark. He frequented Minnie Roberts' Casbah and engaged two Congo cuties at a pop.

A recessed door led to the basement. Dudley took the stairs down. He leaned on a wall panel. It slid open. Fumes hit him straight off.

An opium den. Dim lights and twenty-odd pallets. Water bowls, cups and ladles. Scrawny Chinamen in their skivvies, sucking on pipes.

Dudley counted heads. *Aaaaah*, sixteen fiends adrift.

Dudley shut the panel. The basement conjured labyrinths beneath the Wolfsschanze. Cement walls, mildew, scrolled-iron doors. Ace Kwan's office—an SS bunker.

He knocked and walked in. Uncle Ace squatted over the floor safe. He was sixty-six and consumptive thin. He wore a Santa Claus hat. He conjured atrocity and Yule cheer.

"How's tricks, Dudster?"

"Tricky, my yellow brother."

"How so?"

"There's a dead white man in the lot across the street. Your lads should spread some quicklime and post a guard while the earth absorbs him."

Ace sat cross-legged. He was famously nimble. It was a common heathen trait.

"The lad was last seen with two tong whores."

"Hop Sing?"

"Four Families. You might want to remove the green sedan, as well. I don't want such trivial white business to disturb your clientele."

Ace bowed. "Four Families has been rude to my favorite niece. They are unsavory like that."

"Shall I rebuke those involved? I would hate to see another feud."

Ace stood up. "No, but my Irish brother honors me with the offer."

Dudley bowed. Ace pointed to a side doorway and went *Be my guest.* Dudley opened the door. Ace vanished somewhere. Chinks were stealthy and decorous.

It was his secret room. The pallet, the bowl, the ladle. Compressed tar spread on a bread plate. As always—The Pipe.

He hung his suit coat and holster on a wall peg. The pallet was built for a tall man. Dudley packed and lit the pipe.

The tar smoldered, the burn hit, the smoke funneled in. His shoulders dropped. His limbs disappeared.

The wisps now. *You never know what you'll see.*

Yes—there.

Dublin. Grafton Street, '21. Black and Tans with rubber-bullet guns. They aim for the kidneys. It still hurts when he stoops.

A rally. Patrick Pearse in full cry.

"Irishmen and Irishwomen—in the name of God and the dead generations from which she receives her nationhood—Ireland, through us, summons her children to her flag and strikes for her freedom."

A church rectory. A gun cache in a priest's bedroom. A rifle stock hits his hands. He's on the street now. He's sighting down the barrel. A British soldier's face explodes.

He's on Sackville Street. The recoil subsides. He's looting a Protty-owned shop. Patrick Pearse ruffles his hair.

"She now seizes the moment, supported by her exiled children in America."

Joe Kennedy smiles. He's got satchels full of cash. Irish Citizen's Army men greet him. The Black and Tans murder Patrick Pearse. There's a firing squad. He's got a bull's-eye pinned to his chest.

Joe Kennedy says, "You're a bright boy. You should come to America. Prohibition is a license to steal. You could ferry hooch for me."

He's in Canada, that's Lake Erie, he's on a moored barge. He's holding a tommy gun. Whiskey crates cover the deck.

Boston. A grand house. A Yankee maid scowls at him. He's toddling six-year-old Jack.

Joe Kennedy says, "Dud, this Jew banker fucked me on a deal. Take care of it, will you?"

His limbs are gone. The tar still burns. He knows when to stir the flame. Time is a nickelodeon. It screens through eyes in the back of his head.

He hit the Jew too hard. He shouldn't have killed him. Joe Kennedy is peeved.

"Your future is in Los Angeles, son. I can get you on the police force. You can fuck movie stars and create mischief."

He's standing proud in knife-sharp blues. He's hitting a purse snatcher with a phone book. Jack Horrall toasts him at Archbishop Cantwell's table. He's in Harry Cohn's office. Harry pats a bust of Benito Mussolini. He's outside a Bel-Air manse with a camera. He's got a window view. Cary Grant is engaged in all-male *soixante-neuf.*

Photoplay, *Screen World*—magazine pages aswirl. Bette Davis—aglow with something *he* said.

Switcheroo. Instant travelogue. He's on Coney Island at the Half Moon Hotel. He's hoisting the canary. Don't cry, Lee Blanchard—it's unmanly.

Travelogue. Back to Boston. Young Jack Kennedy's a Navy ensign now. He's due here for Christmas. He wants to fuck movie stars.

Jack starts singing, in Spanish. His voice doesn't go with the tune. Cut to the Trocadero. It's festooned with a banner: WELCOME 1938!

He's at a table with Ben Siegel and Sheriff Biscailuz. Glenn Miller's band plays "Perfidia." Bette Davis dances with a fey young man.

Light streaked in. The nickelodeon jerked. A shutter dropped and killed his travelogue.

He felt his limbs. He saw his coat and gun on a peg.

A Chinese woman appeared. She brought an aperitif. Three Benzedrine tablets and green tea.

Dudley stood up. The room retained a glow.

"What time is it, please?"

"It is 6:42."

"Perfidia" ended off-key. Bette Davis blew him a kiss.

5

LOS ANGELES | SATURDAY, DECEMBER 6, 1941

6:43 p.m.

Bucky was late. He always dropped by the lab on weekends. He trained at the Main Street Gym. Central Station was close.

The lab was dead. Most chemists worked Monday to Friday. Ashida worked seven days and nights.

The captain's office was next door. Elmer Jackson's voice came through a vent. He was boozing with Captain Bergdahl. They discussed the rape lineup with Dudley Smith.

The rapees ID'd the rape-o off a mug shot. Elmer said, "The

guy might be good for the drugstore job this morning, but the DA'll probably have to indict him off a slab."

Bergdahl laughed. Ashida prepped a microscope and the drugstore bullet chunks. Ray Pinker ran *his* tests. He left his report on Ashida's desk. His conclusion: Browning 9mm, shell catcher–equipped.

Wrong. Pinker's comparison text was outdated. *Be certain now. Retest yourself.*

He dialed in close. He got the same characteristics as this morning. Call it conclusive. A Luger slug hits gypsum board.

Bergdahl cracked a joke. The vent amplified his voice. Ha, ha—Come-San-Chin, the Chinese cocksucker.

Elmer said, "Cute, but I already heard it."

Bergdahl said, "Can you tell them apart? The Japs and the Chinks, I mean. I've got a pal on the Feds. He says they've got a roundup list for the Japs, if we get into this-here war. From my white man's perspective, I can't see no difference."

Ashida unlocked his tool drawer. He kept his photographs inside.

There's Bucky. He's crouched in boxing trunks. He's tall. He's lean. His muscles meld more than protrude. He's German Lutheran, with a Jewish star on his trunks. It expressed anti-Nazi sentiment.

He moved sideways on his toes and never tangled up his feet. He had left-hand power off feints. Mariko said he had "Tojo teeth." His dad was in the German-American Bund.

His eyes were small and deep-set. His smile lit up rooms.

There. Those clomps—he's taking the steps two at a time.

Ashida locked up the photos. Bucky walked in and dragged a chair over. He wore flannels and his Belmont letter jacket. The green *B* was pinned for basketball and track.

They shook hands. Ashida said, "Is it true?"

Bucky grinned. "Who told you?"

"Ray Pinker said it's common knowledge, which probably means that everyone knows, except me."

"I'm cleared for the May Academy class. I've passed all the exams, and they told me the background check is pro forma."

Ashida smiled. "You were waiting to tell me. You didn't want to jinx it, so you thought you'd wait until you were sure."

Bucky rocked his chair. "Or after the fight tomorrow. I'll be starved, and I'll buy dinner. We weigh in at noon, and I'll be all butterflies until it's over. I can't drop weight the way I used to. I'm still up at one seventy-nine."

Ashida said, "Take some steam at the Shotokan Baths."

"Nix that. I've got a pass to the Jonathan Club. The DA left a note at the gym. 'Son, I'm betting on you.' "

Ashida slapped his knees. "I could tell you stories about him."

"I've already heard them. He showed up drunk at a Lee Blanchard fight, with two colored girls."

Ashida said, "Junior Wilkins? It's not a very auspicious farewell fight."

"No, but it's one I can win."

Ashida laced his fingers. "Did you read Braven Dyer's column? He said you're running from Ronnie Cordero."

Bucky flinched. "I'm not quitting off a loss, Hideo."

"You wouldn't lose."

"He'd clean my clock. I could take him like I could take Joe Louis."

"I'm sorry you took it the wrong way. I didn't mean to—"

Bucky waved him off. "I ran into Jack Webb. He's selling suits at Silverwood's. He said the Detective Bureau men buy wholesale there."

"Jack's an awful cop buff. He's always bringing the Bureau men coffee and cigarettes."

Bucky stroked his Belmont *B*. "Sentinels forever. Jack should let us buy wholesale. We got him elected class president."

Ashida blurted it. "You've got an admirer."

"Who is she? And what's wrong with her?"

"I've seen her at your fights. She's always drawing you."

Bucky flashed his teeth. "I'm saving myself for Carole Lombard. You think she'll go for these?"

There's the blush. It always happens. Bucky's so gracious that he never sees.

6

KAY LAKE'S DIARY

LOS ANGELES | SATURDAY, DECEMBER 6, 1941

7:03 p.m.

The Strip is swarmed with servicemen. Dave's Blue Room, the Bit O' Sweden and the Trocadero are dishing out free liquor on the sidewalk. I just listened to a news broadcast. The men are being deployed to the Chavez Ravine Naval Base, Fort MacArthur in San Pedro, and Camp Roberts, up near San Luis Obispo. Los Angeles is the deployment hub; the artillery passing through has been consigned to coastal-defense installations and the Lockheed, Boeing, Douglas and Hughes aircraft plants. Ex-Chief Jim Davis runs the Douglas police force; he blathered for a good ten minutes about the need to protect civilian production facilities from Fifth Column sabotage and air-balloon attack. Davis is a vivid local lunatic; I watched him shoot a cigarette out of Lee's mouth at the Bureau Christmas party last year.

I began my diary only this morning. It feels like a remedy to stasis already. I'm looking in at my separate bedroom; the first thing I see are my Bucky Bleichert sketches. They identify my need to engage men anonymously and abstractly. Writing about Bucky forces me to see him in a more critical light.

Lee Blanchard despises Bucky, for his "dance master style" and "handpicked powder-puff opponents." I love Bucky for the ways that he is not Lee, because I am beholden to Lee in confounding ways and need Lee in direct proportion to our shared history.

We had a horrible fight a few hours ago. It pertained to Lee's recent behavior. He's been acting hurt for nearly a month now. He's been sleeping in the Detective Bureau cot room more and more, and spending more and more time with the Bureau's "mascot," a very eager-to-please haberdashery salesman named Jack Webb. He disappeared for a week in mid-November, and explained his absence as "decoy work" in a robbery investigation. I believed it—but only briefly. On a whim, I went through Lee's separate bedroom drawers this afternoon. I found a receipt for a train ticket to New York City and back, November 8 to 15.

I stewed over it. Lee came home and changed out of his civilian clothes. He stated his intention to spend the night at City Hall. I confronted him then.

I demanded an explanation for the receipt and his recent actions. Lee confronted *me* then. He said, "You think you're an independent woman, but you sponge off of *me* and screw guys in *my* house, while *I* foot the bill. You're a dilettante and a parasite, and if you disapprove of my behavior, get the fuck out of *my* house."

With that, Lee stormed out of *his* house, got in *his* car and drove off to live in *his* world—a world that I am subsumed by. A world that I fell into, and want more of.

Brenda Allen, Elmer Jackson and police-sanctioned vice. Lee and his fawning allegiance to Dudley Smith. Bobby De Witt in San Quentin and the scars on my legs. Whatever Lee owed or did *not* owe to Ben Siegel, currently awaiting release from the Hall of Justice jail. The bank heist that Lee planned in large part as a mission to save me. The deus ex machina: a little girl vanishes in 1929.

Lee's little sister Laurie, age twelve. Lee, fifteen then. Laurie disappears. She was at play in a public park one moment and gone forever the next. Lee was supposed to be watching her. He was off screwing the neighborhood round heels instead.

Lee carries the guilt. He hasn't fully touched a woman since that time. It's why he provides me with a comfortable home and does not make love to me. It's punishment sustained and punishment inflicted. It enrages me and moves me to sobs. It's why I love Lee so deeply and refuse to leave him. It's why I sleep with men in his own house.

The houses flanking this house are blaring the evening news; I can hear both broadcasts plainly. FDR is scolding Japan for their vile aggressions. Father Coughlin is scolding FDR and the Jew hegemony.

Both men own posterity. War gives men a plain and simple something to do. There's a brawl down on the Strip. The radios are a low hum under the shrieks.

Lee Blanchard had forty-nine pro fights and engineered a daring robbery. He owns posterity in a way that I never will. That fact infuriates me.

All I have is withering perception. Women write diaries in the hope that their words will beckon fate.

7

LOS ANGELES | SATURDAY, DECEMBER 6, 1941

7:49 p.m.

The news signed off. A talking beaver signed on and pitched toothpaste. Parker kicked his door shut.

Traffic Division was dead. Traffic shit roiled citywide. He was the only man on duty. Nobody else cared.

The division had its own building. 1st and Figueroa—six blocks from City Hall. It was his brainchild. Buy an old warehouse and convert it. Create autonomy. Limit Jack Horrall's access.

Parker prayed. He asked God for the courage not to drink tonight. He asked God to guide him through his incursion.

He was frayed. The Thirst plagued him. West L.A. Patrol snared two soldiers for drunk driving. There were three downed half-tracks at Pico and Bundy. Ten Central Division men got diverted. Central was running a night-watch skeleton crew.

Parker tidied up his desk. Parker stared at the files on his blotter.

Lee Blanchard's personnel file. Carl Hull's files: Claire De Haven, Reynolds Loftis, Chaz Minear, Saul Lesnick. Carl's suspected seditionists' summary sheet on Katherine Ann Lake.

White female American. 3/9/20/Sioux Falls, South Dakota. Prairie stock like him.

Carl called Claire De Haven "the Red Queen." There were no files on the other cell members. The "subsidiary membership" fluctuated. The Queen moved her pawns in and out. She did not know that Doc Lesnick was a long-term Fed snitch.

Blanchard first—a thin file, three pages.

Class B fitness reports. No informant spiel on the Boulevard-Citizens job. Nothing on Blanchard's alleged friendship with Benjamin "Bugsy" Siegel. Four civilian complaints. The complainants accused Blanchard of brutal jail-cell beatings. The complaints were dismissed—the complainants were perverts and hopheads.

No surprises. No new insights. His old instinct confirmed. Blanchard was strictly unkosher.

The Queen and her key pawns—more sinister.

Parker skimmed the files. The gist hit him quick. Doc Lesnick's snitch perceptions felt valid. Claire De Haven was an extortionist. Reynolds Loftis and Chaz Minear were homosexuals. The Red Queen held incriminating photos.

They wore drag gowns at a homo ball. Sheriff's roust sheets corroborated the pix. Loftis and Minear were repeatedly detained during fruit raids. The detentions ran up to 1940. Loftis and Minear habituated queer meeting places and congregated with other degenerates.

The Red Queen dominated them. She told Loftis what movies to act in and Minear how to craft his film scripts. Carl included sample dialogue. It was classic Fifth Columnism.

In the war films: Russian soldiers decry the plight of American Negroes. In the gangster films: hoodlums deride authority and extoll the ghastly charms of relinquishment. In the comedies: sophisticates drop leftist bons mots and vilify Adolf Hitler. The murderous Joe Stalin goes unmentioned.

Parker lit a cigarette. The Lake girl's file ran sixteen pages, replete with photographs.

Here's Miss Lake at Red gatherings. Banners abound. Dubious causes, ragamuffin crowds.

JUSTICE FOR THE SCOTTSBORO BOYS! REMEMBER SACCO & VANZETTI! ROOSEVELT, WALL STREET PAWN! BREAD ON EVERY PLATE NOW!

The crowds were unkempt. Miss Lake was groomed and well-dressed. She *attired* herself.

The photos were crisp black and white. He sensed that she always wore red. She wore a cloche hat to a Ban-the-Klan rally. Men clustered around her. She was not classically lovely. She worked with what she had.

The hat *had* to be red. She was spoofing her own affect. She was distanced from the causes she embraced.

She got straight A's at UCLA. She studied music, literature and political science. Her professors inked comments on her transcripts. They cited her "luminous" term papers. Two profs singled out her essay "Beethoven and Luther: Art and God Within." It was published in a prestigious journal.

Carl Hull secured a list of her library checkouts. It felt emblematic. Left-slanted biography. Romantic-era poetry. Muckraking labor screeds.

Wedges, fulcrums, coercion.

Serendipity.

What was *this* young woman doing with a thug cop like Lee Blanchard? The Boulevard-Citizens job failed to explain it. Carl Hull saw Miss Lake testify at Bobby De Witt's trial. The prosecution foundered until she took the stand. Miss Lake swore the oath between sobs. She closed the show, right there.

He made two calls from Carl's office. He got the FBI first. He wanted to talk to Dr. Lesnick's Fed handler. The man was off fishing in Oregon. He talked to Special Agent Ward Littell instead.

Serendipity.

He knew Ward from church. Ward was an ex-sem boy and a bit of a bleeding heart. Ward knew nothing about Lesnick. Ward leaked a tip.

The Feds were poised to investigate the tapped phones at City Hall. The push would occur in early '42. Ex-Chief Hohmann had snitched off the Department. Fletch Bowron made Jack Horrall Chief. Dimwit Hohmann wanted his job back. The taps and listening posts were an open secret. Fletch and Call-Me-Jack were fake reformers. Jack was 100% on the grift. Jack had a gentler touch than Crazy Jim Davis.

He called Sid Hudgens next. Sid scribed for the *Mirror-News*. Sid confirmed Ward Littell's assertions.

Art Hohmann was a Fed fink. The fucker was lawsuit-happy. Wouldn't *you* be, Bill? Fat Jack is in his chair.

Wedges, fulcrums, coercion.

It was 9:05. Parker grabbed the phone and called the Bureau line.

"Homicide, Sergeant Ludlow."

"It's Bill Parker at Traffic."

"Uh, yeah, Captain?"

"Is Lee Blanchard there?"

Ludlow said, "Yes, sir. He's taking a nap on Dudley Smith's couch."

Parker said, "Don't wake him. And don't tell him I called."

Ludlow mumbled something. Parker hung up. The surveillance pix beamed out at him.

Miss Lake's hat was red. It *had* to be.

9:07 p.m.

Parker shagged his car and cut west on 1st Street. He skimmed the radio and caught newscasts. The news was all *JAPS*.

Japs whiz toward Siam, Japs whiz toward the Philippines. FDR remains embroiled with Jap envoys. Boss Jap Hirohito blows raspberries.

Parker doused the radio. 1st Street swept into Beverly Boulevard. Christmas lights blinked on lawns and outlined doorways. A Schenley's billboard reignited The Thirst. A Maytag billboard got him jazzed.

A family oohed and aahed a gas range. The mom looked like that redhead at Northwestern. Joan something. Homewrecker. He hid out from Helen and *gassed* on *her*.

Parker turned north on La Cienega. The Strip hop-hop-hopped. He swerved around a downed flatbed spilling gas masks. Drunken sailors donned the masks and capered. Two Marines duked it out by the Mocambo. They staggered and capsized a faux Christmas tree.

North on Wetherly Drive. The Lake-Blanchard love nest—halfway up the block.

Streamlined and stylish. Aesthetically landscaped. No kind of cop's house. Too costly, too *good*.

A Packard ragtop was parked in the driveway. Parker pulled in behind it. The house was lit up. Cigarette smoke plumed off a high terrace.

He got out and stretched. He straightened his tie and hitched up his holster. He crossed the porch and rang the bell.

Footsteps responded. She swung the door wide.

She stared at him. She wore gabardine slacks and a man's white shirt. She dressed up to stay home.

"Bill Parker, Miss Lake. I was hoping I could have a few moments of your time."

She checked her watch. It was solid gold. She wore saddle shoes. She cinched her hair with a tortoiseshell barrette.

"It's 9:41 p.m., Captain."

"Yes, I know it's late. If I'm intruding, I could come back tomorrow."

She stepped toward him. It was a block-the-doorway pose.

"It pertains to Lee, then? That's a Traffic Division patch on your sleeve. Has there been an accident?"

She had his prairie twang. He noticed her notice his. She could lose it or modify it. She exemplified *Affect*.

"Officer Blanchard is fine, Miss Lake. It's something else entirely. I'm hoping you'll be curious enough to hear me out."

She stepped aside. He stepped inside. The living room was a movie set. Mauve walls, wingback chairs, tubular chaise lounges. Leftist-message art and a chrome liquor sideboard.

"You have a lovely home, Miss Lake."

She shut the door. "Lee had a successful boxing career. He had good financial counseling, as well."

"Ben Siegel is shrewd with his money. I'm sure he counseled Officer Blanchard himself."

She leaned on the door. The pose covered a pout. For a heartbeat—faux sophisticate, reckless child.

"We've all heard the rumors, Captain. A few of us know that they're false."

Parker pointed to a chair. "Would you mind?"

She nodded and walked to the sideboard. Parker sat down. She spritzed out two club sodas and brought him one. She pulled a matching chair up close.

They touched glasses. She said, "To whatever comes next."

Parker sipped his drink. "Tell me how you knew."

"I attended Mayor Bowron's Easter dinner for Archbishop Cantwell. There was an open bar. You veered between a selection of spirits and the soft-drink tray. In the end, you had a seltzer. You seemed to be both disappointed and relieved."

Parker said, "Do you always observe minor moments that acutely?"

"Yes. And you sense that I do, which is why you're here."

Parker popped a sweat. "You're from Sioux Falls?"

"Yes, and you're from Deadwood."

"How do you know that?"

"Elmer Jackson told me."

"Are you friends with Sergeant Jackson?"

"Yes."

"Are you familiar with the rumors about him?"

"Yes, and I know that they're true, as much as the rumors about Lee are false."

Sweat pooled at his hairline. The goddamn girl saw it. She walked over and opened a window.

A breeze drifted in. Horns honked down on Doheny. The goddamn girl struck a lounge pose.

Fireworks exploded. He caught a wide window view. Illegal Army hijinks. Red-white-and-blue starbursts.

She said, "The war is coming."

"Yes. What do you think about that?"

"I see large events as opportunities. It may not be my best quality."

Parker smiled. "For instance?"

She sat down and crossed her legs. Her bobby sox clashed with her saddle shoes. It was a deliberate *Screw you.*

"The Depression, for instance. It got me out of Sioux Falls."

"What do you think of the eastern-front campaign?"

"I hate the Germans and feel ambivalent about the Russians, if that's what you're getting at."

Parker patted his pockets for cigarettes. The girl reached in her slacks and tossed him her pack. He took one and tossed the pack back.

They lit up. A two-second breather followed. Illegal fireworks went *whoosh.*

"You haven't asked me what I'm doing here."

"You were out clearing traffic jams. You were in the neighborhood, so you thought you'd drop in on a woman you've never met."

"Are you finished?"

"No. You called the Bureau first. You wanted to make sure that Officer Lee Blanchard was asleep on Sergeant Dudley Smith's couch."

Parker gripped the chair and looked around for an ashtray. The girl stubbed out her cigarette and passed hers over. Their hands trembled and brushed.

"*Are you finished?*"

"No, but here's an alternate answer. It's Saturday night, and you thought I might be at loose ends."

"And why would I think that?"

"Because *you're* at loose ends? Because rumors run both ways? Because you read some sort of file on me and extrapolated?"

Fireworks streamed. Sunset Boulevard lit up. Couples jitterbugged on a flatbed truck.

They held a stare. The girl blinked first. She leaned in and plucked the ashtray off his lap.

He flinched. His glasses slid down his nose. The girl pointed to the window.

"What are they celebrating?"

"Opportunity."

"Yes. I'll buy that."

"Will you show me the house?"

She stood up and mock-curtsied. Parker followed her. Such affect—*look.*

Fifth Column art couched in sleekness. Cubism meets oppression. Astonishing—a *cop* lived here.

They walked upstairs. The landing featured deep red walls and floor-mounted lights. Pencil sketches were taped to the red. Breadlines, chain gangs, labor strikes and charging policemen.

She stepped into a room and flipped a wall switch. Light framed a cop still life.

An unmade bed. Discarded blues and desk debris. A .38 Special, handcuffs, spring-loaded sap. Framed wall clips from Big Lee's fight days.

She flipped off the switch. The room went dark. She stood on the too-bright landing and looked in at him. She *posed. He got it.*

She studied movie stars and random photos. She borrowed images to make herself cohere. She was brilliantly good at appearance. She was malleable without it.

The auburn hair, the dark red walls, the klieg lighting. She'll pivot now, that's for—

She pivoted. She walked to a doorway across the hall. He followed her.

The door was shut. A key lock was affixed to the knob. The anomaly stunned him.

He stood beside her. She pulled out a key and unlocked the door. It was her private bedroom. She fed him the cue and saved it for last.

Rose-colored walls, easeled drawing desk. An upright piano against one wall. Busts of Beethoven and Luther.

Pencil portraits arrayed on a shelf. That slick light heavyweight Bucky Bleichert.

Parker pointed over. "He's applied to the Department."

Kay Lake said, "I know."

"Why him? You've got your own fighter."

"You're being disingenuous, Captain. If you tell me that shacking up is forbidden by Los Angeles Police Charter, I'll explain it more provocatively."

Parker walked out to the terrace. The Sunset Strip hopped. Drunken soldiers hobknobbed outside the Trocadero. They whooped and waved sparklers. Traffic was fucked-up from here to kingdom come.

He leaned on the rail. Kay Lake walked out and joined him. He felt light-headed.

She handed him a cigarette and lit it. She lit up herself.

"I stand out here in the rain sometimes. The colors change gloriously."

Parker looked at her. He smelled sandalwood. She sprayed herself back in the bedroom. Affect, appearance—she caught her own sweat.

"What are your immediate plans, Miss Lake?"

"I'm going to enlist."

"Which branch?"

"The one with the snazziest uniforms."

Parker smiled. "You're dead-set?"

She tossed her hair. "Unless you offer me something more enticing."

He flicked his cigarette over the rail. It hit the hood of his prowl car and smoldered.

"There's phone taps and listening posts all over City Hall. I need you to transcribe the wire recordings on the Detective Bureau taps. You'll need to do it at the location."

Kay Lake beamed. "*You're being disingenuous, Captain.* I would say that there's something on the recordings that you want me to hear, and that it pertains to the threat you're holding back on."

Parker flushed. "You can start Monday morning."

She shook her head. "If you make sure Lee doesn't see me, I'll start tonight."

Fireworks blew up twelve o'clock high. The Strip glowed white into pink.

"There's a photograph of you. You were wearing a cloche hat, and I was wondering if it was red."

Kay Lake walked into her bedroom and walked straight back out. She had the hat on.

She posed in the doorway. The hat was no-shit police navy blue.

8

LOS ANGELES | SATURDAY, DECEMBER 6, 1941

10:56 p.m.

Lee Blanchard snored. The lad was shacked up with a lovely lass. He perplexingly slept at City Hall.

Snores drilled Homicide. The squadroom was otherwise still. No Teletypes, no phone blare.

Two boys just rolled to the Congo. A Negro named Jefferson snuffed a Negro named Washington. A Negress named Lincoln precipitated the event. Dudley nixed the job. "Go, lads. The Dudster will be with you in the spirit of impartial justice."

Blanchard snored. Dudley had a small cubicle. The sound boomeranged. Jack Webb picked his snout and perched by the Teletype.

Dudley wrote Beth Short a letter. "Apply yourself more rigorously to your studies, my grand girl. Bring your blind chum Tommy Gilfoyle with you later this month. I will send you a second airplane ticket. I want to watch you describe a motion picture to him, that splendid trick of yours."

Benzedrine still fueled him. A Hop Sing boy guarded the quicklime spill and the bubbling rape-o. He sent the four rapees red roses. He included tender regards.

Blanchard snored. The lad was a constant cuckold. Rumors reverberated.

Dudley picked up *Screen World.* The pages were frayed. He'd read the Bette Davis piece a trillion times. The paper was shredded. Bette's face was ink-smeared.

Harry Cohn found Bette brittle. She refused to leave Warner's for Columbia. Harry said, "I can't understand it, Dud. She must be anti-Semitic." He said, "All good women are. But aren't *all* of you film moguls Yids?"

Harry roared. Harry was an honorary white man. He ran Columbia tightfisted. The studio scrape doc was a lez named Ruth Mildred Cressmeyer. Ruthie owned a dyke slave den with Deputy Dot Rothstein. Ruthie botched a scrape on Bill McPherson's coon squeeze and lost her M.D.'s license. Ruthie's son Huey pulled heists and went to Bund meetings. Huey snitched for him. Huey sniffed glue. Huey was a grand psychopath.

His phone rang. The red button glowed—Lieutenant Thad Brown.

He caught it. "Yes, Thad?"

"I need a favor. It's menial, but you and Blanchard are the only warm bodies I've got."

"Of course."

"We've got a loud party squawk in Highland Park—2108 Avenue 45. The local desk's swamped, and Central's running light. Half the night watch is working that Army traffic grief."

Dudley jotted the address. Static cut Brown off. Sleeping Beauty stirred.

"Rise and shine, lad. There's a task at hand."

Blanchard rubbed his eyes. Dudley fed him coffee. Blanchard dog-yawned.

He slept in his suit coat. He needed a shave. He was a chronic malcontent. He pulled a daring heist in '39 and rescued a dubious maiden. He'd accomplished shit since then.

Dudley grabbed his holster. He steered Blanchard through the pen and watched him shake cobwebs. They elevatored down to the garage and shagged a K-car. They pulled out on Main, northbound.

The dashboard clock read 11:41. Blanchard *yaaaaaawned* and cracked his wind wing.

"Benny's getting out soon."

"Yes, lad. I know."

"He'll probably throw a party."

"He escaped the gas chamber. That's a feat to celebrate."

Blanchard lit a cigarette. "He escaped, thanks to us."

"Don't make me prompt you, lad. Complete the thought that you wish to express."

Blanchard shuddered. "I can still see his face. The canary, I mean. I get dreams sometimes."

Dudley rolled down his window. Cold air juked the Benzedrine.

"Be still, lad. You'd be better served taxing your conscience for those who deserve your regret."

Blanchard gulped and tossed his cigarette. Dudley took Broadway through Chinatown. They bypassed the parkway and caught Figueroa north. Memory Lane: Nightingale Junior High.

Spring '38. A sex fiend holds a girls' gym teacher hostage. The fiend makes her strip in the showers. He sneaks in and blows the fiend's brains out. He sends the hostage lady flowers every Christmas.

They moved through Mextown. Midnight revelers shot dice outside cantinas. They cut over to Avenue 45. The cholos vanished. The street was white and clean.

Wood-frame houses, parkway views, a stiffs' haven. That loud party—up on the right.

The house was bright. Music blared. Jarheads and Waves schmoozed on the porch. A petty officer ladled punch from a soup tureen. The Waves waved American flags on sticks.

Dudley parked. Blanchard got out and stretched. Somebody said, "Cops." Somebody killed the music.

Blanchard walked up to the porch. The revelry froze. Blanchard went *Ssssshhhhhhh*. Nervous laughs went around.

A jarhead said, "I saw you fight this shine down in T.J."

Blanchard bowed. A Wave fed him punch. Blanchard chugalugged it and went *Wooooo!* Church bells chimed midnight somewhere.

Dudley got out of the car. The bell echoes faded. He thought he heard something.

It was faint and high-pitched. It wasn't street noise back on Figueroa.

Blanchard charmed the yokels. The Wave refilled his cup. That shrill noise. Like overlapping violins.

Clock it—one house to the right. A wood-frame job. Tidy. Two floors, covered porch. He pulled out his flashlight and walked over. Shapes crossed the porch.

Coyotes. High-pitched beasts.

Blanchard weaved back toward the car. Dudley crossed the lawn and beamed his light on the porch. Coyotes lapped at the bottom door crack.

The light spooked them. They scattered. Their snouts were bright red.

He checked his watch. It was 12:02 a.m. Blanchard saw him and cut over. Dudley stepped onto the porch.

He flashed the door crack. Of course—blood.

Leaking out the door crack. Stiffening *blood.*

Blanchard jumped on the porch. He wafted cheap rum. Dudley went *Sssshhh.* Blanchard tracked the flashlight beam and went queasy.

Dudley pulled his piece. "Shoulder the door. Watch where you place your feet."

Blanchard aimed at a slack point midway up the jamb. One bump snapped the lock. The door swung in. A stench blew out.

Blood and flesh gout.

"Go inside, lad. Hug the wall and find a switch. Use your handkerchief. Watch your feet, and don't touch anything."

Blanchard covered his nose and went in. Deft boy—he flattened himself to the wall and inched sideways. The front room was midnight dark. Blanchard's feet scraped hardwood.

Light.

A ceiling fixture, bright bulbs, white light on this:

A living room. A wall-to-wall Persian rug. Blood-soaked, blood-*immersed.* Blood from four dead heathens. A yellow brood—papa, mama, daughter, son.

Blanchard said, "Japs."

They were supine. They were eviscerated. They were fully disemboweled. Their entrails flared on the floor. They laid four across. They seemed to be *positioned.* Four blood-caked swords lay beside them.

Long, hooked blades. Thick leather grips. Swords from Jap lore.

Blanchard teetered outside. Dudley heard him puke. He hugged the wall and circled the room. He studied the Japs.

Papa was fifty and trim. Sun-bronzed, rough hands—Jap farmer stock. Mama was plump and papa's age. The boy was twenty-two or -three. He was muscular. He had an insolent spic haircut. The girl was svelte and about sixteen.

Jap lore. Seppuku, hara-kiri, ritual suicide. Dishonor mandates self-annihilation.

Blanchard hovered in the doorway. His knees trembled. A jump tune kicked on next door.

Dudley said, "Call the Bureau and the lab. Tell Lieutenant Brown what we have, and leave a call to Chief Horrall to his discretion. Get Ray Pinker over here, and tell him to bring that bright young Dr. Ashida."

Blanchard talked through his handkerchief. "What about a canvass? You know, door-to-door on the neighbors?"

"Irrelevant, lad. I would say we have suicide. Have Pinker call Nort Layman at the morgue. He's a crackerjack cause-of-death man."

"What about ID's? Do you make them?"

Dudley squatted on the floor strip. "They're not criminals in the classic sense. You don't 'make' insane heathens who outwardly adhere to the white man's law. Brace the owner of the house next door. Determine what he knows. Call the night clerk at the Hall of Records. Inquire about the ownership of this house and find out how long the Japs have rented or owned it."

Blanchard took off. Dudley got out his notebook and pen.

He drew the living room. He eyeball-measured the floor strips and rug. He drew a sofa and two chairs. Blood halfway covered the legs. He called it two inches deep.

Wall décor:

Sepia photos of long-dead Japs and a framed map of Japan. The semblance of a sane family life.

A dining room adjoined the living room. Dudley drew the table, windows and chairs. The blood pools stopped short of the dining room. The living room rug had absorbed all the blood.

Their mouths were locked open. They died gasping for breath. They positioned themselves side by side.

He reached over and poked papa's arm. It stayed rigid. Rigor mortis had settled in.

He walked into the kitchen. It was all white-tiled.

Dishes stacked on a drain board. Jap fare in the icebox. Vegetables, rice, eel and squid.

Dudley drew the kitchen and laundry room. Linoleum floor, washing machine, indoor clothesline. Damp clothes pinned to the line. *Why wash clothes on your suicide day?*

He walked upstairs and stood on the landing. Two bedrooms, left. One bedroom, right. Wall pix of long-dead Japs.

He entered the near left-side bedroom. It was the girl's. It was pure female *Jap*.

The girl slept on a bamboo floor mat. The girl had a potted bonsai tree on her desk. She had slant-eyed stuffed animals. Her closets featured kimonos and normal school attire.

The connecting doorway was padlocked. He prickled at that. He cut around to the bedroom adjacent. It was pure male *Jap*.

The dead boy looked unruly. He sported that spic haircut. Call it—the girl locked the connecting door to keep him *out*.

The hallway doors had key locks. Two locks meant she could lock herself *in*.

The boy's room—unruly and then some.

Two golf clubs propped in a corner. A Franklin High pennant above the bed. Scattered comic books. Note the Nazi-spy covers.

A pitcher by the bed. A piss stink wafting up.

No loos in missy's room and junior's room. No cohabitator's privacy ensured.

Dudley went through the closet and dresser. This was revealed:

Innocuous male clothing. A Franklin letter sweater. Four zoot suits. More comic books. Two switchblade knives. Cheesecake mags and padded jockstraps.

He examined the jockstraps. They were padded with small Jap flags and female underwear. It matched little sister's underwear.

One bedroom left—mom and pop's kip.

He walked in. He checked the bathroom. He saw four toothbrushes in one holder. He saw pachuco hair oil on a sink ledge.

He checked the bedroom. He saw a sheet of paper taped to the wall.

Two lines. Japanese characters. The obvious suicide note.

The closet was packed tight. Mama wore kimonos. Papa favored dungarees and Jap warlord garb. A dresser was jammed into the closet. Dudley opened the top drawer.

Note: stacks of Jap yen and Kraut reichsmarks. Note: a pocket tract titled *The L. A. Oppressor.*

Dudley skimmed all eight pages. It was a goofball polemic. "Mr. Anonymous" assailed anti-Jap rage. He blamed "KKKorrupt fa*KKK*tions within the L.A. political machine." Their minions:

"KKKorrupt KKKops within the Police Department and Sheriff's Office." Mayor Fletch Bowron was pummeled. Sheriff Gene Biscailuz took some shots. Ex-Chief Jim Davis and Chief C. B. "Jack" Horrall got drubbed. The author lashed out at the Jews, the Brits and the Chinks.

Blanchard walked in. He held his pocket notebook and a Lucky Lager. He fucked up downstairs. His shoes were blood-smeared.

"The family's name is Watanabe. Daddy-o's name is Ryoshi. Mom's name is Aya, and the kids are named Nancy and Johnny. The house is in daddy's name. He owns a produce farm out in the Valley, just like every other Jap who don't peddle trinkets or run a fishing boat out of Pedro. The guy next door says they're decent Japs who steer clear of white folks and keep to themselves, and they're supposedly the only Japs in Highland Park."

Doors slammed outside. Dudley walked to Johnny's room and looked down. Two-car pile-out: Ray Pinker, Nort Layman. The Ashida kid and Lieutenant Thad Brown.

They ran up to the house. A big *Oh Shit* boomed. The suave Blanchard walked in. He pawed Johnny's comic books. He belched Lucky Lager.

Dudley snatched his bottle. "Go downstairs and send the Jap up. Chop, chop, Leland."

Blanchard scrammed. Dudley walked into mom and pop's room. Dudley studied the note.

いま迫り来たる災厄は　　われらの招きたるものに非ず
われらは善き市民であり　　かかる事態を知る身に非ざれば

The Jap walked in. It was 1:30 a.m. He was groomed and bright-eyed.

"Do you read Japanese, Dr. Ashida?"

"Yes, Sergeant. I do."

Dudley pointed to the note. Ashida studied it.

" 'The looming apocalypse is not of our doing. We have been good citizens and did not know that it was coming.' "

December 7, 1941

9

LOS ANGELES | SUNDAY, DECEMBER 7, 1941

1:31 a.m.

Dudley Smith said, "Surely a suicide note."

Ashida said, "Yes, most likely."

"Are you Nisei, Dr. Ashida?"

"Yes, Sergeant."

"Have you insights born of your cultural background that might serve to enlighten me thus far?"

The body placement felt wrong. The house was too tidy. Domestic chaos often precipitated seppuku. There should be more disarray.

Ashida said, "The note justified rather than acknowledged dishonor or shame. 'Looming apocalypse' is ambiguous. Most Japanese mass-suicide notes are somewhat more specific and stress the concept of honor regained."

Dudley Smith smiled. He was tall and fit. He had small brown eyes. His soft brogue seduced suspects. The gas chamber ensued.

"I appreciate your comments. I intend to remain in this room and ponder them while you assist downstairs."

Ashida bowed and walked to the stairs. He made the stench: visceral fluids mixed with stale air. He walked down to the living room. Blanchard and Brown stood away from the carpet. They went *P-U* and lit cigarettes.

Ray Pinker snapped body pix. Nort Layman studied the bodies. He wore knee-high waders. He came prepared for liquid rot.

Blanchard said, "I like the girl. If she was alive and kicking, I'd give her a poke."

Brown said, "This could go long. You think Ace Kwan would send up some chow?"

Blanchard said, "Hop Sing and Four Families are back in the shit. Ace has his hands full."

Brown said, "Dudley has truck with Ace. He'll get us some grub."

Blanchard said, "Don't tell Ace we got dead Japs here. The Japs and Chinks got some historical beef."

Two morgue men lugged in blood cans. Layman wrote the time and date on adhesive labels. The morgue men wore rubber gloves and packed metal scoops. Layman pointed to the stiffs.

"Clear a path all around. Seal the cans with tape. Refrigerate the blood, so I can get a peek at the cells."

The morgue men went to it. They scooped blood chunks and canned them piecemeal. Layman tossed them four more cans. The blood was full-caked now. It came loose half-dried.

One man dug a path to Ryoshi Watanabe. One man dug a path to Johnny. They filled six blood cans. They threaded their arms through the handles and hauled them back off the rug.

Blanchard said, "Holy shit."

Layman walked over to the bodies. He picked up the swords. He placed them on the rug. He turned the bodies prone and pulled down trousers, skirts and underwear. Pinker tossed him four thermometers cinched by a rubber band. He inserted them into their rectums and counted seconds on his wristwatch.

Ashida counted off his watch. Layman removed the thermometers and checked the bars. He signaled the morgue men: *Go now.* They peeled off to their hearse.

Layman coughed. "I'd say they've been dead for ten hours. They were disemboweled, so the food in their intestines might have partially dispersed through their blood, onto the rug. If I can get a handle on their digestion, I might be able to pinpoint the time of their death more precisely."

The morgue men wheeled in four metal gurneys. The borders were blood-guttered. Pinker stood over the bodies and snapped posterior shots.

Brown said, "It's suicide. I talked to the Chief. He said to wrap it up and shitcan it."

Dudley Smith walked in. "I lean toward suicide, but we'll make that determination in good time."

The morgue men leaned on their gurneys. Layman signaled *Resume.* They formed a stiff line. The inside man hoisted the stiffs. The outside man grabbed the stiffs and swung them. Layman stretched them out on the gurneys, face-up.

Ashida observed. Ashida gulped and spoke.

"The practice of seppuku entails a ritual meal shortly before the disembowelings. Dr. Layman should be able to determine the amount of food in their digestive tracts."

Layman laughed. "I like this kid. He could call me 'Nort,' but he calls me 'Dr.' "

Pinker laughed. "He's a doctor himself. He's a goddamn Stanford Ph.D."

Blanchard made the jack-off sign. Dudley Smith winked at Ashida.

He fluttered. His legs dipped. Eight white men looked at him.

He walked to the gurneys. He slipped on rubber gloves. The morgue men gave him *Who's this punk?* looks.

Ashida turned Ryoshi over. Yes—instinct confirmed. Ashida turned Johnny over. Yes—there again. Ashida turned Aya and Nancy over. Yes—again, again.

He had the floor. Eight white men stared at him.

"We've got hesitation marks directly below the entrance punctures. It's not surprising, given the enormity of the deed. What's anomalous is the similarity of the marks, given that the four people allegedly eviscerated themselves. In seppuku cases, the hesitation marks are usually straight downward punctures. In all four cases here, the tears go side to side, as if the people were thrashing or resisting the urge to kill themselves, in some way that has never been evidentially recorded in any criminological journal."

Pinker and Layman crowded up. Ashida pointed to the marks on Nancy and Johnny. Layman brushed off blood flakes. Pinker whistled. Layman said, "The kid's right."

Ashida said, "The positioning of the bodies seems wrong to me. I've seen mass seppuku photos in Japanese textbooks. Invariably, family members grasp for one another as they die, even though their original intent was to pose side by side. The bodies are always found in a heap."

Dudley Smith lit a cigarette. "Let's say that we attribute the hesitation marks to papa. He was afraid that his wife, son and daughter would falter at the last moment and be unable to wield the blade. He guided their hands, killed them, arranged their bodies, and then killed himself. He hesitated on himself because the act of killing his family had unnerved him."

Ashida said, "Yes, it's plausible."

Brown shrugged. "We're getting too far afield. It's a goddam suicide."

Blanchard haw-hawed. "It's a back column in the *Mirror*. 'Dead Japs in Highland Park. Emperor Weeps.' "

Dudley Smith said, "Apologize to Dr. Ashida, Leland. 'I'm sorry, sir' will suffice."

Blanchard stared at his shoes. Blanchard said, "I'm sorry, sir."

Ashida stared at his shoes. Layman produced a flask. Pinker grabbed it, took a pull and passed it around. Ashida caught the dregs.

A morgue man laughed. Brown laughed. Ashida laughed. Dudley pointed to the swords and the stiffs.

"We'll print them and run comparisons. We need to determine whose hand touched which weapon."

Pinker shook his head. "The handles are pebbled leather. They won't sustain prints."

Layman said, "Dust the blades. We might get something."

Ashida opened his evidence kit. On top: print powder, print ink, print brush, print cards.

He balanced the kit on Ryoshi's gurney. He examined the four sets of hands. Rigor mortis had set. Their fingers were curled inward. It made the potential print rolls difficult.

Pinker opened his kit. Layman picked up the swords. Dudley walked over and stood by Ashida. They shared a look. It felt telepathic.

Ashida grabbed Ryoshi's left wrist. Dudley bent the fingers and broke them. Bones snapped audibly. Ashida got a stable print surface.

Blanchard said, "Fuck."

Brown said, "Don't go squeamish, son."

Ashida inked the fingers and thumb. Ashida rolled the tips onto a print card and got perfect spreads.

Blanchard said, "Mother dog."

Pinker and Layman worked on the swords. Dudley broke Ryoshi's right-hand fingers. Ashida inked them, rolled them and got perfect spreads.

The room temperature climbed. Ashida started sweating. Dudley broke Aya's fingers. Dudley broke Johnny's and Nancy's fingers. Bones snapped. Slivers pierced skin.

Ashida inked the fingers. Ashida rolled the fingers. Ashida got perfect spreads. Dudley winked at him. Ashida felt himself blush.

Pinker and Layman held up the swords. They were dusted, hilt to tip. Pinker said, "No latents. Just smudges and smooth-leather glove prints."

Blanchard whistled. "Shit, it's homicide."

Brown said, "Not necessarily."

Pinker said, "Someone could have touched the blades with gloves on."

Dudley said, "Toss the premises, Leland. We're looking for smooth-leather gloves. No rough-leather work gloves or ladies' gloves. We're working on suppositions now."

Blanchard scrammed. Brown produced a flask. Layman grabbed it, took a pull and passed it around. Dudley passed it to Ashida. He took a pull. The booze sparked a brainstorm.

"There's a samurai tradition called 'accomplice suicide.' Dishonored patriarchs would bring in close friends or Shinto priests to help them kill themselves and their families. They were the ones who would actually wield the blade."

Brown said, "You're thinking that would account for the hesitation marks and positioning of the bodies."

"Yes, but there's one detail off. The accomplice always leaves family pictures beside the bodies."

Brown shook his head. "Why did I roll out on this one? I'm a ranking police officer."

Layman shook his head. "We don't need Jap homicides with the world in the straits that it's in."

Dudley smiled at Ashida. "As a confirmed isolationist, I would have to agree."

Thumps echoed upstairs. Scrape sounds followed. Blanchard yelled, "No leather gloves! We got cloth gloves, and that's it!"

Ashida felt the liquor. The room was packed. White men with booze breath. Cigarette smoke. Four dead Japanese.

"There's one more thing. The whole family was attired in smooth woolens, from the waist up. If Mr. Watanabe assisted in the suicides of the other three, he would have stood behind them to hold the swords, so he might have left foreign fabrics on their posteriors. A *fifth* person—a suicide accomplice or killer—might have left foreign fabrics on all *four* people, Mr. Watanabe included."

Nods circulated. Yeah, we get it—*but.*

Pinker tossed Ashida a flashlight. He pushed the gurneys up flush and rolled the stiffs on their sides. The morgue men stepped back. Ashida went in two-handed—flashlight and magnifying glass.

He started with Nancy. She wore a thin wool blouse with embroidered snowflakes. In close now. Yes, there—light-colored foreign fibers. They were coarse and brightly dyed. Yes—mauve Shetland wool.

He went at Aya next. Her blouse was a wool-cotton blend. In close now. Yes—identical fibers, on her upper back.

Ashida oozed sweat. He wiped his hands on his suit coat and regripped his implements. Johnny wore a flannel shirt. In close now. Yes—mauve Shetland wool fibers, curlicued.

Ryoshi wore a fine-gauge cardigan. In close now—confirm or refute the thesis—

Yes. Mauve-colored Shetland wool fibers, along his entire back.

Ashida wiped his face. "There are identical fibers on all four of them. It's a common sweater fiber, so it was an easy make. It's mauve-dyed Shetland wool."

Blanchard walked in. He looked slaphappy. He'd stuffed his pockets with comic books.

Dudley collared him. "Toss the place again, lad. Look for mauve-colored Shetland wool garments. Mauve is a light purple shade, in case you were wondering."

Blanchard about-faced. Dudley said, "I want photographs. Create a perspective of the whole house. Let's see if we've missed anything."

Pinker dug in his kit. He grabbed flashbulbs and film. Ashida dug in his kit. He grabbed tweezers and an envelope. He wrote "Watanabe/Avenue 45, 2:17 a.m., 12/7/41" on the flap.

Pinker snapped posterior pix. He got close-ups of the fibers, four bodies across. Brown and Layman walked out to the porch and lit cigarettes.

Ashida tweezed fibers and sealed them. Blanchard thumped around upstairs. He yelled, "I tossed all the dressers and closets! There's nothing like that!"

Dudley watched Ashida work. Ashida tweezed fibers. He filled four envelopes. Pinker waved his camera. It meant *Chop, chop.* Ashida grabbed his evidence kit.

Photo sweep.

Pinker snapped the shots. Ashida carried the film and the flashbulbs. They moved fast. Dudley followed them. They shot, reloaded, shot. The dead bulbs burned Ashida's hands. He tossed them in his kit.

Photo sweep.

Living room, dining room, kitchen. A service porch and damp clothes on a line.

The detail tweaked Ashida. *Why wash clothes on this day? Does this detail logically rule out seppuku?*

Photo sweep.

They moved to the hallway. Floor pix, wall pix, ceiling pix—

Ashida looked down. Pinker looked up. They caught metal shards on the floor. They caught a small hole, directly above them.

Ashida said, *"The floor."*

Pinker said, *"The ceiling."*

Dudley *saw* it. He looked up and down. He said, "I find this compelling."

Ashida squatted by the shards. They had to be silencer threads. They resembled the shards from the pharmacy heist.

"Did you read my report on the drugstore 211, Sergeant?"

"I did, Doctor. It was brilliantly etched and hypothetically rich. You said the bandit who brushed the book rack might not be the rape-o MP."

Ashida nodded. He scooped the shards into an envelope. He wrote "Watanabe/Avenue 45, 2:42 a.m., 12/7/41" on the flap. Pinker pointed to the ceiling. The hole was *bullet* size.

Dudley went *After you.* They quick-walked upstairs. A long carpet strip covered the landing. Dudley grabbed the near corner and pulled. The carpet flew off the floor.

Dudley yanked it to one side. There, on a floorboard—two bullet chunks.

Ashida got to them first. He knelt close. He put his magnifying glass in tight.

The chunks matched the drugstore chunks. It was a sure match or near match. It wasn't a coincidence.

Pinker knelt close. "It's a Luger with a shell catcher. I read your final report, Hideo. I know you did a recheck at the lab. There's just one discrepancy. This bullet had to come from a different ammo batch. I could crush these chunks with my bare hand."

Dudley knelt close. He picked up the chunks and crushed them. Powdered metal sifted off his hands.

He walked downstairs. Pinker went slack-jawed. Ashida *thought* he got it. It brought back his talk with Buzz Meeks. It brought back the green light on the Army rape-o.

Pinker stayed slack-jawed. Ashida walked downstairs. He heard voices in the kitchen. He hugged the hallway wall.

Brown said, "Maybe it's our killer, maybe it's not. All we *probably* have is the same man with a *probable* same firearm at two locations on the same day. Maybe he's a rape-o, maybe he isn't. We don't know for sure that he left those fibers at the drugstore. Yeah, they were an MP's armband fibers, but so what? If you're thinking we've got a rape/robbery/homicide parlay, you might very well be right—but you sure as shit might be wrong."

Dudley said, "It can't be a full parlay. Nort Layman never fucks up his approximate time of death."

Brown said, "Give me a road map, Dud."

Dudley said, "I identified the rape-o off a mug-shot run. Jack Horrall gave me the green light. My boys and I killed the man at 3:30 p.m. yesterday. He couldn't have killed the Japs."

Ashida tingled with it. Another brainstorm sparked. Introductory Forensics: "Instincts *will* cohere."

Deutsches Haus, West 15th Street. That Subversive Squad report. It's a meeting place for pro-Nazis. They allegedly traffic in Lugers and silencers.

10

KAY LAKE'S DIARY

LOS ANGELES | SUNDAY, DECEMBER 7, 1941

3:07 a.m.

". . . and Call-Me-Jack has a standing order in with Brenda. The PD has this private room over at Mike Lyman's Grill, where the ranking guys all hide out from their wives and entertain gash. Brenda sends a girl over, once a week. She blows Jack while he's on the phone with Gene Biscailuz. They discuss jail transfers, who's got the motorcade detail when Roosevelt blows through town, all that horseshit. Get this: The Sheriff's getting blown by one of Brenda's girls, simultaneously. There's a message in all of this, but I'm not sure I want to know what it is."

I held down the lever and squelched the rest of the chat. The device is quite the thing. A thin wire passes through two spools on a machine about the size of a small phonograph. Levers inch the wire back and forth; I wear earmuffs to contain the sound. The preceding conversation typifies the ones I've been hearing since 1:00 a.m. I'm alone in a mop closet, in a blocked-off and empty hallway two floors above the Detective Bureau. It's a cramped space, about eight by eight. I have a desk, a chair, an ashtray, a pack of cigarettes and a thermos of coffee that Captain William H. Parker has supplied. I have only the vaguest of ideas as to why I'm here.

I'm stationed within an "open secret." There are purportedly dozens of these "listening posts" dotted throughout the closed-off and seldom-used hallways here at City Hall. The practice of phone-tapping began under the reign of Jim Davis. Policemen tap phones to learn what other policemen are thinking and plotting. The taps record internal phone calls here at City Hall, and calls to the DA's Office at the Hall of Justice, three blocks away. Policemen monitor the calls on a weekly basis and keep coded logs of the calls that go in and out. There's a stack of these logs on the floor by my desk; shelves hold boxes of wire recordings that match the code numbers for the calls. It is an astonishingly arrogant and heedless practice, perpetrated by astonishingly arrogant and heedless men. How did Captain William H. Parker know that I'd be perfectly at home here?

The preceding conversation is labeled "HD116 to BS014," 6/12/39. I'm sure that it means "Homicide Division to Bunco Squad." Captain Parker has instructed me to identify incriminating conversations, record the code numbers and dates, and outline the gist of what was said. He flushed when I asked him why he chose *this* listening post. He said that he chose it because the logs denoted calls from the Robbery and Homicide squads, along with Central Vice. I found the explanation disingenuous. Captain Parker is entrapping me. He wants me to do something that will further his pious notions of justice and advance his career. He believes that I will hear something that will put me in his power. Until that moment, he knows that I will be entertained.

So, I'm wide-awake at 3:32 a.m. Captain Parker snuck me up in a freight elevator, to make sure that Lee and any Bureau men I might know didn't see me. Lee is most likely asleep on Dudley Smith's couch. I'm here, eavesdropping on covert chitchat from 1939.

I rewound the spool, placed it back in its box and picked up a new spool. It's labeled "BD 214 to DBML 442," 10/6/39. It's an easily ID'd call: Burglary Division to the Detective Bureau's main line.

The caller engaged the callee. It's Bob Denholm at Burglary. He's calling Jim Yardis on the Pawnshop Detail. "Jim, I've got a trace on that old Jew lady's fur coats."

"This coon" escaped from Chino and shagged a car in San Berdoo. He headed to L.A. and 459'd a house in South Gate. He left a fat set of prints, so we made him. We put the car on the hot sheet. The coon hit a house off the Miracle Mile. He got the Jew lady's fur coats and jerked off on her nighties. He pawned the coats downtown and started boozing at a he-she bar on South Main. He was on the wire for auto theft, escape and 459 with perversion. The parlay mandated a "coon hunt." Two bluesuits on a tavern check made him. The coon bolted. The bluesuits slayed his "coon ass."

The conversation continued; I timed it at seventeen minutes and forty-two seconds. Police gossip reigned. I learned which cops were fucking which cops' wives and heard speculation on the quality of the fucking. Call-Me-Jack Horrall would step in the shit sooner or later; Lieutenant Thad Brown or Captain Bill Parker would then ascend to Chief. Officer Larry "the Lizard" Linscott possessed a two-foot penis. DA Bill McPherson fell asleep in City Council meetings and enjoyed Negro prostitutes.

I rewound the wire, replaced it and grabbed another one. I didn't recognize the code letters; the recording was dated 4/9/41. I put the wire on the spool and tapped the lever. I recognized the voices immediately: Call-Me-Jack Horrall and Mayor Fletch Bowron.

They discussed Japanese aggression in the Philippines. Bowron said, "We're going to war, Jack." Horrall said, "Mr. Mayor, you're right as rain. I'm against intervention, but you're sure as shit correct."

Bowron said, "It's this whole Jap angle that troubles me. The Feds have got a detention list a mile long. A colonel in the Fourth Interceptor Command told me the Army's cooking up plans for the long-term imprisonment of all the sketchy Japs they can lay their hands on." Horrall said, "A Jap's a Jap, as far as I'm concerned. They're clannish, and you never know what they're thinking. What's that goddamn word?"

Bowron said, "Inscrutable?" Horrall said, "Yeah, that's it. You want my opinion? They're all Fifth Column. They all breathe, drink and eat Fifth Column, when they're not eating broiled eel." Bowron laughed and said, "Look at it this way. We're going to have a lot of government-confiscated property on our hands, and that means rental revenues if the Japs stay in stir until Armistice Day. L.A.'s a tourist mecca, we'll have lots of servicemen passing through, and they'll need lodging while they're here."

Horrall made cash-register sounds. Bowron said, "That's what I'm thinking. And don't call me a war profiteer, because we can kick back something like 10% to the Japs while they're cooling their heels. I'll keep them in cigarettes and candy bars."

Horrall chuckled and said, "Or broiled eel." Bowron laughed and went into a coughing spell. Horrall said, "Dudley Smith would be a good man to implement a deal like that. He's the smartest man in the Department." Bowron said, "I give the edge to Bill Parker. He's even smarter, and he'd be savvy enough to see something like that as a stepping-stone to Chief."

Static hit the wire. I heard snippets: "Who's got the slush fund?" "Who gets the gash?" "Who'll enlist if we fight this Jew-engineered war?" "Will the PD face a manpower shortage?" "Will FDR sign a wartime draft bill?"

The wire ran out; I rewound it and replaced it. There was one box left. It was marked "3," for three extensions. It noted the Bureau clerical pool, Headquarters Vice, and the Pickpocket Detail. The date: 8/14/39.

I slipped the new wire onto the spool and pushed the lever. The entry talk was garbled; southern drawls eked through. I sensed the voices before I actually heard them. I sensed William H. Parker's intent, as well.

Brenda Allen and Elmer Jackson hailed from Mississippi. Call-Me-Jack let Brenda use the clerical-pool phones. Lee played cards with a Pickpocket Detail lieutenant.

I made the assumption instantaneously; it played out as true. *It was thrilling.* Captain William H. Parker knew it would be.

It was August of '39. The Boulevard-Citizens trial concluded in June. I heard static and *heist* and *trial* a good dozen times. Full voices hit the wire then.

Elmer said, "I know you bought that house for Kay."

Brenda said, "You must have money left over, sugar. You could invest in our service."

Lee said, "I'm not running whores."

Elmer said, "Be smart, hoss. You still owe Ben Siegel. You could cut him in on your part."

Brenda said, "Benny don't play with a full deck, Citizen. That bank was his good-luck charm. You were a damn fool to clout it."

Lee said, "I'm a fool. I'll concede that. And you're right—I still owe Benny favors. But I'm not running whores."

The wire slid off the spool. I started to rethread it; my hands shook and knocked the thermos to the floor. Coffee spilled over the wire. I dried it on my skirt, placed it back on the spool and pressed the lever. Squelch distorted a long interchange. Brenda's voice rose out of it.

She said, "Ben will always be asking you for favors."

Elmer said, "If you owe Ben, he makes you kill somebody for him. Son, you'll get that call sooner or later."

I turned off the machine. Tears rolled down my face and dashed the tabletop.

Lee and I had a routine. We'd devise mock newspaper headlines and pop them at each other to make our points. Parker trusted me to connect the dots on that recording. Now I knew why Lee went to New York. It was on the radio and in the papers. *Here* were some headlines to pop:

SIEGEL TRIAL WITNESS GOES OUT WINDOW! THE CANARY CAN SING, BUT HE CAN'T FLY!

11

LOS ANGELES | SUNDAY, DECEMBER 7, 1941

3:39 a.m.

Snafu:

Wilshire and Barrington. Three-car pileup. Winches, tow trucks, traffic detoured.

A jeep plowed a road-hog Caddy. A '38 DeSoto sheared off the Caddy's rear end. Skid marks, broken glass, street flares. Six injured parties hauled to Saint John's.

They were *all* drunk. The soldier was blitzed off booze from Dave's Blue Room. The squares were still blotto from the Trojan-Bruin game. The soldier had hound blood. He shared ambulance space with a built blonde. She slipped him her phone number.

Parker stood in the intersection. Winches pried the vehicles loose. Tow drivers cinched chains and rolled the cars off.

Poof!—you're alone. *Poof!*—it's your own world at 3:40 a.m.

He doused the flares. He kicked glass down a storm drain. A Plymouth idled by. A redhead had the wheel. She was a Joan-from-Northwestern manqué.

He left Miss Lake at 1:00. She'd probably heard by now. She'd grasp the implied threat, for sure.

Carl Hull clued him in to the specific listening post. Carl had heard a '39 recording. Miss Lake's chums tattled. They jawed with her shitheel lover. Carl called the conversation a "significant wedge."

Cars skirted broken glass and whizzed by him. He sat on the Wilshire curb and lit a cigarette.

He prayed off an urge to drink. He was too charged to sleep. He could brood on his back porch and hit early Mass. Dudley Smith would be there. The Archbishop would suggest coffee and cake.

Parker shut his eyes. A car door slammed. A man coughed and spritzed tobacco juice—he knew that sound.

He opened his eyes. Jim Davis walked up. His coat flapped wide. The hump still wore two big revolvers.

"Don't tell me. You were listening to police-band calls, and you figured I'd be here."

Davis leaned on a light pole. "Got me a swell radio. The insomniac's best friend, as I'm sure you know."

Parker tossed his cigarette. "Insomniacs tend to find each other. The world narrows down at this time of night."

"Yeah. And the world narrowed down when you worked for me. I had a smart lawyer-cop as my adjutant when I pulled my most heinous stunts."

Parker stood up. Davis crowded in. He threw his gut out and walked two-guns-first.

"What's your net worth, Jim? The Mexican Staties were paying you a dollar a wetback to run their trucks through L.A. You let the Dudster sell dope to the coloreds, and it all had to add up."

Davis stepped back. "It's immaterial, son. We're set to fight this war for the Jew bankers, and I got me two big howitzers at my aircraft plant."

Parker laughed. "Maybe it won't come to that."

Davis spritzed juice. "The old Gypsy lady who reads my tea leaves says it sure as shit will."

Parker shook his head. "It's hard to dislike you, Jim. It shouldn't be, but it is."

Davis popped in a fresh plug. He came out of bumfuck Texas. He was a 1916 doughboy. He was Chinese-fluent. He mediated the last Hop Sing tong truce. He ran the Klan out of L.A. and welcomed the Silver Shirts.

"You were always looking over me, son. I'd have pulled a good many more heinous stunts if you hadn't been. I'll be there to tell the world that when they swear you in as Chief."

4:41 a.m.

Parker drove home. The house was dead still. Helen was sleeping. Three hours to 8:00 a.m. Mass.

He poured a triple bourbon and walked out to the back porch. It overlooked the Silver Lake Reservoir. House lights bordered the water. There's twelve lights, predawn.

He sipped bourbon. Please, God—just one.

He thought about Miss Lake. He thought about Joan from

Northwestern. He saw her in jodhpurs and boots once. She shot skeet off Lake Michigan.

Parker turned on the radio. The newscasts were shrill. He tuned in the police band. He caught a tavern stickup. He knew the detectives at the scene.

Police work—a closed circle. We all kneel at the same pew.

An ADW in Compton. A fleeing burglar in Watts. Spectators outside a house in Highland Park. Probable suicide. Sergeant D. L. Smith and Officer L. C. Blanchard at location.

Parker sipped bourbon. Closed circle—the Dudster, Miss Lake's shack job. Two-Gun Jim Davis at loose ends.

The bourbon felt wrong. The standard burn came on lukewarm. A Sheriff's call hit the air.

4600 Valley Boulevard. That county stretch upside Lincoln Heights. Hit-and-run, four down, no suspect-vehicle make. First broadcast: 5:47 a.m.

Parker dumped his glass. Roll on it. You won't drink if you go.

5:48 a.m.

He took his civilian car. The location: a curb stretch off a warehouse block. Big industrial hangars and nothing else.

Crash ropes. Three Sheriff's cars, one meat wagon, four crushed bicycles. Deputies grilling three bruised-up boys. An older man on a stretcher. An ambulance crew standing by.

Parker stopped behind the ropes. His headlights framed the collision point. The wreckage spelled out the incident.

Four bikes. They proceed single file. The older man takes the boys on a predawn jaunt. One adult-size bike at the rear. It's the most damaged. The three bikes in front are *crushed.* They are not rear-impact *smashed.*

No skid marks on the pavement. Pull-away tread smears. The boys were grazed more than hit. Their bikes showed left-to-right denting. The car grazed them on the left and sped away.

The curb was half dirt, half paving. The right-hand tires might have left marks. Plaster molds might reveal the make and model. The bikes were adorned with pennants for the Santa Monica Cycleers.

Parker got out and stood by the ropes. The boys were high school age. Their jabbers overlapped. They left SaMo High at 4:15.

Jim Larkin was their leader. He was English. He was some kind of spy in the Great War. They were riding out to Lake Arrowhead. They sure hoped Mr. Larkin was okay.

Larkin's legs were crushed. Larkin's collarbone was sheared. Larkin trembled from shock.

A deputy signaled the ambulance men. They picked up the stretcher and moved. An object fell from Larkin's pocket. The men tucked the stretcher in the ambulance and pulled out.

The ambulance hauled, Code 3. The boys waved good-bye. One boy started crying. Parker prayed the Rosary.

Dawn came up. Parker walked to the ropes and grabbed that object. It was a pearl-inlaid gun grip. Red stones offset a swastika. The grip was Luger-shaped.

Parker tossed it and drove back home. His errand succeeded. He worked off The Thirst.

He still tasted the bourbon. A stale burn had him parched. He raided the icebox and guzzled orange juice. He vowed to pray for Jim Larkin.

The bedroom door was open. He heard Helen snore. The telephone rang. He walked into the living room and caught it three rings in.

"Yes?"

Miss Lake said, "The threat wasn't necessary. I'll take whatever you have for me."

12

LOS ANGELES | SUNDAY, DECEMBER 7, 1941

6:49 a.m.

Lee Blanchard said, "The natives are restless."

Nort Layman said, "Do you blame them? Your neighbors are up and at 'em one day, going out under sheets the next."

Thad Brown said, "The sheet blew off of Nancy. They got a goddamn good look."

Blanchard said, "She was a dish."

Ray Pinker said, "Yeah, if you like raw fish."

The porch was packed: Blanchard, Brown, Layman, Pinker, Ashida.

Dudley watched bluesuits hold off the crowd. Gawkers filled the street. They eyeball-drilled the house and kicked up a fit.

The stiffs went out at sunup. Early birds caught the show. The hara-kiri rumor ran full speed now. He heard *JAPS* six thousand times. He watched Ashida take it stoically.

The gawkers gawked and jabbered. Men held their kids aloft. The house was rope-cordoned. Eight blues held the line taut. Jejune Jack Webb was out among the natives. He lugged a radio contraption and did interviews.

Some Japs killed themselves. Who gives a shit? No tickee, no washee. Where's Charlie Chan and Mr. Moto? It's Sunday morning—this sure beats church.

The house reeked of fried rice. Ace Kwan sent breakfast up. Dudley barely touched it. He flew on yesterday's Benzedrine.

The job was meddlesome. Jerome Joseph Pavlik could not have snuffed the Japs. He was down in a lime spill at the time of death. The bullet hole and silencer threads might not be a true lead. Pavlik might not be the heist man. The armband-fiber lead might not play. The book-rack fibers might not have been left by the heist man.

The heist man *probably* fired the shot at the house. There were no firearms on the premises. Nort Layman would paraffin-test the dead Japs. The bullet hole looked fresh. The silencer threads were off a fresh fire. Nort would know if the Japs had fired guns recently. Most telling—that note taped on the wall.

Dudley stood on the porch and prepped a logbook. It tallied check-ins and tasks performed. The case could blow wide and go long.

A Helms truck pulled up to the crowd. The gawkers swarmed it for coffee and crullers. A geek pointed to the porch and yelled, "Goddamn Jap!"

Ashida did not flinch. Staunch lad—ever calm.

Blanchard said, "We should be canvassing."

Dudley said, "Cause of death, lad. It's our first priority."

Brown nudged Dudley. They walked inside and huddled. The breakfast dregs were still out.

Brown said, "This job is nothing but shit. It's shit the Los Angeles Police Department and the city of Los Angeles don't want or need."

Dudley said, "Yes, I'll concede that."

That geek yelled, "Goddamn Jap!" It boomed through the house.

Brown said, "*And?*"

Dudley said, "Ideally, we should can it. We should mark it 'suicide, case closed,' and let those heathens rot in hell for their domestic sins."

Brown said, "What sins? They were working stiffs."

Dudley said, "The family strikes me as more original than that. If we proceed, I'll keep you abreast."

Brown snagged an egg roll. "And less than ideally?"

Dudley said, "I think a Japs-killed-Japs solution would make us look good, and allow us time to prepare for Christmas with our families."

The geek yelled, "Goddamn Jap!" Blanchard walked in and beelined to the chow.

Brown nodded. "Japs killed Japs. It's got a good ring."

Dudley snatched Blanchard's plate. "That lad shouting racial slurs may be offending Dr. Ashida. Please take him someplace secluded and kick the shit out of him."

13

LOS ANGELES | SUNDAY, DECEMBER 7, 1941

7:17 a.m.

Ashida crouched outside the window. He caught Dudley's order. Blanchard grabbed an egg roll and took off.

He went outside. He ducked under the cordon. Ashida quick-walked down the driveway and watched.

Blanchard pushed into the crowd. The fools read bad news and stepped back. Ashida watched. He magnetized harsh looks.

Blanchard slammed into the insult man. The man tripped and fell. Blanchard grabbed an arm and dragged him behind a prowl car.

The man flailed. The crowd dispersed. Ashida stood on his tiptoes and watched. Blanchard drop-kicked the man. Ashida heard bones crack.

Compound fractures. Dislocated sternum. Probable shock.

The man went green. Blanchard stepped on his head and muzzled possible shrieks. Ashida looked away. Ray Pinker saw him and tapped his wristwatch.

Ashida walked over. Another shitbird yelled, "Goddamn Jap!"

Pinker got in his car. Ashida got in. He checked the side mirror. He saw Blanchard wipe blood off his hands.

They pulled out. Patrol cops cleared a path. Ashida felt giddy.

Pinker said, "I should be in church. I told my wife I'd start going."

Ashida said, "Dudley killed the rapist."

Pinker nodded. "Who may not be the heist man. *And*, the gunshots, bullets and silencer threads at the two locations do not *conclusively* indict the heist man for the *possible* homicides."

Ashida nodded. "Yes, but it's a significant lead."

Pinker caught Figueroa southbound. Ashida said, "I think it's homicide."

"I lean that way."

"They're going to short-shrift it. Brown will kick it up to Chief Horrall, who'll—"

"—kick it up to that rummy McPherson and Mayor Bowron. I don't see this thing as any more than a one-day headache."

They hit downtown. They cut east and made Central Station. They lugged their evidence kits up to the lab. Pinker grabbed a work sheet.

He wrote "7:49 a.m., 12/7/41" on it. They guzzled hot-plate coffee and worked.

They studied silencer threads. They dye-dipped the threads from the stickup and the house and examined them under full-dialed lenses. The dye magnified metallurgic components. They concluded this:

The threads were *similar*—but not *identical*. Two different silencers were deployed at the two locations. One individual crafted both silencers. Said individual: talented but unschooled.

The tests consumed two and a half hours. Pinker wrote "10:16 a.m., 12/7/41" on the work sheet. The tests prompted questions.

Did said individual *make* both silencers *and* shoot the bullets at either or both locations? Did said individual *sell* one or both silencers? Did he sell them to the heist man and/or a member or known associate of the Watanabe family?

The work torqued Ashida. He was frayed. He crossed a line yesterday. He withheld drugstore evidence. He had no foreknowledge of the Watanabe job.

The job increased the risk of exposure. The job increased his chance to develop his own evidence. He was frayed-wire alert. He got called out at 1:00 a.m. He was nowhere near tired.

Next—the bullet chunks and bullet powder.

Dudley crumbled the chunks at the house. They could crumble the drugstore chunks and spray-dye the powder from both locations. They could look for consistencies or anomalies.

Pinker tore out a new work sheet. Ashida wrote "10:22 a.m., 12/7/41" on top. Pinker crumbled the drugstore chunks in a desk vise.

They spray-dyed both samples and blot-dried them. They placed powder smears under slides and affixed a microscope. They studied the fully magnified characteristics.

Two bullets. Similar metallurgic and powder-grain formations. A Luger was fired at both locations. Small inconsistencies indicated different ammo loads. The cracked bullet chunks at the house indicated faulty ammo.

Ashida wrote "10:39 a.m., 12/7/41" on the work sheet. Pinker futzed with the microscope.

Ashida said, "I'm going back in the house. Something's off. You don't wash clothes on the day you perform seppuku."

"Don't break any rules. Wait until Nort Layman gives us a disposition."

"The dead rapist bothers me. He's Dudley's cat's paw if it's ruled homicide, and they need a convenient suspect with evidential links to the crime. They can write him off as a *vanished* suspect and file on him posthumous."

Pinker smiled. "You're a quick study. You're learning the ways of this man's police department very fast."

Ashida smiled. "Both shots came from Lugers. Dudley found reichsmarks in the house."

"Lugers are from hunger. You know who buys them? Nazi creeps who frequent the goddamn Deutsches Haus."

Ashida prickled. *He'd* keyed on the Deutsches Haus.

Pinker unlocked the gun cabinet and grabbed a Luger. The gun was blue steel. The grips were white pearl. They were inlaid with black swastikas and rubies.

Ashida studied the barrel aperture. He already knew the lands and grooves statistics. He'd memorized his college ballistics texts.

Pinker toggled a bullet into the chamber and walked to the shooting tunnel. He stuck his arm in the chute and fired. Acoustical baffling muffled the sound of the shot.

"It's a froufrou piece. It's for collectors and retired intelligence guys who never saw action."

Ashida walked to the tunnel and dug in the catcher bin. He snagged two bullet chunks.

Pinker rolled his eyes. "Goddamn Lugers. They're not worth a shit."

14

KAY LAKE'S DIARY

LOS ANGELES | SUNDAY, DECEMBER 7, 1941

11:02 a.m.

Sunday brunch with Elmer and Brenda. Decorous, save for the talk.

Brenda owns a lovely home in Laurel Canyon. The furnishings can be seen in *Mr. Deeds Goes to Town*. Harry Cohn enjoys Brenda's girls and gave her free run of the Columbia warehouse.

A Mexican maid laid out huevos rancheros. Elmer mixed gin fizzes. Gary Cooper fucked Barbara Stanwyck on the couch I was perched on. Brenda swore that the rumor was true.

I felt disembodied. It was lack of sleep more than shock over what I'd heard at City Hall. Lee Blanchard, Ben Siegel and Abe

Reles. Captain William H. Parker's belief that I would now be ripe for entrapment. He held me to be a woman who would stand up for her man and do anything to cover his misdeeds. He was gravely mistaken there.

Elmer said, "Lee caught a squawk with the Dudster. It's all over the air. Four Japs in Highland Park."

Brenda dosed her eggs with hot sauce. "You go straight to shoptalk."

Elmer said, "A good host plays to his guests, honey. Shoptalk is the only sort of talk that Miss Katherine Lake enjoys."

I laughed and picked at my food. Brenda and Elmer were nearly ten years older than I. *They* were professionals; *I* was a cop's quasi-girlfriend. The disparity rankled. We all went back to Bobby De Witt and the Boulevard-Citizens job. Open secrets and unspoken truths began germinating there. I wanted to peddle myself to wash the stink of Bobby off of me; Brenda refused to let me do it. She said, "You live by these crazy-girl notions you get from books and movies. I wouldn't be much of a friend if I let you take that nonsense too far."

Elmer handed me a cocktail. I wondered how up-to-date he was on Lee and Ben Siegel. "Bugsy" is now ensconced in a "penthouse" suite at the Hall of Justice jail. Sheriff's deputies serve as valets, flunkies and chauffeurs for visiting starlets. Velvet curtains provide privacy for Ben and his overnight guests. His release is imminent. Abe Reles' "swan dive" scotched the prosecution's case against him.

Elmer smiled and waggled his cigar stub. We possess an odd telepathy and often seem to know what the other is thinking. It always pertains to "shoptalk."

He said, "Lee paid off his chit with Benny Siegel."

I said, "Yes, I figured it out."

Brenda crushed her cigarette on a bread plate. "Tell all, honey. Don't be a C.T."

I said, "No, your lover goes first."

Elmer sprawled in a chair and grabbed Brenda. She fell into his lap and went *Whoops!* He said, "Thad Brown drove Dudley Smith and Lee to Union Station. He read the papers a few days later and put it together."

Brenda said, "How'd *you* figure it out?"

I made that zip-the-lips gesture. Elmer said, "*Give,* sister." Brenda said, "Don't be a C.T."

I played coy. "There's a Traffic captain who knows a lot about Lee."

Elmer draped an arm around Brenda. "How do you know that?"

"Because Captain William H. Parker is courting me."

Brenda hooted. "Honey, that sanctimonious son of a bitch does not court women in any kind of classic sense."

I lit a cigarette. "You mean he doesn't take bribes, beat confessions out of suspects, or screw your girls in the back of Mike Lyman's Grill, where I'm meeting him at 1:00."

Brenda looked aghast. Elmer looked flabbergasted. He said, "Kay, how do you know that Whiskey Bill Parker knows a lot about Lee?"

I blew an imperiously high smoke ring. "Because Parker is courting and coercing me. Because he has me transcribing wire recordings at City Hall before he tells me his play. Because you, Brenda and Lee had a very injudicious conversation on August 14 of '39. You discussed your 'service,' the Boulevard-Citizens robbery and Lee's debt to Ben Siegel. Elmer, you actually said, 'If you owe Ben, he makes you kill somebody for him.' "

Elmer bolted his drink. Brenda waved mock wolfsbane.

I said, "Do you think that William H. Parker is incapable of extrapolating and reaching the conclusion that Lee and Dudley Smith killed Abe Reles? Do you think that William H. Parker doesn't know that half of the Detective Bureau phones are tapped? Do you honestly think that you're as smart as William H. Parker?"

Brenda fished a pack of cigarettes from Elmer's coat pocket. "I can't believe it. You honest to God *like* that son of a bitch."

I felt myself blush. Elmer said, "No more calls from City Hall."

Brenda lit a cigarette and blew her own high ring. "Gossip always comes in droves, Citizens. One of our girls picked up a tip from a G-man she tricked with. Some fellow named Ward Littell."

Elmer said, "Give, sister. Who's the C.T. now?"

Brenda said, "The Feds are going after the Department, strictly on the phone taps. Art Hohmann snitched the listening posts and the whole kaboodle."

I said, "I destroyed that recording I described to you."

Brenda said, "There's oodles more, Citizen. Can you recall what you said on any given phone call from two years ago? *Uh-uh*, you *can't*."

Elmer cracked his knuckles. "I'll tell Jack Horrall. He'll pull the wires with the good dirt, and leave the Feds the pablum."

I heard radio buzz next door. An announcer was almost shouting. The noise was high-decibeled and insistent.

Brenda climbed off Elmer's lap and smoothed out her dress. She said, "Sweetie, please set Sister Lake straight on Whiskey Bill."

Elmer leaned toward me. "Don't hold no goodwill for that Pope-loving bastard," he said. "He's as ruthless as Dudley Smith, he was bone-dirty with Jim Davis, he'll get the Chief's job come hell or high water and take the Department down out of spite if it don't fall his way. He uses people and tosses them away like fucking Kleenex. He's a hatchet man, an extortionist and a fucking prig who gets shit-faced drunk, talks to God and moves his lips while he does it. He ran the 'Bum Blockade' for Two-Gun, he shackled Okies in the back of freight cars and sent them off to the lettuce fields up in Kern County, where the goddamn farm bosses paid Davis a buck a man a day. He ran bag to the Mexican Staties back when Carlos Madrano and Davis were supplying wetbacks to every Jap farm between here and Oxnard. You run, sister. Whatever that man has planned for you ain't nothing you'd ever want for yourself."

Brenda said, "Amen." That radio blasted. I didn't want to address Elmer's pitch. I walked to the window and glanced out.

A man next door saw me. Our windows were wide open. His radio was earsplitting. He reached over and turned it off.

He said, "The Japs bombed Pearl Harbor."

11:34 a.m.

I ran outside. Elmer and Brenda blurred. Radios blared all around me. It was one enraged shout.

I got my car and pulled out, southbound. Traffic was light. I turned on my own radio. The news was all *WAR*.

It was a sneak attack. Japanese air squadrons bombed Hawaii early this morning. The Pearl Harbor naval base was brutally hit. The Pacific Fleet was decimated.

Massive casualties. Vital seacraft sunk. Hickam Field attacked.

Soldiers machine-gunned at Schofield Barracks. Honolulu under siege. Two-faced Jap envoys. Roosevelt's imminent declaration of war.

I turned east on Beverly. The newsstand at Fairfax was swamped. Newsboys ducked into traffic and yelled, "No papers yet!"

I knew I was running. I didn't know where I was going. I knew who I was running from. Elmer's indictment of William H. Parker echoed.

The news was spreading. I saw men affix flags to storefronts. I saw men on rooftops with binoculars and rifles. Police cars sped past me, Code 3. The street tableaux cohered. It told me where to go. I turned off the radio and floored the gas.

Prowl cars swerved across westbound lanes and tore eastbound. I approached downtown. Cops had a dozen Japanese boys spread prone outside Belmont High. They frisked them, kicked them and held shotguns to their heads.

I crossed the 1st Street bridge and pulled into a parking lot. An attendant yelled, "The Japs bombed Pearl Harbor!" I tossed my keys at him and *ran.*

City Hall was under siege. Prowl cars were up on the south-facing lawn. The doorways were flanked with cops armed with machine guns.

I ran. People clustered on the 1st Street curb and played their car radios. I turned north on Spring. Yes, already—men on the Federal Building steps.

The line extended down the sidewalk, a good twenty-deep. The men had mobilized within moments of the news. There were young men, older men and high school boys. One boy dribbled a basketball. I heard *JAPS* and *WAR* ten thousand times.

I got in line. I was the only woman. The men jabbered and smiled at me. I heard *GIRL* along with *WAR* and *THE JAPS.* An olive drab sedan pulled to the curb. A Marine Corps captain, an Army major and a Navy lieutenant got out. The men in line cheered them. They ran up the steps and stood by the ground-floor doorway.

The doors flew open. Three sailors carried out tables and chairs. They positioned them, facing the crowd. The captain and lieutenant sat down. A sailor flashed V for Victory. The major pulled a Japanese flag from his pocket and spit on it. The men in line cheered.

The major tossed the flag into the crowd. A boy grabbed it, spit on it and passed it back. The next boy spit on it and tore off a piece of the fabric. The cheers became a continuous roar. The flag traveled back down the line, shredded and drenched in spittle.

The flag came to me. I spit on it, threw it down and ground it under my feet. The cheers escalated to roars.

Two tall young men picked me up and held me at full arm's length. I floated above the crowd, in my very own swirl. The whole world dipped into me. I yelled, "*AMERICA!*" as loud as I could.

The roar went louder and louder. Motorists whistled and waved. Every man in line looked up and saluted me as I swirled.

The tall young men lowered me; I kissed them as my feet touched the ground. The line pressed toward the recruiting stand. It extended down to 1st Street now. Men impulsively leaped from passing cars, ran up and got in line.

The line inched toward the steps; we were pressed tightly together; we moved as one body, connected. Time went haywire. We lit cigarettes. Flasks went around. Conversations overlapped. I got more and more details. The death toll was mounting. Big battleships went down. *We've got to nip this shit in the bud.*

The line moved. Motorists honked their horns and cheered us. I studied the Marine captain's uniform. The deep green against khaki was a knockout. *Semper Fi.* Screw Captain William H. Parker and his shrouded agenda. I decided to join the United States Marine Corps.

The men in front of me were given forms and told to return for further processing. I was hoarse from cheering and too many cigarettes. The Army major motioned me over. He seemed to be amused. He said, "Sorry, sweetheart. We aren't taking girls yet."

I said, "I'm willing to go now." The major looked at the other officers. They all seemed amused.

The Navy man said, "We didn't make the rules, sister."

The Marine said, "The canteens'll need volunteers. You dance with the boys and send them off happy."

I said, "Give me one of those forms. I'll come back tomorrow. The rules will change between now and then."

Boos and catcalls broke out behind me. The Navy man went *Shush now.* I started to say something. A wadded-up ball of paper hit the back of my head.

A man yelled, "Stow it, lady!" A man yelled, "You had your solo! Give us a chance!"

I turned around. Another paper bomb hit me. A chorus of raspberries blew.

The major thumbed a stack of carbon sheets with photo strips attached. He hit a sheet and went *Aha*. He held it up. I saw myself in a snapshot.

"There's a subversive hold on you, Miss Lake. Some kind of meetings you went to."

Men jostled me off the steps and jeered me. I stared at them and started to walk back toward the sidewalk. A paper ball bounced off my skirt. Men put their thumbs on their noses and made pig sounds. I stopped and stared harder. It made them laugh. Two men spit on me. I balled my fists and went toward them. Then I *sensed* something.

I wiped spit off my blouse. That Something stepped in front of me.

It was a boy-man. He was about six foot six and seemed too big for his clothes. He wore a brown wool suit, a white shirt and a tartan bow tie.

The spitting men looked at him. He grabbed their heads, smashed them and brought a knee up. I heard bones break and saw blood burst like they only had one face.

The spitting men screamed. The enlistment lines dispersed. The recruiters stood up and plain *stared*.

Then the boy-man took my elbow and steered me. Then we were down on the sidewalk and around the corner. Then we were sitting in the Hall of Justice cafeteria.

Where a waitress ran up and said, "The Japs bombed Pearl Harbor!"

Where the boy-man grinned and said, "No shit?"

The waitress huffed and walked off. I said, "My name is Kay Lake." The boy-man said, "Scotty Bennett."

I poured two cups of serve-ur-self coffee. My hands shook. I said, "To victory."

We clinked cups. A radio was bolted to the wall above our table. The broadcast was all *Japs!* Scotty Bennett doused the volume.

"Some day, huh? We'll be telling our kids about it."

I laughed. "'Our' kids, or kids in general?"

He laughed. "It's one of those days where you can't rule anything out."

It was warm. I untied my scarf and unbuttoned my sweater. My body settled back in. I studied the boy-man.

He was one or two years younger than I. He had curly light brown hair and the world's greatest kid smile. No one ever called his bluff. His simple presence was that stunning.

"What do you do, Mr. Bennett?"

"I was about to join the Marines when I met you."

"I was doing the same thing."

"What happened?"

"They aren't signing up women yet. And I went to some socialist meetings a few years ago, which didn't do me any good."

Scotty Bennett smiled. "They should let you in anyway. We can't win this war unless we let bygones be bygones."

I lit a cigarette. "What were you doing before you decided to enlist?"

"I applied to the L.A. Police Department three months ago, but they found out I was shy of twenty-one. What do you—"

"My boyfriend's in the Department. Do you follow boxing? His name is Lee Blanchard."

Deft boy—he put his hands up and mimicked "The Southland's Great White Hope."

"You've seen Lee fight?"

"He kicked the you know what out of that Mex with the harelip. I was four rows back from ringside."

I blew a smoke ring. Quick boy—he reached up and pulled the wisps out of the air.

"Will you stand with me while I talk to the recruiter?"

"Yes. Do you promise not to rescue any more women?"

Scotty Bennett crossed his heart. Rough boy—don't think I can't see you.

"Bucky Bleichert's fighting at the Olympic tonight. Would you like to go?"

"Yes. I certainly would."

"Lee sleeps at City Hall most nights."

Mean boy—he mimicked my pseudo lover catching a right hand.

"My dad came over from Scotland in 1908. He's a minister, and he always says 'God moves in mysterious ways.' I think I just figured out what he means."

I touched his hand. Our knees brushed under the table.

15

LOS ANGELES | SUNDAY, DECEMBER 7, 1941

2:09 p.m.

She was late.

One hour and nine minutes.

She fucking stood him up.

The back room was all his. The back room was the PD's private playpen. Mike Lyman's Grill was open twenty-four hours. Ditto the back room.

Mike Lyman loved cops. Here's why. Buzz Meeks iced a cholo who flashed his *schvantz* at Mike's wife. Grateful Mike anointed the back room.

Spicy wall prints, a full bar, a police Teletype. A private phone line and a foldout bed for woo-woo. Brenda Allen's girls had carte blanche. The back room was open-all-nite. It serviced a ranking-cop clientele.

Parker nursed his fourth double bourbon. He'd been holed up since 8:00 a.m. Mass. The goddamn phone kept ringing. He kept ignoring it. The Lake girl knew he was here. Nobody else did.

Mass was problematic. Archbishop Cantwell had a hangover and suggested a hair of the dog. He acceded. One drink became four. Cantwell harped on Dudley Smith. The fucking Irish stuck together. Dudley missed Mass. Cantwell was fucking stood up.

Dud's got four dead Japs, Your Eminence. It's probably hara-kiri. *Well, William—they'll sure as shit rot in hell.*

He boozed with His Eminence and went to confession. He found a box and waited. He recognized Monsignor Hayes' voice.

His confession ran erratic. He confessed his scurrilous acts on the PD. He confessed his crush on Joan from Northwestern.

Te absolvo ergo sum. Monsignor Hayes was brusque. He was an isolationist mick, like Dudley and Cantwell. Father Coughlin's Sunday broadcast loomed.

Parker nursed his drink. He was half in the bag. The Lake girl was one hour and *twelve* minutes late. The fucking phone kept ringing.

Again and again. Here it comes again. Eight rings, ten, twelve—

Parker grabbed the receiver. Fuzz hit the line. Call-Me-Jack came on.

"Are you there, Bill? I didn't know where else to call."

"I'm here, Chief."

"Good. Now get over *here*."

"Why?"

"Haven't you heard?"

"Heard *what*, Chief?"

"The goddamn Japs bombed Pearl Harbor."

He dropped the phone and ran. He felt the booze evaporate. He ran out the door. He ran up 8th to Broadway and cut north. He caught it all at a sprint.

The radios blaring from storefronts. The people huddled outside a hat shop with their ears cupped.

Squelch, fuzz, static, crackle, hiss.

Hawaii, sneak attack, Pacific Fleet sunk.

Thousands dead, Pearl Harbor, Pearl Harbor.

Vile, atrocious, cowardly. Fifth Column–instigated.

Japs, Japs, Japs, Japs, Japs.

Parker ran up Broadway. His suit coat flapped. He held his hat firm on his head. *Herald* trucks passed him. Newsboys folded quickie editions in the back. He hit 6th, 5th, 4th, 3rd, 2nd. He looked east. There's Little Tokyo. There's Sheriff's bulls in riot gear, swarming the sidewalk.

Up to 1st Street. A lawn hubbub at City Hall. Cops and MPs with riot guns. Black-and-whites and jeeps, parked snout-to-snout. Strafe lights aimed at the sky.

Parker held his badge up. He stumbled on a light cord and ran toward the doors. An MP saluted and stepped aside.

The foyer was all cops and war-jazzed reporters. He walked to a freight lift and pushed 6. The doors closed. He got some breath. The sweat purge sobered him up.

The lift hit the sixth floor. He straightened his necktie and buttoned his coat. He hit the Chief's office, squared-up.

A secretary juggled phones. Her switchboard was full-lit and full-plugged. Parker went through a side door and caught a full house.

Jack Horrall, Sheriff Biscailuz, Mayor Fletch Bowron. DA Bill McPherson—passed out, narcoleptic-style.

Call-Me-Jack was at his desk. Parker pulled a chair up. A Teletype clattered. Jack reached back and pulled out a sheet.

"This is from the Army's Fourth Interceptor Command. There's a fifteen-mile coastline blackout, from San Pedro, Terminal Island and Fort MacArthur north to the southwest edge of city police jurisdiction. Jap fighters could hit us at any minute, and we can't give them lit-up coastal targets to bomb. That's a full-nighttime blackout, in effect until further notice. The only L.A. Police Department divisions affected will be San Pedro and Venice, because they're on the water. We'll have two formal citywide test blackouts tomorrow, 5:00 to 7:00 a.m. and 5:00 to 7:00 p.m. All L.A. residents are required to draw their shades at home and drive with their parking lights only. The Fort MacArthur and Terminal Island gun placements are now operational, and the whole coastline down there is covered by aircraft spotters."

Fletch B. went *Whew!* McPherson stirred and snored. Biscailuz tossed a chair cushion at him.

The room spun. Parker popped a cough drop. Call-Me-Jack said, "We've got the Feds due in a minute. There's some Jap subversives we've got to round up."

Biscailuz said, "I dispatched some boys to Little Tokyo. They're standing ready. We all knew the war was coming, but I didn't see an attack on *us*."

Bowron said, "Cocksuckers. They'll rue the fucking day, believe me."

Biscailuz said, "Yellow bastards. I was hoping for a white man's war. Us versus the Krauts, on foreign soil. This is turning into a shit deal at the start."

Bowron said, "Gene's right. The Krauts are off the deep end with the Jews, but it's not like—"

Jack cut in. "Not like you can blame them?"

Biscailuz laughed. Bowron *roared.* Parker sucked his cough drop. *WAR*—the Krauts, the *Japs.*

The Teletype spit paper. Jack's phone rang. Jack hit the squelch knob and pointed to Parker.

"I'm starting up an Alien Squad. I want my Department in on this shit with the Japs from the ground floor. I'll put together some hard boys to work with Gene's deputies and the Feds. Bill Parker will serve as liaison, and the Department's monitor for any and all blackout-related operations. We're going to be running you ragged, Bill—but I know you can take it."

Parker said, "I'm in, Chief. It's an honor, and I'll carve out the time for the work."

Bowron laughed. "It's ink on your résumé, Bill. It'll look good when you go for Jack's job."

Jack laughed. "Don't talk about me when I'm still in the room."

Biscailuz laughed. "Bill won't mind the work. It means more time to hide out from his wife."

Jack said, "Let's wrap this up. My Moose Lodge has a block of tickets for the Rose Bowl, so we've got to put the quietus to the Japs by New Year's."

Bowron and Biscailuz yocked. Parker sucked another cough drop. Three men walked in. Parker recognized them.

Feds. The L.A. boss, Dick Hood. Special Agent Ed Satterlee. Ward J. Littell, the bleeding-heart Fed.

Introductions circulated. Handshakes and backslaps, ditto. Jack laid out folding chairs. The Feds straddled them. Jack opened a humidor and lobbed cigars.

Bowron arranged standing ashtrays. The gang lit up. The room smoked up, quick.

Hood said, "Let's discuss the roundups. Outside of Tokyo, this is the Jap capital of the known world."

Littell said, "Let's clear the legalities first, Mr. Hood. The three agents in this room are lawyers, as is Captain Parker."

Hood brushed ash off his vest. "Make your point, Ward."

"It's the criteria for identifying enemy aliens, beyond their racial distinction. Roosevelt's going to declare war on Japan tomorrow, and Germany and Italy sometime next week. The Japanese are easily identifiable, Germans and Italians much less so. We don't want to needlessly harass innocent Japanese, and we need to recognize the fact that German- and Italian-born and -derived aliens are potentially more dangerous, due to their enhanced level of anonymity."

Parker smiled. Ward's sidebar was legally and morally astute. The room froze up.

Jack said, "I can't tell the Japs from the Chinks, which invalidates Mr. Littell's concerns."

Biscailuz said, "I can't, either."

Bowron said, "Ask Uncle Ace Kwan. He'll set you straight on that."

Jack said, "Ace is sending dinner over at 5:00. We'll run these sensitive racial matters by the delivery boy."

Satterlee shook his head. "You astound me, Ward. How did someone with your sensibilities get on the FBI?"

Littell blew smoke at Satterlee. Bowron and Biscailuz chortled. Hood said, "The only criteria for the detention of alien Fifth Columnists is the established fact that the fucking Japs bombed a U.S. territory early this morning and killed at least two thousand Americans, and the fucking Germans and Italians did not. And, as I stated a moment ago, L.A. is chock-fucking-full of fucking Japs, so let's cut the fucking shit and discuss the best means to kibosh potential sabotage."

Call-Me-Jack said, "Hear, hear."

Bowron said, "Crudely put, but pithy."

Biscailuz said, "Special Agent in Charge Dick Hood does not mince words."

Satterlee popped his briefcase and removed a pile of folders. Hood grabbed them and passed them around.

"Sixteen pages of Jap names, gentlemen. When it became apparent that we might go to war with Japan, we compiled a list of known and suspected Fifth Columnists for possible detention. These Japs are known fascists, members of suspect fraternal organizations and general Emperor-worshiping bad apples. You'll see that the list is divided into A's, B's and C's. The A's are the Japs considered the most dangerous, and they've been earmarked for immediate detention."

The room was one big smoke cloud. Call-Me-Jack cracked a window. Street noise drifted up. Parker heard *Japs, Japs, Japs.*

He skimmed the file. The A list ran eight pages. There, on page four: "Watanabe, Ryoshi and family/produce farmer/Highland Park."

Hood crushed out his cigar. "Secretary of War Stimson has issued a top-priority bulletin. It mandates the seizure of property belonging to the A-list subversives. The commander at Fort MacArthur has allotted cell blocks at the Terminal Island pen for detention housing. You've got shitloads of Jap fishing boats moored down in Pedro, and the Army's gearing up to tow them in for inspection."

Littell and Satterlee swapped glares. The Teletype kicked out a typed page and wanted-poster set. Call-Me-Jack scanned them.

"Here's one for you, Bill. Apparently, the Federal Building is swamped with men trying to enlist. The state AG sees it as a godsend to fugitive felons looking to flee the country, so he sent some priority wanted listings along. Go over and check faces, will you? I'll have some bluesuits meet you downstairs. If you see any of the poster guys, send the blues in for the rough stuff."

Parker nodded and held up his A list. He pointed to the name Ryoshi Watanabe. He eye-drilled Call-Me-Jack.

"Last night, Chief. The dead Japs in Highland Park. I caught a broadcast. It's Dudley Smith's job, and it's homicide or suicide."

Call-Me-Jack shrugged. "It looks like suicide. I got that straight from the Dudster. Nort Layman's performing the autopsies right now. We'll know more fairly soon."

Parker said, "A Jap homicide case wouldn't hurt us. Mr. Littell might have something. Say we take some guff for the roundups. We're at war, but we still give these dead Japs a full play."

Call-Me-Jack shut his eyes. Parker read his brain waves.

He's weighing pros and cons. He's overbooked. I want his job. Dudley and I tend to clash. He probably wants a leash on Dud. He's more afraid of him than of me.

Call-Me-Jack opened his eyes. "You oversee the job, Bill. I know you're busy and you're not really a case man, but—"

Parker said, "I'll do it."

The City Hall clock hit 3:00. Bowron said, "Two hours to dinner."

Hood said, "I wouldn't mind a drink. And it wouldn't surprise me if Chief Horrall had a bottle."

Call-Me-Jack smiled. "I do, if you call me Jack."

Biscailuz said, "Jesus, the fucking Japs."

3:01 p.m.

The freight lift took him down. Eight blues met him in the foyer. They wore tin hats and packed tear-gas bombs. They were geared for Jap insurrection.

Parker felt stupid. *He* wore his church suit and a snubnose .38. They cut across the south lawn. Jeeps and half-tracks chewed up the grass.

Fool's errand. Ten faces on ten posters. Felony punks—rape, ADW, mayhem. One pachuco and nine white-trash sons of bitches. Fools' odds—these fucks would never try to enlist.

They turned north on Spring Street. The Fed Building was straight up. Parker blinked. A roar hit him.

The enlistment line went down the steps and the sidewalk to the corner. It ran two thousand men. They were singing. "God Bless America" rang.

Parker ran toward it. He dropped the posters. His eyes welled. His glasses slid down his face. The blues ran behind him. Their riot gear slowed them down. They couldn't keep up.

Parker ran. The voices drew him in. They echoed louder and louder. He got up to the steps. He forgot what he was here for. The riot cops caught up and just stood there.

Discordant voices hit him. Parker looked around and saw a commotion. A big white kid beat on three white kids pounding a little Jap. A white woman kicked a white kid sprawled on the steps.

The Jap ran off. The big white kid threw fists and elbows. Parker stood and stared. The two-thousand-voice hymn went dissonant. The white woman turned his way.

It was Kay Lake.

She saw him.

She struck a pose, with chaos all around her.

Parker ran up the steps.

Kay Lake waved and disappeared.

16

LOS ANGELES | SUNDAY, DECEMBER 7, 1941

3:16 p.m.

Four Japs on morgue slabs. Caustic fumes. A big stink in a small room.

Dudley stood with Lee Blanchard and Nort Layman. They smoked to stifle the stink. The morgue adjoined Chinatown. The Chinks kicked up a ruckus outside.

They banged drums. They tossed firecrackers. They *celebrated* the attack. The Chinks hated the Japs, and vice versa. Chinatown would swing and sway tonight.

Blanchard said, "Fucking Japs."

Layman said, "Fucking Chinks. I've got a headache from those fucking drums."

Dudley yawned. He was tired. He'd been up since yesterday morning. He killed a man. He smoked opium and took Benzedrine. He wrote Beth Short a fatherly letter. He honed his plan to meet Bette Davis. He caught this fucking Jap job. The fucking Japs bombed America into a Jew-devised war.

Blanchard blew smoke on Ryoshi Watanabe. "Hey, pops. Fuck your emperor and fuck you."

Dudley laughed. Layman slapped his knees. Firecrackers popped outside.

Blanchard blew smoke on Nancy Watanabe. "Give me some pussy, baby."

Layman said, "You're a troubled man, Leland."

Blanchard said, "I like it when they don't move."

A cherry bomb exploded. The window glass shook. Dudley reached for his gun.

"Sadly, this comic sojourn must conclude. Norton, please report your findings."

Layman said, "Pending toxicology and whatever advanced tests I can dream up, I'd call it homicide or homicide-suicide, and I think the former's more likely. All the blood was intermingled, so individual typings were difficult. I got random chunks of A negative, and the kids would have inherited either mama or papa's blood type, so that muddles things. The wound flaps were shredded, which indicates blade wiggle and a natural hesitation and/or coercion at the moment of the piercings. The paraffin checks on their hands came out negative, so we can't attribute that bullet hole on the second-floor landing to them, at least not in the past forty-eight hours. So far, I'd say this. I've handled four Jap sword suicides, and this doesn't fit my empirical bill. And here's the strangest goddamn thing. I found an oily residue on their feet and tested it. It was shrimp oil."

Blanchard tossed his cigarette. It hit a blood spill and fizzled.

"If it's murder, we lost time on the house-to-house, and now everybody's got a bug up their ass about the bombings, so they won't recall if they saw anything right before the snuffs occurred."

Layman said, "You're right on that. Big events induce a collective loss of memory. More important, who cares? I want to work this job for the pure science of it, but does anybody give a shit about four dead Japs on the day we went to war with Japan?"

The suicide note. The "looming apocalypse." It was grandly evocative. Was it portentous?

Dudley kicked it around. Blanchard was right. A house-to-house would prove futile. Jack Webb was out with the locals. His silly radio chats were their "house-to-house." That angle was *pure* futile.

The wall phone rang. A blue light blinked—police call.

Dudley grabbed the receiver. "Sergeant Smith."

"It's Jack Horrall, Dud."

"Yes, Chief."

"What a day, huh?"

"Surely one to remember, sir."

"I hope you don't have plans to enlist."

Dudley said, "I do, sir. I see a grand career for myself in Army intelligence, and I have an influential friend who could secure me a commission."

"Joe Kennedy?"

"Yes, sir."

Call-Me-Jack whistled. It squelched the connection.

"For now, no dice. That's final, until this war heats up or settles down, and we figure out where the Los Angeles Police Department stands in all of this."

"Yes, sir. And on that note?"

"On that note, what's Nort's take on the Watanabe job so far?"

Cherry bombs blew up outside. Dudley cupped his free ear.

"He leans toward homicide, sir."

"Well, then we'll try to make a silk purse from a sow's ear, to show how impartial we are. I've talked to Mayor Bowron. He's afraid of a backlash if our boys start taking grief for rounding up all these so-called loyal Japs. Are you reading me, muchacho?"

"I am, sir. The implications are quite clear."

"Good. It's a 100% Jap world we're living in now, and I want to make hay out of it while the sun shines."

"The *rising* sun, sir?"

Call-Me-Jack yukked. "That's rich, Dud. I've got some boys here in my office. I'll pass it along."

Flies buzz-bombed the stiffs. Nort aerosol-sprayed them. They dropped dead on Aya Watanabe.

"Please do, sir."

Call-Me-Jack said, "Don't get your dander up, but I've assigned Bill Parker to supervise the investigation. He's a savvy political beast, and I want him to ride a gentle herd on you and your boys."

Dudley lit a cigarette. "Whiskey Bill is bereft of gentleness, sir. He's an administrative drone, he's not a detective, his sole aim is to oust you and become Chief, and his considerable savvy is entirely in the service of personal advancement."

Call-Me-Jack belched. "Parker stays. And don't worry—he won't crowd you. I've got him working the blackouts, the roundups and a liaison job to the Army. He'll be too goddamn *tired* to crowd you."

Dudley said, "Yes, sir. I'm sure that Captain Parker and I will form a nonaggression pact."

Call-Me-Jack said, "Hear, hear."

"May I suggest a fourth man, to supplant Dick Carlisle and Mike Breuning? My choice would be Lee Blanchard. He's been with me since I caught the squawk."

Jack said, "Nix. He's a patrol boy, and I'm forming an Alien Squad to help the Feds out with the rousts. That job's got Blanchard's name written all over it."

Festive music reverberated. Chinks shouted gobbledygook. Dudley looked out the window. Paper dragons whooshed by.

"Yes, sir. I still request—"

"I'll give you Buzz Meeks. He's good muscle when push comes to shove."

Background noise fuzzed the line. The connection sputtered and died.

Blanchard said, "How come the Chinks have this beef with the Japs? They all look alike to me."

3:36 p.m.

The natives were restless.

Dudley blew out of the morgue. He was Chinatown's sole white man. He strolled and enjoyed the show.

Fireworks, dragons, heathen babble. Tong boys with kettledrums. The Hop Sing lads wore red kerchiefs. The Four Families boys wore blue. They beat time like that grasshopper Gene Krupa.

Tojo dummies dangled from streetlights. Tong punks swung hatchets at them. Pillow stuffing swirled.

Dudley walked into the Pagoda. A radio blared *WAR!* Busboys laid down Jap flags as floor mats. City councilmen cheered.

Thad Brown slurped wonton soup. He saw Dudley and waved. Dudley winked and walked down to the basement.

Uncle Ace had redecorated his office. New pix had been framed and hung. FDR adjoined that white actor who played Charlie Chan.

"It is a great day, Dudster. The Chinese man and the U.S. Caucasian will align to slay the Jap beast."

Dudley bowed. "Yes, but we must not lose perspective on our German *Kameraden.* They remain our first line of defense against the Reds and the Jews."

Ace bowed. "My Irish brother seems weary. Might I suggest an invigorating tea?"

Dudley smiled and pulled a chair up. Ace laid out a kettle, powders and cups. *Aaaaaah, so*—Benzedrine and Ma Huang.

The scent invigorated. Ace poured two cups. Dudley sipped and cut through some cobwebs.

Ace said, "I have been thinking."

"Yes, my yellow brother?"

"The folly of the attack on Pearl Harbor presents us with opportunities to exploit the Jap beast. We can hide fugitive Fifth Columnists here in Chinatown and charge them exorbitant rates. We can exploit the white man's native bias toward the yellow man and profit from his inability to discern the differentiating aspects of Oriental physiognomy. White men cannot tell us apart. I see money in that shortcoming."

Dudley sipped tea. "You are quite astute and farsighted on this fateful day. And I would venture that you have a favor to ask."

Ace sipped tea. "That Four Families boy was rude to my niece again. I would hope that my reprisal would not engender a war."

The cobwebs dissolved. His circuitry reconnected.

"I'll kill the boy. We'll broker a truce then. Jim Davis will translate for me."

Ace pointed to a mismatched wall panel. It looked freshly varnished. A Chink flag hung askew.

"I want to show you something. I have new ideas to go along with some work I had done. Please, follow me."

Dudley stood up. Ace opened the panel. A dark hole dropped way underground.

A stairway, wall rails, overhead lights. Ace bowed and went *After you.*

The drop went thirty feet. The stairway featured red carpet. The steps hit a *loooooong* corridor. Hanging bulbs swayed and lit a path.

A generator hummed. The labyrinth was heated and air-cooled. Rooms lined both sides of the corridor. They were prelit. They had that grand model-home look.

Rooms with easy chairs and couches. Rooms with full kitchens attached. Rooms with card tables and wet bars. Rooms furnished with beds and whorehouse peeks.

Secret wall compartments. Hidden camera stations. Movie cameras pointed at two-way mirrors.

Thirty rooms. Wartime chic. The slant-eyed Statler Hilton. A gambling mecca and smut-film set. Chop suey always piping hot. A handy opium den.

Ace bowed to Dudley. Dudley bowed to Ace. The tea hit the back of his head.

Ace said, "I just completed the construction. I had originally planned it as a stag resort. Now, I see it as a luxurious hideout for Jap beasts in flight from prison. I had a fan-tan game here last night. It was profitable. We are at war now, which means that rich folks will need entertainment. Do you see socialites and movie stars coming here to mingle with Jap beasts and other riffraff?"

Dudley laughed. "Yes, my yellow brother, I do."

"Your friend Harry Cohn dropped nineteen G's here. If he lost that much to me, how much do you think he has lost to your friend Mr. Siegel?"

Dudley winked. "Indeed. What exploitable losses?"

Ace started babbling. High-test tea always sent him cross-eyed. He lapsed into pidgin English. He sputtered like Donald Duck.

Aaaaaaaah, yes—the Japs.

Jap roundups, Japs in chains, Japs consigned to luxury cells. Dead Japs at the morgue. Hideo Ashida—that stunningly bright Jap.

17

LOS ANGELES | SUNDAY, DECEMBER 7, 1941

4:11 p.m.

Ashida pulled up to the house. Ray Pinker rode shotgun. The sidewalk was rope-cordoned. Patrol cops held gawkers back.

A tomato hit the windshield. Ashida hit the wipers and thinned out the pulp. Somebody yelled, "Kill the Japs!"

A tomato hit the roof. Ashida and Pinker grabbed their evidence kits and ducked under the rope. The porch was tomato juice. Goldbrick cops and their mascot lounged. Mike Breuning, Dick Carlisle, Buzz Meeks, Jack Webb.

Taking some air. Ensconced with a fifth of Old Crow.

They shook hands with Pinker. Breuning and Carlisle shined Ashida on. Meeks winked at him. Jack said, "What's shaking, Hideo? Your so-called people sure put you in the shit."

Ashida put Jack in a headlock. Jack laughed and swatted him off. Meeks pointed out to the street. Oh, yeah—*the shit.*

The mob was all local yokels. Fools lugged tomato crates, fools burned Japanese flags. Sailors and Waves jitterbugged. A phonograph blared Count Basie.

A tomato hit the mailbox. Meeks said, "I'm getting ticked off."

Breuning said, "You can't blame them."

Jack said, "Sure you can. What did the Watanabes ever do except die? What did Hideo ever do except work for this white man's police force?"

Carlisle said, "You're not a policeman, kid. Don't get your signals crossed on that one."

Breuning said, "Leave the kid alone. The Dudster likes him, and he's only half Yid."

Jack flinched. A tomato hit the porch rail. Pulp spritzed Meeks' coat. Carlisle said, "Look alive. You don't get a show like this every day."

Meeks charged.

He ran straight at the mob. He tore down cordon ropes. The blues stood back and supplied room. He hit a knot of sailors, low.

He pulled his belt sap and arced backhands. He came in low and stayed low. He went for their *faces.* He hit noses, he hit mouths, he hit skulls. The sailors froze. Their gawker comrades stood and watched.

Ashida watched. Meeks was a legendary sap man. His sap featured raised stitching and leather-laced lead.

Meeks dug in low. Meeks grabbed necks and pulled faces close.

Ashida watched. The gawkers shrieked and turned tail. The beat-on sailors covered their faces and stumble-crawled away. One man held a handful of teeth. One man puked blood.

The fools cringed off. Meeks picked up an ice-cream bar wrapper and wiped off his sap. That phonograph was still out there. Erskine Hawkins' band brayed "Uproar Shout."

The needle spun off the record. Ashida caught his breath. Jack passed out cigarettes.

The jug went around. Meeks walked up to the porch. He grabbed the jug, drained it and tossed it. Breuning started to gush. Meeks shoved him flat on his ass.

Ashida walked into the house. He still smelled decomposition. Pinker walked in. They signed the logbook and opened their evidence kits.

The living room carpet was rolled up and cinched. The dining room table was covered with Kwan's takeout.

There was more here. There had to be.

Pinker went *Whew.* "How are you holding up? The Webb kid's right. It's not like you did anything."

Ashida said, "I'm worried about my mother. She's right there at 2nd and San Pedro, with the FBI and Sheriff's coming in. My brother's out at the farm in the Valley. I think he'll be all right for now."

Pinker tapped his arm. "I forgot to tell you, but Bill Parker called me. He's supervising the case for Call-Me-Jack, and he said he wants you on it. Here's the surprising part. He's posted a guard with your mother, a Fed named Littell. Parker said the guy's got no beef with Japanese folks. He hit it off with your mother, and they started playing pinochle right off the bat."

Ashida smiled. "Whiskey Bill."

Pinker smiled. "He's not my cup of tea, but he looks out for the guys who get him results."

"On that note, then."

"Yeah, on that note."

They got out their cameras and flashbulbs. They split up and covered the downstairs. Ashida shot nine rolls of film. He got the kitchen and service porch. He shot the clothesline and hanging garments. *Why wash clothes on the day that you plan suicide?*

Pinker shot the living room and downstairs hallway. Ashida bagged fibers. They got out their print gear and the print cards for the Watanabes. They dusted touch-and-grab planes.

Shitwork. Furniture backing, windowsills, ledges. Smears and smudges. No evidential-quality fragments or full prints.

Ashida felt woozy. He'd been up since the Creation. He withheld drugstore evidence. He saw Bucky and caught this job. His country and ancestral homeland just went to war. His whole world just went blooey.

Jack Horrall quick-rigged an "Alien Squad." He saw the first muster back at Central Station. "Alien Squad" meant "Goon Squad." It was all hard boys.

Strikebreakers, America Firsters, ex-Klansmen. Lee Blanchard and Elmer Jackson were the sweethearts. Call-Me-Jack was working the get-the-Japs gestalt.

The Munson Report was stale news now. It saturated the Japanese papers last month. FDR sent Curtis Munson out to the coast. He visited Japanese enclaves and described what he saw. He called the Nisei "pathetically loyal Americans." The Japan-born Issei:

"Devotedly pro-American, given that they had fled Japan." The Japan-educated Kibei: "Horrified by the onslaught of fascism in their native land."

Ashida print-brushed. Ashida got two full prints. He compared them to the cards and logged them for Aya Watanabe. He dusted a living room window ledge. He got a full print and scanned the cards. He got no matching loops and whorls.

He called it out. "Mr. Pinker, I've got one."

Pinker walked over and eyeballed the ledge. It was an adult-male right-index print. It required a full lift.

"Dudley and Lee Blanchard used handkerchiefs in the house, but I'm not sure about Breuning, Carlisle, Meeks and your pal Jack."

"We should elimination-print them. We'll spare ourselves confusion later on."

Pinker nodded and lugged his kit outside. Ashida walked over and dawdled by the door. Pinker laid print cards flat on a porch rail and inked up the boys.

Avenue 45 was quiet now. The porch reeked of tomato residue.

Pinker rolled Carlisle's prints. Breuning said, "We got fucking Bill Parker riding herd on us now. He's a Bolshevik. Elmer Jackson called me a few hours ago. Parker's got some woman transcribing the Dictograph wires at the Bureau."

Meeks passed Carlisle a Kleenex. Carlisle wiped his hands. Meeks said, "Elmer will lay it all out to Jack Horrall."

Breuning said, "He has, but you know Jack. He'll figure he can ride out whatever Parker's got planned."

Pinker rolled Breuning's prints. Carlisle said, "Parker should watch it. He's on the wires himself. Dud told me that."

Breuning wiped his hands on his trousers. "Pearl Harbor's put a new complexion on things."

Meeks said, "Yeah, yellow."

Carlisle smirked. "Why do you think we're working this shit case? You think it ain't politics?"

Ashida walked back inside. He sprayed the unknown print with ninhydrin and lifted it with clear tape. Pinker walked in with the new print cards. Ashida ran them under his magnifying glass. He got no matches. That meant one unknown print.

They spread out again. Pinker dusted the closet shelves. Ashida dusted the kitchen cabinets and notched grease-coated smears. He noticed two broom whisks below the bottom drawer. He aimed his flashlight at the floor.

He caught broken glass—a small shard pile.

He scooped it up and examined it. He noted an oily sheen on the shards and sniffed it. It smelled like fish oil.

Red dots on the glass—possibly dried blood. He scooped the shards into an envelope and tagged it: "Watanabe/Highland Park/ 5:21 p.m., 12/7/41."

The kitchen reeked of stale egg rolls. Chinese food turned his stomach. He walked upstairs and went through Nancy's and Johnny's rooms. Dudley told Ray Pinker that he found the rooms "engaging."

Ashida tossed the rooms. Ashida got the gist.

Nancy padlocked the connecting door to Johnny's room. Johnny hoarded smutty magazines and Nazi comic books. Johnny possessed padded jockstraps. They were padded with Japanese flags and Nancy's underwear.

Ashida ran his face over them. The smell aroused him. He trembled. He put them back in the drawer.

He walked to Ryoshi and Aya's room. He saw the hate tract on the dresser. He bagged it and tagged it: "Watanabe/Highland Park/5:34 p.m., 12/7/41."

There—the wall note.

Ashida studied the characters and their placement on the page. Pinker walked in. Ashida translated.

" 'The looming apocalypse is not of our doing. We have been good citizens and did not know that it was coming.' "

Pinker said, "We've got *post hoc, ergo propter hoc*, right at the gate. We've got four dead Japanese the day before Japan attacks a U.S. territory. Is that what the note refers to?"

Ashida shook his head. "The 'apocalypse' could mean mass suicide or an inevitable world conflict, with no foreknowledge of this morning's attack itself. 'Apocalypse' could pertain to potential ramifications for individual members of the family or the family as a whole. The note is entirely ambiguous."

Pinker said, "Exactly. And the real question is whether or not the note was coerced, because the consensus is we've got homicide."

Ashida said, "Exactly. The characters are wobbly, it's a male script, and Mr. Watanabe would certainly have been under duress if he were planning seppuku. But, the characters are *extremely* wobbly, even by textbook suicide-note standards."

"We could call it a variant. It's the equivalent of the hesitation marks the swords made when they pierced the bodies."

Ashida studied the paper stock. It was thick and had a cloth content. He tapped dust on his print brush. He ran it over the note and stepped back for more light.

Smears and smudges. One blurred partial. A *badly fragmented* partial—half-eclipsed by a smooth glove print.

Pinker pointed to it. "There. The glove print indicates that someone was guiding the note writer's hand. There's your coercion, right on the page."

Ashida saw a notepad on the dresser. He walked over and studied the top page. It was a grocery list. The characters resembled the characters on the wall note. It was adult-male script. There were no fluctuations, indicating duress.

Pinker came over. "Identical. It has to be Ryoshi."

They walked up to the wall note. A breeze hit the room. Print powder puffed in the air.

Ashida said, "Let's call it coercion. If that's the case, and the killer wasn't Japanese, he ran the risk of Mr. Watanabe writing a note to the police that the killer himself couldn't read."

Pinker smiled. "I know what you're saying, but you should be the one to say it."

Ashida said, "I would surmise that the killer *is* Japanese."

Pinker bowed, mock-solemn. Ashida smiled and bowed back.

That phonograph kicked on outside. Father Coughlin launched a hate harangue, backed by Gaelic lutes. Pinker rolled his eyes and walked downstairs. Ashida stepped into the hallway.

Do the textbook exercise. Let your thoughts disperse and accrue. Let your eyes drift and see.

Stand there. It's a Buddhist practice, 2000 B.C. *Your vile countrymen ignore such traditions. You are of them. You were born to the Samurai class and forged by the Reformation. Japanese customs formed you. Lutheran zealots schooled you. You are equal parts rigid view and the mind untethered. Let this horror house speak to you.*

Ashida stood there. He thought of Bucky's fight tonight. He saw Bucky in the Belmont showers. His old trip-wire gizmo snapped secret nudes. His new gizmo snapped pix at 6th and Spring. That man outside the drugstore. A Bucky manqué. Handsome, but not lovely and—

Ashida blinked. A trip-wire bulb popped.

He noticed a hallway shelf. It was lined with jade knickknacks. A small bottle was wedged behind a small jade temple. Note that frayed label.

Ashida snatched the bottle. A label strip read "Morphine Paregoric." There was no discernible pharmacy name.

Whalen's Drugstore yesterday. The bandit rifles bottles on one shelf. Said bottles: *morphine paregoric.*

Two crimes the same day. Matching details accrued.

Ashida retrieved his evidence kit and dusted the bottle. The smears meant *no more details accrued.*

He stood in the hallway. He heard Dudley's boys bullshitting outside. His eyes traveled. He saw dust motes and a bug on the wall.

The walls, the ceiling. Chipped paint, cobwebs, wait—

Anomaly. Inconsistency. Red-alert flaw.

Note the ceiling-wood strips, laid in lengthwise. Note the parallel seams. The seams disrupt the wood-grain flow. They are crosshatched and barely detectable. They form a two-foot square.

Ashida jumped and aimed his hands. He hit the middle of the square. The square flew back, off an inside hinge. A set of collapsible stairs dropped to the floor.

Metal stairs with rubber foot grips. Soundless, well oiled.

Ashida climbed up them. A slight tug made them retract. The square slid down flat in that movement. The apparatus operated off gears and air-filled cylinders.

A room. Less than an attic. More than a crawl space.

He stood at his full height. He pulled out his penlight and ran the beam. No windows. Lacquered plywood walls. One table, one chair.

On the table: a shortwave radio and ledger. The radio was hooked up to a tape-recording device.

The room was cold. His breath fogged. It was a somewhat cool evening. His breath should not condense. The room was probably soundproofed. Insulation panels trapped cold air.

He turned on the radio. The needle-and-tuning display lit up green. The dial numbers made no sense. He jiggled the volume knob—*be careful now.*

A man shrieked in Japanese. He defamed the United States. It was the "Land of the White Centipedes." He lauded the Emperor's divine triumph in Hawaii this morning.

The tape spools spun. Ashida studied the hookup. It was highly sophisticated. Yes, surely—radio voices activated the tape rig's starter gears. Magnets and radio signals—stunning mechanics.

Ashida pushed a button recessed below the spools. A new Japanese voice fomented. He stated the time and date: 2:00 p.m. yesterday. Chronology: the Watanabes died ninety minutes later.

The man howled. It was rabid-dog propaganda. He spoke native Japanese. Ashida spoke an American hybrid. Phrases slipped by him. The gist was plain. The man described preparations for the attack.

Ashida listened in Japanese. Ashida lost words on a brain spool to English.

He sweated up his clothes. His pulse soared. His breath came out hot and turned to cold steam. The man defamed the United States. It was "a mongrel nation who will die under the hooves of Imperial Japan."

The rant devolved into animal sounds. Ashida turned off the radio. The display light faded to pinpoints. He pushed tape-rig buttons. The spools turned back and forth and repeated the lunatic's words. Yes—yesterday's broadcast was the only recording extant.

He turned off the tape rig. He caught his breath and recited the "Gloria Patria." *Glory be to the Father, and to the Son, and to—*

He forgot the English words. He finished in Japanese. His heart rate settled. He caught his breath and examined the ledger.

Thirty pages. Japanese characters. Dated entries going back three months. Surely *this:* shortwave radio broadcasts, transcribed.

Preparations for the attack. Soliloquies on male honor. A treatise on the erotic throes of kamikaze death.

Glory be to the Father, and to the Son, and to the Holy Ghost. As it was in the beginning, is now, and ever shall—

He lost the rest. He shut the ledger. He flashed his light on the walls. He saw indentations on a wall panel and pushed an edge in.

The panel creaked and opened into a closet. Ashida unplugged the radio and tape rig and laid them in. He curled up the electrical cords and placed the ledger on top. He shut the door and leaned on it.

He slid to the floor. He placed his head on his knees and took one hundred deep breaths. The room spun in time with his exhales and settled back in straight. He held his penlight in his teeth and got out his notebook and pen.

He wrote out a case brief. It was *his* case now. These were notes that no one else would ever see.

"Watanabes on FBI's A-1 Fifth Column list. (Capt. W. H. Parker told R. Pinker this.)

"Hidden shortwave radio at house/foreknowledge of attack on Hawaii.

"Near-identical gunshots and bullet fragments at Whalen's Drugstore and house.

"German & Japanese moneys at house.

"Morphine paregoric bottles disrupted at drugstore/morphine paregoric bottle discarded at house.

"Deutsches Haus: pro-fascist gathering spot. Lugers known to be sold illegally there."

He heard something outside. It got through the soundproofing. That phonograph, out in the street. Muted brass, low woodwinds. A slow-tempo "Perfidia."

Ashida stood up. He felt Shinto calm. He opened the trapdoor and released the steps. The landing looked garish now. He had it all to himself.

He walked down the steps and pushed them back. The door slid into place. "Perfidia" faded. He heard Jack Webb laughing, out on the porch.

He walked downstairs. Ray Pinker buttonholed him.

"Did you find anything else?"

Ashida said, "No."

"I'm hungry. And don't suggest Kwan's, because this place still smells like breakfast."

Ashida smiled. "Will Dudley steer the case the way Horrall and Bowron want it?"

Pinker powdered his print brush. "Unless pious Bill Parker goes on a bender and gets his dick in a twist."

18

KAY LAKE'S DIARY

LOS ANGELES | SUNDAY, DECEMBER 7, 1941

7:13 p.m.

War fever.

The prelims went by, ignored. The national anthem got more applause than all three bouts. A huge flag cinched to a girder fluttered above the ring. The Olympic Auditorium buzzed. Nobody talked boxing. Everybody talked war.

Conversations were impossible; it was just that loud. People talked to one another and at one another, regardless. We were here to be with other people and mark this moment. We were Americans out on the town. We were jazzed up, indignant and proud.

Scotty and I sat four rows back from ringside. Mexican bantamweights held no interest for us. We kept our heads together and whispered; I held Scotty's arm while he rested a hand on my knee.

We spent the day on the Federal Building steps and around the corner at the cafeteria. We traded personal anecdotes and came to the aid of a young Japanese man trying to enlist. Scotty secured his Marine Corps papers. I got a glimpse of Captain William H. Parker and waved him off imperiously.

The man was a rankling presence now. Elmer Jackson had succinctly indicted him. Certain questions troubled me. They undermined this slice of early wartime je ne sais quoi.

Will Elmer tip Chief Horrall to my tap-transcription duty? What specifically does Parker know about me? Will Parker expose Lee for the murder of Abe Reles, and does he even know about it past phone-tap smears? Will Parker cross Dudley Smith over *that* matter? What does Parker want from me?

Scotty squeezed my knee and ran his hand under my hemline. I squeezed his arm and laughed. He said something; I couldn't hear it; I said something back and could not hear my own voice. Scotty smelled like my smoke and his own lime cologne. I wanted to draw him like I drew Bucky. I held my breath for the main event and Bucky's walk to the ring.

Scotty had borrowed his father's car for his enlistment run and had parked it in a lot on Bunker Hill. We walked back to retrieve our cars and caravan to the Olympic. We passed Central Station en route. The newly formed "Alien Squad" was just rolling out. Elmer and Lee were among the cops brandishing pump shotguns. We watched them walk east, toward Little Tokyo. A K-car pulled into the parking lot. Two cops hauled out three Japanese boys and shoved them through the jail door.

A Sousa march came over the loudspeakers and distorted all the raised voices. I heard a commotion and looked around. Bob Hope led a dozen sailors into the ring.

We all stood up and cheered. The music died or merged with the cheers—I couldn't tell which. Bob Hope grabbed the ring mike and laid down a run of jokes. Nobody heard him. We didn't want to hear him. We couldn't stop cheering and living out the moment.

Hope gave up and waved to the crowd. Our cheers became foot stomps and whistles. Hope led the sailors out of the ring and up to a row of back seats. Cops whisked him out to the lobby. His performance ran less than three minutes.

We all sat down. I held Scotty's hands in my lap. I saw a handsome young Japanese man enter the arena and walk to the second row. He wore a Belmont High letter jacket; he attracted a range of curious and plainly hostile looks.

People looked, people whispered, people stared outright. People muttered "*Jap*" and issued catcalls.

The microphone dropped from the rafters again. The announcer entered the ring.

A main event roar smothered further invective; the Japanese man settled into his seat. Yells and locomotive claps covered the introductions. I already knew the statistics by heart.

Ten rounds of boxing, in the light-heavyweight division. Wardell "Junior" Wilkins, the "Sepia Sensation," 22, 4, and 16. And, now, still undefeated at 35–0—Glassell Park's own "Tricky" Bucky Bleichert!

I squeezed Scotty's hand and laced up our fingers. A spindly Negro man jogged out and ducked into the ring. A barrage of boos greeted him. The few Negroes in the colored section gave him his only cheers.

The referee and cornermen hopped in the ring. The young Japanese man turned his head and looked back down the aisle; our eyes met for an instant. He kept looking. I turned my head and followed his line of sight. Bucky popped out of a dressing room and danced on his toes.

He wore his Belmont black-and-green robe. He flashed his buck teeth and raised a glove to salute his dead mother in heaven. I lost my breath, like I always do. Bucky passed by our row. He stopped at the second aisle and stuck a gloved hand out. The Japanese man tapped the glove. Bucky smiled at him. The man's eyes welled with tears.

Some people saw it and booed. Bucky ducked under the bottom ring rope and showed the crowd his teeth. I got frightened for him and hungry for him, like I always do. It always flutters through me the same way.

A cornerman popped in his mouthpiece and removed his robe. *Mine:* the sweet Lutheran boy with the Jewish star on his trunks.

The referee issued instructions. Bucky and the Sepia Sensation touched gloves. I looked up at Greta Heilbrunner Bleichert, despite my disdain for heavenly pap.

The bell rang. Bucky circled, Wilkins charged. Bucky was a good five inches taller. He flicked his jab at the scar tissue above Wilkins' eyes and stayed outside his range.

I squeezed Scotty's hand. It meant *Be still now.* Bucky worked outside-in. He was "taking his opponent's pulse" for a "blind-date introduction." He was "measuring" Junior Wilkins for a "cheap-shot right hand." Lee Blanchard taught me fight strategy and lingo.

Wilkins swung a haymaker. Bucky sidestepped it and left-hooked to the body. Wilkins' knees dipped. Bucky threw a double jab. Wilkins' right-eyebrow scar opened up and leaked blood down his cheek.

The bell rang. Wilkins was winded already. Bucky danced back to his corner and waved to the Japanese man. Scotty said, "Sambo's out on his feet."

I'd squeezed my hand numb. I unlaced our fingers and held Scotty's palm to my cheek. Scotty flashed his stunning kid grin.

The bell rang. I turned back to the ring. The Japanese man diverted me. He mimicked Bucky's feints as he watched him. It was perfectly concurrent mimicry.

Wilkins came in with coagulant smeared to his eyebrow; Bucky flick-flick-flicked jabs at it. I saw intent all over him. I knew the look. It was certainty replacing apprehension. Wilkins' cut opened up and dripped blood; Wilkins pawed at it. He blinked at the precise wrong moment. Bucky measured him for a cheap-shot right and delivered it.

Wilkins went down. He hit his head on the canvas and spit out his mouthpiece. The referee waved the fight over and raised Bucky's hand. Bucky waved to the Japanese man. The crowd stood up and applauded. Wilkins rolled over and crawled up on his feet.

Bucky hugged him. Reporters and photographers ducked under the ropes and eclipsed my view. My legs were weak; I tried to stand and slid back in my seat. Scotty helped me up. We joined the quick march out to the parking lot.

Scotty kept an arm around me. I watched people watching him and noticed them pause. Women were curious. Full-grown men possessed of fine éclat were wary of a twenty-year-old kid.

I turned around and blew Bucky a furtive kiss. The Japanese man diverted me. He was the only one still in his seat.

8:43 p.m.

Scotty got me to my car. I pulled out onto 18th and Grand, ahead of the fight crowd. Scotty drove right behind me. We took Washington west and La Cienega north. Lee was probably out with the Alien Squad or over at Kwan's Chinese Pagoda. I didn't think I'd see his car in our driveway.

Scotty stuck close behind me and played a kid game with his headlights. It was a kind of Morse code: low and high beams, on and off. I watched my rearview mirror and tried to make sense out of it. I think he was trying to spell out "I Love You."

We turned west on the Strip and north on Wetherly. Lee's car was gone. I parked in the driveway and left room for Scotty. I thought about Bucky and a new sketch to draw from memory.

We got out of our cars. Scotty slid on the damp pavement and bumped into me. I steadied him. He put his hands on my shoulders. He said, "Shit, Kay. How come you're so sweet to me?"

I said, "I don't want this day to end. I don't want us to win the war until I learn a few things."

Scotty touched the part in my hair. "I intend to win the war all by myself. I'll ease up until you say it's okay."

"What were you trying to tell me with your headlights?"

"Prom-date stuff. I was trying to get it out before I go to boot camp and you go back to your life."

I touched his cheek. "Not just yet, please."

"Am I going to have to fight Lee Blanchard tonight? He was a ranked heavyweight, and I'm not so sure how I'd do."

"Hush. It's a silly-boy idea."

"I'm full of those."

I said, "We're at war now. You're entitled to be."

We kissed then. I thought of Bucky as we leaned in.

9:21 p.m.

The walk upstairs was all fumbles and half-lit hallways. My bedroom was dark; shadows covered the Bucky Bleichert sketches. We fell on the bed and kissed with our clothes on. We undressed slowly. Snapshots, shutter clicks, discovery.

Scotty saw the scars on my legs. He kissed them, but did not comment. He was too tall for my bed. Passing headlights strafed the Bucky pictures and made him faux-groan. I told him about Sioux Falls. He told me about football at Hollywood High and all the fights he'd been in. I omitted Bobby De Witt, laudanum and coerced prostitution. He revealed that he'd read about the Boulevard-Citizens case. I praised him for not mentioning it at the start.

Midnight came. We made love and talked. Scotty was tender and passionate. He worked hard to please me and succeeded. Sweet boy—thank you for spending this day with me.

I thought about Bucky. Scotty told me about a girl he was with on a visit to his family home in Scotland. His mother died of lupus there. It was 1938. She was only forty-three.

He fell asleep, draped into me. I lay still and blew smoke rings as halos over the bed. Dawn came on; sunlight illuminated Bucky, with Scotty asleep beside me. We woke up and saw each other naked. We silently noted what we'd missed in the dark. We got dressed and had coffee in the kitchen.

I walked him out to his car. We embraced and kissed good-bye. Scotty drove off. I watched him dip down to Sunset Boulevard.

It was cloudy and cold. I looked across the street. Captain William H. Parker stood by a '39 Ford.

December 8, 1941

19

LOS ANGELES | MONDAY, DECEMBER 8, 1941

7:37 a.m.

She saw him and walked straight over. Her hair was mussed. Her lipstick had been kissed off.

She came right up to him. He saw yesterday's clothes and caught her boudoir scent.

"Good morning, Miss Lake."

"You goddamn voyeur. Tell me what you want from me or get the hell out of my life."

"Your amorous ways don't concern me."

"Yes, they do. They concern you and entice you, because you knock on women's doors at night and extort them, because you get your kicks that way, because you have a famously bereft marriage, and you're coming out of your skin with boredom and that slimy, itchy *something* that drives brutal men like you."

Parker leaned on his car. He felt dizzy.

"I won't say it's the pot calling the kettle black. I won't deny that I tend to watch and stare. I won't say that your amorous ways don't intrigue me."

She made fists. "Goddamn you, Captain. Goddamn you for toying with me."

"Or for *seeing* you? Or for recognizing something that you want seen, because you're coming out of your own skin with your idiot attitudes and jejune notions, and your utterly fatuous belief that you're smarter, stronger and better than every other human being on God's green fucking earth, and isn't it a pity that no one else knows it?"

She stepped toward him. Their arms brushed. Her body was warm.

"Say 'yet,' Captain. Say 'no one else knows it *yet*.' Because recognition's a two-way street. Because you can go to war, and I can't. Because you can lock up criminals to sate your petty need for order, and I can't. Because you can rise to Chief, rule your little world and move people around at whim like the shrill martinet that you are—but whatever you do, don't underestimate the fact that *I* see *you.*"

Parker stepped back. "Have I convinced you that Lee Blanchard is dirty beyond your previous imaginings?"

"In your grossly manipulative and circuitous way, yes. The recordings put some things together for me, as you knew they would. But since I've known that Lee is capable of anything for some time, I'm truly not that surprised."

Stay strong, Katherine. Validate my belief in your silly-girl grit.

"I hope you won't confront Blanchard with anything you may have extrapolated from the recordings."

Kay Lake stepped back. "I hope you won't ask me what I figured out or discipline Lee in any manner."

Parker nodded. "I'm assuming that you spoke to your friends Sergeant Jackson and Miss Allen about me, and that you described the task I assigned you."

"I have, but I should tell you that they were nonplussed. And I seriously doubt that whatever you have planned for me concerns Brenda and Elmer or police-sanctioned prostitution. I would say that they have nothing to worry about, and I think you should permit me to tell them not to fret."

Parker nodded. Light rain hit. Wind tossed the girl's hair.

"You know and see so much. I'm astonished at how your actions betray your powers of insight and reveal you to be a reckless child out of her depth."

Kay Lake laughed. "That's a perceptive insight—from a man trying to drown me."

Parker checked his watch. The Bit O' Sweden was straight down on Sunset. Dudley was due at 9:00.

The rain hit harder. Parker opened the driver's door. Kay Lake got in behind the wheel. His cigarettes were on the dashboard. She helped herself.

Parker got in the passenger side. Rain hit the windshield and obscured the street.

"I won't transcribe any more recordings, and I don't think you want me to. We both know that we should keep Brenda, Elmer and Lee out of this, whatever 'this' is."

Parker shook out a cigarette. Kay Lake passed him hers for the light.

"The wedge wasn't necessary, was it? You're just round-heeled enough to take whatever I offer you."

Kay Lake cracked the wind wing. Her hair was wet. The light streaks in with the auburn glowed.

"Test my boundaries, Captain. It may surprise you, but they do exist."

Parker smiled. "*Now*, Miss Lake?"

"Yes. *Now* would be just fine."

Parker said, "You're going to infiltrate a Hollywood Fifth Column cell. They're wholly seditious and deserve to be crushed. They've been investigated by the California State Committee on Un-American Activities and are currently disseminating anti-American and more specifically anti–Los Angeles Police Department propaganda, yet more specifically pertaining to the possible mistreatment and imprisonment of allegedly innocent foreign-born and native-born Japanese, now all the more relevant since yesterday's attack. Dare I say that there *will* be a fair-minded scrutiny of the Jap contingent in Los Angeles. It will be judiciously enacted, and some arrests are likely to occur. The members of this cell are unscrupulous and ideologically insane. They will smear our country and my police force with huge strokes of Red paint. They will toe the Communist Party line and attempt to further the designs of Soviet Russia, once the Allies have won this war, as we inevitably will, and global Communist encroachment emerges as the chief threat to our internal security and the safety of the free world."

Kay Lake said, "It's a mad and presumptuous undertaking. It's as questionable as you consider it to be certain."

"Don't stop there."

"You haven't worked pandemic racial bias into your equation. Since I've seen it already, I would urge you to."

Parker tossed out his cigarette. Kay Lake tossed hers. Their knees brushed. Fucking rain. The car was a steam room.

"Will your concern for our Japanese citizenry prevent you from accepting this assignment?"

"No."

"Am I crossing your boundaries in any way?"

"No."

Parker pointed to the backseat. "Los Angeles Police, Federal and state Subversive Squad reports on Claire De Haven, Reynolds Loftis, Chaz Minear, and some subsidiary scum. We're going to build a derogatory profile on them. We're going to see them indicted for sedition and/or treason and see to the destruction of their cell through coercive means. Your job is entrapment. You are to be a stool pigeon, a snitch, a rat and a fink. If those appellations offend you, *c'est la guerre.* You are an informant. You will collect incriminating information and report it to me. You are a wayward young woman with a traumatically checkered criminal past. I am betting that the Red Queen will find you irresistible."

Kay Lake said, "It's a matriarchy. I like that aspect."

"Paul Robeson is appearing at Philharmonic Hall tonight. You will attend, sans escort. You will meet Claire De Haven and whatever fey men she brings as her escorts. You will steer the conversation to psychotherapy. The Communist Party psychiatrist in Los Angeles is a man named Saul Lesnick. He is a Federal informant. He tends to the psychic needs of Miss De Haven and her slaves, as he concurrently reveals the shallow breadth of those needs to his Federal handler. Dr. Lesnick is also a *coerced* informant, who is quite vividly susceptible to young women. You will endeavor to meet Dr. Lesnick. Do not tell him that you are also an informant. I want him to unwittingly collude with you."

Kay Lake hugged the steering wheel. Her brown eyes were incongruous. They clashed with her auburn hair.

Parker said, "Tell me what you're thinking."

She said, "I'm too thrilled to speak."

8:53 a.m.

He walked down to Sunset. He walked for a chance to view Kay Lake on the sly. She cut across to her porch. He heard a radio. She tuned in Roosevelt's congressional address.

The Bit O' Sweden was overheated. The waitresses wore dirndl skirts. They looked like Nazi cheerleaders five thousand miles displaced. Beer steins dangled off wall pegs. The décor connoted Hitler at play.

Parker grabbed a window table. The sky cleared a bit. The Strip was lined with fake Christmas trees. Mock snow covered the sidewalk.

A tall redhead walked by. She looked like Joan from Northwestern. She was a Navy lieutenant j.g.

The blues, the gold sleeve bands. That stride, maybe it's—

Parker ran outside. The woman was gone. A '36 Dodge pulled away from the curb.

He walked back inside. A zaftig waitress brought coffee. The rain kicked back on. A *Herald* truck drove by. The side-panel blowup read WAR!

Parker sipped coffee. The wall clock tapped 9:00. Dudley Smith walked to the table.

They shook hands. Dudley said, "Good morning, sir." Parker said, "Good morning, Sergeant."

Etiquette. They observed it at work. Catholic fellowship. They called each other "Bill" and "Dud" around Archbishop Cantwell.

Parker said, "You missed Mass yesterday. His Eminence was peeved."

"It was an inconvenient homicide, sir. I said a novena for the dead Japs, in acknowledgment of the Sabbath. I was up late writing you a first summary, by the way. I routed it to your office at Traffic."

Parker stirred his coffee. "I read it this morning, so I assume I'm up-to-date. You lost crucial time on the canvass. Were you waiting for Nort Layman's disposition?"

"Yes. I sent Mike Breuning and Dick Carlisle out belatedly, last night. They got nothing. The dead Japs kept to themselves. They were polite and properly diffident to their white neighbors. They had extremely occasional Jap visitors. They did not string Jap lanterns across their property to celebrate their heathen holidays and did not comport in the mysterious ways we Occidentals have come to expect from our Jap brethren. No one noted anything suspicious near the house during the Saturday-afternoon time frame of the presumed homicides, and given yesterday's events, I would surmise that the white stiffs of Highland Park will not tax their minds for those buried memories that sometimes reappear and solve murder cases."

Parker said, "Background checks?"

Dudley said, "They'll be undertaken, but I'd call them futile. Papa and mama were born in Japan, the children were native-born. They weren't Christian, so you won't find family, birth, death, baptismal and marriage records in any of the conveniently located Jap churches in Little Tokyo. Our bright colleague Dr. Ashida examined the religious geegaws in the house and anointed the dead Japs as of the Shinto persuasion. As Sergeant Turner 'Buzz' Meeks said last night, 'I like broiled eel as much as the next man, but all of this is Greek to me.' "

Parker smiled. "Property-records check?"

Dudley lit a cigarette. "Not applicable, for the moment. They own the house and a truck farm in the Valley, but Secretary of War Stimson has issued a Federal seizure order for the property of the Japs on the A-1 subversive list, which Ray Pinker tells me includes our very own dead Japs. With our country in its current state of agitation, I would say that we won't be able to cut through the Federal red tape necessary to get at those records for some time."

Parker lit a cigarette. "The son and daughter. Your description of their bedrooms was quite vivid."

Dudley twirled his ashtray. "I don't see their implicitly perverted relationship as being germane to the case, but that avenue is being explored. The dead lad and lassie attended Nightingale Junior High and Franklin High School, and Sergeants Breuning and Meeks roused the registrars of those lackluster institutions last night and grilled them per the dead Japlets. The registrars described them as 'decent kids,' 'quiet kids,' 'kids who didn't fraternize with white kids' and 'kids who got average grades and stuck to themselves.' "

Parker kicked it around. Parker looked out the window. Rain, rain and rain.

"The pharmacy heist, the gunshots at the two locations, the silencer threads?"

Dudley said, "We'll be checking gun-sales records and robbery reports, but we'll be coming up against the established fact that only one gun purchaser in six complies with state firearms-registration laws and actually registers their guns. That, and the established fact that Japs are clannish, that Japs sell guns to other Japs exclusively, and that the heist man at the drugstore yesterday was quite obviously a white man. Granted, I consider our dead Japs quite dicey.

That stated, homicide is nearly always a closed racial circle, and I do not see a white heist man as a logical suspect in a feigned ritual-suicide murder case."

Parker shook his head. "Hot potato. You've got forty-three Federal agents, Sheriff's deputies and our Alien Squad working Little Tokyo. Nobody gives a shit about anything but the war, and why should they?"

Dudley said, "Why indeed?"

"Let's go back to 'quite dicey.' I'm thinking of the hate tract and the Axis currency you found at the house."

Dudley shook his head. "Hate tracts are fiendishly difficult to trace. The post office boxes listed on them are often designations for mail drops that hate merchants and pornographers use to muddle the trail of their filth. It's a form of collusion that requires the aid of local postal carriers, and even the most seasoned postal inspectors find this sort of investigation problematic."

Carl Hull knew hate tracts. He should call him and inquire. He should thank him for Kay Lake.

Parker said, "The currency."

Dudley said, "Yes, I find it interesting as well."

"Politics."

"Yes, 'politics.'"

"The A-1 list."

"Yes. I think we should start there. I'll be going down to Terminal Island. The Fort MacArthur MPs have a veritable invasion force of Japs in custody there."

Parker said, "It's our logical first step."

Dudley said, "'Closed racial circle.' We're guided by that concept. We should keep an open mind and still cleave to it."

"You're the homicide man, Sergeant. How likely is a non-Jap suspect for this thing?"

"Very highly *un*likely, sir."

Parker looked out the window. Rain, rain, rain. War headlines, war on the radio. Kill-the-Japs table chat.

"*Cold* potato. The Japs sank the *Arizona.* They're going for the Philippines now. You can't run a homicide case in this kind of atmosphere."

Dudley smiled. His eyes twinkled.

"It's a dead-ender, sir. I'll give it the old college try, but I'm not optimistic. In the end, we'll find that the killings derived from a grave misdeed in feudal Japan. A Jap warlord fucked another Jap warlord's goat without first seeking permission. That transgression has festered for centuries. It finally came to a head on Avenue 45 in Highland Park, the day before the Japs grievously erred and bombed our grand fleet at Pearl Harbor."

Parker laughed. "Keep your boys leashed. Don't frame or kill anyone. This case isn't worth it."

9:46 a.m.

Dudley walked out. Parker kicked blood back in his legs. He was nerve-cramped the whole time.

Rain, rain and rain. Drink, shut the world out, walk back up Wetherly. Sleep it off in the car. She might be out on the porch. She might strike poses.

Parker ordered a double bourbon. The first sip burned. He toasted the Pearl Harbor dead and replayed the test blackout.

He took his black-and-white. He traveled sans headlights. The blackout ran 5:00 to 7:00 a.m. He monitored the Department's two coastline divisions. He drove the coast road from San Pedro to Venice and caught dawn on the sea. No streetlights or traffic lights. House lights and car lights were off. Aircraft spotters were out on the beach. No Jap planes hovered or streaked. They had no glow to sight by and no targets to seek.

He cruised inland and checked individual houses. They were per-guideline dark. He peered through window-shade gaps. He saw strips of light and heard radios. FDR defamed the Japs—over and over.

Twenty-odd houses, all guideline dark. Let's reprise Deadwood in 1916.

Voyeur. The Lake girl called him that. He was fourteen in '16. He peered in brothel windows while his father fought the Great War. William H. Parker II came home with The Thirst. He reprised William H. Parker I, after the Civil War truce. Two Army captains. Antietam and the Argonne. War begets The Thirst.

Parker stared out the window. The zaftig waitress brought refills. He thought about Joan and the Lake girl. He fed The Thirst and watched their faces merge.

20

LOS ANGELES | MONDAY, DECEMBER 8, 1941

11:17 a.m.

Visit cell block 9 at T.I. It's *the* Jap hot spot in Pedro.

Four tiers. Twelve cells per. Two hundred and sixteen men and forty-two women.

Dudley brought Mike Breuning, Dick Carlisle and Buzz Meeks. They rehearsed interrogation skits on the ride down. The boys were war-fevered. Dudley nixed their enlistment plans.

"We're the home-front vanguard, lads. We have meddlesome tasks to fulfill before we can run off to glory."

They hogged a guard stand. They skimmed subversive lists. MPs lounged nearby. A catwalk adjoined the stand. Male Japs were sardine-packed, six per cell. They looked forlorn and fucked-up.

Breuning said, "This is a humbug job. The action's in the Philippines. Who gives a shit who killed the fucking Watanabes?"

Carlisle said, "Jack Webb's going for the Air Corps. He'll be bombing Tokyo before we clear this case."

Meeks said, "There's Jap subs off the coast, as far south as Santa Barbara. KFI ran a spot on it this morning."

Dudley skimmed the "A" summary. The Watanabes were listed. They were "known fascist sympathizers." Two known associates were named.

Hikaru "Tachi" Tachibana. Born 4/29/03—Kyoto, Japan. Suspected Japanese spy. Popped near the Douglas Aircraft plant in Santa Monica. The date: 3/12/40. In his possession: a peewee camera loaded with infrared film.

Tachibana was released on bail and slated for deportation. Judicial proceedings occurred. Tachibana absconded. He was rumored to be lost in Mexico.

"Frequently seen at the Watanabe produce farm (San Fernando Valley) prior to his disappearance."

KA no. 2: James "Jimmy the Jap" Namura. Born 11/9/07—L.A. "Known criminal and pro-fascist." Preston Reform School grad, grifter, dope peddler. Pushed maryjane at Nightingale Junior High.

"Frequently seen at the Watanabe produce farm (San Fernando Valley) early 1941."

Breuning said, "The check mark by Namura's name means he's in custody here. And the Watanabe kids went to Nightingale."

Dudley said, "Find the tier sergeant. Have Mr. Namura placed in that interview room we passed on our way in."

Breuning scrammed. Carlisle said, "The Feds are all over Little Tokyo. They're tossing the Japs in our divisional jails. I talked to a guy on the Alien Squad. He said the Sheriff's are clearing out the horse paddocks at Santa Anita. Call-Me-Jack thinks we'll be at our booking capacity by next week."

Meeks spat chaw juice in an ashtray. "It ain't right. Most of these fuckers just want to eat broiled eel and put the boots to mama. This is one big upscut that don't have to be."

Carlisle *slooooooow*-burned. Breuning whistled and waved. They ambled to the sweat room.

The door featured a two-way mirror. Inside: a floor-bolted table and chairs. On the table: a fat phone book. By the table: Jimmy the Jap Namura, perched in a chair.

Note the duck's-ass haircut and swastika tattoo. Note the hophead gaze.

They walked in and locked in. They hovered by the table. Jimmy the Jap giggled. Dudley signaled the lads.

Meeks said, "Remember Pearl Harbor."

Breuning and Carlisle grabbed Jimmy the Jap and threw him against the wall.

He crashed and bounced. He was thin. It made a flyswatter sound. Breuning snatched the phone book and smacked him in the head. He curled up, centipede-style.

Meeks said, "Enough of that. Mr. Namura is an American citizen."

Carlisle said, "Bullshit. This is a kangaroo court, and he's the kangaroo."

Jimmy the Jap pissed his pants. The lap lake spread to his knees.

Breuning arced the phone book. Dudley pulled his arm down and got in whisper tight.

"Have the tier sergeant locate Mr. Namura's arrest log. It should include an inventory of the items found at his dwelling. We're looking for phenobarbital, morphine paregoric, Axis monies, hate tracts, a silencer-fitted Luger and tools to fashion silencers."

Breuning lammed. Meeks dumped Jimmy the Jap back in his chair. Carlisle smacked him with the phone book. The swat dislodged a gold tooth. It fell on the table and spun.

Jimmy the Jap giggled. Dudley signaled Carlisle and Meeks. Carlisle fed Jimmy the Jap a cigarette. Meeks fed him his hip flask. Jimmy the Jap sucked on the tit.

Note the grateful shudder. Note the now slow-pulsing veins.

Dudley straddled a chair. "Your known associate Ryoshi Watanabe and his family were killed Saturday afternoon. The manner of death was simulated hara-kiri. I'm looking for a convenient Japanese scapegoat, and recent geopolitical events have convinced me that you fit the bill. Your job is to dissuade me. Begin by exonerating yourself. Continue with a primer on the Watanabe family. Entertain me with your knowledge and perception, or you will die in the green room at San Quentin Prison within three months' time."

Jimmy the Jap sucked bourbon. His heathen pallor flushed.

"I was at a graduation party up at Preston. A kid I know topped out a three-spot. We got some Tulare gash and fucked them."

Carlisle said, "Where did you fuck them?"

Jimmy the Jap giggled. "Where do you think? In the snatch."

Dudley said, "The location, lad."

Jimmy the Jap tee-heed. "The Sleepytime Lodge, right off the 101. It's a dodge the bulls at Preston work. They peddle twat for graduation parties. The girls cut them in for 20%."

Meeks said, "What time did you check in?"

"About noon, Tex. I've seen you in pictures, you know. You're always the fat guy on the spotted horse who never says anything."

Dudley smiled. "Sergeant Meeks enjoyed a career as a cowboy-film extra before he became a policeman. He had a grand speaking role in *Shootout at Crested Butte*."

Jimmy the Jap tipped the flask. "I was in a two-reeler once. It was down in T.J. We fed a Mex girl some Spanish fly and got her all hopped-up. She took on me, two beaners and a Doberman pinscher named Rex."

Meeks said, "What time did you check out of the lodge?"

"Rex had a big dick. It looked like a dousing rod."

Carlisle waved the phone book. Jimmy the Jap mock-cringed.

"We checked out about 9:00. We clouted a '36 DeSoto at an auto court off the ridge route and drove to L.A. We hit a Bund rally at Hindenburg Park and gassed on the fräuleins and beer. The gash and my pal peeled off in the DeSoto. I caught a ride with a Nazi cat named Fritz. We smoked a reefer and discussed the Jew question. He dropped me at my place about 1:00. I was still asleep when the Feds popped me. They said, 'Your people bombed Hawaii, punk!' I said, 'So what? What's that got to do with me?'"

Breuning walked in. He signaled Dudley: *Nix, nein, nyet.*

Carlisle said, "Give us some names. Your pal, the girls, the Nazi guy's last name."

Dudley flashed the cutoff sign. "The Watanabes, lad. What can you tell us about them?"

Jimmy the Jap went *Light me.* Carlisle fed him a cigarette. Jimmy the Jap drained the flask and tossed it to Meeks.

"Ryoshi was in with half the fraternal societies on the West Coast. You know, all those old-country feudal cats. I met him at a track meet at Lincoln High. We used to drink Ma Huang tea and gas on world events. Ryoshi was off the deep end on the Emperor, eugenics and eradicating the Chinks. He was gone on the notion of the worldwide Japanese hegemony. I told him all we needed was Asia, let the *Führer* take care of the Reds and the Jews, and don't fuck with the United States. I'm embarrassed, boss. I got no beef with the American white man. Pearl Harbor wasn't my idea."

Dudley grinned. "You are a charming witness, Mr. Namura. Please continue with your intriguing discourse on the Watanabe family."

Jimmy the Jap rocked his chair. "He was a secretive cat, Ryoshi. He went to meetings here and there, but he never spilled on who he saw or what he knew. He figured the Hitler-Tojo boys would win the war, so he converted all his U.S. coin into reichsmarks and yen, which may have been premature, given the latest news from the Russian front. He was running his farm on a shoestring, and he brought me up for a couple of weeks last winter, to ride herd on his slaves. His pickers were all wetbacks. The Mex Staties supplied them. Ryoshi told me the jefe was a Statie captain named Carlos Madrano. He pushed heroin down in Baja and was some kind of crime boss down there. I saw him once. He wore this snazzy outfit. Black shirt, jodhpurs, jackboots. He was *muy fascista, ándale pues.*"

Grand Carlos, adroitly observed. Wetback runner—old news. *Heroin? New news.*

Dudley signaled the boys. They got out their notebooks. Breuning tossed the change-up.

"What about mama? What have you got on her?"

"What's to get? She wore kimonos and bowed a lot. She walked out of rooms backward. She limped because Ryoshi made her bind her feet."

Meeks said, "What about those fraternal societies? What have you got in the way of names?"

Jimmy the Jap laughed. "I've got nothing, because I don't speak Japanese. I dig the lore and the politics, but those fraternal guys take it all the way to the Middle Ages. What's the point of establishing a new world order if you can't accommodate a new generation? It's like I said. Ryoshi knew those guys and went to those meetings, but he kept it zipped up."

Carlisle said, "Cousins, uncles, other known associates?"

"Nix, boss. Ryoshi and I drank tea and gassed on world events, but that was all that *we* fraternized. I worked up at the farm and saw *El Fascista* nosing around, but I did not partake of the Watanabes' private lives, outside of that."

Breuning said, "Hikaru Tachibana. Ring a bell?"

"Nix, boss. No bells there."

Meeks said, "You pushed maryjane at Nightingale. Did you push to Johnny and Nancy?"

"*Nein, mein Herr.* Some Narco cops kicked the piss out of me in '37, so I put that dodge down and got into politics. I've got a front on Alameda. If you're in the market for rising-sun flags or Nazi armbands, call me."

Breuning said, "Johnny and Nancy. Give on that."

"What's to give? Nancy was a yawn. She wore kimonos in the house and bobby sox to school. Johnny was a snot-nose punk. He was gassed on all of Ryoshi's far-right hoo-haw and dressed like a cholo, but he was strictly a cream puff. He had a pervert streak. He used to peep Nancy. He said she had a thick bush."

Meeks said, "Silencer-equipped Lugers. What's the first thing you think of?"

Jimmy the Jap yawned. "I think 'from hunger.' Guns don't yank my chain, Tex. If you're asking me about that kind of gun or *any* kind of gun and the Watanabes, all I can say is 'I don't know' and 'It doesn't jibe with my truck with them.'"

Breuning said, "You didn't seem surprised when we told you the family had been killed."

Jimmy the Jap scratched his balls. "Nothing surprises me these days. I'm sleeping it off when the Feds kick in my door and tell me I'm Fifth Column. Fifth Column *what*? I sell fascist trinkets, gas on hop and chase cooze. Yeah, I dig the Emperor—but when push comes to shove, give me the old U.S.A."

Dudley slapped his knees. "Mr. Namura, you've exonerated yourself to my satisfaction. Lads, do we have a consensus?"

The boys nodded. Jimmy the Jap said, "I've got one more thing."

"Go ahead, lad. We're listening."

"Ryoshi told me that *El Fascista* and some 'white stiff' owned their place in Highland Park. It was some kind of 'phantom ownership,' 'unofficially recorded,' all that surreptitious jive. *El Fascista* and the stiff were buying lots of Japanese property and were 'planning big things,' which Ryoshi did not elaborate on."

Ryoshi was on the A-1 list. The War Department ordered all A-1 property seized. The property records would be Fed-sealed. Carlos Madrano was tight with Call-Me-Jack. *El Fascista* could not be braced—

Yet.

Dudley stood up. "I will try to get you released, Mr. Namura. In exchange, I will ask that you attempt to determine the verifiable ownership of those Japanese properties you mentioned. My name is Dudley Smith, and I can be reached at City Hall."

Jimmy the Jap went *Sieg Heil!* Dudley *Sieg Heil!*ed him back.

Breuning and Carlisle yukked. Meeks fish-eyed Dudley. The *Okie* fish eye—quite severe.

Jimmy the Jap said, "*Mein Führer.*"

Dudley bowed. "You honor me, lad. But I must insist that you stop."

21

LOS ANGELES | MONDAY, DECEMBER 8, 1941

1:07 p.m.

The farm was way northeast. Dudley's report included a map. The Watanabes grew lettuce and cabbage. A wood carving marked their property line.

日本への門

"Gate to Japan"—carved in kanji script.

Ashida idled his car by the fence. The far-east Valley was Japanese farm turf. The acreage stretched up to the San Gabriels. The soil components sustained vegetable crops.

The Watanabes were dead. Their *braceros* worked on. Scrawny Mexicans. Stoop labor. Plunge that grub hoe, hack those roots.

"Wetbacks." Probably run by Carlos Madrano. *El Capitán* supplied the Ashida farm's workers. Their low pay assured borderline profits. *El Capitán* provided slaves for most of the East Valley farms. He was hooked tight with the PD.

Mexican Staties straw-bossed the Watanabe slaves. They wore starched khakis and SS-style hats. The Feds were out bagging Nisei and Issei. The Staties flaunted fascist garb.

Ashida stepped out of the car. A smell hit him—anomalous, distinct.

It was fish oil. He caught the same smell on broken glass at the Watanabe house. He read Nort Layman's autopsy protocol. It noted shrimp oil on the four victims' feet.

A work boss noticed him. He wore a cross-draw piece and a belt sap. Ashida got in the car and gunned it. He couldn't talk to the workers. It would get back to Dudley.

なぜこのことが気になるのか。*Why do you care about this?*

He was thinking in his native tongue. It was really his *second* tongue. He was birthright American. He was racial-code Japanese. The answer was this:

理由を知らなければならないからだ。*I need to know WHY.*

He cruised perimeter roads. He saw the same setup four times. Japanese farms, Statie slave drivers, desiccated labor crews. Akira was the sole boss at *their* farm. The Statie bosses felt like a new Medrano mandate—*trabajo muy difícil.*

The roads curled southwest. He passed carrot fields. Skinny *braceros* stooped and cut roots. A non sequitur loomed up ahead. Healthy pickers, no *fascistas* in view.

He pulled up to the fence. A Japanese man lounged across the wire. He wore short pants and a pith helmet. He leaned on a long-handled hoe.

Ashida tried native tongue. It felt garbled, straight off.

どうも、芦田という者です。"Do you know Ryoshi Watanabe? He has a farm nearby."

The man spoke Japanese. He mauled nouns and dropped connecting verbs. "Have not seen Ryoshi lately. Quiet man. Sold farm. Don't know who to."

Ashida held up his ID card. The man dead-eyed it. He had no English. Ashida deployed native tongue.

"I'm a police chemist. When did Ryoshi sell his farm? What can you tell me about his family and friends?"

It sounded off-kilter. He was native-tongue rusty.

The man mumbled in Japanese. Ashida fumble-caught the words.

"Family kept to itself. Sold farm recently. Got no cash. Got percentage of crop."

Ashida built a response. He started to talk and lost words. The man spat at his feet and walked off.

A breeze stirred up dirt. It rose off crop furrows and swirled. Ashida got in the car. *His* farm was close.

He drove though dirt clouds. The road was half-visible. He skittered on gravel all the way there.

His illegals looked fit. *They* had a heated bunkhouse and got Sundays off. *Akira* straw-bossed them. Black-shirted Staties—verboten.

Ashida parked by the truck shack. The breeze leveled off. Dirt clouds went *Poof!*

Akira walked up. He brought Coca-Colas. Ashida slid out of the car and grabbed one.

They clinked bottles. Akira said, "Mariko's driving me crazy. She hasn't figured out that it's a new world now."

"The FBI has a list. There's agents and city cops rounding people up."

"If there's a list, her name's on it. She called me this morning. She was half-gassed, and this time you can't blame her. They're knocking on doors and hauling away whole families. Half the doors on her floor have been padlocked. It was going on all night."

Ashida sipped his Coke. It was lukewarm. He tossed it in a trash can.

"She's got an agent baby-sitting her. A captain on the PD set it up. He wants to mollify me, for now. There's a multiple homicide I'm working."

Akira tossed his Coke. "Special Agent Ward J. Littell. Mariko kept saying his name. He knows the way to the old girl's heart, I'll give him that. He boozed and played pinochle with her until 2:00 a.m."

Ashida smiled. "You only call her 'Mariko' when you're angry with her."

"She thinks Father Coughlin's the Pope. She calls the president 'Franklin Double-Cross Rosenfeld.' She told me Pearl Harbor is a 'Zionist encampment.' "

Ashida toed the trash can. "Has anything odd occurred with Captain Madrano? Has anyone tried to buy this place?"

Akira shook his head. "No. Madrano supplies the slaves, and that's it. He gets his cut, says '*Gracias*' and comes back with his hand out the next month. And *nobody* wants this place. The topsoil stinks, and we're harvesting second-class crops."

The wind kicked up dirt. Ashida got back in his car. Akira leaned on the driver's door.

"We're in the shit, Hideo. The goddamn Emperor pops his cork in Tokyo, and we're paying for it in L.A."

Ashida said, "I'm working on something. It could benefit the Department. If I benefit the Department, they'll make efforts to benefit us."

Akira laughed. "*Really?* You trust that calculation like you trust some chemical formula you got from a textbook? You're the only Japanese on the Department. Do you think you'll get civil service protection in all of this?"

A gust rocked the car. Pebbles raked the windshield.

Akira said, "That man Littell told Mariko that the FBI's bringing in Bucky Bleichert. They think he's got some dirt on Nisei subversives. He knows Mariko backward and forward. Do you think he won't squeal? Do you think they won't hold his police appointment over him?"

Belmont. The showers. The trip-action camera clicks. Bucky stands under the stream.

Ashida shook his head. Swirling grit stung his eyes.

"Mother never liked Bucky. She's blowing it out of proportion."

Akira said, "There is no proportion. Pearl Harbor took care of that."

2:21 p.m.

He saw random words in kanji script. They bounced off his windshield. He pulled away and made the perimeter road.

He felt like a pilgrim fresh off the boat. Don't speak Jap—speak American.

I must become indispensable. I must be essential to the Los Angeles Police. I must act boldly. I must abet justice and secure the safety of my family—whatever it costs, whatever it takes.

Dirt roads to blacktop. The Cahuenga Pass to Hollywood. Flags at half-mast. Christmas decorations. No colored lights—it violated blackout codes.

Ashida took Sunset east. He kept the windows up. His car buffered him. Motorists might see him and yell, "*Jap!*"

It hit him then. He missed something at the house. Something very obvious. Something that the killer missed.

He was restless. The lab felt like a ball and chain. He bypassed Figueroa and cruised Chinatown. He saw tong boys in colored kerchiefs. He saw Mayor Bowron and Sheriff Biscailuz outside Kwan's.

The Chinks hate the Japs. There's good reasons why. The Rape of Nanking—1937. Japanese soldiers behead Chinese babies.

Chinatown adjoined Little Tokyo. The local Chinese are jubilant, the local Japanese are bereft. There's four dead Japanese in Highland Park.

Close quarters begets combustion. Now, there's *no* Japanese in Highland Park.

The crime felt racially circumscribed. The crime felt geographically contained.

Ashida cut south on Alameda. He rolled down his window and caught some cool air. A tin can hit the windshield. He blew a red light and slow-crawled to Little Tokyo. Fed sedans were double-parked along the east edge.

He slow-crawled up 2nd Street. American flags adorned storefronts. Broken windows, padlocked doors, seized-property bills attached. White men in dark suits with gun bulges. A roust outside Saji's Fish Mart.

Four Alien Squad bulls. Six Japanese boys. Lee Blanchard tossing wallets and car keys. Thad Brown and Elmer Jackson with shotguns.

He slow-crawled by his mother's building. The widow Nakamura stood outside, cuffed. A Sheriff's paddy wagon was up on the sidewalk. Mariko was on her fire escape. She was standing with a tall Fed. They laughed and sipped cocktails.

A Japanese man sprinted west. He held a bloody toupee and a piece of his scalp. Cal Denton chased him. Cal Denton was notorious. He once bodyguarded Two-Gun Davis and kicked a Negro pimp to death.

There's Captain Bill Parker. He's measuring traffic skid marks. He looks exhausted. He looks like he might need a drink.

Ashida passed a building draped in crepe red, white and blue. A window sign read ANTI-AXIS COMMITTEE. It was a pipe shop in the '30s. It was empty on Saturday. It's a patriotic hot spot now.

Ashida slow-cruised Main Street and looped back east on 1st. Dusk came on, *sloooooow*. A siren smothered street noise. 4:55—five minutes to the test blackout.

He pulled to the curb. The siren blare extended. He timed it off his watch. The repetitions stopped at 4:59.

Window lights went off. Drapes were drawn. Shutters were pulled. Motorists doused their headlights and hit their parking lights. Traffic lights went dim.

Soft dark, more dark, full dark. A commensurate street hush. Traffic thinned. People moved indoors. The Feds piled into their Fed cars and drove off.

It came to him. He didn't say it, see it or think it. He just knew.

The spot was a mile and a half southwest. He ran his parking lights and drove alleyways. There's no neon, no building light. The world is dark and flat now.

Shapes slid across 3rd Street and 6th Street. They were low-lit somethings. They had to be cars.

They drove too slow. He drove too slow and felt himself blend in. He turned west on Wilshire. Stop and go lights hardly beamed. He swerved south on Union and almost plowed a truck. The spot was right there at 15th.

No sound, no lights. *Wilkommen*, Deutsches Haus.

Ashida parked and looked over. No sound, no light. He heard a car crash somewhere.

His dried-blood scraper might work. His penlight, for sure.

He grabbed them. He walked over and banged on the door. The adjoining window glass shook.

The world is dark and flat. There's no one here. It's a simple 459.

You know it's wrong. You know you must hoard evidence unilaterally. You know you must produce your own quantifiable results.

Ashida stuck the scraper in the keyhole. Call it a scalpel now. Probe the tumblers, *click-click*.

He did it. The keyhole was well oiled. The scraper blade had give.

Wait for the clicks. Wiggle the blade. Once more, that's—

The lock snapped. The door popped open.

Ashida stepped inside and shut the door behind him. He clamped his teeth on the penlight. The Watanabes' attic, now *this*.

He arced his penlight. The beam hit on this:

Swastika wall flags. Framed photos atop bookshelves. Hitler in brownshirt, Hitler in short pants, Hitler with wildly tossed hair.

Mein Kampf on the shelves. The screed in English and German. Clothbound books with blank spines.

Ashida grabbed a book and flashed the pages. It was all photographs.

Ravaged men in striped pajamas. German soldiers holding severed heads. Pigs foraging in a corpse pile.

He replaced the book. He went light-headed. *Penlight first—breathe as you walk.*

He stepped into an office. It was twelve feet square. Note the trinket-packed shelves.

Hitler and Hirohito key chains. Jewish skullcaps with toy propellers. Swastika-embossed poker chips.

A desk and swivel chair. Six sliding drawers.

He tried the drawers. They were locked. There were no keys on the desktop. He scraper-stabbed the keyholes. His hands dripped sweat, the scraper slipped, he popped one drawer.

It was empty. He left tool marks. They revealed the break-in.

He took a breath. He kept at it. He jimmied, he yanked, he gouged, he pulled, he jiggled, he shoved, he pried. His hands slipped. He wiped them on his suit coat. He sweated through his shirt cuffs.

There—two, three, four, five, six drawers popped. There—wipe your face, smear your fingerprints, catch your breath.

His jaw ached. His teeth ached. The penlight ratched his mouth.

He went through the drawers. Three were empty. The fourth held a big wad of reichsmarks. The fifth held a velvet drawstring bag.

He picked it up and laid it on the desktop. The heft aroused him. He pulled the string and dumped the bag on the desk. Four crude silencers and four Lugers fell out.

Blue steel automatics. Pearl grips with onyx swastikas.

He touched the guns. He stroked the guns. He held the guns to his cheek. He placed the guns and silencers back in the bag and cinched it.

Look for paperwork. Member lists, receipts, transaction books.

He looked under the desk. He checked the adjoining bathroom. He disrupted the shelf knickknacks. He made too much noise.

Nothing. No paperwork, no—

He went fluttery light-headed. He grabbed the bag and ran. His limbs felt disconnected. He bumped bookshelves and toppled Hitler busts. He went back out the door. It was 6:29. The blackout was still on. The world was still dark and flat.

Cars crawled up 15th Street. Clouds hid the moon. L.A. felt submerged. The a.m. *Herald* ran a headline—SOUTHLAND BRACES FOR JAP SUB ATTACK!

His car was a U-boat. The front seat was the cockpit. He took Union to 6th to Grand. Other submarines passed him. The water was too thick. They all maneuvered too slow.

He still felt disconnected. He checked the dashboard clock: 6:38, 6:39, 6:40. The world would relight at 7:00 p.m.

Grand to 1st, east to the station.

The building was underwater. He parked and locked the bag in his evidence kit. He walked in the rear door. The trapped-in light burned his eyes.

The booking desk was swamped with *JAPS* and Alien Squad goons. Lee Blanchard held a boy by the neck.

Ashida walked up to the lab. The lights were off. He hit a wall switch and tripped the ceiling bulbs. The window shades were taped to the glass.

Ashida locked himself in. Nobody would notice it. He was the night-owl Jap. He had no personal life. He always worked late.

He cleared table space. He laid out the Lugers and silencers. He opened the storage drawer and retrieved his two photo sets. He placed them by the Deutsches Haus swag.

Two shots of dye-dipped silencer threads. Shot no. 1: the pharmacy. Shot no. 2: the Watanabe house.

He scraped threads off the Deutsches Haus silencers. He dipped them in a vat of aniline dye. He pat-dried them and studied them under a full-dialed microscope.

Confirmed. *Yes*—the same metallurgic components. *Yes*—the same minor inconsistencies. *Yes*—his earlier conclusion, updated.

Different silencers were deployed at the pharmacy and the house. They were made from the same metal. Deutsches Haus was the source of the silencers used at both locations.

Horns honked. Whoops went up outside. Ashida checked the wall clock. 7:00 p.m., on the snout.

He pulled the tape off the window shades. Downtown L.A. was lit up. Building lights, neon lights, car lights. Motorists rode their horns and flashed V for Victory.

He opened the ammo drawer and grabbed four bullets. He loaded the Deutsches Haus Lugers and screwed on the silencers. He secured the ballistics tunnel and laid out the guns. Ready, aim, fire.

Four guns, four silencers. Four shots, four muffled thuds. Eyeball confirmation no. 1:

The silencers shed threads from a single firing. They curled and dropped off like the threads at the pharmacy and the house.

Ashida studied the pix from the pharmacy and the house. Ashida retrieved and studied the rounds he just fired.

Confirmation.

The new rounds deteriorated identically.

Deutsches Haus, Whalen's Pharmacy, the Watanabe house. Identically malfunctioning Lugers. Probable firing pin and ejector flaws. Sheared and bifurcated rounds. Brazen armed robbery. A faked ritual slaughter. Deutsches Haus guns fired at both locations.

I must become indispensable. I must continue to act boldly and unilaterally.

Ashida thought of Bucky. Ashida held a Nazi gun to his cheek.

We're at war.

The world is dark and flat.

Cars are submarines.

22

KAY LAKE'S DIARY

LOS ANGELES | MONDAY, DECEMBER 8, 1941

7:57 p.m.

The audience is tense and poised for the moment. We're at war with a fascist enemy. An American Negro with leftist cachet and snob appeal will soon appear and validate our enlightened good taste. I'm six rows back from the stage, in an aisle seat. I'm the unescorted young woman in the stunning red wool dress. This will not be as much fun as last night's Bucky Bleichert fight. I am not here with Scotty Bennett. The stripped-to-shorts Bucky will not wave to the crowd and flash his big buck teeth.

I am here to advance Captain William H. Parker's presumptuous agenda. The Red Queen and her male consorts are one row in front of me. I know them from the photo-affixed files that Captain Parker gave me this morning. Claire De Haven is quite patrician. Her trembling hands and a wet sheen on her neck denote the drug habit mentioned in her file. She is a tall and handsome woman in her early thirties, a debutante who took a postcollege fall for the Left and astonished the Left by continuing to show up. Flanking her: the homosexual actor Reynolds Loftis and his lover, Chaz Minear. The two men form the nucleus of the Red Queen's cell. They are prissy, venomous, smug. I am close enough to hear their conversation and close enough to geopolitical reality to be guardedly sympathetic to their goals. The Queen's "subsidiary members" sit to their right. They are a blur from Captain Parker's crib sheet—the type of men who rush to agree, fetch drinks and light cigarettes. The Queen hosts grand parties at her home in Beverly Hills. Male guests often wind up in her bed. The subalterns empty ashtrays, carry glasses to the kitchen and lock up the house while their queen ruts.

I have been supplied with a primer on their dissolution. Narcotics, promiscuity, dry-out cures at a Malibu health farm run by a dubious plastic surgeon. Brilliant Captain William H. Parker. He read the subversive file on me, assessed my part in the Boulevard-Citizens case and perceived the outré nature of my relationship with Lee Blanchard. He understood that I am of these people and thus so appalled that I will entrap them, betray them and destroy them. We are of the Dakota prairie, Captain Parker and I. We see profligacy in ourselves and indulge and recoil from it in erratic measure. Captain Parker took a moral leap with me. He assumed that I would go at the Queen from a sense of self-vindication. He is entirely correct.

They are speaking with raised voices now; there's aggression in their tone. Conversations are buzzing all around me. It's predictable precurtain chatter. When will FDR initiate the massive wartime draft? What will be the numbers and who will be exempt? The Japanese have overrun the Philippines, the Hawaiian death toll mounts. The Queen and her consorts disdain the talk aswirl. Their talk is more elitist. It pertains to the "illegal mass imprisonment" of "innocent Japanese." It's gadfly chat in the middle of a war-bond rally. It's starkly illustrative of who they are—because I know it to be true.

I drove through Little Tokyo this afternoon. Lee is an Alien Squad cop, so I had to see. I saw arrests, confiscations, shackle chains of compliant Japanese. Lee walked up 2nd Street, twirling a billy club. I saw the Japanese man I noted at the Bucky Bleichert fight, observing the scene from his car just as I was. He was a thousand times more potently intent than the fussbudgets seated one row in front of me.

The houselights began to fade; it felt like the blackout, reprised. I was driving away from Little Tokyo when the 5:00 siren blew. Natural dusk and darkness by law spawned a contained chaos. I saw two auto wrecks in a minute's time; I witnessed a skirmish in Pershing Square. The dearth of light prompted the altercation—I'm sure of it. Placard-waving rightist factions fought. It was Catholic Coughlinites versus Gerald L. K. Smith's Protestant-Nationalist goons. They swung signboards and fists until they couldn't see whom they were hitting.

The houselights went all the way off. Stage lights replaced them. The curtain rose. A pale woman carried a massive stringed instrument over to a chair. She acknowledged mild applause. Paul Robeson walked onstage, bowed and stood under a spotlight. Frantic applause burst out. Claire De Haven cued her slaves to stand. The bulk of the audience took it as their consent to rise.

I remained in my seat. The moment was inimical to subversion. Robeson bowed and raised his hands: I'm honored, now sit. The Queen and her slaves complied first. The rest of the audience sat and fell quiet. The accompanist strummed an introduction. Robeson launched "Ol' Man River."

The tall Negro with the huge basso. The Broadway showstopper-cum-slaves' lament. The dilettante leftists. The wayward girl from Sioux Falls. The unhinged police captain and his anti-Red pogrom.

I giggled.

It just happened. It popped through all my calculation. The people around me heard it. I sensed scowls in the dark.

Robeson wrung the song dry and brought it to crescendo. The workers' troubadour and Princeton alum goes showbiz! White swells and Fifth Column hacks go wild!

I giggled. It registered above all the cheers. A man went "*Sssssbhbhb.*" I giggled louder. I was nine years old and cutting up in church, the Sunday after the stock market crash.

The audience cranked out bravos and slowly simmered down. Robeson made with the dutiful bows. A dowager glared at me. I rebuffed her with a little wave. Robeson segued to the labor ditty "Joe Hill."

I got antsy. I was to make contact with the Reds, and no more. It felt insufficient. A Princeton-educated Negro extolled class revolt; a frail woman with runs in her stockings strummed an oversize lute. I laughed and covered my mouth. The dowager whispered, "*Be still, child.*"

Poor Joe Hill. He was railroaded and snuffed by the powers that be. Fear not—his message lives on. I held my hand over my mouth. Robeson soaked up adulation and segued to Verdi's *Otello*. He was the tormented Moor now. He went from Trotskyite recitalist to Milanese hambone. I *clamped* my mouth. I felt Claire De Haven's pissy gaze.

I shut my eyes so I wouldn't roar outright. Pictures clicked through my internal nickelodeon. I worked up the dialogue. I predicted the outcome and knew I was right.

Robeson laid on the torment. I thought of the Japanese man at the Bucky Bleichert fight and rose to my feet.

"No human being deserves to be entertained with a world at war and a city engaged in repressive actions directed against innocent people, simply because of the barbarism performed by their native countrymen."

It was spoken as a polemic; it was issued just short of a shout. The Moor sang through it. The accompanist dropped her lute. People rustled, hissed, whispered, *ssshhhh*'ed, booed. House lights snapped on. I became aware of individual movement. A speck appeared in my vision—but I did not react. The Red Queen was the first to stand and *Look at Me*.

"No human being deserves to be entertained while policemen and Federal agents harass and illegally detain innocent Japanese-Americans in the spirit of racial hysteria and overreaction to a fascistic display of aggression, and—"

In one instant:

The mad Moor shut up and *Looked at Me*.

All the houselights went on.

All the Queen's consorts stood and stared.

Boos, shouts, garbled admonitions—building to a roar.

"Goddamn Bolshevik!" "Goddamn fascist!" "Get out of here, you whore!"

I yelled a response; the roar smothered it; an usher grabbed my arm. I balled a fist and hit him in the face. I caught the tip of his nose and felt it crack. Blood burst into his eyes.

Everyone stood. The usher weaved and made hurt sounds. *Everyone looked at me*. Their shouted censure filled the hall. I looked straight at Claire De Haven as a group of men charged me. Men in silly uniforms—grabbing me, clutching me, picking me up as I thrashed.

Men carried me. I enjoyed it as it occurred. I stayed in character and squirmed in resistance. We went up an aisle and out to the lobby. I jerked and hit my head on a door frame. I saw a wall clock that read 8:19.

8:20 p.m.

The Biltmore clock read 8:20. I opened my eyes in the backseat of a prowl car. I had a topsy-turvy view. Pershing Square, the Biltmore, Philharmonic Hall. A whoosh as the prowl car pulled out.

I didn't recognize the two cops; they'd cuffed me during my unconscious moments and ignored me now. The driver went north on Hill Street. Central Station was a minute away; Lee worked out of it; I was a noted police girlfriend. My performance got me *this*. I had hoped for a firm scoot to the lobby and a tête-à-tête with the Red Queen. I didn't think I'd be arrested and run the risk of alerting Lee.

A call hit the two-way radio; the cops grumbled about a B & E on Bunker Hill. Central Station was on the way; the passenger cop checked his watch and told the driver to gun it.

They continued to ignore me; we got to the station in less than a minute. The driver idled outside the jail door. The passenger cop led me inside and locked me into a cell on the women's row.

It was the middle cell on a five-cell tier; I had single lodging. The other cells held Japanese women. They were squeezed in four to a cell, each equipped with two bunks and exposed toilets. They looked away from one another. They gave no indication of acquaintance outside of this jail. There were young women, old women, women somewhere in between. There was no conversation. There was no camaraderie or commiseration. They registered the white girl in the bright red dress and felt the shame that she didn't feel for herself.

I turned away from them. I sat on the bottom bunk and lowered my eyes. I got it then.

They were a collective. They assumed one façade in solidarity. They were as sure-minded and composed as the Red Queen's collective was fretful and shrill.

The *Mirror-News* was partially wedged under my mattress. I read the front section.

The Pacific war. The Russian front. The Japs on an island-hopping rampage. A Sid Hudgens piece on Bucky Bleichert on page eight.

The banner was BUCKY BOY IN BLUE? A snide two columns followed.

Sid recapped Bucky's farewell fight and stressed his pending appointment to the Los Angeles Police. But is said appointment "pryingly predicated" on his supplying Federal agents with "insidious info" on "jungled-up Japs" aligned with that "heathen hellion Hirohito"? The piece described Bucky's Belmont High athletic career and friendship with fellow green-and-blacksters in the "slant-eyed community." Sid's trademark kicker: Isn't Bucky the son of German immigrants, and thus potentially suspect of Fifth Column leanings himself? "Whither goest thou, *Herr* Bleichert?"

I balled up and tossed the newspaper. I shut my eyes to blot out the cell row and all the Japanese women. They were still standing still, and they still despised me for my folly of self.

I was hungry. I wanted a big steak dinner and a cigarette. I wanted to watch Scotty Bennett take his shirt off. I wanted to dance with Bucky in his police dress blues.

A woman one cell over stifled a sob. I kept my eyes shut and prayed for her. I indulge prayer when the world seems incomprehensible and only a plea to the incomprehensible makes sense. The Reformation, the prairie, solidarity. The war and the Jewish star on *Herr* Bleichert's trunks.

The mattress settled under me. My prayer dislodged a piece of the earth and sent me spinning. No dreams, please. No Scottish pastor's boys, no war, no mad Moors—

7:38 a.m.

"You were stunning, Miss Lake. You upstaged Paul Robeson."

I tilted my head and opened my eyes. The women were gone.

"Were they released? They were here when I fell asleep."

Captain Parker unlocked my cell. He was in uniform and looked exhausted. He tossed me a pack of cigarettes and a lighter.

"Your bunk mates? They were transferred to the Lincoln Heights jail. The desk sergeant told me you slept through it."

I lit up. "Where were you sitting?"

"Two rows behind you. I knew you'd pull something when you laughed that first time."

"Why didn't you get me out of here sooner?"

"Because I knew you'd want the experience."

"You were right."

Parker said, "I think our next—"

I curtailed him. "I won't allow you leverage on anything pertaining to Lee Blanchard. You can indict him for the Boulevard-Citizens robbery or for murders he may or may not have committed for Ben Siegel, as you deem fit."

He leaned against the wall bars. "What are you telling me?"

"Not to assume that I'll fold behind coercion. Not to assume that I'll do everything that you demand without compensation."

Parker patted his knees; I tossed him his cigarettes and lighter. He lit up and blew a smoke ring higher than this girl ever could.

"*What are you telling me?*"

I folded out yesterday's newspaper. Page eight was crumpled, but legible. I tapped the middle columns and handed it over.

Parker read the piece. He crushed his cigarette on a bar hinge and smiled.

"I'm recalling those sketches I saw at your house. I would guess that you're quite smitten."

"Is the article accurate?"

"Yes. Apparently, Mr. Bleichert is acquainted with some dubious Japanese. I don't know who they are, but Federal agents will be interviewing him shortly. The results of the interview will determine the status of his appointment."

I tossed my cigarette in the toilet. "I'd like to observe the interview."

"I'll arrange it."

"I want Bucky to get on."

"Quid pro quo. Call Dr. Lesnick's office and request a 2:00 appointment this Wednesday. You'll see the Queen on her way out. I'd say she'll recall last night and cite serendipity."

I laughed. Claire, darling! I'm out to destroy you, but *do* tell me first. Where did you get that *gorgeous* dress you wore to the Robeson bash?

December 9, 1941

23

LOS ANGELES | TUESDAY, DECEMBER 9, 1941

7:49 a.m.

Parker walked off the tier. Exhaustion rehit him. He'd been up since the Japs bombed Pearl Harbor.

Not quite.

He cadged naps in his black-and-white. He got booze sleep in his new office. Jack Horrall gave him a Detective Bureau room. He was now the PD's "wartime emergency planner."

It covered his Traffic duties. It acknowledged his lust for hard work. He was the armed forces liaison. He collated Teletypes on war matters. He oversaw the Alien Squad and kept them leashed. He slack-leashed Dudley Smith and the Watanabe case.

He should wrangle the case some ink. Sid Hudgens could provide it. Sid owed Call-Me-Jack five yards in card losses. Tractable Sid.

Parker walked up to the muster room. He had five minutes with Kay Lake. It revived him and wrung him dry. He was alone in their deal now.

Carl Hull called him last night. He'd joined the Navy. Call-Me-Jack granted him a war-service leave.

In the meantime:

"I'm out of this deal of yours, William. It feels imprudent and untimely. We're in an actual war, and it's based on a great deal more than ideology. The Reds are our allies, and they've been dying in great numbers and bleeding Hitler dry. I subscribe to your prediction of an ideological conflict after we win *this* war—and, of course, domestic Reds will need to be interdicted. But, *presently*? *Presently*, your operation seems like quite a mad crusade. And, frankly, the notion of you and young Miss Lake troubles me."

He hung up. He hurled his telephone. It hit an auto-wreck wall map and shattered.

The muster room was chalkboard-walled and covered with masking paper. He came in at 5:00 a.m. and chalked up his pitch. He'd spiel officialese, verbatim. They'd be impressed.

He walked in. They beat him there. Call-Me-Jack smoked a morning stogie. Gene Biscailuz wore two six-guns. Fletch Bowron reeked of perfume. Bill McPherson snoozed.

Parker circled the walls and pulled off the paper. Six chalkboards glowed.

Jack said, "Bill was up early."

Biscailuz said, "Bill never sleeps."

Bowron said, "Bill's forgotten what his wife looks like."

Jack said, "Bill forgot that the day Adam fucked Eve."

Biscailuz laughed. Parker tapped chalkboard no. 1.

"We're at war, gentlemen. No one can say that the city of Los Angeles isn't taking it seriously. And if I look tired, I'm not the only one."

Biscailuz said, "I'm *hungry*. We should get Ace Kwan to send up some egg foo young."

Jack said, "I got blotto at Kwan's last night. Ace sent me home in a cab."

Bowron slapped his knees. "Go ahead, Bill. Strut yo stuff."

Parker grabbed a pointer and walked board to board. His block print was perfectly aligned. He filled in the abbreviations and expanded the officialese.

"Governor Olson has called for the immediate internment of all Jap nationals and suspected sympathizers. Attorney General Warren expects industrial sabotage. State guardsmen are now patrolling power lines and aqueducts statewide. New York City Mayor Fiorello H. La Guardia has been appointed director of the U.S. Office of Civilian Defense. He will fly to Los Angeles today, accompanied by Mrs. Franklin D. Roosevelt. They'll be briefed by state guard officials."

One chalkboard down. One city bigwig dozing. Three city bigwigs alert.

"Four hundred Japs on the 'A' list are in custody. Forty-two Federal agents are interrogating them. The Japs are being held at the Terminal Island pen, the Fort MacArthur stockade, the Hall of

Justice jail, the Lincoln Heights jail, and the jails at six of the Los Angeles Police Department's geographical divisions. Suspicious Jap fishing boats in San Pedro Harbor are being boarded, searched and towed to port. Navy PT-boat patrols are being deployed from Santa Barbara on the north to the Mexican border on the south. There is a high probability that Jap submarines are patrolling these waters."

Three chalkboards down. Parker deployed a monotone and excised his prairie drawl.

"Coastal defense batteries are being manned twenty-four hours. Coastal highways have been closed to all nonmilitary traffic. The Board of Supervisors has declared a state of wartime emergency."

Four chalkboards down. No hiccups or speaker's gaffes.

"Los Angeles is on a full-time blackout alert. Yesterday's a.m. and p.m. test blackouts were successful. There was no significant rise in the local crime rate, and traffic accidents increased by a mere 6%. There will be a citywide test blackout Wednesday night. The dusk-to-dawn time span will supply civic officials with valuable statistics."

Five boards down. There's the finish line.

"Per the Watanabe case. I met with Sergeant Dudley Smith yesterday. Sergeant Smith submitted a comprehensive first summary report. Sergeant Smith and three other detectives are working the case, full-time. I will approach *Mirror-News* scribe Sid Hudgens myself and will exhort him to portray the investigation in a laudatory light. The Watanabe case may prove to be a significant propaganda tool, should the PD's Alien Squad or the Sheriff's deputies working the roundups attract accusations of brutal treatment, or if the roundups and property seizures themselves come to be morally questioned."

Parker caught his breath. Fletch Bowron applauded.

Biscailuz said, "Get Bill a White Man of the Week Award."

Jack said, "Shit, get him a double highball at Mike Lyman's."

Bowron said, "Eleanor Roosevelt's coming. She'll probably want a parade."

Biscailuz said, "I heard she's a lezbo. My deputy Dot Rothstein told me. Dot's on the lezbo grapevine. She's the one who told me that Barbara Stanwyck licks snatch."

Bowron said, "I'm taking the bull by the horns on this Jap deal. Get this. I'm going to can all the Japs on the city payroll. They're all Fifth Column, and cream puffs don't win wars."

Parker said, "I don't think that's a sound idea, Mr. Mayor."

Blurt. Speaker's gaffe. Hear that pin drop?

Parker suppressed fidgets. Ward Littell opened the door.

"Sorry to interrupt, gentlemen. Captain, we're about to start with Mr. Bleichert."

Call-Me-Jack went *Shoo.*

Bowron said, "Comrade Bill. Saved by the bell."

Parker about-faced and followed Littell. They walked to the detectives' squad bay. Mirror-front sweat rooms lined the back wall.

Kay Lake stood outside no. 1. She could look in. The men inside couldn't look out.

Parker and Littell joined her. She ignored them and stared through the glass. Littell said, "These are gutter tactics. They're like Stalin's show trials."

The room was small and tight-packed. Ed Satterlee, Dick Hood. Dwight "Bucky" Bleichert. A table-and-chairs tableau.

Parker flipped a wall switch. Speaker static crackled. Sound merged with sight.

Bleichert rode his chair backward. Hood and Satterlee paced. Kay Lake wore her up-all-night look. Her dress was rumpled. Her hair was mussed.

Satterlee said, "Here's what interests me. When you shave in the morning, do you see a German or an American in the mirror?"

Bleichert grinned. "You mean, like the mirror on that wall over there? The one with two sides to it?"

Hood said, "You can't score a knockout here, son. We're on the points system. You've got to say the right things and win by decision."

Bleichert pointed to the mirror. "Who's on the other side, J. Edgar Hoover? Does he really care if I get on the L.A. Police?"

Hood said, "Answer the question, please."

Satterlee said, "German or American? Pick a country, pick a loyalty."

Bleichert said, "My parents were born in Germany. I was born here. I was born in 1917, which gives me an alibi for the Great War."

Kay Lake smiled. Parker smelled her stale perfume.

Hood smiled. "I see your point, but our job is to investigate people with German and Italian bloodlines who might find their loyalties strained."

Bleichert said, “You’re reaching, Mr. Hood. And I don’t know about ‘bloodlines.’ You can’t tell a Kraut or a dago just by looking at him.”

Hood and Satterlee swapped signals. Satterlee snapped his suspenders. Hood said, “Yeah, I know. It’s not like they’re Japs.”

Bleichert drummed the table. “German bloodlines are diffuse. It’s not like Germans are Japs.”

Parker studied Bleichert. Kay Lake hugged the wall. She stuck her hand in his pocket and grabbed his cigarettes. Her hand was warm. His leg fluttered. She lit up and blew high smoke rings.

Satterlee said, “Do you *like* Japs?”

Bleichert said, “I don’t give a shit one way or the other.”

Hood said, “You went to Belmont High.”

Bleichert shrugged. “Class of ’35. The Sentinels, green-and-black forever. What’s all this have to do with me getting on the Los Angeles PD?”

Hood said, “We started compiling intelligence three years ago. We learned that the Jap kids from Little Tokyo went to Belmont. We checked the registration rolls and discovered that this fight phenom was a Belmont alum, and that he sure had a lot of Jap friends. We thought, If this goddamn war comes, our bright boy Bucky would be a good one to talk to, because he just might have the lowdown on some Jap Fifth Columnists.”

Satterlee crowded the table. “Then we learned that our bright boy applied to the PD here. I won’t mince words, son. If you give us some names, you get on. If you refuse, your application is marked ‘null and void.’ ”

Bleichert wetted up. It was sweat, tears or both. Kay Lake pressed the mirror.

Bleichert said, “I know two brothers named Ashida. Akira runs the family farm, and Hideo’s a chemist with the PD. Their father’s dead, and their mother’s named Mariko. She’s a drunk, and she’s crazy about the Emperor and that Tojo guy. She’s got a Jap flag in her living room closet, for all that’s worth.”

Kay Lake shut her eyes and laid her head on the mirror. Parker white-knuckled his gun belt.

Littell said, “Mariko’s harmless, and Hideo’s a brilliant kid. I’ll tell Hood that.”

Kay Lake said, “Men are so goddamned weak.”

24

LOS ANGELES | TUESDAY, DECEMBER 9, 1941

10:29 a.m.

Opium.

The world was his channel. His pallet was a lifeboat. The pipe was his guide.

He flicked across lovely postcards. He welcomed fellow travelers. Bette Davis joined him. They're lovers in London. They're straphangers in the Tube.

Opium.

The pallet, the pipe. Ace Kwan's basement. He's here one moment, gone the next.

It's the Blitz. Ireland has stayed neutral. Joe Kennedy is an isolationist. He's the ambassador to England, but he knows things. The Nazis will win the war. The British beast will fall. Black and Tans killed Dudley Smith's father and elder brother. It left Maidred Conroy Smith widowed and prone to beat her young son.

Time evaporates. Blitzkrieg. It's September 1940. The Germans firebomb London. Dudley and Bette. Uncle Joe gets them a private car in the Tube. Uncle Joe resigns his posting later that fall. The British press dubs him a coward. The Blitz terrifies him. Irish lads drive him to Kerry and nurse him with booze and whores. Dudley and Bette. Uncle Joe got them this private car and ran home with his nuts shriveled up.

Opium.

His senses merged. London burned. Furtwängler played Beethoven's Ninth. He'd meet Bette Friday night. The Shrine Auditorium. The newsboys' bash. He'll wear his best tweed suit.

London becomes Nanking. Ace Kwan told him stories. Jap soldiers behead Chink soldiers. Jap hordes take a monastery and sodomize the priests.

Bette sees it and sobs. He consoles her. *War is the dark grandeur of forfeit, my child. It engages the hellhound within me.*

The Tube car entered a tunnel. Nanking went *Poof!* He's back in Kwan's basement. *Yes, please*—the pipe.

He explained it to Bette. Anesthesia, supplication. *I am all thought and act. My habitude is connivance. I must halt and renew myself in this maddening rush.*

Opium.

Joe Kennedy reappears. He repeats words from 1927.

"Your future is in Los Angeles, son. I can get you on the police force. You can fuck movie stars and create mischief."

A projector clicks and sends film through a slide. Uncle Joe shares his smut fixation. Tijuana, '33. They're in a whorehouse, watching movies screened on a sheet. Two grand lezzies attend them. Dot Rothstein and Ruth Mildred Cressmeyer are honorary men. Dot's a Sheriff's matron and pimp for Gene Biscailuz. Ruth Mildred's a scrape doctor for Jewboy Harry Cohn. It's a grand and odd confluence.

Uncle Joe bankrolls smut films. Uncle Joe has a piece of Carlos Madrano's wetback-running schemes. Uncle Joe keeps a hand in the rackets. It reminds him of his origins.

The projector clicks. A Mex girl becomes Bette in *The Letter.* He got a letter from Beth Short this morning. Yes, she's coming to L.A. Yes, she'll bring her blind friend Tommy Gilfoyle. She hints at that "horrible thing" that happened last year. He'll call Tommy and inquire.

Uncle Joe says, "Devilish men require families, Dud. They keep you safe while you do what you damn please."

Felicitous words. Uncle Joe has his own bastard daughter. She's the spawn of Joe and Gloria Swanson. Laura Hughes is now fourteen. Joe secretly supports her. She took the name Hughes to ridicule Joe. Howard Hughes fucked Joe on a movie deal, circa '31. Unbidden children represent unbidden fate.

Laura lives at the Immaculate Heart Convent. Archbishop Cantwell knows her story. He has a lurid crush on the girl.

Opium.

The projector clicks. Wisps become faces.

Jack Kennedy smiles. He's a Navy ensign. He's coming to L.A. He wants to fuck Ellen Drew. He wants to fuck Gloria Swanson better than his dad did.

Click. There's that shift within him. His normal state is Thought and Act. His habitude is connivance. The postcard tour has refreshed him. He's returning to Thought and Act.

Mike Breuning once worked as a film tech. Ace Kwan has peek rooms within his labyrinth. Harry Cohn loses fortunes in tile games there. Harry owes Ben Siegel more money. Abe Reles is dead. Ben will leave jail soon. Ben loves to carve capital from perverse ventures. Harry Cohn produced a short film eight years ago. It was a suck-up ode to Benito Mussolini. Harry has a bust of Il Duce *on his desk. Has he dumped it in Sunday's aftermath?*

Thought and Act. The war. A realist's perspective.

The Japs won't bomb L.A. They're island-plundering insects. The Pacific is their ant farm. It's their habitude.

They'll lose the war. They'll stagnate as Yankee industry outstrips their material might. They fight to die and ascend to slant-eyed Valhalla. That dubious motive condemns them. Hitler is the Western world's mad lover. Wagner wrote the *Führer*'s ghastly end.

Tristan und Isolde. Unresolved harmonies. The world as the strings drop.

Thought, Act. War as opportunity. Ah, there it is.

Mass internment bodes. Ride along with it. Imprison local Japs for the war's duration. Leverage their property and charge them caretaking fees. Bring in wetbacks to fill vacancies in scut-work employment. Recruit Mex Staties to collect work kickbacks and oversee the wets. Jimmy the Jap Namura has been released from T.I. He would make a grand liaison to the Jap community. Empty out Little Tokyo and other Jap enclaves. Move in thousands of jigaboos too addled to pass conscription tests. Create a circumscribed vice zone built from confiscated Jap holdings. Keep the coons close at hand and contain their antics. Punish aggressions against the white race with instant death. Move rich Japs into Ace Kwan's tunnels and charge them stay-out-of-jail rent. Make the comely ones act in anti-Axis smut films geared for a white clientele.

Opium.

The pipe—once more, yes.

Projector clicks. Thought and Act restored. Memory Lane—New Year's, '38.

The Trocadero. Bette on the dance floor and "Perfidia." That moment he saw her and caught fire.

25

LOS ANGELES | TUESDAY, DECEMBER 9, 1941

11:44 a.m.

They won't report the break-in. They won't reveal the thefts. They sell illegal weaponry. They peddle fascist filth.

The lab was a.m. busy. Chemists logged fiber samples and worked microscopes. Ashida rode his desk. He was keyed up and woozy. He got no sleep.

Ray Pinker walked up. "I've got bad news, kid. It was on the radio. Fletch Bowron's fired all the Japanese on the city payroll. I hate to say it, but that means—"

Ashida opened his top drawer and grabbed a leather pouch. Pinker said something reassuring. Ashida ran out of the lab. He took the stairs three at a clip. He made the front door and sprinted.

He cut across 1st Street. Cars swerved around him. City Hall was two blocks down. He ran there in his lab smock.

He went in the Spring Street door. He took the front stairs four at a clip. The Bureau buzzed. Robbery and Bunco—stuffed with desk-squatting cops. Vice—just Elmer Jackson.

Elmer grinned. "Hey, I know you. You used to work here."

"Captain Parker? I heard he has an office now."

Elmer waved his cigar. "Try 614. If the door's closed, he's sleeping it off."

Ashida walked. It was pushing noon. Homicide emptied out. Bunco and Robbery, likewise. A cop swarm swarmed to the lunchroom.

They all saw him. They all knew him. None of them greeted him. They hit the elevators and pushed DOWN.

Homicide was wide open. Twelve cubicles and one office. The main phone line and twelve extensions.

He shut himself in. He wedged a chair back under the doorknob. He opened the pouch and examined his tools.

Burglar's tools. Confiscated evidence. Three small lock picks and a blunt-edged pry.

The main phone sat by the Teletype. He eyeball-tracked the cord to a wall-mounted fuse box. Beside the box—a smaller box, smeared with wall paint.

A narrow cord connected the boxes. The phone was Dictograph-tapped.

Ashida placed his tools on the Teletype. He picked up the phone receiver and heard a dial tone. He took a skinny-head pick and pried off the talk and hear disks. He saw perforated diodes and glued-in microphones.

He screwed the disks back on. He eyeball-scanned the east squad-room wall. Four cubicles, four phones, four legitimate fuse boxes and piggyback boxes adjacent. Small boxes, painted over. Innocuous. Brazen. Two fuse boxes—who cares?

Ashida replaced his tools and unhooked the chair. He stepped into the hall. Sid Hudgens idled outside the cot room. The Sidster saw him and hooked a finger. Ashida walked over and looked in.

Sssshhh—men asleep.

Twelve cots, five sleepers. Alien Squad boys. Tin hats and gun belts dumped on the floor. Shotguns propped against the wall.

Hudgens closed the door. "Bund, Silver Shirts, Thunderbolt Legion. Care to comment, Dr. Ashida?"

Ashida said, "No comment."

Hudgens poked his ears with a paper clip. "Call me jaded, but I think the whole deal is fishy. The Feds are freezing assets and closing banks, habeas has been suspended, and now Fletch the B. has pulled all you folks off the city tit. Tojo and his boys took Manila, but that don't mean you should lose your job."

Ashida said, "No comment."

Hudgens chortled. "Did you read my piece in yesterday's *Mirror*? If you didn't, the postscript is a scorcheroo."

Ashida said, "I'm listening."

"It's about your old pal Bucky the B. The Buckster wants to mothball his mitts and come on this white man's police force. I suggested that he might have to fink out some Fifth Column fucks in order to secure the gig."

Ashida flushed. "*And?*"

"*And*, Bucky snitched you and your family. *And*, he starts the Academy next May."

The hallway shook—avalanche, earthquake, flash flood.

Hudgens ghoul-grinned. Ashida about-faced. Room 614 was two doors down. He walked over and straight in.

Parker stood near a wall map. Hammer-and-sickle pins covered Russia. Swastika pins covered Deutschland. A bottle and shot glass were out in plain view.

Ashida cleared his throat. Parker turned around. His gun belt slid down his hips.

"Yes?"

"I was hoping I could talk to you, sir."

"I'll venture a guess. You think I can help you retain your city employment."

"I know you can."

Parker tapped his wristwatch. "One minute, Doctor. Brevity affords you your best chance to convince me. Don't repeat yourself. I find repetition taxing."

Ashida said, "I overheard two detectives talking. They said that you had a woman transcribing the Dictograph taps here at the Bureau. They found it amusing, because you were on the recordings yourself, which implies that you made self-incriminating statements. The two detectives went on to say that Chief Horrall had been informed of your actions, but that he was too cocky and lazy to intercede. The implication was that the taps were an open secret, which does not negate the verifiable evidence of your easily identified voice on the recordings."

Parker poured a shot and downed it. He's the Man Who Would Be Chief. He's belting hard liquor at 12:16 p.m.

"Who were the detectives?"

Ashida said, "Mike Breuning and Dick Carlisle. Since they know, it's safe to assume that Dudley Smith knows the gist of your statements."

Parker tapped his watch. "Tell me what you want. Do not employ flattery or threats."

"I want to thank you for stationing Agent Littell at my mother's apartment. I want to prove myself essential to this police department. I want to keep my job and remain on the Watanabe case."

Parker took another pop. "What can you do for me?"

"I can pull the taps, trace the wires to the listening posts and erase the recordings."

Parker dug through his desk and pulled out a folder. Circuit diagrams, certainly.

"Do it now, Doctor. Do it openly. I'm too valuable for Jack Horrall to fuck with. I'll try to impart that same value to you."

Ashida bowed.

Parker threw the folder at him.

Parker said, "You heathen cocksucker."

26

KAY LAKE'S DIARY

LOS ANGELES | TUESDAY, DECEMBER 9, 1941

12:21 p.m.

It's worse today. It feels more embittered. There are more Federal men and more cop sentries stationed on 2nd Street rooftops. I saw FBI agents swarm a vegetable market. They shackled the proprietor and dragged him to a paddy wagon. A Fed fired his shotgun into the sidewalk vegetable displays. Rock salt shredded rows of cabbage into pulp.

I walked up 2nd Street. I felt invisible as a white woman and anomalous as a police-world provocateur. I'd called Dr. Lesnick's office and secured an appointment. I'd rehearsed my mock-impromptu meeting with Claire De Haven. 2nd Street registered as official chaos. It was sanctioned by justified outrage and perpetrated in the spirit of racial bias and war hysteria. I was here as Captain William H. Parker's pawn. I needed to see this within that context.

2nd Street was packed with pedestrians and prowl cars. Sheriff's deputies milled outside the Sumitomo Bank and loaded money bags into a van. The deputies held machine guns and scanned the sidewalk; an FBI man nailed a government-seizure notice to the door. "God Bless America" echoed from a storefront one block west. I saw red-white-and-blue bunting draped across the façade and men distributing pamphlets by the doorway.

I heard an explosion. It was a shotgun blast. I heard a second burst and saw two Japanese boys prone in the street. They were directly across from me; their trouser legs were torn to bloody strips.

A third boy dashed across the street. I caught a side view of a cop raising his shotgun. Then Captain Bill Parker stepped out of a crowd and yanked the cop's arms into the air. The rock-salt round exploded at nothing but sky; the boy escaped into an empty building.

The boys in the street flailed at their wounds; a man and woman ran over with rolls of gauze. Captain Parker snatched the cop's shotgun and ejected the remaining shells. He looked outraged. The cop trembled at his display of assertion. Captain Parker threw the shotgun at him and stepped back out of sight.

He never saw me. It happened very quickly. I walked toward "God Bless America" and the tricolored bunting. I hardly felt my footsteps.

The storefront was the "Anti-Axis Committee." It was a dispensary for pro-American regalia. The merchandise could not have been made from scratch since Sunday's attack. Shelves held stars-and-stripes armbands, Uncle Sam hats and anti-Emperor polemics. Browsers browsed. There were Japanese locals, robe-clad Shinto priests and Japanese pastors in dark suits with Protestant collars. A man and woman stood behind a case full of geegaws. They wore AVENGE PEARL HARBOR buttons. Hawaiian leis were draped around their necks; the flowers had been dyed mourning black. The Anti-Axis Committee and everything in it had to have been planned and executed well in advance of Sunday's events. It did not indicate foreknowledge of the attack. It acknowledged the bloodthirsty designs of Imperial Japan and predicted this moment of response.

The music came from a phonograph perched by the door. A pastor manned the recording disk. "God Bless America" repeated, loud and close-quarters shrill.

A man waved a jar at me; I dug into my purse and dropped in a twenty. The man tossed a red-white-and-blue lei over my head. I bowed and felt idiotic.

The man bowed off and accosted other browsers. I dawdled by a revolving book rack filled with tracts. The place felt like a vaudeville tent.

Reynolds Loftis and Chaz Minear walked in.

I looked down and feigned interest in a "Nisei Heroes" screed.

Loftis and Minear saw me; little nods and nudges affirmed it. *That crazy girl from the recital. She sure caused a scene!*

The jar man sideswiped me again. I sensed Loftis and Minear within range and performed an encore. I deployed a stage whisper this time.

"These tracts are inherently unradical and fail to critique the systematic bigotry that has fueled this counteraggression for the past two horrible days. This cravenly jingoistic display of yours is an insufficient response to the injustice currently being perpetrated on this very street."

The man cringed. Loftis and Minear heard every word.

I walked outside and turned north on Main. My car was parked at City Hall. I recalled then—the gas gauge was down near empty, and I just gave all my money away. Lee was probably holed up at the Bureau. I could dun him for gas money or visit Elmer Jackson at Vice.

Downtown L.A. was all war and Christmas. Flags, faux fir trees, Salvation Army Santas. Aircraft spotters surrounded City Hall. They resembled dotty bird-watchers. They brought picnic baskets and wore funny hats.

I walked up to the Bureau. The cot room and Vice squadroom were dead. A crowd hovered by the Homicide pen. Call-Me-Jack Horrall, Gene Biscailuz, Sid Hudgens.

I joined them. They ignored me and stared into the squadroom. I tracked their eyes and saw a man disassembling a desk phone. He wore a lab smock and had his back to us. The floor was strewn with detached parts.

The man was removing tap mounts. It was weirdly synchronous. It brought back Bill Parker's tap-transcription ploy.

The man pulled wires. He turned around and faced the hallway. I recognized him immediately.

The young Japanese. There at Bucky Bleichert's fight. There in Little Tokyo yesterday.

Sid Hudgens noticed me. "What gives, Katherine? And what's with the lei? Were you over at Pearl for the fireworks?"

I removed the lei, dropped it over Sid's head and pulled him to a spot down the hall. Sid said, "Not here, sugar. Big Lee could show up any second."

Call-Me-Jack and Gene Biscailuz drifted. I said, "Sid, what is this?"

Sid sniffed the lei and leered. "I'm writing it up as a pro-Horrall piece. Bill Parker talked the Chief into letting that Jap kid do a little wire pulling. The Feds are planning some kind of *farkakte* probe. The Bureau's full of recording posts, and the shit on the wires could get half the Department indicted. Parker's plan is to plant some phony taps and wire rigs after New Year's and lay in some innocuous jive, which'll send the Feds home with *buppkes.* The Jap kid's name is Hideo Ashida. The Department's in a bind, 'cause he's the best crime-lab man in the West, but in case you ain't noticed, he's a *furshtinkener* Jap."

Hideo Ashida. Hideo Ashida at Bucky's fight. Bucky rats out *Hideo Ashida. I* transcribe Bureau taps Sunday morning. *Hideo Ashida* removes them *now.*

"Another time, huh, sugar? You, me and a bottle of Courvoisier while Lee's out of town with the Dudster?"

I blew Sid off and walked into the squadroom. Hideo Ashida snipped wires on a fuse box. He saw me. His smock and pants were grease-smeared and streaked with Spackle dust.

I said, "My name is Kay Lake. Captain Parker had me transcribing the taps."

Form of address seemed to stump him. A bow or a handshake? This girl discomfits me.

He said, "Dr. Ashida." He stuffed his hands in his pockets—*so there.*

"Is your doctorate in electrical engineering?"

He said, "I have two doctorates. I'm a research chemist and a microbiologist. I'm also a criminologist, but that's a self-bestowed title."

The whole business vexed him. The Homicide pen was a junk heap. Three detectives lurked by the door. *What's Lee Blanchard's twist doing with this haughty Jap?*

Hideo Ashida squirmed. Decorum flummoxed him. His limbs were impediments. He was diverted from his task.

I said, "I could show you the listening post I worked in."

"Captain Parker gave me a list of the locations. I have all the information I require."

He would refuse all offers. I had to state my intent.

"There's a good deal of work here. I'm going to help you."

He twitched. He almost bowed. He almost screamed "*No.*"

He said, "Yes. As you wish."

2:06 p.m.

It was hard work. I worked in a tweed skirt, silk blouse and cashmere sweater. My stacked-heel pumps slid on the floor. I kicked them off and worked in my stockings.

We unscrewed telephone disks, pulled cords and removed microphones. We worked at close quarters. Dr. Ashida retained an ever-decorous distance. He explained the task of tap removal entirely with gestures. His gestures were ever graceful and fluent.

We went from squadroom to squadroom, listening post to listening post. We lugged boxes; we filled them with transcription logs and yanked wires. Jack Webb followed us for a good two hours. He was a Belmont High chum of Dr. Ashida and Bucky Bleichert. Dr. Ashida went queasy every time Jack mentioned Bucky; I wondered if he knew of Bucky's betrayal. Jack managed the Belmont track team. "High-Jump Hideo" and "Bucky the Bullet" went to the All-City finals.

Dr. Ashida was deft. Athletics partially explained it. I screened mental snapshots of Bucky and Hideo, Belmont '35. Pep rallies, cheerleaders, laps on that hilltop track. Locker-room camaraderie and soapy Bucky in the showers.

It was filthy work. I tore my nails, ravaged my stockings and stained up my sweater and skirt. We communicated with nods and hand signals. I smelled his sweat and my own sweat; we lifted, yanked, carried and hauled. Bureau men dropped by and made conversation; they looked askance but refrained from editorializing. I explained the work as Bill Parker's gambit to thwart a Fed probe; I heard "open secret" a good dozen times. The taps went back to Two-Gun Davis. Cops kept tabs on other cops in a corrupt copocracy. The taps were a perennial pain in the ass. Good riddance to bad rubbish.

Dr. Ashida clenched every time I said "Parker." Bucky Bleichert was the phantom male presence in my life; Captain Parker was the most provocative. Dr. Ashida possessed histories with both men. He was wet-eyed at Bucky's farewell fight. His association with Captain Parker was all police intrigue.

I wanted his perceptions. I wanted to crack his reserve. I was the interrogator and cop with the rubber hose. *Who are these two men? You must tell me what you know.*

We worked. We pulled wires, removed microphones, cleaned out listening posts. The kibitzers drifted off at end of watch. I was jittery, hungry, exhausted. We blitzed through and finished our work.

We were disheveled. We were one collective mess.

I suggested a drink at Mike Lyman's. Scotty was meeting me there later. I knew exactly what Dr. Ashida would say.

He said, "Yes, as you wish."

5:51 p.m.

We took the freight lift. We went out the 1st Street door as the Hill Street bus pulled up. Dr. Ashida stood aside and let me board first. I dropped two nickels in the fare box. We stood at the front and held the rail. Every passenger on the bus stared.

We were dirty and dramatically unkempt. Yellow man, white woman, war. Did they think we were plotting treason or fucking on the City Hall lawn?

The driver turned south on Hill. We made good time. I yanked the cord and signaled a stop at 8th Street. The driver pulled over and let us off.

The bus pulled away. A man yelled, "Goddamn Jap!" A woman yelled, "White whore!"

We walked into Mike Lyman's. The supper rush was just starting; Thad Brown stood at the bar. He did a double take and waved to us; I curtsied and waved back. Dr. Ashida preferred seclusion. I *knew* that. I led him to a back booth.

We settled in. Dr. Ashida said, "Black coffee," and sanctioned me to fetch it. He didn't want to risk a pissy waiter. I *knew* that. I walked to the bar, ordered the coffee and a Manhattan.

The barman served me quickly. I carried the drinks to the booth and interrupted Dr. Ashida. He was daubing his shirt collar. He saw me and dropped the napkin. I stifled a laugh.

"Cheers, Doctor."

"Yes . . . Miss . . ."

"Lake. My name is Katherine Lake, and I've gone by 'Kay' for years."

Dr. Ashida said, "Cheers, Miss Lake." He fiddled with his cup and saucer. He spilled coffee and doused his hands. He wiped them and tucked them under his legs.

I asked him where he attended college. He said, "Stanford." I told him that I went to UCLA and waited for a response. He nodded. It told me this:

He knew nothing of my Big Lee's shack-job reputation. He knew Lee but had no dirt on the Boulevard-Citizens job.

"I saw you wave to Lieutenant Brown."

"I know him through my boyfriend. He works Central Patrol, and his name is Lee Blanchard."

"Yes. I know Officer Blanchard."

I said, "Not 'Lee,' Dr. Ashida? You certainly outrank him in the police hierarchy."

He shook his head. "I only use first names by invitation. I know you're thinking it, so I'll say it. It's a commendable Japanese trait."

I laughed and raised my glass. "Yes, it occurred to me, but I was thinking of that commendable trait within the context of police work."

"Yes?"

"You have a hierarchy and nonmeritocracy, offset by a paramilitary ethos and casual social codes. Close personal and professional bonds are formed within this oddly flexible structure."

Dr. Ashida sipped coffee. "Captain Parker commands formality. I would always employ the most rigorous form of address with him."

I said, "Captain Parker is subtle. He's using me for an intelligence foray, and 'using' doesn't begin to tell the story. He knows that my loyalties will be stretched, because he recruited me with a certain foreknowledge of my likely ambivalence. He's banking that my ambivalence will grant me credibility with the people I've been engaged to entrap."

Dr. Ashida sipped coffee. I was baiting him. He knew it. He was aroused by the challenge of provocation and response. But, he didn't see the point. But, the notion of rapport vexed him. He was a scientist. He scorned everything but quantifiable results.

"You transcribed the taps for Captain Parker. I'm wondering how he convinced you to do it."

I lit a cigarette. "That's all I'll be telling you, Doctor. I wanted to see if police intrigue interests you as it does me. You confirmed that it does."

Dr. Ashida smiled. It delighted me. I sipped my cocktail and smiled back.

He said, "I think Captain Parker has misgivings about the roundups. He assigned an FBI man to look after my mother."

"I witnessed his misgivings today. And his action with your mother must mean that he values your work."

"I'm hoping to prove myself indispensable."

"Yes, but you're employed by the city, so you'll be losing your job."

"I think my position is safe. For now, Captain Parker is my guardian—"

He stopped. I traced his eyes and saw why. Lee was standing there. He was wearing civvies and holding a highball. His shirt was darkly spotted. It looked like congealed blood.

He said, "Aloha, baby. You too, Hirohito."

I said, "Go home, Lee. Sleep it off. There's a roast you can heat up."

"Go home to *what*? My girl's out entertaining the Axis powers."

A hubbub began building close by us. Lee's slur, my raised voice. People looked over. They poked one another. They strained for better views.

I said, "Shut up, Lee." Dr. Ashida stared at his hands. Lee pointed to the stains on his shirt.

"Jap blood. A guy named Takahashi ran on me. He's at Georgia Street Receiving now."

I stood up. The hubbub built and spread to a whole string of tables. Two waiters stopped to look.

"*Go home, Lee.*"

"Really, sweetheart. I'm enlightened when you keep to white men. But a goddamn Jap?"

I slapped him. My nails raked his cheek. He leaned into my hand and made it worse. Blood trickled over his lips.

Somebody gasped. The whole room gasped. Somebody said, "Oh," and dropped their drink. I heard glass shatter. Somebody said, "Shit."

Lee walked out. He bumped a waiter and capsized his tray. A birthday cake with glowing candles fell.

I sat down and looked down. Dr. Ashida bolted my drink.

The hubbub subsided. I heard exhales and dish clatter. A man went *Whew!*

Dr. Ashida looked at me. His eyelids fluttered. The veins in his neck pulsed dark blue.

"I've seen you at the Olympic. You're always drawing pictures of my friend Bucky."

"Yes. And I saw you at the fight Sunday night. Bucky waved to you."

"We've been friends for years. We went to high school together."

I said, "I have a very bad crush on him. It's all too unseemly."

A hand touched my shoulder. My rough boy—prompt and dear.

Scotty loomed. Dr. Ashida stood up and stood dwarfed. Scotty said, "Hello, sir. My name's Bennett."

Dr. Ashida muttered good-byes. He kept his eyes down and walked away. I nuzzled Scotty's hand.

He said, "Lee Blanchard's out on the sidewalk, crying. I'm not complaining, but you sure spread yourself thin."

The war was two days old. I consorted with suspect aliens and created public scenes. Pinch me—I could be home practicing Chopin.

27

LOS ANGELES | TUESDAY, DECEMBER 9, 1941

7:09 p.m.

Mayor Fletch served prime scotch. Parker pledged just *one* and quick-marched to *three*. The office was geared for bullshit and booze. Walnut panels, green leather chairs and spittoons.

Jack Horrall said, "The Bureau looks like the Philippines is supposed to look. The fucking Japs invaded today."

Bowron said, "I heard it was 'Jap,' singular."

Jack said, "Lee Blanchard's girlfriend was helping out. Jesus, there's stories on *her*."

Parker sipped scotch. His world was upside down. He was losing weight. He'd been living on cigarettes and pretzels.

The roundups verged on unkosher now. The Alien Squad was running amok. Those kids with the rock-blasted legs.

He said, "We can't fire Dr. Ashida. He's essential to the Watanabe job."

Bowron said, "So, it's '*Dr.*'? Jesus, they'll let anyone into Stanford."

Jack said, "You've got to concede this one, Fletch. The Jap kid pulled us out of this shit on those taps. We were *all* on them. I used to call Brenda Allen from Homicide."

Bowron sipped scotch. "I don't like it. I already issued the order. 'All Japs city-employed' means 'all Japs city-employed.' It doesn't mean we make Charlie Chan an exception."

Parker sipped scotch. "He pulled all the taps and erased all the wires. The Feds will be coming through in February. He spared us a lot of grief."

Bowron nibbled a pretzel. "'Fed probe,' shit. Any probe that isn't directed at Fifth Columnists will be laughed out of town at its inception."

Parker said, "We owe the kid, Mr. Mayor. And that means we can't roust his mother and brother."

Bowron laced his scotch with Bromo-Seltzer. He rubbed his stomach—goddamn ulcers, shit.

"All right, I'll concede. Never let it be said that Mayor Fletcher Bowron isn't an enlightened white man."

Call-Me-Jack said, "Hear, hear."

Bowron belted his voodoo drink. The Feds were due at 7:30. Dick Hood, Ed Satterlee, Ward Littell.

Bowron belched. "Lay it out, Bill. You know what we're here for. The roundups and tomorrow night's blackout."

Parker lit a cigarette. "It's been all over the papers and the radio. The curfew, the specific instructions, the works. Our officers will be working the checkpoints, along with Army sentries. Fleeing vehicles will be fired upon. That's straight from the CO at Fourth Interceptor."

Jack whistled. Bowron flashed V for Victory. Spotlights swooped off the City Hall lawn and crisscrossed the windows.

Parker said, "We've got Sheriff's reservists stationed at key intersections. They'll be looking for drunks and erratic drivers. On the roundups, we've got T.I., the Hall of Justice jail, the city jails, and the county honor farm booked to near capacity. It's starting to feel out of hand. Given the volume, I don't see how the Feds can accurately assess the innocence or guilt of these people, and we need to accept that it's highly likely that most of the people being detained are in fact blameless."

Jack whistled. Fletch B. rubbed his temples—goddamn headache, shit.

"As mayor of the great city of Los Angeles, I am officially anointing Captain William Henry Parker the Third as 'Comrade Bill.' "

Jack went *Take a bow*. Parker bowed sitting down.

"I think we're headed for a full-scale wartime internment. From what I've read, Roosevelt's leaning that way. This poses the question—where do we house the goddamn Japs?"

Bowron belched. "We implement Federal property-seizure laws and grab all their houses and land. We lease it out and use the money to offset the cost of stockade-type housing."

The Feds walked in. They filled the doorway. Homo Hoover favored tall men with jawlines. These men personified that.

Bowron served up booze and club chairs. It set a gabfest tone.

Dick Hood said, "The Navy sunk two Jap destroyers, and the Reds are bleeding Hitler dry. We're on the rebound."

Bowron sipped scotch and Bromo. "The Navy's got the high seas, but we're landlocked in L.A. So, gentlemen, if it goes to internment, where do we house the goddamn Japs?"

Ed Satterlee futzed with his cuff links. "Wherever we put them, they pay for it. And why mince words? If they've got dough, we house them commensurate with their ability to pay. If they're short on cash, we fill up the Marine Corps brigs."

Ward Littell shook his head. "There's job furlough. The women work in defense plants for a suitable wage. FDR gets his draft bill through Congress, and the men have the option to enlist."

Hood mimed masturbation. Satterlee rolled his eyes. Littell lit a cigarette and blew smoke his way.

Call-Me-Jack laughed. "The fucking draft. We'll lose all our best men. All we'll have left is illiterate thugs."

Parker said, "That's all we've got now, Chief."

Everyone laughed. Everyone slugged scotch. Parker's glow went to a flush.

Satterlee said, "We seized sixty grand at the Sumitomo Bank. A Sheriff's van is taking it down to the T.I. vault tomorrow night."

Littell crushed his cigarette. "Is the money itemized? Will it be properly returned to the account holders?"

Satterlee said, "Who gives a shit? We're at war with these fuckers."

Hood went *Ixnay*. "I hate to say it, but Ward's right. We'll itemize."

Satterlee sighed. Bowron mixed a fresh scotch and Bromo. Parker jumped on Hood's concession.

"All our jails are hitting capacity, and we're only two days into this. I think we should have the agents conducting the interviews compile a list for habeas. If we release some low-risk Japs, we'll have more jail space if the real shit hits the fan."

Bowron said, "I like the sound of it. You divert overcrowding and get the low-risk Japs to go home and snitch the bad apples."

Hood went *Comme ci, comme ça*. "It flies, up to a point. Habeas might work, but if we go to full-scale internment, they're all going back in stir anyway."

Parker checked his watch. It was pushing 8:00. A Dudster briefing loomed.

Littell said, "You should transfer over to our shop, Bill. We need more clear thinkers."

Satterlee said, "Comrade Ward, meet Comrade Bill."

Hood said, "He's not Mr. Hoover's type."

Call-Me-Jack said, "The head G-man's a fairy. I still can't get over it."

Parker winked at him. "There's no way I'd transfer. There's a job I want right here."

7:59 p.m.

The briefing was set for the cot room. Hurricane Hideo had blitzed the squad pens. Parker took service stairs down. Dudley sat with Ashida and Buzz Meeks.

Parker took a cot. Meeks passed him an ashtray. Dudley said, "Your play with the taps was brilliant, sir. You were both muckraker and protector of the corrupt status quo. You furthered your personal agenda and enhanced your reputation as a company man. Bravo, sir."

"Thank you, Sergeant. It was a two-edged sword as a compliment, but I'll take it."

Dudley smiled. "Did you play the recordings, sir? Were you stricken by the sound of your own voice and dismayed that you didn't hear mine?"

Parker winked. "Is that a roll of phone slugs in your pocket, or are you just glad to see me?"

Dudley roared. Meeks yawned. Ashida sat prim.

Parker said, "We're going back to fundamentals. Yes, the Watanabes possessed an anti-American tract. Yes, Dr. Ashida presents a vivid case for the alleged suicide note being coerced. Yes, the note refers to a 'looming apocalypse,' which might indicate either Sunday's attack or the inevitable American-Japanese conflict. I would doubt that the family had specific foreknowledge of the attack, and the crime itself seems to be more of a familial blood feud than a geopolitical matter. Dr. Ashida, would you care to offer comments from a Japanese-American perspective?"

Ashida nodded. "I would agree and disagree, Captain. The killer or killers had to have been Japanese-fluent, or they wouldn't have been able to read the suicide note. The 'looming apocalypse' line might have been a ruse within a ruse, and one intended to shift attention from a family motive to a political motive, should the suicide come to be revealed as having been staged. More pressingly, we have the spent round and the silencer shards, along with the astonishingly unlikely coincidence of the spent round and silencer shards at Whalen's Drugstore the same day."

Dudley beamed. "Doctor, you are a very bright penny."

Ashida blushed. Meeks unwrapped a cigar. Parker said, "The Watanabes were on the 'A' list. I don't consider it applicable, because I believe the Feds were overzealous in compiling the names in the first place. There were two known associates of the family listed. The first was a reputed spy named Tachibana, who allegedly fled to Mexico. The second was a man named Namura, who's in custody at Terminal Island. Sergeant, did you follow up on this during your visit to T.I. yesterday?"

Dudley said, "We interviewed Mr. Namura, sir. In point of fact, he was not a KA of the family, and had no true Fifth Column leanings himself. The sergeant of the guard had been complaining of overcrowding, so I took it upon myself to secure his release."

Meeks eyeballed Dudley. Meeks emitted strange brain waves. Meeks scowled a bit.

A patrol cop walked in. He said, "Phone call for you, Sergeant Smith."

Dudley followed him out. Searchlights strafed the windows. Somebody outside yelled, "*Banzai!*"

Meeks high-signed Ashida. "Don't take it rough, kid. It's your fucked-up people, not you."

Ashida blushed. "We keep coming back to the silencers and Lugers."

Parker said, "Yes, compounded by the fact that Sergeant Smith and his lads killed a man on Saturday afternoon. The man might or might not have fired the gun at the pharmacy, and he was dead himself by the time the Watanabes were killed. It's a pity, because he might have given us some insight as to that bullet hole on the second-floor landing."

Meeks whooped—*mother dog!* Ashida sat prim.

Parker said, "There's a lesson here. Don't abrogate due process. The act creates more problems than it solves."

The Dudster walked back in. Meeks fish-eyed him. Ashida sat prim.

Dudley smiled. "Did I miss anything?"

Parker lit a cigarette. "I told Nort Layman to do advanced blood work on the bodies, and I want Dr. Ashida to do molds on the loose dirt in the Watanabes' driveway. We had rain yesterday morning, but there's a corrugated roof over the driveway, so we might get some protected lifts. Fundamentals, gentlemen. I want detailed biographies on the victims and a backup house-to-house canvass."

A Teletype clattered somewhere. The echo dispersed. The sixth floor was an evacuation zone.

Parker yawned. "There's been a good deal of anti-Japanese rancor in Los Angeles lately."

Meeks said, "Imagine that."

Parker said, "I want Dr. Ashida to have a full-time bodyguard. I was thinking of two men in twelve-hour shifts. Meeks, do you have any ideas?"

Meeks said, "How's Lee Blanchard and Elmer Jackson grab

you? Lee drools for plainclothes jobs, and Elmer's tired of standing around 2nd Street, sniffing broiled eel. It's sitting-down work, and both them boys enjoy a good magazine."

Parker nodded—done. Meeks waved his cigar.

"On the gun angle. One, we know it was a silencer-fitted Luger at both locations. Two, dead heist suspect or no dead heist suspect, it's the only real lead we got. Three, let's take a leap and say there's a fascist slant to this job. The Deutsches Haus over on 15th Street sells Lugers illegally. It's all over a whole shitload of Subversive-Squad reports."

Ashida twitched a tad. Parker blurry-eye yawned.

"We'll raid the place later tonight. I'll call the Feds. Sergeant Smith, I want you and your boys."

Dudley smiled. "I bear our Teutonic kin no animus, but we'll be there with bells on."

Meeks goose-stepped off his cot. Dudley went *Lad, you slay me.* Parker shut his eyes.

Get it? I'm half in the bag. I'm bored. I've had enough.

Footsteps moved out. Somebody killed the lights. The room spun. The floor dropped under his feet.

The drop might have been a dream. The drop might have been sleep.

28

LOS ANGELES | TUESDAY, DECEMBER 9, 1941

8:34 p.m.

Tong skirmish—Four Families versus Hop Sing.

They fought behind Kwan's. Dudley parked his K-car and watched.

He knew the opponents. Dewey Leng pumped gas at Chuck's Chevron. He was Four Families. Danny Wong fry-cooked at the Pagoda. He was Hop Sing.

The lads parried with switchblades. They grunted in their brusque language. They scampered and slashed.

Dewey Leng closed the gap. Danny Wong was winded. His knife hand fluttered. Dewey Leng feinted and chopped at his fingers. Danny Wong screamed.

Uncle Ace bossed Hop Sing. Danny was a stellar cook. No killing, please.

Dudley pulled his piece and fired above them. A fence board exploded. The noise spooked the lads. They scurried away.

The kitchen door was off the alley. Dudley opened it and followed a large rat in. Cooks and busboys bowed. He bowed back. Cats chased rats across scrub sinks. Peking ducks cooled.

Dudley walked down to the basement. Ace lounged in his office. A woman hand-stitched armbands. They were red, white and black—pure Deutschenationale. "*I am not a Jap!*" replaced the swastika.

Ace said, "We sell them to Chinese, Koreans and Jap beasts trying to pass. I foresee brisk business."

Dudley laughed. Ace signaled the woman: *You go.* She vanished like female slaves worldwide.

Ace said, "What gives, Dudster?"

"I have many grand notions to share with you, my yellow brother."

Ace rubbed all ten fingers. "You tell me. Grand notions mean money."

Dudley snatched the desk chair and swirled it. The office went *wheeeee.*

"A few questions, first. Tell me again, what does Harry Cohn owe you?"

"Jew cocksucker. It is still nineteen grand. The Jew beast owes Ben Siegel forty-eight."

"Two grand sums, two grand Jew beasts. Second, have you found the Four Families boy who insulted your niece? Your rivals have been misbehaving of late, and I had pledged death to the lad."

Ace said, "My boys find him, Dudster kill him."

Dudley tilted the chair. "In due time, my brother. Most pressingly, a Jap lad named Jimmy Namura will be visiting us in a half hour. We spoke on the telephone a short while ago. I hope I wasn't precipitous in extending the invitation."

Ace rubbed his palms. He was aglow. Greed became him.

Dudley said, "I believe that the entire Jap population of our city will be interned within sixty days' time. This provides us with an opportunity to implement your own grand notion to provide them with room and board in your tunnels and coerce them into performing in naughty films. It had occurred to me that the Japs would feel better if they actually looked Chinese, and that you know a morally sketchy plastic surgeon named Lin Chung. He's no Terry Lux, but he's a competent man."

Ace said, "Sounds like a dud deal, Dudster. Japs, Chinamen—the white man cannot tell us apart."

Dudley said, "Yes, but you had told me that Dr. Chung was a noted eugenicist who had studied racial surgery as performed by Herr Hitler's regime. I thought he might appreciate a chance to indulge his curiosity."

Ace shrugged and grabbed the phone. Ace dialed a number and spieled rabid Chink. A busboy walked in Jimmy Namura. Jimmy the Jap wore khakis and a silk bowling shirt.

He *Sieg Heil!*ed Dudley and scowled at Uncle Ace. The busboy scrammed. Uncle Ace dumped the phone and scrammed with him. Japs brought home the Rape of Nanking.

Jimmy the Jap clicked his heels. Dudley said, "You've worn out the joke, lad. It was amusing the first time, but no more."

"I've learned something, boss. I told you you wouldn't regret springing me."

Dudley pointed to a chair. Jimmy the Jap got comfy. He had that eager-snitch look.

"Here's the windup and the pitch, boss. *El Jefe* Madrano isn't a partner with that white stiff buying up all the Japanese properties. All that skinny I told you about the stiff owning the Watanabe house and all that 'phantom ownership' jive *es la verdad*, but *El Jefe*'s just a scout, and there's really *two* white stiffs. The 'phantom ownership' is officially recorded somewhere, but that's all I've got on that."

Dudley said, "Continue, please."

"That first pitch was a strike, boss—and I got another fastball coming. You've got *two* white stiffs, but I've got no names. They've bought city properties and farms from families named Ugawa, Hiroki, and Marusawa. They own the Watanabe farm and their flop in Highland Park, all through some 'dummy corporation.' That cat we talked about, Hikaru Tachibana, was the two guys' bird dog, and he allegedly got the deal on the Watanabe farm done. Tachi was out on bail and had some deportation hearing pending, but he absconded and started running a string of chippies up in Hollywood. Now, he gets arrested under a phony name, gets bailed and goes absconding again. Remember, he's supposed to be hiding in Mexico—but I heard that a Japanese guy snuffed him right after he brokered the deal on the Watanabe farm. So, allegedly, Tachi's *muerto*, anchored with lead weights and buried in some dirt-covered well hole out there in that farm stretch."

Dudley savored it. "And how did you secure this information?"

"My lips are sealed, boss. I'm a Jap on the Jap grapevine. I know Japs who know Japs who know Japs. If you start bracing them for corroboration, my Jap goose is cooked."

Uncle Ace walked Lin Chung in. Dr. Chung packed a large satchel. Ace brought a frosty mai tai on a tray.

Dudley said, "Drink up, Jimmy. Mr. Kwan is quite the swell host."

Jimmy the Jap shrugged and snatched the goblet. It featured almond bitters, high-volt rum and morphine.

He took a jolt and went pie-eyed. Jolt no. 2 dropped his lids. Jolt no. 3 put him supine.

9:07 p.m.

The floor served as a bed. A tablecloth served as a sheet. Dudley jammed a chair cushion under Jimmy's head. Lin Chung disinfected his instruments with Old Crow. Ace smoked cigarettes to cover wayward scents.

Scalpels, cutting knives, catgut sutures. A bone saw with serrated teeth.

Lin Chung built a mouth vent with paper clips and duct tape. Dudley called Mike Breuning at the Bureau. Mike confirmed Whiskey Bill—the Deutsches Haus, 11:30.

Dudley dug through Ace's closets. Ace was a big tunnel digger. Yes, he's got all the tools.

Large shovel, small shovel, pickax. U.S. Army Geiger counter.

Dudley packed them into a duffel bag and carried them out to his car. His evidence kit was stashed in the trunk. Like the Boy Scouts—be prepared.

He walked back to the office. The tablecloth was soaked red. Jimmy the Jap's brows were cut and clamped wide. Lin Chung wore goggles. He worked through Ace's smoke.

He cut cheekbone to chin and blotted blood with cocktail napkins. Dudley stayed clear of the spritz. Lin Chung plucked tendons with pencil tips.

Dr. Chung was a witch doctor of subwestern repute. Indeed—no Terry Lux. Dr. Terry owned a dry-out farm in the Malibu Hills. He did movieland plastic jobs and booze and dope cures. Dr. Terry dried out jigaboo jazzmen and Hancock Park swells.

Lin Chung poked Jimmy the Jap. Lin Chung said, "So far, I pessimistic. Physiognomy incompatible, I think. Might not work on mass scale like Uncle Ace propose. Eugenics wave of the future, but still in its infancy. Require thought and study. This cocksucker still look Jap to me."

Jimmy Namura woke up and screamed.

9:29 p.m.

The screams chased him outside. Dudley hit the parking lot, hellhounded. He bagged his car and tapped the siren. The sound smothered fading screams.

Dublin, 1919. Black and Tans fire into a Grafton Street crowd. His brother James dies. He hides in a refuse bin. He's fourteen. His world is all sirens and screams.

He took Broadway to the Arroyo Seco. The parkway shot him straight north. He dry-swallowed two Benzedrine.

Mass surgery might prove untenable. It might be a eugenic conceit. Finer hands might make it work. Terry Lux *loved* to cut faces. Terry was America First and perhaps further right. Lin Chung could provide cut-rate cuts.

The Watanabe case was *his* case. The outcome was irrelevant. The case was his laboratory. It sanctioned him to exploit the dark races. The case shadowboxed the war.

He cut through Pasadena and Glendale. He took dirt roads to the northeast Valley. They were rutted and rock-strewn. He dropped into low gear.

Jap farmland. Fertilizer stink. Night irrigation. A constant subterranean hiss.

He had a Watanabe farm map. He'd disinterred before. Dublin, '22. He located buried British guns outside Galway. Joe Kennedy supplied his cell with metal detectors.

There's the Watanabe farm. There's the kanji-script sign. It means "Gate to Japan."

The bennies tapped his bloodstream. It was all one big long shot. The lead weights on the body rang credible. The "dirt-covered well hole" narrowed it down. Jimmy the Jap might have been conned. The body might be elsewhere. It was worth an hour's time.

Clouds covered the moon. Dudley parked behind a scrub bush and saddled up. The duffel bag, the Geiger, a flashlight. His full-dress evidence kit.

He lugged his gear to the fence line and trampled down a stretch of chain links. He turned on his flashlight. He saw cabbage rows and smelled fertilizer. He flicked on the Geiger. The dial lit up, the needle hovered at zero.

There—a low hill ahead. No crop furrows—just green-brown grass.

Dudley trudged over. The load slowed him down. The bennies supplied extra oomph. The Geiger led the way. The needle stayed low. The clicker *click-clicked.*

He read the clicks. He made them. Metallic soil traces—innocuous.

The hill was a trudge. His heart rate bollixed his breath. He saw a stonework well up at the top. He low-beamed his flashlight and caught scurrying bugs.

The needle jumped. The clicker clicks clicked click-by-click *loud.* The intervals shortened. Follow the clicks, follow the needle, look for inconsistent topsoil.

Click, click, click, click, click.

A click-jabber, persistent. See the needle? It's jumping, *click-click-click.*

There—*that* patch of ground. Bugs are digging into it. There's soil exposed. They want that edible moss and that *something* underneath.

The needle shot to the end of the dial. The clicker clicked *LOUD.* The *click-clicks* said *DIG HERE.*

Dudley turned off the Geiger and got out his tools. Dudley anchored his flashlight and aimed it at the ground. Dig, now—there's something there.

Bugs skittered away. He sank his shovel into the swarm and killed the fuckers en masse. He chopped through them and hit soft dirt.

He tossed it away from his gear. Underground bugs squirmed. He smelled corpse-dissolving quicklime.

Dirt—one shovel's worth. *Dirt*—two, three, four, five, six. Yes—a flesh underscent.

Yes—yellow skin. Yes—brown dirt in black hair. Paradoxical quicklime. It liquefies flesh, it preserves flesh, it perfumes flesh and emits ghastly scents. It pervades soil and leaves metal traces. It alerts Geiger counters.

Dudley dug through soft dirt and quicklime. Dudley dug around a dead man's outline. His head's on top. He was dumped feetfirst. He was stripped nude to hasten the rot.

It had to be Hikaru Tachibana. Loose dirt engulfed him. A stone well space loomed underneath.

The flesh stink outstunk the quicklime. Dudley tied his handkerchief over his nose and mouth. Tachi's skin still adhered to his bones. It was a grab-and-pull job.

Dudley grabbed. Dudley pulled. The head and torso came out of the hole. The legs and entrails were gone.

Look at the Jap. There's half of him left. His eyeballs have dropped from his face. There's maggots atop his leg bones.

Note his bony chest. Note his rising-sun tattoo. Note the needle marks on his arms. Note the seven odd knife wounds on his biceps and abdomen.

Well preserved. Seamless cuts. An overall starburst effect.

Dudley got out his evidence camera. He attached the flash gizmo and screwed in a bulb. He laid Tachi out and held his flashlight close.

He aimed the camera one-handed. He shot the belly wounds first.

The bulb exploded. He ejected it and popped in another bulb. He shot the mid-left bicep wound. He squatted and went contortionist. Lucky seven, seven wounds, seven bulbs in his kit. He got seven tight close-ups.

The bennies ratched up his heart rate. He gouted sweat.

Dudley kicked Tachi back in the hole. Tachi's left arm dropped off. Dudley refilled the hole and smoothed out the dirt. Bugs reconverged.

Clouds passed over. Dudley made like a hellhound and bayed at the moon.

He packed up his gear. He brushed himself grime-free. He walked to his car and placed the gear in the trunk. He got in the car and drove back to flatland L.A.

It was late. He made the Cahuenga Pass, quick. The pass to Hollywood. La Brea to 15th and east.

The Deutsches Haus was lit up, gemütlich. The raiding party stood out by their cars.

Breuning, Carlisle, Meeks. Whiskey Bill Parker. Ed Satterlee and wet-blanket Ward Littell.

Dudley pulled up behind them. Breuning and Carlisle flashed V for Victory. Parker popped his trunk and dispensed shotguns. *Was ist das im Deutschen Haus?* It's *Tannhäuser*, too loud.

Parker said, "In the door and spread out."

They racked their shotguns. They ran over and flanked the doorway. Dudley kicked the door off the hinges. *Tannhäuser* soared, unconstrained.

The Haus was a shithole. Five men sat around a Victrola. It was Pabst Blue Ribbon and Nazi armbands on loden coats.

Flying wedge.

Breuning, Carlisle and Meeks went right. Littell and Satterlee went left. Dudley and Parker took the chute.

The *Kameraden* just sat there. They ranged thirty to sixty. They looked innocuous. A Munich rally, the guys selling peanuts.

Parker kicked over the phonograph. *Tannhäuser* crashed and died. Littell aimed at a Hitler bust and blew it up. Stray pellets took out a window. Breuning and Carlisle cheered.

Meeks and Satterlee went in butt-first. They head-smashed the Huns. They knocked them out of their chairs. They kicked them prone and cuffed them facedown on the floor. Shrieks, yells and protest slogans—all gobbledygook.

Littell pumped in a fresh round and blew up the Victrola. Tube glass exploded. Dudley scoped the room—this sissy's Berchtesgaden.

Herr Breuning stomped Hun to Hun. He raged in German and kicked the Huns in the balls. Dudley watched Parker watch him. They traded eyeball clicks.

The Huns squealed. Parker yelled, "Toss the place! We want silencers and guns!"

"The place" was blitzkrieged. Shattered *Führer*, shattered glass, shotgun-pocked walls. Five *Übermenschen*, five piss-your-pants pools.

Dudley walked up to Parker. The pious pest looked haggard. His blue suit hung off of him. Hate tracts were stacked on a bookshelf. Dudley examined them.

"They look like the tract at the Watanabe house, sir."

Parker examined them. "They look like a left-wing tract in an outside deal I'm working."

The lads hit the back office. Flying wedge—two Feds, three city cops. Dudley heard five shotguns rerack.

Explosions overlapped. Wood sieved through the doorway. Parker ran back to the office. Meeks whooped—*mother dog!*

Lads, did you blow up a desk?

Satterlee yelled, "Nothing so far! No silencers and no guns!"

A Hun bleated something. Dudley caught "silencer."

He squatted beside him. The man looked vaguely Semitic. The man was seedy-debonair.

"What was that you said, lad? I'll loosen your handcuffs if you repeat it."

The man gasped. The man said, "We got burglarized last night. We lost our Lugers and silencers."

There's a lead—snag it.

"And your name, lad?"

"Robert Noble, Esquire. Order of the Iron Cross and the Thunderbolt Legion."

Dudley patted Esquire's leg. "And before you anglicized it? Speak in a whisper, so your friends won't know you possess mongrel blood."

Esquire rasped it. "It's Moskowitz."

"And how many silencers and guns did you lose?"

"Four."

"Does this grand establishment *sell* silencer-equipped Lugers?"

Esquire squirmed. "I'm the ordnance lieutenant. I consigned two silencers and two pieces to a heist guy. He wanted to lay the goods off on some Japs he knew. He was a young, snotty guy. I don't know his name."

Dudley uncuffed Esquire. "Did you tell this lad how to demonstrate the silencers and the guns?"

"I don't read you."

"Think, Robert. Did you advise the young man as to how he might best demonstrate the effectiveness of the ordnance?"

"Oh, yeah. I told him to fire into roofs or ceilings, that that would impress the Japs good."

Crash noise echoed. Cops run amok. They're dumping shelves and punching through wallboards.

Dudley whispered. "My colleagues will be busy in your office for the next few minutes, which will allot me the same amount of time. I think you have a business ledger stashed on the premises. Tell me where, or I will kill you. I will unlock your handcuffs, pull a gun from my back pocket, fire it and place it in your hand. I will then blow your brains out and cite self-defense."

Satterlee yelled, "American money! We found a hidey-hole!"

Dudley patted Esquire. "Your answer, lad?"

Esquire whispered. "I don't truck with the ledger, but it's behind that high shelf with the *Mein Kampf*s."

Dudley walked over and stood tiptoed. He reached behind Herr Hitler's screed and pulled out a clothbound binder. He stuck it in his waistband.

He brushed a pile of swastika pins. He laughed and pocketed them. Archbishop Cantwell was a Coughlinite and loved a good trinket. Shamrocks were passé.

December 10, 1941

29

LOS ANGELES | WEDNESDAY, DECEMBER 10, 1941

12:04 a.m.

A wind kicked through. Broken glass shattered. Door padlocks thumped.

Ward Littell called it a "pogrom." Mariko had her very own bleeding-heart Fed. They played cards and swilled cocktails. Her son's old room was Ward's room now. Mariko was living it up.

Because Bill Parker pulled strings.

Ashida stood on the fire escape. Sleep was a pipe dream. He'd been up since Monday morning.

He was woozy. Bucky finked him to the Feds. Kay Lake knew it. She knew things that other people didn't.

Because Bill Parker pulled strings.

The wind escalated. Broken glass flew. Cops paced adjacent rooftops. Ward left an hour ago. Captain Bill ordered a Deutsches Haus raid.

He had the guns and silencers. They were stashed at his apartment. He hid them with his Bucky photos.

Elmer Jackson stood one rooftop over. His cigar bobbed and glowed. Elmer and Lee Blanchard were his new bodyguards. Ray Pinker called and told him. He said Bill Parker pulled strings.

Police work. Kay Lake's male hierarchy. Kay Lake, the sorority girl Mata Hari. She was keyed in on Bucky. He'd seen her at Bucky's fights. They shared a certain reverie.

They worked together. He pilfered a tap disk. He took it to his apartment and played it. He heard four ghastly phone calls.

All from mid-'39. Fletch Bowron/Two-Gun Davis/Call-Me-Jack Horrall. They discussed the "Jap issue." It prophesied *now*.

The inevitable war. The inevitable internment. Property seizures, bank raids, confiscations. Lists compiled and names named.

The "Chinks" as potential enforcers. Chinatown and Little Tokyo are *this* close.

Two-Gun Davis spoke Chinese. He mediated tong truces. His negotiations always favored Hop Sing. The Chinks stood ready to assist the local white man.

Casual chat. Tong-snuff cover-ups and Ace Kwan's dope den. The Dudster pitched a Four Families lad off a building. A passing truck severed his head.

Bowron called the Chinks their "storm troopers." They'd be the ones to steamroll the Japs.

Ashida walked down the hall. Mariko snored in her room. Ward drove off to the raid and left his door open. The room felt magnetic.

Ashida picked up Ward's pajamas and held them to his cheek. He caught a scent and memorized it. Ward's briefcase was out and open. Ashida stroked it.

He skimmed a carbon sheet. It was the top page of the "B" list. The names ran from Akahoshi to Aridosho. He knew half of the people. They were all fine citizens.

He walked back to the fire escape. Ward's car pulled to the curb. The wind felt good. He heard, "Hey, Hideo!" out in the dark.

Elmer Jackson waved his shotgun. Ashida yelled, "Hey, Elmer!" back.

30

KAY LAKE'S DIARY

LOS ANGELES | WEDNESDAY, DECEMBER 10, 1941

12:37 a.m.

The basement is full of Lee's boxing memorabilia. There's a passel of publicity stills, along with framed posters for Lee's "Big Money" bout with Jimmy Bivens. The fight was fixed. Lee "went in the tank." The poster is dated July 16, 1937. It precedes Ben Siegel and the Boulevard-Citizens heist.

Lee will probably spend the night at City Hall. He will show up here when he damn well pleases, and right at the point that I begin to miss him. He'll apologize for his loathsome conduct at Mike Lyman's. He might heap praise on Dr. Hideo Ashida.

Who possesses a remote sort of courage. It's the courage I once mistakenly ascribed to his friend Bucky. The intersection of these two men fascinates me. I keep thinking, Why now? and go to the war as the only explanation. In the meantime, I can't sleep and remain hungry for Scotty Bennett. In the meantime, Captain William H. Parker has sent me a movie.

I'm set up to watch it. The screen is a roll-down contraption hooked to the rear basement wall. Lee bought it to view old fight films, and I've learned how to run the projector. I was there for the first show of *Gone with the Wind.* I want to see this movie much more.

I loaded the film and thought about Scotty. We left Lyman's in the wake of Dr. Ashida's embarrassed exit; we checked into the Rosslyn Hotel and made love. I wanted to spend the night—but Scotty said that he couldn't. He'd borrowed his father's car and promised to return it by midnight. My rough boy remained in the thrall of the Reverend James Considine Bennett. I resisted the urge to comment. I said, "You can go, but I'm not done with you yet."

It angered Scotty. He brought that anger to our good-night kiss; I started wanting him all over again.

I stuck the first piece of film under the slide, hit the switch and turned off the lights. There it was—*Storm Over Leningrad.*

I steadied the spools and leaned into the speaker. An overture covered the titles. The fascist dissonance was stolen from Prokofiev; the heroic harmonies were stolen from Brahms. A polemical folly unfolded; the real Russians and Germans were staining the steppes workers' red as I watched.

I was too tired to laugh. My clothes were filthy. My muscles ached from hours of grubby work in police squadrooms. My heart just plain dropped.

Claire De Haven and company cared for the plight of the world. Claire De Haven and company extolled tyrants and lived for adversarial cliché.

I recognized the Russian-front exteriors. They were the grounds of Terry Lux's sanitarium. The PD had their summer picnics there.

I'd read Captain Parker's files. The Red Queen was the uncredited writer and director. The movie was shoddily improvised. The actors tripped over one another. The battling soldiers shot BB guns. The windbag oratory was flabbergasting. Most of the Nazis appeared to be Mexican, Jewish or Greek.

I felt sick. Captain William H. Parker sent me *this*. He viewed my performance at the Robeson recital and assumed my derisive laughter here. He did not stop to think that I might feel kinship with a woman this touched by the world's horror.

Enough.

I turned off the projector and turned on the lights. *Storm Over Leningrad* swooped and died. I stood in front of a wall mirror and performed.

The mirror was Claire De Haven. I was myself speaking to her and myself as her in reply. I ridiculed her movie for its artlessness and praised her courage in wearing her staunch heart on her sleeve. She voiced skepticism. My prairie-girl/police-consort persona was unconvincing. I was too young and feckless to have shed blood for the Red Cause. She called me a child sophisticate and critiqued my performance at the recital as artfully realized sophistry. "Are you a police informant, Katherine? You whored for a pimp and excoriated him at trial. You live with cops and off of cops and come to me with your revulsion for them as the stated basis of your credibility. Where have you been before that? I have stood before official committees and have been pilloried for my beliefs. I do not see one iota of self-sacrifice in you."

It was *my* best self-indictment as *her* best moment. I would meet her tomorrow, at Dr. Lesnick's office. Her slaves would tell her that they saw me at the Anti-Axis Committee. She would be impressed that I recalled lines from *Storm Over Leningrad* and would not know that I had watched it the previous night. I looked in the mirror and saw myself as her. I aged ten years and became slightly dissolute and much more patrician. *I lacerated myself*. I outcritiqued Claire De Haven's critique.

It was enough to take with me. I couldn't hold my mirror pose a moment longer. I had his mother's number memorized and wanted to talk to him. I dialed the number and barely heard it ring.

Hideo Ashida said, "Yes?"

I said, "It's Kay Lake."

"Yes, I know."

"Tell me what you mean."

"I'm saying that when the phone rang this late, I knew it was you."

"Were you awake?"

"Yes."

"I don't think I'll ever be able to sleep."

He said, "It's the war. Everyone is like that."

I said, "I saw Captain Parker yesterday afternoon. He was exhausted."

"I saw him several hours ago. He fell asleep in a briefing."

"I think—"

"I don't want to talk about Captain Parker. It seems inappropriate."

I said, "Tell me something. Give me an insight or provoke me. Tell me what you're thinking."

He said, "I've been assigned two bodyguards. I think you're acquainted with them."

"Tell me who."

He said, "Sergeant Elmer Jackson and Officer Lee Blanchard."

I said, "Meet me tomorrow night. Give them the slip. We'll have a drink somewhere."

He said, "Yes, as you wish." The phone went dead then.

The receiver slipped out of my hand. Nobody could sleep. Some of us could think as our eyes blurred.

Captain Parker knew the movie would instill empathy. He was creating confusion and a fanatic's fury within me. He knew I'd never back down. I was his sister in fury.

31

LOS ANGELES | WEDNESDAY, DECEMBER 10, 1941

12:37 a.m.

Traffic death. Shoreline job. Windward and Main.

Parker stood in the intersection. A lab man chalked the body and measured skid marks. The driver never saw the old lady. He was driving per blackout regs. The old lady stepped out of nowhere.

The driver was all boo-hoo. He said he was fucking exhausted. The fucking Japs bombed Pearl Harbor. He hadn't slept since Sunday morning.

Parker sent him home. Sleep, brother. We'll call you for the coroner's inquest.

A morgue van hauled off the body. The bluesuits resumed patrol. Parker wrote the report in his car. His clipboard blurred.

He got the call outside the Deutsches Haus and drove here. He played the radio on the ride over. A newscast gave him the blues.

That man James Larkin died at Queen of Angels. He got sideswiped on his bike Sunday morning. He was leading the Santa Monica Cycleers. The kids survived, he didn't.

Parker prayed the Rosary. His voice cracked. He vowed to pray for Larkin's recovery and forgot to enact the vow. The Japs bombed Hawaii. It induced mass amnesia.

Parker recalled an odd detail. Larkin's going in the ambulance. A Luger grip falls from his lap.

It was dark and cold. Hide-and-drink conditions excelled. Dudley's boys were booking the Krauts at the Hall of Justice jail. He should be there.

Parker drove downtown. He left the blackout zone and hit lit-up L.A. A woman jaywalked at Temple and Hill. She wore a Kay Lake–style red dress.

Parker double-parked outside the Hall and took the cop lift up. The thirteenth floor was Axis-packed. The holding tank was all Jap.

The booking desk featured Dudley's boys and the five Kraut fucks. They were shackled to a come-along chain.

Breuning said, "The skipper's back."

Carlisle said, "I'm hungry. Let's head over to Kwan's."

Meeks said, "It's Shotgun Bill."

Parker checked the arrest log. The *Schweinehunde* were penciled in. Max Affman, Robert Noble, Max Herman Schwinn. Ellis Jones and a dentist named Dr. Fred Hiltz.

They were bruised up from the raid. Their snazzy armbands drooped.

A jail deputy hovered. Parker said, "Book them for sedition and hold them for the Federal grand jury. No habeas, no bail. Place them on the colored tier. They might learn a few things."

A tall *Schweinehund* grumbled. Breuning backhanded him. The desk phone rang. The jail deputy got it.

A fat *Schweinehund* said, "I don't bunk with no coons." Breuning backhanded him. The jail deputy passed Parker the phone.

"Yes?"

"It's Nort Layman, Bill. You should meet me at Homicide. I've turned up something on Nancy Watanabe."

32

LOS ANGELES | WEDNESDAY, DECEMBER 10, 1941

1:52 a.m.

His favorite nightcap—coffee and Benzedrine.

Dudley cigarette-chased them. The squadroom was empty. Dr. Ashida and Miss Lake left the place disarrayed. It kept the night-watch lads out.

His cubicle was spotless. *He* remained untapped. *He* made his dicey calls from pay phones. A Jew locksmith sold him slugs.

His desk phone blinked. *Aaaaaah*—the photo lab.

The night-shift man pledged a rush job on his snapshots. The man was a pervert parolee. He would not reveal the dead Jap in the pix.

Dudley twirled thoughts. One thought persistently twirled. *He missed something at the house. It was something very simple. The killer might have missed it himself.*

He twirled thoughts. One thought niggled. Call-Me-Jack burdened him with a stray job.

The draft would deplete the Department. Cops would be conscripted willy-nilly. It would mandate emergency hires. He had to scan recent reject files for men fit to serve.

It was niggling work. It cramped his brain waves. The Watanabe case ran full-time. *It* was his brain-broiler.

He missed something at the house. He should consult bright Dr. Ashida.

Dudley restudied the book. It was Ray Pinker's knife-wound text. It included photographs.

Yes—multiple blade marks. Yes—the central puncture and starburst effect. Yes—the same incision perspective.

The photos matched the stab points on Hikaru Tachibana. He was almost certain. The lab pix would cinch it.

Two phone lights blinked. Dudley strolled to the doorway tube chute and stuck his hand out. That whoosh *whooshed.* He grabbed the canister and strolled back to his desk.

Next—the comparison test.

Ray Pinker's knife photos. His own knife-wound photos. Twelve text photos and seven flashbulb shots.

He studied both sets. He went back and forth. Identical? *Yes.*

Pix confirmed. Go to Pinker's historical text.

A Jap war knife caused the wounds. The knife derived from eighteenth-century Japan. Feudal warlords dipped the blades in slow-acting poison. Superficial wounds rarely proved lethal. Warlords superficially wounded their men to test their courage under duress.

Deep stab wounds always proved fatal. Deep stab wounds and the poison caused slow and tortuous death. Warlords often stabbed the arms of their victims. This ensured that no pierced organs would cause instant death. Warlords often pierced their victims' abdomens. This transmitted poison to the lower intestines. This brought about slow and horrid death.

Dudley closed the book and stashed the photos. His brain twirled. He should study the Deutsches Haus ledger. His brain retwirled. Buzz Meeks caught the Whalen's job. *That* case aspect perplexed him. Meeks might have items desk-stashed.

It was 2:12 a.m. Robbery would be dead. Dr. Ashida's photo gizmo snapped evidence pix. Meeks might have duplicates.

Dudley walked over to Robbery. The squadroom was tombsville. Meeks had a horseshoe paperweight on his desk.

The top drawer was open. Pencils, paper clips, erasers. One roll of evidence film, with a note attached.

"T.M.: Sorry, but it wouldn't develop."

Dudley crossed out the note. Dudley wrote below it, "Try again. Return the photos to me. Try harder. You're a lazy fiend son of a bitch."

He walked to the tube chute and stuffed the film and note in. He hit the photo-lab switch and heard the *whoosh.* He walked back to his desk and studied the ledger.

The Deutsches Haus. Sedition as pratfall. Illegal weaponry sales. Buyers would use pseudonyms. It was a long shot.

Yes—block-printed columns. Dates and ordnance lists. Pseudonyms, as predicted.

H. Himmler, J. Goebbels, H. Göring. "A. Hitler"—that's rich.

Dudley scanned pages. There's Hirohito, Tojo, Mussolini. There's more puerile humor, up to—

A real name.

Huey Cressmeyer.

Ruth Mildred's perv son. Ruth Mildred, Dot Rothstein's lez frau. Ruth Mildred fucked a man to have a child that she and Dot could pervert.

Dudley skimmed the rest of the ledger. It starred Field Marshal Rommel and A. Hitler's squeeze, Eva Braun. He locked up the ledger. His brain Geiger-counter clicked. Two desk-phone lights blinked.

He walked to the tube and snatched up the goodies. He walked back to his desk and unloaded them.

The lazy fiend delivers. It's prompt. It's wildly serendipitous.

Dudley examined the photos. He hypothesized the fuckups that gave him these shots.

Dr. Ashida's wizardly gizmo. It's applied to the task of photographing license plates. A malfunction occurs. Car wheels hit the wire and make the shutter trip. Something jams the lens upward. Four blurred images of Huey C. result.

It's Huey. He's about to heist Whalen's Drugstore. *They're blurred* images. They're courtroom invalid. It's Huey—but only if you know him.

He heard foot scuffs. Bill Parker and Nort Layman walked up.

Layman said, "Nancy Watanabe was recently pregnant. She'd had an abortion. I did advanced blood work and found stray tissue cells. The father had AB-negative blood."

Dudley said, "A delightful surprise."

Parker said, "It explains the morphine paregoric at the house. It's prescribed for cramps in early pregnancies."

Layman said, "The Whalen's guy pawed around in the paregoric. It's in Buzz Meeks' report."

33

LOS ANGELES | WEDNESDAY, DECEMBER 10, 1941

2:34 a.m.

Ashida wrote in kanji.

He summarized his private findings. He sprayed his paper with a preflammable mist. Direct heat would burn it.

He was relearning his mother tongue. Translation came slowly. Words came in fragments.

He worked at the kitchen table. Mariko and Ward Littell gabbed in the living room. Bookies' "flash paper." It spawned his idea.

He botched dual-language clauses. His pen skipped.

渡辺邸にあった短波ラジオ。あれを盗め。新たな放送を聴くべし。

English to Japanese and back again. Kanji to Arabic script.

"Shortwave radio at house. Steal radio. Play new broadcasts."

His mind misfired. He omitted parts of speech.

"Broken glass with fish smell at house. Shrimp residue on victims' feet. Fish smell on man at farm property."

He translated and *re*translated. It assured accuracy. He blew on the pages and dried the ink. He trembled. He had to sleep. He knew he'd never sleep. Kay Lake's phone call got to him.

It unnerved him. It made him think fantastically. Kay Lake had interdicted his brain waves. She seemed to be clairvoyant. She was immersed in Bucky Bleichert. Her erotic view of Bucky disturbed him. It granted her insight and deductive force. He was afraid that she could read his mind and decode his shameful thoughts.

Mariko walked in. She was stinko. Ashida covered his notepad.

"Mother, did Captain Madrano or any of the other Mexican policemen inquire about our farm labor? About replacing them or buying our farm?"

Mariko shook her head and snatched an ice tray. Ashida heard noise outside. He tilted his chair up to the window.

The Sumitomo Bank was open. Deputies loaded cash bags into a van. Thad Brown held a tommy gun and watchdogged the transfer.

The van pulled out. Brown nailed a seizure bill to the door.

Ashida went back to work.

Kanji, Arabic, kanji. "*What did I miss at the house?*"

He yawned. It hurt. He stood up and saw spots. He had to stop. He couldn't drive home. He had to fall down somewhere close.

His bedroom was Ward's bedroom now. His chemistry gear was packed in the closet. He could *brew* sleep.

He weaved down the hall. The door was open. He grabbed vials of fo-ti and liquid valerian. He took them to the bathroom and ran sink water into a cup. It tasted like astringent mud. He got it down in one gulp.

The spots returned. He braced himself on the walls and made it back to the kitchen. Mariko's rocking chair glowed some strange color.

He fell down in it. He rocked himself to some strange place. It looked like a bank vault. The money was purple, not green. The Lake girl and the Bennett boy committed seppuku. Their blood was the color the money should be. The Bennett boy stood under a shower. Water splashed on a secret camera. He tried to form a stop sign in kanji. Kay Lake blew smoke in his face.

He heard gunshots. His eyes burned. He opened them and saw daylight out the window. The last gunshot was the bank bell clanging. He squinted and saw the bank clock. The big hand and little hand said 1:30.

The gunshots were the doorbell. The water was his own sweat and urine. The world was the rocking chair on the floor.

He stumbled to the door. He opened it. Bucky Bleichert stood there.

"Hideo, I'm sorry. I just couldn't—"

He hit him and hit him and hit him. Belmont '35, green-and-black forever. Bucky stood there and took it.

He hit him. Bucky's blood was some strange new color. He hit him until he couldn't hold his hands up.

34

KAY LAKE'S DIARY

LOS ANGELES | WEDNESDAY, DECEMBER 10, 1941

1:38 p.m

The oppressed-workers prints were predictable. The comely receptionist affirmed that Dr. Lesnick enjoyed young women. I was the only analysand in the waiting room; I wore a college-coed ensemble designed to tweak the doctor's susceptibility and introduce myself as a swoony huntress of the Left. Wool skirt, white blouse, fitted navy blazer. Scuffed saddle shoes for collegiate bonhomie, and bright red knee sox. A black beret pinned with a FREE THE SCOTTSBORO BOYS button. Most of the boys *had* been freed, and several of the boys were by all accounts guilty. It didn't matter. I was impervious to political reason and giddy with my own neuroses.

I was early for my appointment. I came early to acclimate to my huntress' habitat. I had created a narrative for my first session, based on Jung-like archetypes. I would thus designate the men in my life and both enchant and enrage Dr. Lesnick. He would be impressed that I possessed some knowledge of Jung and appalled that I had co-opted his theories so self-servingly. The sexual subtext would drive him mad and get me in like Flynn.

A radio broadcast served up distraction. U.S. flyboys sank two Japanese destroyers. President Roosevelt would soon initiate the wartime draft. Japanese submarines were now prowling our shoreline waters. Fletch Bowron weighed in on tonight's all-city blackout. Captain William H. Parker will meet with civil defense authorities later today. Mrs. Franklin D. Roosevelt will attend the wingding at the Hollywood Plaza Hotel.

The inner-office door opened. Dr. Lesnick entered the waiting room and looked at me.

He was sixty-five years old, frail and thin. He wore a Freud beard. His fingers were nicotine-stained. He had that haunted-Jewish-refugee look. He said, "Miss Lake?" and ushered me into his office.

The analyst's chair, the analysand's couch, the WPA murals. Beverly Hills meets the Dust Bowl. Lesnick closed the door behind us.

I took the couch; Lesnick took the chair. We lit cigarettes and pulled ashtrays close. Lesnick said, "May I ask who recommended me?"

"I went to some Young Socialist Alliance meetings a few years ago. There was a consensus that you were very good at interpreting dreams."

"Would you say that your dreams possess consistent themes?"

I shut my eyes and crossed my legs at the ankles; I wanted the doctor to ogle me and gauge my suitability for the Red Queen's cell. We were both police informants. I knew that he was; he did not know that I was. I had the upper hand.

The office was pleasantly cool. I blew smoke rings and burrowed into the couch. I said, "The unifying theme is sex."

A long silence percolated. I had preannounced my faux narrative off the doctor's first query. Lesnick gave the Feds intimate dirt on Claire De Haven. His informant role surely suffused him with self-loathing. I represented a quid pro quo. He could vouch me to the Red Queen and recoup on his perfidy.

The silence extended. I pictured the doctor enjoying my college-girl-recumbent pose. *Sex equals social consciousness equals politics. I'll tie it all up inextricably. He's astonishingly arrogant. He's every intelligent man who's not really brilliant and must convince the world that he is. He'll tell Claire De Haven all about me. He'll turn my pre-scripted monologues into disengaged ramblings. He'll tell the Queen that he rapidly deduced the key to my soul.*

He said, "Describe your dreams."

I put out my cigarette and laced my hands behind my head. I said, "Five men from my life pass through my dreams, interchangeably. I've given them archetypal names, based on my survey of Jung. There's 'the Chaste Lover,' 'the Boxer,' 'the Unruly Boy,' 'the Authoritarian' and 'the Japanese.' I live with 'the Chaste Lover.'

We've had a few dashed sexual encounters and have settled into an arid domesticity. The Chaste Lover is a policeman, and I'm incongruously very much a part of his world. The Unruly Boy is a recent conquest, who may be going off to the war. The Boxer is a local celebrity, and a man I've been drawn to for some time. The Authoritarian and the Japanese are men I am in no way sexually compelled by, but they are the most gifted of the men, and gifted men compel me more than any other male type."

Lesnick said, "You think in types, then? Your survey of Jung has led you to organize your internal life in that manner?"

I said, "Yes. I think in types. I grew up in the Depression, and I've seen how the inability to think clearly and act decisively has hobbled our leaders and sustained oppressive conditions in this country. I made up my mind not to be that way. Thinking in archetypes has helped me grasp political situations as well as personal ones."

Another silence followed. My incomplete response laid the bait. *Nail me, Doctor.*

He said, "Your critique of oppression is quite incomplete. Especially so, given that button you're wearing."

He took the bait. I let him win. I made him think, *This callow child, she's so* young.

"I was only citing an example of how I think. I organize my external life rigorously, but my internal life and dream life are quite something else."

"It's very rare to have a patient begin analysis with their dreams. They usually begin by describing a current crisis or with a short autobiography."

I shifted on the couch. I was off in a stage performer's calm. I said, "My dreams undermine my self-confidence in the world. That's why I decided to begin a course in analysis. My external state remains static, but my unconscious state is currently in upheaval."

He said, "Do you see the exterior world as a manifestation of your thoughts?"

"My personal world or the world at large?"

"Both."

"My personal world, certainly. The world at large, quite often."

"Would you explain 'the world at large,' please?"

I seized the moment. We had unconsciously colluded; it had forged his archetype of me. I was the Child Megalomaniac.

"I've comported in the world erratically and come to a point of self-knowledge that has given me uncanny insight. There are certain people who carry fire in the world and cause the world to shift in dramatic, inexplicable and rarely detectable ways. People like that, *like me*, create political shifts and effect changes of the social climate. So you see, Doctor, that is why the contradictions of my dream life are so disturbing."

Lesnick shifted in his chair. I sensed him keying up. He said, "Tell me about your dreams, then. Why is sex the unifying theme?"

This was my time to soliloquize. Lesnick's snitch duty had secured his daughter's prison release. Wayward Andrea Lesnick, wayward Katherine Lake. A drunken girl drives her car into a car filled with Rotarians. A South Dakota girl steals money and catches a bus to L.A. Politics, dreams, sex. Newly revealed megalomania. A clock was ticking toward the end of my fifty-minute hour. I performed with brevity.

I went straight to my archetypes and stitched them up. They were all policemen and policeman manqués. Why am I so drawn to men who rule by hobnailed boot? I'm a megalomaniac, but I'm confused.

I'm a woman in a man's world. They won't let me in. I tried to join the Marines on Sunday; I was smeared with red paint and rebuffed. I'm surrounded by atrocity and am enraged that I cannot make it stop. I carry fire in the world and sense my own complicity in the horror we all live as one soul united. My inner and outer worlds have merged. I make love with and fixate on all these men because it's all women have to make the horror stop.

I interpreted my own interpretations. I exuded megalomaniacal self-absorption. I described my girlhood, my sojourn with Bobby De Witt, my relationship with Lee Blanchard. *Get it, Doctor?* My external life is chaotically disordered and has led me to a point of intransigent mental resolve. Aren't people like me malleable at their core? Don't you think that Claire De Haven will go for me and see how faithfully I will serve the Red Cause?

Captain Parker was there, expurgated. I portrayed him as a police-world acquaintance and ghastly rightist theocrat. Hideo Ashida exposited my enlightened racial stance and outrage over the roundups. Scotty Bennett gave me raw sexual details; I merged them with some choice Bucky Bleichert fantasies. I held my voice to a monotone. It told Dr. Lesnick that this intimate revelation in no way discomfited me. *I give good value, don't I, Doctor? You don't know that it's all by design and all for effect.*

Lesnick interrupted me. He said, "Our time has concluded, Miss Lake."

I stood up. Lesnick stood and faced me. I couldn't read his expression.

"I'd like to schedule another appointment."

He said, "Please call my secretary."

I said, "Thank you, Doctor," and opened the door. Claire was sitting in the waiting room.

She had a new upswept hairdo and wore a tan twill suit. Her eyeglasses subverted her patrician look. One man in twenty would *get* her—and she always knew who those men were.

She looked up from her magazine. I caught a blink. *Oh, really—it's you.*

I dug in my purse, pulled out my cigarettes and looked in mock vain for matches. I pretended not to see her stand or to sense her shadow. Then she pounced with a gold lighter and a ready flame.

I accepted the light. She smiled just as I looked up and started to thank her. She caught my Scottsboro Boys button.

"I saw you at the Robeson concert. You brought down the house."

I blushed on cue. A drama teacher taught me the trick. Think mortifying thoughts and hold your breath.

I said, "I ended up in jail. I had a cell all to myself. The other cells were filled with Japanese women. They were too embarrassed to use the toilet. I watched them squirm all night."

The Queen lit her own cigarette. "Until the morning? When your parents bailed you out?"

I said, "No. Until my cop lover came to the station and the jailer told him his crazy Bolshevik girlfriend was in the you know what again."

She smiled and slipped the glove off her right hand. I extended my hand as she extended hers; it was gorgeously synchronized. She said, "Claire De Haven." I said, "Kay Lake."

She said, "Robeson sang 'Ol' Man River' again, after they carried you out. The standing ovation acknowledged you more than him."

I said, "It was foolish of me. No political good came of it."

Claire De Haven shook her head. "It was provocative and theatrical. You raised a valid grievance and may have caused people to consider it."

She's older and more worldly. Social class divides you. Feign subservience.

I studied my scuffed saddle shoes. Cheerleader Kay, Phi Delt fuckup. Claire De Haven said, "I'm having some people to my house tonight. It's the white Colonial at Roxbury and Elevado. 9:00 would be lovely, and I do hope you'll come."

I smiled. "Will Mr. Robeson be there?"

She smiled. "Not if you are, dear."

The doctor's door opened. Claire De Haven touched my elbow and walked away. I stepped out to the hallway; a tall man was leaving the office next door. I recognized him. It was Preston Exley, the policeman turned construction king. He smiled and stepped aside. I walked downstairs and outside.

It all caught up with me and sent me giddy. Preston Exley walked to the curb and talked to another tall man. I looked up at Dr. Lesnick's window and saw the curtains part.

Claire De Haven scanned the sidewalk. She saw me and studied me. I resisted the urge to blow her a kiss.

35

LOS ANGELES | WEDNESDAY, DECEMBER 10, 1941

2:54 p.m.

Parker primped in the bathroom. He wore his best suit. Call-Me-Jack said, "I want you looking sharp, Bill. Roosevelt's lezbo wife will be there."

Fletch B. wangled the Presidential Suite. It was football-field big. The bathroom adjoined the main room. The door was cracked. Chitchat drifted in.

Sheriff Gene told DA McPherson not to snore in his seat. Eleanor Roosevelt gabbed with Fletch. Franklin's raising the draft age to forty-three. He wants six million men.

Parker ducked into a powder room and snatched the phone. The suite lines bypassed the switchboard. He dialed Thad Brown at City Hall.

"Homicide, Lieutenant Brown."

"Bill Parker, Thad. I'm calling from the Plaza."

Brown whistled. "Be convincing, boss. The Feds think we'll screw up the blackout."

Parker buffed his shoes with a Kleenex. "Pass this on to Horrall. Roosevelt's raising the draft age to forty-three. Per manpower, it's twice as bad as we thought. We're going to have to recruit draft-exempt men and go to the reject files."

Brown said, "Jack's got the Dudster on it already. *And*, he's setting up an 'Auxiliary Police Program,' to augment the sworn personnel."

Parker cleaned his glasses on his necktie. "Winos, derelicts and pensioners with nothing to do. We don't have the personnel to run security checks."

Someone tapped the door. "You're on, Captain."

Brown coughed. "What goes with the Watanabe job? Can we trust Dudley not to short-shrift it?"

"He's on for the whole ride, and Horrall trusts him. That said, I don't think Pinker and Ashida will rig evidence just to give Dud a solve. Nancy Watanabe had a recent abortion, which is the only fresh lead we've got."

Brown said, "*Sayonara*, Bill."

Parker said, "*Banzai*, Thad."

Applause rippled. Parker quick-primped and stepped into the room. Eighty people looked up.

Bigwigs hogged the first row. The First Lady, Mayor Fiorello La Guardia, L.A. city hotshots. American flags flanked the lectern. Parker positioned himself.

Fletch B. tapped his watch. Gene Biscailuz yawned. Bill McPherson looked sleepy.

Parker introduced himself. He notched mild applause and plagiarized Bob Hope.

Get this, folks:

A Jap submarine drifts into the Silver Lake Reservoir. The crew disembarks. They battle pachucos in Echo Park. They march to Griffith Park. Giant Bengal tigers escape from the zoo and eat them. "Wars are won with the resources on hand—remember Pearl Harbor, folks!"

The audience dead-eyed him. He got *no* smiles, *no* chuckles, *no* punch-line yuks.

Parker segued to preparedness. Motorist safety, pedestrian safety, power-outage tips. Blackout rules, driver etiquette. Plans to suppress vandalism. Mobilization strategy for air and sea attack.

It's our duty, ladies and gentlemen. Citizen support spells V for Victory!

Mild applause, bored applause. The First Lady, with her hand up.

"Yes, Mrs. Roosevelt?"

"On a related topic, Captain. Are you confident that everything possible is being done to safeguard the civil liberties of the Japanese people being detained in Los Angeles?"

Parker gripped the lectern. He saw that cop sandpaper those kids.

"Yes, Mrs. Roosevelt. I *am* confident."

3:22 p.m.

He ran.

He backed away from the lectern and ducked out. He nixed the handshake line and a schmooze with Frau FDR. He took service stairs down to the bar.

He ordered just-one-bourbon and snagged a window booth. He watched the world drift down Vine Street.

Autograph hounds lurked outside the Brown Derby. Newsboys ducked into traffic and hawked papers. Four Navy women piled out of a cab. They wore the winter blues with officers' braiding.

Parker hugged the window glass. He checked their rank braids and studied their faces. Two ensigns, two full lieutenants. No lieutenant j.g.'s, no tall redheads, no possible Joans.

"What are you looking at?"

Hurricane Kay—fucking unsummoned.

"I thought I saw someone I knew."

"Those Navy women?"

"Yes."

"I sense a story here."

"It isn't much of one, and I'm not going to tell it to you."

She sat down. She snatched the cherry out of his drink.

"Dr. Lesnick is smitten. I met the Queen, right on schedule. She invited me to a party at her house tonight."

Parker studied her. "Your outfit is too broad and satirical. I'll tell you how to dress from here on in."

She sipped his drink. She lipstick-smeared the glass.

"Suppose I don't have the clothes you require?"

"Then I'll buy them for you."

His cigarettes were there on the table. She helped herself.

"How should I behave at the party tonight?"

Parker sipped his drink. "Act like you're not impressed by the glamour, but betray that you really are. Don't create another scene, under any circumstances. Keep track of conversations pertaining to upcoming meetings, rallies and political functions. Sneak into rooms and check the closets and drawers. I'm assuming that you'll visit the house on subsequent occasions, so I'll get you a concealable camera. I want photographic evidence of seditious literature or anything of a perverse nature that you might come across."

Kay Lake smoked and drank. *His* cigarettes, *his* liquor.

"I borrowed your persona for my session with Dr. Lesnick. We discussed archetypes and susceptibility. He has to tell the Queen that I'm malleable. She has to think that she's using me, or none of this will work."

Parker nodded. "I want you to wear a black cashmere dress tonight. I'll buy it and have the shop deliver it. Wear the stacked-heel pumps that I've seen you in."

Kay Lake blew smoke rings. "I'm a four. Make sure the waist is properly darted."

Her eyes deflect light. She's immune to doubt. It's her strength as a snitch and her flaw as a cognizant being.

"Were you flattered that I made you an archetype?"

"Don't flirt with me, Miss Lake."

"If I flirt with you, you'll know it."

Her eyes are so dark brown that they're black.

36

LOS ANGELES | WEDNESDAY, DECEMBER 10, 1941

3:56 p.m.

Il Duce. Mussolini, *molto bene*. The scowl and huge head.

Harry Cohn lugged *Duce* to a closet. The bust weighed eighty pounds. Jewboy Harry was fat and had a bum pump. His office was fascist moderne. A fairy set decorator dolled it up, *Führeresque*.

Dudley said, "You're a bright lad, Harry. I admire the dandy dago as much as you do, but it's best to keep him cloistered until this unnecessary world conflict concludes."

Harry glowed sclerotic. He dumped the *Duce*. The floor reverberated. He huffed back to his chair and lit a cigarette.

"Tell me what you want and give me the dirt. You never visit me just to schmooze."

Dudley settled into his chair. It was Pontiff size. It featured a built-in ashtray.

"You owe Ace Kwan nineteen thousand, Harry. You owe Ben Siegel an additional forty-eight. I can get you the nineteen tonight. I have a business opportunity pending."

Harry glowed. His standard fuchsia went to claret. The man radiated poor health.

"You mick cocksucker. You never come just to schmooze."

Dudley slapped his knees. "Jack Kennedy's coming to town. I'm sure you know what the lad has in mind."

Harry scratched his balls. His desk resembled Pharaoh's tomb. A perch permitted starlets to kneel and blow him.

"I've got some hot numbers that Jack will appreciate. Remember Joe the K and the T.J. smut days? Dot and Ruth Mildred got in a beef over that WAC major. Those were some rollicking times."

Dudley said, "I have some grand ideas along those lines."

"You always have grand ideas, Dud. But I produce quality motion pictures for a motion-picture public that demands quality, so you won't see me peddling one-reelers of diseased twat and pimply guys with big schlongs."

Dudley smiled. "Our friendship is based on extortion, Harry. We've never issued ultimatums, because we both understand that. I should add that you produced a nearly forgotten documentary on Herr Mussolini in 1931, and that I possess celluloid evidence. Don't you think that the current world situation would serve to cast disapproval on your fawning tribute to that dago beast?"

Harry throbbed. His neck veins pulsed. See those arteries swell?

"I'll consider your 'idea,' you mick cocksucker."

"Grand. And since we're engaged in the process of barter, what can I do for you?"

Harry chained cigarettes. "I've been getting strike threats. My slaves are getting antsy, and I might need some hard boys to quell all this Red-inspired grief."

Dudley said, "I'll be seeing Ben Siegel tomorrow. He'll be released from jail soon, and he'll set you up with some stellar strikebreakers."

Harry stabbed out his cigarette. "You're a cock tease, you fucking mick *ganef*. Give me the dirt."

Dudley winked. "You shall have it. And I have a grand assortment for you today."

There—the ritual begins.

Harry's right hand leaves the desktop. Harry's zipper scrapes. Harry's right shoulder dips.

Dudley said, "Rita Hayworth is playing hide the ham with a heroically hung drifter named Sailor Jack Woods. Barbara Stanwyck remains butch. She's known as 'Steamy Stanny' in all the lez hot spots. Carole Lombard has been palling around with District Attorney Bill McPherson, who has been spotted dozing at official confabs pertaining to the detention of subversive Japs. DA McPherson is covertly known as 'Darktown Bill,' a nod to his penchant for jungle-bred trim. DA McPherson has been frequently spotted at Minnie Roberts' Casbah, a noted coon whorehouse. Miss Lombard, a mud shark herself, accompanies him and enjoys Zulu warriors while the DA enjoys dark girls."

The ritual nears crescendo.

Harry's right arm jerks. Harry's right shoulder spasms. Harry gasps and tissue-blots his face.

Dudley lit a cigarette. "Ace Kwan wants to shoot smut movies. They'll express anti-Jap sentiment, and perhaps feature Jap talent. I'd like to bring in you and Ben S. I can get you the money to cancel your debt with Ace. You'd be clean, and you'd be a grand one to assist us in this venture."

Harry swabbed his brow. "I'll consider it, you mick cocksucker."

"Grand. And to an unrelated topic, then. Does Ruth Mildred do all your scrapes? I was thinking of an unfortunate Jap girl. Do you let Ruthie work freelance?"

Harry shook his head. Moisture spritzed. His arteries groaned.

"Ruth Mildred is my abortionist. She does the scrapes *I* tell her to, and no more. I have the exclusive medical rights to Ruth Mildred Cressmeyer, ex-M.D."

Dudley smiled. "A final question before I leave you to your work. Do you credit the rumor that our swell chum, *der Führer*, is slaughtering Jews by the millions?"

Harry said, "I don't give a fucking shit. He can kill all the fucking Jews he wants, as long as he doesn't kill me."

4:31 p.m.

"King Cohn must go! King Cohn must go!"

Chants boomed outside Harry's office. Dudley walked down Gower and scoped the Red riffraff.

Seedy placard wavers. Kikes and coons predominant. A picket line up Gower Gulch. Cowboy extras milling by Rexall Drugs. Rightist lads geared for counterattack.

"King Cohn must go! King Cohn must go!"

He was parked down at DeLongpre. Doltish drudge work loomed. He was tired. The bennies wore off at dawn and dumped him in the cot room. Three hours' sleep did not suffice.

"King Cohn must go! King Cohn must go!"

Dudley walked to his car and tucked in. Huey C. lived nearby. He was tied to *two* sets of apron strings. He stuck close to his dyke mommies.

Drudge work. The reject file weighed in heavy. Dudley balanced sheets on his lap.

Abbott, Adams, Allsworth, Arcineaux, Arthur. Drunks, wife beaters, all-around cretins. Atterbury, M. and Atterbury, S.—twin brothers and too-zealous Klansmen. Babcock, Bailey, Baltz. Consumptive physiques and suspect bonds with children. Beckworth—two jail jolts. Begley—a harelip. Bennett, Robert Sinclair—what's this?

R. S. Bennett, nickname "Scotty." Applied in August '41. Twenty years old then. Lied about his age. Aced the physical and written exams. Extremely high intelligence marks.

Six five, 220. Hollywood High grad. All-city fullback and class valedictorian. All-state debater. Accepted at Yale's divinity school. Father: the Reverend James Considine Bennett. Born: Aberdeen, Scotland, 1894. Mother: the late Mary Tierney Bennett. Liar Scotty, rejected for service. Note the principal's cautionary aside.

"This boy has gotten in numerous fistfights since his freshman year. He has achieved a very high scholastic and athletic standing, but he seems to overly relish his reputation as the toughest boy in the Los Angeles City School District."

Current address: 218 North Beachwood.

"*King Cohn must go!*" The demonic chant carried.

Dudley drove to Waring and El Centro. Huey lived in a shabby bungalow court. Slatterns sunned naked toddlers out front.

Dudley parked and tipped his hat. They swilled sneaky pete and ignored him. He walked back to Huey's flat.

Knock, knock—who's there? Dudley Smith, so fiends beware.

He pushed the buzzer. Huey opened up. He's nineteen, six two, 140. He's got dandruff and cystic acne. There's model-airplane glue congealed on his face.

Dudley shut the door and locked them in. Huey mumbled something. The room was four-walled with Kraut banners. Balsa-wood Messerschmidts dangled from the ceiling.

Huey mumbled anew. Dudley picked him up and threw him into the wall. Huey pinwheeled and crashed a shelf of toy panzer tanks. He fell face-first on a sofa. He was too glue-addled to shriek.

Dudley pulled five bennies out of his pocket and jammed them in Huey's mouth. Huey gagged and swallowed. Dudley brushed glue crusts off his hand.

"You'll revive in a few minutes, lad. We're here to discuss the Whalen's Drugstore heist Saturday morning, the Lugers and silencers you procured at the Deutsches Haus, and the recently dead Watanabes. You know me, lad. Your mothers and I are great chums, which will not prevent me from killing you if you dissemble."

Huey mumbled, precoherent. He wore a Luftwaffe jumpsuit. Dudley swallowed three bennies and cigarette-chased them. The smoke stifled a pervasive glue stench.

Hubert Charles Cressmeyer II. Ruth Mildred named him after her dermatologist dad. Huey doted on mama's squeeze, Dot Rothstein. The Dotstress was Jewish. Huey graciously overlooked it.

Dudley pulled a chair up. The room spun a bit. He was skipping meals and losing weight.

One, two, three cigarettes. Smoke clouds over low-hanging aircraft. Dudley cracked a window. Huey yawned and stirred.

He rubbed his face. He stretched. The Night Creature, revived.

"Hi, Uncle Dud."

"Begin with Whalen's, Huey. I'm ill-suited for amenities today."

"Them Watanabe humps are dead? *I* didn't do it."

"I believe you, lad. The county grand jury might not."

"It's a Jap caper. The Japs mind their own paper, just like the Chinks. That shouldn't cause no work for your white man's police force."

Dudley said, "A cogent analysis, but irrelevant. Start with Whalen's, lad. Omit nothing."

Huey said, "Okay, I clouted Whalen's on Saturday, but that was the only time. I knew the store was a patsy, and nobody could place me there for the first four or five jobs, which half-ass alibied me for my slot. I got some wallets and some phenobarb to give to my mom for her scrape gigs, and I poked around in the morphine paregoric. This babe I knew had been pregnant and got her doctor to script her the morph for her cramps. She shared it with me, and I started appreciating it. I was about to clout some, but I thought, Uh-uh, you'll build a habit. I brought an Army MP's armband with me but forgot to put it on. See, I read about this MP rape-o in the papers, and I wanted to put the onus off on him. I had the Luger all silencered up, and I popped off a round for grins."

Credible. Quintessential Huey. Adroitly conceived and shoddily done.

"And the pregnant girl was Nancy Watanabe? You didn't know she had a scrape?"

Huey picked his nose. "Nancy. How'd you know that?"

"Did you impregnate her?"

"Shit, no. You know my MO, Uncle Dud. I like older stuff. Anything under fifty is jailbait to me. I lick snatch like a hound dog on a biscuit, but I never put it in. You won't see me slammed with no paternity suits. My mama taught me better than that."

Still credible. "And your blood type, Huey?"

Huey patted his hip. "It's O plus, Uncle Dud. And I got my reform school donor card right here in my pocket."

The bennies kicked in. Dudley's cells reawakened. His bloodstream went *aaaaaaaaaahhh*.

"The Deutsches Haus. Are you well established there? Are the fools in residence chums of yours, or just acquaintances on the right flank?"

Huey said, "The latter, Uncle Dud. Fifth Column's Fifth Column, but only the real die-hard guys make a religion out of it. I'd see them guys at Hindenburg Park and rallies here and there, just enough for them to trust me and consign me them suppressors and guns. But I'm a heist boy and a lone wolf at heart. I didn't want them political types sniffing around my illegal shit."

Pure Huey. Self-preserving, self-deluded. He signed the Deutsches Haus ledger in his own name.

"Do you recall specific Deutsches Haus employees or habitués? Can you relate telling incidents or give me specific names?"

Huey shook his head. "*Nein, Obersturmbannführer.* They were all 'Fritz' and 'Wolfgang' to me."

A radio squawked next door. Try the "Blackout Special" at Blackie's Lounge. Black-tie cuisine at a workingman's price!

"Tell me about the Watanabes. Again, omit nothing."

Huey sighed. "I got the same answer for you, Uncle Dud."

"Which is?"

"Which is Fifth Column's Fifth Column."

"Elaborate, lad."

"Fifth Column's Fifth Column. Which means everybody knows everybody, and everybody's all linked up in these ways they ain't revealing to nobody else. You got the Bund, America First, the Silver Shirts with them snazzy getups. The fucking Watanabes always spoke Jap around white folks, even them they were simpatico with. I knew Johnny a bit on his own, and Nancy likewise. Old man Ryoshi and old lady Aya? Them as a fucking *family*? I didn't know them from hunger."

Dudley said, "Really, lad?"

Huey reptile-flicked his tongue. "I offered Aya twenty scoots to let me lick her snatch. She slapped me. Jap women don't take it the French way."

Dudley smiled. "Proceed, please."

Huey bummed a cigarette. "I ran with Johnny W. He was one of those wild-on-the-outside, live-with-mom-and-dad kind of Jap kids. We clouted a few liquor stores, and Johnny held his mud, so that made him a white man to me. Johnny knew an older guy named Hikaru Tachibana, who up and vanished one day. He was about to get deported to Japan, but he scrammed on his bail and started running prosties, and then he plain disappeared. Johnny played his shit close to the vest, but I got the feeling that he knew lots of strange-o Japs like Tachi."

Huey—credible, snitch-frenzied.

"And you shot your silencered Luger into the ceiling at the Watanabe house."

"Yeah, last Friday. Ryoshi said he was in the market for a piece, so I gave him a demonstration. You know me, Uncle Dud. I get trigger-happy sometimes, and I go a bit crazy. The silencer dropped threads, so Ryoshi nixed the sale."

Dudley lit a cigarette. "Let's discuss Nancy."

Huey reptile-flicked his tongue. "I licked her snatch at the Nightingale prom. This Mex kid I know spiked the punch."

"Can you offer me anything more substantial?"

"How's this? I didn't knock her up, and my mom didn't scrape her. She shared her morph with me a few times, but that was it. Okay, I rifled that shelf at Whalen's with her in mind, 'cause I didn't know she got scraped. But I didn't knock her up, although I got a pretty good line on who did."

Dudley said, "I'm listening."

Huey picked his nose. "Johnny introduced me to this fucked-up crowd of Japs he ran with, but I pretty much steered clear of them. They carried these poison-dipped knives that had all these different blades on them. Johnny said there was four of them, young guys, with these beliefs that were too crazy even for him."

Dudley got goose bumps. They were bennie-enhanced.

"Please continue."

"All right. The guys pulled heists, worked shit jobs and donated all their moolah to the Imperial Jap Cause. I met this scary-shit Jap-Mex half-breed who was part of the cell. He had bad cysts on his back, worse than mine. He bragged that he knocked up a Jap girl, and I'm pretty sure he meant Nancy."

"His name?"

"I never got it, and Johnny told me the guy lammed back to Mexico. The guy bragged that he killed a family in Culiacán, but I thought he might have been pulling my pud."

"Please continue."

"That's it. You've got these four fucked-up Japs who live in Griffith Park, 'cause they give all their money to the Emperor. They hate the Chinks more than the Krauts hate the Yids. They think you got to rape and kill the female relative of a tong boss to achieve 'transcendence,' but they ain't got the nuts to do it."

Call Huey credible. Call his tale unverifiable. Call his knife spiel corroborative and tangential.

"I have a task for you, Huey."

Huey gulped. "What task?"

"The city will be blacked out tonight. I concede the short notice, but you're a resourceful lad. A Sheriff's van carrying a great deal of money will be traveling southbound, en route to Terminal Island. I would call 74th and Broadway the ideal spot to take it. You are to rouse your ascetic Japanese chums, set up a diversion and rob the van. You will carry the pump shotguns and use the rubber bullets that I know you stole from the Preston Reformatory. I will allow you to keep five thousand dollars for yourself, and to pay your pals one thousand apiece. You are to subtly interrogate them about the Watanabe family, Hikaru Tachibana and the esoteric knives they carry. They sound too mercurial to have killed the Watanabes, despite your speculation on young Nancy's pregnancy, but they may be good for Tachi. Failure to perform this task and bring me the balance of the money will mandate your premature death."

Huey picked his nose. "Suppose the Japs won't do it?"

"Then round up a band of your fellow Preston grads."

Huey grinned and ate his pickings. What a resilient lad.

6:04 p.m.

It was dark. The slatterns and tykes had decamped. The blackout would begin at 7:00.

Dudley walked through the courtyard. Thought and Act, Benzedrine. The van heist was impromptu and high-risk.

He got his car and cut south. Army sentries stood at Melrose and Gower. They manned a searchlight and packed carbines. Beverly and Larchmont was fortified. Sheriff's bulls cradled tommy guns.

Dudley stopped at 1st and Beachwood. The house was '20s Spanish-style. Tile roof, casement windows, brushed adobe walls. He walked up and rang the bell.

R. S. Bennett opened the door. This big Celtic Brownshirt. A hammer hurler. Bred for kilt-clad brawls.

Dudley flashed his badge. "Mr. Bennett, my name is Smith. I've come to recruit you for the Los Angeles Police Department."

Scotty Bennett said, "I've been rejected, sir. I'm only twenty."

Dudley said, "We're at war, lad. Extreme circumstances provide for a stretching of the rules. We need you more than you need the United States Marine Corps."

Scotty Bennett smiled. The doorstep glowed. The boy was born to fight crime and break hearts.

"Would you consent to an audition? It will save time and spare you ten weeks at the Police Academy."

Scotty snatched a sweater off a wall peg. Note the big *H* pinned for basketball and football. Note the seven rings on the left sleeve.

"Tell your dad you'll be out late, and not to wait up. There's mischief in the air."

Scotty shut the door. They walked to the K-car and piled in. Dudley unhooked the two-way and roused the Bureau. Thad Brown counseled Call-Me-Jack. He should see this.

The radio crackled. Thad picked up.

"Lieutenant Brown. Who's calling me?"

"It's Dudley, Thad. And it's not a frivolous call."

Brown whistled. The line went *screeeee.*

"I can read tone, Dud. Tell me what you've got."

"Can you be across the street from the liquor store at 74th and Broadway in half an hour? What you see will be self-explanatory."

Brown said, "Sure, Dud."

The radio *screeed* and went on the fritz. Dudley hooked it up and kicked the gas. They pulled out, southbound.

Hollywood, Hancock Park. Big blackout-ready houses. We're thirty minutes shy. Pull your shades, dim your lights.

Scotty said, "Green or orange, sir? I know you're from over there."

Dudley smiled. "Green everlastingly, lad. I'm a separatist, a militant papist and more."

"Dublin?"

"Yes, Dublin. And how did you discern that?"

"I'm quick to learn, sir. I understand things instinctively."

"Don't call me 'sir,' call me Dudley."

"All right, 'Dudley,' then."

They took 6th to Vermont and cut south. Car traffic *de*creased. Foot traffic *in*creased. It was 6:53. The siren would blast at 7:00.

Scotty stared out his window. *Bright lad—you see everything.*

"I'm orange, sir. I wear the color on Saint Patrick's Day, but I've got no grudge with the green. I got in a fight at Blessed Sacrament in '38, but that's as far as it went."

"And how did you fare in that engagement?"

"The orange prevailed, sir. I hope that doesn't make you think less of me."

"On the contrary. And don't call me 'sir,' call me Dudley."

Wilshire, Olympic, Pico. Venice, Washington. We're approaching the Congo. There's the—

It was fucking *loud.* Pole-mounted horns squawked. Shades went down. Neon signs vanished. Traffic lights flashed through cellophane. Car lights beamed amber and low.

BLACKOUT.

Scotty cracked his knuckles. Dudley hit his parking lights. Coontown came on, dark and *slooooooow*.

Dark folk on de sidewalk. Dark sky, dark streets, dark skin. Washington to Broadway and south. *Say what, what's dis?*

BLACKOUT.

72nd, 73rd, 74th. Hear the tom-toms and *oooga-booogas*? It's de *deep* Congo now.

The Dark Continent. *Blackout* dark. Dark desires sizzle here.

There's Lew's Liquor. It's dark, inside and out. The clerks wield flashlights and peddle hooch. Clock their all-spook clientele.

Thad Brown stood across the street. Dudley pulled up and idled by the parking lot. Eugenics. Note the natives at play.

A blackout crap game. Four jigs with flashlights and dice. A dollar bill–dotted blanket. Swerving light on hot dice.

Scotty studied it. The jigs wore yellow satin jackets. Gang scum. The Rattlesnakes. They whooped and waved their flashlights.

Dudley said, "We have an unlawful assembly. Will you require a sap or handcuffs?"

"No, sir. You might call an ambulance, though."

Dudley whooped. Scotty stepped out of the car.

The jigs capered. Thad Brown watched. His white fedora marked him. His cigarette glowed.

Flashlight beams crossed the lot. It was all dipsy-doodles. A jigaboo shot snake eyes. Cheers and groans went up.

Scotty walked to the blanket. Scotty swiped the dollar bills. The jigs saw it. *Oooga-boogas* rose. A jig swung his flashlight.

Scotty grabbed his arm at the wrist and snapped it. Dudley heard bones break.

The jig screamed. More jigs came in. *Ooga-booga.* They're packing flashlights and fists.

Scotty snapped their wrists. Scotty broke their hands. Scotty sidestepped blows. Flashlights fell, glass cracked, light did crazy things. Fists hit Scotty and did not budge him.

The jigs screamed. Scotty went in close.

He grabbed their necks and hoisted them. He held them high and hurled them. They hit the ground. They thrashed and tried to crawl.

Scotty kicked them prone and stepped on their faces. They ate gravel and dollar bills. There's a cracked-light close-up. See that severed ear?

Are you watching, Thad? The screams are like Dublin, 1919.

7:14 p.m.

The noise seared him. He left Scotty to Thad and his Welcome Wagon spiel. He pulled into a vacant lot just south.

The noise faded. He fluttered. He felt his mother's fists and smelled his own blood.

Blackout. Dublin, 1919. L.A., 1941.

He hit a switch and got some roof light. The headliner reeked of a recent suspect's pomade. He grabbed his chessboard and pieces off the backseat. His pulse subsided.

His play was half risk, half calculation. Huey might not rouse the four crazy Japs. Huey might get dirt on Tachi and the Watanabes. Tachi was sliced with that feudal knife. *Fetch, lad. Tell me about that.*

Dudley set up the chessboard. The bennies brain-fueled him. He toppled pawns and rooks.

The Jap-Mex breed might be good for the Watanabe job. The Jap-Mex breed probably knocked Nancy up. Huey said the breed killed a Mex family. Huey said it might have been brag.

Call-Me-Jack wants a Jap killer. The house was too tidy for a full-bred lunatic. The Griffith Park boys packed that feudal knife. Said knife killed Tachi. The breed felt right for the Tachi job. Everything else felt wrong.

And—where's the profit? And—something's missing from the house.

Knights down, bishops down.

The DA felt wrong. Bill McPherson was wet-brained. Bill McPherson fucked jungle cooze. Bill McPherson snored in briefings and nursed a Red grudge. He might not rubber-stamp a Watanabe indictment.

It was 7:56. Dudley rolled down his window. L.A. was blackout black. He heard noise across the street.

Prompt Huey. Appropriate that vacant lot. Night Creature, fetch.

Car doors slammed. Stray moonlight lit up Huey and his gang.

There's four men. They're wearing bandannas. Note their exposed foreheads. That's yellow skin—Huey roused the Japs.

Huey wore Sheriff's duds. Makeup hid his acne. He was grandly disguised.

The Japs lugged cans into the street. They oil-doused the cement and skulked back to the lot. Huey walked to the middle of the street, with a flashlight.

Cars approached, north and south. Oil spill. Deputy Huey waved them around it.

The cars slowed and dipped by. The street went carless. Parking lights approached from the north.

Wide-spaced lights. *Van* lights. 7:59 p.m.—the Sheriff's, on time.

Huey stood his ground and waved his flashlight. The van braked and stopped short of the spill. Two deputies got out. Huey braced them.

Sorry, fellas—we've got an obstacle. The deputies huffed and checked their watches.

BANZAI.

The Japs reconnoitered. They wore crepe-soled shoes. They

crept up behind the deputies. They raised shotguns and let rubber bullets fly.

The sound was *whoosh/thwap*. Four Japs, two cops, four nonlethal loads. The deputies pitched and hit the oil spill. They fucking gasped that I-need-air rasp.

Huey pulled out fabric tape and glued their mouths shut. Two Japs cuffed them and dragged them into the lot. Two Japs jumped in the back of the van. Huey got in the van and drove it into the lot.

No motorists eyeballed the incident. No pedestrians walked by.

The lot was blackout black. Dudley relied on sounds.

Car doors slammed. Van doors slammed. Rustles, foot scrapes, grunts. The looting, the sacking, the tossed money bags.

Two car doors slamming. Tires spinning on dirt. Then "*Sayonara*"—yelled out pure Jap.

37

LOS ANGELES | WEDNESDAY, DECEMBER 10, 1941

8:21 p.m.

They were cuffed up. A short chain linked them. Bodyguard Lee Blanchard, cop stooge Hideo Ashida.

It was Ashida's idea. Hit T.I. with a bang. Spook the inmates, wow the guards.

San Pedro was twenty miles from L.A. proper. The ride down was tense. Blanchard was still scratched up from his Kay Lake tiff.

Ashida sold the trip to Bill Parker. *I'll do interviews in Japanese. I'll query the inmates per the Watanabes. The Nisei community is tight-knit. I'll probe and feign empathy.*

They entered the sally port and hit the guards' station. An MP buzzed them in. They walked down a corridor and snagged their sweat room.

Ashida rubbed his wrist. He'd jobbed Parker. He planned to stress his private leads. The farms, the buyouts, the wetback workers.

He spoke Japanese. Blanchard barely spoke English. He'd overhear the interviews and register zilch. They loitered outside the sweat room. Blanchard smoked and fouled up the air.

Takagawa, Kuradasha, Mikano, Murasawa. He got the names off the "A" list. They were North Valley farmers. They had to know the Watanabes.

The cuff gouged his wrist. He stepped back and put slack in the chain. The smoke congested him.

The sweat room adjoined a cell block. The cells were jam-packed. Men paced and bumped the bars. They looked malnourished. *Stir-crazy* said it all.

Blanchard rattled their chain. "I think we should bring in Mr. Moto. He always solves the case in an hour and a half."

The smoke was brutal. Ashida tugged at the chain.

Blanchard said, "You know what gets me? They hire this white guy to play him. Peter Lorre's a hophead, in case you didn't know. Wilshire Vice has got a green sheet on him."

Ashida looked down the catwalk. A guard escorted Hiroshi Takagawa. A mug shot was clipped to his file. Ashida had the facts memorized.

Blanchard nudged him. They took their seats and slacked up the chain. The guard walked Takagawa in.

Ashida stood and bowed. He spoke prepared text and translated back to himself.

"I apologize for this grave injustice inflicted upon you. You see, the same has occurred to me. I have questions pertaining to Ryoshi Watanabe that will serve the greater cause of justice for the Japanese community."

Takagawa stared at him.

Takagawa spit on the table.

Takagawa pulled a newspaper from his pocket and threw it in Ashida's face.

Blanchard said, "Tough luck, Mr. Moto."

The guard said, "I like Charlie Chan better. You always get some wisecracks and some girls."

Takagawa said, *"Traitor."* He trembled. The guard recuffed him and shoved him out of the room.

Ashida scanned the paper. It was in kanji. A piece excoriated the Ashida family. They were collaborators. The son was an informant.

He was the only Nisei on the PD payroll. Nisei blood signed his paycheck.

Pictures included. Hideo Ashida at Stanford. Mariko Ashida with Agent Ward Littell.

Blanchard said, "You're fucked, Mr. Moto. You ain't going to find *any* Japs willing to talk to you."

Ashida jerked his cuff chain. Blanchard haw-hawed. They walked through the sally port and back outside. The MPs snickered. Ashida's knees dipped and held.

Blanchard uncuffed him. It was shoreline-blackout overcast. The harbor air stung.

Ashida got in the car. Blanchard got in and gunned it. They drove the connecting bridge and hit the mainland. Traffic was light. The moon played hide-and-seek.

Blanchard kept it zipped. Elmer Jackson was set to relieve him. Ashida kept it zipped. His thoughts scattergunned.

He spoke to Ray Pinker, back at the lab. Pinker knew radio. He queried him, disingenuously.

Can shortwave broadcasts be transmitted to individual sets? Pinker said yes.

The Watanabes' secret attic. Their radio gear. It's transmitting straight to him.

Blanchard said, "Kay and I don't have your standard deal going. I give her a long leash with men, so she keeps wiping the slate for all the rowdy shit I do with the Department. It's a good deal most of the time. It's worth giving up all the racy stuff just to have it."

Ashida studied Blanchard. The pitch played oddball. Blanchard touched the scratch marks on his face.

"Don't get in too deep with her. She'll use you and cut you loose. She's always looking for something she can't have, and she don't let people get in the way."

Ashida looked out his window. It was Monday night, redux. *The world is dark and flat. Cars are submarines.*

Blanchard skimmed the radio. It was all blackout spiel. He killed the sound and cut over to Broadway. They hit a snag at 74th Street.

Sheriff's cars, swarming cops, lab vans. Arc lights in a vacant lot.

Blanchard waved and went through. Ashida rolled down his window. He heard a fracas up ahead.

The blackout dark amplified sound. Pitch resonated higher. He heard shouts and breaking glass.

Blanchard hit his high beams. He caught the scene. Negro looters, up at 66th.

Men in yellow jackets. Running leaps through store windows.

Blanchard hit his siren and drove straight at them. They dropped truncheon sticks and scattered. Blanchard bumped the curb and drove up on the sidewalk.

He plowed trash cans. He clipped a slow-moving fat boy. The looters hurled rocks at the car.

Ashida laughed. Blanchard laughed. He killed his lights and pulled back on the street. Pissed-off shouts faded.

Blanchard said, "Fucking niggers."

Ashida said, "I used to be friends with Bucky Bleichert. He's an ex-boxer, like you."

"He's a cream puff. Kay wets her drawers for him. He's coming on the Department."

"I know."

"He finked you to the Feds. He's got a snitch jacket already."

"I know."

"We'll win this war before too long, Ashida. This bad deal of yours won't go on forever."

Blackout L.A. whizzed by. Blanchard dangled an arm out his window. They hit Central Station. Blanchard stopped the car by the back door.

Ashida got out. He saw Elmer Jackson first thing. Elmer dozed in a parked black-and-white.

Blanchard said, "Watch out with Kay."

Ashida said, "Thanks for the ride."

Blanchard brodied out of the lot. Elmer snored on. Let sleeping dogs—

He had the blackout. He had the door keys. He had his penlight.

He got his car and cut north. Chavez Ravine, Mount Washington. Smudged hillsides and shit shacks. No parkway hum. Blackout drivers stayed home. Twisty pavement was a rough go in the dark.

It was 9:42. Highland Park was dark-past-dark. Ashida parked and walked up to the door.

The lab keys got him in. He had the floor plan memorized. He ignored the check-in log. He stood in the dark. He felt the Watanabe House Gestalt.

He missed something here. He's a gifted scientist. He should not miss simple things.

He walked upstairs and stood on the landing. He jumped and released the stairs. He went up them and retracted them. Rats skittered back in their holes.

He flashed his penlight on the cubbyhole and tapped it. The panel opened up.

There:

Radio, tape rig, ledger. Still in place—Sunday to Wednesday.

Now:

Work from recent memory. Tap the radio. Flick the right switches. Watch the metric bands glow.

There:

The bands illuminated. He goosed the volume and got sound. He kept it low and geared up to translate.

A lunatic ranted. He stated yesterday's date and announced the time as 2:41 p.m.

Think in English. It's faster that way. The lunatic rants. Don't miss his words.

And record them first.

"Secret military maneuver tomorrow. Submarine attack at dawn."

Ashida turned on the tape rig. The spools jammed. Tape shredded. He could not record this:

"Pocket sub" / "California coastal waters" / "Tomorrow at sunup." "Goleta Inlet, above Santa Barbara." "Collaborationist fishing village, Chinese-Japanese allied." "Torpedoes." "Punish traitors." "Aligned with our blasphemous enemy."

A rat zipped by. Ashida jumped and brushed a cobweb. A spider fell into his hair.

Ashida went *Eeeek.* The spider hit a wall plank. Ashida went *Eeeeeek.* It scared him. It sounded feminine.

The lunatic ranted. He ballyhooed Nanking, '37. Soldiers make women drink pus. Soldiers make children eat shit. Soldiers shove dynamite up a Chinaman's ass.

He unplugged the radio and tape rig. He grabbed the ledger. He released the stairs and went down them. His hands were full. He was sweat wet. The penlight ratched his teeth.

He carried the load outside. His car was right there. He locked his swag in the trunk. He retraced the floor plan all the way back. He double-checked the cubbyhole.

There—cobweb-covered. A stack of kanji-script tracts.

Ashida grabbed the tracts. He had X-ray vision now. He went down the steps and retracted them. He walked outside and back to his car.

A '38 Dodge was parked behind him. He touched the hood and felt engine heat.

"Hello, lad."

Ashida shivered. His teeth clacked. He told his brain to make it stop.

Dudley Smith appeared. He touched Ashida's arm. It sparked electric shocks.

"Why are you shaking, lad?"

"Because I'm afraid of you."

Metal touched his hands. He opened his right hand and released his left hand. Dudley took the tracts and passed him a flask.

His eyes adjusted. Sight merged with sound. Dudley leaned on the hood of his car.

"Drink, lad. It's 1919 vintage. I killed a British soldier and raided his stock."

Ashida took a pull. "Why did you kill the soldier?"

"I made inquiries and determined that he was the one who shot my brother."

"How old were you then?"

"I was fourteen."

Ashida tipped the flask. "Do you still hate the British?"

"Not individually. I hate them as a race given to imperial misconduct."

"I hate the Chinese that way. I can cite historical grievance to justify it, but the balance of atrocity always tips back to my own people. I hate them simply because of what I know them to be."

Dudley laughed. "Do you hate them individually?"

"No, of course not."

Dudley took the flask. His hand was warm.

"Are you an authoritarian, Dr. Ashida? Do you have an abiding allegiance to the cause of an ordered society?"

The liquor warmed him. "Yes. It defines my racial view and sense of the civil contract. I despise sloth and disorder. Racial exclusivity facilitates the social code. The natural instinct to exclude must be codified by law."

Dudley sipped brandy. "Lad, you are the brightest of bright pennies."

It was dark. It covered him. He let himself blush.

"Thank you, Sergeant."

"Dudley, please."

"Yes, as you wish."

Dudley passed the flask. "The roundups are unnecessary and reductive. They've created a self-perpetuating chaos that will serve to undermine the social order we both wish to preserve."

Ashida held the flask. Dudley's hand had warmed it.

"It's a remarkable policeman's insight. And, of course, I agree."

"Have last Sunday's events stretched your loyalties and induced ambivalence?"

"Yes. The attack constitutes misconduct, and now the roundups do."

Dudley said, "Per exclusion. Do you feel more American or more Japanese at this moment?"

Ashida sipped brandy. "More of both, actually."

Dudley held out his hand. Ashida passed the flask.

"Have you withheld evidence, lad?"

"No, I haven't."

"Why did you come here?"

"Because I've missed something very simple."

"It was my reason, as well."

Lie now. You have an opening. Let the brandy speak.

"I found the tracts in a crack behind the kitchen cabinets."

"It's more than that, lad. We're two bright pennies, and we both missed something significant and staggeringly obvious. We must surmise that the killer missed it, as well."

Ashida nodded. "You said 'killer' singular. Do you think it was one man?"

Dudley said, "I do, lad. The crime reeks of individual animus."

Ashida said, "There were four victims. It would have been logistically taxing for a single man."

Dudley said, "We have a sexual motive and a political motive. The sexual motive derives from Nancy and her recent abortion.

The political motive is deeply obscure and most likely stems from internecine fascist intrigue, of an incomprehensible nature. One man did it, lad. I'm sure of that."

Ashida took the flask. "Do you think Captain Parker is a capable man for this job?"

"I do not, lad. He's not a rank-and-file case man. I know that he's done well by you, but he's not someone you should look to as a mentor. He'll sell you out the moment that it suits his needs."

Ashida gulped brandy. "And you won't?"

Dudley said, "I'm a detective. Bill Parker is an administrative drone. I have a long-term need for a brilliant criminologist, Bill Parker does not. I am impervious to frivolous rules, Bill Parker is hamstrung by them. I suspect that you and I are quite alike in that way."

Ashida said, "He saved my job. He's kept my mother out of jail. For now, he's vouching our freedom."

Dudley touched his arm. "Say it, lad. I know you're thinking it. 'What can *you* do for *me*?' "

A peekaboo moon passed over. The big Irishman took on a glow.

"Yes, I was thinking it."

A woman walked a dog by. Dudley tipped his hat.

"My good friend Ace Kwan has a plan to provide comfortable shelter to harassed Japanese and safeguard their holdings until the hysteria subsides. William H. Parker will always comport within legal guidelines, even if it means enforcing racial bias. I am in no way constrained by the law."

The moon vanished. Ashida felt moonstruck. He had bodyguards. He had patrons. He'd called Kay Lake and arranged to meet her later. He was tête-à-tête with the Dudster.

"All these covenants and agendas. They supersede common human logic."

"It's a confounding world we live in, lad. It makes the loyalty of gifted men that much more essential."

38

KAY LAKE'S DIARY

LOS ANGELES | WEDNESDAY, DECEMBER 10, 1941

10:19 p.m.

The black cashmere dress was a knockout. Captain William H. Parker: couturier to stylish informants. Pinch me—am I really here?

The Red Queen's home was magnificent and filled with gilded folk celebrating themselves. The windows were covered with velvet drapes specifically purchased for blackout revels. Light itself had been redesigned for this one evening. We cavorted in slashes of light; we were extras in a German Expressionist film about the captives of the Beverly Hills Blitz. *This* was a bunker! *These* were some guests for the end of the world!

The lighting scheme was designed by Gregg Toland, the cinematographer who shot the current Hearst-censured film *Citizen Kane*. Toland went on a bender when *Citizen Kane* tanked. He ended up in a Tijuana whorehouse; Claire De Haven and Orson Welles rescued him. They got him to Terry Lux's dry-out farm and brought him down off Cloud 9. This lighting gig was occupational therapy.

I circulated, I listened, I talked when compelled. I heard praise for Uncle Joe Stalin and his brave Red troops; the Japanese roundups received properly outraged attention. I left a trail of conversational bait. I dropped my name, my leftist résumé, my anomalous cop-world credentials. Remember me. I'm young and unaccomplished. I'm desperate to impress you.

The party was now in high gear; I hadn't yet spoken to Claire De Haven. We drifted in overlapping circles and tracked each other with looks that said *Let's talk later.* She'd already researched me—I was certain of it. Dr. Lesnick would have spilled everything that he knew and might have suspected. We needed time alone—and I knew she wanted it.

I circulated, I listened, I talked when compelled. Dr. Lesnick saw me, acknowledged me and ignored me. Kurt Weill and Lotte Lenya appeared and created a stir. Vladimir Horowitz played a Bach partita on a piano bathed in a searchlight. The sound was smothered by people talking.

They talked about the war, exclusively. They urgently made their points and were heedless of the points of their interlocutors. It was one huge roar of venomous insight. Everyone had to be more acute in their critique of worldwide slaughter. They were all of the Left and all seeking to upstage their companions and a reigning maestro. They were shrill, didactic, correct about most things. They were heedless of the fact that they'd gain more converts if they just stopped talking.

Bertolt Brecht cruised by and made a pass at me; I told him *The Threepenny Opera* was a yawn and sidled off. Reynolds Loftis cruised by and mentioned seeing me at the Anti-Axis Committee. I gave him a my-big-mouth-again response and blushed with a blackout spotlight on me. Loftis seemed charmed; I segued to the war and milked it. Egalitarian L.A., the fellowship of shared catastrophe. Loftis praised my performance at the Robeson show; I told him how the evil cops blasted the Japanese boys—but did not mention the gallant intervention of Captain William H. Parker.

Loftis left me abruptly; I saw that a handsome young man had magnetized him. I got an idea. It took hold and flourished. Thoughts of Hideo Ashida had sparked the brainstorm—and it would surely ingratiate me with the Red Queen.

I looked around for her and found her. She stood alone, in zigzagged light. The light was in her eyes; she couldn't see me watching. She had to have gone to a hairdresser directly from Dr. Lesnick's office. She wore a Joan of Arc do now; it was straight out of the Dreyer movie. The short crop, the fuck-you bluntness. She wore a velvet dress earlier; she wore a peasant shift now. I scanned the room and gauged her audience. Terry Lux was watching her. Gregg Toland was aiming a camera.

Her pose, *my* poses. I got the urge to *do something now*.

I took side stairs up to a second-floor landing. The bedrooms were off a long hallway. I tried all four doors; just one was open.

It was her bedroom. I knew it immediately.

The room was a clash of color and fabric. The bedspread was plum satin; the walls were flocked green. The armoire and dresser were ebony. The dress she'd worn earlier was there on the floor. Her stockings had been rolled off and tossed.

Four pewter-framed movie stills centered the room. They displayed Renée Falconetti in *The Passion of Joan of Arc.* That hairdo/*her* hairdo. Falconetti's martyr eyes; Claire posed in zigzag light.

I felt it. I felt *her.* I touched the discarded dress and saw that Claire had sweated it through. *I* was sweating—dark cashmere in a warm room.

I rifled the nightstand drawers. I found a political tract and tucked it into the back of my dress. I saw a hypodermic syringe and a dozen ampules.

Falconetti. The short hair, the fierce eyes. Claire's light-show homage.

I left the room and brazenly walked downstairs. Claire was gone. Her slaves were setting up a movie screen and projector. I struck a Falconetti pose under those zigzag lights.

It was my homage to Claire's homage. I gazed up at the infinite. Someone tossed a shadow on me. It was Claire. She'd changed clothes again.

She wore a dark skirt and an elegant cardigan. She seemed floaty. Her blue eyes popped with much too much black.

She said, "*La Grande Joan.* I'm not surprised that you got it, and that you had to try it yourself."

I stepped out of the light. "I'm a ham, but I can't compete with you in the role."

Claire said, "You may or may not be a ham, but you're like the bad penny. You keep turning up."

"I'm here at your invitation."

"The Robeson concert, the Anti-Axis Committee, Saul's office. Where next? I first saw you on Monday, and you're satirizing me in my own home Wednesday night."

I reached into her pocket and stole her cigarettes. I lit up and extended the pose.

"Invite me to another party. I'll never turn down anything this seductive."

Claire smiled. "Who referred you to Saul Lesnick?"

"I heard some YSA people discussing him."

"Are you a police informant?"

"I wouldn't betray my beliefs for the sheer adventure of it. And the few cops who might know that you exist wouldn't risk putting us together."

Claire motioned for her cigarettes. Our hands brushed as she took them. She lit up. I leaned in and cupped her hand.

"I'm having another party, next Monday night."

"I hope you'll invite me, and I hope there'll be another blackout."

Someone whistled. Someone yelled, "It's movie time!" Chaz Minear yelled, "I wrote the script, so Reynolds and I will act all the parts!" Vladimir Horowitz called out, "I will provide the all-Russian soundtrack. It will be Prokofiev and Rachmaninoff!"

Claire's slaves arranged floor cushions facing the screen. Claire steered me over to a front-row seat. A man flipped a switch and killed Gregg Toland's light show. The projector rolled. Oh shit—*Storm Over Leningrad.*

Applause, whistles. Good-natured raspberries, boos. The film rolled. Loftis and Minear read over the dialogue; Horowitz soared over them.

Claire sat close beside me. I moved my lips in sync with the actors and felt her watching me. She *understood.* I *knew* the film. It was a cultural artifact of my youth.

She touched my arm. The gesture meant *Thank you.* I leaned toward her and whispered.

"I want to make a documentary exposing the roundups. I have a friend. He's Japanese. He has police protection, and he could help us."

Claire squeezed my hand. Loftis and Minear kowtowed to Horowitz and shut up. The maestro killed off the rest of the movie. The Rachmaninoff *Études-Tableaux* transcend pap.

The lights went on. Claire was gone. A handsome young man had replaced Horowitz at the piano. Bertolt Brecht said, "That's Lenny Bernstein."

I went over and stood beside the keyboard. Lenny Bernstein said, "Pick a composer."

I said, "Chopin."

Lenny Bernstein made room on the bench. I sat down and started playing one of my slow nocturnes. Lenny placed his hands over mine and dictated the tempo. His hands interpreted, my hands made the keys drop.

December 11, 1941

39

LOS ANGELES | THURSDAY, DECEMBER 11, 1941

12:08 a.m.

The back room bounced. Waiters laid out booze and corn chips. The PD ran 'round the clock now. Blackouts, late-night briefings.

It was all justified. The war turned time topsy-turvy. *This* was unjustified. Dudley had a new pit dog. Ergo—his service oath.

Call-Me-Jack waved a cocktail and Holy Bible. Parker stood with the gallery. The Dudster, Buzz Meeks, Hideo Ashida. The ratlike Jack Webb.

Hurricane Kay. She stirs, ubiquitous. Dud's pit dog was her Sunday-night lover.

Call-Me-Jack held out the Bible. The pit dog placed a paw on it and held a paw high.

"Do you, Robert Sinclair Bennett, solemnly swear to protect the lives and property of the citizens of Los Angeles and uphold the bylaws of the Los Angeles Police Department, so help you God?"

Scotty Bennett said, "Yes, sir. I do."

Dudley clapped. Jack Webb whistled. Ashida fish-eyed Scotty. Meeks picked his nose.

The kid was twenty. He radiated pliability. The Dudster hits paydirt.

Call-Me-Jack passed out goodies. Scotty grabbed his badge, cuffs and .45. Handshakes circulated. Call-Me-Jack high-signed Dudley and went out the door.

Webb built highballs. The gang flopped on couches and chairs.

Scotty was starstruck. *Don't I go to police school? No, you're a war cop. You break heads for Dudley Smith.*

Parker straddled a chair. "You read my memo. Nancy Watanabe was recently pregnant and had an abortion. So far, the father's unknown. Let's take it from there."

Meeks said, "We canvassed again. Everybody said the same thing. 'They're good wholesome folks.' "

Parker nodded. Scotty looked bewildered. Ashida sat prim.

Meeks said, "What about that tract we found at the house? It laid all that Bolshevik shit on the PD."

Parker said, "I don't think it's germane. It looks like a left-wing tract I've seen recently, and I think you'll trace it to a post office box and determine that it's nothing but some unscrupulous guy who writes tracts from all positions for a buck. Mail fraud's Federal, and it seems like a dead end to me."

Dudley said, "I agree, sir."

Parker said, "We're four days in now. Sergeant Smith, I want a second summary report. List everything that you and your men have learned. Feel free to extrapolate and state your impressions."

Dudley sipped his highball. "Yes, Captain."

Meeks sipped his highball. "I talked to Doc Layman. He told me he's frozen the stiffs. He thinks he might learn some new shit that way."

Ashida said, "Stray histamines lie dormant in dead tissue. Freezing cadavers serves to isolate cells. Dr. Layman might be able to tell us something about their degree of panic. We might be able to surmise how long they had foreknowledge of their deaths."

Parker lit a cigarette. "Where's your bodyguard, Dr. Ashida? I want you covered at all times."

"I couldn't locate Sergeant Jackson, sir. I've been alone since I got back from T.I."

Meeks said, "Elmer was off somewhere, sleeping. He gets all tuckered out auditioning Brenda's girls."

Dudley laughed. Scotty looked dumbstruck. This shit was all Greek to him.

Meeks lit a cigar. "There's a rumor floating around, from about a year ago. The pitch is that some folks were looking to buy the Watanabes' house and their farm in the Valley. We've got a second rumor that the house and farm were sold, but it wasn't officially recorded nowhere, and since the Watanabes were on the 'A' list, the Feds have seized all their property records. The Hall of Records didn't log it, but that don't mean it didn't occur. The Watanabes were the only Japanese folks in Highland Park, so I canvassed the Japanese folks in

Glassell Park and South Pasadena. I got vague scuttlebutt that some guys—and nobody could put names or races to them—were throwing out sales feelers to the Japanese folks in them areas."

Dudley tensed up. He glanced at Meeks and glanced away. It went by *rápidamente*.

Meeks waved his cigar. "I took a run by that whole stretch of farmland, out in the Valley. You got Mex Staties riding herd on the Watanabes' wetbacks and a whole lot of others. Since the Watanabes are *muertos*, it makes me think that someone else owns their property."

Dudley winked at Parker. "I have wonderful friends on the Mexican State Police, just as our dear captain did at one time. It would serve us poorly to harass them. They are invaluable to our extradition efforts."

Open secret. He ran bag for Two-Gun Davis. Dudley knew it. They both ran bag to the Staties. It's his self-loathing sin. It's the Dudster's blithe status quo. Call-Me-Jack and Two-Gun had yachts stashed in Puerto Vallarta. Carlos Madrano maintained them.

Meeks said, "The Watanabes' phone bills were a bust. They called their farm suppliers and nobody else. They made some calls to pay phones in Santa Monica, which I can't figure out, but it's probably just a fluke."

Parker looked at Ashida. "Again, Doctor. I want you to do molds on the tire tracks in the Watanabes' driveway. Their car's in the city impound, and there's a Teletype exemplar on the tire treads. Let's see if we can get some fresh lifts."

Ashida nodded. Jack Webb raised his hand.

Parker said, "You're not a policeman, Mr. Webb. You've ingratiated yourself at the Bureau, but please don't interfere in this."

Jack Webb gulped. His Adam's apple bob-bobbed.

"You should hear me out, Captain. I was doing some man-in-the-street interviews yesterday morning, and I think I picked something up."

Parker sighed. "Go ahead, then. Air it, and get it over with."

Jack Webb gulped. "A sailor told me he saw a black car pull up in front of the Watanabe house at about 2:30 p.m. on Saturday. A middle-aged white man got out and entered the house. He was heavyset and was wearing a purple sweater."

The room froze.

Dud's first summary. Mauve fibers on the victims. Dr. Ashida's theory. The killer stood behind the victims and guided their hands on the swords.

The room *un*froze. Meeks relit his cigar. Scotty went *I don't get it.* Ashida sat prim.

Dudley said, "Purple is not automatically mauve."

Webb said, "I didn't get a better description, and the sailor shipped out of L.A. last night."

Scotty said, "I don't understand any of this."

Meeks said, "Why should you? You were at the Hollywood High prom when the Watanabes bought it."

Scotty evil-eyed Meeks. Dudley grinned. His pit dog showed fang.

Meeks shot Parker a *look.* Call it Okie-shrewd.

Dudley stood up. "I have an engagement, gentlemen. I will bid you a late good evening and take my leave."

It had to be Kwan's. Mark it late chow and collusion.

The Dudster walked out. Jack Webb shuffled his feet. Scotty stared at his badge. Ashida sat prim.

Parker said, "Dismissed."

The room thinned out. Parker got Meeks alone. Meeks shut the door. Parker walked to the bar and poured bourbons.

Meeks said, "I never know when you're on the wagon."

Parker said, "Don't be impertinent. Tell me what the look meant."

Meeks slugged bourbon. "I'm thinking Dud wants to bury this. More than we all do, with a war on."

Parker slugged bourbon. "You're giving me old news."

"Bowron and Horrall want a Jap-on-Jap killer. They're afraid of a backlash on the roundups, which you can't blame them for."

"You're giving me old news."

Meeks booze-dunked his cigar. "Here's the new news, for what it's worth. I saw Pinker and Ashida's full run of trip-wire photos from the pharmacy heist. Aside from the picture that caught the license plate, all the photos I had in my desk were too blurred to make sense. I came into the squadroom yesterday and saw that the negatives had been disrupted, so I braced the photo-lab man. He told me that Dudley went through my desk and had him take another stab at developing them pictures. The guy struck gold that second time, and I saw dupes of the pix. The heist guy is Dudley's snitch, Huey Cressmeyer. That punk is well known in certain circles."

Parker bolted his drink. Meeks refilled him.

"Is he heavyset and middle-aged? Does he fit for the purple-sweater man?"

"He don't, Cap. He's nineteen, and he was in the Lincoln Heights jail when the Watanabes got sliced. He blew a traffic light and got popped for twelve unpaid tickets. That Sheriff's butch Dot Rothstein bailed him out at 6:15. She's Huey's mama's main girl."

Parker bolted his drink. Meeks refilled him.

"I got more news, Cap. You ready for it?"

"Don't string me along, Meeks."

"I wouldn't dream of it. That stated, did you read that bulletin on the Sheriff's van robbery last night? It's a Fed job. You've got the blackout, a hijack and sixty grand in Jap cash gone."

Parker said, "74th and Broadway. I saw the Teletype."

Meeks licked his cigar. "The gang fired rubber bullets, so the deputies survived just fine. Here's the kicker, Cap. Huey the C. was a suspect for the 459 of a guard shack when he was up at Preston. You know what got clouted? Rubber bullets and 12-gauge riot guns."

Parker kicked it around. "You're a Robbery man. I'll get you a liaison spot on the job. I'll see if Dick Hood will bring in my friend Ward Littell."

Meeks said, "Dudley?"

"It's a check and balance. There's no stopping him in the short run, but we can minim—"

Meeks jabbed Parker's chest. "Minimize the grief to your career?"

40

LOS ANGELES | THURSDAY, DECEMBER 11, 1941

12:57 a.m.

Call-Me-Jack snarfed Pearl Harbor duck. It was Peking duck dolled up with pineapple rings.

"I like the kid. Thad told me he dusted those shines with aplomb."

"He did, sir. He's a fearsome young man, and I hope we won't lose him to the draft. He'd put in his papers for the Marine Corps, but I think our friend Fletch can get him declared 'Police-essential.'"

Call-Me-Jack yocked. "Send him to the Philippines. He'll dust those Japs with aplomb."

Kwan's was deadsville. They dined by themselves. The blackout deterred late-night trade.

Dudley tossed an envelope on the table. "A business venture bore fruit, sir. I want you to share in it, but I shouldn't divulge the details."

Jack palmed the pouch. "Thanks, Dud. I appreciate the thought, and you know I never require the details."

Dudley sipped bennie tea. Jack snarfed egg rolls. He was fat and prone to night sweats.

"Give me the rundown, Dud. What have you got, where's it going, and how can we wipe this off our plate?"

Dudley said, "It's going nowhere, but I'd be remiss if I didn't mention the possible opportunities that may well appear."

"Music to my ears, so keep going."

"Two unidentified white men have been buying up and attempting to buy up Jap house and farm property, which may prove or not prove to be germane to the case. I'm the only one who has up-to-date knowledge of this, although my boys and the blabbermouth Turner Meeks know some of it. Meeks spilled information to Whiskey Bill tonight, but nothing alarming. Grand William requested a second summary report from me, which I will supply him with in due time. The report will be a masterpiece of ellipsis and omission. Grand William will be satisfied and nullified."

Jack picked his teeth. "You've always had a bug up your ass about Parker. Why do you think I assigned him to ride herd on this case? You and your boys are constrained to a certain point, but you and I pull the strings. I blame the Catholic Church for Bill Parker. He's blotto on altar wine, and he's out to punish the world for his own fucked-upedness."

Cogent, but heretical.

"Parker knows that the Jap internment is a fait accompli, sir. He seems to have some misgivings about the roundups, but he will comply with all official orders and the Department's version of events, which includes the Watanabe case. It is not within his moral makeup to take any kind of vigilante action. He understands the necessity of a Jap-on-Jap solution, and further understands that failing a wholly verified arrest and indictment, the only proper outcome is to bag a vile Jap pervert and interdict his certain future perversions with Murder One and a gas-chamber bounce. The evidence must be compellingly doctored. The pervert must be a horrifying individual, who must explicate the mad designs of the entire Jap race and thus justify a full-scale racial imprisonment."

Call-Me-Jack clapped. "Two things, Dud. One, I applaud your summation and wholeheartedly agree. Two, you couched the whole fucking thing in Bill Parker. I blame the Catholic Church again. You men are fucked-up on mystical juju straight out of papist Rome."

Dudley laughed. *Ho, ho—you cocksucking heretic.*

Call-Me-Jack said, "The roundups are a crock of shit, and we both know it. Most of your local Japs are fine folks, but they should be sequestered until the war veers our way. What I fear is a press backlash. We shouldn't have to take it—not at a time when the draft will be taking our best men. I'm not worried about losing my job, to Whiskey Bill or anyone else. As long as Fletch B. is in, *I'm* in. And when I'm *out*, the City Council will rubber-stamp Thad Brown. What I want is the fucking Japs tucked away, a peaceful wartime city and jerkoff reformers like Parker stalemated until I retire, head to Puerto Vallarta, get shit-faced drunk every night and fuck comely señoritas on my yacht. I want the fucking press to extoll our fucking clean city and clean police department, and I wouldn't mind making a few bucks out of it. We both know how to carve a buck, Dud. We want the same things, straight down the line, and you've got free rein, *within reason*, to get us what we both want."

Dudley clap-clapped. "A brilliant summation, sir. I will inform you, to the proper degree of accountability, as events progress."

Jack wiped duck grease off his necktie. "I want the Watanabe case solved and a grand jury indictment rubber-stamped by New Year's."

"You shall have it, sir. Although, I should add that our narcoleptic district attorney troubles me. Mr. McPherson is shamefully compelled by the dark races. He frequents bar-b-q establishments south of Jefferson Boulevard, and enjoys the company of Negro prostitutes. I fear that he might dally or equivocate on our indictment."

Jack went *So?*

Dudley said, "I would like your permission to sandbag him."

Call-Me-Jack nodded. "*New Year's,* Dud. I want a closed-chambers, four-count grand jury indictment. Throw in kidnapping, because the perv held the Japs hostage before he chopped them. That way we get Little Lindbergh and another gas-chamber bounce."

"You shall have it, sir."

"New Year's. That's unequivocal. That Fed probe on the phone taps is coming up, and I want the Department looking squeaky clean on all matters specifically Jap in advance of that."

"You shall have it, sir."

Jack burped. "Parker trumped us and saved our bacon on those phone taps. It's a fucked-up world we live in."

Dudley smiled. "It is, sir."

"Is there anything else I should know?"

"The prospect of a white suspect has emerged, but I'm sure the lead will play out as fruitless."

"I *know* it will."

Dudley lit a cigarette. "Sid Hudgens should write up the case, sir. There's been no ink on it thus far. The war has very badly upstaged us."

"I'll talk to Sid. Brenda's having a poker game tomorrow night. I'll tell Sid about McPherson. He'll love that."

"He's a grand columnist, our Sid."

Jack said, "Parker. Any final words?"

"We'll be having our monthly dinner with Archbishop Cantwell tonight. Whiskey Bill will be playing host. I'll take gentle digs at him and reinstill a sense of our stalemates."

Call-Me-Jack smirked. "Will Cantwell wear red robes? Will he tell you how he keesters little boys?"

Nun-raping Protty beast. Vile spawn of Luther and his vile church.

"No, sir. His Eminence is far too secularized for all of that."

Call-me-Jack lit a cigar. "What can *I* do for *you,* Dud? It's a two-way street we've got here, and you're doing a damn good job on your side of it."

"I want to go to war, sir. I have some designs that I'll share with you in due time, but I'll leave the implementation to Ace Kwan and my boys. Joe Kennedy has pledged me a commission in Army Intelligence."

Call-Me-Jack drummed the table. "*New Year's*, Dud. Fulfill your duties for the Department, and I'll grant you a leave of absence."

A bennie wave hit. He's in uniform. He's twirling Bette Davis at the Coconut Grove.

Jack thumbed the envelope. *That's five grand, you Prod fuck.*

"Carlos Madrano is embroiled in the case, sir. He's playing scout for the men buying the properties and running wetbacks to Jap farms."

"Carlos is sacrosanct, Dud. Don't rattle his cage."

Gunshots popped outside. Call-Me-Jack said, "Fucking tongs. The fucking Chinks are worse than the fucking Japs."

1:49 a.m.

Tongs, indeed.

He left Kwan's. Tong jalopies rolled down Broadway. They flew tong antenna flags. Tong boys rumbled in a gas-station lot.

Dudley got his car and U-turned. He smelled tong stink bombs. He saw a tong chain fight. The tongs are restless. They're all mischief.

He was all mischief. He dropped by Huey's place before Lyman's. Huey's Jap cohorts had lammed somewhere. He told Huey to fetch them and set up a powwow. He had some questions to ask.

Tachi, the Watanabes, deadly feudal knives. Please elaborate on that.

Rain hit the windshield. Dudley pulled into the Hall of Justice lot. A door guard ran over with an umbrella. Ben Siegel had a staff of flunky cops.

The guard served as a lift operator. They elevatored up to the jail. White piss bums and Fifth Column Japs shared cell space.

They turned a corner. There—the Penthouse.

Six cells combined. No bars. Wall-to-wall carpets and cashmere-tufted chairs. A privately enclosed bathroom. Paneled walls and a four-poster bed.

A fully equipped wet bar. The pajama-clad lad himself.

Handsome Ben. Don't call him "Bugsy." He's the Jew Cary Grant.

They shook hands. Ben slid the guard a sawbuck and dismissed him. Dudley lounged on the catwalk wall. Ben stretched out on the bed.

"You're gaunt, Dud. Jack Horrall must be working you."

"He is, Ben. I could use a grand retreat, such as this."

"Gene Biscailuz is the best innkeeper in town. All this for three yards a night. McPherson stalled my release papers, but I'll be out at noon. I could have stayed to New Year's, but they don't celebrate Hanukkah here."

Dudley laughed. "Ben, you're a pisser."

"'The canary has wings, but he can't fly.' I was looking at a gas-chamber jolt. You and that Blanchard hump put the skids to it."

Dudley said, "An honor, Ben. Superb compensation and train fare. I bought my daughters Indian beads in Bisbee, Arizona."

"They're dumber than the *schvartzes*, the Indians. They sold Manhattan Island for peanuts. I should have bought L.A. off the beaners when I had the chance."

Brass tacks now. It's late. He knows it's about gelt.

"I'll be paying off Harry Cohn's debt to Ace Kwan, and I have a way for Harry to get you your forty-eight. It will most likely take some finagling, but I should have it to you soon."

Ben studied the ceiling. Salvador Dalí painted the mural swirling across it. Rabid unicorns fucked naked gash.

"Finagle away, Dud. It's what you do best."

Dudley lit a cigarette. "I have a bone to pick with the DA. He stalled your release, and I'm sure you'd like to see him compromised."

"I would, Dud. Spare me the details before, so I can enjoy them after. You'll have a favor on the books while you finagle me the forty-eight."

"Harry needs to break some union heads at Columbia."

"I'll send Mickey Cohen and Hooky Rothman over. They'll pull Harry out of the shit lickety-split."

That bennie tea *surged.* Dudley caught a dizzy spell.

"There are five domestic Nazis two tiers over. They were entombed here on Tuesday night. I would like to have Mickey and Hooky briefly jailed on gun-carry charges. While ensconced, they will beat the Nazis to the point of near extinction. I am attempting to secure the names of every Bundist, Silver Shirt, Klansman and pro-Axis shitheel on my Department and the Sheriff's."

Ben studied the ceiling. Dalí owed him. He was stretched thin with cocaine. Ben set him up with Terry Lux. Dr. Terry dried him out.

"Sure, Dud. It'll inconvenience Mickey and Hooky, but the Dudster will owe them one. It's all quid pro quo with us guys, and it all comes out in the wash."

"There's one more thing, Ben."

"There's always 'one more thing' with you, Dud."

"It directly pertains to our chum Lee Blanchard."

Ben cracked his knuckles. "That cocksucker does nothing but owe me. If he thinks Reles paid it off, he's got another fucking think coming."

Dudley said, "I have a swell acquaintance on the Feds, a man named Ed Satterlee. The Feds have a leftist psychiatrist reporting to them, and Agent Satterlee told me that Lee Blanchard's girlfriend, one Katherine Lake, was seen leaving the good doctor's office. She has apparently been befriended by a seditious shrew named Claire De Haven, who threw a swell party last night and was overheard inviting Miss Lake to a second party upcoming. You know the Hollywood crowd, Ben. It would please me to get an advance peek at the party invitations."

Ben cracked his thumbs. "Quid pro quo?"

"Of course."

"I want to watch Mickey and Hooky slug on the Nazis. I want them to wear sap gloves."

41

LOS ANGELES | THURSDAY, DECEMBER 11, 1941

2:19 a.m.

JAP hordes overrun Philippines! U.S. fliers sink *JAP* destroyer! *JAP* parachutists swarm Luzon!

The radio blasted it. Linny's all-night deli—blackout Beverly Hills.

Kay Lake smoked and ignored her food. She wore a black dress and a trench coat. People stared at them.

Ashida sipped coffee. The British soldier's brandy had worn off. He still smelled Dudley Smith.

Kay said, "You're distracted."

Ashida said, "I have to leave soon. There's something I need to see."

"At this time of night? In a *blackout*?"

"Time has a new meaning now. It's why there's so many people here. They can't sleep, and they're afraid they'll miss something."

Kay stubbed out her cigarette. She ignored the radio and the gawkers. It was *très* Kay.

He checked Bureau Teletypes and got the word on Goleta. The sub attack *did* occur. A fishing village got blitzed yesterday morning. It was *très* hush-hush. The Santa Barbara Sheriff's sealed it there at the spot.

He took a big risk. He called the Sheriff's Office and impersonated Ray Pinker. "Can I send a man up?"

They said sure. He didn't say the man was a *JAP*.

Kay said, "Thanks for meeting me. I know it's not really your style."

"I don't have a style. I met you because I knew I wouldn't be able to sleep, and because we have engaging conversations."

Kay smiled. Her teeth were lipstick-smudged.

"You'll say 'What do you want?' to me sooner or later. If I've figured it out, I'll tell you."

Ashida heard *Jap* and *white girl.* The place was full of late-night touts. The place reeked of steamed meat.

"I know what you want. You want to trade perceptions about the world we live in and discuss Captain Parker. He's given you a task that makes you feel important, and he's proven himself important to me. You were invited to a party in Beverly Hills, and you knew you wouldn't be able to sleep. You don't know what you want from one moment to the next, and now the war's gotten under your skin."

The radio erupted. Ashida heard *dead* and *JAPS*. The touts cheered and flashed V for Victory.

"I'm acquainted with both of your bodyguards. That fact intrigues me."

"Yes. Because you see everything as *you*."

"On that note, then. I know some people that you might find

engaging. We want to film a documentary exposing the roundups, and I thought you might like to help us."

Ashida shrugged. The radio blared an advertisement. *Hacienda Homes in Sherman Oaks! Another Exley Construction smash!*

The newscast resumed. *JAPS perish as bombed destroyer sinks!*

Ashida said, "The City Council approved a building plan last year. It was a proposed block of homes in Baldwin Hills, and Exley Construction was given the contract. The buyers' covenant permitted the Nisei to bid on home sites, but the City Council redlined the provision. The Nisei sued in district court. They won, and a few families moved in. They saw they weren't wanted and sold their homes back to Exley Construction for a pittance."

Kay looked around. Ashida traced her eyes. One wall featured Jewish-fighter photos. Barney Ross, Benny Leonard, Maxie Rosenblum. The Lutheran Bucky Bleichert, crouched below them.

Kay blew him a kiss. "I saw Preston Exley, just yesterday. He was leaving an office four blocks from here."

Their booth adjoined a window. Ashida pulled up the shade. Beverly Hills was blackout dark and flatland flat.

Kay looked out. She stared at a parked car. A big man leaned against it. Ashida recognized him—Officer R. S. Bennett.

It startled Kay. Ashida lowered the shade.

"He's on the Department now. I was at his swearing-in a few hours ago. He's our first emergency hire."

"Do you think he's following me?"

Ashida smiled. "He's twenty years old, and you're nothing but seduction. It wouldn't surprise me if he were."

Kay laughed and touched his hand. It shock-waved him. He pulled his hand back. He stood up and toppled his chair.

He walked outside. *JAP, JAP, JAP* trailed him. The Bennett boy was gone. Beverly Drive was 3:00 a.m. still.

He got his car and drove west. He kept the windows down. It dried his sweat and rewired his adrenaline. Beverly Hills, Westwood, Brentwood. Blackout-dark enclaves.

Santa Monica, the coast road. A clear shot north.

Soldiers patrolled the beachfront. They manned searchlights and scanned the wave break. Sandbagged bunkers, machine-gun nests.

He was risking coastal checkpoints. There's a blackout, he's a *JAP*, he's got a hot radio in his trunk.

He hid the radio gear from Dudley. They sat in his car and talked. Their shoulders brushed. He skimmed the *JAP*-language tracts and lied per their contents.

They were anti–L.A. Police. He soft-soaped that aspect and harbored the lead for himself.

Ashida drove north. Raw nerves and sea spray kept him revived. He passed Zuma, Oxnard, Ventura. He saw beach sentries and aircraft spotters. He lucked out on checkpoints—none, none, and none.

He passed Santa Barbara. Dawn was two hours off. The Goleta Inlet was close.

The Sheriff's man said they'd sealed it "on-site." That meant an evidence shed off the water. The attack occurred at dawn yesterday. Expect cops and Army Intelligence. Expect catastrophe display boards. Expect cadavers and debris.

Expect rancor. Expect suspicion. Explain yourself. You're a brilliant forensic chemist. It's an early-wartime ambush scene. *You had to see.*

But, it's a JAP *sneak attack. But, you're here unsanctioned. But, you're a* JAP.

It wouldn't work. He'd risk detention. Parker, Pinker, Smith—name drops wouldn't work. He had tenuous patrons back in L.A. He was a low-down *JAP* here.

He started to turn back. He saw beachfront lights ahead. He pulled up on a landside bluff and grabbed his binoculars.

He looked down. The site was eighty yards off. Arc lights framed an open-front shed.

He saw body tubs. Odd limbs extended. Dry-ice fumes blew out. He saw severed legs in a washtub.

He saw forensics pix clipped to clotheslines.

He saw trash bins full of charred wood.

The shed was lit bright-bright. One detail was off. Cops and Army brass should be hovering. Cars and jeeps should cover the beachfront and blacktop.

He saw one jeep only. He saw legs crossed at the ankle, sticking out.

One guard on duty. Goldbrick, predawn snoozer. There's nobody else around.

Risk it, Mr. Moto. He might be asleep. Try it, Mr. Moto. If he's awake, you're fucked.

Those bright-bright lights. You don't need flashbulbs.

Ashida grabbed his camera. He had sixteen exposures. He pinned his ID card to his jacket and crossed over to the blacktop.

He smelled charred wood and flesh. Salt spray merged with it. He walked straight to the jeep. He heard snores, straight off.

He looked in the cab. *Sweet deal, Mr. Moto.* The soldier wore earplugs.

The shed was decked out haphazardly. The attack was unexpected. Torpedoes hit the beach. It's a fishing village. It's "Collaborationist"—*JAPS* and Chinks allied.

Torpedoes hit. Explosive fire follows. It explains the charred wood in the tubs.

Cops and soldiers swarmed the scene and built this shed. They culled evidence haphazardly. They stuck around all day and got bored.

Think fast, Mr. Moto. You've got five minutes.

Ashida paced the shed. He paced quadrant-to-quadrant in strict crime lab–style. He photographed debris and the evidential photographs. He reconstructed the attack.

Torpedoes hit. The dock and fisherman's huts blow up and fall down. Fishing boats burn into wave-scattered bits. Waves crash, waves recede. Severed arms and legs bob on the crests.

Men stumble out of rubble piles. They're on fire. They scream and thrash. They fall down dead at the water-sand line.

Five dead men. Forensic photo–captured/body tub–confirmed. A stray foot on the sand. Note the photo. Note said foot right here in a tub.

Ashida studied the foot.

He examined it. He photographed it. He got in close and smelled it. He caught early decomposition. He caught a fish-oil scent. He revised his ID to shrimp oil.

It was anomalous. It was familiar.

Nort Layman's autopsy brief. Shrimp oil on the soles of the Watanabes' feet. Blood-dotted glass shards at the house. Said shards reeked of *FISH.*

His trip to the Nisei farms. That worker he spoke to. He smelled *FISH* on him.

Five dead men here. In wet sand yesterday. In body tubs today.

Collaborationists. Note the pix and snap your own shots. *Say what, Mr. Moto?* Two men look Japanese. Three men look Chinese. Racial distinction runs close. *You could be right, you could be wrong.*

Ashida paced the shed. Ashida snapped pix of pix and pix of dead men *right here.*

Dead men on dry ice. Two men badly flame-charred.

He rolled them onto their backs. He brushed off black skin. One man was scorched down to his rib cage. One man was marked by a faded stab wound.

It was old and knife-inflicted. The scar was symmetrical. The knife had to be multibladed. The scar resembled a starburst. Note the single deep puncture.

Ashida paced the shed. Ashida reloaded his camera. He heard a wave crash. He heard the soldier snore five yards away. He heard his own heart beat on overdrive.

He touched all the dead men. He noted their physiques. He matched their missing limbs to the limbs in the severed-limb tub. He said Shinto and Christian prayers for them.

Four minutes down. *Go, Mr. Moto.*

He hit the last quadrant. He photographed photographs.

Small cans in a rubble heap. The labels read "Chopped Shrimp." Charred paper. Kanji-script notations. Money tallies. A Japanese-yen-to-U.S.-dollar play.

Thirty seconds, Mr. Moto. That dozing soldier might wake up.

Ashida braced the last limb tub. He knelt and aimed his camera. He shot a sheared penis arrayed on dry ice.

42

KAY LAKE'S DIARY

LOS ANGELES | THURSDAY, DECEMBER 11, 1941

7:23 a.m.

I brought my sketch pad and pencils to the restaurant. Captain Parker called at dawn and requested a meeting. I hadn't slept, couldn't sleep, and assumed the same for him. I was going from public place to public place, to meet police chemists and policemen I hadn't known the week before.

My table overlooked La Cienega, just south of Wilshire. Dick Webster's smelled of lemon pies and war-alert tension. I went home after Claire's party, then left for my truncated klatch with Hideo Ashida. Hideo left abruptly; I went back home to ponder the vicissitudes of entrapment. Captain Parker was now twenty-three minutes late; I filled up sketch-pad paper.

My pencils moved near randomly. I drew the woman behind the counter and segued to passing cars on La Cienega. I moved to Scotty Bennett in police blues, to Hideo Ashida, naked, with Bucky Bleichert's body. Then I was back in Claire's bedroom with Renée Falconetti.

I saw the Joan of Arc film as a high school frosh; a fey teacher took a group of students to the only foreign-movie theater in Sioux Falls, South Dakota. The Silver Shirts got the theater closed down the next week. Sioux Falls was a nativist hotbed; the theater served up moral turpitude imported from Catholic countries. Religious ecstasy akin to coitus and a short-haired woman burned alive. Falconetti's depiction of a woman consumed by cause and a supplicant's desire for transcendence.

I drew Falconetti as Joan and Claire as Joan; I incorporated their features in a seamless Claire-Joan. A truck drove by and made the window glass rumble. A man and a tall red-haired woman got out of a car and began walking toward Wilshire. Bill Parker pulled his black-and-white up behind them. He stepped out and started following the couple. The woman swiveled to adjust her skirt and looked straight at him. Captain Parker appeared to be stricken. I read the look on his face.

She wasn't *Her*, whoever *She* was. *She* wasn't among those Navy women I saw him staring at yesterday.

He entered the restaurant. I slipped out of my trench coat. He purchased my dress and should see me in it.

A waitress swooped by and refilled my coffee; I pointed to the other cup on the table and had her fill it. Captain Parker sat down; I noticed the pilled lint on his uniform. I knew that lint-on-cop-blue stamp very well. Captain Parker had slept in the Bureau cot room.

He warmed his hands on the coffee cup. He said, "Good morning, Miss Lake."

I closed my sketch pad and placed it under the table. I said, "Sunday afternoon. Outside the Federal Building. You saw me with a very large young man."

"Yes, and I saw him leave your house Monday morning. His name is Robert Bennett, the Department just signed him on, and he has all the earmarks of Dudley Smith's latest pet thug. I'm sure you find him alluring, which speaks more to your susceptibility than your judgment."

Touché.

I said, "I was being disingenuous. I thought you might know things about Officer Bennett that I don't."

"I witnessed his oath of service last night. I would venture that you know him somewhat more intimately."

Touché. Et pour la robe en cachemire noir?

"I had a splendid time at Claire De Haven's party. She invited me to a second party next Monday night."

"Please continue."

"I sneaked into her bedroom, rifled the drawers and saw a hypodermic syringe and several vials of what I assumed was morphine. I stole a political tract, but I haven't read it yet."

"I'll get you a concealable camera. I want photographic evidence of illegal narcotics and paraphernalia."

"Terry Lux was at the party. He was watching Claire very closely. I'm assuming that she dries out periodically at his ranch, when the PD isn't using it for softball games and picnics."

"So, it's 'Claire' now? Have you established a bar of friendship?"

"All betrayals start with friendship, don't they? Isn't there always a filial basis for entrapment?"

"I'm going to fit you with an undetectable microphone. You're going to get Miss De Haven to advocate the violent overthrow of the United States Government, and we're going to have an audial record."

"Will you get me another snazzy frock while you're at it? *This* one turned some heads."

"I want photographs of every pill vial in her medicine cabinet. I want photographs of all her recent phone bills and photographs of every page in her personal address book."

"We're going to make a documentary movie exposing the Japanese roundups. I proposed the idea, and Claire went for it. I'll make sure it's less outlandish than *Storm Over Leningrad*, so the jury won't bust a gut and laugh it out of court."

"Juries do not appreciate subtlety, Miss Lake. If you create a filmed document, it must be bluntly and vilely seditious and unequivocally state Miss De Haven's ideological designs."

"Is ideology unequivocally anything? Doesn't she have to blow up an aircraft plant first? Should I encourage her to do it, and should I bring along a noted cinematographer?"

"Treason is ideology and free speech perverted. Seditious thought and its reckless public expression is a grave criminal offense that fully sanctions me in this action that you allege to be precipitous, presumptuous and subversive in and of itself, so help me fucking God, I know it to be true."

I was dizzy. He *looked* dizzy. My cigarettes were on the table. He helped himself and tossed me the pack. We lit each other up.

I said, "Who is she, Captain Parker?"

He said, "Who is *who*, Miss Lake?"

I said, "The tall red-haired woman you keep looking for."

He stood up and banged the table. The silverware jumped a foot. William H. Parker looked schoolboy hurt and old-man haggard. He'd lost ten pounds in the five days I'd known him. His gun belt pulled his trousers halfway down his hips.

He ran away from me. I looked out the window and watched. He got into his car and swerved into traffic. Motorists honked their horns. Captain William H. Parker stuck his arm out the window and held his middle finger up.

In uniform. In his police black-and-white.

I laughed. The prowl car peeled out; I saw middle fingers salute him back and heard horn honks peak and fade. It made me laugh and left me exhausted. Just sitting at the table hurt.

Restaurant sounds subsided to a hum. I shut my eyes for one second and opened them just as quick. A wall clock told me I'd been asleep a full hour.

I rubbed my eyes and looked out the window. The tall red-haired woman stood out at the curb.

I reached for my sketch pad to draw her. I put the pad down just as abruptly and did something I'd never done before.

I prayed for the woman's safe passage through this war.

43

LOS ANGELES | THURSDAY, DECEMBER 11, 1941

9:14 a.m.

Parker paced his den. It was men's club–furnished. Framed certificates honored him.

His law school degree. His state Bar plaque. His Phi Beta Kappa key. Thirty-four police commendations.

The certificates covered three walls. The fourth wall was masking-papered. Inked headings denoted this:

Blackouts/Traffic Statistics.

Alien Squad/Subversive Roundups.

Watanabe Case/Details-Chronology.

Lake/De Haven.

Parker paced. He was doomsday exhausted. His glasses slid down his nose.

He was stretched Mass-wafer thin. He threw a fit in full uniform. He was afraid that he was missing things. That meant *write them all down.*

Blackouts/Traffic Statistics. Jot graph notes.

Last night's blackout spawned a Negro riot. Five people died in car wrecks. A soldier shot a society dame at a checkpoint. She did not hear his *"Halt!"* warning. He drilled her dead.

Alien Squad/Subversive Roundups. Jot graph notes.

"Feds go to 'B' subversive list. Details to come." "Hold squad briefing. Urge officers to curtail strongarm methods."

He'd seen War Department Teletypes. FDR had full-scale internment plans. Army teams were scouting sites throughout the Southwest. The local jails were Japped to the tits. A mass evacuation boded. Hold for the Jap diaspora.

Watanabe Case/Details-Chronology. Jot graph notes.

"White man/purple sweater. Black car outside house, 12/6/41, near time of death."

"H. Ashida to do tire molds/most likely futile."

"Watanabe calls to Santa Monica pay phones."

Lake/De Haven. Jot graph notes.

He raised his pen. The world dipped off its axis. He was that fucking tired.

Lake/De Haven. It's all in his head. There's nothing to jot on the graph.

Kay Lake was working both ends of it. She was a swoony unfulfilled artist. She saw her film as a luminous polemic. She wanted to entrap Claire De Haven. She had to win his "fatuous" and "presumptuous" war. Her courtroom testimony settled the Boulevard-Citizens case. He would put her on the witness stand and doom the Red Queen. He would craft her oratory. She would explicate his theocratic resolve.

She senses his misgivings per the roundups. She thinks she can instill apostasy. Their meetings leave him tense. He thinks of her more than he should.

Parker laid his head on the graph. His arms and legs were rubberized. The wall held him up.

The door creaked. Helen walked in. She wore her gardener's jumpsuit.

"You're a wreck, Bill. You should take the day off and sleep."

He kept his head down. It hid the *Lake/De Haven* graph.

"I can't. I have to collate Teletypes, and Horrall wants a briefing on the blackout."

"The world can do without you for a day. You didn't start the war, and I don't think you'll be the one to finish it."

"Helen, *please.*"

"*Bill*, please. Please rest, please don't sleep in the cot room at City Hall, please tend to yourself, and please don't run away from me like you've been doing."

She looked perky. She always looked perky. She was born perky.

"I'll take Sunday morning off. We'll go to Mass and get breakfast at Lyman's."

Helen laughed. "Where you'll disappear into the back room and read Teletypes. Where you'll gab with Thad Brown and joke about ousting Jack Horrall. Where—"

"Helen, please—"

"Bill, *please* stop neglecting your marriage. Bill, *please* curtail your brusque behavior with my family and friends. Bill, *please* take the pledge again, because I can't stand seeing you drunk. Bill, *please* don't work so hard and learn to have some simple fun, so you won't have nightmares and sweat up the bed on the few nights we share it. Bill, *please* quit praying aloud when you think I can't hear it, because I don't want to know what you're saying to God. Bill, *please* stop getting crushes on college girls when you have a woman who—"

Parker ran.

He made the back porch. He covered his ears. It didn't kill this:

Helen stomps through the house. Helen slams doors. Helen gets her car and guns it. Helen lays rubber down the driveway.

He kept a jug in the toolshed. He walked over and snatched it. He took three good pops.

He got the burn and the shudders. He got the bright colors. He got that moment you go somewhere else.

He stashed the bottle. He got an idea. He went back inside and snatched his desk phone. An operator plugged him through to Chicago.

Northwestern U. The campus cops. He had cachet there.

The Chief came on the line. Parker laid it out.

Joan. A biology major. About twenty-five. Tall and red-haired. He saw her shoot skeet off Lake Michigan. She owned a vent-rib 12-gauge.

The Chief said he'd jump on an ID. Parker hung up.

He felt sandbagged. Doomsday, Armageddon. Booze begets instant misconduct and regret. He walked to the couch and fell down.

Deadwood.

Yeah, that's it.

It's 1916. Those are brothel windows. Now it's '24 L.A. He's beating up his first wife. They're at the hospital. She's bandaged up and spiteful. She's hitting him back.

Church processions. He's shaking a mitre box. Pope Pius XII in *Deadwood*? no, that can't be.

Church bells. No, doom bells. Bloody thorns or his gun belt gouged him awake.

He opened his eyes. His wristwatch read 8:14.

Not the Pope—the *Archbishop.* Jimmy and Dudley—the mad micks.

He got up and opened the door. They saw him disheveled and roared that mick way. His Eminence favored golf togs outside the rectory. He wore a pink sweater and kelly green slacks.

Dudley said, "Our future Chief, roused from sleep."

J. J. Cantwell said, "We're three Catholic men relieved of our duties. We're going to get shit-faced drunk and defame the Prottys and the kikes."

Parker ushered them in. His Eminence was sixty-six and rambunctious. Dudley doted on him. They met in Ireland, circa 1919. Dudley killed British soldiers. Cantwell funneled gun money.

Dudley said, "I smell Helen Schultz Parker's corned beef and cabbage, warming in the oven."

Cantwell said, "*Schultz?* Bill married a *Hun*? We might have to intern her, along with all the heathen Japs."

Dudley said, "She's a fine Catholic lass, Your Eminence."

Cantwell said, "We'll have to have Bill explain this new war to us, Dud. Father Coughlin lays the blame on the coons and the sheenie bankers, and I tend to agree with him."

Dudley said, "America and Ireland first, Your Eminence. You know where I stand on that."

Cantwell said, "Let's get shit-faced drunk and defame that Jew shitheel in the White House. Franklin Double-Cross Rosenfeld, his name is."

Parker yawned. He was hungover. He craved a hair of the dog.

The phone rang. It hit him as gunshots.

He grabbed it. "Yes?"

"It's Thad, Bill. Please put Dudley on."

He passed the receiver. Dudley took it and dispensed winks.

He said, "Sergeant Smith." He listened. He said, "Certainly." He passed the phone back.

"There's devilish mischief in Chinatown. My presence is required."

Ignore the tone. Read his eyes. Dear God, such glee.

Part Two

THE CHINKS

(December 11–December 19, 1941)

44

LOS ANGELES | THURSDAY, DECEMBER 11, 1941

8:33 p.m.

White man's fellowship diverted. Murder One in Chinatown.

Dudley shagged his K-car and ran Code 3. His roof lights strafed lawn lights and nativity scenes. The siren hurt his ears.

Back roads were best. Silver Lake and Echo Park—the hill route. It should go seven minutes, door-to-door.

It took six. His siren got him through bottlenecks. He skirted Chavez Ravine and hit Ord Street. Tong balloons bobbed sky-high.

This heathen custom. String balloons to fire escapes. It means *War*.

A crowd was cliqued up. Tong boys ran predominant. Three black-and-whites at the location. A four-floor building, all Chink.

Dudley skidded up, Code 3. Bluesuits flanked the entrance. The place was tight-sealed.

Firecrackers popped. Paper dragons flew. War with the Japs, and now *this*?

Dudley walked over. The bluesuits pointed up to the second-floor hall. He sailed there. He squeezed by a morgue man. Cigarette smoke blew out a doorway. It meant boocoo cops.

They spilled into the hallway. Thad Brown and Nort Layman. Mike Breuning and Dick Carlisle. Scotty Bennett with his gorgeous big-kid look.

Jim Davis was there. Two-Gun was Too-Fat now. His two .45's bulged wide.

The gang greeted him and backed off. It's the Dudster's show.

He tipped his hat and sailed by them. Ace Kwan stood by the bedroom door. He saw Dudley and pointed him in.

Requiescat in pace. Dear girl, heaven-sent.

She was on the bed, naked. She was positioned facedown. Blood ran from her hips to her neckline. Note the blood-drenched coverlet. Note the blood-drenched sheets.

Ace said, "My niece. We were too late with our measures. The Japs fucked us up."

Dudley embraced him. The old man was all sinew.

"I will avenge her, my yellow brother. I will be merciless."

Ace squeezed Dudley and stepped back. Dudley signaled the living room. Breuning, Carlisle and Scotty B. ran up.

Dudley said, "We're throwing out a dragnet for Four Families. Mike, call Elmer Jackson at the Bureau. Vice has sheets on all the known members. Get me ten patrol boys from Central, ten from Hollywood, and bring Elmer with you. Dick and Scotty, rouse the coppers downstairs. I want a display of force. Go out and roust all the blue-kerchief punks you see and string up a grand shackle line. I want four paddy wagons. We're going to fill them with Four Families fucks and drive them to Temple and Alameda. There's a grand vacant lot there. It's a perfect interrogation spot."

Breuning scrawled up his notebook. Carlisle buffed his glasses. Scotty plain loomed.

Ace knelt by the bed. He touched the dead girl's hair. He fondled colored beads.

Dudley squared up Scotty's tie. "Your suitability for this profession will be tested tonight. Can you assure me that you will rise to your tasks?"

"Yes, sir. I can."

"Don't call me 'sir,' call me Dudley."

Scotty grinned and cracked his knuckles. Jim Davis waddled up.

"Can I help, Dud? I was listening to radio calls and thought, That's sure as shit a touchy homicide, in my old stomping grounds."

Dudley bowed, Chink-style. "Of course, Chief. It's going to be quite the heathen night, and I would be honored to have you join us."

"It's been 'Jim' since I retired, Dud."

"The grand jury forced you out, sir. It was a heinously coerced retirement."

Davis chomped a plug. "You're very gracious, Dud."

Ace screeched at the dead girl. Davis joined him and screeched in full Chink. Breuning and Carlisle ignored it. Scotty studied it. The dead girl left him unfazed.

Dudley said, "Lads, Chief Davis will be chaperoning you. Do what he says at all times. He will serve as your interpreter. The tong truce that he brokered has been violated, and we are witnessing the upshot now. Go, lads. God be with you on this garish night."

The lads smirked and moved. Ace touched the dead girl's hair and stood up. The blood on the sheets had gone stiff maroon. Ace bowed and stepped out of the room.

Dudley shut the door. Dudley circled the bed. Sirens *scree-scree'd* outside. He willed the room quiet. He got down and *looked.*

Her neck was unmarked. Her eyes were shut. He pulled up the lids and checked the pupils. No petechial hemorrhage. No exsanguination. The fuck did not strangle her.

The bedsheets were tucked smooth. Sex did not precede the death. It was not a lust crime. He stripped her to humble her. He wanted to humble the men who loved her. He wanted to violate them.

The dark races declared *WAR* in this manner. Ravaged women meant *WAR*. It was ghastly and cowardly.

Dudley studied the girl's back. The blood had firmed up. The darker patches indicated severed arteries. Dried blood and wet blood covered the stab wounds. It was high-volume spill. It indicated numerous thrusts. It exceeded the standard kill-the-whore two or three thrusts.

He bent over the girl. He got out his handkerchief. He blotted up a dark blood patch. It soaked his handkerchief. He tossed it and grabbed a pillowcase. He swabbed the patch blood-free.

Multiple cuts, off a central puncture. A starburst pattern.

Just like Tachi Tachibana. Just like the photos in Ray Pinker's book. The feudal warlord's knife. Eighteenth-century Japan. Huey Cressmeyer's spiel, yesterday.

Huey knew four crazy Japs. They packed knives that made this precise wound. They lived in Griffith Park. They hated the Chinks. They hated tong chiefs. They believed you must kill their female kin. This vile act bestowed transcendence.

Four Families did not kill Rose Eileen Kwan. Huey's Jap pals did. Huey used the Japs in last night's van heist. *He* made Huey do it.

Dudley slow-eyed the room. He went quadrant-to-quadrant—floor, walls, furniture. He caught a metal glint under a chair.

It was a knife. It was slick with Rose Kwan's blood. Note the six blades. Note the starburst pattern. It's not feudal vintage. It's recently manufactured.

Dudley ripped off a sheet swatch and wrapped the knife up. The evil thing bulged his pocket.

Toss the room. Be thorough, be slow.

He rifled the closet. He went through every drawer. He pulled up the rug and looked under the bed. He saw clothes, books, phonograph records. He opened the books and ruffled the pages. One book, two books, three—

A photograph fell out. It was four by six and in color. The print had faded. It showed a young man.

He had dark hair. He was a pallid non-Caucasian. He might be a Jap-Mex half-breed.

Huey C., yesterday.

A Jap cell guy pregged up Nancy Watanabe. Said guy possessed acne cysts. He said he killed a family in Mexico. It might have been brag. He might have fled back to Mexico. *He might be a Jap-Mex half-breed.*

The Watanabe job was tidy. The Rose Kwan snuff was sheer sloth. The Watanabe job reeked of singular animus. This was an evil-boys mob. There were probably four killers. The death pose suggested it.

The wrists and ankles were not abraded. She did not thrash. Four boys subdued her. She was stripped, pinned prone and stabbed. She wasn't gagged. One boy pushed her face into the mattress and quashed her screams.

Dudley pocketed the photo and walked out to the hall. Nort Layman and a morgue man perched there. He motioned them in. Ace leaned on the wall.

"What gives, my Irish brother?"

Dudley lit a cigarette. "It's not Four Families. It's a cabal of renegade Japs. We will kill them, and Four Families will provide us with a scapegoat that will serve to enhance your power."

Ace bowed. Dudley grabbed the hallway phone and dialed the Bureau. He heard two rings and one click.

"Homicide, Breuning."

"Yes, and Johnny-on-the-spot."

Breuning laughed. "Go up on the roof and look north on Broadway in a few minutes. I wangled the vehicles and the manpower, so it should be some show."

Dudley said, "I will surely savor it, lad."

"What else have you got for me?"

"Find Huey Cressmeyer and make him available. Call Carlos Madrano in Tijuana and tell him to drive to Los Angeles immediately."

Breuning rogered it. Dudley hung up and walked back in the bedroom. Ace waved his beads at dead Rose.

She was up on her side. Nort Layman held a speculum and a mirror. He mouthed "No rape."

The living room was noisy. Crazy laughs bounced down the hall. Thad Brown swapped Jap jokes with some Chinamen. They were straight off a Bob Hope broadcast.

Dudley stepped out on the fire escape. A paper dragon sailed by him. He climbed up and stood on the roof.

Twenty blues quick-marched up Broadway. They packed shotguns and nightsticks. They smashed windows. They were advance-briefed. We're out to get Four Families. Tell their affiliates that.

The cops surged north. Four paddy wagons tailed them. Southbound traffic U-turned and vanished.

They smashed windows. They rock-salted fleeing Chinks. They pulled tong punks out of gin mills and nigger-knocked them. Fireworks, dragons, festive music. *Forget the Japs. Here comes the L.A. Police.*

Cops tossed tongsters in paddy wagons. Cops stomped tongsters on the street. "Display of force." Festive music and screams.

There's Scotty Bennett. He's got two punks by the neck. There's Jim Davis. He's a grand pistol-whipper. There's some rooftop folk enjoying the show. They're flying the red flag of Hop Sing.

Dudley lit a cigarette. What's this? A blue-kerchiefed dragon, floating straight at him.

Nose-to-nose now. A fierce reptile. Curled lips and bared teeth.

Dudley held up his cigarette. The dragon bumped into it. Burning embers to dry paper—an instant flame. The dragon exploded. Dudley pushed him out toward the street.

The dragon flew four stories high. Chinks looked up and shrieked. Chinamen grabbed their Chinklets and held them on their shoulders. The fiery dragon swayed in the wind.

Dudley hopped the fire grates downstairs. Broadway reeked of spent cherry bombs. His K-car was unmolested. He got in and swooped to Temple and Alameda.

The lot was pure quiet. He perched there. He reclined his seat and went someplace hazy. He felt that postbennie wooze.

The world disappeared. Time went in a bucket. He heard engine rumble and opened his eyes. The world had relit, all too soon.

Mike B. had Huey C. cuffed. Four paddy wagons idled up ahead. Dick C. and Scotty B. stood with Jim Davis. Two-Gun's shirt was blood-soaked.

Dudley got out and stretched. Huey quaked. Breuning shoved him in the backseat.

He moaned for his dyke mommies. The lad possessed initiative but lacked male dignity.

Dudley said, "Send the paddy-wagon boys home, Mike. They've served their purpose, and they might lack the stomach for this."

Breuning lammed. Huey boo-hoo'd. Dudley got in the backseat and uncuffed him. Huey pulled out a Mars bar.

"Your Jap chums killed Ace Kwan's niece. Do you know where in Griffith Park they reside?"

Huey unwrapped the Mars bar. "The hiking path up from the Observatory."

"Would they be harboring evidence from the van job? Specifically, evidence that might come back to you?"

Huey munched the Mars bar. "Naw. I took everything incriminating with me. And they're broke already. They gave all their gelt to some radio swami who's gone on the Japs."

The paddy wagons rocked on their axles. Dudley heard muffled screams.

"I'm treating you to a Mexican vacation, lad. My friend Carlos Madrano will be escorting you down. You are to remain out of sight as all of this resolves."

Huey wolfed the Mars bar and licked his fingers. The paddy wagons shook on their axles. Dudley heard muffled screams.

He hit the roof light and held up the photograph. Huey eyeballed it.

"Is this the half-breed with the acne scars? The lad who bragged that he killed a family in Culiacán?"

Huey squinted. "I can't tell, Uncle Dud. Maybe *ja*, maybe *nein*."

The paddy wagons shimmied on their axles. Dudley heard muffled screams.

He cuffed Huey and walked over. The wagons stood four across. They swayed and banged one another. The screams got worse.

Dudley entered the first wagon. Six tong boys were cuffed on the bench. Dick Carlisle packed a rubber hose. The grip was friction-taped. The business end dripped blood.

Dudley stepped out. Dudley entered the next wagon. Eight tong boys were cuffed on the bench. Mike Breuning packed a beavertail sap. It was lead-stitched.

Dudley stepped out. Dudley entered the next wagon. Five tong boys were cuffed on the bench. Jim Davis packed a billy club and shrieked in Chinese.

Dudley stepped out. Dudley entered the next wagon. Nine tong boys were cuffed on the bench. Scotty Bennett packed his fists.

Scotty looked at Dudley. A skinny tong boy gave Dudley the finger. Dudley laughed. The skinny tong boy spit blood on his shoes.

Dudley said, "Uncuff him. Bring him outside for a bit."

Scotty unhooked the boy. Dudley stepped outside. Scotty shoved the boy toward him. The rascal spit blood and swayed on his feet.

Dudley said, "Kill him."

Scotty pulled his .45. Scotty blew his brains out, point-blank.

December 12, 1941

45

LOS ANGELES | FRIDAY, DECEMBER 12, 1941

12:19 a.m.

Mold work. Tire-tread casting.

Difficult in the lab. Add this outdoor setting. Add the cold night and arc light. Add the kibitzers.

Lee Blanchard and Jack Webb. With a jug scrounged at the El Sombrero.

Ashida plastered up a tread trough. Arc light beams singed his neck. He had exemplar pix of the Watanabes' car. They owned a '36 Dodge.

He was two hours in. Bill Parker called and ordered the work. He called from Lyman's. Sid Hudgens was with him. Parker said, "Nobody can sleep, so we might as well be working. I've talked Sid into writing a piece on the case. I'm working—so you should be, too."

He didn't say "And you're drinking." He didn't say "And you're buying off a corrupt newsman."

Ashida worked. Dirt-and-gravel driveways made for good lifts. He'd confirmed the Dodge with six molds.

It was *elimination* work. He was looking for *suspect* car moldings. The odds: ten thousand to one against.

It was half-ass quiet now. The Chinatown ruckus had lulled. They heard shotgun blasts a mile southeast. Jack checked his police-band radio.

The Dudster ordered twenty cops out on a riot sweep. The fracas extended. It featured fireworks and high-flying debris.

Ashida daubed plaster. Lee Blanchard and Jack Webb were liquored up. Blanchard was scratched up from Kay Lake.

Jack said, "Scotty Bennett's on the PD now. You know, that big fullback from Hollywood High."

Blanchard said, "I think he's messing around with Kay, not that I give a shit. I saw him going into Lyman's after that scene she pulled with me."

Jack said, "I don't get it. You're shacked up with Kay."

Blanchard said, "You're too young to get it. You ain't figured out that the world is a strange and fucked-up place."

Ashida daubed plaster. Yes—strange and fucked-up.

Submarines. The Goleta Inlet shed. He drove back to L.A. and developed the photos. He succumbed to fear. He destroyed the Watanabes' radio with a ball-peen hammer. He burned the ledger. He mixed a sedative and slept for ten hours. He woke up, terrified.

It was everything.

The roundups. His thefts. His lies. Crazy Kay and her crazy-girl agenda. Dudley Smith versus Bill Parker.

He studied the shed pix. Physiognomy, eugenics. Three dead men looked Chink. Two dead men looked Jap. They might all be mixed-race. He thought in racial slurs now. *The world was this fucked-up place.*

Blanchard said, "Hideo's pals with Kay. They made quite the pair at Lyman's. Thad Brown damn near shit a brick."

Jack said, "Quit needling Hideo."

Blanchard said, "Hideo's okay. It's Kay who ain't—but I love her, anyway."

Jack said, "Let it go, brother."

Blanchard tipped the jug. "Scotty Bennett. Another cop. And now your old pal Bucky's coming on the PD. Kay'll have her hands full."

It was cold. They wore their high school jackets. Belmont and Manual Arts. *Track meets, the showers, Bucky.*

Jack said, "I screwed up at the briefing. I shouldn't have mentioned the purple-sweater guy. I think Dudley's peeved at me."

Ashida said, "You did the right thing. It's a good lead."

Blanchard tipped the jug. "It's a *shit* lead. Nobody wants a white killer. That's straight from Horrall."

Jack snatched the jug. "I heard Mike Breuning and Sid Hudgens talking. I think they're cooking up something with the DA."

Blanchard unsnatched the jug. "McPherson's a mud shark. He used to bring colored girls to my fights and cause a big stink."

Jack resnatched the jug. "I did an errand for Mike, but he told me it was shitwork at the gate. I called PC Bell and checked those pay-phone calls that the Watanabes made. The clerk gave me the locations. The booths were out by those aircraft plants. You know—Lockheed, Douglas, Boeing."

Blanchard said, "You're right, shitwork. You follow these leads, and all you get is shit."

Ashida braced a new tread set. It was a grass-gravel imprint. He adjusted the arc light. He laid down his calipers and tape.

He squatted low. He got naked-eye bingo: *Something's different here.*

It was *diamond* tread. The Watanabes' Dodge had *sawtooth* tread. This was *separate-car* tread. He was naked-eye sure.

Something's familiar. He'd seen it before. He knew that tread.

Ashida ran out to his car. He dug in the glove box and skimmed his bulletin stack. He knew it was recent. The diamond-tread Goodyear—

December 11, 10, 9, 8—

There:

Sunday, December 7, 5:45 a.m. A Sheriff's car-on-bicycle job. 4600 Valley Boulevard. Four-person hit-and-run.

It's dark out. They're clipped from behind. Three teenaged boys survive. The group's leader expires.

Jim Larkin. Dead at Queen of Angels. The bulletin photo matches the driveway tracks. The same tread. The same wear pattern. The same impression depth.

December 7. Pearl Harbor morning. 5:45 a.m. The morning *after* the Watanabe snuffs.

That car, in *this* driveway. The driveway was roped off from Sunday a.m. on. *That* car, *those* tires, *this* driveway—sometime before that.

Ashida read the whole bulletin. His hands shook and jumbled the words. An eyeball witness said this:

The suspect's car hit-and-ran. It almost looked deliberate. The car was black. That's it for vehicle ID.

But:

A white man's arm dangled out the window. The man wore a purple sweater. End of description—that's all of it.

46

KAY LAKE'S DIARY

LOS ANGELES | FRIDAY, DECEMBER 12, 1941

2:16 a.m.

Scotty fumbled with me.

He showed up an hour ago. His hands were bruised; his suit was wrinkled; he wore a shoulder-holstered gun. My wartime lover. The "first emergency hire" of the Los Angeles PD.

He had surveilled me late Wednesday night; he had observed my date with Hideo Ashida. I should have been furious—but something made me step back from it.

My rough boy was distraught. He bolted three quick scotches, carried me upstairs and went at my body. He'd start to kiss me, stop and burrow into me. He'd get up and adjust the curtains to further contain us.

The bedroom is dark. We can't read each other. It's as if we're back in the blackout.

I put my hand on Scotty's chest and felt him pulsing. I said, "Tell me."

He said, "I was waiting outside here, way late Wednesday night. I'd just got sworn in. I wanted to tell you before someone else did. You came home, but you went out again, and I wanted to get things straight in my mind before I told you. Then you drove to Linny's and met Ashida. He was at the ceremony, so I knew you knew."

I smoothed his hair and undid his holster. He relaxed a bit. I placed his holster on a bedside chair.

"I was angry at you for following me. But I understand it now."

Scotty said, "I like Ashida okay, but he's a Jap. I wanted to tell you, but when you saw me outside Linny's, I knew he'd tell you and take it away from me."

I said, "I'm sorry. And you know I couldn't have known."

"I know. But there's a war on, and he's a Jap. It's like I said the other night. You spread yourself pretty thin."

I touched Scotty's face. His eyes were wet. I brushed away tears.

Scotty trembled. He said, "I killed a man. I thought I'd join the Marines and shoot Japs on some island. I killed a Chinaman instead."

His tremors moved to my body.

"What happened? How did it happen?"

He said, "Ace Kwan's niece was killed. The guy who did it went after Dudley, so I shot him."

"And?"

"There's no 'and,' Kay. That's all I'm supposed to say. You can read about it in the *Mirror.* Dud gave Sid Hudgens the exclusive."

I rolled away from him. There was Dudley Smith and Lee; Dudley Smith, Lee, and Abe Reles. "The canary can sing, but he can't fly." Coney Island and a drop out that window. A dead Chinaman now.

Scotty rolled into me. His breath subsided. He'd said it.

The bed was disarrayed. I pulled the covers over us and felt the hitch that signified Scotty's drifting to sleep. A five-day love affair and this body's knowledge already. The hitch felt safe.

Scotty slept. I turned on the bedside lamp and moved the beam away from him. I got out the tract I stole from Claire De Haven's.

The title was *Fascist Harvest.* An L.A. policeman's badge was pictured below it.

The prose style was luminous by propaganda-tract standards. The introduction rehashed beefs pertaining to Chief Jim Davis. It was stale stuff—but then the author riveted me.

Davis was abetted in his repressive enforcement schemes. The brains and "oppressive mind-set" behind them belonged to his administrative aide. The aide was a ruthlessly ambitious and incandescently brilliant lieutenant named William H. Parker.

Lieutenant Parker was an exceedingly gifted attorney-at-law. Lieutenant Parker utilized his legal prowess to enhance his personal power within the Los Angeles Police Department and to increase political autonomy for the Los Angeles Police. These measures were couched within a disingenuous and entirely self-serving populist stance. They restricted political influence as it regarded day-to-day police work. They dashed all notions of civilian oversight on the Los Angeles Police. They set the stage for greater political-police collusion, once compliant politicians with "quasi-reformer" credentials were lured into the PD's fold. The tract predicted the current reign of Mayor Fletch Bowron and Chief "Call-Me-Jack" Horrall, and laid the blame on the then Lieutenant William H. Parker.

Lieutenant Parker was a sterling long-term thinker. His legal mind was attuned solely to his own goals. He despised the Davises, Bowrons and Horralls of the world and facilitated their power solely to pave the way for his own ascent. He created the police regimes that he purported to despise and intended to reform at that far-ahead moment when power came to him. The author praised Parker here. He employed Marxist methods with magisterial aplomb. His city charters greatly increased the civil-service protection granted to Los Angeles police chiefs and gave them a free rein to ignore civilian interference and rule for life. Lieutenant William H. Parker was no less than the creator and sustaining force behind Police State Los Angeles and the theocrat's utopia that he planned to build from scratch. The author of the tract knew it: "As a victim, as a citizen engaged in revolt, as an affluent woman rendered a casualty in Whiskey Bill Parker's war."

So, it's personal. So, it's all about the two of you.

The text went to memoir. Claire De Haven described an anti-police rally in Pershing Square. The date was October 11, 1935. Claire was twenty-five and organizing for the Socialist Workers Party. L.A. cops beat a Negro prisoner to death at the Lincoln Heights jail. Protests ensued.

Police influence quashed a rising hue and cry. Lieutenant Bill Parker extorted newspapermen citywide. He pledged favors if they suppressed their coverage. They did. The incident faded from public consciousness. The SWP called for a rally on October 11.

Claire was there. The rally was peacefully run. Mounted cops attacked the protesters. Lieutenant Parker commanded them. Claire saw him in jackboots and World War tin hat. She was beaten, kicked to the ground and tossed in a paddy wagon. She was locked up on the women's tier at the Central Station jail. *I* was in the jail Monday night. *I* was locked up with a score of Japanese women. *They* were commandeered in a moment of racial hysteria.

Sheriff's matrons tended to the female prisoners. They were stripped and sprayed for lice. A very large matron with a Jewish surname took her time with Claire. She fondled Claire's breasts, shaved her hair close, dressed her in a scratchy smock and threw her in a cell. Claire saw herself in a mirror. She had been beaten and molested. Her mirror image brought to mind Renée Falconetti in *The Passion of Joan of Arc.*

Claire's lawyer father bailed her out. She fixated on the man in jackboots and glasses. She talked to a Police Department plant. The man said, "That's Whiskey Bill. Let me tell you about him."

Joan of Arc. William H. Parker.

Claire kept her hair short. She viewed *The Passion of Joan of Arc* repeatedly. The Protestant-reared atheist converted to Catholicism. She attended Mass at Saint Vibiana's. Lieutenant Parker worshiped there. She observed him every Sunday morning. She watched Lieutenant Parker comport with an Irish-born policeman named Dudley Smith. She saw Lieutenant Parker and Sergeant Smith laugh and joke with Archbishop Cantwell. Monsignor Joseph Hayes became her confessor. He was also Lieutenant Parker's confessor.

The rest of the tract was pure indictment.

William H. Parker's intent was to place Los Angeles under martial law. His reforming zeal was the fascist ethos of subordinate and control. His Catholicism was the male vituperation of the Borgias. Her Catholicism was the ecstatic revelation of Joan of Arc.

I put down the tract. Officer R. S. Bennett slept beside me. I turned off the lamp. My bedroom went war-blackout dark.

The tract was never publicly issued—I sensed that very strongly. None of the information was documented in Claire's file. The relationship was impersonal on Parker's side—I sensed that even more strongly. He never saw the tract or saw Claire in church. It didn't matter. She saw Parker, just as he saw me.

Claire's middle name was Katherine, my full first name. I had lived a version of her life. The lover beside me killed a man this very night. His presence consoled more than disturbed me.

I have lain still for hours. I am aswirl in madness and magic. I don't know what to do next.

47

LOS ANGELES | FRIDAY, DECEMBER 12, 1941

7:20 a.m.

Parker annotated his graphs. He felt refreshed. He fell asleep drunk and woke up sober. He reinstated The Pledge.

Blackouts/Traffic Statistics. Jot graph notes.

Status quo here. He called the Bureau an hour ago. A secretary checked his Teletypes. There was a Jap sub attack Wednesday. Goleta, north of Santa Barbara.

A "hidden" fishing village was torpedo-bombed. Dead Orientals were found. They appeared to be Chinese. The local Sheriff's Office and Camp Roberts provost were on it.

Alien Squad/Subversive Roundups. Jot graph notes.

Status quo, again. One cross-reference.

Ward Littell was the FBI's rogue conscience on the roundups. Ward called them a "catastrophic injustice." He got Ward assigned to the Sheriff's van-heist job. He called Dick Hood and wangled the assignment. He did not say the names Huey Cressmeyer and Dudley Smith. Dick called the heist "a no-leads baffler."

Watanabe Case/Details-Chronology. Jot graph notes.

Status quo again. Four dead Japs. No news is good news. Who gives a fucking shit?

Dudley left his house last night. He stayed home and got blotto with the Archbishop. A tong kid killed Ace Kwan's niece. Dudley lit up Chinatown. Scotty Bennett killed the niece killer. Dud gave Sid Hudgens the exclusive. It derailed *his* plan to co-opt Sid for Watanabe-case ink.

He packed off the Archbishop and met Sid at Lyman's. He pitched him the notion. Sid was wowed. Sid consulted his editor and called him back this morning.

"Sorry, Bill. Ace Kwan's *Chinese* and tight with Fletch Bowron. Scotty Bennett's a good-looking kid. The Watanabes were *Japs* in hate-the-*Japs* L.A. We've got space for one piece of slant-eyed ink—and Ace and Scotty are it."

Buzz Meeks was on the van heist *and* the Watanabe job. Buzz

Meeks was uncowed by Dudley Smith. The alleged house and ta purchases troubled Meeks.

Who gives a shit? It was Dudley's case. Dudley was Call-Me-Jack's boy.

Lake/De Haven. Jot graph notes.

He couldn't. It was all invisible. The Fifth Column worked invisibly. His challenge was to render their treason coherent. Kay Lake was his vehicle. She will show how words and thoughts poison the human spirit with systematically criminal intent. Kay Lake will say *This is the Evil of the Mind. This is how mass murder evolves from sordid dramaturgy. This is God reviled in the name of social critique*.

This redeems him for the squalor he himself perpetrated. This redeems him for his actions under Jim Davis. This is how he will cleanse this great city.

The phone rang. Parker unhooked the receiver.

"Yes?"

"Fred Kalmbach in Evanston, Bill. I hope you've got a pen handy."

Parker said, "Go ahead, please."

"She's Joan Woodard Conville. That's C, O, N, V, I, L, L, E. She's twenty-six, with a date-of-birth of 4/17/15. She graduated from the West Suburban Hospital Nursing School in '37. She got her B.S. in biology at Northwestern, while you were here in '40. She's from Tomah, Wisconsin. The most recent lead I've got is that she moved to Los Angeles, which seems like it might make you happy. That's all I've got for current whereabouts."

Parker scrawled it on *Lake/De Haven*. The doorbell rang. He jerked and dropped his pen. The phone connection died.

The bell persisted. Some fool leaned on it. Parker walked out and opened the door.

It's Hideo Ashida. He's the sole Jap on the city tit. He's holding two photo bulletins up.

Ashida looked at Parker. He held the bulletins side by side. He went *Look, Captain, look*.

Parker looked. He saw two bulletins. They showed two tire tracks. Identical tread patterns, wear patterns, declivities.

An L.A. Police photo: the Watanabes' driveway, an un-ID'd car. A Sheriff's photo: "Larkin, James/4600 Valley Boulevard."

Parker studied the photos. Parker linked the dots.

b, the older man, the kid cyclists. He was there. He He went just to look.

ped the bulletins. "The car that hit Mr. Larkin was Watanabes' driveway. Note the soil erosion. I'd say the made the week before they were killed."

Par leaned on the door. He felt weightless. The door held him up.

"I was there that morning. I heard the squawk and drove over. An object fell out of Larkin's pocket as they put him in the ambulance. It was a Luger grip embossed with a swastika."

Ashida tapped the Larkin photo. "There's an eyeball-witness description of the man driving the car. He was white and wearing a purple sweater."

Parker crossed himself. "Why did you bring this to me?"

"Because you outrank Sergeant Smith. Because I thought you'd find it more compelling than he would."

"Finish the thought, Doctor."

"Because the notion of a white suspect intrigues me."

Parker said, "It's vehicular manslaughter. The Sheriff's should have a full package."

Ashida said, "It's threadbare. They've got no suspects and no more information. It's like it is with our Department. They're swamped by the blackouts and roundups. They can't give this job a fair shake."

"Tell me what you're thinking."

"I'm thinking that war regulations will constrain us. Larkin was a British Intelligence man, but the British embassy and Scotland Yard won't release information without a month of back-and-forth and writs. They'll say, 'There's a war on.' They'll say, 'We're being bombed, and you aren't.' "

Parker said, "Tell me what else you're thinking."

Ashida pointed to his car. "I'm thinking that I have Mr. Larkin's address. He lived in Santa Monica Canyon, and I doubt if the Sheriff's have searched his house."

Parker grabbed his house keys and shut the door. He walked straight to Ashida's car and got in.

Ashida got in. They took Silver Lake Boulevard to Sunset. Hollywood, the Strip, Beverly Hills. *Shut-the-fucking-world-out-so-you-won't-back-down.* Parker glued his eyes shut.

Sunset Boulevard went twisty. Westwood and Brentwood twisted by. The Pacific Palisades twisted by. Parker smelled the ocean.

Ashida swung south to SaMo Canyon. Those fucking monkeys. *Hear-no-evil/see-no-evil. Shut-the-fucking-world-out.*

Ashida stopped the car. Ashida said, "We're here."

Parker opened his eyes. *Here* was *this:*

A Japanese-style house. Low roof, cement façade, louvered windows. A sliding front door. Bonsai shrubs on the walkway.

High shrubs enclosed it. Shut-the-fucking-neighbors-out-and-get-inside-*now.*

They walked up to the door. Parker rang the bell and got reverberation. They waited ten seconds. Ashida jimmied the lock with some lab tool. The door slid open.

They stepped inside and slid it shut. Ashida flicked a wall switch. Here, look at this:

A small living room. A bisecting koi stream. A flat cement floor and walls lined with teak bookshelves. Japanese art and architecture. Japanese history. Sitting mats, paper lanterns.

Ashida took the lead. Parker followed him. The house was small. The connecting hall was flat cement. The one bedroom was twelve by twelve.

The bed was a floor mat. A glass wall framed an outside garden and a koi pond. Jim Larkin lived in stark beauty. Jim Larkin shut-the-fucking-world-out.

Ashida opened a closet door. Bam—just like that:

Four suits on hangers. A fuckload of German Lugers, hooked to a wallboard.

They dangled by their trigger guards. Parker counted seventeen. Ivory grips embossed with black swastikas. Red rubies inlaid.

A dresser below the guns. Two drawers only. Ashida opened the top drawer. *Bam!*—just like that:

A money stack. U.S. dollars, British pounds, yen and reichsmarks. Allied/Axis gelt—a fortune.

Ashida tapped the bottom drawer. Bam—just like that:

A loose-leaf binder—and nothing else.

Ashida opened it. The contents: two sheets of paper covered with Japanese script.

Jim Larkin was a white man. Jim Larkin knew Japanese.

Ashida studied the pages. Parker studied him. He's translating now. His lips don't move. His eyes barely do. It's word stew to thoughts sustained. He respects the house. He'll speak softly.

Ashida said, "I think it goes back to what Buzz Meeks brought up at the briefing. It pertains to buyouts or potential buyouts of Japanese-owned houses and farms. I'm extrapolating here, but I trust it. There's no Japanese names listed, just initials—but the initials by and large conform to the initials of Japanese men whose names I've seen on the subversive lists. The addresses listed are all in Glassell Park and South Pasadena—with one exception—and that's 'R.W.,' for Ryoshi Watanabe, with his address in Highland Park. Based on the tenses of the verbs, I'd say that some houses and farms were actually purchased, while, in other cases, the approaches were made, but the house and farm owners refused to sell. The amounts paid or offered are well below market value, and I have a theory about that."

Parker said, "Tell me. I'll extrapolate with you."

Ashida said, "We all knew the war was coming. I would posit that the men who tried to purchase the houses and farms had foreknowledge of when and/or where the Japanese forces would attack. I would further posit that they knew there would be a massive roundup of native-born and foreign-born Japanese, and a massive confiscation of their assets. We're headed for a large-scale internment, and I think the men knew that."

Parker said, "The Watanabes were killed the day before Pearl Harbor."

Ashida said, "Jim Larkin was mowed down at 5:45 Pearl Harbor morning. The news didn't hit L.A. until just before noon."

Parker said, "He knew something. The hit-and-run was premeditated. I'm certain of that."

Ashida scanned the room. The house was crazy serene.

Parker crossed himself. "I vowed to pray for him, but reneged on it. I caused his death."

48

LOS ANGELES | FRIDAY, DECEMBER 12, 1941

9:49 a.m.

Ruth Mildred loved cheesecake. The office celebrated her Sapphic bent and rogue-doctor status. Note the medical diplomas and framed glossies.

She pointed to Rita Hayworth. "I scraped her. She had a thick bush."

Dudley laughed. He felt fit. He slept at home and played patriarch. The visit would hold his brood to Christmas.

Ruth Mildred ogled Jean Arthur. "I scraped her. I licked her snatch while she was anesthetized."

Dudley roared. Ruth Mildred lived to entertain. Nice girls in a jam flocked to her. She did King Cohn's scrape jobs. Dot Rothstein lured in outside work. Ruth Mildred was L.A.'s scrape overlord.

She ogled Ginger Rogers. "I scraped her. The baby had two heads."

Dudley smiled. Ruthie was big at Columbia. She had a chic corner office with a waiting room. The latter was packed now. Dot and Huey C. Mickey Cohen, Hooky Rothman. Carlos Madrano, up from T.J.

He spoke to Carlos. He quizzed him per his Jap-farm schemes. Carlos refused to divulge. He quizzed him per the Jap house/farm buyouts. Carlos said, "*No más*, my friend. I will not talk about that."

Ruth Mildred ogled Carole Lombard. "I scraped her. The daddy was a jigaboo."

Dudley rocked his chair. "Did you scrape a Jap girl named Nancy Watanabe?"

Ruth Mildred lit a cigarette and threw her feet up on her desk. Her skirt flew wide.

"I don't scrape Japs. That species of gash in no way intrigues me."

"You're not freelancing at MGM? I heard rumors about that stunning lass who played Scarlett O'Hara."

Ruth Mildred said, "Okay, I did a job for Warner's. Bette Davis missed two cycles, and I treated her for a miscarriage."

It sandbagged him. His breakfast curdled. He heard chants out on Gower.

"End the feudal system! King Cohn must go!"

Mike Breuning called him. Sid Hudgens was bird-dogging *Baaaad* Bill McPherson. He'd been on a cooze run at Minnie Roberts' Casbah. He might return today.

Ruth Mildred ogled Barbara Stanwyck. "I scraped her. I sold her snatch hair to Frank Capra."

Dudley lit a cigarette. "Huey pulled a caper. I'll need to stash him in Mexico for a while."

"My baby never works single-o."

"There's a grand chance that his partners will evaporate."

"Keep him safe, Dud. My baby's frail."

"King Cohn must go! King Cohn must go!" This Red roar in Gower Gulch.

Dudley zipped to the waiting room. Mickey and Hooky sulked. Captain Carlos read *Time* magazine. Huey quaked. The Dotstress thigh-massaged him.

Dudley said, "Bid good-bye to your mothers, son. You'll be leaving in a moment."

Carlos said, "You'll love Tijuana, Huey. We will go to the donkey show tonight."

Huey ran to Ruth Mildred. Dudley admired his speed. Huey threw his arms around her. Ruthie consoled him. Note her tongue in his ear.

Harry Cohn walked in. Mickey and Hooky stirred and displayed brass knucks. The gang adjourned to Ruthie's office. Ruthie slid Huey off her lap and opened the curtains. The gang peered out.

Picketers and chanters. Raggedy exemplars of specious discontent.

Mickey and Hooky slid out the door. Harry lit a cigarette and flushed sclerotic. Standing room only. Exclusive sneak peek. *Red Riot on Gower Gulch!*

It stars Mickey and Hooky. They're two-fisted Jewboys, wielding steel knucks. *"King Cohn must go! King Cohn must—"*

The Hebrew hard-ons hit. They ducked their heads and came in low. Picket signs flew. Picket fucks fled. Dudley saw ripped cheeks and hairlines. Someone's dentures bounced in the street.

Harry said, "Thanks, Dud. And thank Ben Siegel for me. I'll consider your smut deal."

The gang enjoyed the show. Dot tittered. Huey burrowed into Ruth Mildred.

She ogled Lupe Vélez. "I scraped her. The daddy had a two-foot schlong. I had to stitch Lupe up."

10:18 a.m.

The Dotstress ran interference. She led them through the studio and up to the Sunset gate. Mickey and Hooky flexed their hands. Their shirts were bloodstained.

Dot waved bye-bye. Dudley smooshed Mickey and Hooky into his car. They pulled out east. The Red riot dispersed. Traffic noise covered the shrieks.

"It's your day to curry favor with influential men, lads. I applaud your fine work for Mr. Cohn, and offer applause in advance for your work for Mr. Siegel."

Mickey flexed his hands. The *Herald* called him a "pint-size plug ugly." The *Herald* knew their shit.

"We're supposed to tune up some Nazi humps. What's the drift on that, Dud? You've got no beef with the Krauts."

Dudley said, "You will enjoy humbling men who condone the mistreatment of your grand people. They will reveal the names of other Bundists and like-minded souls in the Sheriff's Office and Los Angeles PD. I will coerce those men into working for me. They will assist a roundup of potential witnesses for a case I'm investigating. It will not be a job for the frail of heart."

Hooky massaged his hands. The *Mirror* called him a "vicious strongarm thug." The *Mirror* knew their shit.

"So we get fake-popped on a gun charge and lounge around in stir? That's the drift here?"

"It is, lad. That stated, I think you'll find the accommodations engaging."

Mickey and Hooky relaxed. Dudley highballed downtown. His best suit was stashed at Kwan's. Bette Davis, tonight at the Shrine.

South to Temple. There's the Hall of Justice. There's the Welcome Wagon—two deputies in Santa Claus hats.

Mickey and Hooky yocked. Dudley pulled up to the jail door and idled. A Santa cop grabbed the sled. Mickey slipped him a C-note. The Santa cop swooned and peeled out.

A Santa cop escorted them up. Hooky slipped him a C-note. He swooned. They hit a Jap-infested catwalk. There's the Penthouse. It's been redecorated. It's a bookie front now.

Blackboards. Chalked-on results for Pimlico and Bay Meadows. Fourteen phones. Ben Siegel—holding two pairs of sap gloves. Palm-weighted. Twelve ounces of solid lead per.

Benny hugged Mickey and Hooky. The gloves changed hands. Ben wore a swell blue suit. The boy nearly glowed.

He said, "A little break for you. I'll have you out by Hanukkah."

Dudley said, "Ace Kwan will cater your meals. Keep your ears perked for jailhouse chat that Mr. Siegel and I might find alluring."

Mickey and Hooky donned the gloves. They were fetishist's black.

Ben said, "You're down to four, Dud. That Dr. Fred Hiltz guy finagled bail somehow. He's jungled up with that anti-Semite preacher, Gerald L. K. Smith. They're in some sort of hate-tract biz."

"Not all Smiths are as benevolent as I am. I should add that the Reverend Smith is a Protestant."

Ben pointed down the catwalk. It was empty-cell Siberia. The deputies tuned up rape-o's and child molesters there.

Dudley said, "I want names. Currently employed policemen. The Bund, the Silver Shirts, the Klan, the Christian Front, the Thunderbolt Legion. I doubt if they will withhold the information."

Mickey and Hooky flexed their gloves. Benny bowed. Proceed, *meine Kameraden.*

They walked over. The fucks were cuffed against a bar row. They stood behind-the-back cinched.

Tuesday night. The Deutsches Haus. The same lads, minus Fred Hiltz. In jail denims now. Denied bail. FUCKED in war-fevered L.A.

Scared. Trembling. Face-to-face with vicious Yids.

Dudley said, "My friends and I want names. Local policemen on the far-right flank that you've encountered. You'll be returned to your cells once you provide those names."

Ben Siegel gleamed. Zionist Ben. He was big in the Jewish Orphans Fund.

He nodded. Mickey and Hooky stepped in.

They slapped. Palm weights delivered the hurt. They employed shoulder pivots. They looked mean. Jews, racial scapegoats, *Kristallnacht.*

The Nazis thrashed and shit their shorts. Mickey and Hooky laid in love taps. The taps dislodged teeth. Lips split. Bridgework fell. The Nazis squirmed against the bars. They contorted. They started screeching names.

Dudley stood up close. The Krauts snitched names. He heard "Dougie Waldner, Sheriff's, Firestone Station." He heard, "He's Klan and Shirts, and he knows Gerry Smith."

Mickey and Hooky moved back. Benny embraced them. The Nazi fucks coughed up teeth and names.

Dudley heard "Fritz Vogel" and "Bill Koenig." Dudley heard "Bund." Dudley heard "77th Street Station." The blood became untenable. Dudley moved back. A Santa cop shoved a phone in his face. He heard Dick Carlisle on the line.

Carlisle said, "McPherson, Casbah, outside on Temple, *now.*"

Dudley ran.

He made the freight lift. He made the ground. He made the parking lot. A '39 Chevy rolled by. Bill McPherson had the wheel.

A '38 Cadillac rolled up. Sid Hudgens had the wheel. Dick C., Mike B. and Scotty B. rode with him. Dudley jumped in back.

Carlisle said, "The DA's up ahead, and he's stinko."

Sid said, "I've got my camera."

Scotty said, "What do *I* do?"

Carlisle said, "What do you think? You *loom.*"

Breuning said, "He just up and ducked out of his office. I called Minnie Roberts and got the lowdown. He ordered the 'Mudbath.' It's three colored girls."

Carlisle went *Uuuuugh.* Sid went *Oooh-la-la.*

The Chevy hooked onto Broadway, southbound. Sid stuck in, bumper-tight.

Dudley caught his breath. He pulled out his notebook and scribbled. He wrote "Waldner/Sheriff's/Firestone." He wrote "Vogel/Koenig/77th."

The Chevy made time. The Sidster hovered in pounce range.

The complexion bronzed at Jefferson Boulevard. Dudley smelled white missionary *en croûte*.

The Call of the Jungle doomed the DA. There's the Casbah—a strip of rooms above Sultan Sam's Sandbox.

The Chevy pulled to the curb. Darktown Bill got out and primped his way upstairs. Sid braked and parked. Dudley counted off sixty seconds. Sid flashbulb-prepped his camera. Breuning and Carlisle smirked.

Scotty was dumbstruck. He killed a Chink last night. He slept with a woman. His suit was rumpled. Note the fading perfume.

Dudley said, "Now."

They piled out and laid tracks. They went up the stairs, single file. Minnie met them on the landing. She flashed four fingers to denote room no. 4. Dudley led them over. Breuning and Carlisle kicked in the door. It sheared and flew off the hinges.

Bad Bill was poking a darky girl. Two high yellows stood by. They held switches and wore Cleopatra gowns. All hail the "Mudbath."

The Sidster popped a flashbulb. Glare torched the room. It made the mudbathers blink and—

Halt.

It's a shakedown.

Bill, stop fucking. The Mudbath is over. Put down those switches, girls.

The rutters froze. The cops ran into the room. Sid flashed photo no. 2. Breuning and Carlisle grabbed the switch girls. Scotty pulled the DA out of the saddle and tossed him on the floor. The girls squealed and beat feet down the hall.

McPherson sobbed. Breuning threw a blanket on him. Dudley hovered, close in.

"You will be presented with a suspect in a multiple homicide case sometime between now and New Year's. You will have a confession, superbly corroborated by eyewitnesses and forensic evidence. You will facilitate the filing of a grand jury indictment. The matter will be expeditiously adjudicated. You will secure a four-count conviction. It will buttress your reputation as a jurist of sterling repute."

McPherson soiled the blanket. McPherson went *Yes, yes, yes, YES!* Sid shot photo no. 3. The room glared bright white.

Dudley signaled the boys. They scrammed the room and vacated the Casbah. They walked back to the car. Sid screeched a U-turn and pointed them north.

The boys laughed. The boys whooped. The boys exhaled steam. Scotty played it sotto voce. He looked shell-shocked.

Sid drove west to Figueroa. The scenery improved. Mock-snow Christmas trees and REMEMBER PEARL HARBOR! signs. Klieg lights outside the Shrine Auditorium. Hold for Miss Bette Davis.

Dudley chain-smoked and brooded. His dope-peddling Armenians vexed him. Their heroin source had dried up. It induced a coontown panic. They've pled for help. He has no answers.

Ensign Jack Kennedy will hit L.A. tomorrow. Beth Short and Tommy Gilfoyle will hit shortly. Beth at seventeen—more and more cut from his cloth.

Beth's letter vexed him. He got it right before the Watanabe snuffs. Her "horrible thing" last year. She must reveal that event.

City Hall appeared. His lads disembarked. Sid went *Where to?* Dudley made slant eyes. It signified Kwan's.

Sid drove him there. Dudley winked and got out of the car. Black-bordered business fronts ran up the street. They were Four Families affiliates. They were heathens in mourning.

Hop Sing boys flanked the Pagoda. Their coat bulges concealed big gats. They got the door for him. He ducked to the basement. Ace had prepared his room.

The pallet, the bowl, the tar. The pipe for enhanced *Thought and Act.*

Dudley shrugged off his suit coat and holster. He lit the pipe. He held the smoke. He breathed *ouuuuuut.*

Something quashed stray imagery. He went straight to the Watanabe house.

That simple detail overlooked. He shouldn't care. The case would be fallaciously solved.

He inhaled again. He walked in the front door and circled the bodies. His sketched map merged with his memorized floor plan. The overlay encompassed brain camera and animation.

The dining room, the kitchen. The damp clothes on the line. It indicates homicide. The killer forgot to remove the clothes and/or dry them. It indicates a mental lapse.

He inhaled again. He walked through the house three times. He smelled all the food in the icebox. He touched all the furniture. Downstairs, upstairs, the note. "Looming apocalypse." Did it prophesy Sunday's attack or the current roundups?

He inhaled again. He stepped outside and conversed with Dr. Ashida. A truth sideswiped him. It's why they have to know *Who* and *Why*.

Dialectic. The lad embodied great utility and insight. Scientific application meets baffling event. Eugenics and racial identity. Add lurid psychopathy. Add the native-born Japanese and foreign-born Irish. Their compatible and conflicting visions. Their shared need to know *Who* and *Why*.

He spoke to Ashida, outside the house. The lad relinquished his pilfered tracts. Tracts were a difficult trace. Ed Satterlee cued him in to Lee Blanchard's girlfriend, Kay Lake. Miss Lake meets the Red Claire De Haven. Miss Lake attends a party at her home. Miss De Haven invites Miss Lake to a second soirée. Ben Siegel is procuring a guest list.

Whiskey Bill's "outside deal." Whiskey Bill's strident anticommunism. Chart the possibilities.

Miss Lake might snitch Reds to Bill Parker. That might explain Whiskey Bill's "left-wing tract" and "outside deal." It was all hypothetical. It was worth strategic scrutiny.

Ed Satterlee told him this: Parker got Meeks assigned to the Sheriff's-van heist. The move was suspicious. It might mean nothing. It might bode as Parker-Meeks collusion. The van job was watertight. Parker could not suspect Huey Cressmeyer.

The Watanabe house faded to pinpoints. Dr. Ashida waved good-bye. Light jumped through a door crack. He heard footfalls and smelled fortified tea.

A cup touched his hands. The footfalls retreated. He sipped the tea. It supplied the high voltage he'd need.

His body recalibrated. His watch said 6:18.

He got up. He put on his suit coat and hooked on his gun. He walked into the office. Ace greeted him. Note the ordnance on his desk.

Two .45's. Silencer-fitted and loaded with poison-dipped dumdums. Two short-handled axes. Note their razor-honed blades.

They bowed to each other. Ace wrapped the tools in a gunnysack. Dudley pulled out his switchblade. The business end popped up.

Ace said, "My Irish brother."

Dudley said, "My yellow brother."

He held out the knife. Ace held out his right index finger. Dudley cut it and passed him the knife. Ace cut Dudley's finger. Blood dripped over their hands.

They clasped hands. They formed a lace-fingered fit and merged blood. They wiped their hands on the gunnysack and walked outside.

Ace owned a Packard sedan. It was warlord size. They took Broadway to Temple, Temple to Vermont. Christmas lights blinked everywhere.

They took Vermont to the Griffith Park road. Plush homes, green hills, the Observatory dome. That stunning city view. No other parking-lot cars.

The hiking trail. A dirt pathway. It's steep and shrub-bordered. There's a fluttering light fifty yards up. Smoke denotes a cookout.

Ace passed him his pistol and ax. Ace armed himself. They stepped from the car. Dudley followed Ace.

They walked up the trail. A roasting-meat smell hit them. The light grew bright. The trail leveled off. Yes—the light signifies cooking flames.

Dudley saw three men. There should be four. Huey had four heist helpers. There's only three men here.

Voices now. It's that Jap bark-and-grunt. Two men look pure Jap. One man's a verified Chink.

Dudley recognized him. He was a Four Families initiate. Call him a "Collaborationist." He probably fingered Rose Kwan.

It's suppertime. They're roasting rats impaled on ice-cream-bar sticks.

Ace stepped into the clearing. He struck a pose—the aging Bringer of Death. The fucks saw him. One fuck tittered. One fuck muttered. One fuck dropped his skewered rat.

Ace aimed above the flames. Muffled thuds became holes in their faces and brains out the backs of their heads. They pitched away from the fire. Dudley stepped up and mouth-shot them. Teeth and bone exploded. Ace dropped his gun and raised his ax.

The old man *desecrated*. Dudley watched him. Ace chopped off heads and legs. Ace quartered the fucks. Ace monkey-moaned through it all.

Ancient sounds. Heathen desecration. Blood, fire, burned rats on sticks.

49

LOS ANGELES | FRIDAY, DECEMBER 12, 1941

7:27 p.m.

T.I. again. The same cell block and sweat room.

Ashida sat with Elmer Jackson. A cuff chain cinched them up. They were working the same ploy.

I'm Japanese, like you. I serve the police. Still, they oppress me. Aren't I sympathetic? Answer my questions, NOW.

Captain Parker sent him down. The ploy derived from their 459 at Jim Larkin's bungalow. The ledger. The assumed link to the house/farm buyouts.

Ashida and Parker discussed the ledger. Parker showed him the Feds' subversive lists. They cross-checked them with the T.I. arrest log. Ashida matched up four initial sets.

T.A. equaled Thomas Akahara. G.Y. equaled George Yamato. W.O. equaled William Okamura. R.M. equaled Rollo Moriyama.

Elmer said, "This cuff routine is bullshit. I'll unhook you if you want."

Ashida smiled. "There's a point to it. I'll tell you about it someday."

"I did a hitch in the Marines, and it was from hunger. I don't want to go back, war or no war."

Ashida said, "You'll be draft-exempt. You're friends with the Chief and the mayor."

"You mean Brenda is. I just run bag and do the scut work."

"You'll be declared 'police-essential.' I'm sure of it."

Elmer relit his cigar. "This white man's police force has been good to us. You, especially. Remember that when they start carting your people off to some hellhole, and you get rightfully inclined to hate me."

Ashida checked his notepad. He had opening questions prepped. Who approached you about your property? Why was the sale or potential sale attempted and/or recorded in secret? Were the buyer or buyers in any way suspicious to you?

Elmer smoked up the room. An MP walked in Thomas Akahara. Mr. Akahara seethed. He was fat. He sported a Hitler mustache.

Ashida stood up and rattled his cuff chain. Ashida dredged up Japanese phrases and dispensed a formal hello.

The MP uncuffed Akahara. He pulled out a news clip and spit on it. He bared Tojo teeth and glared.

Elmer hooted. The MP shrugged and recuffed Akahara. They about-faced and scrammed.

Elmer said, "Dr. Hideo Ashida. Reluctantly notorious and despised by his own kind. The only yellow man on the Los Angeles PD."

"Let's go back, Elmer."

"Okay, but let's stop at Lyman's first."

The guard captain poked his head in. "Telephone call, Sergeant."

Elmer uncuffed Ashida and followed him. Ashida teethed on that missing *something* at the Watanabe house. He missed *something* at Larkin's place. Two *somethings* tweaked him now.

He brain-walked through both locations. He walked room-to-room. He got something/nothing a dozen times over. Elmer walked back in.

"We got to put a rain check on Lyman's. There's three dead Chinamen in Griffith Park, and Bill Parker wants you."

7:54 p.m.

They double-timed down the catwalk. Inmates held newspapers up to the bars. Ashida caught peripheral views.

Mariko ran her mouth again. The papers spieled the gist. *Viva J. Edgar Hoover! God Bless the L.A. Police and Special Agent Ward J. Littell!*

They shagged to Elmer's car and peeled northbound. They crossed the bridge. The shoreline blackout swaddled them. It pressed down the sky. It smothered the ground. You got white pavement lines and no more.

Elmer said, "I can add, and I can go 'one plus one makes two.' That Scotty kid pops a Four Families boy last night, and now we got three dead Chinks. That adds up to 'tong war' in my book."

Ashida stared out his window. They hauled north. The blackout lifted six miles up. Elmer tapped his headlights and siren.

They caught a long dead stretch and made Western Avenue. The siren bored them straight to L.A. proper. They cut west to the park road.

Note the door-to-door canvass. Note the blues holding back civilians. Note those lights in the Observatory lot.

A sentry waved them up. Elmer killed the siren. See that? It's night arc-light glow.

Outdoor homicide. Follow the glow.

They made the lot. City vehicles packed it. Prowl cars, K-cars, meat wagons. Morgue men trudged a hiking path.

Follow the glow.

They parked and hiked up the path. The glow built to a blaze. A shitload of cops talked dead-man talk. Their voices boomed.

A clearing. Four bluesuits, three morgue men. Thad Brown, Buzz Meeks. Captain Bill Parker, civvy-clad.

Arc lights pointed *down.* Flashlights pointed *down.* Dirt soaked blood maroon. Entrail stink. No bodies, per se.

Ashida counted limbs. Six arms and legs meant three dead men. Four bedrolls in plain sight. That meant a fourth man snuffed somewhere else or plain gone.

Three heads. Forehead entry wounds, rear-head exit wounds. Mouth wounds. Exploded jawbones and teeth. They're shot in the forehead first. They gasp for air. Second shots go straight in their mouths.

Ashida studied their faces. Ashida studied the severed limbs and matched up skin tone. Eugenics. Race science. Asian racial distinctions.

Skin color. Physiognomy. Hair density. He could subdivide Asians by race. Most Asians thought they could—but could not.

One victim was Asian mixed-blood. Two were Japanese. He based his ID's on racial instinct. Scattered shells. Obvious .45's. Dumdum bullets. Mouth wounds that blew noses up.

A cop said, "Check Tojo. He's got his snout all over this."

Thad Brown said, "Shut up."

Bill Parker said, "Meeks, what are you doing here?"

Meeks said, "I caught the Bureau squeal. Slant-eyed homicides interest me these days."

Ashida scanned the ground. Spilled blood oozed past the clearing. The path dirt was hard-packed. It would not imprint footsteps.

Three heads. No personal gear with the bedrolls. A rising-sun tattoo on one arm. A shotgun-size rubber bullet.

A knife beside the bedrolls. Unbloodied and undeployed here. A short handle. A central puncture blade. Six smaller blades welded to a metal strip.

Crude manufacture. Anachronistic. A torture weapon—vaguely feudal-style.

Ashida knelt by the bedrolls. He recalled the Goleta Inlet. The blade marks on the dead man. Similar to these blades.

A cop said, "Charlie Chan's on the job."

Thad Brown said, "Shut your mouth."

Ashida studied the knife. Cigarette smoke diffused the death stink. A cop puked in the bushes. A cop squeezed prayer beads.

Elmer said, "I see a Four Families scarf. We got ourselves a tong war."

Ashida stood up. Parker and Meeks scoped the rubber bullet. It was riot-gun knock-you-flat size.

Meeks said, "Makes you think of Huey C., don't it, Cap? There were four other guys on the van heist, but we only got three here. Is this all a little close for you?"

Parker walked up to Ashida. He hopped a severed leg and gestured down the path. The arc-light poles swayed. Arc-light heat juked up the stink.

Ashida followed Parker. They found a quiet spot. Ashida felt arc-light burns on his neck.

Parker said, "Preliminary impressions. Tell me what you think."

Ashida said, "They're Japanese, not Chinese. One man may be mixed. It's imprecise science, but I'm reasonably sure of it."

Parker lit a cigarette. "Meet me at Nort Layman's office later. He's got something new on the Watanabes. He called over for Dudley, but I picked it up."

Ashida said, "I missed something at Larkin's bungalow. It's driving me crazy."

Parker tossed his cigarette. "Break in again."

"Elmer Jackson's driving me. I don't have my car."

Parker handed him a key ring. "Take mine. The plate number is QF-661."

Morgue men wheeled gurneys past them. Parker turned tail back to the clearing. Ashida walked down to the lot.

QF-661 stood by the park road. A half-full jug was there on the seat.

Ashida got in and U-turned. The park road got him past the sentries. Vermont got him to Sunset and that twisty shot to the beach.

The K-car was unwieldy. The shift lever stuck. The clutch squeaked and slipped. He drove west and got synced with it.

Hollywood to the Strip. The Strip to Brentwood. Brentwood to the Palisades.

He hit SaMo Canyon. He got out and walked to the door. He was 459-proficient now. One pick tweak got him in.

He shut the door. His penlight carved a path. Living room, kitchen, bedroom. He studied the koi stream and pond. The koi spoke to him.

There's no telephone.

There's no address book with names and phone numbers listed.

Lyman's back room. The Wednesday-to-Thursday-midnight briefing. Stray talk. The Watanabes called Santa Monica pay phones.

Nearby pay phones. Near the SaMo aircraft plants—Boeing, Douglas, Lockheed.

There was one other *something*. It was seemingly prosaic.

Ashida shut his eyes. He went someplace calm. He smelled powdered fish food. The koi spoke to him.

The Sheriff's bulletin. An inventory. Items found on Jim Larkin.

"Right-front trouser pocket. Three pay-telephone slugs."

Something or nothing? Connecting thread or non sequitur?

Ashida walked back to the K-car. He U-turned to the coast road and Sunset east. He drove downtown. He's a Jap in a cop sled. Colored fish talk to him.

He parked outside the morgue and walked in. Gurneys lined the central hallway. Body parts were gauze-wrapped and paper-pinned. Arms, legs, heads. All tagged "Griffith Park/12-12-41."

He smelled thawing flesh. He traced it to Nort Layman's exam room. Nort and Captain Bill had a jug. Ryoshi Watanabe was stretched out on a slab.

Ryoshi was six days and seven hours dead. Nort had sliced his back into chunks. The cuts were ten by ten. Freezing facilitated the slicing. Nort pointed to a chunk. It was tagged "upper-right posterior."

The thawing revealed an old wound. It was etched in subcutaneous tissue. It was barely detectable.

It was a knife wound. It was a *multiple-blade* wound. It reprised *the knife* in the clearing and the *knife scar* on the Goleta man.

Nort said, "It's a very old wound, so it wasn't visible on the surface of the skin. I looked up the blade pattern in Ray Pinker's weapons text. It's a knife out of eighteenth-century Japan. Warlords poison-dipped the blades. It was quite the perverted thing."

Parker said it first. "We just found a knife like that in Griffith Park."

50

KAY LAKE'S DIARY

LOS ANGELES | FRIDAY, DECEMBER 12, 1941

10:37 p.m.

The gang's all here.

I knew some of the men at the bar personally, and some by their pictures in the papers. They were drinking and casually speaking; they ignored the people seated in booths a few feet away. I was waiting for Scotty and had secured a room at the Rosslyn Hotel. He was ninety minutes late, but I didn't care. I was observing a blithe collusion.

Mayor Fletch Bowron, Jack Horrall, Sheriff Gene Biscailuz. FBI men Dick Hood and Ed Satterlee. Scorn for the Jap Whipping Boy. Brenda Allen's regulars as war profiteers.

They discussed the seizure of Japanese holdings; they cracked jokes about the Jap woman who committed suicide in the Lincoln Heights jail. Satterlee hatched a plan to issue armbands to all local Japanese. Chat turned to the Watanabe case. Jack said DA McPherson had been "keestered." Biscailuz laughed and said, "Dudley Smith?" Jack poked his middle finger through the circle of a forefinger and thumb. Mayor Fletch said, "Ouch."

I nursed a Manhattan and eavesdropped. Fiorello La Guardia entered the grill and joined the *Kameraden*. He praised the blackout-monitor work of Captain Bill Parker. Jack and the FBI men held their noses. I thought of Claire De Haven's tract and saw Parker done up in jackboots.

The group broke up. Dudley Smith entered the PD's back room a few minutes later. He carried a tweed suit in a cellophane wrapper. He'd lost weight—he reminded me of Captain Parker that way. His appearance didn't surprise me. L.A. had been running on insomnia, cigarettes and liquor since last Sunday. People appeared at whim and vanished; I hadn't seen Lee since our fight here Tuesday night. People comported with a new sense of allegiance. Everything was new. Many people embodied surprise; a few embodied revelation.

Scotty left my bed and returned to duty. The a.m. *Mirror* brought him right back. Sid Hudgens wrote the piece. Officer Robert S. Bennett, the Los Angeles Police Department's first emergency wartime hire, proved his mettle during a murder dragnet in Chinatown last night. The niece of noted restaurateur Grover Cleveland "Uncle Ace" Kwan had been brutally murdered; "anonymous tips" led to a search for Four Families tong fiend Chiang "the Chinaman" Ling. Sergeant Dudley L. Smith and Officer Bennett cornered Ling. The Chinaman broke free and made an attempt on Sergeant Smith's life. The inexperienced—but bold—Officer Bennett shot and killed Ling before he could "snuff" Sergeant Smith with "heathen aplomb." A photograph of Scotty in football garb ran with the piece.

The article reeked of collusion. I juxtaposed it to Claire's account of her journey with Whiskey Bill and teethed on my own wartime allegiance. I ran for my car and drove to Beverly Hills then. Claire's Packard was parked in her driveway. I parked across the street and waited.

She walked out a half hour later. A scarf covered her Joan of Arc hair. I followed her to a Catholic church in Brentwood. She attended Mass there.

Comrade Claire, Supplicant Claire. I studied her from a dozen pews back, the same way she once studied the worshipful Bill Parker. Such adroit symbiosis. How perfect to merge with her perfect adversary on his own mystical plane. How perfectly unconscious for Parker to pick Claire as his target. His inner life perfectly mirrored the chaos that Claire so proudly displayed to the world.

I ducked out of the church before she saw me. Claire left the service and returned to her car ten minutes later. She took Bundy to Wilshire and drove all the way downtown. I stuck behind her, and ran a series of yellow lights keeping up.

Claire turned north on Main Street. I sensed her destination as Little Tokyo, and pulled up directly behind her. She turned east on 2nd Street and slowed down to observe. I watched her point a camera out her window and snap photographs.

I tracked her eye and camera lens. She snapped a sad-eyed man outside a fish market. She snapped the children with American flags on sticks and Cal Denton beating a man's teeth in. And now she's stopped her car. And now she sees Whiskey Bill Parker, standing at the corner of 2nd and San Pedro.

He jotted notes on his clipboard; Claire pulled up on his blind side and photographed him. She rested her arms on the window ledge and anchored the camera quite securely. She framed portraits of the man. She caught his superhuman focus and lunatic rectitude. I wondered if she noticed his slack uniform and the pathos in his eyes. How perfect. Her photographs indicted the man who sent me out to entrap her.

Wartime allegiance. Collusion.

Claire reloaded her camera three times. Parker reeled from exhaustion. He fell into his black-and-white and reached for his bottle. Something astonishing happened then.

Claire lowered her camera. She allowed the moment to go unrecorded. She felt pity or decided not to risk documenting it. I drove away then. I felt them both in the core of my bones.

Scotty was an hour and fifteen minutes late. Thad Brown and Jim Davis walked in and stretched out at the bar. They ignored the diners a few feet away. I lit a cigarette and listened to them talk.

Collusion.

Jim Davis ran security at Douglas Aircraft. They discussed the prospects of Fifth Column sabotage there. Thad changed the subject. Three Chinks were slaughtered in Griffith Park earlier tonight. Two Japs and one Chink-Jap, really. The breed was Four Families. Chinatown was running a fever. "That Scotty Kid" blew up that Four Families punk and stirred up a shitload of shit. We've got to avoid a full-scale tong war. We've got to whitewash the snuffs in the name of a Chinatown peace.

Bill Parker entered the grill. He saw me but did not acknowledge it. I waved and blew him a kiss. I regretted it instantly.

Parker joined Brown and Davis. I eavesdropped. The PD was mobilizing in Chinatown at midnight. The Dudster's display of force had the Chinks all hopped-up. Davis spoke in singsong Chinese and stretched his eyelids for added effect. Thad told the tale of Come-San-Chin, the Chinese cocksucker. The bartender poured a double bourbon and slid it over to Parker. Whiskey Bill downed it and white-knuckled the bar rail.

Thad tapped his watch; the three men dropped dollar bills on the bar and walked out. Scotty was late. Now I knew why. Scotty was needed in Chinatown.

I was all-of-a-sudden bored. There were no more provocative men to distract me. Tableside war chat resounded that much more predictably. The eastern front, the Japs. My son's draft deferment. I heard Hitler's gassing Jews. Well, *someone* has to! Eleanor Roosevelt's a lez—the shoe-shine boy at the Jonathan Club told me.

Hideo Ashida walked in. I knew he was looking for me.

I stood up; he pretended not to see me. It would acknowledge that he came here *to* see me and would put him at a perceived disadvantage. I waved and forced his hand. He made a disingenuous show of noticing me, walked over and sat down.

The ruse was unlike him. He wore subterfuge unconvincingly. He carried a whiff of formaldehyde. He'd been to the morgue.

He said, "Hello."

I said, "Who were you looking for?"

"I thought Jack Webb might be here. I know he comes by when he has the chance."

The waiter walked over. He saw the Jap with the white girl and about-faced. I slid my drink across the table; Dr. Ashida took a more than healthy belt. It was a wartime play. Normally abstentious Japanese had a newfound yen for the sauce.

"Go find Jack. You'll have a better chance of being served with him."

"That's all right."

"I'm happy to sit with you, but I think you'd be more comfortable with Jack."

Dr. Ashida slid my drink back. "You're trying to make me uncomfortable. You're trying to get me to say something I don't want to say."

"You don't have to say anything. I'm happy to see you, and I'm pleased that you came here looking for me."

"All right."

"I'm sorry you're uncomfortable. We could go someplace else if you'd like."

"All right."

" 'Go someplace' has connotations. I don't want to make you any more uncomfortable than you already are."

He said, "I'll go wherever you suggest. I'll be uncomfortable wherever it is, but since you enjoy my discomfort, it shouldn't concern you."

Touché.

I said, "Room 314 at the Rosslyn. I'll go over first."

He just sat there. I walked outside before he could say, "All right." I dodged traffic across 8th Street, went in a side entrance and rode a back elevator up. The room smelled of freshly laundered sheets. The pillowcases were clean, but faded lipstick stains could be seen. There was just the bed, a sofa and a bathroom. It was a purposeful hotel room.

I smoked and paced. Other women had preceded me. Their heels had dug holes in the carpet.

My mind went blank. I couldn't think it through past a no-show or knock on the door. I fought the urge to run someplace safe. A string quartet played itself out in my head.

The door buzzer startled me. I blotted my lipstick on a tissue and smoothed out my hair. The buzzer blared again. I walked to the door.

Hideo Ashida was mussed up. His cheek was scratched. He smelled like my left-behind cocktail. He stepped inside. Our shoulders brushed. My legs fluttered; I leaned on the door so he wouldn't see.

"What happened to you?"

"I knew Mrs. Hamano. She would escort my brother and me to church."

"Yes?"

"She hanged herself at the Lincoln Heights jail."

"Yes, I know that."

"Some frat boys at the bar were telling jokes. I told them to stop it. There was some shoving, and Mike Breuning saw it and stepped in."

I touched his cheek. He flinched. I ran my thumb over his eyebrow. He trembled. I put my whole hand on his face.

He said, "Why are you doing this?"

I said, "Because we're alone in a hotel room, and because I want to."

He didn't pull away from me. So, I brushed his hair back. He didn't pull away from me. So, I said this:

"Say my name, Hideo. Say 'Katherine' or 'Kay.' "

He said, "All right. Katherine, then."

My hand trembled. He didn't pull away from me. So, I kissed him.

Our lips barely touched. He raised his hands to hold me back; his arms brushed my breasts.

We stayed that way. Our foreheads touched. It was a fit of sorts. His shirt was partially unbuttoned. I felt his pulse through it. I slid my hand under the fabric and placed it on his heart.

He shuddered. I moved in under his arms and found a closer fit.

He said, "Katherine, please."

I said, "Please, what?"

He said, "No, Katherine, please."

I pulled away from him. He went loose. I was the only thing holding him up.

He leaned against the wall and slid down it; he sat on the floor and drew his knees to his chest. I stood over him. He touched my legs and steadied himself. I moved closer. He pulled his hands back.

So, I sat on the floor beside him. So, I put an arm around him. So, we listened to a band concert on the radio next door.

I didn't want to lose the fit. I didn't want to say anything or do anything that would scare him away. The music was part of the fit; the raucous numbers and ballads merged. It ended, slow-tempoed. Hideo asked me to tell him a story.

All I had was a recounting of pratfall and eros. It started in a 1920 snowstorm and stopped when a police captain knocked on my door. I smelled the prairie on him. I would end my story there.

The radio was kind to us. Our next-door neighbor put on a night-owl serenade. The music was perfect for storytelling. We sat on the floor, in our fit.

My heroine was a dubious huntress; she was far too self-serving to ever be Joan of Arc. I described my early stay in L.A. and my time with Bobby De Witt. I euphemized Lee and the Boulevard-Citizens robbery. I spilled everything that Bobby had done to me. Hideo asked to see the scars on my legs. I pulled up my skirt, rolled down my stockings and showed him. He ran his fingers over the ridges and pulled his hand away. I wanted more of him there but said nothing.

His hand left me warm, so I told him about Bucky. I described my desire to capture a man and render him mine by seeing him. Hideo touched my leg then. He told me about a camera he'd devised to photograph people covertly. Bucky Bleichert hovered. Hideo's eyes went somewhere. It was Bucky's betrayal writ horribly deep.

So, he told me about Bucky. It was Belmont High, green-and-black forever, the Mighty Sentinels. The Kraut boy from Glassell Park, the Little Tokyo Jap. Half-Jewish Jack Webb—there with the jokes and along for the ride.

Track meets, pep rallies, the All-City cage finals. His crazy fascist mother, Bucky's Bundist dad. The boys packed tight in a deuce coupe. That long ride to a big game in Fresno.

The story receded into secret-camera snapshots. What Bucky wore on prom nights, how Bucky rescued Jack from pachucos. How Bucky chewed raw steaks and swallowed the blood before his fights. That time he drove the drunk Bucky home and tucked him into bed. Bucky's Sportsman of the Year award, bestowed at the L.A. Press Club. The rented tuxedo, the legs too short, the terribly clashing corsage.

I heard all of it. Hideo kept his head on my shoulder and a hand on my leg. I believed all of it and none of it. I felt heartsick in a way I never had before.

Silly girl. Idiot seductress. Now you know what he is. Don't cry while he tells you his story.

51

LOS ANGELES | FRIDAY, DECEMBER 12, 1941

11:58 p.m.

Tong hordes and cops. A rope line between them. Face-off at Ord and North Main.

Sixty Four Families punks. Sixty Hop Sing. Thirty cops culled for their penchant to cause pain. Darktown bruisers. Alien Squad goons. Scotty Bennett—in uniform tonight.

The punks jabbered. The cops held parade rest. Parker stood on the balcony at Daddy Wong's Chow Mein. Thad Brown and Jim Davis stood with him. Two-Gun held a plugged-in bullhorn.

The blues guarded stacks of brass knuckles. It was Two-Gun's idea. State the terms of truce and let the Chinks blow off steam. Clear out the jail ward at Queen of Angels. Reserve ten ambulances. Chinatown would flow red tonight.

It felt cumulative. It felt overdue. Somebody snuffed Ace Kwan's niece. Scotty B. snuffed the real somebody or some convenient Chink. A Four Families punk got snuffed in Griffith Park. That put Hop Sing one death up. Ace Kwan was the PD's favored warlord. The situation mandated parity.

Parker scanned the cop line. He noted Lee Blanchard. He noted Fritz Vogel and Bill Koenig—77th Street thugs. Thirty cops. Two Kay Lake lovers. The war had L.A. all fucked-up.

Brown said, "The natives are restless."

Davis said, "Now, Bill? Jack Horrall gave me carte blanche."

Parker said, "Now, Jim."

Davis raised his bullhorn and spritzed Chinese. He sounded like Chiang Kai-shek inbred with Donald Duck. Parker knew the gist. No more killing, boys will be boys, let's joust before the truce. No rackets enforcement through 1942!

The punks tossed a heathen fit. The cops distributed knuckle dusters, one per punk.

The rope went down. Male nurses pushed gurneys out of bars and chop suey pits. Firemen screwed hoses into hydrants. High-pressure water knocked rioters flat and washed away blood.

Parker walked away. He took rear stairs down to the alley and headed for Kwan's. Crazy jabber trailed him. He cut through the kitchen and muted it.

Brown and Davis beat him there. They sat with Uncle Ace. Lychee nuts and rumaki were laid out.

Parker pulled a chair up. Two-Gun said something in Chink. Ace made the jack-off sign. Thad slapped his knees.

Two-Gun said, "No more grief with Four Families. They'll reciprocate if you give your word."

Ace said, "I agree."

Thad said, "They've agreed to pay you ten grand in reparations for your niece."

Ace said, "I accept."

Thad waved a rumaki stick. "Chief Horrall is adamant about no more killing. He'll close Chinatown down if even one more killing occurs."

Ace said, "I will comply."

Two-Gun said, "No investigation on the Griffith Park killings. That's straight from Jack Horrall."

Ace said, "It is the best for all concerned."

Two-Gun grabbed *two* rumaki sticks. "A Chinaman killed himself at the New Moon Hotel. We can pin the job on him."

Uncle Ace beamed. Parker made fists and stared at him. Ace made the jack-off sign.

Ambulance sirens kicked on. Hydrant water whooshed. It all reeked of Dudley Smith.

December 13, 1941

52

LOS ANGELES | SATURDAY, DECEMBER 13, 1941

12:42 a.m.

Meeks said, "You're dressed nice, Dud. Am I keeping you from doing something you'd rather be doing?"

The paperboys' bash was over. Grand Bette was surely long gone.

"You are, lad. I won't pretend I'm not miffed. I'm sure your 'urgent matter' could have waited for the morning."

The back room was musty. The Teletype clacked. That Chinatown truce abets mayhem.

Meeks said, "Where's the wink and the blarney, boss? Tell true, now. I ain't never seen you without them."

"State your intent or make your request. Refrain from threats or suffer the consequences."

Meeks lit a cigar. "I'm caught between you and Whiskey Bill. I'm sort of like the Ashida kid that way."

Dudley cracked his knuckles. "State your intent or make your request. This prelude is vexing me."

Meeks fumed up the room. "I went out on the DB call. A park ranger rang it in. Parker was talking to Ashida. They seemed chummy to me."

"Again, for the last—"

"I saw a rubber bullet on the ground. It reminded me of that Sheriff's-van job I'm working, which Parker put me on for some goddamn inexplicable reason. I dusted the bullet and got a ten-point print on Huey Cressmeyer, but I '*refrained*' from telling Whiskey Bill. I can count, Dud. You had four men plus Huey on the van job, and three dead in the park. I'd say that one guy—probably a Jap—had already scrammed off. That leaves two Japs and a Jap-Chink half-breed who can't be traced to the heist. They're dead, and I'll bet you got Huey stashed someplace."

Dudley lit a cigarette. "You have my attention. Finish your recounting, please."

"Here's what I've got. Huey boosted the bullets and some riot guns from Preston. I didn't put that in my report to Parker and Ward Littell, just like I left out the print."

"*And*, lad?"

"*And*, I saw Ashida's trip-wire shots, because I leaned on your pervert pal up in the photo lab. *And*, it's Huey again. He pulled the pharmacy job last Saturday, and for all I know, he's got a whole shitload of dirt on the Watanabe clan."

Dudley said, "Is there more?"

Meeks said, "Huey and his Japs clout the van. I go by the House of Lem Mortgage Company and learn that Ace Kwan paid off the loan on one of his buildings the next day. You always share your takes with Ace. Ace's niece gets killed, and your boy Scotty kills a handy suspect. It's getting tight as a tick, so here's what I'm thinking. Huey's Japs killed the Kwan girl, and you and Ace took them out."

What a shrewd detective. The Dust Bowl Charlie Chan.

"I wish to purchase your silence on these matters, through to New Year's. That includes your continued dissembling to Captain W. H. Parker."

Meeks wiggled three fingers. "I got me a slew of pregnant girlfriends. Your pal Ruth Mildred sure could help me out."

Dudley said, "Done."

Meeks walked to the bar. He poured a shot of bourbon and dunked his cigar.

"Call-Me-Jack wants a Jap to swing for the Watanabes, and I can't say I disagree. But I'm working the job, so I got a stake in it."

"Make your point."

"If it's a frame, I'd like to see some true pervert son of a bitch who really deserves it to go down."

As you will, you hayseed fuck.

"He'll be morally appropriate for the gas chamber, I assure you."

1:07 a.m.

The Shrine was the Tomb now. She was long gone. He ran anyway.

He ran to his K-car. He ran lights-and-siren southbound. He cut the noise at Washington and swung west. He pulled into the lot. A sea green Rolls-Royce almost grazed him.

His headlights strafed the windshield. He recognized the driver from a *Screen World* spread. Boston stiff Arthur Farnsworth—grand Bette's second hubby.

He's teary-eyed, swerving the Rolls, wringing a hankie. Harry Cohn told all. It was a studio-dictated marriage. Hubby was a whips-and-chains queer.

Hubby fishtailed down Washington. Dudley parked by the stage door. It was a *loooooong* long shot. He patted on cologne and chewed a pastille.

He walked to the door. A firm shove got him in. The houselights still glowed.

The Taj Mahal West. A plush-mosque motif. Wall tapestries and a thousand empty seats.

An elevated stage. The Mosque, the Crypt. Discarded programs everywhere. The Shrine, postmidnight. A stand-still-and-catch-your-breath spot.

Laughter. Overlapping peals. Behind the curtains, stage right.

Dudley jumped onstage and tracked it. He parted the curtains and sidestepped klieg lamps in the dark. He saw light down a corridor. He heard boys' voices. A woman laughed, contralto-pitched.

The boys squealed. Dudley stretched tall and walked over. He unbuttoned his suit coat. His shoulder rig showed.

She was down on her knees. She wore a pale blue gown. She was shooting craps with three paperboys.

They were starstruck. They hovered, they attended, they swooned. They wore their bargain-basement church suits. Everybody laughed and plain carried on.

His shadow hit them. The boys looked up. They were poor lads and wise to the world. They saw copper, straight off.

She felt their eyes leave her. Stray eyes discomfit the diva. She saw him and made him in a blink.

She saw the gun, the tweeds, the cordovan shoes. *Hold my eyes for a heartbeat, please.*

She did. He smiled and looked away first. He knelt beside her and dropped a C-note on the floor.

The boys looked at him, looked at her, looked at them both. She pointed to the fat boy with the dice. He passed them to her. She blew on them and rolled.

Snake eyes.

The thin boy said, "House take."

The blond boy scooped up the C-note and some singles. His cohorts squealed. Miss Davis opened her clutch and took out her cigarettes. Dudley lit her up.

The boys gawked. Dudley doffed his hat and dropped it on the blond boy's head. It covered his eyes and nose. Everybody laughed. *State your name now. She knows you know hers.*

He said, "Dudley Smith."

She blew a smoke ring his way. He laughed and passed her his flask. She took a belt and passed it to the blond boy. He took a belt and passed it to the fat boy. He took a belt and passed it to the thin boy. He took a belt. He went *Holy cow!* and passed it back to Dudley.

Bette Davis blew smoke at the boys. They made mock gagging sounds and mock-thrashed on the floor.

Bette Davis said, "They have to start sometime."

Dudley said, "I'm pleased to have shared their initiation with you."

"Mine was somewhat less refined."

"Would you care to set the stage?"

"A speakeasy in Harlem in 1924. That's as far as I'll go."

Dudley laughed. The fat boy snatched the flask. His cohorts chortled. The blond boy passed Miss Davis the dice.

The thin boy said, "Blow, Bette."

Miss Davis said, "I've heard *that* before."

Dudley roared. Bette blew on the dice and rolled lucky seven. The boys tipped off the flask. A babble went up. The boys laid down bets. *Bette's point, Bette's point, Bette's point.*

Dudley dropped a yard on the singles. Bette rolled and crapped out. The boys whooped and grabbed the take.

The boys looked at her, the boys looked at him. They made goo-goo eyes over his gun. He undid his holster and tossed it to the thin boy. It went *thud* in his lap.

Laughs circulated. The gun circulated. It landed in Bette's lap. She pulled it from the holster. She looked straight at Dudley.

"Should I?"

"I'd be quite disappointed if you didn't."

Bette stood up. Her gown was smudged. She flicked off the safety and aimed at the ceiling. She kicked off her shoes and got a grip on the floor.

She said, "Remember Pearl Harbor."

The boys whistled and cheered.

She squeezed off the full clip. Seven rounds, lucky seven, big noise. Muzzle smoke and cordite stink.

Plaster chips blew down from the ceiling. Dudley stood up and brushed silt out of her hair.

Bette's smile acknowledged his touch. The boys applauded. He took off his suit coat and laid it down. Bette took his arm and curtsied to the floor.

She said, "Mr. Smith."

He said, "Miss Davis."

They shook hands, mock-formal. The boys made with the oooh-la-las.

They returned to the game. Dudley emptied out his wallet, Bette emptied out her clutch. Dudley engineered their losses. The throws went boy to boy. House take, house take. The boys got nigger rich. They were up on Cloud 9.

His flask went around. Her flask replaced it. Bette brushed plaster off his trousers. Sweet intervals, then her touch.

The boys started yawning. They were boozed and too lucky to live. Dudley cited the time. The boys groaned. Bette laid down a long and sweet brush-off.

Dudley passed out toy badges. The boys hugged Miss Davis. She hugged them back and urged them to buy war bonds. She left big lipstick prints on their cheeks.

They were wobbly-kneed. They wheeled their bicycles out to the parking lot and pedaled off, whooping. Dudley helped Bette into her coat and walked her outside. His prowler was the only car in the lot.

He lit cigarettes. They stood close and looked at the sky. "Perfidia" ebbed someplace soft inside him.

Well, then.

They tossed their cigarettes. They brushed bullet dust from each other's hair and came in tight for the kiss.

53

LOS ANGELES | SATURDAY, DECEMBER 13, 1941

2:24 a.m.

Ashida wrote on flash paper. Invisible ink, flammable page stock. His own secret language.

It was his secret document. It would scald in common sunlight. Kanji script, English, shorthand. Five layers of obfuscated text.

Mariko's kitchen table did desk duty. Mariko geisha-girled in the living room. Elmer Jackson was stinko. Ward Littell ballyhooed Bill Parker. Captain Bill secured his berth on the Sheriff's-van job and shitcanned his roundup work.

The roundups disgusted Ward. He insistently critiqued the FBI's "racial agenda."

The roundups disgusted Elmer. He called them a "plain old raw deal."

Mariko disgusted Ashida. She blabbermouthed to the Japanese papers. Both his T.I. trips proved fruitless.

Kanji, English, shorthand. Impromptu hieroglyphics.

He drew the knife scar on the man at Goleta. He drew the knife found in Griffith Park. He drew the faded knife scar on Ryoshi Watanabe.

He drew the severed foot at Goleta. He drew wavy lines off the sole. The lines signified the smell of fish oil.

He smelled fish on the man at the farm. He caught a fish-oil scent on broken glass in the Watanabes' kitchen. Nort Layman noted shrimp oil on the Watanabes' feet.

Ashida drew shrimp. His pen wandered. He drew Kay Lake at the Rosslyn Hotel. He drew Bucky and Kay as phantoms, intertwined. He drew Jim Larkin's koi. He wrote 渡辺邸で何を見逃したのか? He translated: "What did I miss at the Watanabe house?"

Mariko toasted Nao Hamano. Good American, good mother. Dead at the Lincoln Heights jail.

Elmer said, "Hear, hear."

Ward said, "The Navy's calling me. Maybe sub duty. I could hibernate and fight the war."

Mariko tee-heed. "Ward ladies' man. Girl in every port."

Explosions on 2nd Street. *Ploosh*, *blam* and screams.

Elmer said, "Rock-salt rounds."

Ward said, "They're lacing it with bird shot now. It knocks anything human flat."

Mariko tee-heed. "No girls on submarines. I send Ward dirty books."

Ward and Elmer haw-hawed. Ashida looked out the window. He saw two boys with shredded jackets, knocked flat in the street.

Two cops dragged the boys to a K-car. Bucky Bleichert weaved across the street.

Ashida walked downstairs. Bucky was blotto on the front steps. He beat Bucky up on Wednesday. He still bore contusions.

Ashida said, "Hello, champ."

Bucky said, "You're the champ, and I've got the lumps to prove it."

Ashida sat beside him. Their knees brushed. Ashida slid back.

"You've been to the Shotokan Baths. The Harada brothers had a bottle. You've been talking boxing for hours."

Bucky said, "I retired undefeated. I'm either a chickenshit or the world's luckiest white man."

Ashida smiled. "You're a little of both."

Bucky smiled. "The brothers think I could take Lee Blanchard. I told them they're nuts."

Ashida said, "It's a toss-up. He's stronger, you're faster."

Bucky smiled. "Beat me up again, will you? I said I'm sorry, but it sure as shit wasn't enough."

Ashida smiled. "You'll pummel yourself from here on in."

Bucky drew his legs up and rested his chin on his knees. It was such a lovely thing.

"I'll graduate the Academy in July. We'll be working together then."

Ashida said, "I'll be in prison. Unless the right white man owes me."

54

KAY LAKE'S DIARY

LOS ANGELES | SATURDAY, DECEMBER 13, 1941

2:36 a.m.

I tended to Lee in the kitchen. His back and arms were covered with small cuts. He stood over the sink, stripped to the waist. I stood behind him with alcohol, tweezers and swabs.

The new tong truce was rigged for Hop Sing. Many Chinatown residents knew this. They gathered on rooftops and hurled bottles down on the cops. A dozen men were rushed to Queen of Angels; Lee's uniform shirt was now rags.

I extracted a shard and daubed the cut. Lee said, "It hurts, but it feels good. Tell me what that means."

"It means that your nerve endings were injured in a certain way. Your brain is receiving conflicting signals of pleasure and pain."

"Sioux Falls or UCLA? Where you learned it, I mean."

"I read an anatomy text. I studied the diagrams of the skin."

Lee smoked. I held his head down to get purchase on his wounds. I kept thinking of lovelorn Hideo. Bucky was in the room with us then, Bucky stayed with me now. Hideo was crucial to my documentary-film plan. He was my inside source and device to shape the film into a conflicting political statement. Parker wanted the film to explicate Claire De Haven's seditious designs. It would do that—while it showed these designs manifested as the exposure of a grave injustice. The film would portray the roundups as systematic brutality, war profiteering and racial hysteria of inescapable dimension. I would convince Claire to shape the film sans editorial comment. She and her comrades would not be permitted to speak on film, and thus validate Parker's assessment of their treasonous intent. I saw the film as *my* film and *my* codicil to Claire's tract defaming Parker himself. One person would speak to the world in *my* film—and that would be Dr. Hideo Ashida. He would exposit my ambivalent view of the police world I both loved and despised; he would speak from deep professional knowledge and his deeper personal experience as an oppressed Japanese. This film would nullify Parker's attempt to further maim Claire De Haven and would liberate Claire from her grandiose martyrdom.

Lee said, "Scotty B. wasn't hurt. I bet you're happy to hear that."

"Don't move your head. I've got a deep one here."

Lee said, "Did you screw him?"

I said, "Yes."

"Did you screw Hideo Ashida?"

"I offered, but he declined."

Lee laughed. "He probably goes for Jap girls exclusive. I'll hand it to him there. He knows there's lines you don't cross."

I pulled out the sliver and swabbed blood off the cut. Lee said, "The war's this license to fuck like rabbits. Not that you've ever needed one."

55

LOS ANGELES | SATURDAY, DECEMBER 13, 1941

2:42 a.m.

La Guardia said, "These Japs are fat and sassy. I see no mistreatment here."

They toured the Fort MacArthur stockade. It was all politics. Mayor Fiorello, Mayor Fletch, dipshit Ed Satterlee. A 1:00 a.m. call roused Parker.

The gang was up at Brenda A.'s trick spot. They'd worn out the girls. They still felt jazzed.

Fletch insisted. "I know it's late, Bill—but nobody sleeps these days. And it can't do your career any harm. This guy's got Roosevelt's ear."

Hence the tour. Hence the Pedro jaunt. Hence the bored MPs and gloomy Japs.

They were two tiers in. Most of the Japs slept through it. La Guardia jived with the insomniacs. He called them "papa-san." He said he *loooved* Mr. Moto. He'd seen all those movies.

Parker walked with *El Jefe*. Bowron and Satterlee hung back with the MPs. Parker detailed his blackout work. La Guardia gassed on him. Bowron and Satterlee bristled.

La Guardia said, "That Jap lady who killed herself had a Jap war bond on her. It sounds Fifth Column to me."

Parker said, "It was an unnecessary death, sir. I'm sure she was despondent, but that doesn't justify the act."

La Guardia said, "Live by the sword, die by the sword. The Navy just sank three more Jap destroyers. Those cocksuckers will rue the day they dropped those eggs on Pearl Harbor."

They hit the last tier. Parker felt sandbagged. Griffith Park, the morgue and Chinatown. No sleep and this bullshit.

Bowron said, "All the commandeered Jap real estate will leave the city fat and sassy. So you tell me. Where do we house the Japs?"

Satterlee said, "The Army's got scouting teams combing the Southwest. You've got abandoned Army installations that can house six thousand Japs at a pop."

Bowron said, "I ran into Preston Exley in Beverly Hills yesterday. We see the same doctor for migraines. You know Preston, right? He was on the PD, and now he's a land developer."

Satterlee said, "Right. The retired inspector who made good in real estate. I've jawed with him a few times."

Bowron said, "Right. And if you've jawed with him recently, you know that he presents a persuasive case for interning some high-line Japs within the L.A. city limits, because a mass incarceration of that magnitude will promote a civilian job boom and keep the Japs close at hand for interrogations."

Satterlee said, "Preston's got the Midas touch. He knows what to buy and where to buy, and he knows how to squeeze a buck."

Bowron said, "His people may go back to the *Mayflower*, but I think he's got some kike blood."

Satterlee said, "He thinks there's money in Jap property. The question is, Who oversees the property while the Japs are in stir?"

Parker yawned and kept pace with *El Jefe*. Bowron and Satterlee yawned and lagged back. "Hey there, papa-san!" "How's the world treating you?" "That Mr. Moto—ain't he a sketch?"

They killed off the cell block and hit the fresh air. They lit cigarettes and got revitalized. *El Jefe* pressed to see a gun placement. Mayor Fletch and Agent Ed suppressed groans.

They piled into their jeep. Shoreline blackout—the driver drove by roadway Braille. They got up flush to a cliffside. They hit a sandbagged bunker perched there.

Six men with binoculars. Two tripod-mounted machine guns. Radar gizmos. Deck chairs prearranged.

The gang piled out of the jeep and into the bunker. La Guardia backslapped the soldiers. Bowron and Satterlee crashed into chairs. Parker lugged a file box Call-Me-Jack gave him.

He grabbed a chair. *El Jefe* lubed the soldiers with raw jokes. Fletch and Agent Ed dozed. Parker cracked the file box. He brought a small-beam flashlight.

Oh, shit. Call-Me-Jack's new brainchild. The "Wartime Auxiliary Police."

Application forms. Applicant dossiers.

Parker scanned the pages. Call-Me-Jack plays Uncle Sam. He wants *YOU!* He wants air-raid wardens, airplane spotters, parking-ticket drones.

The applicants were low-tide. Pensioners, cop buffs, draft dodger types. Boris "Frankenstein" Karloff. Bantamweight Manny Mendez. Nightclub buffoon Lou Costello and the "Hearst Rifle Team."

Eight sharpshooters. Regulars at tycoon Hearst's San Simeon shack. Sheriff Biscailuz endorsed the team. They assisted his mounted posse and corralled jail runaways. All eight men were in the San Berdoo Klan.

Misanthropes, movie monsters, misfits. The wartime Keystone Kops. Call-Me-Jack drooled for publicity. He'd sign up every one.

Parker shut his eyes. He tried to doze. It was hopeless. *El Jefe* had some live ones. He wouldn't let go.

Joan Woodard Conville, white female American, age 26.

She wouldn't let go. She kept sideswiping him. He called the Motor Vehicle Office and tried to trace her address. No go—she had no driver's license. He called four nurses' directories. No go—she wasn't listed.

It felt foolish. He felt foolish. He called the Northwestern cops back. He told them to send an ID pic of Miss Conville. It was police-sanctioned peeping.

His graph work stood in arrears. He was behind on *Watanabe Case/Details-Chronology*. He'd been disrupted. Tangential cases stacked up. The Griffith Park triple. The Larkin hit-and-run.

It was fucked-up. *He* was fucked-up. The Watanabe case *got* to him. He cared more than he should.

A guard hut adjoined the bunker. Parker walked over. The guard boss was out. Parker grabbed the desk phone and dialed the morgue.

Nort picked up. "Morgue, Dr. Layman."

"It's Bill Parker, Nort."

"You can't let it go, can you? It's only been four hours."

Parker laughed. "Let's just say I can't sleep."

"You're not alone there. We're at war, or haven't you noticed?"

Parker said, "You're still thawing the cadavers, right? I thought you might have more information."

Layman said, "Roger that. You read my initial report, right? Shrimp oil on the victims' feet?"

"Right, I remember."

"All right, then catch this curveball. The freezing and thawing isolated particles in the subcutaneous tissue, under the soles of their feet. I found ground glass covered with shrimp oil on eight feet out of eight. Their feet were heavily callused, which isn't surprising, because Japs tend to walk around barefoot. What did surprise me was the even distribution of the particles. It was as if they were walking on the glass deliberately."

Curveball. Sinker. Wild pitch.

"Will you issue a statewide coroner's bulletin on that? Hospitals, infirmaries, doctors' offices. It's a long-shot parlay, but put my name and office number on it for callbacks."

Layman said, "You're way out in center field on this one, but I'll do it."

Parker said, "Thanks, Nort. You'll be rewarded, in this life and the next."

"I've already been rewarded, Bill."

"How so?"

"It's a hell of a treat to see you obsessed."

56

LOS ANGELES | SATURDAY, DECEMBER 13, 1941

5:09 a.m.

This grand manse, this grand lady.

They made love and talked. The bedroom was tucked in a parapet. Fireplace, dark beams, brushed-cement walls.

The bed was four-postered. The sheets were peach satin. Casement windows overlooked the Brentwood hills. A handsome Airedale lolled beside them.

The house was mock medieval. Stained glass and rough wood loomed throughout. Bette loved to fight. Her home portrayed her as embattled.

Her husband lived above the garage. Bette caught hubby blowing the chauffeur on their wedding night. She banished him then. He escorted her to events and attended queer masquerade balls. He fulfilled her studio morals clause. The chauffeur had a big dick.

Bette said, "Dudley Liam Smith. Are you surprised to be here?"

Dudley stroked the Airedale. "Delighted, more than surprised. I would have contrived another form of introduction if tonight hadn't resolved so serendipitously."

The Airedale stretched and kicked up his legs. Bette scratched his back.

"Do you miss Ireland, Dudley?"

"No, lass. I do not."

"No family there?"

"British soldiers killed my father and brother. My mother drank herself to death. My one aunt ran off to London with a Protestant. He was quite the dashing fellow. He looked like Leslie Howard in *Gone with the Wind.*"

Bette laughed. "I screwed Leslie Howard. He looks like a fairy, but I assure you he's not."

Dudley laughed. "Who else have you screwed?"

Bette said, "Most of the men on the *Photoplay* eligible-bachelors list. Warner's made me host the Hamilton High prom party. I was bored, so I screwed the president of the Lochinvars Social Club."

The Airedale curled up between them. Dudley laid an ashtray on his back and lit cigarettes.

"I'm picking Jack Kennedy up at noon. His dad and I go quite far back."

Bette laced up their fingers. Dudley stretched the full length of the bed.

He'd kissed off her lipstick. She was smaller than he thought she'd be. She thrashed a way he'd never seen before.

"Joe Kennedy made a pass at me once. He was running RKO then. I heard Jack's an even bigger chaser, but he's hung like a cashew."

Dudley laughed. It shook the bed. The Airedale glared at him. Bette snatched the ashtray and scooted him down to the footboard. He flashed his fangs and went to sleep.

"Dear girl. How did this occur?"

"You got lucky. We shouldn't mince words about that."

"Should we give a nod to the war? I sense appetite in the air."

Bette kissed him. "My appetite preceded the war. Ask the boys in Lowell, Massachusetts."

"I'm afraid they would make me quite jealous."

"I wouldn't want to see you jealous."

"And why is that?"

"Because you're brutal. Because you're all enticement and threat."

Dudley kissed her. She held his face and rubbed their noses, Eskimo-style.

"When I saw you, I thought, Oh, the big cop with the crush on me. And he dressed for the role."

Dudley crushed their cigarettes and put the ashtray on the nightstand. Dawn beamed outside. The big backyard glowed.

"Are you always that quick-witted?"

"Yes. I live by immediate perception. It's how I've survived."

Dudley smiled. "On Broadway? In Hollywood?"

Bette smiled. "You've killed British soldiers, and don't tell me you haven't. I've told the Jewish mama's boys who run my part of town, 'No, I won't blow you,' and got the part anyway. Aren't we both lucky to be that way? Aren't you glad you're not like the rest of the world?"

He trembled a tad. He wetted up a tad. Bette wetted up and touched his eyes.

"Dear man. Step away from your life and be sweet with me for a while."

Dudley pulled her hands down and pinned them to the bed. Her wet eyes were up against his. She hooked a leg over him and brought them just *that* close. It went to a thrash and stayed in a thrash. The thrash made her shut her eyes. The thrash let him look at her.

Her arms were soft. Her breasts pulled flat with the thrash. He kissed her neck. She showed her teeth and bit her lips. The thrash built to a flush all over her body. Then the arch above the thrash, a clutch and thrash, a plummeting something.

9:46 a.m.

The Airedale slept between them. Dudley stirred and saw the dog first. He marked the moment—*Bette Davis snores.*

He kissed the dog's snout and kissed Bette's shoulder. He walked to the bathroom and shaved with a dainty razor. He dressed and rigged the curtains to light up Bette's hair. He kissed her arms and walked downstairs.

The Airedale showed him out. He nuzzled the grand beast. He walked outside and took in the morning.

Brentwood north of Sunset. Tudor mansions, French châteaux, Spanish haciendas. Dudley Liam Smith—*fate favors you.*

He got his K-car. He hooked out to the Valley and east to Burbank. The airport cops let him perch on the runway. He had two hours to kill. He smelled Bette on his shirt cuffs.

He had time to scheme and strategize. He had time to craft a disingenuous report to Bill Parker.

Watanabe/multiple homicide/12-7-41. Second summary—one week in.

He popped three bennies. He padded redundant information. He layered in futile background-check dirt. He heaped on the dead-end leads and stressed the clannish Jap culture that constrained the job.

The bennies kicked in. He shoveled cop officialese and underlined his detective's frustration.

Record checks were impossible. The war dashed all normal avenues of approach.

Can you read between the lines, Captain? Call-Me-Jack wants this job shitcanned by New Year's. He will get what he wants—but this damnable case intrigues me.

The Boston flight taxied in. Baggage men rolled stairs to the door. Dudley got out and stood by the gate. Jack was the first down the steps.

He wore his Navy blues. He saw Dudley and beelined. They hugged hello and shoved apart. They pushed each other out to arm's length.

Jack said, "You mick cocksucker."

Dudley said, "The pot calls the kettle black."

They got in the K-car. Dudley tossed Jack's bag in the back. Jack futzed with the two-way dial and stirred up a hum. Dudley pulled off the runway.

Jack said, "Where are we going?"

"How did your father once summarize Los Angeles?"

"He said you come here to fuck movie stars and create mischief."

"Well, then. Harry Cohn has an introduction for you."

Jack twirled his hat on one finger. "I wouldn't say no to Rita Hayworth or Ella Raines."

Dudley said, "Lad, you'll have to. Miss Hayworth is out of town, and Jewboy Harry has designs on Miss Raines himself."

"Which makes me the low man in a Mongolian cluster fuck."

Dudley laughed. "Ellen Drew, lad. She's a stunning new contract player, and she's waiting at the Los Altos Apartments."

Jack messed with the radio. Code numbers and locations overlapped. 390, Little Tokyo. Prowl cars requested.

Jack said, "What's going on at East 1st Street?"

"It's Japtown, lad. The locals are being detained."

"Can you believe it? We knew it was coming, but we didn't think they'd hit us first."

"It's a new world we live in."

"I fly to Pearl on Monday. I've got briefings, and then it's a jump to some shitty little island full of cannibals."

Dudley lit a cigarette. "Your dad came through. I'm free to be commissioned at New Year's. Army Intelligence. Mexican duty, most likely."

Jack said, "Dad's still got some pull. That 'Jittery Joe' talk didn't do him any good, though. Come on, Dud. *You'd* bail on the Blitz. A little drive up to the Emerald Isle and some sweet Irish cooze."

Dudley skirted the Hollywood Bowl. "Ireland's a place you don't leave. I'm surprised Joe came back at all."

"His money and his kids are here. Given that, you'd come back yourself."

Christmas was coming. The faux trees were up. Salvation Army kettles cluttered Sunset.

Dudley flicked his cigarette. "Does your dad still have that yen for dirty movies? He hasn't lost it at his advanced age?"

Jack laughed. "Ask him yourself. He'll be at Ben Siegel's party on Sunday. That said, he's always called the smut business 'high pulchritude with low overhead.'"

Dudley laughed. Jack tipped his hat over his eyes. Dudley took Highland to Wilshire. The Los Altos flanked a gas station and a South Seas–motif lounge.

It was a wayward starlets' haven. Contract players turned tricks in rent-by-the-night flops. Dot Rothstein ran the dyke dens. Eleanor Roosevelt munched muff in 419.

Dudley parked in front. Jack dug in his bag and spritzed on Lucky Tiger. The lad was comely but frail. He looked vaguely inbred.

"Ellen Drew, right?"

"Yes, lad. She's in 332. Mention *The Château in Montparnasse.* She played the French maid."

Jack said, "This won't take long."

"I know, lad. Your reputation precedes you."

Jack yocked and scrammed. Dudley cogitated. The Watanabe house. Mental walk-through no. 9,000.

He walked the floors and checked the closets. He looked under the sink. He peered behind the icebox. He retrieved two memories.

He recalled mouse shit by a drainpipe. He recalled spilled detergent near the washing machine.

Jack hopped in the car. A hickey bloomed on his neck.

Dudley said, "You weren't long."

Jack winked. "Nice kid. Tell Harry to be good to her."

"Where to, lad?"

"The Delfern place. Dad's got an envelope for Gloria."

Dudley drove northwest. Jack shut his eyes and forestalled chitchat. Gloria Swanson lived in Holmby Hills. Joe K. was her way-back-when lover.

Joe looted her bank accounts. Gloria hatched their love child in '27. Joe pooh-poohed his patrimony and provided covert support.

The house was small-hotel size. Dudley brodied into the *porte cochère* and roused Jack. The lad looked startled. He grabbed his hat and rolled out of the car.

The backyard gate was open. Jack strolled over. Dudley cogitated.

He studied his report. He beefed up his canvassing notes. He ran mental walk-through 9,001. He recalled more mouse turds and spoiled lettuce in the icebox.

Jack walked back. His zipper was down. He tumbled into the car and tipped his hat. Dudley pulled out to the street.

Jack said, "I hate him."

Dudley said, "Yes, I know."

"Joe Junior fucks her, I fuck her. Bobby's too pious to fuck her, and Teddy's too young."

"Yes, lad. I know."

"It doesn't do any good. I still hate him. She made me fuck her out by the pool, and now my ass is sunburned."

Dudley laughed and turned onto Sunset. Holmby Hills Christmas trees loomed skyscraper high.

Jack said, "He rapes the world and shits all over decent people, then runs when the chickenshit Krauts drop a few bombs. I'm a chickenshit for feeding on his money, and you're a chickenshit for driving me around."

Dudley smiled. "Immaculate Heart, then?"

Jack smiled. "Immaculate Heart, you mick cocksucker."

They tootled down Sunset. Jack stared out the window and scratched his balls. Dudley turned north on Western. The convent and school were built up a hillside.

The Archbishop's limo was parked across the street. J. J. Cantwell liked to perch and peep schoolgirls.

Dudley pulled up behind him. Jack got out and walked over to the playground. It was recess. Laura sat by herself. She looked like a Kennedy, one genetic beat removed.

She saw Jack and ran up to him. J. J. Cantwell stepped out of the limo. He wore linen golf slacks and a pink sweater.

Dudley joined him. Cantwell stared at Laura and Jack.

"He's too thin, Dud. Isn't Joe feeding him?"

"He takes his sustenance from love, Your Eminence."

Cantwell giggled. "I won't live to see a Catholic president. Joe has designs for his sons, I've been told."

"He does, Your Eminence."

"A Catholic police chief. That's more within my grasp."

Jack and Laura chucked a baseball. J. J. Cantwell stared.

"How long does Chief Horrall plan to stick around, Dud?"

"Until the war concludes, Your Eminence."

"And his preferred successor would be the capable, but dismayingly Protestant Thad Brown?"

"It would be, Your Eminence."

"Can Horrall avoid scandal for the remainder of his term?"

Dudley did the wavy hand. "A toss-up, Your Eminence. The FBI will be conducting a wiretap probe next February, and the Chief could be besmirched. He's taking payoffs from a Vice sergeant named Elmer Jackson, who is quite embroiled with an enterprising madam named Brenda Allen. I would not like to see it become public news."

Cantwell said, "Bill Parker is afraid of you."

Dudley said, "I know that, Your Eminence."

"Are you afraid of him?"

"No, Your Eminence. I am not."

"Do you have something on him?"

"Yes, Your Eminence."

"Does he have something on you?"

"No, Your Eminence."

Cantwell stared at Laura and Jack. They tossed the baseball. His Eminence caught every move.

"I am pleased by this balance of power between two fine Catholic laymen, and I am equally fond of you and Bill Parker. I would like to see a Catholic Chief in my lifetime, and would hate to see this balance dashed unnecessarily."

57

LOS ANGELES | SATURDAY, DECEMBER 13, 1941

1:14 p.m.

A warehouse block. Innocuous. 4600 Valley—hit-and-run homicide scene.

The impact point had eroded. Monday's rain drenched the tread marks.

Ashida walked outside the rope line. He held the Jim Larkin DB file. Ray Pinker shagged it for him.

A black-and-white skidded up and grazed Ashida's car. Bill Parker got out. He wore a too-loose uniform. He had that frayed I-can't-sleep look.

He walked up. His glasses fit cockeyed. He probably passed out on them.

"It's a premeditated vehicular homicide. The man possessed dexterity and nerve. He smashed Larkin hard enough to kill him and barely touched the boys. It all feels professional."

Ashida said, "And he was wearing a purple sweater, just like the white man outside the Watanabe house."

Parker said, "*Mauve* sweater. Those were *mauve* fibers you found on the victims' posteriors. *Mauve* and *purple*. It's ambiguous."

Ashida nodded. "The Sheriff's checked all the car-repair and paint shops, and got nothing. He had to have damaged his car, but he's kept it garaged."

Parker lit a cigarette. His gun belt flopped down his hips.

Ashida said, "It was an obvious cause of death, so there was no autopsy. I found one interesting note in the file, though. The impact sheared off a chunk of flesh from Larkin's rear thigh. The examining surgeon noted a 'circumscribed, uniformly configured series of stab wounds embedded in a muscle group,' but there's no photograph."

Cars whizzed by. The black-and-white spooked them. They braked and crawled.

Parker said, "The fucking knife. We've got the faded wound on Ryoshi Watanabe, and now we've got this."

Cars crawled close. Parker stood too close to them. Ashida stepped back.

"Yes. The whole thing keeps growing."

Parker's two-way squawked. Garbled speech issued. Parker walked over and snatched the receiver. The squawk leveled off.

Ashida studied the impact point. He noted loose molding. He saw a single sawtooth tread.

Parker walked back. "That was the Bureau dispatcher. I had Nort Layman put out a statewide bulletin on the glass particles and shrimp oil on the Watanabes' feet, and we just got a kickback from Lancaster. A hospital treated a 'Japanese derelict' for cut feet and released him an hour ago. We've got no name on the man, but there's half a connection. The deputies up there had fielded complaints from five local groceries. Customers found glass particles in cans of Japanese-caught and -manufactured shrimp. It's Sheriff's jurisdiction, and Gene Biscailuz saw the bulletin. He thinks it's Fifth Column sabotage, so he's going up."

Ashida gripped the rope line. Car whizzed by, too close.

Parker said, "Dispatch gave me the scoop on the canning distributor. His name's Wallace Hodaka, and he's in the Fort MacArthur stockade."

Ashida said, "We have to."

Parker nodded yes. They looked at each other. They eschewed more preamble. They walked to their cars and peeled out.

They convoyed, southbound. Ashida took the pole slot. Parker bird-dogged him.

They hit Main Street. They caught Lincoln Heights. Ashida checked his rearview mirror. Parker rode his back bumper and sucked on a flask.

They laid tracks to Pedro. Parker bumper-locked him and nipped on his flask. Downtown, darktown, Gardena. Salt air and Army trucks—San Pedro up ahead.

They hit Fort MacArthur. They hit the stockade. Ashida saw Parker stash his flask and gargle mouthwash. The gate guard fish-eyed Ashida—*Hey, you're a Jap.*

Ashida flashed his ID card. The guard clocked the black-and-white and waved them in. They found slots by the door. They got out and stretched. Parker teetered and held.

MPs flanked the door. They saluted Parker and fish-eyed the Jap. Parker pointed Ashida ahead. The sally port was a full-barred enclosure. The desk guard squint-eyed Ashida—*Hey, who's this Jap?*

Parker braced him. "We're here to interview an inmate named Wallace Hodaka."

The guard checked his desk book. "We just logged some L.A. boys in and out. A Sergeant Smith called down and said he had Chief Horrall's okay. We logged in Sergeants M. Breuning, R. Carlisle, and Officer R. S. Bennett. They examined our inmate list and left a few minutes ago."

Ashida gulped. Parker gripped his gun belt and cinched his loose pants. The guard unhooked a wall phone and gabbed officialese. He hit a button. Two bar doors slid wide.

"Interview room no. 3. He's a tubby little Tojo guy, and he don't speak English."

Parker walked ahead. His gait was off. His feet looked wrong on the floor. Ashida walked behind him.

He ignored the cell rows. Inmates saw him and hissed. It escalated cell to cell. They spat at him. He stuck to the middle of the catwalk. The spit globs fell short.

Number 3 was an eight-by-eight sweat room. The door was open. Wallace Hodaka wore jail khakis and straddled a chair.

Ashida shut the door. Hodaka stood and bowed. They shook hands. Hodaka rebowed. Parker popped a tin and swallowed six aspirin.

"Interview him, Doctor. You know what we need. Promise him habeas if he cooperates."

Ashida straddled a chair. He stacked up mother-tongue phrases and cut loose. Hodaka cut loose in reply.

He talked fast. He *wanted* to talk. It was a listen-now/translate-as-you-go deal. Ashida nodded—*Please, go ahead.*

Wallace Hodaka was perceptive. He spoke in direct sentences and did not digress. Ashida listened and mentally translated at his speedy clip.

Parker leaned on the door. His eyes were bloodshot. He was half in the bag.

Hodaka ran out of breath. He bowed to Ashida and Parker. Ashida bowed back and laid out the gist.

"Mr. Hodaka knows nothing about the particles of glass found in the canned shrimp that he produces, and he seems credible to me. He was detained here because he manufactured Emperor Hirohito souvenir dolls up until three years ago, when the Emperor's warlike agenda became evident. The shrimp canning is done at a San Fernando Valley truck farm owned by Hodaka family cousins. A rotating workforce of Japanese transients does the canning work. If glass got into his shrimp, it was inadvertently, and due to the sloppy efforts of his workers—or from errors that derived from the fishing-boat source of the shrimp. San Pedro–moored boats sell him their shrimp catches. Mr. Hodaka was very clear on this one point—and, again, I find him credible. He's always paid cash for the shrimp, and he's never kept records of the transactions. He can't honestly give you any names for his shrimp providers."

Parker said, "Keep going."

Ashida said, "Mr. Hodaka *does* know about the white men attempting to purchase Japanese-owned houses and farms, but he doesn't know their names. Their 'front man' was allegedly a man named Hikaru Tachibana, who was rumored to have been murdered—but Mr. Hodaka has no more details on that. A cousin visited Mr. Hodaka here a few days ago, and told him that a man named Jimmy Namura was seen in Little Tokyo and the Valley early last week, asking about the men attempting to purchase the houses and farms. Namura was seen again on Thursday, also in the Valley and Little Tokyo, asking the same questions. This time, Namura was facially lacerated and wore bandages that seemed to indicate a recent surgery. Mr. Hodaka knows nothing more about Jimmy Namura, has never met any member of the Watanabe family, and knows nothing about them. Again, Captain, I find Mr. Hodaka entirely credible."

Parker rubbed his eyes. "Tachibana and Namura were Watanabe family KAs. They were in the 'A' subversive index."

Ashida said, "I know. And Dudley Smith got Namura released from T.I."

"I'd bet that Dudley is hiding him. If it's anywhere, it's Chinatown. And if anyone knows, it's Ace Kwan."

Hodaka fidgeted. He fretted his jail wristband. He'd chewed his cuticles raw.

Ashida smiled. "You'll get Mr. Hodaka habeas."

Parker said, "Not today. He's more useful here."

3:12 p.m.

More hissing. More spit globs. More synchronized this time.

Traitor, traitor, traitor.

They reversed their way back down the catwalk. Parker took the lead. He ignored the taunts and spittle. His feet still looked wrong on the floor.

They walked through the sally port and out to their cars. Parker peeled off first. He fishtailed and kicked up grit.

Two-car convoy.

Parker took the lead. Ashida trailed him. He had a choice rear-window view.

Parker sucked on his flask. Parker *weeeeaved* his black-and-white. Ashida bumper-lock tailed him. They kept their windows down. Parker played his civilian radio. It was soaring Bruckner, too loud.

Northbound. Pedro, Gardena, mainland L.A. Over to Broadway. Chinatown, straight ahead.

Parker U-turned and swerved up to Kwan's. Ashida braked and got out of his way. Parker bumped the curb and stalled dead by the entrance. Ashida parked across the street.

The Pagoda was gussied up. The doorway dragons wore Christmas wreaths. A Santa sled was perched on the roof. A sled banner read REMEMBER PEARL HARBOR!

Parker stashed his flask and gargled up some mouthwash. He spit it out the window and spritzed a passing Ford. A passenger lady evil-eyed him. Parker flashed his middle finger and lurched from the car.

Ashida watched. Parker got a grip on the street and pushed off. He stumble-walked. He entered the Pagoda. Ashida ran up behind him.

The dining room was cryptsville. Busboys lounged near the kitchen. Uncle Ace sat at his favored table and read a comic book.

Parker used chair backs as handholds. He stitched a course and made it over. Ashida walked a step back.

Uncle Ace looked up. Parker slid into a chair. Ashida sat down beside him.

Uncle Ace said, "Yes?"

Parker said, "We have several questions."

He slurred it. His breath reeked. Uncle Ace hitched his chair back.

"Yes? I hope I have the answers for you."

Parker pulled out his cigarettes. Three match swipes got one lit. "A man named James Namura. His moniker is 'Jimmy the Jap.' We need to know his whereabouts."

Uncle Ace slid his ashtray over. "I do not know Mr. Namura, or know of him."

"I think you do."

"I assure you that I do not."

"I think you do."

"It insults me that you repeat yourself. Describe Mr. Namura, so that I may better understand why you so persist."

Ashida watched. The busboys watched. They cleaned their fingernails with switchblades.

Parker said, "Here's your description. He was seen a few days ago, and was noted as being 'recently facially scarred.' A plastic surgeon named Lin Chung is a ranking member of your tong, I know that you're friends with a plastic surgeon named Terry Lux, and that you supply the opiates that Dr. Lux employs at his clinic in Malibu. Chief Horrall is indebted to you, but at this moment, I don't care."

Uncle Ace shook his head. "You are out of your depth, Whiskey Bill. I advise you to go home and sleep it off."

Parker flushed. Uncle Ace pulled out a stiletto and scratched his neck with the blade. Parker pointed to Ashida.

"This man is Japanese."

"Yes, and he is locally celebrated and honored for his forensic expertise."

Ashida blushed and sat on his hands. It always quashed swoons.

Uncle Ace said: お会いできて光栄ですよ、芦田さん。あなたが苦しい立場におかれていることは理解しているつもりです。

Ashida quick-translated. *"I am happy to meet you, Doctor. I understand your embarrassment in this moment."* It was perfect Japanese.

He stood and bowed. Uncle Ace stood and bowed. Parker went cardiac red.

He poked Ashida. It hurt. Ashida's arm went numb.

"You hate the fucking Chinese. Don't tell me you don't. Run this interrogation and get the information we need."

Ashida said: わたしにはあなたに対して含むことは何もありませんよ、クワンさん。Ashida brain-translated back. *"I bear Mr. Kwan only goodwill."*

Uncle Ace smiled.

Parker said, "You dirty yellow savages. How fucking dare you?"

Uncle Ace winked at Ashida. Uncle Ace resumed his knife manicure.

Parker said, "Hit him."

Ashida said, "No."

Uncle Ace smiled.

The busboys watched. Ashida watched them. They held their knives against their legs.

Parker said, "Hit him."

Ashida said, "No."

Uncle Ace smiled.

The busboys stepped forward.

Parker said, "Hit him. You're a fucking Jap coward if you don't."

Ashida said, "No."

Uncle Ace laughed and winked. Parker stood up.

His knees bumped the table. The ashtray jumped. Cigarette butts flew. Parker jumped and went for Uncle Ace. Parker fell on the table, face-first.

Uncle Ace slid his chair back. Parker's weight dumped the table. The legs snapped. The table hit the floor. Parker rode it down, face-first.

Uncle Ace smiled at Ashida and walked to the kitchen. The busboys followed him in.

Parker flailed and tried to stand up. His glasses had shattered. Ashida knelt and held him down. The table creaked under their weight.

He's disordered and ruled by puerile emotion. He's not Dudley Smith.

58

KAY LAKE'S DIARY

LOS ANGELES | SATURDAY, DECEMBER 13, 1941

3:39 p.m.

I drew Scotty as he slept. I kept the bedroom dark and used the nightstand lamp as a framing device. It's midafternoon now; Scotty arrived in a state of up-all-night exhaustion. We live in an around-the-clock city. The sleeping Officer Robert S. Bennett exemplifies it.

Scotty's muscles are bunched and plainly reveal his recent exertions. He worked a Chinatown rope line last night, got fitful sleep in the Bureau cot room and went back to duty with his fellow Dudster goons Mike Breuning and Dick Carlisle. It was hours of file work on the "chump change" Watanabe murder case, which has planted a "wild hair up the ass" of Chief Jack Horrall. A trip to the Fort MacArthur stockade followed. It all inexplicably pertained to shrimp oil, fish oil, glass shards and the Watanabe house. Goons Breuning and Carlisle checked an arrestees' log, secured the address of a fish-canning setup operating out of a Japanese truck farm, and hustled Goon Scotty out to the far-east end of the San Fernando Valley. Goon Scotty found the journey south and precipitously north perplexing; it all pertained to "these white guys" trying to buy "Jap" property—sheer gobbledygook to him. Goon Breuning and Goon Scotty strongarmed the Japs as Goon Carlisle cleared out canning equipment to avoid a "public safety hazard." Goon Breuning spoke pidgin English to the Japs, who revealed "goose egg." Goon Scotty was ordered to slap the Japs around, while Goon Carlisle exhorted them to silence. Goon Scotty still didn't know what the Dudster and his lads were after. My sweet boy didn't like slapping around passive Japs, although he'd killed a "Chinaman" Thursday night.

Early-wartime Los Angeles and around-the-clock adventures. My rough boy, clenched in his sleep.

I shifted the lamp and threw light on the bed space beside Scotty. I drew Claire De Haven as herself and Claire as Joan of Arc. I placed the two hers beside my naked lover. I studied the drawings and saw how Claire achieved such seamless transformation.

It was all belief. She did not exist beyond her imagination. Thinking things so made them so. She feigned irony and possessed only zealotry. She seized on William H. Parker and me because we were both of her ilk. We were both her enemies and her only blood kin.

It was dusk now. I turned off the lamp and got back into bed beside Scotty. My rough boy was deeply asleep. I put my head to his chest and felt the cadence of his heartbeat.

Lee came home. I heard him enter his separate bedroom and shut the door behind him. Dance music drifted from clubs down on the Strip; a bright moon skittered through storm clouds and lit Scotty up at odd moments. I thought of Claire's party coming up next Monday night and wondered why Dr. Lesnick's office hadn't returned my call requesting a second appointment. The probable answer? Claire had spoken to the traitorous doctor. She said, "Let it go, Saul. She's mine."

Such sleep. Robert Sinclair Bennett, such a spell you're in. You're off in the shadow play of Dudley Smith. You're in as deep as I am with William H. Parker.

I lay there for hours. The music began to soften as 2:00 a.m. neared. "Moonlight Serenade" always announced last call at Dave's Blue Room. How many times had I dreamt that Bucky and I would dance to that tune? Where did Hideo Ashida's dreams of Bucky take him?

"Moonlight Serenade" ebbed away from me. I opened my eyes in a daylight-bright bedroom. Scotty was gone.

The door was half-open. Scotty was out in the hall. He was dressed in yesterday's clothes. He was talking with Lee.

Scotty, in his shoulder holster and tartan bow tie. Lee, in his uniform.

They stood too close to each other. Lee said, "I could take you." Scotty hooked a thumb back to me. He said, "You know where I'll be if you'd like to try."

Rough boys—neither one blinked.

December 14, 1941

59

LOS ANGELES | SUNDAY, DECEMBER 14, 1941

7:27 a.m.

Helen went to Mass. He should have gone. Dudley Smith scared him away.

Parker stood in his den. He sipped an eye-opener and stared at his graphs. *Watanabe Case/Details-Chronology* hexed him.

Dudley shot him a second summary. It hit his tray before that outburst at Kwan's. It was verifiably accurate. It might be fraudulent.

He should have gone to Mass. He could have asked Dudley. Ace Kwan would have briefed him per the scene.

Parker sipped vodka with lemon juice and cayenne. Jesuit priests developed the formula. It was a prepledge purgative. It followed quixotic missions and mortifying acts.

He'd stumbled out of Kwan's. He got to his car and radio'd the Fort MacArthur stockade. He got an address for the Hodaka cannery and drove out there.

He found the workers cowed. They refused to talk. His guess? Dudley's boys preceded him. They extracted information and blocked future access.

The priests' brew burned his guts. It alleviated withdrawal pain. It postponed The Pledge.

Parker jotted up his graph. He thought of Uncle Ace. The fuck blinked just once.

He tossed out a parlay. Jimmy Namura/facial scars/Lin Chung and Terry Lux. The toss-out made Ace blink. Parker annotated the moment and added question marks.

The priests' brew slaked his craving. It got dangerous here. He had to prevent The Warm Glide.

Parker drew swastikas and Lugers. Parker drew swastikas embossed on Luger grips. The grip falls from Jim Larkin's hand. The

Lugers in Larkin's bungalow. Alleged Lugers at the Deutsches Haus. The Lugers fired at the pharmacy and Watanabe house.

The graph hexed him. Ditto the priests' brew.

Parker killed the brew and grabbed his briefcase. The pepper burn doubled him over. He walked out to his car and sat through a jolt of cramps.

He found a radio prayer show. A priest extolled self-restraint as a duty. He drove west and lost track of the time.

The beach. Army trucks and new seaside bunkers. Santa Monica Canyon. Larkin's bungalow.

Quixotic mission. Do it anyway. That trick you learned way back. Twist the knob and hit the jamb, just so.

He walked to the door.

He did it.

The bends returned. The Thirst returned. The door popped—just so.

He stepped inside and shut it. The living room koi stream charmed him. He walked to the kitchen and found some algae flakes. He walked back and fed the koi.

They darted and gorged. Parker fought off cramps and walked to the bedroom. He fed the terrace koi. He opened the closet. Seventeen Nazi Lugers—right there on pegs.

He pulled them off and stuffed them in his briefcase. He broke a sweat. It smelled like grain booze and lemon juice. He walked outside and closed the door. Hideo Ashida stood by his car.

The bends. Seventeen guns in his briefcase. They banged and scraped. They weighed fifty-odd pounds.

Parker lugged the guns over. They banged and scraped. Ashida stood prim.

"I took Larkin's Lugers. We can test-fire them at the lab and compare the rounds to the spent round at the house."

Ashida said, "The spents at the house and pharmacy were too degraded to serve as specific exemplars. If we test-fire these guns, we'll get similar erosion, and any results we obtain will be unverifiable. I'm reasonably sure that all the guns in this welter of cases came from the Deutsches Haus. We'll have to settle for that assumption."

Parker said, "You can print-dust the guns. We don't have a print card on Larkin, but we could place him, or *someone*, inside the house.

The evidence would serve to corroborate the car in the driveway and the hit-and-run."

Ashida said, "Yes. I came back to steal the guns for that purpose."

Parker lowered the briefcase. Ashida reached in his pocket and pulled out a lozenge. *Sir, your breath stinks.*

He forked it over. Parker unwrapped it and popped it in his mouth. Clove and licorice. A kid's palliative. Deadwood, 1910.

Ashida said, "The Sheriff's hardly worked the job, so I canvassed the block here myself. I learned that Mr. Larkin was friendly, garrulous, enjoyed the company of younger people, and loved to bicycle. He did not entertain at his home. His neighbors did not know that he was fixated on Japanese culture, or that he harbored Axis moneys and German firearms. The radio reported him to have been a British Intelligence agent in the first war, which I find credible. None of his neighbors knew it, which I find revealing."

Parker crunched the lozenge. Ashida passed him a stick of Beemans pepsin gum.

He unwrapped it. "The lone wolf with the secret life."

"Yes. Who made calls from public booths and carried telephone slugs."

Parker chewed the goddamn gum. "The Watanabes called booths in Santa Monica."

"Yes, and I checked the specific locations. They were all on Lincoln Boulevard, no more than two miles from here."

"It's all Fifth Column. It reeks of it. The secretive old intelligence man, the secretive Japanese."

Ashida said, "We don't know who called those pay phones or who they talked to."

Parker said, "I'm going to subpoena the phone records on those booths. Outgoing calls are recorded, and maybe we can get a take on the incoming ones."

Ashida shook his head. "It's a very long process you're suggesting. PC Bell is buried in War Department work now. Any legal request will attenuate."

Parker spit out his gum. "I fed the koi."

Ashida passed him a fresh stick. "I was going to."

Parker unwrapped it. "We'll find them a good home when all this is over."

"Yes. I was thinking that."

Parker pointed to their cars. They eschewed more preamble. Ashida nodded yes.

They got in, they U-turned, they convoyed downtown. Ashida took the lead. Parker bumper-locked him. He chewed the fucking chewing gum dry.

They made Central Station and walked up to the lab. It was theirs, solo. Ashida locked them in.

Parker wedged a chair under the doorknob. Ashida cleared off an exam table. Parker laid the Lugers out.

Ashida laid out a pack of gum and a box of cough drops. Parker nodded—*Yeah, okay*.

Ashida tagged the Lugers—nos. 1 to 17. Parker chewed gum and watched him work.

The bends subsided. Latent booze evaporated. The cayenne burned his mouth. The shakes might or might not come today. The Thirst Denied would start tomorrow.

Ashida worked. Parker watched. He chewed gum and sucked cough drops. He drank left-behind coffee.

Ashida donned rubber gloves and earmuffs. He loaded all seventeen Lugers and toggled in test rounds. He held them lightly to avoid print smears.

He fired all seventeen Lugers. The ballistics tunnel vibrated. He retrieved the spent rounds. They were all cracked in half.

Parker watched. Ashida eyeball-checked the firing-pin marks. He lit up and bowed.

"I was right. These guns, the gun in the pharmacy heist and the gun fired at the Watanabe house all came from the same ordnance batch. We have the same firing-pin malfunctions on all three sets."

Parker recalled something. "I was booking those humps from the Deutsches Haus raid. One of them said the place had been burglarized Monday night. He said silencers and Lugers were stolen. We didn't find any during the raid, so that absolved them on illegal gun-sale charges. I thought he was just covering up on that, so I let it go. Now, I'm thinking there really was a 459."

Ashida gulped and flinched. Ashida looked away. Parker eagle-eyed him. *See those neck veins pulse?*

"All five of the men made bail. The *Mirror* ran a piece on it."

Ashida kept his eyes down. Parker stepped up close to him. Ashida backed away.

He did it. He B & E'd the Deutsches Haus.

Parker backed away. Parker looked down. Parker looked up and smiled. Ashida looked up and saw him. Ashida smiled. They bowed in formal sync.

Parker turned away. The moment needed air.

He chewed gum. He sucked cough drops. He turned back around. Ashida was back in his prim skin. Parker watched him work.

His print gear stood ready. Powder/brush/ninhydrin/Scotch tape. He laid the Lugers out beside them. He tape-tagged them—1 to 17.

He held pencils down the barrels. He dusted and sprayed surfaces. Smudges and streaks appeared. Ashida eyeball-scanned the surfaces. Guns nos. 1 to 5: smudges, smears and streaks.

Ashida worked. Parker watched. Ashida dusted gun no. 6. More smears, more smudges. Spray now. Spray that smooth grip first.

He did it. Parker tracked his eyes and caught the BINGO. *Pop!*—there's a right-index fingerprint.

Ashida rolled tape over the print and got a transparent lift. He stuck the tape to a print strip. He opened a drawer and pulled out a file exemplar. "Watanabe/12-7-41/unknown right-index print."

Ashida studied the exemplar. Ashida rigged a microscope and examined the new lift. He went back and forth three times. He was stranglehold intent.

Parker held his breath. His chewing gum went dry. Ashida tapped the file card.

"It's a match. I lifted an unknown print at the house last Sunday. There's no way to know if it's Larkin himself, because we've got no sample on him. This new print is a perfect fit. A man touched one of Larkin's guns, and we've placed him in the house now. We're closing it all in."

60

LOS ANGELES | SUNDAY, DECEMBER 14, 1941

8:08 p.m.

It was elegant. It was egalitarian. It was a most star-studded bash. Ben Siegel beats the rap. The Trocadero swings tonight!

Jimmie Lunceford and his Orchestra. Tantrum-tossing Harry Cohn. "Jittery Joe" Kennedy. Joan Crawford, ogling Scotty Bennett. Sheriff Gene Biscailuz, news nabob Sid Hudgens, three dozen jarheads.

Benny invited the lads. He oozed patriotic largesse. He waltzed on the "Big Greenie" Greenberg snuff. Benny showed off shakedown snapshots. Bill McPherson hosed a darky girl in boots.

Dudley circulated. Mike Breuning and Dick Carlisle jawed with Dot Rothstein. Jack Webb dogged Sheriff Gene and plagued him with kid bullshit. Ellen Drew and Elmer Jackson bobbed for apples in rum punch.

Jack Kennedy fucked Ellen yesterday. Ellen whored for Brenda Allen between ingénue stints. Benny lined up Brenda girls for the jarheads. Herr Siegel, the Jew Santa Claus.

Dudley circulated. Jimmie and his boys launched a raucous "Lunceford Special." Clarinets swayed. Trombone slides waggled. The Troc was all bonhomie.

Packed dance floor, swamped tables, standing-room-only bar.

Time tipped. New Year's, '38. He saw Bette here that first time. She was perched in a booth now. They'd shared lovers' looks. It was we'll-meet-later semaphore.

Bette sat with her froufrou hubby. He eager-eyed a waiter. Will homo hijinx ensue?

Dudley orbited. Benzedrine and Macallan '24. He chatted up Jewboy Harry. My smut-film plan—say ye yea or nay? Harry said he leaned toward yea—don't crowd me, you mick fuck.

Dudley circulated. Jittery Joe waved him over. Dudley hovered by his booth. They gabbed old times in Dublin and Boston. Yak, yak. Dudley's Army commission. Jack's L.A. gash run.

Joe brought up their smut jaunts to T.J. The Dotstress and Ruth

Mildred were grand company. Dudley outlined his smut scheme. Joe pledged twenty-five grand.

Joan Crawford and Scotty Bennett necked. Elmer Jackson and Ellen Drew jitterbugged. Brenda Allen swooped by and pulled Joe up to fox-trot.

A Benny goon sidled close. He handed Dudley an envelope. Dudley slit it and read the note inside.

That party list. Benny delivered the dish. Claire De Haven's do Monday night. Notable Reds had RSVP'd. It was a Commie conga line.

Miss Katherine Lake would be there. Miss Lake was spotted at Red Claire's last bash. Whiskey Bill's "outside deal." The Parker-Smith stalemate. *All allegiances must be scrutinized.*

Bette hit the dance floor. Dudley caught a flash of her green dress, aswirl. It was *kelly* green. She wore it for him.

She danced with a tall Marine. A short Marine cut in. She danced with him. A stout Marine cut in. She danced with him and waved to Dudley.

The room weaved. It reprised the '33 earthquake. Bette placed his world on springs.

The short Marine walked up. Dudley saluted him. The short Marine delivered a note. Dudley unfolded it.

"*D.S. I keep a suite upstairs. Join me after the festivities, please. Ever yours, B.D.*"

The short Marine vanished. Dudley kissed the note and caught patchouli. He orbited—Benzedrine and Macallan '24.

Scotty Bennett necked with Joan Crawford. Brenda Allen necked with the short Marine. The Dotstress and Ruth Mildred saw it and went *Uggggh*.

The wingding wound down. Jimmie Lunceford blared the national anthem and shooed folks to the doors. Bette headed for a staircase. Dudley watched her dress trail up the steps. Hubby and a swish waiter swapped anxious looks. They walked toward a cloakroom, seconds apart.

Hubby opened the door and ducked in. The waiter ducked in moments later. Dudley strolled over and peeped the keyhole. Hubby had the waiter's prick in his mouth.

This grand war. The world on springs. D.S. + B.D.—the heart and arrow.

The room evaporated. Couples swerved outside, entwined. Joan C. had Scotty B. fuckstruck.

Dudley walked up the staircase. Her door featured a cupid's-quiver knocker. He banged it. She opened up, sans pause.

They kissed in the doorway. Dudley unhooked the green dress. The straps caught on Bette's shoulders. He slid them off and pulled the green to her breasts. She wriggled the door shut. She stood on her tiptoes and kissed him. Champagne and tobacco—he knew her breath now.

Her mouth on him. His mouth in her—he wanted that. He picked her up and carried her. He looked for a kneeling spot.

A velvet-tufted sofa. Yes—that's your spot.

He put Bette down. He pushed up her dress. Her stockings were hooked to a garter belt. She said, "Dudley Liam Smith." He bit at her stocking snaps.

He bit them off. He ripped her stockings and dainties down to her feet. Bette said, "Dudley Liam Smith." She pulled at his hair and brought her hips up.

He found that her he wanted. She said his name. He learned that taste. She held his head down and pushed her hips up. He pulled at her breasts. She pulled his hair.

She pushed her hips and said his name. She thrashed and lost his name and went to gasps. She arched and pushed the sofa up against a wall. Her last thrash knocked over a lamp.

11:23 p.m.

"Dudley Liam Smith. Are you tired of hearing it?"

"No, darling. I am not."

"You can't be comfortable where you are."

"I'm a Church-bred lad. You can't imagine how familiar this is."

"I wouldn't want you to regard me as familiar."

"Consoling, then. Familiar only in the sense that I've imagined this moment a great many times."

"Dear, dear you. The big Irish cop with four daughters, while I'd give anything for just one."

"I have a fifth daughter, of illicit birth. She's living in Boston now. She's my favorite daughter, but I would lovingly bequeath her to you."

"Tell me about her."

"Her name is Elizabeth. She's seventeen, and quite gifted and lovely. She has evolved a peculiar narrative form with a blind friend of hers. She describes the action in motion pictures to him, as he concurrently hears the dialogue. It's quite a grand collaboration. She never falls behind in her description, and thus a young blind man is given God's gift of sight."

"I would like to meet that girl and witness that gift of hers."

"She'll be in Los Angeles, with her friend, for Christmas. I'll arrange an outing."

"Is she a sympathetic lapse between your bouts of brutality, Dudley? I say this because it reminds me of myself."

"Your perceptions honor me, darling. I imagined you as vividly lucid, but you are lucid in excess of your most potently imagined self."

"Such recognition you grant me. I'm jaded, you know. I outgrew fatuous acclaim some time ago. 'It takes one to know one.' I see that adage at work here."

"I won't belabor the point. I wouldn't want you to consider me familiar."

"You're redefining 'familiar' for me. This unseemly posture of ours has me questioning concepts and acts."

"Dear, dear girl. You're getting sleepy, I can tell."

"I am sleepy. And I'm a selfish woman who has every intention of falling asleep right here."

"I would not want to keep you from that."

"My God, those young Marines. I do not want one single one of them to die. I don't want it, and I will not permit it. Shit, those fucking Japs."

"You're yawning, lass. Say something grand before you fall off."

"Dudley Liam Smith, please kill a Jap for me."

11:54 p.m.

Bette slept. He didn't. He was Church-bred. He shifted his knees and refined the posture. He reached that toppled lamp and killed the room light.

The Macallan '24 wore off. The Benzedrine stayed. Bette slept, he didn't. Cars backfired out on the Strip. Doors slammed down in the Troc. Pictures flashed off their echoes.

His mother hit him. His mother snapped a razor strap. He held his gun and kept his head on Bette's breasts.

The sounds dwindled. The sky went second-by-second bright. He stood up and rubbed his knees alive. He arranged Bette head-to-toe on the sofa. He placed his suit coat over her and walked to his car in shirtsleeves.

The world rolled on springs. He smelled Bette all over him. He took Sunset east and cut south on Virgil.

The Melrose stoplight stalled him. He looked around and saw a lanky Jap in a phone booth. He was making Jap-like gestures on a call.

The light went green. Dudley pulled to the curb and got out. The Jap blathered on. Dudley walked to the booth. The Jap noticed him.

What's this? Where's your coat? What's with that gun?

Dudley pulled that gun and shot the Jap four times in the face. It blew out the back of his head and the back of the booth.

Dudley said, "For Bette Davis."

December 15, 1941

61

LOS ANGELES | MONDAY, DECEMBER 15, 1941

6:17 a.m.

Football practice. Early-morning scrimmage. His standard window view.

His apartment provided the view. He rented it for the view. All roads led back to Belmont. Green-and-black 4-ever.

Ashida watched a block-and-pass drill. He made the two receivers Bucky. Both boys fumbled. He shut his eyes and made them *more* Bucky. *His* Bucky snagged the ball and ran through the goalposts.

He walked to the living room closet. His early trip-wire gizmo was stashed on a shelf. He kept his photo box beside it.

The pictures were paper-sheathed and sequestered from sunlight. He'd hidden the camera behind a ledge, facing the showers. A tight-sprung wristwatch tripped the shutter.

Basketball practice ended at 4:00. The camera clicked at two-minute intervals. Lucky clicks caught Bucky, stripped.

Ashida studied the photos. He held them by the edges and left no fingerprints. He recalled his lab work with Bill Parker. They turned up that one print. He dusted the other Lugers, with nil results. Parker nailed him for the Deutsches Haus 459. They eschewed an explicit exchange.

The photos were perfect. *Bucky* was perfect. The black-and-white was perfectly etched. Kay Lake tugged at him. He assumed her perspective. The silly huntress mooned for Bucky Bleichert. What would she think of *his* Bucky, nude?

She called him last night. It was all about that crazy film. A muckraking exposé. Roundups as pogrom. It derived from her maneuverings with Bill Parker.

She invited him to a party tonight. "Comrade" Claire was tossing a do. He agreed to go.

Ashida replaced the photos and studied the gizmo. The lens mount was firm. The shutter wire was taut. The switch mechanism had chipped over time. It rendered the gizmo *un*perfect.

The new gizmo was still stashed outside Whalen's Drugstore. Secondary switch gears were tucked in. It was early. He could remove the backup gears and refit the old gizmo.

He walked downstairs. He got his car and drove downtown. Traffic was light. It supplied a cognitive window. He brain-walked through the house.

Watanabe/187 P.C. Room by room, quadrant by quadrant. Nine days since the murders. His ten thousandth walk-through.

6th and Spring was morning quiet. He parked outside Whalen's and studied his gizmo. The casing held firm. The gizmo remained protected. He pulled the secondary switch gears and drove off.

He turned on the radio. The police band kicked in. Code 3—homicide at Melrose and Virgil.

Dead man in a phone booth. Gunshot wounds, close range. Lab men and morgue men requested. Ray Pinker and Thad Brown there now.

Ashida drove home. He walked upstairs and grabbed the a.m. *Herald.* He saw a news pic below the fold.

A Fed roust. A curio shop—1st and Alameda. Dick Hood, Ed Satterlee, two unknown Feds. One frightened Japanese man.

Two Feds held large swords. Two Feds held matching *SCABBARDS*. There it was. Hot off a fluke. Right at mental walk-through ten thousand.

Here's what he missed. Here's what Dudley missed.

There were no *SCABBARDS*. There were no *HOOKS* or *WALL PEGS* to hang the swords on. They were display items. They were always left out to see.

Ashida vibrated. Camera shutters clicked.

No scabbards.

No hooks or wall pegs.

No spackling or wall indentations. No wallpaper inconsistencies.

CLICK—ten thousand times. *CLICK*—ten thousand and one.

CLICK—the world's revving up now. *CLICK*—it's at silent-movie speed.

Ashida walked back downstairs. He got his car. The car drove him. He made Avenue 45 in one second. The house glowed ten thousand times too bright.

He let himself in. He stood still and reduced all that speed.

He walked through the living room. He scrutinized and confirmed. He walked through the dining room. He scrutinized and confirmed. He walked through the kitchen. Yes, scrutinized and—

"Hello, lad."

Ashida turned around. Dudley wore plaid suit pants and no coat.

"You embody revelation, lad. You have quite the large eyes at this moment."

"I know what we missed. That 'very obvious thing.' I came here to confirm it."

Dudley smiled. His neck was lipstick-smeared.

"Were you going to tell me? Or were you going to share the insight with Bill Parker exclusively?"

Ashida said, "I hadn't decided yet."

Dudley laughed. "How much evidence have you withheld? I'm curious about that, and about the extent of your collusion with Bill Parker."

Ashida gripped the sink ledge. "I'm not telling you."

Dudley said, "Tell me what I missed, then. Dazzle me with your circumlocutions."

Ashida smiled. "There were no scabbards. There were no wall pegs or hooks. I don't understand how we both overlooked it."

Dudley bowed. "Extrapolate, please."

Ashida said, "The killer brought the swords inside, in some form of conveyance, or had secreted them here on a prior visit. The act was premeditated, and conceived and embellished in a state of escalating psychosis. The family complied out of a racially and culturally regressed sense of shame, deriving from Nancy Watanabe's sexual misconduct and recent abortion, and Johnny Watanabe's incestuous voyeurism and probable molesting of Nancy. The motive for the killings is tripartite. The killer was driven by sexual animus, a sense of personal betrayal, and insane ideological conviction. The entire case rests on the distinction between the shade of mauve and various shades of purple. The mauve fibers on the victims' posteriors conclusively indict the killer, regardless of what you and Chief Horrall want. It might be the heavyset white man, seen in a purple sweater. It might be a Japanese man, wearing a much lighter-shade garment. Ceremonial swords are quasi-illegal. The curio shops that sell them keep no records. White collectors purchase the swords, along with Japanese patriarchs eager to celebrate their feudal heritage. We remain at an evidential dead end. The overall *motives* are becoming clear to me."

Dudley sniffed his shirt cuffs. Ashida smelled an orchid-content perfume.

"I will not require you to divulge what you've withheld from me. I will ask if you have suspects."

Ashida said, "I think I understand the crime, but I have no inkling as to who committed it. It feels very much like an open-file case to me."

"You said it yourself, Doctor. Chief Horrall and I would very much prefer a Japanese killer. I'm sure you've discussed our wishes with Captain Parker."

Ashida said, "Yes. We've discussed it."

"Have you discussed official versus unofficial justice? Has Whiskey Bill extolled the virtues of expedient justice to you?"

Ashida stepped close. Dudley Smith reeked of a woman.

"*You* explain it, Sergeant. *You* tell me what it means."

Dudley stepped closer. Their hands almost touched.

"A Japanese killer indicted by New Year's. A man so vile that the injustice of his conviction is monumentally overshadowed by the sheer monstrousness of the acts he's already committed, and fully justified by the interdiction of the future acts he will most assuredly commit. The real killer, perhaps uncovered at a later date, perhaps not. Anonymously extinguished, regardless of his race."

Ashida bowed. "That statement in no way offends me."

Dudley sniffed his shirt cuffs. The mad creature, moved by scent.

"I commend you for your actions at Kwan's Pagoda. Your composure in the face of Whiskey Bill's boorishness did not go unnoticed by Jack Horrall."

Ashida said, "The Chief's patronage is important to me."

Dudley said, "As it should be. The Chief will be meeting J. Edgar Hoover at Union Station this afternoon. Mr. Hoover is here to further implement his plans to abrogate the civil liberties of your people. Japanese radios and firearms will be confiscated. A good many more Japanese businesses will be forcibly closed. There will be a massive seizure of Japanese property and financial assets, and it is likely that your people will be made to wear demeaning armbands. I condemn these actions, even as I attempt to exploit them. I am grateful that my lawless streak allows me the latitude to maneuver, and to offer opportunities and protection to my colleagues and those who serve to further my designs. I feel that you have begun to emerge as a colleague."

Ashida went dry-mouthed. The kitchen went gas-stove hot.

Dudley said, "A Japanese man was murdered early this morning. His name was Goro Shigeta, and he was shot in a phone booth south of Hollywood. He appears to have been heavily in debt to bookies in Little Tokyo, and Thad Brown thinks he was killed to settle a gambling debt. I would disagree with that hypothesis. I think a white man motivated by misguided patriotism and racial hatred killed Mr. Shigeta, and I think that a good deal more of such hatred will be inflicted upon your people. I would like to spare you and your family the horror of it."

Ashida white-knuckled the sink ledge. "And, in return?"

"In return, I would like you to weigh the pros and cons of my patronage versus Bill Parker's."

Ashida said, "Yes, I'll keep an open mind."

Dudley half-bowed. "Grand. And, along those lines, I would like to show you something. It entails a trip to Malibu, tomorrow afternoon, and it pertains to a plan that Ace Kwan and I are working on. We are determined to assist members of the Japanese community in avoiding internment."

"Well-heeled members?"

Dudley winked and about-faced. He grabbed the dining room phone and dialed a number. Ashida heard a pick-up sound.

Dudley laughed. The phone line crackled. Dudley said, "Dr. Ashida" and "witness the procedure." Dudley listened and smiled.

Dudley said, "Our surgeon chum, Terry Lux." Dudley listened and smiled. Dudley said, "He's drying out Miss De Haven? Yes, I've heard of her."

"Comrade" Claire. Kay Lake. The party tonight. Some odd confluence.

Ace Kwan brayed on the telephone. It was surely *his* bray. Dudley winked and turned away. Ashida ducked out the kitchen door.

There—one last glance. A telling one—Dudley sniffs his shirt cuffs.

9:24 a.m.

He walked around the house. Neighbors evil-eyed him. *Who's that Jap? Oh, yeah—he's with the cops.*

Ashida bagged his car. He felt light-headed. The car drove him. It bypassed the lab. It drove him to Virgil and Melrose.

The booth was roped off. POLICE SEARCH AREA, NO TRESPASS, KEEP OUT. Black-and-whites, K-cars, meat wagons. Thad Brown, Nort Layman, Ray Pinker. Three morgue jockeys, poised with body sacks.

Ashida parked across the street. He pushed his seat back and watched.

Goro Shigeta had a face and no head. His rear skull was obliterated. His ears blew out with his brains. The killer stood close to him. The powder burns on his forehead indicated that. The shots shattered the rear phone-booth wall.

Ray Pinker bagged shell casings. They were fat. They were probably .45 ACPs. The morgue men scooped up brains.

Ashida watched. Simple details held him. The day slipped away.

The morgue men hauled off Shigeta. Thad Brown directed a canvassing crew. Bluesuits swarmed Virgil down to the south horizon and worked their way back. They buttonholed Brown. They went *Nix*, *nothing*, *nyet*.

Brown sent them home. The scene dispersed. A bluesuit lagged back and watchdogged the booth.

Ashida took off. The car drove him. He thought of Dudley Smith. Some woman marked the Mad Creature. *He* knew her scent, secondhand.

Ashida drove downtown. He double-parked outside the station and ran up to the lab. He was late for Claire De Haven's party. He kept spare dress clothes in his locker.

He beelined over. A note was taped to the door.

Hideo,

Per Watanabe/187 P.C.

Nort's got more on the bodies. (The thawing revealed an irregular threading on the wounds, & now Nort's convinced the swords found at the scene couldn't have made the incisions.) Also, he found minute traces of a rare Japanese narcotic poison in the victims' livers.

R.P.

It came at him, jumbled. He sifted it forensically. He layered in case logic. He shook it all out.

The killer brought the swords and smeared blood on them postmortem. He didn't kill them with the swords. The swords made the hesitation punctures only. The punctures were inflicted postmortem and were solely obfuscation. The narcotic poison anesthetized the Watanabes. It left them compliant and immobilized at the moment of their deaths. The killer killed them with a prosaic foreign implement or *THE KNIFE.*

Japanese narcotic poisons induce near-immediate retching. Predeath euphoria and narcoleptic states follow. The killer knew the Watanabes. The killer served them tea. They retched on their clothes. He made them change clothes in a euphoric state. Ryoshi wrote the suicide note then. The killer *was* Japanese or *knew* Japanese or decided to *risk* Ryoshi's predeath warning to the police. Ryoshi might have considered it all a prank and might not have known they were doomed. The purple-sweater white man was middle-aged and heavyset. Jim Larkin knew Japanese. Jim Larkin was a gaunt sixty-seven. The purple-sweater white man pulled up in a car. Jim Larkin had no driver's license and did not own an automobile. Jim Larkin was Fifth Column. The Watanabes were Fifth Column. Foreknowledge of Pearl Harbor defined all five deaths.

The Watanabes were dead. The killer lingered in the house. He washed their soiled clothes and hung them up to dry. *Why wash clothes on the day that you intend to die?* This hypothesis answered that question.

The killer served them tea in the kitchen. They retched onto slick linoleum. The killer wiped their vomit up. Feudal warlords dipped their knives in slow-acting poison. This killer did not. Japanese narcotic poison absorbed rapidly. It evaporated more rapidly in spilled blood. The poison should not have been identified. The killer did not bank on Nort Layman's near-insane persistence.

Ashida thought it all through.

Ashida thought, *THE KNIFE.*

62

KAY LAKE'S DIARY

LOS ANGELES | MONDAY, DECEMBER 15, 1941

8:09 p.m.

Comrade Hideo was late. The swell party went on without him.

I came in red. I'd dipped by Bullock's Wilshire and purchased a twin to Bill Parker's black cashmere dress. My dress matched the living room curtains. I wore it so that I could stand beside them and pose.

Claire's slaves were in attendance. Dalton Trumbo, Abner Biberman and John Howard Lawson represented the more feted Hollywood Left. I met them, traded war chat with them and moved on. An imperiously tall neighbor appeared and walked straight to the piano. It was Sergei Rachmaninoff—who appeared to be drunk. He attracted a range of comments on the Russian-front war; he said, "Fuck the men of the brave Red Army," and banged out loopy Scriabin.

Claire came as herself. Her red dress complimented mine; her Joan of Arc hair had grown out into a charming bob. She was gaunt. Claire, the martyred crusader. Claire, the dry-out-farm habitué. Claire, with the carriage to make dissolution stylish. Claire—who swirled around me and met my eyes like we were the only two in the room.

Claire, who was saving me. *We'll talk later, dear.* I represented *opportunity*. Her every look told me that.

Hideo was late. It discomfited me. He was the crux of my entrapment-seduction of Comrade Claire De Haven. I stood by the red drapes in my red dress and sipped a red-tinged Manhattan. It was my second party in as many nights.

I heard Jimmie Lunceford blasting from the Trocadero last evening and walked down to catch the occasion. Five scoots to the doorman got me in. Ben Siegel had been released from jail and had invited numerous cops, Marines and film colony folk to mark the moment. I played wallflower and observed. I thought I saw Scotty

Bennett duck out a side door, but couldn't be sure. The astonishing thing I saw was Dudley Smith trading looks with Bette Davis.

It was unmistakable and altogether romantic. Their glances were very much synchronized. Miss Davis danced with a series of Marines and played eye music with the Dudster. They are most certainly lovers.

I left then. There was no way to top *that* party favor. Early-wartime intermezzo—my dear God.

My current party favors were less glamorous. Andrea Lesnick stood across the room; she was a young and female version of her father, with identical nicotine-stained fingers. I recalled Bill Parker's brief. The Feds sprung Miss Lesnick from Tehachapi and used that wedge to turn Dr. Saul as a snitch. The doctor walked in the door a few minutes ago. He went directly to the bar, spritzed a highball and talked to a Chinese man dressed in a physician's white coat. I could tell that it was shoptalk. Reynolds Loftis mistook the Chinese man for a waiter and hit him up for a cocktail. The Chinese man gave him what for.

I was antsy. I had a small camera and miniature wire recorder in my purse and intended to put them to use. They were the filched property of Officer Lee Blanchard; Lee had used them during a loan-out assignment to Central Vice. I wanted Hideo Ashida to be here, and wanted Comrade Claire to see us together. I was quite anxious to make things occur and even more anxious to cause trouble.

Rachmaninoff segued to a dank piece by Karol Szymanowski. It eloquently rebutted the chirpy talk all around us. The late Mrs. Hamano got significant play. Likewise, the Japanese man shot in the phone booth. It was all over the radio. Chaz Minear pegged it as "escalating racial juju, jingo-imperialist style."

I was antsy. I felt ignored. I walked to the bar and mixed myself another Manhattan. Saul Lesnick and the Chinese man were still at it. The Chinese man's coat was embroidered with Asian symbols and "Lin Chung, M.D." The two men discussed eugenics. Lesnick called it "quite the compelling and inaccurate science, and surely the justification for ghastly racial misdeeds."

Lin Chung vehemently disagreed. He said, "Science very precise! Science very precise!"

Lesnick looked away from him. I followed his eyes to the patio. His daughter was summoning him.

Lesnick walked over. I trailed him and loitered near the door. Father and daughter lit cigarettes together and coughed in unison. Andrea said, "Bad this time, Daddy."

Lesnick said, "I'll run you out to Malibu, after the party. Dr. Terry will wean you. He's been doing day retreats with Claire. See how much better she looks?"

They looked for Claire and saw me. I turned and walked back into the living room. Claire crossed my line of sight. *Day retreats?* She was floatier than I had ever seen her.

It made me that much more antsy. I cut through conversational cliques and entered the downstairs bathroom. Parker wants evidence of Dope Fiend Claire? Let's toss the medicine chest.

I opened the chest and got out my camera. Parker wants it, Parker gets it. A row of pill vials. Morphine, phenobarbital and Dilaudid. All prescribed by Saul Lesnick, M.D.

I snapped three close-ups and noticed a small bottle on the shelf. The label bore Japanese characters. I unscrewed the top and looked in.

The bottle contained black hair dye. I photographed it, stashed the camera in my purse and went back to the party. Rachmaninoff had passed out on the piano keys. The front door opened; Hideo Ashida walked in.

He closed the door and stood poised. Lovely Hideo, in a navy hopsack blazer and gray slacks.

Stand there, darling. Be tentative. Your people are raping the civilized world. Jingo-imperialist L.A. is unjustly retaliating. Stand there and look handsome. Let the party swells take note. This audience was made for you.

Hideo stood by the door. *Yes—be forlorn and apprehensive. Be controversial, be* oppressed.

The jabber commenced. People looked over. Who's *He*? What's *He* doing here? He's not Chinese, like that doctor. That's right—he's Japanese, he's a *JAP.*

People touched one another. People gestured and looked at the door. I watched eyes travel. *Claire, darling—please look.*

She was talking to Reynolds Loftis. He watched eyes travel. *His* eyes went to the door. Claire followed his eyes. *Yes, love—please look.*

She did. I watched her dip and swoon—just a little. She set the stage for me.

I dropped my purse and ran to Hideo. I shouldered partygoers out of the way and knocked over drinks. I claimed the room and owned the room. Hideo saw me. He held out his arms. He wanted to hold me off—I knew it. I couldn't have that. I flew into him and kissed him before he could move.

He put his arms around me. It wasn't passion—he did it to hold himself up. I held his head and put my tongue in his mouth; he moved his tongue because he'd heard that men and women did that. It looked like a lovers' kiss. I put everything I had into it. Hideo went numb. The kiss tasted like mint mouthwash.

His arms went slack and dropped to his sides. I broke the embrace, to make it look synchronized. I slid an arm around his waist and swiveled us to face the party head-on. Hideo followed my lead perfectly.

We claimed the room. That brash girl and her shy lover. Aren't they sweet together? And *so* brave—with the war eight days old!

Everyone looked at us. Everyone clapped. Claire yelled, "Bravo!" Reynolds Loftis and Chaz Minear went *Woo-woo-woo!*

Hideo smiled. He was knock-kneed and seemed to be both keyed up and exhausted. We walked into the crowd. Handshakes, back claps and embraces engulfed us. People stated their names. The overlay went to cacophony. Hideo stated his name and let strangers touch him. I stepped back to let it all happen. Claire stepped into the fawners' circle and winked at me. I winked back; Claire slid an arm around Hideo's waist and led him out of the crowd. She hijacked my man with aplomb. I watched as she steered him to a divan.

The crowd watched. I ducked past the piano and the snoozing Rachmaninoff and retrieved my purse. I went up the staircase to the second floor as Comrades Hideo and Claire held center stage.

That hallway again. Those closed bedroom doors.

I went down the hall and jiggled knobs. Claire's bedroom and the bedroom beside it were unlocked; I entered the latter one first.

It was strewn with male clothes and toiletries. Shirt monograms gave it away. Reynolds Loftis and Chaz Minear shacked up here.

An armoire flanked the door. The first drawer was stuffed with male underwear; the second drawer held homosexual paraphernalia. There were spiked collars and a program for a transvestites' ball at Leo's Love Nest. There were photographs of W. H. Auden, naked on a beach with Reynolds and Chaz. There were matchbooks for the Tradesman and Knight in Armor bars, with men's first names and phone numbers jotted on the inside covers.

I photographed all of it. I went through the bottom drawer and found a single tract, stuffed under a sock pile.

The title was *J'accuse: The Los Angeles Police Reich, Volume III.* It ran twelve pages; I knew immediately that the lucid Claire was not the author. This tract defamed a Red Squad lieutenant named Carl Hull.

I skimmed the text and shot close-ups of the pages. Lieutenant Hull was a close friend and ideological consort of the then Lieutenant W. H. Parker. I added *alleged* to the indictment. Parker was surely prejudiced, but did not actively purvey racial hate. Lieutenant Hull was possessed of a scholarly mien during his on-duty hours. Come dusk, he became a "Night-Riding Nativist Nabob" and dragged Mexicans back over the border from the hindquarters of his white stallion. Lieutenant Hull asserted that *Mein Kampf* was the lost book of the Bible and that Jesus Christ was an Aryan and not a Jew. Lieutenant Hull was also a speechwriter for the Christian Nationalist Legion and the most infamous offshoots of the America First Committee.

I replaced the tract, dropped the camera into my purse and stepped back into the hall. No one saw me; all the revelry remained downstairs. I moved into Claire's bedroom and closed the door. I saw it, first thing—a new martyr had joined Joan of Arc.

Claire had pinned newspaper photos to the wall beside Joan. They depicted Nao Hamano, alive and smiling—and dead in the jail cell where she killed herself. I reached for my camera, then dropped it back in my purse.

No. Claire did not indict Bill Parker at his most self-damning. I had to extend the same reprieve.

I studied the pictures. Claire had pencil-stroked Nao Hamano's hairline. Little arrows revealed her intent. The black dye made sense now. Claire as Joan, Claire as Nao Hamano. A new transformation—immediate and of this war.

I walked back to the party. Admirers thronged Hideo; they ran monologues as he listened and played ethnic novelty act. Claire was sitting alone. She was holding a drink and a cigarette. I walked over and took them from her; our hands trembled as they brushed.

She said, "You create memorable moments, disappear and reappear. I'm not accusing you of anything. I'm commenting on your deliberate nature."

I finished off Claire's cigarette and scotch with bitters. I said, "I'm out of my depth with this crowd of yours. I've found my early-wartime boon companions, but two parties in one week is taxing. Your people are fascinating, but I have a limited capacity to observe and do nothing."

Claire pointed to Hideo. "Is he red-blooded? I see you as a woman of appetite, and I'm wondering if Dr. Ashida is up to your needs."

I laughed and doused the cigarette in her glass. It bought me a heartbeat. Claire found the entrance scene contrived—I knew it.

I said, "He isn't my only lover. I have a weakness for rowdier men, and Hideo fulfills me in ways that they can't."

"You're saying that he's socially relevant. You're saying he's a diffident lover, and a grand foil in your ongoing stage show."

She nailed you. Concede it. Allow her that triumph. Express chagrin.

"Yes. That's pretty much it."

I went to *crestfallen.* My shoulders sagged. I leaned back on the couch and fell into Claire's shadow.

She said, "Reynolds has an eye on him. I think he senses susceptibility and/or inclination."

Be blasé. Express mild titillation. You appreciate risqué address.

"I think not. Tell Reynolds I'll keep an eye on him, though. If Hideo loses interest in me, I'll attribute it to that and play Cupid for him."

Claire said, "Deft girl. So quick with the answers. I've known you less than a week, but you've quite captured me."

I said, "It's the war. Everything feels immediate. Relationships reveal their purpose over time, but the war won't allow for that. I'm going mad with a sense of purpose unfulfilled. I would assume that you are, too."

Claire touched my knee. "Bright girl. So alert to my moods. I'm enjoying day retreats at Terry Lux's clinic. Come out tomorrow. We'll take a mud bath and discuss purposeful things."

"That would be lovely."

"Andrea Lesnick will be there. We'll be representing the Wartime Female Disenfranchised."

"Will you come as Joan of Arc, then? I would hate to see you crop your hair again, but I'd be intrigued to watch you extend the performance."

Claire lit a cigarette. She snatched up a heavy lighter and replaced it with a too-brusque thud. *Dope.* I could tell that she needed it; I saw her drift off with the urge.

I said, "Our film idea is the closest thing I have to a purpose. I think we should film the roundups covertly, and refrain from editorializing. Our polemical strength rests in the imagery itself."

Claire said, "We'll discuss the matter tomorrow." She looked away from me and scanned the room. She blinked as she saw Saul Lesnick holding a medical bag.

Claire looked back to me. She said, "I'm committed to the film. I hope the lovely Dr. Ashida will participate."

We stood up to say good-bye for now. I stepped into Claire's shadow and let her be altogether more woman than I. She whispered, "Red becomes you, Comrade," and touched my waist.

She vanished then. She dipped between two men and reappeared on the staircase with Saul Lesnick. Her good-bye trumped me and left me breathless. I sat down and shut my eyes.

The room spun. Beverly Hills became Pearl Harbor eight days ago. I'd stopped at the Beverly Canon before the party. I caught the newsreel sandwiched between the two features. I saw footage of the *Arizona* aflame and Japanese planes strafing Wheeler Field. They mowed down a little boy who could have been Japanese.

A Marine was hawking war bonds in the lobby; he told me he was shipping out for Pearl the next week. He saluted a Navy ensign sharing a bag of popcorn with a woman. I recognized them from the *L.A. Times* society page and the backwash of my own life. The ensign was Jittery Joe Kennedy's playboy son; the woman was Ellen Drew. She costarred in Paramount turkeys and part-time whored for Brenda Allen. Ellen looked at me. She whispered, "That little boy," and started crying. It embarrassed Ensign Jack.

The room spun; I kept my eyes shut; I had a sense of Hideo Ashida adrift, a few feet away.

"I spoke to Mr. Rachmaninoff. He isn't very nice."

It was Andrea Lesnick speaking. I opened my eyes and motioned her to sit down. She kicked off her shoes and sat with her legs tucked under her. She wore nose-pinching glasses. I sensed her sensing us as jilted girls at loose ends.

I said, "He's the maestro. He doesn't have to be nice."

"All I did was ask him to play a favorite piece of mine."

"If it was the C-sharp Prelude, you probably touched a nerve."

"I might have confused him with another composer."

"That couldn't have helped."

Andrea laughed and lit a cigarette. Her movements precisely mimicked her father's. It was astonishing to observe.

My purse sat between us. I reached in and tapped the switch on the recorder. Andrea failed to notice it.

I said, "I'm in analysis with your father. I don't know if I should be talking with you. It might comprise an ethical breach."

Andrea said, "Don't be naïve. Papa's driving me to Malibu after the party. All I'll have to do is say, 'Your analysand, Miss Lake. Give me the goods, pretty please.' I'll know more about you than you know about yourself by the time we get to the beach."

"Well, now I know who to go to for gossip."

Andrea said, "It isn't me. I've been to the penitentiary, so I hate snitches. The Feds tried to get me to snitch Claire and her people, but I refused. Papa snitched to get me out, but he doesn't know that I know. I'm impolitic, you see—but I'm not an informant. It's not betrayal if you supply the information voluntarily, and without malice. I've been to the Lincoln Heights jail and Tehachapi, so I understand these things. Papa thinks I'm naïve, but I'm not. He blames himself for me going to jail, but I settled my own hash on that one. He's just a self-absorbed little Communist, and he thinks everything evolves from him. I'm horrible, aren't I? I play on my papa's guilt and get everything I want out of him."

She talked with her hands and waved her cigarette in time. Her dress was dusted with old ash burns.

"Does Claire know that your father informed on her? Do any of her people know?"

"Of course not. It's not betrayal if you hold your mud and don't say anything. Hold your mud is a penitentiary term. I got it from the lezzies at Tehachapi. They all looked liked Dust Bowl refugees, except that they're fat. They liked to watch the regular girls take showers, so now I only take baths when Papa tells me to. The worst lezzie was this Sheriff's matron named Dot Rothstein. She tried to get the regular girls to do things with a bar of soap shaped like a prick."

I shut my eyes. *Please stop talking. Please don't think I'm like you.*

Andrea said, "You think you're unique, but you're not. Everybody shuts their eyes when I talk about lezzies and the penitentiary. Everybody thinks I'm crazy, so don't think you're unique. It doesn't make me bad that I did it with girls. You think I'm crazy, but I'm just impolitic. I only did it with girls a few times, and I'm not a snitch."

I opened my eyes. Andrea's dress was covered with ash; I started to brush it off, then pulled my hand back. A waiter walked by with a drink tray. Andrea stood up and grabbed two whiskies. She said, "Don't think you're unique," and walked away.

I shut my eyes. I pretended that I was out on the town with Ellen Drew and Jack Kennedy. We went to the Trocadero; Dudley Smith and Bette Davis twirled by us on the dance floor. Ellen, Jack and I—quite the cutups. We had a late supper at Dave's Blue Room and rice cakes in Little Tokyo. There were no Jap roundups. There was no Andrea Lesnick, no Bill Parker, no Claire De Haven. I was very far away from this goddamn room.

The party noise subsided. I opened my eyes and saw the two Lesnicks walk out, draped around a comradely Sergei Rachmaninoff. He kissed the tops of their heads and made way for Hideo Ashida to walk out in front of them. I'd wanted to kiss Hideo good night, with an audience present. It didn't matter now—because I was a snitch.

Claire was gone. There was no one I wanted to bid good night or felt compelled to entrap. I gathered up my purse and coat and walked outside with a group of alleged Fifth Column strangers. The strangers dispersed in front of the house; I walked across the street to my car.

William H. Parker stepped out of the car parked behind mine. William H. Parker, in his slack uniform. William H. Parker, unsteady on his feet. William H. Parker, with no place to go at 2:00 a.m. William H. Parker, with nothing to do—except entrap me.

I walked up to him. William H. Parker, with his bourbon breath. William H. Parker, unshaven. William H. Parker, with his skivvies exposed and his shirt on inside out. William H. Parker, with his drooping gun belt.

I said, "How fucking dare you." I said, "I'm more Red than Claire De Haven, so indict me." I said, "If you saw me kiss Hideo Ashida, I meant it."

I called him a voyeur and a malicious martinet. I cursed his malevolent God and his sexless marriage. I was *this* close to him. I smelled the stale urine on his trousers. I asked him how often he passed out and pissed himself. I damned him for knowing how lonely I was and for exploiting my grotesque need for adventure. I was *this* close to him. I saw the spit bubbles on his lips and the caked grime at his collar. I saw the chain for the cross around his neck. I saw a film of tears over his eyes.

I must have shouted. House lights went on behind us. Parker did not move, Parker did not speak, Parker did not flinch or offer rebuttal.

More house lights went on. I willed Claire's lights to flare and expose us—and failed. I called Parker a parasite and a vampire. I brought up fresh invective and felt my voice crack. Parker was *this* close to me. I knew that he would never flinch or lower his eyes. I had no voice to extend the indictment.

I snapped first. I wheeled and got into my car as Parker stood mute. I smoked and watched the house lights dim over X number of minutes or hours. I checked my rearview mirror and saw that he'd gone. I cursed him for leaving me.

Two upstairs lights flared within Claire's house. I stared at the window brackets and willed movement. I succeeded this time.

Reynolds Loftis and Chaz Minear kissed. Claire pranced in a kimono. She had dyed her hair jet black.

They walked out of the light and left me alone. I became frightened. I conjured Bucky, Lee, Scotty, Hideo, Brenda and Elmer to keep me company. William H. Parker pushed his way in with them. I cursed him and banished him. He refused to go away.

I thought of Andrea Lesnick. I played the recording of her crazy remarks and indictment of me. It was worse than being scared and alone. I'd forgotten to turn off the device; the recording included a long pause and my tantrum spewed at Bill Parker. I sounded picayune and entirely ununique.

My voice faded into hoarse whispers and silence. I turned off the device and laid my head on the steering wheel. I didn't want to go home. I tried to sleep and grasped for consciousness every time I got close.

X number of hours brought dawn. Milk trucks made their rounds; children skipped off to school. Music drifted over from Claire's house. A small ensemble played "Perfidia."

December 16, 1941

63

LOS ANGELES | TUESDAY, DECEMBER 16, 1941

8:17 a.m.

Women.

Joan Woodard Conville and Kay Lake—persistent distractions. Bette Davis—hard to ignore.

Parker stood on the parade lawn. The Academy was hosting a *biiiiig* war-bond rally. Miss Davis was the surprise emcee.

Flags galore. A big lawn crowd. A dais packed with local hotshots. There's Miss Davis—sprinkling ruby dust.

Call-Me-Jack sucked in his gut. Two-Gun Davis leered. Bill McPherson stayed awake. Thad Brown and Archbishop Cantwell tittered. A *biiiiiig* question loomed. Why is Dudley Smith here?

Miss Davis strolled the dais. She moved man to man. She touched arms and left lifelong crushes. She curtsied for His Eminence. She moved on to Dudley. He stroked her leg under the table.

It can't be. It shouldn't *be. How COULD it be?*

Folding chairs covered the lawn. The crowd was half cops, half paying stiffs. Parker took his seat. He was dead-to-rights, far-gone shot to shit.

The sun burned his eyes. His head throbbed. His uniform chafed. Miss Conville and Miss Lake crawled around inside him.

He crawled away from Miss Lake and drove to Saint Vibiana's. The night watchman unlocked the sanctuary. He prayed for three hours straight.

He invoked the Holy Trinity and revoked The Thirst. He recited abstinence prayers. He emptied his backup jug outside the church.

He drove to the Bureau and cleaned up. He was emaciated. He'd worn his uniform shirt inside out.

He put on a fresh uniform. He brushed his teeth bloody. The duty sergeant brought him an envelope.

He opened it. His hands shook and tore the flap. The Northwestern cops delivered. There's Joan Woodard Conville.

There was one snapshot. It was backside-annotated. "Bowler, Wisconsin. 5/23/39."

She sat on a split-rail fence. She wore a plaid shirt, high boots and jodhpurs. Her hair was cinched and center-parted. She radiated a severe and breathtakingly implacable beauty.

He peeled the envelope at dawn. He'd frayed the picture already.

Bette Davis walked to the microphone. Cheers went up. She glanced at Dudley. Did the Dudster just *blush*?

Miss Davis spoke. The loudspeakers futzed and distorted her words. The men at the dais swooned.

". . . and three wonderful new members of the Los Angeles Auxiliary Police—the Hearst Rifle Team! They will now perform a daring trick with my very own unrelated namesake, James Edgar—"

The loudspeakers refutzed. Jim Davis hopped to the lawn and fired two .45's in the air. The crowd locomotive-cheered. A Negro man in jockey silks walked up a palomino. Parker recognized him. He played slaves in plantation films.

He helped Two-Gun Davis up on the horse. Davis kicked his spurs and charged the nag down to the edge of the lawn. He dismounted and stuck a cigarette between his lips. The crowd went nuts.

Parker scanned the dais. Call-Me-Jack wooed Miss Davis. Miss Davis smiled and rebuffed his binoculars. A balloon drifted by her. She stabbed her cigarette and popped it. The dais bigwigs cheered.

There's the riflemen. They were crouched out of sight, hambone eager. They're wearing ceremonial robes. They're packing .30-06's. They radiate *Klan*.

The crowd went all-the-way nuts. Parker got a jolt of the pre-shakes. Dudley stepped off the dais and vanished. Miss Davis waited ten seconds and scrammed off his cue. The Klan shits formed a line and aimed at Crazy Jim's cigarette.

Ready, aim, fire.

Three shots went off. Tobacco exploded forty yards out. The fucking cheers hurt.

Dudley walked toward the rose garden. Miss Davis hovered a discreet distance back. The garden was gussied up with DON'T TREAD ON ME flags. MPs flanked a table stacked with war bonds.

The Klan shits went to port arms. Parker quick-walked down to the parking lot and puked in a hedge. He heard rifle shots and covered his ears.

He saw Jim Davis drill a Mexican, back in '33. The shot missed the cigarette and took off his nose. He bled to death on the eighth hole at Wilshire Country Club.

He heard more shots and more cheers. He heard horses' hooves on the lawn. He heard "God Bless America," loudspeaker-canned.

He dropped his hands. He sucked in air and caught a wave of the bends. The lawn crowd dispersed and formed a bond-purchase line. He slow-walked around to the lawn.

Thad Brown was up on the dais. Call-Me-Jack and the Negro jockey traded quips. The Negro did a soft-shoe and promoted a buck off the Chief. Thad signaled Parker: *See El Jefe now.*

The Negro took off with his swag. Thad trailed him. Parker bolted the steps. Call-Me-Jack slid him a chair.

"You're off the Watanabe job. Your stunt with Ace Kwan queered it. You're lucky Ashida had a leash on you. Dud reports directly to me now. I advise you not to protest."

Parker said, "Yes, sir."

Jack scratched his balls. "You stay on the blackouts, the round-ups, and all our war-planning work. Chinatown's still iffy, so I'm sending Jim Davis in to lay some voodoo on the Chinks. You and Jim go back, so I want you to watchdog him."

Parker gripped the chair slats. "I want to enlist. You'd like to get rid of me. This is your chance."

Jack grinned. "Comedian. The fucking Marx brothers combined. First, you fuck us on those phone taps and save your pal Ashida's job. Now, you want to blow town while the Feds crawl up our ass."

Parker shut his eyes. Call-Me-Jack belched scotch and bitters. It reinstilled The Thirst.

"You screwed us and did us a shitload of good, Bill. We've got a leg up on the Feds because of you. Sid Hudgens will do a feature on the Watanabe mess when Dud clears it, which'll notch us some publicity to offset this Fed snafu. All in all, I'm ahead on you. Don't queer it with me like your queered it with Ace."

Parker said, "Yes, sir."

Sid H. waltzed the Webb kid by. Call-Me-Jack winked at them.

"Go home, Bill. You've got one, remember? Reacquaint yourself with the lovely Helen Schultz Parker. Remember her? I danced with her at your wedding."

Parker stepped off the stage. Wet grass put him into a slide. He caught himself on the railing and walked to the parking lot.

Simple sunlight hurt. His uniform felt like a bug swarm. He got out the picture and caught new details.

Her teeth were slightly crooked. Her hands were as big as most men's.

Thad Brown walked up. Parker said, "Horrall canned me."

Thad shrugged. "Dud'll get us a clean solve or hang it on some fiend who should have burned for deals ten times as bad. One of us will be Chief after the war, Bill. We'll thank our lucky stars we've got guys like the Dudster shoveling the shit for us."

"It rankles, Thad. Don't tell me it wouldn't rankle you."

Thad shrugged. "Dud's got four dead Japs in Highland Park. I've got a dead Jap in a phone booth. Dud's got no leads because there's a war on, and the Japs won't talk to white cops. The same shit applies to me. A solve's a solve, and the same thing goes for no-hopers. A dead Jap's a dead Jap, and white cops didn't start this war."

Sunlight hit the photo. Most redheads had freckles. Miss Conville did not.

Thad said, "Who is she?"

Parker got out his notebook and pen. His hand trembled. Thad noticed it. Parker jotted her particulars.

"Find her for me. Will you do that?"

Thad nodded. "Go home, Bill. Dead Japs are dead Japs. Pretend that you're like the rest of us for a while."

64

LOS ANGELES | TUESDAY, DECEMBER 16, 1941

9:50 a.m.

Call-Me-Jack said, "You and Bette Davis. Jesus."

Dudley said, "Yes, sir. Our Savior indeed."

"How did you finagle it?"

"Gaelic charm, sir."

"*She's* the charmer. Jesus, the line's backed up all the way to Chavez Ravine. Gene B. thinks she'll sell fifty G's."

"I took her for a spin through the ravine, sir. Mexican peasants swarmed the car. It was as if the Virgin of Guadalupe had appeared."

Call-Me-Jack belched. "Sid Hudgens is writing it up. 'Diva Davis Wows Boys in Blue. Grown Men Fall at Her Feet.' Jesus, and you're *screwing* her."

The Chief had an on-the-grounds hideout. It featured reclining seats scrounged off a train wreck. Ben Siegel donated the bar supplies.

A window overlooked the parade lawn. A wall peek scoped the officers' lounge. Dudley walked over and peeped the slot.

Mike, Dick and Scotty were there. Ditto the porcine Buzz. Three other men stood around. They were plainly vexed.

Jack lit a cigar. "What gives, Dud?"

Dudley leaned on the wall. "We're nine days in on the Watanabe case, sir."

"I read your second summary. The gist is 'Fuck those Japs, it's going nowhere.'"

Dudley said, "That's correct, sir."

Jack pinched a neck cyst. He was double-wide fat. Brenda Allen fucked him most Tuesdays. She said he was hung like a flea.

"I get the picture. It's a baffler, which fucking stews you. You'd like to close it out kosher, just to say you did it. Boo hoo, boo hoo. The war upstaged you, and now I've got you on a clock."

Dudley smiled. "Yes, sir. New Year's is sixteen days off."

Call-Me-Jack waved his cigar. "I canned Bill Parker."

"A wise move, sir."

"He fucked with Ace Kwan. We can't have that. Ace is the number-one Chinaman in this white man's town."

Dudley said, "He is, sir."

"The Ashida kid keeps popping up and making himself useful. He's like a fucking jack-in-the-box. He helped us on the phone-tap deal, and he threw down against Parker with Ace. He's chummy with Parker, then he comes in for the other guy. They had to be working rogue on the Watanabe job, which constituted another good reason to cut our fucking losses."

Dudley lit a cigarette. "Ace and I have conceived a wartime plan, sir. You'll be in for 5%. Young Hideo is essential to our endeavors."

Call-Me-Jack ghoul-grinned. "Tell me as much as you think I should know. You understand how I operate. I'm a see-no-evil/hear-no-evil sort of guy."

Dudley glanced out the window. Bette's bond line covered the lawn.

"The internment will produce a significant backlog of affluent Japs, indignant and anxious to avoid incarceration. Ace has tunnels under the Pagoda. They could house a hundred Japs, easily."

Call-Me-Jack sniffed the air. "I smell green. Give me a little taste, and cut me off before I start drooling."

Dudley smiled. "I know you know Terry Lux, sir. He hosts our softball games and dries out the film colony elite."

"Sure. Terry does nose jobs for Yids trying to pass. That, and he's a do-gooder. He did free work on those kids who got scorched in that pileup on the coast road."

"Terry's a face man, sir. He has quite the avid interest in eugenics and other advanced forms of racial science. My plan is to have him cut Japs to look Chink, which may or may not work, given that most white folks can't tell them apart. The fees will be quite lucrative, and the cut Japs will be able to comport openly in Chinatown, under Ace's high-priced protection. The procedure itself has not been perfected, but I am optimistic. There's also a smut-film angle that will certainly play out."

Jack buffed his badge. "I'm on the hook, Dud. Get to Ashida before I know too much."

Dudley said, "He is an astonishingly gifted forensic scientist. His gifts far exceed the legendary Ray Pinker's. I do not wish to see Dr. Ashida or any members of his family imprisoned, and I wish to vouch his sub-rosa employment with the Los Angeles Police Department for the duration of the war. I intend to ensure Dr. Ashida's services and employ him in my endeavors with Ace Kwan. He is unpopular in the Japanese community at this moment, but that will change when the Japs are hauled off en masse, and a handsome young Japanese man appears to explain the alternatives."

Jack tapped his wristwatch. "See-no-evil/hear-no-evil. That fucking stated, I will reiterate. I want a Jap killer indicted by New Year's—

no-tickee, no-washee, and I'll sign your Army release papers the second the grand jury complies. I talked to Sid H. before the rally. He's going over to the *Herald.* The Hearst Rifle Team boys are tight with Mr. Hearst, and they set it up. Mr. Hearst has been running hot since that *Citizen Kane* picture came out, and he's got a thermometer so far up his ass that it hurts. He's looking to make friends with some cops not adverse to cracking heads in Hollywood, and your name quite naturally came up. Sid plans to write some front-page spreads once you've got a suspect, so don't shilly-shally. He's bringing Jack Webb in as his legman, so we've got a friendly press on this one."

A ruckus erupted next door. Dudley checked the wall peek. Mike Breuning waved a Nazi flag. The new men had that caged-beast look. Call-Me-Jack waddled over.

"What gives? What's with the goddamn flag?"

Dudley said, "You know my boys, so I'll introduce the other lads. Left to right, we have Bill Koenig, Fritz Vogel and Douglas Waldner. The former two work the 77th Street DB. Waldner is on the Sheriff's. Their early-wartime loyalties are suspect, and properly so. The Bund, the Shirts, the Klan, the Christian Nationalist Crusade. I would say that my boys have just fulfilled their worst fears of exposure."

Jack went *Tut-tut.* "You're co-opting muscle. It's slick, son. Dudley Smith knows you fight fire with fire, so he brings in reinforcements."

"Just so, sir."

"Go to it, then. I've got an early lunch with Mayor Fletch and Ed Satterlee. We've got our own Jap shit to sort through."

Dudley clicked his heels, Kraut-style. Call-Me-Jack yukked and went out a side door. Laughter drifted up. Bette wooed the yokels. Men stretched tall. Their wives glared.

Call-Me-Jack sucked in his gut and stretched to his tiptoes. Bette saw him and made with the smiles. Dudley opened a connecting door. The lounge ruckus died.

He didn't know the new lads. They made him, fast. It's the Dudster. He's Jack Horrall's hard boy.

Koenig was Scotty Bennett size. Vogel exuded mean. Waldner had that fetching storm trooper look. It urged Jews to flee.

Dudley strolled up to them. He snatched the flag from Breuning and ripped it to tatters. Nobody moved, nobody breathed.

"You've heard the threat, and you know that I'll implement it. Raise your hands if you're in."

Vogel raised his hand. Koenig raised his hand. Waldner raised his hand. Scotty stood by and looked young. Meeks stood by and looked sullen. Breuning and Carlisle stood by. They issued subdued mean.

Dudley said, "You are now detached to the soon-to-be-celebrated Watanabe homicide case. You will work under my supervision and the direct orders of Sergeants Breuning and Carlisle. Your job is to locate and help us select a range of suitably coercible eyewitnesses, along with a range of suitably perverse Japanese suspects. For the latter, you will scour the Fort McArthur stockade, the Terminal Island penitentiary, the Hall of Justice jail, the Lincoln Heights jail and the various L.A. Police and Sheriff's divisional jails for politically incarcerated suspects with no alibis for the afternoon of Saturday, December 6. See Sergeants Breuning and Carlisle for more specific details."

They took it in. Koenig cracked his knuckles. Vogel snapped his suspenders. Waldner went *Ja, mein Führer.*

Vogel said, "I'm not squawking, and I don't mind this kind of work. You coming down on us feels indiscriminate, though. I know a lieutenant at Wilshire who's twice as jungled up as any of us."

Dudley said, "You're speaking of?"

"Carl Hull. I worked the Red Squad with him, under Jim Davis. He's a 100% America First. How's this? He wrote that speech that put Charles Lindbergh in the shit."

Indeed.

Hull was Bill Parker's confrère. Hull was a scholarly rightist. Bill Parker peruses a Deutsches Haus tract: *This looks like a left-wing tract in an outside deal I'm working.*

Waldner went antsy. Dudley goosed him. Waldner said, "Hull was in the Shirts. I used to see him at rallies."

Indeed.

Koenig went antsy. Dudley goosed him. Koenig said, "I saw Hull with that twit Bill Parker, over at Wilshire. It was the day before the Japs hit Pearl. It looked like they were cooking something up."

Carlisle said, "Nobody move. I know that look. The boss's wheels are turning."

Dudley winked at him. "Dick, lad. You and Mike find a copy of

Colonel Lindbergh's grand speech of September 11, and deliver it to Lieutenant Hull at Wilshire Station. Tell him to meet me at the Malibu Rendezvous restaurant at 4:00 p.m. today."

Breuning and Carlisle lit out. The new lads went *Huh?* Dudley shut his eyes. It quashed distractions.

He'd talked to Ed Satterlee. Ed said the L.A. Feds owned a fink psychiatrist. Kay Lake was seen leaving his office. A Red shrew named Claire De Haven befriended her. Kay Lake attended a party at the shrew's home last week. The shrew invited her to a second party held just last night. He was initially tweaked. Ben Siegel got him a guest list. Ace Kwan said Terry Lux was drying out Claire De Haven. Parker. Initial suspicions, strategic concerns. Confluence—the Feds and Dr. Saul Lesnick. The De Haven shrew and Kay Lake. Carl Hull and Bill Parker, "cooking something up." "Outside deal I'm working." All instinctive—and all unverified.

Dudley opened his eyes. Scotty Bennett loomed.

"Yes, lad?"

"I've got to tell someone. It's driving me nuts."

Dudley said, "Tell them what, lad?"

Scotty said, "I fucked Joan Crawford."

11:06 a.m.

He just missed Bette. He stepped outside and saw her Packard laying tracks.

She left the place gaga. Men fanned themselves—*whew!* Little boys compared lipstick-smacked cheeks.

Dudley lit out. He took the parkway-Valley route. He chased three bennies with cold coffee.

He hooked through Pasadena and Glendale. Ranch roads shot him to the Malibu hills. Ace Kwan and Lin Chung did the advance work. Terry Lux approved their guinea pig.

A Jap wino. Strong Jap physiognomy. A eugenicist's dream.

He phoned Hideo Ashida and told him 1:00 p.m. He said, "Lad, you can't afford to miss this show."

The Malibu hills played peekaboo with the ocean. The Channel Islands dipped off a cloud bank. The hill road hit the coast road and dead-ended. Dudley drove north to the spot.

Pacific Sanitarium. Right there, on the land side. Quite the grand spot.

A converted hacienda. Plush acreage. Lovely lawns and a putting green. Robed patients, out strolling. Lourdes for the dissolute rich.

Dudley parked in the *porte cochère*. Dr. Terry strolled out. Dressed in tennis whites, per always. Terry could *play*.

Terry closed out Big Bill Tilden once. Big Bill was in for shock treatments. It failed to curb his yen for young boys.

Dudley got out and stretched. Terry ambled up. Women found him enticing. He allegedly bounced both ways.

They shook hands. Terry dispensed a bone crusher. He squeezed tennis balls for a Grip of Steel.

"Dud. Always a pleasure."

"For me, as well, Doctor."

"Lin Chung said you observed the cut on a man named Namura."

Dudley lit a cigarette. "I did, yes. Lin was less than satisfied with the results."

Terry said, "Lin's a nose-job man. If your Jew daughter's got a big beak, Lin's the surgeon for you. Beyond that, he's a butcher. Beyond that, I don't know if mass-scale cuts on fugitive Japs is feasible. It might end up being a three- or four-step procedure, with ambiguous results. What I dig is the psychology and race science. The Japs and Chinks hate each other, and it's virtually impossible to tell them apart. You know the drill on Nanking, right? The Japs dumped Chink babies out of *airplanes. All* Japs feel superior to *all* Chinks. Now, you cut Japs to look Chink. I'm a eugenicist. The potential ramifications here wow me."

Dudley smiled and tossed his cigarette. Terry went *After you.*

They toured the grounds. Terry furnished narration. Hopheads and boozehounds strolled by them. They sipped purgative potions and cleansed their sapped souls.

There's Lupe Vélez. There's that L.A. loop. Ruth Mildred Cressmeyer scraped her. There's Ellen Drew. Jack Kennedy breezed through her life last weekend.

There's a frail quail. She's Andrea Lesnick. Her daddy's a psychiatrist and left-wing race man. Race science crossed political lines. God was dead. Let's build *Übermenschen* to replace him.

That loop again. Saul Lesnick, M.D. Kay Lake was seen at his office.

They entered the main building. Note the long corridor. Note the swank bedrooms and wide-open doors. Note the hopheads lashed to their beds. Watch them writhe and kick white horse.

That loop again. White horse was scarce in L.A. now. His coontown pushers were vexed. Carlos Madrano ran horse in Mexico. That loop—an insiders' cluster fuck.

The corridor hooked into an ell. Both sides were lined with steam rooms. Note the portholes. Dr. Terry liked to peep.

Dudley peeped. The patients' names and allotted times were taped to the doors.

There's Raoul Walsh. He's gouting sweat in the buff. There's Anita O'Day, pacing in steam clouds. There's a tall woman, perched on a ledge.

She's desiccated but regal. Her ribs show on one side only. Her breasts are asymmetrical. She's awash in sweat.

"Claire Katherine De Haven."

Kay Lake's new friend. Saul Lesnick's analysand. That loop as ratchet gear.

Click, one more notch. Claire De Haven, leftist dilettante. Fed informant Lesnick. Enter Miss Lake. Click—she could be a snitch herself.

Click—the irregular loop. Click—let's brace Carl Hull. Click—do I sense Bill Parker here?

He studied Claire De Haven. Her nipples were dark for such a fair woman. Dark veins ran through her breasts.

Terry smiled. *Who's the peeper now?* They walked down the hall. The cut room was small. A wizened Jap was strapped to a table-bed.

He was out cold. A plastic bag and feeder tube were hooked to his left wrist. Cutting tools were laid out on a tray.

Hideo Ashida stood by. He clasped his hands that classic Jap way.

Dudley said, "Dr. Lux, Dr. Ashida."

Terry said, "Doctor, a pleasure."

Ashida said, "A mutual pleasure, sir."

Terry donned rubber gloves. "Stand back five feet. There'll be blood."

Dudley stepped back. Ashida stepped back. The Jap wino dozed on.

Terry quick-raked his hair with barbers' shears and got close to his scalp. Terry alcohol-daubed his face and grease-pencil marked it. Terry clamped his head in a vise gadget clamped to the table.

He poked the man's face. A nurse walked in. Terry mock-growled at her.

She blushed. She placed a sponge tub between the wino's legs. Terry nodded. She rolled the tool tray over.

Knives, scalpels, skin peelers. Four bone saws. Skin clamps that resembled hair clips.

Terry dispensed winks. He flexed his fingers and picked up a scalpel. He leaned in and cut.

He peeled cheekbone flesh down to muscle strands and rolled it onto a clamp. The nurse sponged blood. Terry studied the strands.

"Maybe, maybe not. If you're looking for a quick assessment, you're out of luck. For this to work, we might need something like an assembly line. I think this man might need resinous injections to puff out his cheeks and alter his skin tone—and even then, you'd have more luck fixing him up with a 'Joe Wong' ID card."

A fly buzzed through the room. It circled Ashida's face. Ashida ignored the fly and studied the wino.

Terry went back in. He cut and stretched tendons. He sopped up blood and fixed studs to ledged bone. The nurse smeared absorbent putty below the wino's eyes.

Ashida watched. Dudley watched him watch. His eyes dipped to a window at precise intervals. The lad embodied astounding *focus.* Dudley checked his watch and timed the glances. Three minutes, exactly. Eyes right, eyes left. The procedure to the window and back.

The window framed a picnic lawn. Robed hopheads lingered. The lad glanced out with intent.

Terry cut and sawed bone. Blood sprayed the room. Ashida tracked the window. Five, six, seven times. There, now—see him blink.

There's Kay Lake, at a picnic table. She's embroiled with Andrea Lesnick.

Young Hideo and round-heeled Kay. Still chummy past their phone-tap pulls. That loop. Another ratchet click.

Terry sawed. Loose skin hit Dudley's shoe. He shook his foot and divested it. He walked out to the hallway.

Ashida walked out. Dudley read his gleam.

"Are you impressed? I would assume that this part of our plans would work to safeguard a fair number of your people."

Ashida said, "It can't possibly work, but I'm impressed."

Dudley lit a cigarette. "Tell me why, please."

"I'm impressed because it's a bold and radical measure. I'm impressed because it both acknowledges and plays hell with racial purity, and because it affirms the ultimate separation that defines race."

Dudley tingled. "You are a very bright penny, Hideo."

"Thank you, Dudley."

The saw noise escalated. Terry said, "Shit."

Ashida said, "I would like to shoot some movie footage with a friend of mine. She gave me a camera. Our intent is to expose the injustice of the roundups."

Ratchet click.

"They are indeed unjust. Proceed, then. You have my consent."

The saw noise escalated. Terry said, "Shit. I nicked the occipital ridge."

Ashida hovered close. Their coat sleeves brushed.

Dudley said, "My Japanese brother."

Ashida said, "My Irish brother."

3:41 p.m.

The saw noise got to him. Malibu '41 meets Dublin '19. Grafton Street—screams and sirens. The noise quashed his good-byes and pushed him outside.

The Malibu Rendezvous was straight across the road. Dudley jaywalked over. Army spotters had commandeered the parking lot. They manned machine guns and searchlights.

Dudley walked in. The motif was lacquered trophy fish and driftwood. Carl Hull had the place to himself. His head poked above a back booth.

A jukebox blared noise. Dudley pulled the plug. The *bam!* silence spooked Hull. He looked over and saw the Dudster. He bolted his drink and waved on a refill.

Dudley sat down across from him. Hull wore Navy ensign's blues. Call-Me-Jack okayed his enlistment. He'd heard the scuttlebutt.

"The getup surprises me, Carl. I didn't think you approved of this war."

The barman brought a triple. Dudley waved him away. Hull knocked back half of the juice.

"You don't, either. You don't sit things like this out, though. You know how it works."

"I do, yes."

Hull said, "So does Colonel Lindbergh. I wrote that speech for him, and so what? We both know the Jews engineered this war to put us in hock to the Reds. Your implied threat isn't much of a threat, and I can't figure out for the life of me why you're shaking me down."

Dudley smiled. "We weren't at war when you wrote that speech, but we're at war now. That fact renders my implied threat golden. The Jews are the Jews, and they are a grand scapegoat for all manner of the world's ills, although I hardly think that their shoddy business practices mandate genocide. You are politically sound only up to a point, Carl. You do not possess the sterling mind and brilliant acumen of your dear friend Bill Parker, and you are blinded by unintelligent hatred in a way that he is not. You flinched when I said 'Bill Parker,' Carl. I'm wondering why."

Hull jiggled his glass. Booze sloshed on the tablecloth.

"Wonder away, Dud."

Dudley said, "I'm monitoring Parker. I have no intention of upsetting the applecart of anything he or the two of you may be running outside of your normal duties. You hitched your star to the man a long time ago, and I am simply gathering intelligence to vouch my autonomy in the unfortunate event that grand Bill becomes Chief."

Hull unclenched. He stirred his drink and licked the swizzle stick.

"You're tweaking me for a reason. Tell me what you've got."

Dudley said, "I have a left-wing psychiatrist turned out by the Feds, and his dope-fiend daughter sprung from Tehachapi. I have a leftist woman named Claire De Haven, and Officer Lee Blanchard's inamorata, Katherine Lake."

Hull smiled. "We're operating the Lake girl. It was Bill and I, but I pulled out. We wanted to build a sedition profile on the De Haven woman and these Reds she lords it over. The real war starts when this one ends. You know that as well as I do. We wanted to get our feet wet and lay the groundwork for what's coming. I had a pink sheet on the Lake girl. We knew she was out for kicks and malleable beyond our wildest dreams. We sent her in to collect dirt on Claire De Haven, but I had second thoughts."

Dudley smiled. "And your second thoughts pertained to?"

Hull said, "Bill himself. The operation was a sweet deal, and justified all the way. Bill was out on a limb with it, though. He'd lost his sense of proportion, and I could tell that he was off the deep end on the girl."

Dudley shook his head. "Such zealotry saddens me, Carl. It is always naïvely conceived and fatuously executed. I would call Miss De Haven and her cell harmless. They may prove to be convenient scapegoats for aesthetic reasons, but I find 'sedition' an uncomfortable stretch. I may or may not ask you to monitor this silly pogrom for me. If you inform Bill Parker of our conversation, I will kill you."

65

LOS ANGELES | TUESDAY, DECEMBER 16, 1941

4:34 p.m.

Sentry posts ran down the coast. MPs scanned southbound traffic. The beachfront was jammed with machine-gun nests.

Ashida felt *Jap* and looked *Jap.* He was too *Jap* to get cut and look *Chink.* It wouldn't work anyway. The Lux-Smith plan was madness. He told Dudley that. The Japanese and Chinese were one race. Nationhood divided them. Biology did not. Terry Lux knew that. He simply wanted to *cut.*

The notion remained tantalizing. It was a controlled experiment spawned by world war. How would racially altered people behave? An all-new discipline of eugenic psychology results.

Ashida swerved inland. He couldn't risk a stop-and-frisk. He was stretched thin. He might blurt the names of his many white patrons. They were the ones stretching him.

He said good-bye to *Dudley* and huddled with *Kay.* She was soon to join *Claire* for a mud bath. *Claire* gave *Kay* camera gear for *Comrade Hideo.* He secured permission to film the roundups. *Comrade Dudley* granted consent.

The canyon was narrow-laned and twisty. He oversteered and induced fishtails. His foot slipped off the clutch.

He was exhausted. He'd been up since dawn yesterday. Every moment stretched him.

Kay's love charade stretched him. Claire stretched him. She cogently analyzed the roundups. She said, "Will you shoot some film for us, darling? Your eye would be invaluable."

He said, "Yes." It was easy. That fact astonished him.

He went home. He tried to sleep and failed. He got up and worked the Watanabe case.

He canvassed Japanese curio shops. He pressed on swords purchased by white men. Half the shop owners recognized him. They refused to converse. The other half said they knew zilch.

The roundups were on overdrive. He choked on the hate and fear. He saw Bill Parker, couched in his car. He appeared comatose. The Sunday-morning Parker was all raw-sober nerves. The Tuesday-morning Parker was half-dead.

He called the War Department and tried to track Jack Webb's lead. Jack said a sailor saw the purple-sweatered white man. The sailor shipped out of L.A. that night. He pressed a clerk on troop movements for December 6. The clerk refused to divulge.

He called PC Bell. He requested records for the Santa Monica pay phones. The clerk told him to submit the proper forms.

He went to the morgue and talked to Nort Layman. They discussed The Knife found at the Griffith Park scene. They reexamined the wound photos of the four dead Watanabes. They reexamined the frozen cadavers nine days postmortem.

They agreed. It might be The Knife, replicated. The Knife might be the murder weapon.

They discussed the poison found in the victims' livers. He detailed his tea-and-soiled-clothes theory. Nort found it credible. Nort identified the poison by its bond components. It was anachronistic and was not mass-produced under a brand name.

It could not be purchased wholesale or retail. A skilled chemist could manufacture it in large or small quantities. The killer was a skilled chemist or knew a skilled chemist. Said chemist was adept at ancient Asian chemistry.

The cut-through hit the Valley. Ashida took ranch roads to the Cahuenga Pass. Hollywood traffic was light. Full dusk was on. He could shoot Little Tokyo at twilight.

Sunset downtown, Alameda south. A sawhorse roadblock at 1st Street.

He pulled up short of the barricade. He rolled film into the camera. He screwed on a mid-range lens.

Metal wheels crunched. He tracked the sound to the far side of the roadblock. Four cops pulled a jumbo handcart into view. It was piled high with rifles and shotguns.

Small radios fell off and shattered. A fat Fed trailed the cart. He held a cocked revolver.

Ashida heard screams and smelled tear gas. A Japanese boy ran toward the cart, rubbing his eyes. The fat Fed fired over his head and blew out a second-floor window.

J. Edgar Hoover leaned on a government limo and watched. Hoover wore a camel-hair topcoat. His hair was pomaded. He was diminutive.

Ashida noticed a black-and-white parked three car lengths up. He knew that license plate. He walked up and checked the front seat.

Bill Parker sleeps again. He looks beyond half-dead now. A photograph rests on the dashboard.

A woman. Quite the stern beauty. Plaid shirt, jodhpurs, high boots.

Ashida studied the photo. It was sharp-contrast black-and-white. The woman was probably red-haired.

66

KAY LAKE'S DIARY

LOS ANGELES | TUESDAY, DECEMBER 16, 1941

6:41 p.m.

My separate-bedroom terrace blazed with light. Lee had strung up Christmas bulbs and laid out scuffed furniture meant to be rained on. The motif acknowledged the weather and the war. I wanted to perch here on winter nights and watch festivities down on the Strip; I wanted to kill the lights on the blackout nights that were sure to come. Sirens would sound; the city would go dark within moments. I wanted to be here for that.

Scotty and I sat in deck chairs and sipped bourbon. Tinseled Christmas trees and REMEMBER PEARL HARBOR! signs were interspersed and backlit all along Sunset. We linked hands every so often and stayed in our separate selves.

We had both been out in the world today. I'd sat naked in steamed mud and plotted revolution with a woman I intended to betray; Scotty had plotted a "pervert sweep" with Dudley Smith's boys. It was drudge work for the Watanabe case, an unfolding event that bewildered him—the boy who became a policeman less than a week ago. Still, he was a quick study. He was learning the rituals of the Los Angeles Police Department, and had begun to employ its vernacular.

Mike Breuning, Dick Carlisle and Buzz Meeks were "strong-arms." Three new cops had been co-opted for a stint of "heavy work." Their new duty was to "haul in Jap sex fiends," "ex-cons with perv jackets" and "ding-farm runaways." Bright boy, troubled boy—part pastor's son, part thug. You'd be tussling with Catholic lads and fucking me at the best hotel in Aberdeen if you weren't here with me now. The Bureau's New Year's dance is coming up. Wear your kilt and formal dinner jacket; I'll wear a black silk dress and a tartan sash to match your ensemble. Rest your hand on my leg and call me "Katherine," darling. You're imperiously tall. You make me wish that I was as tall as Claire *Katherine* De Haven.

Claire and I removed our robes and stepped into the mud bath; the mud was warm and caused us to get goose bumps. We took in each other's bodies as we slid in.

Claire was depleted from her dope-purging treatments and was quixotically alive with notions of apostasy. I thought she'd try to draw me out and trap me in falsehoods and contradictions. I was wrong. She wanted to discuss our movie.

I wanted to make a film devoid of stated text. That tactic would foil Bill Parker's attempts to deploy the film as evidence of sedition. It would nullify Parker's mission, while I made his mission my grand moment in the overall grand moment of the war. Claire was fixated on the roundups as a grave and immediate injustice. She considered Hideo Ashida to be the deus ex machina of the male Japanese psyche, and believed that he should editorialize on film. I agreed, but stipulated that anything he said must be void of inflammatory content. Claire said she planned to speak at a rally in Pershing Square Thursday morning. The rally loomed as a populist free-for-all. Gerald L. K. Smith would spew hate for the Christian Nationalist Crusade; the Young Socialist's Party and Bund would be there. Claire and Reynolds Loftis would speak themselves.

She said, "Darling, *you* should speak. I'm playing a hunch here. You could fire up our crowd, and the crew could film their reaction. You're right about actual speeches undercutting the force of the mise-en-scène. But you can *give* the speech, and we can capture the response."

I enthusiastically agreed. I would tell the crew to film my speech with full sound; I would make certain that that moment ran unexpurgated in the movie. The segment would mark my defiance of William H. Parker and would strike a blow to the heart of Claire's tormentor. Claire would never know the intent of this design. The film would invalidate me as a courtroom witness and accuser. Parker would not risk the embarrassment of my official dishonor. He would never know that I conceived this plan while naked with the woman he sought to destroy.

I looked down at the Strip. Scotty kept a hand on my knee and brooded. I heard Lee park his car in the driveway. He stabbed the keyhole a half dozen times and unlocked the front door; I could tell that he was drunk.

Scotty stretched and laced his hands behind his head. Lee walked upstairs and stepped out on the terrace. His uniform was rumpled; I knew he'd been scrounging at Kwan's.

Scotty turned around and looked at him. He said, "Hey, bub. How's the world treating you?"

Lee said, "Not so good."

Scotty said, "Why's that, bub?"

Lee said, "Don't call me 'bub,' you punk cocksucker."

I started to step in. Scotty squeezed my knee and stopped me. Quick boy—he reached back and unhooked his holster.

"*Blanchard*, then. How's the world treating you, *Blanchard*? How's tricks in Little Tokyo, *Blanchard*? It's a nice night, *Blanchard.* Why are you so bent on fucking it up?"

Lee unfastened his gun belt and lowered it to the floor. "Dudley hasn't uttered a fucking word to me since he started creaming for you, *Bennett.*"

Scotty said, "You sound like a fucking homo."

Lee balled his fists. Scotty stood up and gave me a look. It said *I'm sorry/things go this way/it wasn't my call.* I moved to the far edge of the terrace. My legs fluttered and held.

Scotty pointed to me. "Any man who'd skate on a woman like that is a fucking queer in my book."

They were three feet apart. I felt the pull go both ways. Scotty let his shoulder rig drop. They went for each other right there.

It was a three-foot charge and collision. They came in with their guards down and made no moves to block blows. Lee dropped two body shots below Scotty's arms, ducked his head and let Scotty swing high. Scotty swerved off balance; Lee threw a right uppercut and snapped his head back. Scotty staggered; Lee threw a hard left elbow straight at his nose. I heard bones break. Lee raised his head and caught a faceful of Scotty's blood. It blinded him. He flailed and rubbed his eyes. Scotty grabbed his head and bit off a piece of one ear. Lee screamed. Scotty spit the piece in his face and head-butted him. Lee's nose cracked and gouted blood. He screamed again; his arms were low; he was wide open.

Scotty took one step back and dug his feet in. He threw a left hook to Lee's rib cage and a right cross to his head. They connected; Lee reeled and stayed standing. He weaved and ducked his head. Scotty swung high and wide again, and got tangled up in his feet.

Lee had openings. Every Bucky Bleichert fight I'd seen gave me the diagram. I wanted it to end and didn't care how. The science of it moved me and felt ghastly all at once.

Scotty stumbled and tried to gain his balance; Lee threw left-right body shots and an in-tight uppercut. Scotty reeled and hit a chair back. Lee cocked a wide left hook. He launched it, missed Scotty's head and stumbled into him. Scotty had his balance now; they grappled and held each other upright.

Scotty jammed a knee between Lee's legs and jackknifed him.

Lee screamed and coughed blood. Scotty launched the wide left hook that Lee failed at. He aimed high and caught Lee's head coming up.

His head snapped at a near-right angle. I heard bones *shear* and started to scream "*No.*" My throat closed up; I choked on that single word.

Lee pitched forward. His eyes rolled back. Scotty threw left-right body shots. I heard Lee's ribs crack. He fell facedown on the terrace. Blood and tooth stubs poured from his mouth.

67

LOS ANGELES | TUESDAY, DECEMBER 16, 1941

8:21 p.m.

Church inhibited The Thirst. He had The Shakes now. He sequestered himself and fought off Desire.

The sanctuary was all his. That night watchman let him in. Saint Vibiana's, again.

Parker hogged a front pew. He gripped the pew back in front of him and numbed his arms. He was booze-free since Miss Lake's tirade.

He couldn't go home. Helen would be there. She'd see his tremors and propose a cure at some rummy priests' farm. He couldn't have it on his record.

Tremors hit his legs. He dug his feet into the floor and quashed them. He was ten times past exhausted. He spent the day dogging the Alien Squad. He kept falling asleep in his car.

His body and brain got disconnected. It induced all-day brainstorms. He called PC Bell and demanded the Santa Monica payphone records. A shift boss said they were buried in war work. Parker persisted. The shift boss caved. Look for a reply in two weeks.

His knees spasmed. Parker regripped the pew ledge. The Sweats would start soon.

He had an 8:00 a.m. meeting. He had eleven hours to ride The Hurt out and prepare. Fletch B.'s office. The now-standard Feds and politicos. J. Edgar Hoover and Preston Exley.

The Big G-man. The ex-cop turned construction king.

Preston ran Homicide during the mid-'30s. His cop son Thomas was killed on duty. Preston buried his grief in work. Preston gutted out recurring migraines. He built the Arroyo Seco Parkway. He built low-end houses for Negroes and high-end houses for whites. He's got a local internment plan—and he's got some high-level ears.

The Jitters hit. Parker roamed the pew rows. He picked up Bibles and read his way through the Psalms. He prayed for his neglected wife. He prayed for the success of the Lake/De Haven incursion and the destruction of Claire De Haven's cell. He prayed for the courage not to drink. He prayed for Miss Conville and Miss Lake.

His prayers consumed seven hours. He roamed pews and worked his legs numb. He walked to the altar. He lit candles for his lost ones.

His congressman granddad. His irresolute father. The Okies he drove out of L.A. The people he hurt in his craven reign under Jim Davis.

He stretched out on a pew. He bypassed sleep and got up at dawn. He walked outside and got his black-and-white. The Shakes were internal now.

He drove to City Hall. He cleaned up and changed uniforms. Strong coffee stirred his blood. He wrote a manpower-shortage report. He hit Fletch B.'s office, on time.

The door was open. The office swelled.

Fletch, Call-Me-Jack, Sheriff Gene. Ward Littell and Ed Satterlee. Fey Mr. Hoover. Handsome Preston Exley.

His skin itched. His bones ached. The de rigueur handshakes scared him. Here they come now.

He endured bone crushers. He endured de rigueur laughs. Mr. Hoover flashed cold eyes.

Preston said, "You're working too hard, Bill. Demand a month's vacation. I've got pull with the mayor."

Fletch laughed. Hoover shot him a look. Fletch snapped to and arranged chairs.

Hoover took the lead chair. Preston sat beside him. The rest of them got bleacher seats. Parker dug his feet into the floor. Muscle cramps loomed.

Hoover said, "Tangential matters first. The van robbery of December 10 interests me. The Sumitomo Bank is in the Federal Reserve System, and its Jap provenance is irrelevant. Mr. Littell, you have the floor."

Parker looked at Littell. Buzz Meeks had solved the case, sub rosa. The rubber bullets. Huey Cressmeyer's prints.

Littell said, "It's dead-stalled, sir. I don't see a solve on this one."

Hoover bristled. His nails were buffed. His shirt was stiff-starched. His Masonic pin was pink gold.

"No significant criminal cases directly or indirectly related to Federal cases or even remotely related to the current roundups of Japanese subversives are to go unsolved. No significant criminal cases directly or indirectly related to the internment of all Japs in the greater Los Angeles area are to go unsolved. The Bureau will be going after the Los Angeles Police Department in February of next year. The matter of the illegal phone taps strewn throughout City Hall will become public news. I am prepared to exonerate, absolve and push dirt under the rug in this matter. I would be more inclined to pursue that course if you heed my admonishings here."

Jack said, "We all swim in the same stream, sir. What's good for the goose is good for the gander, and municipal and Federal law enforcement will be well served to present a unified front. You may or may not know that an entire Jap family was murdered here in L.A. the day before Pearl Harbor. The lead investigator thinks the case will be wrapped up by New Year's. We've got a scribe for the Hearst rags by the nuts, and he's going to run a series of puff pieces in the *Herald*. I'll tell him to work in an FBI angle. Pork barrel, sir. One hand washes the other. *Comme ci, comme ça* on the phone-tap imbroglio. We fucked up, so now we pay the piper. That stated, I think we've come to a meeting of the minds on this one."

Fletch said, "Amen."

Sheriff Gene said, "Hear, hear."

Satterlee went Comanche. "White man smoke peace pipe. Wisdom prevail."

The shtick drew laughs. Parker fought stomach cramps. Hoover puffed his pocket square.

"The roundups, Ed. Update us in one minute or less."

Satterlee said, "We're going after the fishing boats in San Pedro Harbor, and we've got the Coast Guard backstopping us on that. We're confiscating Jap firearms and running ballistics tests to compare to the evidence in preexisting Federal and local cases. We're getting ready to deploy agents to search the houses, apartments and businesses of the Japs we've already got in custody."

Fletch said, "This is a well-oiled machine you're describing."

Jack said, "We're feeding Hirohito a shit sandwich."

Satterlee said, "There's a Jap bantamweight I like. 'Tornado' Tagawa. He's fighting Manny Gomez at the Legion Stadium next week. I've got money on him. Don't make me pop him before he takes that beaner out."

The shtick drew laughs. Hoover smiled at Satterlee. Parker sensed a simmering crush.

Sheriff Gene said, "I rolled on a coroner's bulletin last Saturday. It pertained to that homicide case that Chief Horrall brought up. Our boy Nort Layman found glass particles covered with shrimp oil on the victims' feet, and he requested information from hospitals and groceries statewide. I rolled to a grocery-store call up in Lancaster. Sure as shit, they'd been consigned an order of Jap-caught and -canned shrimp, and it was sure as shit full of crushed glass. The lead went dead there, but it sure as shit felt like Fifth Column stuff to me."

Jack said, "You're talking Greek here, Gene. I don't know about this aspect of the case, but I'll pass the information along to my man, Dudley Smith."

Satterlee shivered. "The Dudster. There's a piece of work."

Fletch said, "Amen, brother."

Jack said, "He's fucking Bette Davis. That's no shit. It's one for *Ripley's Believe It or Not.*"

Sheriff Gene looked at Parker. Telepathy, half-assed.

That bulletin. It ordered kickbacks to Parker himself. Sheriff Gene might know that. Call-Me-Jack dumped him off the case. Sheriff Gene might know that. Sheriff Gene was juked on Fifth Column grief. The Watanabe case? Outside his purview.

Hoover sniffed his boutonniere. It was early-morning fresh.

"We're running afield of our purpose here. Canned shrimp and Jap murder cases are not national-security priorities, while housing

Japs for the duration of the war is. You're at bat, Mr. Exley. I advise you to hit for the stands."

Preston winked. "Mr. Hoover demands brevity, so I'll get to it. A contiguous stretch of the eastern San Fernando Valley is dotted with Japanese-owned truck farms. The farms could be purchased from the Japs outright, leased for the length of the war, or legally confiscated under state or Federal security-seizure laws after the owners themselves have been detained. Internment camps could be erected on those sites, utilizing California state laws on eminent domain. The detainees would work the existing farmland under the direction of a private guard force employed by my firm. Profits would be dispersed to my firm and to local government, which would help to defray the cost of our part of the overall mass internment. Leased farms that generate *substantial* profits would pay out a *nominal* percentage of those profits to the incarcerated owners themselves. 'Trusty' Japs would be allowed the privilege of participating in a furlough program, where they would be bussed to factories in downtown L.A. to work under armed supervision, and returned to their compounds at night. They would pay for their room and board and would be rewarded for their cooperation by being permitted to retain a small portion of their paychecks. The linchpin of all aspects of this proposal is *proximity*. The San Fernando Valley adjoins L.A. proper. The initial transporting of interned Japs is thus expedited. The trusty-Jap shuttle is a simple, day-to-day milk run. The farm camps themselves will create a large-scale employment boom and resultant economic boom for the city and county of Los Angeles."

Feasible. Adroit. Casually malevolent. FAMILIAR, in that it—

Ward Littell made fists.

Hoover said, "Superb, Mr. Exley."

Call-Me-Jack said, "A grand slam, in my ballpark."

Fletch said, "Kudos, Preston. It lets us house and feed our own Japs, while we keep them close at hand."

Sheriff Gene said, "It takes the pressure off the county jails and those big internment centers the War Department is planning. My deputies could run shackle chains from the Valley to the job sites. The Japs are a green-thumbed race. They turn out high-quality produce, we sell it to every class eatery in town."

Satterlee said, "Ward Littell and Bill Parker look glum, so we know we're on the right track."

Ward said, "It's ghastly. It's depraved. It's something we'll all live to regret."

Fletch said, "Ward and Bill seem to be forgetting Pearl Harbor."

It's usurious. It's exploitative. It's FAMILIAR, in that it—

Parker fought off gut cramps. Parker thought it through.

It suggested the Watanabe case. It suggested the house and farm buyouts that Buzz Meeks revealed. Actual buyouts. Rebuffed buyouts. Rumored buyouts. Secretly recorded—in no way criminal.

It all played tangential. Preston's plan played insidious and legally sound. There were no farm-buyout links to murder.

The meeting broke up. Parker's brain waves dispersed. His cramps doubled down. His legs were gone. The crowd filed out. He waved from his chair.

Sheriff Gene walked back in. "How's the boy, Bill?"

"I'm all aces, Sheriff."

"I know you requested the kickbacks on that bulletin, and that Jack pulled you off the Watanabe job."

"That's right, Sheriff."

Sheriff Gene twirled his hat. "I'm still tweaked on that canned shrimp. I had a lab man examine that sample we got up in Lancaster. He said it was full of toxic human oils."

Parker yawned. "I'm off the case, sir."

"Sure, but you could hoof it down to Pedro and hook up with the Coast Guard. They're boarding some Jap shrimp boats today. It still reads Fifth Column to me. You could scoot down there and quench both our curiosities, if you've got a mind to."

Call-Me-Jack whistled. It was wicked shrill.

"Chinatown, Bill. Riot gear. You and Jim Davis, for old times' sake."

9:42 a.m.

"Riot gear" meant the tin hat and shotgun. "Riot gear" meant rock-salt rounds.

He took the elevator. The Bureau hallway buzzed. Lee Blanchard and that Bennett kid traded swats last night. The kid put Blanchard in Queen of Angels. Blanchard's shack babe inspired the grief.

How's *this* per cooze? Dud S. is sticking it to Bette Davis. *Es la verdad, muchacho.* Elmer Jackson saw them smooching at the Academy.

The briefing rooms buzzed. There's Dudley and his boys. Note the nose splint on Scotty Bennett. Note Sid Hudgens and Jack Webb, sitting in.

There's Thad Brown and a *Mirror* hack named Morty Bendish. Morty drooled for the dead-Jap-in-the-phone-booth caper. He wanted to lay in Pearl Harbor. The dead Jap fingered the attack. A Jap spy chilled his Jap ass and muzzled him. Thad said he found it far-fetched.

Parker signed out his riot gear. He suited up in the hallway and flexed his legs on the stairs. He made it to the garage. He drove to Chinatown.

He saw Jim Davis, outside Kwan's. Davis wore Army fatigues and packed a king-size shotgun. Uncle Ace stood beside him. His FDR cape drooped on the ground.

Parker ditched the car and walked up. Ace spit just short of his shoes. Davis said something in Chink. Ace replied in Chink and ambled off.

"Good morning, Bill."

"Chief."

"Like I always say, it's been 'Jim' since the grand jury sacked me."

Parker said, "All right. You're an ad hoc conscript. You're not the Chief."

Davis said, "You're boiling it out, I can tell. We'll get you a tonic at that herb joint in Ferguson's Alley."

The Hurt smothered him. He wore lead shoes. His shotgun weighed ten tons.

"Let's go, Jim. I want to get this day over with."

They walked Broadway north. Davis buttonholed passersby and dispensed Chink bons mots. Parker yawned through it. The Hurt paved new paths.

His legs fluttered. Sweat pooled and soaked his socks. Davis ran his mouth. *Aaah*, the old days.

The Bum Blockade. The vag sweeps. Jew-pawn FDR's campaign trips. Carl Hull and the Red Squad. Remember that Kraut hard-on, Fritz Vogel? Red riots in Pershing Square.

Bill, you stood tall there. We brought in mounted troops. We were the Cossacks. They were the rabble. Bring on the balalaika music and swords.

They waltzed. Tong boys jabbered and tong-eyed them. The Hurt moved to his head. His hat was too big. He sweat-soaked the band. The visor fell over his eyes.

Bill, you were good. How's Helen these days? You brought in Carlos Madrano. You finessed our extradition deal with the Staties. Bill the Brain. You walked me through depositions. You wrote my grand jury spiel. You brokered our strikebreaker agreement. The merchants' cabal still owes you.

They waltzed. The Hurt gored him. Davis wooed kids with bubble gum. They stopped at the herb joint. Davis ordered him a potion. It tasted like frog shit and dirt. It gave him X-ray eyes.

It put ants in his pants. It contained ground roots and mystical powder. They left the shop and stopped at a call box. The world took on pastel hues.

Parker called Sheriff Gene. He rogered that mission to Pedro. Sheriff Gene said to hit Pier 16. Ask for Lieutenant Duguay.

They waltzed. Parker popped sweat and weaved. His taste buds popped. He exhaled mystic dirt.

North Broadway buzzed. The tong truce was five days in. It felt abrogated already. Tong boys congregated. They wore their tong kerchiefs and switchblade-cleaned their nails. They fell in behind the fat Chink-o-phile and the sweaty cop.

Parker and Davis strolled. Shop owners braced the Big Bwana and whispered tips. Dewey Lem's a 459 man. Joe Chen's a 211 man. A Chinaman plugged that Jap in the phone booth. There's a tile game at Kwan's right now. It's high stakes, it's marathon. It's drawing Hollywood folk.

They waltzed. Parker waltzed behind mystic dirt. The creeping tong boys closed the gap. They're twelve yards, ten yards, eight yards back.

Hop Sing crept straight behind them. Four Families crept, right across the street. Parker kept looking back. The fucking tong fucks crept.

Parker got scared. The Hurt and that mystic dirt had him quivered. The Hop Sing fucks were *six* yards back. Four Families was straight across Broadway.

Davis said, "They're too close."

Mystic dirt. The Fear and The Hurt. They're creeping on rubber-soled—

Parker raised his shotgun. The fucks crept on. *Four* yards now. He jacked in a round and fired.

The shotgun buckled. Rock salt blew. He nailed four Chinks in one spread. Davis aimed across the street and tripped both triggers.

He launched bigger rounds. *His* Chinks went airborne. Parker's Chinks caught the salt chest-high. Their tong threads vaporized. Shards sliced straight through to their skin.

They screamed and turned tail. Parker pumped rounds and aimed at their backs. He sighted in tight. He squeezed the trigger, slow. He knocked them down and strafed the clothes off their backs.

The blasts spooked the locals. They turned tail and ran. Jim's Chinks screamed double-loud. One punk lost two fingers. One punk groped for chunks of his ass.

Screams. Tong fucks and locals, all high-decibel. Language-stew gobbledygook.

Jim Davis whipped out his dick and wagged it. Jim Davis yelled Chink insults.

The punks crawled. They were salt-sheared and shredded. They crawled through diced clothing and blood.

Davis walked across the street. Parker followed him. Davis wagged his dick at the punks on the ground and doused them with piss.

"It's an old-country custom, hoss. I own their souls from here on in."

11:16 a.m.

He bolted. Mystic dirt, pissed-on hoodlums. The ex-Chief, wagging his dick.

Parker cut down an alley. His shotgun weighed six tons. His sweat smelled putrid. His head felt wrung out.

He ran straight to Kwan's. Some shithead had egged up his car. The windshield was yolk-spattered. He ran the wiper blades and thinned out the splats.

The car started and rolled. Nobody slashed his tires. The brakes worked. Nobody cut the linings.

He drove south. Broadway ran direct to Pedro. He saw tear-gas clouds above Little Tokyo. Bluesuits swarmed low rooftops.

He thought about The Case. Sheriff Gene sanctioned him to work it. He teethed on The Case. He teethed on Dudley Smith and Hideo Ashida. He highballed it straight to Pedro.

Salt air announced the harbor. Parker skirted Fort MacArthur and the Terminal Island Bridge. A checkpoint blocked off harbor access. Duty MPs saw his black-and-white and waved him in.

The docks were hodgepodged with Coast Guard cutters and skunk-wood fishing boats. Search teams boarded the boats, six men per. The dock road was packed with jeeps and black Fed sedans.

Japs wheeled fish barrels. They looked scared. MPs strolled with M1's and leashed police dogs. The dogs growled at the Japs and drooled for their fish.

Parker drove to Pier 16. A cutter was moored there. It was rigged with grappling hooks and prow-mounted machine guns. Two Coast guardsmen and two Sheriff's deputies stood on deck. They wore slinged carbines and scanned the horizon.

An officer spotted the prowl car and walked over. He wore fatigue blues with lieutenant's bars. Parker stepped out of the car. Salty air fogged his glasses.

They shook hands. Parker stamped blood in his legs.

"Did the Sheriff call ahead?"

The lieutenant said, "He did, Captain. I told him that if you hauled tail, you could see something interesting."

Parker said, "What have you got?"

"We've had our eyes on two shrimp boats that range north, up the coast to Santa Barbara. They fish north and berth here, full-time. The skippers and crews are on the Feds' A-2 list, and their residences have been vacated. They're all sleeping on the boats and making their fish drops covertly, at night."

Parker considered it. "Is their canning done at a truck farm in the Valley? I'm thinking of a place owned by a Jap named Hodaka."

The lieutenant said, "No, sir. We were tipped that these guys drop their catches at a plant in Little Tokyo."

Parker considered it. "I read a bulletin. A Jap sub torpedoed a fishing village at the Goleta Inlet, just north of Santa Barbara. It was last week. Do you think these boats could play in somehow?"

The lieutenant shook his head. "Nix on that, sir. I read that bulletin. The boats we're looking at are deep-sea jobs, and that Goleta village was nothing but burned-up shore-fishing craft. And, there's this. We're going after all-Jap crews, but that bulletin said the village humps were Japs and Chinks in cahoots, which is odd—given how those humps hate each other."

A pierside siren *screeeed.* A guardsman dropped his ship-to-shore phone and tore up to the lieutenant.

"We've got a spotting-plane report, sir. That first boat anchored in Ventura, and the Sheriff's up there raided it and said it was clean. It was all some kind of snafu. The skipper said they've been going out for albacore for over a year, and he had the records to prove it. They sleep on the boat because they're all track fiends, and they blow their coin on the nags. Nobody can make a case for these guys as Fifth Column. There's all that, plus the fact that they dump all their loads on Lou's Fish Grotto in Long Beach."

The lieutenant made the jack-off sign. The onboard men grabbed life jackets. It smelled like a rollout. Parker sniffed hullabaloo.

The lieutenant said, "Don't tell me. The other boat's coming in."

The guardsman said, "Aye, aye, sir. It's headed our way."

The lieutenant blew a whistle and ran up the gangplank. Parker fast-walked behind him. A deputy lobbed life jackets. Parker snagged his. Two guardsmen retracted the anchor. The cutter pushed off.

The engines whirred and caught. It happened too fast. Parker stagger-walked to the prow and hugged a gun mount.

A telescope was fixed there. It pointed straight ahead. He took his glasses off and put an eye down. He squinted and caught the hubbub.

A two-mast fishing boat. Maybe two miles out. Tiny figures on deck. Maybe yellow men.

The cutter churned straight ahead. Waves drenched the deck. Engine noise muffled all shouts and yelled commands. Parker hugged the gun mount and kept that eye down.

The lens compressed the horizon. The cutter-to-fishing-boat gap closed. The tiny figures expanded.

Yellow men—yes.

They look scared. Their boat is stalled. Two men are priming rear-deck motors.

The cutter cut waves. The cutter cut close.

Close.

Closer.

Close now.

VERY CLOSE.

Twenty yards or knots or clicks or whatever—

Parker kept that eye down. The yellow men looked scared and mad. Parker slid his glasses on and squinted.

"Hands up, now! All hands up! All hands up, all hands on deck!"

Parker straightened up and braced himself. The boat-to-boat crash knocked him flat. His view went all upside down.

A guardsman tossed a grappling hook. Parker saw it upside down. Men with tommy guns jumped. Parker saw it upside down. Four Japs raised their—

Parker stood up. His view recalibrated. He wobble-leaped and jumped on the boat. The sea cops drew down on the Japs. The Japs raised their hands up, up, *up.*

The boat rocked. A wave hit Parker. He went sea-blind and grabbed a mast rail. He thought he saw—

The Japs reach in their pockets.

The Japs raise their hands and open their mouths.

The Japs bite down and fall down.

The Japs convulse and puke foam and—

One Jap thrashed right by Parker. Puked foam hit Parker's shoes. Parker made a crazy noise and jumped back.

He was still close. The Jap was *too* close. The Jap had smooth fingertips. The Jap had *no* fingerprints. Smooth tips meant carbolic-acid dips and—

A sea cop panicked. He arced his tommy gun down and let *go.*

Deck wood exploded. A Jap's head exploded. All the sea cops arced down and let *go.*

The Japs blew up, the deck blew up, it all blew into wood scraps and smoke.

Parker ran.

He ran from the gore and the noise. He ran toward the rear of the boat. The boat lurched. Parker tumbled down a stairwell. He went upside down and rolled belowdecks.

He hit a small compartment. He saw a might-be Jap or might-be Chink torching currency and tracts. Parker was *this* close to him. The money and paper flared into black ash.

Parker was *this close* to him. The gelt was reichsmarks and yen.

The tracts were in Jap script and English. *They were just like all the tracts in this crazy mix of—*

The fucker bit a pill and thrashed. Parker stepped on his hands and broke his fingers flat. The fingertips were smooth tissue. Parker saw it. He was *this* close.

December 17, 1941

68

LOS ANGELES | WEDNESDAY, DECEMBER 17, 1941

2:07 p.m.

Kwan's basement. It's hotsy-totsy. It's egalitarian.

Everybody rubbed shoulders. The tile game was unstoppable and eighteen hours in. The war justified the misconduct. Everybody knew it. This went unsaid:

Life's short. Easy come, easy go. There's Jap subs off the coast. Those swabbies at Pearl didn't know what hit them. *We* could be next.

Benzedrine tea kept it going. Uncle Ace supplied a full bar and around-the-clock buffet. Hopheads packed the "O" den. Lin Chung morphine-soothed losing players. Brenda Allen peddled cooze at her new wartime rate. Salvador Dalí's pet leopard roamed. He mauled a busboy and snatched chow mein off Count Basie's plate. Nobody gave a shit.

The minuscule meet the mighty. The elite meet the effete.

Clark Gable was there. He displayed a pic of Cary Grant with a dick in his mouth. There's Call-Me-Jack Horrall. There's Nort Layman and Ed Satterlee. There's Stan Kenton. He's with the "Misty" June Christy. She's got eyes for Scotty Bennett—all bruised and contused. Tough luck, sister—that's *Joan Crawford* draped all over him.

It was sardine-packed standing room only. The basement trapped smoke from ten thousand cigarettes. It was one big iron lung.

Dudley stood with Bette. They watched high steppers throw tiles. He'd been up since yesterday morning. Pervert patrol. They'd been rousting potential eyeball wits and death fiends.

Records checks. A new canvass. Where's that Jap-needle-in-a-haystack? Where's that perv-to-end-all-pervs?

He was near-shot exhausted. A sleepover date boded. Ace prepared them a room upstairs. Bette's hubby was occupied. He was hosting a houseboy named Man-Oh-Man Manolo. Man-Oh-Man serviced film folk. His short arm was more like a foot.

Dudley watched the game. Ace dealt tiles. Elmer Jackson played watchdog. He held Jim Davis' boss shotgun.

Jim and Whiskey Bill had indulged misconduct. They rock-salted two tong cliques. One lad developed septicemia. One lad lost three fingers. Uncle Ace was miffed.

The game was eons in. Players came and went. They succumbed to gambling fatigue and scorched pleura. Harry Cohn was sixteen hours in. He played bantamweight stiff Manny Gomez and three Chink dentists.

Harry was fifty-three grand down. He'd repaid his previous debt with van-heist money. Harry owed Ben S. forty-eight. Ben watched the game with Jew-payback eyes.

The game was incomprehensible. The players threw tile-tossing fits. Bette steady-eyed Miss Crawford. They loathed each other. Such bitch-goddess fury.

She pointed to the buffet. Clark Gable and the leopard noshed spareribs.

"Clark's a silly boy. He collects women's snatch hair. He'd fuck that beast if someone held its tail."

Dudley roared. The basement was a tinderbox. A roving waitress passed him a mai tai.

Bette said, "I'm going to use the upstairs loo. The one here is occupied. Brenda is blowing Sheriff Biscailuz."

Dudley kissed her neck. Bette ducked into the crowd. People faded out small in her swirl. Dudley lost her in a low smoke cloud. His fucking lungs burned.

The game continued. Manny Gomez cashed out. Jewboy Harry lost four straight bets and eight grand. Dudley winked at Ben Siegel. Jewboy Ben winked back.

Harry cashed out. Kibitzers booed the famous misanthrope. Harry grabbed his crotch and booed back.

Dudley steered him to Ace's office. Harry was damp and florid. The office was blessedly smokeless. Harry crashed into a chair.

"I owe Ace sixty-one G's. Why do I do this to myself? I'm a powerful man with a heart condition. Why am I such an inveterate slum crawler? The Germans are slaughtering my people, and I'm powerless to stop it. Why do I add to all the world's sorrow and grief?"

Dudley leaned on a towel rack. "You owe Ben forty-eight, Harry. You have a hundred and nine thousand in gambling debts outstanding. You can bemoan your unnecessary losses or allow me to offer you relief."

Harry said, "Fuck you, you mick cocksucker. Don't think I don't know where this is going. Don't think I'm incapable of saying 'I'm not in the smut biz these days.'"

Dudley coughed. "You saw me with Bette Davis."

Harry coughed. "Don't gloat, you mick cocksucker. I know you're *schlamming* her, and I'm not impressed. I also noticed that punk goon of yours with Joanie. That don't impress me, either. Gash like that goes for anything beefcake. Bette and Joanie are the town pumps, and given that the town is L.A., that's saying something."

Dudley grinned. "Shall I convince Bette to leave Warner's for a few months, to facilitate her appearance in a film for Columbia? Would my proposition cause you to reconsider, in that case?"

Harry said, "On my hands and knees, you mick cocksucker. In such a case, I would grovel and thoroughly enjoy it."

Dudley winked and walked back to the party. Ben S. saw him and went *So?* Dudley nodded and popped through a smoke cloud. Scotty and Joanie necked in a doorway. Clark Gable and the leopard snoozed on a couch.

Sycophants and sinners. *What* world conflict? The brave and the wrong.

Dudley walked up to the restaurant. Bette owned it now.

Tonged-up busboys hovered. Patrons pushed autograph books. Bette dished out hugs and posed for snapshots. A line went out the door and down the block.

Bette dispensed cards. *Call my secretary. Buy war bonds. I'll sign glossies and kiss them. I'll send them to you.*

She shook their hands. She talked to them. She gave them her eyes. She met them one by one and engaged them. She did not brush a single one of them off.

She looked over and saw him. She blew him a kiss. Dudley's eyes welled.

The line grew. Radio trucks screeched to the curb. Bette Davis wows Chinktown. Brother, *that's* news!

Dudley walked upstairs. The room was small and tidy. He stretched out on the bed.

The wallpaper blurred. The leopard jumped on the bed. He tried to pet him. The beast dispersed into spots.

He went in and out. The leopard jumped back on the bed. In and out. The leopard purred and pawed at his feet. Out and in. There's Bette. She flopped on the bed and pulled off his shoes.

"I got a hundred and sixty-eight thousand dollars in pledges. The line went on for six hours."

Dudley yawned and touched her leg. She pulled her dress up to her garter belt. He slid his hand in.

"You embody metamorphosis, darling. You were a leopard just a moment ago."

Bette flashed her claws. "I'm a tigress, really. They're much more deadly."

Dudley undid the straps. Her stockings fell slack.

"I'm close with Harry Cohn, you know. Would you ever consider doing a film for Columbia?"

Bette said, "You're crossing the line with me, sweetie. Please don't do that."

Dudley flinched.

His eyes blurred.

Tears ran down his cheeks.

LOS ANGELES | WEDNESDAY, DECEMBER 17, 1941

10:23 p.m.

A siren kicked on. Ashida woke up. He rolled over and looked out the window.

L.A. went black. The Belmont bleachers vanished. Searchlights reared up and swooped.

The siren blare escalated. The fear moment passed. No Jap Zeros swooped.

Ashida dressed in the dark. He got an hour's sleep. The morgue was a short walk. Nort Layman lived there and never slept.

He stepped into the hallway. Someone painted *JAP!* on his door. He got home at 8:30. It happened between then and now.

Ashida locked up and walked downstairs. The street was blackout black and searchlight yellow. He walked due east. The sirens sustained a high rev.

He thought of Goleta. He thought of cut-Jap eugenics and muckraking films. He passed the Hall of Justice. Night clerks perched on the roof and enjoyed the show.

He hit the morgue. Hearse drivers shot craps on the roof. A guy pissed over the edge.

The morgue ran 'round the clock. Ashida walked back to Nort Layman's exam room. It featured disinfecting tables and body vaults. Nort added a couch and clothes rack.

Nort sat on the couch. A gurney played footrest. Ashida took the one chair.

"I hope you're staying out of phone booths. I did the Shigeta autopsy. He was blown to shit. It feels like a race job, more than anything else."

Ashida said, "Tell me why."

Nort said, "His face was obliterated. I think the killer intended to make that statement, either consciously or unconsciously. He eradicated all external evidence of the man being Japanese."

Ashida considered it. "Racial science, in a way. A malevolent form of eugenics."

Nort shrugged. "You've got progressive eugenicists who want to build healthier people, and Nazi humps who want to wipe out the races they don't like. The Shigeta deal interests me, though. It feels like a crime of opportunity, with a random victim. And I have a very strong hunch that the guy plugged Mr. Shigeta to impress someone."

"Like a cat bringing a mouse home to its master?"

Nort lit a cigarette. "Exactly."

Ashida said, "The Watanabes. We're ten days in now."

Nort pointed to a body vault. "I've been going through wound texts for days. Not only were the swords at the house too dull to have made the incisions, but no goddamn ceremonial sword in existence could have made them."

Ashida said, "Let me extrapolate, please. You liked my theory that the killer had the Watanabes drink poison tea. It would account for that rare poison found in their livers. There's that, and that knife that Captain Parker and I saw in Griffith Park, which significantly matched the faded wound on Ryoshi Watanabe, which—"

"—which *could* have been the weapon that killed the Watanabes, but not dipped in poison, the way the warlords did. Which *could* have been used, one blade at a time, to both kill the Watanabes and simulate hara-kiri."

Ashida smiled. "Is it feasible?"

Nort smiled. "It's feasible, working on possible. And, if I continue to suffer from insomnia, I'll probably think up some new tests I can run."

The all-clear sirens blew. Nort retracted his window shades. Outside lights flared.

They talked crime and science. Nort teethed on the Shigeta job. Ashida thought of Kay Lake. She called him before he sacked out. She talked up a planned Pershing Square rally. Comrade Claire booked a camera crew. It was their opening film salvo.

Crime and science. Eugenics. Nort brought up Dr. Lin Chung. Dr. Lin was a race man and nose-job provider. Ashida brought up Terry Lux and stayed mum on the cut job he saw. Nort disdained Dr. Terry. He went to med school with him. Terry pandered to rich dope fiends. Terry was tight with Ace Kwan. Terry knew the Dudster. Ace supplied opiate base for Terry's dope cures. The Dudster mediated a southside dope trade. Some Armenian fucks peddled white horse under his flag.

They talked. They teethed. Biology and chemistry. Newfangled spectrographs. The sun popped to life. Nort dozed off in mid-discourse. Ashida stood up.

Nort stirred. Nort said, "Stay out of phone booths."

7:28 a.m.

The morgue left him woozy. Decay and pestilent vapors. He walked outside and sucked in fresh air.

Pershing Square was close. He cut through Little Tokyo and tallied padlocked shops. They ran about 68%. A fat man leaned out a window and hissed at him.

He hit Hill Street. Pershing Square was packed and 8:00 a.m. rowdy. A platform flanked the bronze J. J. Pershing. A microphone was wired to loudspeakers hooked into trees.

A hambone harangued a big crowd. Ashida joined the fray. He was skintight with the great L.A. unwashed.

Speakers huddled on the platform. That's Dr. Fred Hiltz. He's been in the papers per the Deutsches Haus raid. Hiltz chatted with Reynolds Loftis. Claire and Kay chatted with a colored man. Ashida made him off a Vice sheet. He was the local *Burgermeister* of the Negro Nazi League.

The ham was Gerald L. K. Smith. He was a Disciples of Christ cleric and noted Jew baiter. Ashida kept his head down and tried to blend in. Smith whipped up the crowd.

German atrocities have been overplayed. The Red Control Apparatus ladles on the boo-hoo. Hitler mollycoddles the Jews. He's a heartwarming humanist. Join the Christian Nationalist Crusade. Derail the "Jew Deal" of President Franklin "Double-Cross" Rosenfeld. Write to P.O. Box 8992/Glendale, California. Purchase our informative tracts.

The crowd cheered. The crowd booed. The crowd tossed paper cups. A water-filled condom hit the platform and exploded. Gerald L. K. Smith hugged the Negro Nazi. They faced the crowd and *Sieg Heil!*ed.

More cheers. More boos. More water-balloon bombs. The crowd grew. Ashida got compressed. A skullcap man brushed by him and mouthed "*Goddamn Jap.*" He saw the film crew. They stood on benches at the back of the crowd.

Kay Lake walked to the microphone. She wore a police blue dress. The crowd simmered down. Ashida caught the gist.

Let her talk. She's a girl. *Feed us some shit we can work with, doll. We're here to act up.*

Ashida scanned the crowd. He saw Bill Parker back by the film crew. Parker stood on a trash can and leaned upside a tree. He wore civilian clothes. He had a high balcony view.

Kay placed her hands on the mike stand. Kay looked straight at the crowd.

"We live in a time of the vile act justified. Vile acts spawn immediate and reactive injustice. Such reaction is often obscured by righteous intent. The empathic bond of shared catastrophe creates an unshakable will to power that binds each and every one of us to a world outside of and most deeply within ourselves. We comport in this shared world at great moral peril, and understand that this is the moment that calls us to self-sacrifice. The name that we give to this moment is History, and that moment is now."

She paused. Ashida read it. She's catching her breath. She's got them for one instant.

Kay said, "History afflicts both individuals and nations. History assumes the form of a mass debt that common people pay in blood. History *is* this moment, and *at* this moment we are charged to love and hate on a mass scale, as we act as individuals called to the best within ourselves, as we react to atrocity by euphemizing atrocity, for atrocity assumes forms both subtle and strident and obliterates everything within its path, and as individuals we are thus charged to the near-impossible task of enacting love that much more ruthlessly, and with a self-sacrifice that would have been unknowable had History not summoned us. At this moment, our options become do everything or do nothing."

She paused. Ashida read it. She's still got them. She knows they won't hold off much—

Kay said, "War is the mass imprisonment of the individual will and the paradoxical liberation of the individual voice. Thus, self-sacrifice oft becomes the voicing of unpopular sentiment within more popular outrage. History is this moment. This moment must acknowledge the merger of the individual voice and our nation's will to power, and bring it to a more specific moment of conscious and contrary statement. We must avenge the Japanese attack on Pearl Harbor with the full assumption of our mass will to power, which will be in the end our individually enacted wills to fight and risk death. Because we are honorably called to that duty, we must honorably call ourselves to the recognition of the sordid fact that we are now perpetrating a blood libel on the honorable Japanese people of this city, that our best selves have been countermanded by fear and irrational hatred, and—"

Boos. Jeers. Catcalls.

Shouts, yells, shrieks.

Kay moved her lips. The crowd yelled over her. Lowlifes dumped the loudspeakers. Kay moved her lips. No sound came out.

She had no voice. They stole her voice. Somebody yelled, "*JAP!*" It was right up close to him. A man jumped in and hit him.

He pitched forward. He flailed and stayed upright. He heard *Goddamn Jap!* a million times.

A man hit him. A boy hit him. A girl kicked him. He raised his hands and covered his face. A woman yanked at his arms.

Ashida went down. People hit him and kicked him. He lost sight of Kay. People hit him. People kicked him. People spit on him. He felt beat-on and shit-on and fucked-up anesthetized.

Something hit the people.

They stopped. They stumbled. They tripped. They fell down themselves. Something hit them and made them run.

It's hard to see. There's blood in his eyes. It might be Scotty Bennett and Bill Parker. They're hitting the people. They're hitting them and kicking them and making them run.

December 18, 1941

70

KAY LAKE'S DIARY

LOS ANGELES | THURSDAY, DECEMBER 18, 1941

8:36 a.m.

I kept speaking. No one heard me. The microphone and loudspeakers provided no sound. I had no voice. The crowd's voice was obscenity.

I kept speaking. Paper debris and water balloons hit the platform. Everyone jumped off. Garbage spattered me.

I held the microphone and kept speaking. My lips moved and made no sound. I spoke with undiminished intent and could not hear my own voice. The crowd was directly below and right in front of me. I heard a thousand *Japs* and saw a savage beating.

Someone was down. People were kicking him. People were beating those people and forcing them to disperse. I couldn't see faces. It was all punches and kicks. I held the microphone and kept speaking.

I delivered my indictment. The platform rattled and skewed my line of sight. People ran in front of me. I thought I saw Ed Satterlee. Bill Parker and Scotty Bennett might have run by. They were disheveled. The might-be Parker lost his glasses. The might-be Scotty wore ripped clothes.

I looked to the 5th Street sidewalk and blew a line of text. Mike Breuning and Dick Carlisle eased Hideo Ashida into a K-car. Hideo brushed the back window and left blood streaks.

The car pulled out. *The lie that race defines human beings. The lie that dissent defines sedition.* The car turned north on Hill Street. I watched it disappear. A paper bag full of food scraps hit me. *The definitive lie of fearful hatred.* Rotten fruit in my hair.

A man hurled a trash can at the platform and cracked a foundation strut. The boards listed to one side; the microphone stand tipped over; I stumbled and fell down with it.

The platform collapsed. I crashed to street level. A man ran up, kicked me and ran back into the crowd. Saul and Andrea Lesnick walked through the rubble. They grabbed my arms and began to hoist me; I felt how frail they were and pushed myself upright.

They were frail. I was jarred and battered. We stumbled to the Hill Street curb and a double-parked Chrysler. Saul got in the driver's side; I got in beside him. Andrea slipped and fell into the back.

Saul pulled into traffic. Andrea said something about her nerves and Queen of Angels.

We drove north. I brushed apple pulp out of my hair. Traffic was stalled in front of us; I saw the whip antenna on the K-car above the traffic line. Hideo stepped out of the backseat and began walking east. He held a bloody handkerchief to his face.

Saul cut through Bunker Hill and got us to the hospital. He parked by the side entrance; he helped Andrea out and gave me a look. It meant *You've done enough*. They walked in the door together—frail comrades, arm in arm.

Lee's room was on the third floor. I smoked a cigarette in the car and walked inside to the washroom. I tended to myself and reread Saul's look. *Brittle child, chaos attends you, so impervious to others.*

I took the elevator up to Lee's room. Lee was asleep, with his bed cranked into a sitting-reclining position. He had metal studs and sutures in his jaw. His chewed-off ear had been retrieved and stitched back into place. Criss-crossed stitches secured his nose.

He'd left the house, arm in arm with Scotty. *No hard feelings, huh? Jesus, that Kay. It was like the first Louis-Schmeling fight. You stay here, sweetie—this is man's stuff.*

They drove off together. Of course, I stayed behind. Chaos attends but does not subsume me. I don't stick around to view the cost.

I pulled a chair up to the bed and watched Lee sleep. Leland Charles Blanchard, "The Southland's Great White Hope." Ex-contender, policeman, bank robber–killer. I'd known him for three years. This is where we were now.

I watched Lee sleep. He never stirred. A medical chart was hooked to the wall above his bed.

"You were brilliant, Miss Lake."

He'd let some prairie into his voice. Deadwood and Sioux Falls—that short distance apart.

I turned my chair around to see him. His face was nicked, his jaw was bruised, his eyes were huge without his glasses.

"Did you follow me here?"

"I saw Lesnick drive off with you. I had an instinct as to where you were going."

"My movie is unprecedented. It will stand as an unbiased document, whatever you do to Claire and me."

"Don't cast yourselves as martyrs. It's not who you are. She's a traitorous dilettante, and you're the biggest opportunist since me."

"I may be that in spirit, but I lack your résumé. You can't blame me for that. You had Two-Gun Davis for a mentor, but all I have is you."

"Your résumé is the men you've screwed to get what you want. It exceeds my résumé in sheer volume."

"Who's the tall red-haired woman? What will you do when you find her and she sees how little you have?"

"What will you do when your 'unprecedented' movie is labeled Exhibit A in Federal court?"

"What will you do when the world steps aside and you don't get what you want? What will you do when Russia remains our ally after we win this war? What will you do when the world decides that you're not worth the trouble and throws in with some other man less furious and more presentable than you?"

Lee coughed. I turned away and looked at him. He twitched in a dream; his eyes fluttered; he rolled onto his side.

I shifted my chair back around. He was gone—and the room was too bright and quiet without him. I opened a window and saw Scotty down on the sidewalk. He was disheveled and reading the Holy Bible.

I'll make love with him again.

I horrify myself.

Only William H. Parker knows my heart.

71

LOS ANGELES | THURSDAY, DECEMBER 18, 1941

10:19 a.m.

Occupied territory.

Miss Lake would know the term. It dovetailed with "blood libel" and made dialectic sense. Cops and Japs ran equal here. The cops had increased. The Japs had *de*creased.

It vibrated in plain view. Door-to-door rousts. Street frisks. Gun confiscation.

Parker pulled to the curb. The warehouse was off 1st and San Pedro. That Coast Guard lieutenant supplied the address. He called from City Hall and got no answer. He opted for a 459 then.

The canning plant. The shrimp boats dumped their catches here. This three-story warehouse. This bolted-padlock door.

He had a tire iron and flashlight. He had one full day sober. He slept in the Bureau cot room last night and woke up tremor-free. He smashed his glasses in Kwan's Pagoda. He lost them in Pershing Square. It was 459 with a squint.

He walked over and snapped the lock. It was his first solo 459. Hideo Ashida partnered him on the Larkin-bungalow raids. Ashida vanished from Pershing Square. He's beaten-on one moment, gone the next.

Parker stepped inside and slid the door shut. He ran his flashlight over the floor and walls. One floor/four walls—all smooth cement. It was dead empty. Call it dead certain. The place had been cleaned out.

It was damp. It was musty. He caught a subscent. He couldn't place it.

He walked along the walls. He held his flashlight close. He saw floor-to-ceiling streaks and made the source.

Washcloth marks. The walls had been wiped. The practice erased fingerprints.

Parker touched a streak mark. He felt slight condensation.

The place was print-wiped *yesterday. After* that botched harbor raid. Word got back to the owners or renters.

He walked to the second-floor landing. He saw floor-to-ceiling wipe marks. He caught that subscent again.

He nailed it. It was shrimp oil.

He saw charred paper on the floor. It was charred like the tracts and money on the shrimp boat. See *that*? *Japanese characters.*

Now extrapolate.

The warehouse was pre-1900. The buying and selling went Jap-to-Jap. That wartime paper backlog. His rogue police status. It impeded records checks.

He walked to the third-floor landing. He saw more wipe marks and caught more subscent. He saw an empty can on the floor. It was unlabeled. Note the shrimp oil and glass specks.

Now extrapolate.

Last Saturday. His talk with Nort Layman. The glass in the canned shrimp up in Lancaster. Sheriff Gene investigates. He thinks it's Fifth Column work.

Nort eschews that conclusion. Nort extrapolates.

Four dead Watanabes. Glass particles flecked with shrimp oil on all their feet.

Heavily callused feet—"Japs tend to walk around barefoot."

"What did surprise me was the even distribution of the particles. It was as if they were walking on the glass deliberately."

Parker walked back to his prowl car. He left the warehouse door ajar. It was a fuck-you/I'm-a-rogue-cop-now move.

He unhooked his two-way and roused the morgue, direct. Nort picked up.

"Dr. Layman. Who's this?"

"Bill Parker, Nort."

Nort said, "I'm not surprised, and I bet you've got questions."

"I do, and it's a parlay. Glass particles and shrimp oil. Is there efficacy here? What would that combination *do*?"

Nort cleared his throat. "I'd been wondering about that myself, so I did some research. I came up with one thing, which hits me as a non sequitur. The oxide componentry of the glass, in concert with shrimp oil, would create a level of toxicity that would prove deleterious to urban topsoil and many forms of foliage and grass."

Huh?

"That's it, Bill. I know it's a head scratcher, but so's the goddamn case. It's a head scratcher and a dead-ender, and I'm running out of tests I can run."

Parker said, "Thanks, Nort."

Nort said, "You know where to find me."

The connection fritzed and died. Parker hooked up the radio and notched his seat back.

Shitwork bodes. There's Call-Me-Jack's report stack. "Assess this shit, Bill. You know it's not my style."

He thumbed the top folder. It detailed Preston Exley's Jap-housing plan.

Predictive statistics. Potential internee-employment sites. A *Mirror* piece on Exley Construction and the Arroyo Seco Parkway. Notes on proposed Highland Park on-ramps. Hoo-ha on Preston's cop career.

Boring shitwork. Assess *what*?

Parker lit a cigarette. He thought about the shrimp-boat slaughter. Mass suicide, scorched paper. Links, links, links. Dead Japs and one maybe-Chinaman.

He thought about Pershing Square. He fought beside Scotty Bennett. They rescued a fickle Jap.

He prayed off a jolt of The Thirst. He thought of Miss Lake.

Her lovely dress. Garbage-spattered and trashed. He should buy her a new dress just like it.

72

LOS ANGELES | THURSDAY, DECEMBER 18, 1941

11:37 a.m.

Dudley walked through Mike Lyman's. Cops and local bigwigs tossed the shit. Dire shit—that Santa Monica sniper.

It was late-breaking shit. The fiend sniped Army sentries on the Palisades. The fiend *fatal*-sniped a Jap a mile from the beach. Maybe it's Fifth Column. It's a fucked-up fiend, sure as shit.

Sniper talk now outrevved war talk. The fiend sniped soldiers *and* Japs. The cops got it. Chaos is king. It perplexed the bigwigs.

Dudley hit the back room. Mike B. and Dick C. oozed *eager.* Scotty B. snapped to. He wore that unfetching nose splint. Buzz Meeks smirked—ever shifty and porcine.

They sprawled up the furniture. Carlisle worked the buffet. He served coffee and ham sandwiches.

Dudley said, "Report, please."

Carlisle said, "We've been at it since Tuesday morning, and we've turned up nine fools who'll stand as eyeball wits. They've all got parole-violation sheets and bench warrants we can squeeze them with. They live inside a tight radius of the Watanabe house, and they'll ID any suspect we tell them to."

Breuning said, "Six white men, a beaner and two Japs. We snagged the Japs out of South Pasadena, but they were at a block party on Avenue 44 that day. We tried, but we couldn't dig up any women."

Dudley said, "It will be a closed grand jury proceeding, which means that our witnesses' criminal records will be sealed. Thankfully, saints are not required for this part of our endeavor. If Vogel, Koenig and Waldner provide us with a properly loathsome and unhinged suspect, he'll be deemed unfit to stand trial, sentenced to death in a negotiated manner and held incommunicado until such time that a suitably pliable psychiatrist declares him competent. The Feds have a Jew doctor named Saul Lesnick in their pocket. He would be a grand one to pronounce our lad sane and fit for the gas chamber. What we must avoid is a well-publicized trial, where our unruly eyeball wits might be discredited."

Meeks unwrapped his sandwich. "I got us a Jap kiddie-raper. He's got no alibi for December 6 and 7, and he's about as low as human beings get. We could pack him off to the green room and not lose any sleep over it."

Dudley sipped coffee. "I'll keep that under advisement, lad. I want Vogel, Koenig and Waldner to report their findings first."

Scotty raised his hand. "Listen, I'm new to this. We brief the eyewitnesses? Is that it? We lead them through their depositions?"

Breuning and Carlisle laughed. Dudley winked at Scotty.

"I *dictate* their depositions, lad. I layer in discrepancies to impart verisimilitude."

Breuning and Carlisle *re*-laughed. Scotty grinned. Vogel, Koenig and Waldner showed. Carlisle dispensed lunch.

It was SRO now. The new lads slouched by the door.

Dudley said, "Report, please."

Vogel lit a cigarette. "Bill and I dug up four Jap sex creeps, all at large and all with stat-rape sheets. If you want my opinion, it goes like this. Our guy knocked up Nancy Watanabe and snuffed the whole family to hush it. He got Nancy a scrape down in T.J., but it all went blooey in his head anyway. Doc Layman said the daddy had AB-negative blood. I checked jail records on all four of our guys, and one guy's AB neg."

Dudley raised a hand. *Be still, please.* Waldner opened his yap. Carlisle shushed him.

He talked to Huey Cressmeyer. It was eight days back. Huey snitched the Griffith Park cell. Huey said this:

The guy who made Nancy preg was a Jap-Mex half-breed with bad acne cysts on his back.

"The cat bragged that he killed a Mex family down in Culiacán."

"The cat headed back to Mexico."

The original cell was four men. He and Ace killed three. The cell was "Collaborationist." They snuffed two Japs and a half-breed. The Jap-Mex half-breed was a wild card. He was probably still in Mexico. He would not derail their full-Jap plans.

The lads wolfed their sandwiches. The lads kept it zipped.

Dudley said, "I would very much prefer AB-negative blood, but it may not be essential. Any paramour of poor Nancy Watanabe would be subject to intensive personal questioning per the lass herself, and all our coaching might fail to provide him with the answers. I see blood type as corroborative, rather than primary evidence. What we want is a raving lunatic motivated by incomprehensible lust."

Waldner said, "I've got him."

Dudley smiled. Waldner was an avid thug. Waldner did not indulge whimsy.

"He's a transient knife sharpener named Fujio 'Fuji' Shudo. He did a six-year jolt at Atascadero and got paroled on Wednesday, December 3rd. He was seen going door-to-door with his tool cart in Highland Park on the 4th and 5th. I lost track of his movements then, but I'm betting he's clear for Doc Layman's time of death on the 6th. He's been holed up at a fleabag hotel in Little Tokyo since

Pearl Harbor day. The Kyoto Arms, a real dive. He's afraid to go out—because of the roundups, I'm guessing. I paid Elmer Jackson to keep tabs on him. Elmer's working the Alien Squad, so he's in the area a lot. Fuji's still holed up in his room, belting terpin hydrate."

Dudley said, "Please continue."

Waldner said, "I've got no blood type, but I like him. He's a knife man and a nut-farm inmate, and he did that Atascadero bounce for mayhem. His moniker is 'Bamboo Shoot' Shudo. He kidnapped some wetbacks in '34 and stuck bamboo shoots up their keesters."

Breuning winced.

Carlisle said, "Ouch."

Vogel said, "That smarts."

Scotty gulped.

Koenig said, "Bend over and touch your toes. I'll show you where the wild goose goes."

Meeks said, "Bon voyage, sweetheart. The green room's coming up."

Dudley said, "I assume that Mr. Shudo remains in place?"

Waldner said, "Right there, boss. Elmer J.'s his watchdog. If Fuji bolts, Elmer will call me."

"Have the witnesses at City Hall for a 7:00 p.m. show-up. I'll brief them before we bring in Mr. Shudo."

Grins circulated. *Woo-woo-woo*s followed. Breuning and Carlisle twirled their saps.

Dudley opened the door. Sid Hudgens and Jack Webb were close by.

"We've identified our suspect, lads. Be at the Kyoto Arms Hotel at 8:00 tonight. Mr. Hearst will get the exclusive."

12:29 p.m.

The lads filed out. He hit the couch. He was tired. His bones hurt.

He was losing weight. The bennies depleted him. He forgot his wife's name yesterday. He's fucking Bette Davis. She instills tremors in him.

She upbraided him last night. He faltered. She made herself soft and tried to rescind the rebuke. She saw weakness in him. He tore off her clothes and went at her to regain his edge.

They have a truce now. He must trump her as he trumps all men. The method eludes him.

Beth Short and Tommy Gilfoyle are due. Bette will meet them. He's running too many people. He's thinking at a frantic pace. He flails for consciousness when he needs sleep.

Dudley yawned. Dudley reached for a thought and missed it.

The couchside phone rang. Dudley grabbed the call.

J. C. Kafesjian blathered. Their "H" source got popped in bumfuck Honduras. J.C. harped on his tight bond with Call-Me-Jack Horrall. "It don't mean shit if there's no shit to sell to the jigs."

Dudley baby-talked him. Dudley proffered no solution. He *oversaw* J.C. He did *not* procure his dope. Dudley mollified him. J.C. fumed and hung up.

Dudley yawned. Dudley reached for a thought and missed it. The Teletype clacked. He reached for a thought and reeled it in.

He called a downtown florist. He spieled his police credentials and said he'd send a check. He ordered three dozen red roses. He gave them Bette's name and address. The clerk whistled. Bette Davis, *whew!* The card? "Sign it 'Your Secret Irish Admirer.'"

The clerk hung up. Dudley yawned. He felt schizy and itchy. He popped three bennies and popped his briefcase.

Watanabe/187 P.C.

He skimmed reports. He keyed on the tracts at the house. The case hexed him. They had Fuji Shudo now. A true solve was irrelevant.

Still—

Dudley repacked his briefcase. Thad Brown walked in and pulled a chair up.

"I've got a Teletype coming. The Fourth Interceptor Command's got me on those snipings."

Dudley said, "It appears indiscriminate. He's shooting Japs *and* soldiers."

Brown lit a cigar. "*He's* indiscriminate. It's like the phone-booth snuff. Some crazy fucker sees a Jap and 86's him. You want my opinion? It's all a nutty string of dead-enders."

The Teletype clacked and spooled paper. It's a ballistics sheet. There's a photograph. Lands and grooves on a spent bullet.

Dudley grabbed the sheet. A margin note grabbed him. ".30-06 carbine/sawed barrel."

He saw the land-groove pattern. He saw the barrel nicks common to sawed-offs. He passed the sheet to Brown. He ID'd the sheet, he *made* the gun, he *made* the assailant right there.

Brown studied the sheet. "Sawed-off rifles are from hunger. The shells tumble. I'm betting on some Army punk with a hard-on for the world. You check armory thefts and take it from there."

Dudley said, "I should be going, Thad."

"Go, Dud. Get Jack H. his solve on your Jap caper. We should get at least one Jap solve before this fucking war ends."

Dudley waltzed. The bennies kicked in and perked him. He ducked out the side door and shagged his K-car. He drove to City Hall and elevatored up to six.

The Bureau was lunchtime-lulled. He hit his cubicle and unlocked the bottom-left desk drawer.

Aaaaah—

His throwdown guns and spare handcuffs. His Huey Cressmeyer file.

He had Huey's rap sheet and reform-school transcript. He injected Huey with Pentothal last summer. The dope made him talk. Huey blabbed all his 459's and 211's. He recorded and transcribed the confessions. He test-fired Huey's fourteen pistols and four rifles. He had the result sheets right—

Here.

Huey's sawed-off carbine. Identical lands and grooves. A match to Thad Brown's sheet. Trigger-happy Huey—back from Mexico.

His tests were run covertly. Thad's sheet would never match any on-file gun.

Dudley locked the file up and elevatored back down. He popped two more bennies and ran to his car.

He took 1st Street to Boyle Heights. The Heights was a grand weave of kikes and cholos. Ruth Mildred ran her scrape clinic there. *Right* there—an ex-warehouse behind an auto-wreck yard.

Two full floors—all Girls, Girls, *GIRLS.* Girls-on-benders, girls-on-the-run, girls-in-a-jam.

Floor no. 1 was a dormitory. Ruth and Dot rented rooms to lezbo Marines. They went AWOL from Camp Pendleton. The lezbo grapevine drew them here. Hey, Butch—Ruth and Dot want *You!*

Floor no. 2 was a scrape shack. It was cop-protected. It featured deluxe scrape gear and recovery rooms. It catered to Harry Cohn's stars and the L.A. elite. The exam rooms featured wall peeks. Sapphic sisters paid to watch.

Dudley parked in the auto yard. CARRO MONTEZUMA—SE HABLA ESPAÑOL. He walked through the dorm. Girls with crew cuts scowled. He went up to the waiting room. Plain janes with bulging bellies pitched boo-hoo.

He knew the receptionist. He always forgot her name. They coupled in a parked car once. It lingered for her.

"Huey, darling? I know he's here. Where else would he go?"

"Number four, love. I've never been able to say no to you."

Dudley winked and walked down the hall. The door was shut. He pushed it open. The room was Huey's lair now.

Note the bedroll on the table. Note the skivvies hooked to the stirrups. Note the *der Führer* pinups. Note the model airplane–glue stench.

Note Huey. He's building a toy panzer tank by the scrub sink. He's wearing a jockstrap and a Nazi armband. Note the Mossberg .30-06, propped on the wall.

Huey saw Dudley. Huey *guuuuuuuulped.* Huey said, "Please don't hurt me, Uncle Dud."

Dudley grabbed Huey and slapped him. Dudley ripped off his armband and crushed the toy tank. Huey squealed. Dudley picked him up and threw him against the far wall.

The effort taxed him. He gasped for air. Huey crashed and fell on the floor. Huey crawled up on mommy's gyno table.

Dudley said, "Carlos Madrano stashed you in Mexico, last Friday. You were instructed to stay there, without complaint. You have returned, against my wishes, and you have performed a string of unconscionable misdeeds. Explain yourself. Be thorough."

Huey burrowed into a blanket. He tucked his knees up to his chin. The blanket was fluffy pink.

I was holed up in T.J. I was going squirrelshit. I was drinking 151 rum and sniffing cocaine. I was going to the donkey show every night. I was reading comic books and anti-Jew tracts. Uncle Carlos gave me films of bossman Hitler's speeches. I bought a projector and screened them on my Klan sheet.

I got the urge to KILL. I shot a Jew tourist outside the Agua Caliente racetrack. He was wearing a beanie, so I knew he was a Yid. I got the

URGE TO KILL a jigaboo. I drove to San Diego and shot a coon outside the El Cortez Hotel. I read about that Jap who got shot in that phone booth. I got the URGE TO KILL a Jap. I drove to Oceanside and shot a Jap mowing some white stiff's lawn.

I got the URGE TO KILL soldiers and at least one more Jap. I drove up to L.A. and cruised Santa Monica. I shot a Jap sitting on a bus bench. I sniped some soldiers on the Palisades, but the cocksuckers survived.

Dudley pulled down the blanket. Huey sucked his thumb. Dudley ruffled the lad's hair.

"No more, son. I can't have you causing such grief."

"Okay, Uncle Dud."

"I'll have to destroy your trusty rifle. We can't risk it being traced back to you."

Huey said, "I brought you a gift from Mexico. It's something you'll like."

Dudley said, "A souvenir trinket? A key fob shaped like a sombrero?"

Huey blew his nose on the blanket. "Better than that. Something you want."

Dudley jabbed his arm. "Get to it, lad."

"Okay. It all goes back to what we were talking about last week. You know, I was trucking with some Japs on the far-right flank."

"Yes. Including the late Johnny Watanabe."

"Right, Johnny. There's him, and there's this guy that said he got Nancy preg. I said I didn't know his name. Remember? I told you he was a half-Jap, half-Mex breed."

"I recall it vividly, lad."

"Okay, so here's the rest of the drift. I get a bee in my bonnet down in T.J. I think, I should locate this halfbreed fucker, shanghai his ass and bring him home to Uncle Dud. Maybe he sliced the fucking Watanabes, maybe he didn't. It don't matter, because kicks are kicks, and I've never pulled a kidnap before. However it plays out, I'll bet Uncle Dud sure would like to talk to him."

"Continue, please."

"Okay, so I go out looking. It don't take too long, because Jap-spic half-breeds stand out. I find the guy in a whorehouse in Ensenada, and I Mickey Finn his ass and toss him in the trunk of this jalopy I bought for thirty clams. Then I drive him over the border and up here to L.A. His name's Tojo Tom Chasco, and I've got him stashed in the next room right now. This lezzie nurse has got him knocked out on a morph and phenobarb drip."

The Night Creature fetches. Such initiative.

Dudley scanned the room. He saw syringe kits on a shelf. He saw a wall-bolted phone.

He grabbed the receiver and dialed-up the Bureau. He went straight to Mike Breuning's desk.

"Homicide, Sergeant Breuning."

"Send Scotty to Ruthie's clinic, lad. I've got an errand for him."

Breuning said, "Roger, boss."

Dudley hung up and snatched a syringe. Huey plucked at him. He resembled Renfield in *Dracula. Master, come look.*

They walked next door. Dudley looked.

Tojo Tom was friction-taped to a gyno table. He was stripped to his boxer shorts and out cold. He was muscular and about twenty-eight. Eugenics. He was equally Jap and Mex.

¿Qué pasó, Tomás?

They needed a *full-blood* Jap killer. *Fuji Shudo* fit that bill. The case was twelve days old. Tojo Tom was their first hard suspect.

Huey hovered and made like Renfield. Dudley jammed the syringe in Tojo Tom's arm.

He hit a fat vein. He extracted a full sample. Tojo Tom slept through it. He was off on Cloud 29.

Dudley reached in his pocket and pulled out a handful of bennies. He made a fist and crumbled them to powder. He poured it into Tojo Tom's drip bag. It merged with the extant liquid. Rise and shine, Tojo Tom.

Huey patted Tojo's dick. He went Greek in reform school. It complied with the Ruth-Dot gestalt.

Tojo Tom slept in hophead heaven. Dudley and Huey stood by. Young Scotty walked in. Huey swooned, just a tad.

Dudley passed him the syringe. "Good Samaritan, lad. There's a lab man named Samuels. Get me a quick typing and call me back here."

Scotty vamoosed. Huey sulked and picked his nose. Dudley watched the dope-bag liquid recede. He felt slightly *off.* His pulse stuttered. His breathing hitched.

He stared at the dope bag. The liquid drained. The wall phone rang and startled him. He snatched the receiver.

"I'm listening, lad."

Scotty said, "It's O-positive blood. He couldn't have impregnated Nancy, if that's what this is about."

Dudley said, "Go back to the Bureau, lad. We've a busy night ahead."

Scotty hung up. Dudley hung up. The dope bag drained out. Tojo Tom twitched.

His veins pulsed. He broke a sweat. He electroshock-spasmed. Dope contravention. He's on a snootful of new hop.

Tojo Tom opened his eyes.

Tojo Tom flexed his body.

Tojo Tom saw his old pal Huey. Tojo Tom saw an obvious cop.

He eyeball-tracked the room. He's getting it. He's been shanghaied. It's not Mexico. It's not a whorehouse. It's some rogue hospital.

He flexed. He thrashed. He sprayed piss and soaked his shorts. He thrashed a strip of tape loose. Blood trickled down his arm.

He gleamed a tad. He eyed the drip bag. He's getting it. *Why do I feel gooooood? Because there's a needle stuck in my arm. Because there's hop in that bag.*

He coughed. His eyes traveled. He zeroed in on the big cop. He *Jap*-zeroed in on Huey. He said, "You sandbagged me, you hump."

Dudley said, "*Hola, Tomás. ¿Qué pasó? Ojalá que se mejore pronto.*"

Tojo Tom coughed. "White cops who speak Spanish don't impress me. There's lots of you. You always want information, and you always say there's an easy way and a hard way. If you want to impress me, speak Japanese."

Dudley smiled. "I'm Spanish-fluent, lad—but that's as far as my linguistic gifts go. I'll bring in my friend Ryoshi Watanabe, if you like. I'm sure he'd be willing to translate for me."

Tojo Tom said, "*Ryoshi es estúpido. Es el pinche cabrón.*"

"You've employed the present tense, Tomás. I find that interesting."

"It's correct usage, *pendejo*. I'm half-Mexican, so I know. And what's with that funny accent of yours? Are you some limey homo?"

Dudley laughed. "Did you impregnate Nancy Watanabe, Tomás? Huey told me you knocked up a Japanese girl."

"Huey licked Nancy's snatch at the Nightingale prom. *He* told *me* that. I knocked up a twist named Shirley Yanagihara in '39, and I've got mongoloid triplets somewhere to prove it. Why are you so hipped on the *estúpidos* Watanabes, *pendejo*? There's a war on. Why aren't you off fighting for the wrong side?"

"Huey thought you meant Nancy Watanabe. Huey also said that you bragged of killing an entire family in Culiacán."

Tojo Tom laughed. "I remember that night. We were drinking with some Collaborationist boys in Griffith Park. I said I killed a family in Culiacán and fucked Betty Grable. Huey said he pistol-whipped Clark Gable and raped Carole Lombard. This Chinese-Japanese half-breed said he firebombed a nigger church in 1912, but I don't think he was born until 1918. These Collaborationist boys ended up getting snuffed, but that's the only action of that sort that any of us ever saw."

Dudley smiled. Huey pouted. Wild-goose chase. The Night Creature, disdained.

Tojo Tom said, "You've got me on some sort of rocket-ship fuel. I feel so good that I'm not half as pissed off as I should be. I'm in a whorehouse in Ensenada one moment, and strapped to a table at some undisclosed location the next. I was drinking mescal one moment, and now I'm jawing with my ex-pal Huey and some limey cop. I'm curious about all of this, but I don't want to spoil the fun."

Dudley said, "The Watanabe family was murdered on Saturday, December 6. The crime occurred here in Los Angeles. I'm sure you didn't kill them, so I will apologize for the outrageous inconvenience of your abduction, which Mr. Cressmeyer undertook without my consent. While I have you, I would love to hear your insights on the family itself."

Tojo Tom tee-heed. "Live by the sword, die by the sword."

"I understand the concept, but please elaborate."

"It means they were Fifth Column. It means they pissed off some Fifth Column humps, who took it out on them. Fifth Column's Fifth Column. None of us do much, except meet on the sly and jaw treason. Once in a while, you get rivalries. You want my bet, limey? Somebody said something or did something that didn't seem like anything, but it festered. That's the way it is with Fifth Column humps. They know someone who knows someone who knows someone who plants a bomb. Something happens once in a blue moon, but most of it's all in our minds."

Dudley said, "You're a bright penny, Tomás."

Huey huffed. "He's not as bright as me, Uncle Dud. If he's so bright, how come he's here?"

Tojo Tom squirmed. "I need to go to the bathroom."

"Momentarily, lad. In the meantime, please tell—"

"—tell you the book on the Watanabes, which isn't much of a book. If it was a book, the title would be *Screwy Jap Family*. Nancy was a round heel, and Johnny was window-shopping all over the far right. He was palling with those Collaborationists, pulling crimes and donating the takes to the Emperor's cause. Ryoshi and Aya pushed hate tracts and laundered Axis money. They were shortwave-radio pals with some white American and English fascists whose names I don't know, but all they did was talk, talk, and talk. The only thing I could ever give them credit for was knowing that Hirohito would hit Pearl Harbor first. It was the last time I saw them, about eight months ago. Ryoshi said something like 'We will strike first at the naval base in Hawaii.' I had the feeling that he picked it up off his radio chats. Then what he said came true, and now you're telling me the whole family got clipped the day before."

Huey said something dumb. Dudley shushed him. Huey clammed up.

The Watanabes possessed no shortwave radio. The Watanabes possessed no radio at all. The house had been tossed. The garage had been tossed. There was no basement. There was no attic. There was no shortwave hookup.

Tojo Tom said, "My teeth are floating. I need to use the can."

Huey said, "I'm hungry. Do you think Kwan's delivers this far?"

Dudley said, "Think, Tomás. Where did the Watanabes keep their shortwave set?"

Tojo Tom said, "Ryoshi had a hidey-hole rigged to the second-floor ceiling. He kept all his secret stuff there."

Ransack the hidey-hole. It might be undisturbed. It might have been tossed already. There might be no radio. That would mean this:

Hideo Ashida got there first.

Ashida might have heard broadcasts. Ryoshi might have kept broadcast logs. Ashida might have read them. Ashida might have suppressed crucial leads from the start.

"Secret stuff." Irrelevant stuff. Fuji Shudo would burn. A true solve was irrelevant. Tojo Tom supplied a relevant lead. The lead rendered him irrelevant.

Dudley pulled his ankle piece. It was silencer-rigged. The ammo pierced skulls and lodged in brain tissue. Minimum leak resulted.

Huey giggled.

Tojo Tom shit his shorts. A big stink resulted.

Dudley cocked the gun.

Tojo Tom said, "I know where there's money."

Dudley aimed the gun.

Huey squealed.

Tojo Tom said, "I was running horse for Carlos Madrano. I know where he stashes his money and dope."

Dudley lowered the gun.

Huey pouted.

Captain Carlos and heroin. That rumor, redux.

"Is there more, lad? You've been credible up to this point. I would advise you to continue."

Tojo Tom said, "Carlos has got some kind of land-grab deal going with some rich gringos, here in L.A. I've got no names for them. I think it's a good tip, but that's all I've got."

Land grabs. That rumor, redux.

Dudley walked to Huey's room. He grabbed the wall phone. He called his man at PC Bell and placed a rush order.

Trace job. Long-distance calls. Start at the Mex Statie HQ in Baja. Check Carlos Madrano's line. Cull all L.A. calls, going back three months.

He pledged a C-note. *Rápidamente, por favor.* Huey taunted Tojo Tom next door. Dudley hung up and walked back.

Huey said, "Let me kill him, Uncle Dud. I've never killed a half-breed before."

Dudley threw Huey against the far wall. Huey pinwheeled and crashed. Tojo Tom whooped.

"You may not kill Mr. Chasco, or anyone else. You will baby-sit Mr. Chasco while I attempt to verify his statement. I am quite busy, and will call for an expanded statement later. You will *cater* to Mr. Chasco, Huey. I will kill you if you do not."

2:51 p.m.

The dorm lezzies blew kisses. He hit the auto yard and walked up to his car.

He dry-swallowed three bennies. His brain perk-perk-perked.

Hate tracts, redux. Across all case lines. Ashida filched the Jap-language tracts. Did he lie about the contents?

Dudley popped the trunk. The Jap tracts were stashed there.

He scanned them page by page. His brain perk-perk-perked. He saw that tract at the Deutsches Haus. They popped Fred Hiltz at the Deutsches Haus. Hiltz was a hate-tract man.

Link *that* tract to *these* tracts. Different languages and print styles.

Wait.

There's a lost memory. *That* tract to *these* tracts. *Perk, perk—there it is.*

Identically glued bindings / identical paper stock.

Dudley walked to a phone booth. City directories were chained to an inside peg. *Perk, perk.* Go in alphabetically.

The northeast directory. The *C*'s first. "Christian Nationalist Crusade": 2829 Chevy Chase, Glendale. On to *H.* "Hiltz, Dr. Fred": 2831 Chevy Chase, Glendale. On to *S.* "Smith, G. L. K.": 2829 Chevy Chase, Glendale.

The detectives' craft. Instincts confirmed. Disparate wisps cohere.

He snagged his car and laid tracks. He took the 1st Street bridge to Broadway. He took Broadway to the parkway. He popped two bennies and hit Avenue 45.

He parked in the driveway and walked across the lawn. Some fuck painted *JAPS!* on the door.

He let himself in. He walked straight upstairs. He paced the second-floor landing and stretched tall. He tap-tap-tapped the ceiling. He noticed inconsistent grain. He tapped that exact spot.

Presto—folding stairs dropped to the floor.

He walked up them. He lit a match. He lit up a snug crawl space.

No shortwave radio. One table and wall outlet. The radio *was* plugged in there.

Dusty footprints by the table. Note the heel and toe marks. Hideo Ashida always wore shoes with *taps.*

Hideo Ashida was here. Hideo Ashida stole the radio. Hideo Ashida stole the tracts. You drove up then. You should have searched his car.

Dudley got chills. Benzedrine. This detectives' competition. His quixotic regard for the lad.

He walked down the steps and retracted them. The ceiling panel slid in place, flush. He walked out to his car and drove to the parkway.

He felt off-kilter. He should eat something. The thought sickened him.

Mr. Smith, Sergeant Smith.

The Brit Smith, the mick Smith. The Prod, the Papist. Gerry was Huey Long's protégé. He was a share-the-wealth Red then. The Kingfish was snuffed. Gerry turned hard right. He was one florid Jew baiter.

Dudley swung off the parkway. A bridge put him up on Chevy Chase. He caught the edge of a golf course and read address plates.

Right there. Two mock Tudors, by the driving range.

He parked curbside. 2831 was range-flush. The backyard was grassed in. Fred Hiltz sailed irons. Gerald L. K. Smith cued up his balls.

Dudley ambled over. He came at them sideways. They were copwise. Hiltz knew him from the Deutsches Haus. Smith provoked discord routinely. They were copwise.

There—Hiltz sees him. There—he nudges Smith. They're a Mutt and Jeff team. Hiltz is short, Smith is tall. Convergence. Mike Breuning said he saw them at Pershing Square.

Note the pitcher of lemonade. The dark hue says that it's spiked.

Hiltz cranked a three-iron. The ball sailed two hundred yards.

Gerald L. K. Smith said, "Well, sir."

Dudley said, "Pastor, it's an honor to meet you."

Hiltz twirled his iron. "He's Alien Squad, Gerry. He was there at the Deutsches Haus. The Jew Control Apparatus sent some hard boys in."

Smith said, "Friend or foe? Come on, out with it. You're smiling, but you're a harness bull in mufti. That brogue is disarming, but I wouldn't want to get on the wrong side of it."

Dudley cranked up his smile. His mouth twitched. He felt off-kilter.

"My name is Smith, Pastor. I answer to it proudly, as I'm sure you do. I'm Dublin-born, I'm Catholic, I'm a sergeant with the

Los Angeles Police. Some pamphlets that I believe you to have published have come to my attention as collateral evidence in an already-solved homicide case. I have a few perfunctory questions along those lines, but the true purpose of this visit is to solicit your advice on a business matter."

Hiltz sailed off a high one. Smith hoisted his trousers. He had stock moves. He was a grand stage ham.

"I bear no ill will for Catholics or the Irish, sir. The Irish lit bonfires so that Luftwaffe airplanes could get a better fix on London and blow it to smithereens. English Jews wrote *The Protocols of the Learned Elders of Zion.* The Jew Control Apparatus has its own special entrance at number 10 Downing Street."

Dudley bit his tongue. Hiltz walked to a sideboard and poured three lemonades. Smith went *After you.*

They pulled up chairs, facing the golf course. Hiltz dispensed lemonade. He was Gerald L. K.'s flunky. Gerry collected stooge protégés.

Hiltz raised his glass. "*L'chaim.* It's a Jew toast. If you can't beat 'em, join 'em. I like a good pastrami sandwich as much as the next Christian white man."

Dudley *Smith* roared. Gerald L. K. *Smith* roared. He had the lion head common to stage hams.

They sipped lemonade. It was laced with high-test bourbon. Dudley broke a sweat.

Smith said, "Huey Pierce Long, R.I.P. The sour mash that you are now imbibing came from his private stock. It's 168-proof. The Kingfish appreciated a fast push out of the gate."

Hiltz said, "That Jew dentist massacred him. I was in dental school then. Carl Weiss, DDS. That Jew cocksucker defamed my whole profession. I heard the news on the radio, and joined the Shirts the next day."

Smith said, "Ask your questions, sir. 'Perfunctory,' you stated. That means *three* questions to me."

Dudley said, "A Jap family named Watanabe was killed on December 6. They possessed one English-language and a score of Jap-language tracts that I believe you to have published. Did you know this family? Did you sell them tracts? Do you know or think you know anyone who might have known them?"

Smith said, "Well, that's three questions."

Hiltz said, "We've got no 'Watanabes' and no Jap names, period, on our mail lists. We consign our Jap tracts to a newsstand guy at 2nd and San Pedro. Who knows where they end up."

Smith said, "They get killed December 6. Pearl Harbor takes it up the shorts the next day. No wonder I haven't seen it in the papers."

Dudley said, "Fainthearted people might call your pamphlets hateful, but I do not. It does not perturb me that some of your published screeds are vociferously anti-American, anti-Catholic, anti–Los Angeles Police, pro-Japanese and more than occasionally written from a Communist perspective. These extraordinary times have created a radically comingled populism, and your pamphlets serve to give it voice. I am possessed of extreme viewpoints that most of our fellow Americans might consider reprehensible. I laud you for having the courage to put forth such a diverse range of thought."

Smith and Hiltz gawked. This mick can *talk*!

Hiltz said, "The bad pamphlets pay for the good pamphlets. We're proponents of First Amendment discourse, and we revere our native right of free speech. Also, it's fun to stir up shit from conflicting perspectives, and see how it all comes out in the wash."

Dudley sipped lemonade. It burned going down. It merged with the bennies and sparked tingles.

"Who writes the tracts? Who receives them? How extensive are your mail lists?"

Hiltz said, "This guy's bearing down with the questions, Gerry."

Smith said, "There's a pitch coming, son. Smitty ain't here to waste our time."

No, you vile Prod sack of shit—I am not. "Smitty"? I have killed men for less.

Dudley said, " 'Smitty.' That's rich."

Hiltz said, " 'Smitty's' a potato eater from way back. The Irish breed with the dagos every chance they get. It's eugenics. They produce good-looking people with dark hair and blue eyes. Potatoes are an aphrodisiac. Smitty's probably got half-dago whelps scattered all over the country."

Dudley went for his sap. *No, no, no—don't.*

"I will readily admit my fondness for potatoes, Doctor. It is surely in my eugenic blood."

Smith said, "Don't rile Smitty, son. He's got more than potatoes in his blood."

Dudley sipped lemonade. Dudley faked a cough and popped three bennies.

Smith said, "To answer Smitty's questions, then. I write the right-wing tracts, Dr. Fred writes the left-wing tracts, and an old British fascist guy who was Jap-fluent wrote the Jap tracts, but he got killed in a hit-and-run accident on Pearl Harbor morning. The Jap-tract market has slowed down since we got in the war, but I'm considering hiring a Chink writer to write anti-Jap tracts and a Jap writer to write anti-Chink tracts in their own languages, which will cover a lot of bases and buttress our pro–First Amendment stance. There's a socialite Commie woman named Claire De Haven who buys our Red tracts in bulk, and she even wrote an anticop tract herself. She distributes the tracts to Hollywood Jews, labor agitators, bleeding hearts, jigaboos, welfare creeps, queers, lovers of President Franklin 'Double-Cross' Rosenfeld, Jap lovers, Klan haters, Fifth Columnists and the Red parasites who pollute the minds of our young at American *Jew*niversities."

The stage ham pooped out. Hiltz rolled his eyes. *He's always like this.*

Dudley said, "Pastor, how many names do you have on your mail list?"

Hiltz stirred his lemonade. "Now, he gets to it."

Smith said, "Let's allow him his moment. He hasn't been brusque so far."

Hiltz said, "He was brusque at the Deutsches Haus."

Smith slurped lemonade. "Smitty, I'm not a bragging man—but Dr. Fred and I are currently blessed with 68,981 names on our list."

Dudley whistled. It came out dry. *He* was dry. The golf course swirled.

"Gentlemen, I represent a cadre of investors who stand to reap significant profits from the upcoming Japanese internment. Among our many plans, we intend to shoot risqué movies with an anti-Axis political content, featuring Jap performers. This war is a free-for-all, gentlemen. If even 15% of the people on your list have the predilection or wartime je ne sais quoi to partake, we would all earn significant monies."

Hiltz said, "And that's only one of your plans?"

Dudley said, "Yes."

Smith slurped redneck lemonade. "And you're telling us it's police-protected? I used to drink and worship with Two-Gun Davis, so I know police protection when I see it."

"Chief Horrall is less flamboyant than Chief Davis, but no less willing to capitalize on unfortunate situations that he himself did not create."

Hiltz said, "The Japs lost me with Pearl Harbor. I wouldn't mind turning a buck off the upshot. We could tithe 10% to the Crusade and wash our hands of the seamy side."

Smith winked. "Dr. Fred's been known to enjoy a racy two-reeler every once in a blue moon. He draws the line at tykes and animals, though."

"We all do, Pastor."

Smith said, "How much seed money are you looking for, Smitty?"

Dudley said, "None, sir."

Hiltz said, "The magic words. You can't trust a man who arrives with his hand out."

Smith said, "It's all about selecting the proper names on the list. You can't send out 68,981 smut brochures and remain confident of a high sell-through and no Christian censure."

Hiltz said, "Amen."

Dudley sipped redneck lemonade. His vision fritzed. His shirt collar seeped.

"There are a great many details to be worked out, gentlemen."

Smith said, "You're looking peked, Smitty. It's not attractive on a ruddy guy like you."

Hiltz said, "Huey Long's private stock is not for weak sisters."

A golf ball hit the house. Dudley flinched and reached for his piece.

Hiltz said, "Goddamn Jews. They're gunning for us, I can tell."

Smith said, "It's a restricted club, Freddy. You can't blame this one on the kikes."

Hiltz said, "You're right, Chief. It's *Smitty* who's gunning for us. He's got a case of the yips."

Dudley stood up. He saw spots in front of his eyes.

"Gentlemen, I'm afraid I must leave. I have a murder suspect to arrest."

Hiltz said, "Did you hear the one about Pope Pius and the Dalmatian? Just a quick one before you go."

Smith said, "You shoo, Smitty. I can tell you've been working too hard."

6:03 p.m.

He got to his car. Caddies lugging golf bags blurred by him. He clutched his Saint Chris. Martin Luther taunted him. He started the car and got rolling downhill.

A canyon, a golf course, a white pavement line. He concentrated on his front tires and that white blur. He squinted. His clutch foot went numb. The car jerk-jerk-jerked.

He turned on his lights. Bugs crawled over the windshield. He ran the wipers and killed them.

He drove too fast. He drove too slow. He popped four bennies. He lost track of where he was. It looked like Dublin. Street signs said GLENDALE.

He stayed in second gear. He stalled out traffic behind him. He lurched up to red lights and fishtailed through greens. Christmas trees and American flags made him cry.

It might be raining. It might be his tears. He ran his wipers and brushed off more bugs. He weaved by the Silver Lake Reservoir. Front tires/white pavement line.

He saw double and triple. He passed Melrose and Virgil and saw that phone booth. Goro Shigeta waved at him. He yelled *You're dead, and I'm not.*

He made Temple Street. His vision discombobulated and normalized. He checked the rearview mirror and saw Dudley Liam Smith. He recognized a hot dog stand.

He test-fired his mind. He recalled his daughters' names. He recalled sporting events. The second Louis-Schmeling fight, 6/22/38.

Temple to Spring. Spring to City Hall.

The garage was near empty. He parked with great care. He wobble-walked to the lift and pushed 6. His feet were all pins and needles.

The lift stopped. He made the Bureau hallway. It was suppertime dead. The wall was a pavement line. His feet were front tires. He made it to the men's room.

He threw the bolt and locked himself in. He slid down the door. The floor tile induced shivers. He crawled to the sink and pulled himself up.

He soaked a paper towel and doused his face. The mirror was a mirror. It was not a bug habitat.

Dudley Liam Smith. Dear Lord, that's a scare.

He walked back out to the hall. He walked to his cubicle and fell into his chair. He stifled a screechy child's sob.

Cigarettes settled his pulse and rewired his blood. Twenty minutes to the show-up. The eyeball wits were being briefed now.

He sucked pastilles. His pulse raced and subsided. The desk phone rang. He snatched the call.

"Homicide, Sergeant Smith."

"Larry at PC Bell, Dud. You wanted fast, so you got it."

"You'll be compensated, lad. You know I reward rapid service."

Larry said, "The only consistent run of Ensenada-to-L.A. calls that Madrano made over the past three months were to three local numbers. You've got the home number for a man named Preston Exley. That's E,X,L,E,Y and WEbster-4821, which is a Hancock Park exchange. The second number is Exley Construction, 6402 Wilshire Boulevard, OLeander-2758. We've got Beverly Hills for the third number. It's the office line for one Pierce Patchett. That's P,A,T,C,H,E,T,T. The number is CRestview-7416. I don't know what sort of business Patchett is in, but the address is 416 Bedford Drive."

Dudley wrote it down. His hand trembled. The pencil snapped.

Larry nagged him. You owe me a C-note—blah, blah. Dudley hung up. Evidential links and tweakers overlapped.

He *knew* Preston Exley. He *served* under him. Preston ran Homicide for a spell. He read an inter-Bureau memo. Exley Construction had proposed internment-prison plans. The Madrano-to-Exley calls *suggested* Watanabe-case links.

Carlos Madrano fed wetbacks to Jap truck farms. Add the "two white stiffs" embroiled in the buyouts. Exley and Patchett might be those stiffs.

Patchett's address hit familiar. 416 Bedford Drive. There's more overlap.

Ed Satterlee supplied it. They were gabbing at Kwan's. *"We've got this Red psychiatrist turned. He's got an office on Bedford, across from Klein's Pharmacy."*

He knew Klein's. His wife got her asthma pills there. The address was 419 Bedford. He always parked by 416.

Overlap.

Preston Exley suffered from migraines. They discussed it at a Bureau lunch last year. Preston said a Jew doctor worked wonders for him. The man was deep off in eugenics. His office was right by Marv's Hofbrau. A pal in the same building recommended him.

Marv's Hofbrau. Across the street from Klein's Pharmacy. Right by 416 Bedford Drive.

Exley. Doctor-snitch Saul Lesnick. The unknown Pierce Patchett. Evidential leads and overlaps.

The phone rang. He fumble-snatched the receiver.

"Homicide, Sergeant Smith."

"It's Bette, and I will not tolerate one single interruption or line of blarney while I tell you that my husband was there when the flowers arrived, as were Willie Wyler, Myrna Loy and John Huston. My husband began weeping, in full view of my friends. John said, 'Who sent them, Bette? Some stagehand you're fucking?' I was mortified, I was inconvenienced, I was made to look picayune. Do not cross the line again with me, Dudley—because I will not let you inconvenience me one more time."

He trembled. Bette hung up. He fumble-lit a cigarette. The match singed his hand.

Buzz Meeks walked up. He struck a pose. He oozed insolence. He wagged a cigar.

"You look dicey, Dud. The Dudster with troubles. It's one for the books."

"Is there a point to your comments?"

"The point is you owe me three scrapes. My girlfriends are squawking, and I know you got to book Ruthie in advance."

Dudley scrawled up a note slip. "Pierce Patchett/416 Bedford/ Beverly Hills." He tore it off the pad and gave it to Meeks.

"Get me all you can on this man. I'll pay you five hundred. No delays, no cornpone asides. You've *inconvenienced* me, lad. I will not let that happen again."

Meeks gulped. There—the fucking balance regained.

Dudley stood up. He got anchored. He weave-walked to the show-up room. It was elbow-to-elbow tight.

His lads. The nine eyeball wits. Low-life Meeks, waddling up.

A sideshow. A fashion show. Punks in slit-bottom khakis. Sideburns and duck's-ass haircuts. A Mex in a full-drape zoot suit.

Jabber. Oppressive smoke. Dudley went light-headed. Dick Carlisle went *Pipe down, now.*

Dudley said, "Good evening, and thank you for your cooperation. We are forgoing the show-up we had originally planned, in favor of a more expeditious two-step procedure. You will view the suspect's image on a mug-shot strip, and will later view the man himself through a blacked-out interrogation room mirror. In recompense, you will be given ten-dollar food and beverage chits for the much honored Kwan's Chinese Pagoda."

The lowlifes stomped and cheered. Dudley raised a hand and squelched it.

"To further express our appreciation, all of your extant bench warrants and parole holds will be rescinded."

More cheers, more stomps. Dudley went queasy. Bette berated him. He shook his head and muzzled her.

Dougie Waldner passed out mug shots. The strips featured full-face and side-angle views. Bamboo Shoot Shudo ran pudgy. He had a *loooooow* hairline.

The mug shots went around. The wits scoped the slayer. *Woooo*, he's ugly. *Woooo*, he's scary. *Wooooo*, he's *evil—and dat's no fuckin' shit.*

The strips ran back to Waldner. The Mex said, "He looks like a werewolf."

Dudley said, "December 6, gentlemen. That was twelve days ago, and memories tend to falter with the passage of time. Paradoxically, memories cohere in the proximity of important events. We all remember where we were when we got the word on Pearl Harbor. That horrible occurrence has forever fixed the sighting of our suspect in your minds."

Nods went around. The Mex howled like The Werewolf. It promoted boocoo laffs.

Dudley signaled Scotty: *It's you and me.*

A black-and-white was prestashed downstairs. Ditto a throwdown piece and two Ithaca pumps.

They took side stairs down. Dudley went on-and-off weavy.

Scotty fiddled with his nose splint. It looked ridiculous. It marred his boy-man élan.

They piled into the sled. Dudley took the wheel. Scotty scanned the backseat ordnance and whistled. The Kyoto Arms was two-minutes close—1st and Alameda.

Dudley pulled out and goosed the lights and siren. Bette said "*You inconvenienced me.*" He went pins and needles. He kept hearing her.

They cut southeast. It was late-fall cool. Local business fronts were broken-windowed and dark. Little Tokyo had been raped. Unimprisoned Japs stayed indoors. It was a howlers' night. *No one out but us werewolves, boss.*

Sid Hudgens and Jack Webb beat them there. They brought a camera geek along. The Kyoto Arms was a two-story fleabag. There's Elmer Jackson on the fire escape.

Dudley pulled up across the street. Sid and Jack trotted over. He shook his legs limber. Scotty loaded the shotguns.

Sid said, "I'm glad you brought the Bennett kid. Our female readers will go for him. Mr. Hearst knows that beefcake sells papers."

Jack said, "Mike Breuning showed me a mug shot. The cocksucker looks like a werewolf."

Sid howled. "*Jap Creature Apprehended! Fearless Cops Storm Monster's Den!*"

Dudley laughed. He felt fine-all-of-a-sudden. Scotty passed him a shotgun.

Sid said, "You're a swell-looking kid, Scotty—but I don't like that splint."

Jack said, "Have you been off to Mars? Scotty KO'd Lee Blanchard."

Dudley ripped off the splint and tossed it in the gutter. Scotty went *Ouch!* Blood trickled down his cheeks.

Sid and Jack went *Ouch!* Elmer yelled, "He's in 216!" He waved his Ithaca pump.

Dudley grabbed the throwdown piece. The camera geek walked up. He said, "Watch the birdie." He snapped the Dudster and the swell-looking kid.

Sid said, "*Hollywood High Fullback Scores Crime Touchdown! Werewolf Slayer Sacked!*"

Jack said, "Holy shit, this is kicks."

Sid said, "Blast a few rounds, will you, Dud? Mr. Hearst likes action pix."

Dudley winked at Scotty. "I'll take the door. If he makes any sudden moves, kill him."

The geek hooked a flashbulb strip to his camera. They ran across the street and went in the front door. No lobby, no desk man. Straight-up stairs to the second floor.

They ran up, single file. Elmer stood outside 216. They formed a crash line. The camera geek took the rear slot.

Dudley kicked in the door. There's The Werewolf.

He's on the bed. He's dolled up in skivvies. He's slurping muscatel.

Note the bamboo shoots, propped on the nightstand. They're covered with dried blood and shit.

They ran in. They stood three across. A flashbulb popped.

The Werewolf snarled. Dudley triggered a round and blew out a window. Bulb no. 2 popped. Elmer triggered a round and blew up a wall. Scotty triggered two rounds and blew up the bed legs. The mattress and Werewolf crashed to the floor.

Bulb no. 3 popped. Dudley charged Bamboo Shudo and kicked him in the head. Shudo screeched. Elmer crowded up and stepped on his neck. Bulb no. 4 popped. The room went phosphorescent. Dudley went light-headed and glare-blind.

Scotty crowded up and grabbed Shudo's wrists. Dudley heard bones shear. His head cleared. Scotty cuffed Shudo's hands behind his back.

They dragged him.

They dragged him facedown. It was clumsy. Their shotguns got in the way. Dudley grabbed a foot. Elmer grabbed a foot. Scotty grabbed an arm and walked backward.

Shudo screeched and ate floor wood. They dragged him down the hall and down the stairs. His face bounced off the steps. Tooth stubs hit Scotty's shoes.

Dudley saw a crowd outside. He dropped the foot and pulled Shudo up by his hair. Elmer and Scotty held his arms and steered him. Dudley got the door and shoved him outside.

Local Japs ghoul-shrieked. White squares cheered. They steered Shudo up to the black-and-white. Sid and Jack stood by.

The photo geek snapped a shot. *Pop!*—he got Dudley's mitts in The Werewolf's mane and The Wolf in full snarl.

Shudo flailed. Elmer sapped him in the balls. Shudo gasped and went two-second meek. Dudley laid down his shotgun and popped the trunk.

Elmer shoved Shudo in. Scotty slammed the door. City Hall—Code 3.

Dudley drove. Scotty rode up front. Elmer took the backseat. The Werewolf thrashed in the trunk.

Dudley lit a cigarette. Scotty chewed gum and blew a big bubble. Dudley stabbed his cigarette. The bubble blew all over Scotty's face.

Scotty laughed. Elmer laughed. They all laughed and went *WHEW!* The siren whooped *loud.*

They made City Hall. Dudley idled the car by the lift. Elmer and Scotty popped the trunk and hauled Shudo out.

They kicked his legs wide. They manhandled him and got him into the lift. The doors slid shut.

Dudley sat in the car. He popped sweat and felt it freeze. He blinked and saw Bette. She said, "*You inconvenienced me.*"

He tasted Huey Long's booze. His breath was off. His trousers fit slack. His feet swam in his shoes.

Rest, now—just a bit.

He parked the car and worked the seat back. Bette said those words again. He said, "Hush, dear. I've work to do."

He caught his breath. He wiped his face and walked to the lift. He pushed the button. The doors slid wide. *Dudley Liam Smith—a task beckons you.*

He went up six floors. He primped and stepped into the hallway. His audience awaited him. They jammed the sweat-room row.

Now, they turn. Now, they applaud. Now, they honor you.

Call-Me-Jack Horrall. Lieutenant Thad Brown. Ray Pinker and Hideo Ashida. A glum Bill Parker.

The eyeball wits. All his lads. Sid Hudgens and Jack Webb. Werewolf watchdog Elmer Jackson.

He walked over. They pumped his hand. They clapped his back. They attaboy'd him. He heard *Werewolf! Werewolf! Werewolf!* He looked in mirror-front no. 1.

Fuji Shudo was cuffed to a bolted-down chair. He dripped blood on a bolted-down table.

Dudley smiled at his colleagues. Dudley winked at young Hideo and dour Whiskey Bill. He tapped the speaker above the mirror. Shudo's breath eked.

Breuning lobbed a syringe. Dudley snapped it out of the air. He motioned Scotty over. They stepped into the room.

Shudo stuck out his tongue and wagged it. Scotty huddled close. He smelled like fresh bubble gum.

Dudley said, "Walk the witnesses by the look-see, individually. Get their eyeball confirmations and write the precise time and date in your notebook. Go to the property room and filch a pair of Nancy Watanabe's panties and one of Aya Watanabe's brassieres. Go back to Shudo's room, drag the articles over the floor and create a coating of particles. Place the articles in one of Shudo's coats, return here and talk to Sergeant Jackson. Tell him that he's green-lit to toss the room."

Scotty walked. The steno rolled in his machine. Shudo tongue-wagged him. The steno said, "*Really*, sweetheart."

Dudley roared. The steno arranged his machine. Shudo studied him and rattled his cuff chain. Dudley blindsided him.

He grabbed Shudo's head. He jammed the syringe into his neck and siphoned blood. Shudo screamed. Dudley pulled out the spike and waved at the mirror.

Breuning walked in. Dudley tossed him the syringe.

"Good Samaritan, lad. The fastest typing you can get."

Breuning scrammed. The steno slid his chair outside spit-glob range. Dudley straddled his chair. Shudo sat two feet away.

Dudley reached under the table. Flip—the hallway-speaker switch.

Shudo queer-eyed the steno. Dudley laid his cigarettes and matches on the table. He faked a cough and popped three bennies. Shudo shook his chain.

Dick Carlisle rolled in a coffee cart. He poured two cups and left the cart close. The steno grabbed his. Dudley grabbed his. Carlisle left the room.

Dudley lit a cigarette. Shudo made *gimme* eyes. Dudley slid the pack and matchbook over. Shudo lit up.

His lips were lacerated. His teeth were cracked bloody. He smoked stylishly. He was almost-but-not-quite effete.

Dudley said, "To begin, I am Sergeant D. L. Smith, assigned

to the Homicide Division of the Los Angeles Police Department. The stenographer is Mr. George T. Eggleton, a licensed and board-certified employee of the county of Los Angeles. It is now 9:23 p.m., on Thursday, December 18, 1941. We are in the Detective Bureau offices of the Los Angeles Police Department. This is our first interview of Mr. Fujio Shudo. Mr. Shudo's local address is 682 East 1st Street."

Shudo killed off his cigarette. Dudley slid him the ashtray. Shudo crushed the butt.

"I want to go home."

"To the Kyoto Arms, Mr. Shudo? To Imperial Japan?"

"No. Atascadero. I had a sweet berth there. I didn't have to think about nothing. I think too much when I'm on the outside."

"What do you think about, sir?"

"Crazy things. You wouldn't understand."

"I would, sir. My enlightened perspective might surprise you."

Shudo said, "Okay, then. I did it."

Dudley said, "Did what, sir?"

Shudo said, "I bootjacked three rumdums from a he-she bar on East Fifth. I fed them terpin hydrate and got them all sleepy. I stole a car and took them up the ridge route. There was a pretty forest outside of Castaic. I was in the honor farm there. You know my MO, chief. I'm the Sheriff of the Brown Trail."

Dudley said, "Would you explain your last comment, please."

Shudo said, "Bamboo shoots. The dirt road. Figure out the rest for yourself."

Dudley said, "Are you admitting sodomy or other forms of sexual deviance, sir?"

"Okay, chief. If that's what gets me back home, I admit it."

"And where did you go after you performed the sexual assaults that you have just elliptically, but colorfully, described?"

"I left the winos in the pretty forest. I gave them a buck each for car fare and got a pizza pie at a diner on the ridge route. The old bat behind the counter was real friendly. She said she didn't usually like Japs, because we were in with the Krauts, and she was a Jew. She said she liked me because I look like a werewolf, and Lon Chaney flirted with her at a sneak peek in Burbank back in '34. She didn't charge me for my coffee. She was nice, so I left her a big tip."

Dudley said, "And then, sir? You presumably left the diner. Where did you go then?"

Shudo said, "Back to the hotel."

Dudley said, "The Kyoto Arms Hotel, at 682 East 1st Street?"

"Right."

"You've described the abduction and its aftermath quite concisely. Will you tell me when it occurred? The *date*, sir. Do you recall the date or the day of the week?"

Shudo scrunched up his face. Dudley slid his cigarettes and matches over. Shudo lit up.

"Two weeks ago. Wednesday. They kicked me loose at Atascadero. I got off the bus and rented that hotel room. I started drinking terp and got the hankering. My dick started talking to me, so I went to the Murakami Nursery and got some shoots."

Dudley said, "That's Wednesday, December 3rd, that you're describing. You were released from Atascadero on that date. You rented a room at the Kyoto Arms on that date, you purchased bamboo shoots at the Murakami Nursery on that date, you abducted the three men and performed the sexual assaults that you described on that date, you returned to your hotel room after you left the diner, on that date?"

Shudo pouted. "That's right, chief. You don't have to be so quick with the questions, though. It's not like I don't want to go back. That, and you and your pals didn't have to be so rough. I had a sweet berth at the Big A."

Dudley said, "I apologize, sir, but you do resemble a werewolf. My colleagues and I were unprepared for your fearsome appearance, and acted out of sheer panic. Again, sir, my deepest apologies."

Shudo grinned. His cracked teeth wobbled. His lips oozed blood.

"I like you, chief. You got that funny accent, and you talk nice."

Dudley said, "Thank you, sir. You are a man of considerable insight, and I appreciate your kind regard for me. On that note, I would like to discuss your apprenticeship in the knife-sharpening trade."

Shudo said, "That's me. 'Fuji, the Werewolf.' 'Fuji, the Knife Man.'"

Dudley lit a cigarette. "How long have you practiced the trade, sir? As I understand it, you peddle your wares door-to-door."

Shudo said, "'Fuji, the Knife Man.' I've been at it since '31. I was in Preston for 459 and indecent exposure. I learned the trade in metal shop."

Dudley blew a smoke ring. It sent him light-headed.

"You were out with your cart two weeks ago, weren't you, sir? That would be Thursday, December 4th, and Friday, December 5th. You were in Highland Park, a few miles north of Chinatown, on the west side of the parkway. Is that correct, sir?"

Shudo yawned. "Yeah, that's correct. But I don't get it. I told you what I did. I *confessed.* I told you I bootjacked them winos and had fun with them. You don't need to talk so much. I'm ready to go back, and all you got to do is give me the paper, so I can sign it and go to my cell and go to sleep."

Dudley crushed his cigarette. He felt bilious. His wedding band slipped off and hit the table.

He grabbed it. He saw spots in front of his eyes.

"I'm curious, Mr. Shudo. You were released from Atascadero on Wednesday, December 3rd. You rented a room in Little Tokyo, kidnapped three winos and sexually assaulted them at a remote location sixty miles north of Los Angeles, ate a pizza pie at a nearby diner and returned to your room, all on Wednesday, December 3rd. The following day, Thursday, December 4th, you were spotted in Highland Park, with your knife-sharpening cart. I'm curious, sir. You're fresh out of a mental institution, and you've been quite the busy lad. My question is, where, when, and from whom did you secure the knife-sharpening cart you were seen with?"

Shudo yawned. "Too many dates. Days and dates get blurry, you know? I'm a terp man. I drink terp and lose track of things. It's not my fault. Nobody's that good with dates. People don't remember what they did on Tuesday, three weeks ago. This is all Sanskrit you're talking."

Dudley drummed the table. "Normally, you would be correct about that, sir. But the Japanese attack of Sunday, December 7th, has served to embed a unique sense of chronology within all of us. We recall our movements preceding and following that event with enhanced clarity. Do you understand that, sir?"

Shudo yawned. "Too many words. Too much talk and too many dates. You got to slow down, chief. I'm a terp man. I'm losing track of things."

Dudley saw spots. Bette said, *"You inconvenienced me."* The spots dispersed.

"The cart, sir. Where did you buy the knife-sharpening cart?"

Shudo yawned. "Outside the Shotokan Baths. This old nip named Kenji. He sold me the cart, wheels, sample knives, the megillah."

"And when was this?"

"The morning. I was hungover. I thought, Shit, I'm back here again. Shit, I should go home."

Dudley smiled. "And that would be the morning of Thursday, December 4th?"

Shudo yawned. "That's right, chief. The Werewolf's at the Shotokan Baths, and he's one day out of stir."

The door light blinked. Dudley walked over. Breuning and Scotty B. stepped inside.

Scotty said, "I planted the items. I gave Elmer the green light on the toss."

Breuning said, "We hit paydirt on the typing. The Wolf's AB negative, so he could have knocked Nancy up. I called Atascadero, on a hunch. Get this. The Wolf was out on a work furlough at the approximate time that Nancy would have been impregnated, so we're golden there."

Dudley smiled. "Reserve a padded cell at Central Station. Call the jailer. Tell him it's a straitjacket deal."

The boys tore off. Dudley walked back to the table.

Shudo said, "I'm hungry. I'll cop to the Lindbergh baby job if you get me a pizza pie."

The steno hooted. Dudley drummed the table.

"Let's return to Thursday and Friday, December 4th and 5th. You're on your knife-sharpening rounds in Highland Park. What drew you to that particular area? Was there any specific reason?"

Shudo shrugged. "Instinct, I guess. I was on the Figueroa bus, and it looked like a good place to work."

"Instinct." A sure grabber. Lunatics succumbed to wisps.

"You say 'Instinct.' Had you been drinking terp at this time? Would you say that it contributed to your 'instinct'?"

"I don't know. I guess so."

Dudley drummed the table. He went light-headed. He lit a cigarette and saw spots. He saw Bette in the wall mirror. He shook his head and shooed her off.

"Would you be more specific, please? Were you drinking terpin hydrate, and do you think it contributed to your 'instinct' to peddle your wares in Highland Park?"

Shudo pouted. "I want a pizza pie and medical attention. You and your pals kicked the shit out of me."

"In due time, sir. We have the matter of your knife-sharpening rounds in Highland Park to discuss first."

Shudo said, "Highland Park and *Glassell* Park. Them neighborhoods confuse me. It was the first two days I was out of the joint, and maybe more. I was belting terp. Things get fuzzy when you belt terp. You get hazy and lose track of the time."

Missing time. Terp blackouts. Lunatic gems.

"You were on your rounds in Highland Park and possibly Glassell Park, on that Thursday, that Friday and possibly that Saturday, right?"

"Right."

"You made some sales and talked to some customers, right?"

"Right."

"Do you recall any specific sales that you made?"

"No. But I made sales, because I woke up in my room and had money in my pocket."

"Do you recall any specific incidents that occurred on your rounds? Any specific people you might have talked to?"

Shudo giggled. "I talked to a little girl. She said I looked like The Wolfman. Her dad took a picture of me."

"And when was this, sir?"

"It must have been Saturday, maybe noon or so. Her dad said a college football game was coming on the radio."

"And this was in Highland Park, sir?"

"Yeah, one of them avenues with numbers. Forty or fifty something."

"And *then*, sir? Do you recall any incidents or interactions that might have occurred *after* you talked to the little girl and her father?"

Shudo shook his head. "It all got fuzzy then. Terp, man. It gets into your noggin."

The door light blinked. Dudley got up and walked over. The floor dipped. He reached for the wall.

The door popped wide. Call-Me-Jack beamed. A thin man stood beside him. He looked like a lox jock. He wore a Phi Beta Kappa key.

"Dud, this is Ellis Loew. He'll be presenting the case to the grand jury. He went to Harvard, and he's a comer. Bill McPherson calls him 'the Hebrew Hammer.' "

Loew cringed. Dudley laughed—*That's rich, sir.*

"A pleasure, Mr. Loew."

"Mine entirely, Sergeant."

Jack pointed to Shudo. "He's The Werewolf Slayer. Can you smell the wolfsbane? Sid Hudgens is writing that angle up."

Loew drifted off. He screamed wet blanket. He was no shtick-meister Yid.

Jack said, "He's a stick-in-the-mud, but he's damn good in court. He's got the ethics you'd expect from one of his kind."

Dudley popped a sweat. The walls compressed. He loosened his necktie.

"Close him, Dud. Close that fucker and get this off our plate. Sid H. sees this caper as a Sunday-supplement series. It'll take us straight up to that Fed probe and have us looking so good that that fucking pansy Hoover will drop the whole thing. The Japs got Pearl Harbor, but we got The Werewolf. He slayed his own kind, but we're blind to racial horseshit, so we fucking slayed *him*. Close him, Dud. I'm going over to the tile game at Kwan's. Meet me there later. We'll belt a few."

Dudley walked back. Call-Me-Jack shut the door. Shudo yawned. Dudley tossed a change-up.

"I'm still curious about something, Mr. Shudo."

"So am I. I'm curious about Thursday, Friday and Saturday in Highland Park, when you got me for grief up the ridge route on Wednesday."

"Then our curiosities overlap, sir. Your 'instinct' took you up the ridge route on Wednesday, and to Highland Park for the following three days. I don't think we can entirely attribute your 'instinct' for Highland Park to the consumption of terpin hydrate, do *you*, sir?"

"I don't know. Maybe not. Instincts are strange. It's this word we use to explain things we can't explain."

Yes—like brainstorms. He could enlist Hideo Ashida. The lad could craft a Jap-script note. Fuji Shudo writes to Ryoshi Watanabe. A friendship preexists.

The note bolsters hazy memories. He rolls The Werewolf's prints on transparency tape. He plants a print at the house.

"Did you belong to any Japanese fraternal societies before you went up, Mr. Shudo?"

"I went to the clubs. Why? I don't get this, and I want to go home. The clubs were all Japanese, and the guys I keestered were white. I'm losing track of all this, and my head hurts, and you promised me medical care and a pizza pie."

Dudley went light-headed. Dudley leaned across the table.

"I realize that things are often quite hazy for you, sir, given your long-standing consumption of terpin hydrate. However, I *do* know that you were often seen in the social clubs on 2nd Street, as far back as the early '30s, often arguing politics and racial issues with a man named Ryoshi Watanabe. Do you recall Ryoshi Watanabe, sir?"

Shudo yawned, Shudo shrugged, Shudo rattled his cuffs.

"I don't know. I used to go to those clubs, sure. I knew a guy named Ginzo Watanabe and a guy named Charlie Watanabe, and—"

"—and it all gets hazy after that, doesn't it? It all gets hazy and instinctive, and you wake up in your hotel room with knives missing from your cart, and you wonder where your instincts took you before you passed out, and why there's shit and blood on bamboo shoots, and what vile thing did you do with this or that sharp implement, when instinct led you to this or that house, where these hazy memories of arguments you had years before exploded, and you just couldn't help yourself, so—"

Shudo spit at him. The glob hit his eyes. He saw spots. His eyes burned. He heard *"You inconvenienced me."*

The Werewolf showed his teeth. Dudley pulled his sap and went for his mouth.

He hit him. He tore his mouth at the corners and crushed his stubbed teeth. He heard the door swing. He heard foot scuffs. He grabbed The Wolf's mane and pulled him in tight. Something blocked his arm. It was Bill Parker, all red-face flustered.

He *flicked* his arm and *flicked* him aside. The *flick* tossed Parker sideways. The *flick* put him down on the floor.

The Wolf spit at him. It burned the spots in his eyes. The door crashed in. Thad Brown ran in. Mike Breuning and Dick Carlisle got to him first. "Go slack, boss"/"Go slack, boss"/"Go slack, boss—we've been here before."

He went slack. He let go. They grabbed his sap and wrestled him out to the hall. The temperature dropped twelve thousand degrees. Some brain shutter doused his lights.

He heard, "Go to Kwan's." Everything tumbled. An elevator dropped.

He saw green numbers: 5, 4, 3, 2, 1. The doors opened. He saw marble walls and Main Street up ahead.

He walked outside. Lawn sprinklers twirled and sent up a mist. He anchored his legs and walked through the wet.

The water felt good. He slid on the grass. His trousers slid down his hips. He felt like Bill Parker looked.

Parker was frail. He *flicked* Parker off. It brought back '38. He beat a Mex dead at Newton Station. His lads said, "Go slack, boss."

"You inconvenienced me."

He dashed the words and erased Bette's picture. *El Pueblo Grande* at midnight. That howler's moon and Chinatown straight ahead.

Dudley Liam Smith—the world tumbles.

He walked straight to Kwan's. He wolfed all the gumballs at the counter. He's werewolf-famished. The counter girl says, *Dudster, you claaaaazy.*

He weaved down to the basement. The tile game was sputtering out. Ace dealt to Harry Cohn. Clark Gable and that leopard snoozed on a couch.

He made the office. He made the den. There's the pipe, the bowl and the tar.

He shut himself in. He removed his suit coat and holster. He kicked off his shoes.

Opium.

Go slack, boss. We've been here before.

Wisps and The Werewolf. His Army commission. *Captain* D. L. Smith. Parity with *Captain* Bill Parker.

That pesky bug. He *flicked* him.

Dudley smoked opium. His pallet flew over America. He visited his loved ones.

Stopover, Boston. Say hello to Beth Short. She's laughing. She's satirizing her rogue-daughter status. She's calling him "Dad."

Stopover, L.A. He nuzzles Bette's Airedale. Bette's naked, Bette's loving him, Bette's a crone in a flash. *He inconvenienced her.* She throws red roses in his face.

Dudley smoked opium. Stopover, Central Station and The Werewolf's padded cell.

The Wolf wears a straitjacket. Terp vials dot the floor. The cell is lined with blood-and-shit-streaked bamboo. The smell drives him out. It's a quick hop to the morgue.

He goes by Nort Layman's office. He steals a vial of Ryoshi Watanabe's blood. He revisits Fuji Shudo. He prints him and creates a tape transparency. He visits the house and finds an overlooked surface. He rolls on the bloody print.

Opium.

Create a note for me, Hideo. Link the victim to the killer in 1933.

Stopover, Nowhere.

He went blank. He reached for thoughts and snagged nothing. He reached for pictures and got empty frames.

"You inconvenienced me."

Stopover, Dublin. A gallery on Sackville Street. At that location—portraits in gilt frames.

His mother. His dead father and brother. His wrathful Bette.

He heard "Perfidia." He smelled roses. He felt sharp thorns on his face.

Dudley smoked opium. The pallet under him dropped.

Dudley said, "Don't hit me."

December 19, 1941

73

LOS ANGELES | FRIDAY, DECEMBER 19, 1941

1:57 a.m.

They kissed.

It was Claire's idea. Film it at the Anti-Axis Committee. Show the mixed-race lovers in a postmidnight clinch.

It was a post–Pershing Square kiss. It refracted his beaten appearance and Kay's barn-burning speech. The shoot was running in high gear now. Kay laid out her latest intrigue.

She *wanted* the film to come off broad and parodistic. She *wanted* it to scotch Bill Parker's loony crusade.

The kiss required umpteen takes. Kay was eager. Ashida faked urgency. Claire played director. The open doorway served as their set.

An arc light beamed down and prickled them. Two cameramen and a light man hovered. Reynolds and Chaz stood with Claire. Saul Lesnick brought his black bag. The Japanese extras got a dollar each.

They kissed again. Kay went in with her tongue. The cameramen shot the kiss from umpteen angles. They got the shelves stacked with antifascist pamphlets. They got the walls draped with AVENGE PEARL HARBOR! signs.

They kissed again. Kay caressed his bruises. Claire said, "That's good, kids."

The setup drew attention. Ashida saw a Fed sedan parked across the street. They broke the clinch. Claire said, "Once more, please."

A car rumbled by. A man yelled, "Goddamn Jap!"

Ashida flinched and bumped the arc light. Kay steadied him. He brushed free and walked to the back of the room. He stood by a jingoist toy shelf. Kabuki dolls were dolled up red, white and blue.

It was escalating.

Pershing Square. Goro Shigeta. The Japanese man shot in Santa

Monica. Nao Hamano's suicide. A suicide at the Fort MacArthur stockade.

Claire talked to a cameraman. Their voices carried. She bribed a cop at the Lincoln Heights jail. They could film the Hamano cell.

Little Tokyo was decimated. Twelve days, then to now. Incarceration, confiscation, liquidation. It was common knowledge—the internment flies in February.

Fait accompli. One possible way out.

Dudley Smith. Brutally revealed tonight. Stunning and endearing.

It started with Pershing Square and impotent Bill Parker. Whiskey Bill came solely to ogle Kay Lake. The attack on Hideo Ashida disturbed his sense of order. Scotty Bennett's intercession was something else.

Dudley knew the hate was building. Dudley knew that he'd ducked his bodyguards. Dudley sent men out to loose-tail him. *They* extricated him. Bill Parker flailed for his glasses and punched at the air.

The scene replayed at the Bureau. Parker witnessed Dudley's lapse and reacted again. The civil forfeit offended him more than the brutality. Parker hated disorder. That hatred created disorder in him. Parker's intervention was prissy and indicative of the man. Dudley's lapse showed the raw man beneath the glib skein.

Ashida studied the Kabuki dolls. Kay glanced back and saw him. She blew him a kiss.

He tried for a Dudley Smith wink—and failed. *Nobody* winked like Dudley Smith.

Kay laughed. Ashida thought of Bucky. He got that flutter and walked to the parking lot. A Fed was checking license plates. He carried a flashlight and strolled.

It's 2:26 a.m. *There's no one out but us Feds and Reds.*

Ashida got his car and drove home. That *JAP!* was still there on his door. He went straight inside and straight to his picture trove.

He got out the photos and his gizmo prototype. He went *all* flutters. He placed the Bucky pictures on his lap and nickelodeon-fanned them. He made Bucky dance in the nude.

He kept old photos loaded in the gizmo. The lens glass magnified details. He clicked levers and slid photos by. Shutter stops and Bucky, in the nude.

He scrolled pictures. They began to blur. It wasn't attrition caused by exposure. The pictures rarely met light.

Ashida studied the gizmo. Diagnostic scrutiny, prognosis.

A too-tight lens mount. Upward pressure. Hence, tears in the film.

The housing gears had rusted. The blurs were not pronounced. A new lens mount would halt the blurs at this point.

He had one new lens mount. His new gizmo was still affixed by Whalen's Drugstore. He could switch mounts. The new gizmo had run out of film. It was a twenty-minute drive, door-to-door.

He ran back out. He drove to Whalen's and braced the new gizmo. He pulled wires and detached the generator. He grabbed the new gizmo and drove straight back home.

All right. Prognosis to procedure.

Ashida studied both gizmos. Ashida figured it out.

It's a scroll-through. Go back to the first day the new gizmo clicked film. It's thirteen days ago. It's Saturday, December 6. It's that drugstore 211.

Scroll film until it runs out. Pull the lens mount then.

Ashida tapped levers. Click—car wheels hit a rubber strip stashed curbside. Click—the shutter snaps. Click—an image appears under glass.

Click—that first car parks. Click—the man looks like Bucky. Click—there's the robber's car. Click, click, click—throughout the day.

Click—the gizmo *works.* The precise time and date are clock-marked below each image.

Click—cars pull up and park. Click—there's a double exposure and blurred image. The gizmo jerked off the pavement. The lens jerked upward and snapped foot traffic. See the passersby on Spring Street?

Ashida scrolled photos. Click/snap/picture—all 12/6/41. 1:46 p.m., 2:04 p.m., 2:17 p.m. A rattled-lens run—note the blurred foot-traffic pix.

2:36 p.m., 2:42 p.m. Clear pix off an upward-right image. 3:08 p.m., 3:18 p.m., 3:19 p.m.—*WAIT.*

Hold it now. Wait, wait, wait.

Click/snap—a downtown street scene.

That's *FUJI SHUDO* in the foreground. He's stagger-gaited and visibly bleary. He's zorched on terpin hydrate. The people around him look agitated and downright scared.

They should be. He's evil. He practices bamboo-shoot rape.

It's 3:19 p.m. He's three and a half miles south of the Watanabe house. He's out among refuting eyewitnesses. It's Nort Layman's precise time of death.

The fearful people will recall Shudo. He's that outré. Coerced eyewits have placed Shudo in Highland Park at this time. These eyewits countermand those eyewits. Sure, it's a frame. Sure, The Werewolf will burn. Yes, it's justifiable. But that brings up this:

The Hearst papers will blast the case. Evidential details will be spilled nationwide. The real eyewits will recall The Werewolf and fuck it all up.

Ashida studied the image. Earthlings walk with a werewolf. He terrifies them.

Call-Me-Jack ran late stags most Thursdays. He should hear this.

Ashida rolled. He ran down to his car and burned tread to City Hall. He double-parked in a City Council space and ran up to 6. He heard dirty-joke snippets, straight off.

He tracked it. "Dudster this," "Dudster that." "What do you call an elephant hooker? A two-ton pickup that lays for peanuts."

Ashida walked to the briefing room. It was cops and Feds, intertwined. Note the Hearst Rifle Team boys. Note Brenda Allen by the all-Kwan's buffet.

Highballs and a dice game. A Jap flag for a craps-rolling felt.

Ashida stood in the doorway. Call-Me-Jack waddled over. The lipstick smear on his neck matched Brenda's shade.

"Dr. Ashida. What brings *you* here?"

A rifle man said, "Banzai."

Thad Brown said, "Shut up, he's ours."

Jack gestured out to the hallway. Ashida complied.

"I'm sorry for the intrusion, sir. I wouldn't be here if I didn't consider it urgent."

"*Urgent* always gets my attention. Remember, though, I'm jaded. It was the Dudster versus The Wolfman a few hours ago."

Ashida said, "This pertains to that, sir."

"Okay, kid. Impress me. The Dudster versus The Wolfman. Take it from there."

Ashida said, "Fujio Shudo was outside Whalen's Drugstore at

6th and Spring at Nort Layman's precisely estimated time of death. The trip-wire device that Ray Pinker and I installed that morning authenticates this quite plainly. Shudo was surrounded by five people who were obviously quite frightened of this fearsome individual. Those people will not forget Fujio Shudo, sir. They will come forth as newspaper and radio publicity accrues, they will contradict our eyewitnesses, and they will be credible."

Jack shrugged. "So what? Five eyewits aren't nine eyewits. Your device is something out of Buck Rogers or *Tom Swift and His Flying Saucer from Mars*, and you and Ray Pinker are the only two white men on earth who understand how it works, and you aren't even white. There's that, and there's a kicker. Yeah, Dud blew up at a bad time, but he picked himself up off his heinie, quick. He went back to the Watanabe house and turned up an eight-point print on The Wolf. You want a final kicker? The print was in Ryoshi Watanabe's blood."

Ashida reached for the wall. It wasn't there. Jack steadied him.

"You missed a fingerprint. So what? I don't blame you. Dud blows his cork, you blow an eight-point latent. We're all human, right? The important thing is solidarity. This police department has stepped way out on a limb for you, Doctor. You're too damn smart not to know that, and there's one other thing."

Ashida said, "Which is, sir?"

"Which is this. Dudley Smith is real fond of you."

74

KAY LAKE'S DIARY

LOS ANGELES | FRIDAY, DECEMBER 19, 1941

4:14 a.m.

The cell.

It was drab. There was a metal bunk, a sink and a lidless toilet. The jailer had vacated all the women's cells. A thin wall separated this tier from the men's tiers. They were brimful of Japanese "subversives" and general riffraff.

The crew moved their gear into the cell and began setting up. I stood with Reynolds and Chaz; Claire and Saul Lesnick gabbed with a light man. Nao Hamano died in the cell. The sequence would feature Claire, speaking directly to the camera.

She would address the powers that be and soliloquize from Mrs. Hamano's perspective. I wanted her to be loopy and bombastic. I feared that her eloquence would supersede bombast and convince a jury that she was indeed plotting treason. We were shooting two sequences here at the jail. The second was Hideo Ashida's stroll down the tier. Hideo, the police chemist. Hideo, the tenuous survivor of a horrible pogrom. Hideo, beholden to his white cop masters and despised by his own people for playing the game so goddamn well.

We needed Hideo here—but Hideo was gone. He broke off a filmed kiss with me and walked away, two hours ago. Claire said, "His kisses are quite tenuous, dear. Perhaps I should rent you a hotel room where you might rehearse." Staged kisses and my gender might have driven him away. Or perhaps he sensed peril—as I was beginning to.

We were under Federal "lockstep" surveillance. Our equipment and developing trailer was outside in the lot; Ed Satterlee and Ward Littell were parked across the street. Littell was Mariko Ashida's protector and was opposed to the roundups; Littell was a Federal agent charged with conducting them, nonetheless. I sensed peril. My cop-wise antennae kept twitching.

Our shooting schedule ran frenetic. It was wholly determined by the contents of Saul Lesnick's black bag. Claire kept saying, "I need to do this and *get away* somewhere." I was determined to shape the content of the film and prevent it from granting her the martyrdom she so desperately craved.

I was tired. My 'round-the-clock life since Pearl Harbor was catching up with me. The tier was strewn with cords and camera dollies; temporary telephone lines had been installed. Claire was skimming news clippings on Mrs. Hamano. Immersion, transference, identity assumed.

There was a daybed in the equipment trailer. I needed a moment's rest and more than a moment alone. I walked out to the parking lot.

I saw Hideo enter the jail. He wore his particular look of harried and prim.

I stepped into the trailer, kicked off my shoes and lay down. I heard thunder and hoped for dawn rain. Late autumn in Sioux Falls brought electric storms. I loved them passionately. I spent my girlhood on our front porch, imploring God to bring downpours.

The phone rang. I grabbed the receiver and pulled the cord over to the bed.

"Hello."

A man's voice came on the line. "It's Ward Littell, Miss Lake. I got this number from a police source. I'm sure you know who I am, and that this call constitutes a risk for me."

"I do know who you are, Mr. Littell. I know that you've been helpful to Hideo Ashida and his mother, but you haven't said anything risky."

Littell said, "I'm about to, and so I'll be brief. I would advise you to destroy the existing footage of the movie you're filming. Mr. Hoover is in Los Angeles. He's quite concerned that your movie is abetting the Japanese war effort."

I began to reply. Littell hung up on me. The hang-up noise became a pick-up click. Someone was making a call from an inside-the-jail line. The two calls were moments apart. Something tweaked me. I tapped the connector button and listened in.

I heard a moment's static and "News travels fast, lad." The brogue announced Dudley Smith. A man said, "I didn't know where you were, so I went to Chief Horrall." It was Hideo Ashida.

Their voices were hushed. Hideo was twenty yards away. He was making the call within range of Claire and the crew.

Dudley said, ". . . your grand photo device."

Hideo said, "I had no intention of interfering in your case against Fuji Shudo. I was simply pointing out a glaring time discrepancy."

"Did the Chief tell you that I uncovered a corroborating print? I lifted it off a patch of dried blood."

Hideo did not respond. His silence extended. I read some kind of shock in his pause. The conversation made no sense to me.

Dudley said, "You haven't asked me 'Whose blood,' lad."

Hideo said, "Ryoshi Watanabe's. The Chief told me that."

The Watanabe case. They had a suspect. They had solid leads.

Dudley said, "It's winding down, lad. I'll be crafting a chain-of-evidence brief for our lawyer chum, Ellis Loew. Shudo is AB negative, so I think we can attribute Nancy's pregnancy to him."

Hideo did not respond. His silence extended. I read some kind of censure in his pause.

Dudley said, "Are you feeling ambivalent, lad? Are you torn between the notion of a just exoneration and the degree of expediency required to ensure your safety? Am I witnessing a dithering expression of fatuous Japanese solidarity?"

Hideo said, "I simply acted on instinct."

Dudley said, "You're being disingenuous. You're far too circumspect to fall prey to the hot blood that 'instinct' implies, and I would venture to guess that your only instinct *is* circumspection."

Another pause. "Exoneration," "expediency." "Ambivalence," "interference." It felt like dialogue on a frame.

Dudley said, "Are you *there*, lad?"

Static hit the line. I shook the receiver and cleared it. Hideo said, "I've become involved in that movie I told you about. Remember? You gave me permission."

Dudley said, "Yes."

Hideo said, "Ward Littell told my mother that Mr. Hoover is here now, and that there'll be a Federal raid on the movie. I called you to tell you that. I'm sorry I bypassed you on the Shudo matter, but my intention was to bring the issue of the discrepancy to the attention of someone as far up the chain of command as possible, as soon as possible."

Traitor. Coward. Perfidious deviant in the thrall of a bold man he would dearly love to fuck.

"That is indeed a good tip, lad. I would caution you not to share it with Miss Lake, Miss De Haven, and the sundry dilettantes involved in this idiot venture. I assure you that your participation in the venture will be persuasively explained away, by me, at my most immediate opportunity. We are embroiled in the backwash of Whiskey Bill Parker's lunacy—and, as such, I would caution you to continue to treat the man with perfunctory kid gloves."

Hideo said, "Yes, Dudley. You have my word on all of that."

Vile, simpering, craven. Emasculated, frigid, vapid, picayune—

An air-raid signal blasted. I fumbled the phone back into the cradle and ran outside. Dawn was just breaking. The City Hall searchlights swooped across the southern horizon.

Red lights flashed above the jail. Uniformed jailers ran out and piled into their cars. The film crew followed them. Claire, Reynolds, Chaz and Saul Lesnick *walked* out. They were determined to appear unfazed by an air raid. Comrade Hideo *strolled* out. He was *smiling*.

They got in their cars, pulled out and made for the parkway. I was almost-but-not-quite alone.

Ward Littell and Ed Satterlee were parked across the street. A black-and-white was parked a half block behind them. It was too dark to see through the windshield.

It had to be *him*. *I* was here, and where else did *he* have to go?

I stepped back inside the trailer and locked myself in. I gathered up four reels of unedited film and dumped them in the service sink. A shelf above the sink was lined with bottled solvents; two were marked with skull and crossbones. I poured the contents over the film strips, watched them bubble and burn.

A rough-edited cut of the film had been fed into a glass-topped device. It allowed the editor to view it, frame by frame. The shoot had been rushed and haphazardly implemented. Still—it was *my* film that had to be destroyed. I had to see some version of it.

The editor's desk was covered with film strips; I went though them and straightened them into one long trail. The trail covered the floor up to my ankles. The commencing image was already clamped into the device. I held a lamp down and squinted.

It was a black-and-white negative, rendered white-on-black. The first frame portrayed a peaceful 2nd Street.

I'd seen the editor work and had a sense of how to operate his machine. I stood over the desk and fed film strips under the glass.

The process was slow. Air-raid sirens provided a soundtrack. Frame by frame and image by image—*my movie*.

The reversed black and white. The roundups in miniature. L.A., a week and a half after Pearl Harbor.

Street rousts. Japanese men and cops with shotguns. Cut to a white-on-black Claire, speaking to camera. Cut to clips from *Storm Over Leningrad*.

William H. Parker is right: they are didactic buffoons. William H. Parker is wrong: the roundups are barbaric and Claire is courageous in attempting to expose them. William H. Parker is right: the film indicts the filmmakers as provocateurs out to exploit injustice. William H. Parker is wrong: expressed outrage does not equal treason and any succor that it provides to our enemies must be seen as incidental and not actionable in any sane court of law.

I went through the film, frame by frame. I lived my movie and my moment in History. I became adept at identifying the people I already knew. I quickly spotted reverse-print snips of familiar figures and garb.

That's Thad Brown—I see his light fedora. That's Elmer Jackson—I see his ever-jutting cigar. That's my own speech yesterday. That's the riot in Pershing Square.

I caught the front of a building off 1st and San Pedro. Yes—I know those rounded pillars and that narrow stoop. Yes—that's Ed Satterlee. He's talking to an Asian man.

Their headgear identified them. Satterlee was tall and wore flat-topped hats with feathers; the presumed Asian man wore a coolie-type hat. I scrolled frames and saw what looked like an exchange. The men were close enough to be embracing.

Something made me stop. It was an *I-see-something* moment. I ran the subsequent frames through the glass, fast. I knew what I was seeing before I actually saw it.

Their hands touch. Their hands withdraw. Satterlee places something in his pocket. Both men wheel. Both men walk off. They head out in opposite directions.

It was a handoff. It was a covert exchange.

I grabbed a pair of scissors and snipped the appropriate frames. The trailer came with a darkroom. I'd studied photography and knew how to develop film.

I stepped into the darkroom. The red light above the door went on automatically. The developing tray was filled with solution. I laid the strip in and let the solvents go to work.

The enclosed space muffled the air-raid sirens; caustic chemicals made my eyes sting. The film-strip images reversed their shades and slowly came to life.

I pulled out the strip and held it up to dry. Yes, it was Ed Satterlee. The red light on his face ID'd him. I stepped out of the darkroom. The red light became normal light. I identified the Chinese man. It explained the whole furtive vignette.

It was a payoff. It was filmed inadvertently. The Chinese man passed Agent Satterlee money. They concluded their business then.

The Chinese man was a Hop Sing enforcer. Lee pointed him out to me at a Bureau Christmas party. He delivered Ace Kwan's holiday baskets to Call-Me-Jack and the boys. Cask-strength scotch and dry-rubbed ducks. Neatly folded C-notes.

Lee riffed on the man. His name was Quon something; he'd witnessed the rape of Nanking. He was a vociferous Jap hater. His rage far exceeded Ace Kwan's.

I stepped outside and lit a cigarette. The sirens went off; those dark clouds looked ready to burst. The Fed car was gone. The black-and-white was still here. *I* was here. Where else did *he* have to go?

I walked over. Parker stepped out of the car. He was fresh groomed and wore a neat uniform. His glasses were lost in the riot. He wore wire-rimmed spectacles now.

He said, "Miss Lake." I said, "Captain Parker." He reached into my skirt pocket and removed my cigarettes. I lit him up.

"Dudley Smith knows about your operation. I overheard him talking to Hideo Ashida. They're colluding on the Watanabe case. I determined it from their conversation."

Parker said, "I've been relieved of my stewardship. I lost face with Ashida, and he threw in with Dudley. He's a farsighted young man in a terrible bind. His interests are better served with Dudley. I can't fault him for that."

We smoked and looked at the storm clouds. Traffic hummed on the parkway. I glanced south and saw the Federal Building. The morning enlistment line swelled.

"The FBI is going to raid us and confiscate our film. We'll all be arrested."

"Will you warn your comrades?"

"No."

"Because your cause will be better served by anointing them as martyrs?"

"Yes."

"Will you reveal this operation?"

"Under no circumstances."

"Do you believe that your own martyrdom will tip the balance of credibility away from me and toward you and your friends?"

"Yes, and there's one more thing."

"Which is?"

"You've given me myself, and I will not betray you."

It began to rain. Parker stared at the sky and held his hands out to touch it. We looked at each other. I walked to the middle of the parking lot and let the rain come down on me.

Black clouds eclipsed the City Hall spire. Lightning streaked over the Hall of Justice. I thought of the prairie. Flash floods and tornadoes. Drunken Indians, drowned in their lean-tos. That short havoc that takes witless lives and lets ruthless dreamers start up anew.

The black sky was overwhelming. I let time dissolve. I felt William's hand brush my leg. I held that moment close and stood still in the rain.

75

LOS ANGELES | FRIDAY, DECEMBER 19, 1941

8:29 a.m.

Sleeping beauties. A cot room slumber party.

Call-Me-Jack and Jim Davis dozed. Mike Breuning and Lee Blanchard, likewise. Jack and Jim were stag-night refugees. Breuning was bushed from the frame job. Note Blanchard's fistfight wounds. Blanchard was hiding out from Kay Lake.

A.M. *Herald*s covered the floor. COPS STORM WEREWOLF'S LAIR! JAP FIEND APPREHENDED! BAFFLING JAP WHODUNNIT—FULL STORY REVEALED!

Front-page news. A big photo spread. The Dudster and The Wolf. The "Demon's Den." Scotty Bennett, dragging Fuji Shudo. Scotty Bennett, chomping bubble gum.

The boys slept. Parker stepped out to the hallway. Thad Brown braced him.

"I've got a partial trace on Joan Conville. She's a home wrecker and more than a bit of a wild one."

Parker said, "Tell me."

Brown said, "I've got no location on her now, but she was shacked with a man at 8th and New Hampshire up until Pearl Harbor. He joined the Army that day. She joined the Navy, was commissioned as a lieutenant j.g. and was ordered to stay put and wait for her training papers. She's on the loose now. She was working as a research biologist at a lab in Culver City, but she grabbed her last paycheck on the 8th and skeedaddled. She broke up the Army guy's marriage and cut him loose the day they enlisted. You want my opinion? She's a shitload of trouble that you'd be well advised to avoid."

Parker smiled. "That's *it*? That's *all* you've got?"

Brown said, "Isn't it *enough*? There's all *that*, and there's the disappointing fact that she's a Protestant."

Parker laughed. Call-Me-Jack and Two-Gun lurched to the washroom.

Brown said, "One of us will be Chief after the war, Bill. When the City Council grills us, I swear that I won't mention the big redhead in your closet."

Parker grinned. His last drink was 2:00 a.m. Tuesday. He'd marked sober days in his Bible. He'd pledged five clams per day to the church.

Brown said, "We should go. It's Mr. Hoover's show."

They ran the back stairs. Call-Me-Jack and Two-Gun beat them. Fletch Bowron sat with Hoover and Preston Exley. Chairs faced a speaker's stand and easel. A San Fernando Valley map was propped up.

Hoover wore a fresh carnation. Preston fiddled with a pointer. Call-Me-Jack and Two-Gun sipped Bromo.

Parker and Brown took seats. Hoover tapped his watch. Nobody smoked—Hoover disapproved.

Jack said, "Eleanor Roosevelt's jungled up with that colored mammy from *Gone with the Wind.* They shack at the Los Altos Apartments when FDR blows through town. Gerald L. K. Smith hosted a shindig at the First Christian Church of Glendale, and Gerry does not speak with forked tongue."

Hoover said, "Pastor Smith is a long-standing FBI informant. He rats out his rivals in the alarmist-pamphlet business. He's very well connected along the right flank."

Parker studied the easel map. It depicted the Valley's east edge. Circles denoted farmland. Check marks denoted farm structures. They were Jap properties. It went with Preston's internment plan. It *suggested* that rumor per the Watanabe case.

Hoover said, "The floor is yours, Mr. Exley."

Preston walked up to the easel. "In essence, what I am proposing is a separate cog within the larger cog of the Federal government's wartime internment planning, which mandates the housing of hundreds of thousands of suspect Japanese in massive centers throughout California and Arizona, and as far north as Wyoming and Montana. My proposal allows us to cull inmates selectively, house them locally and see to it that the accretion of revenue remains local, so that it might boost the specific wartime and postwartime economy of Los Angeles. When I say 'selective,' I am implying a judicious application of eugenics, or racial science. The Japanese are a gifted people, an industrious people, and a compliant people. We would be well served to keep a number of them here, close at hand. Keep in mind that they themselves will benefit from a postwar economic boom, once they've been released from custody."

Jack said, "I get it. The Japs have got green thumbs, so we put them to work on their own farms and their neighbors' farms, to work along those lines you've already described. I don't like the word *kickback*, but it applies here. There's potential profits for all those concerned. We take a sizable number of Japs off the Federal government's hands, which benefits Mr. Hoover's people. We police our own Japs, so we see the lion's share of the wealth."

Fletch said, "Where's the 'racial science' part, Preston? What do you mean by 'selectively'?"

Hoover said, "Since Mr. Exley and I have already discussed it, I'd like to answer that question. My agents have been the driving force behind the roundups of Japanese subversives over the past twelve days. As such, they have observed a great many Japanese, and have compiled individual dossiers on them. I see this as a controlled experiment in both penology and eugenics. Japan has remained a feudal culture, running parallel to ours, but hamstrung by atavistic social codes, up through the Industrial Revolution, as free societies have come to flourish in the West. Now—despite or because of their native atavism—they have mobilized and nationalized their resources almost on a par with our own white country's. The Japanese threaten the worldwide Western hegemony at this moment—but we will, of course, crush them in the end. Why not exploit their native cunning and brainpower as we destroy them militarily, in the hope that our experiment casts light on a race both inferior and oddly superior to ours, most tellingly differentiated by their mad drive for power? Why not ply them with intelligence and mental and physical aptitude tests, and select our potential Los Angeles–based prisoners on that basis? Why not study these people while we imprison and productively employ them?"

Davis said, "Mr. Hoover don't speak with forked tongue. I'm a race man from way back. This angle of the plan has got me licking my chops."

Preston said, "Don't stop licking there, any of you. I'm thinking we can run those tests and come up with a select few within the select few, give them high-security clearances and allow them to work at those defense plants out in Santa Monica. You've got Lockheed, Boeing, Douglas and Hughes out there in one tight stretch, and Jim's running the Douglas police force already. We could expand Jim's jurisdiction to all the plants and deputize a special group of men to police our worker Japs exclusively."

Prescient. Lucrative. Usurious past moral reason. Blood libel. Slavery reestablished on American soil.

Parker stared at his hands. *Don't look up, they'll read your mind—*

Preston said, "The draft will saddle us with a citywide shortage in menial employment. I propose that we create a guest worker program with the Mexican State Police. They will supply us with peons to fill the shortages, we house them in Chavez Ravine, Shore Patrolmen from the Chavez Ravine Naval Base can do the policing there. Again, the entire operation remains localized and fully indigenous to L.A."

Hoover sniffed his carnation. "I need a touch of fresh air. I would like to observe some arrests in Little Tokyo, and I would like to do so now."

Call-Me-Jack said, "I've got two cars waiting."

Davis said, "Some Reds are shooting a movie. Dick Hood's getting ready to put the quietus to it."

The boys jumped on cue. Parker got up and followed them. They took the mayor's private lift down.

Two Fed sedans idled in the basement. Ed Satterlee and Ward Littell drove. Parker got in beside Ward. They swapped looks. Call-Me-Jack and Jim Davis piled in the back.

The other boys hitched with Satterlee. The cars pulled out, snout-to-tail. Parker shut his eyes and squeezed his holy cross.

He felt the ride over. Every bump jarred him. The two-way radio squawked. The Anti-Axis Committee—one minute to go.

We've got Hearst Rifle boys up on rooftops. There's four Feds already there.

Street bumps, left turns, right turns. We're inside Little Tokyo. One minute to go.

Parker counted right turns. Ward braked and pulled over. Parker opened his eyes. Satterlee's car idled flush in front of them.

The Hearst fucks manned neighboring rooftops. They packed scope-mounted Mausers.

More Hearst fucks hogged the sidewalk. A photo man, Sid Hudgens, Jack Webb. The target storefront blazed red, white and blue.

Ward squeezed Parker's arm and stepped from the car. Satterlee got out. Four Feds jumped from a surveillance van.

They pulled sidearms. They walked to the doorway. It was wide open. They went in, guns first.

Parker got out. The Hearst geeks blocked his view of the door. The storefront was sotto voce. No protests, no slogans, no shouts.

Parker waited. He strained to hear her. He heard handcuff ratchets click.

She walked out ahead of the others. He left her standing in the rain. She wore a brown ensemble then. Now she wore bright red.

Part Three

THE FIFTH COLUMN

(December 19–December 27, 1941)

76

LOS ANGELES | FRIDAY, DECEMBER 19, 1941

10:19 a.m.

Meeks sat down. Halitosis fogged the booth. He decided to kill him in 1946.

The war would be *pffft*. He'd be rich. Meeks would rot in Ace Kwan's lime pit.

Vince & Paul's was dead. They sat by the exit. A waiter brought coffee and vanished.

Meeks said, "I turned up some racy scoop on Pierce Patchett. You owe me five hundred."

Dudley dropped five yards on the table. Meeks snatched it up.

"I'd say he's about forty. He's a big, impressive-looking guy who's good at jujitsu, for what that's worth. He's an 'Orientalist,' which means he goes for shit that emanates from that godforsaken part of the world. He's a land developer, and he's turned significant coin with deals here and there. He's also a chemist by trade, some kind of closet fascist, and a budding sugar pimp. He's got a plan that involves plastic surgery, which sounds like outer space to me. He wants to cut girls to look like movie stars, which'll probably tickle your funny bone, given the true-life stuff you're getting. The scoop is that he wants to run a telephone-service operation, like our chums Brenda and Elmer."

Dudley sifted it. "Continue, please."

Meeks drummed the table. "I see circle jerk and cluster fuck all over this guy, and a whole flotilla of other guys he knows. I ran Patchett's house and office phone records. There's lots of calls to our old pal Preston Exley's house and office, and calls to your beaner pal Carlos Madrano, down in Ensenada. Patchett's office is in the same building as a doctor named Saul Lesnick, who just happens to be treating Preston for migraine headaches. More fucking over,

I learned that Lesnick is a Fed informant, and that he's infiltrated some kind of Red cell. More fucking over on that, I went to the cop you always go to to get the dirt on Fifth Column types."

Dudley sifted it. "Continue, please."

Meeks said, "I cracked union heads under Carl Hull, so I know how to read him. As soon as I say 'Lesnick,' he starts dropping his drawers. Okay, I know that you braced him. Okay, I know that Bill Parker's running Lee Blanchard's girlfriend in that cell that Lesnick's in. I know that you're always keeping tabs on Parker, and that you told Hull that you'd let Parker's deal with the Lake twist go forward. 'Circle jerk,' Dud. The Lake cooze is fucking Scotty Bennett and might be fucking Hideo Ashida. 'Cluster fuck.' Exley, Patchett and Madrano aren't hooked up on that anti-Red thing, but they're hooked up on something bigger and better."

Dudley *re*sifted it. "Continue, please."

Meeks hunkered in. Note his gold watch. He killed three shines in a blastout at Slauson and Broadway. He stole that watch off a dead coon.

"You smell money in the Watanabe job. I've known it since I spilled that scoop on those farm and house buyouts at the briefing last week. *Now*, you've got Exley, Patchett, and Madrano. You've got the Mex Staties strawbossing the wets at those Jap farms out in the Valley. You've got these allegedly 'unknown' white stiffs buying and trying to buy farm and house properties from the Japs, secretly recorded sales, and Exley's plan for internment sites on confiscated Jap land, which is all over every inter-Bureau memo floating around the PD and the mayor's office. It's a circle jerk and a cluster fuck, and you smell money, and my bet is that you haven't figured out all the angles, and that Ace Kwan is in this with you, and you're waiting until Shudo is indicted and off your plate, and then you'll kick your schemes into high gear, and you wouldn't mind knowing that Whiskey Bill won't get some anti-Red or anti–Dudley Smith wild hair up his ass to complicate your already too-complicated life."

Dudley clapped. Meeks, with halitosis. Meeks, with his gold watch. Meeks killed two spics in a blastout at Wabash and Soto. Meeks stole God knows what off of them.

"It's a brilliant, lucidly reasoned and accurate précis, lad. It prompts the question 'How much do you want?' "

Meeks unwrapped a cigar. "5% of whatever you and Ace might

be cooking up on any kind of land deal you're looking at, and whatever else you might have going on the internment end."

Dudley said, "Done."

Meeks said, "It must gall you to know that you can't kill me."

"Yes. I'll concede the point."

Meeks stood up. "Take care of yourself. You blew your cork with The Wolf, and I know you're stretched thin. You're the horse I've got my money on, and I need you fit for the race."

11:36 a.m.

Meeks waddled out. The 5% deal goosed his date of death. The shit would go in 1942.

Dudley doodled up cocktail napkins. He crumbled a bennie and goosed his coffee.

The war caught up with him yesterday. Today announced a new campaign. He thought of Bette. She bridged both days as his sorceress.

He *conjured* her. He bore the mad grit of the Irish dispossessed. He *summoned* her. She did not know it yet.

The bennies tickled his brain. Memo: call Huey and prepare to brace Tojo Tom Chasco. Memo: send Ellis Loew a grand bottle. Apologize for the Werewolf dustup. Welcome him to the Hearst-hurrahed Watanabe Case.

Dudley doodled. He sifted Meeks' spiel and shorthand-transcribed it. Circle jerk, cluster fuck. Collusive connections revealed. No real murder leads. The house/farm buyouts take shape.

Shorthand. Equals signs and excised parts of speech. Quotation marks, question marks, boldfaced proper nouns. See how the names repeat?

"E.'s internment-housing plan." "W. house directly off Arroyo Seco Parkway." "Parkway blt. by E. Construction." Take this conjectured leap:

"Presumed buildup of L.A. after war."

Cocktail napkins. Detectives' hieroglyphs.

Meeks lays out Pierce Patchett. He wants to run cut whores. Who's the King of the Cut Men? Terence Lux, M.D.

Dudley drew Jap faces and Jap faces cut to look Chink. He saw no eugenic difference. He drew Terry Lux with a scalpel. He drew

Claire De Haven. He drew Claire De Haven nude in Terry's steam room.

He drew Hideo Ashida. Hideo's watching Terry cut that Jap wino. He finds the cut scheme dubious, but enjoys eugenics.

Hideo's gizmo play troubled him. It felt recklessly unconscious. His "corroborating-witness" pitch was far-afield contrived.

He drew question marks and a map. The map denoted proximity.

The Arroyo Seco Parkway. Downtown L.A. to Pasadena. An Exley Construction contract. Lincoln Heights to the east. Highland Park to the west. South Pasadena at the north terminus.

He drew the twisty blacktop. He X-marked on- and off-ramps. He fanned his pencil to indicate hillsides and undeveloped land.

He caught a bennie surge. He got up and left the restaurant. He shagged his K-car and drove to the parkway.

Chavez Ravine marked the south edge. Lincoln Heights stood due east. The Heights was all scrub hills and shack rows. There's a drainage creek running parallel north.

There's Highland Park, to the west. There's fewer hillsides and on- and off-ramps. Undeveloped land abuts the west side. There's no meddlesome creek.

There's barren land on the west flank. There's meddlesome houses interspersed. They abut the parkway safety fence.

Dudley got off at Avenue 64 and looped south. He noted topography and counted vacant lots. He drove to Avenue 45 and The House.

He parked in Their Driveway. He strolled to Their Backyard.

It overlooked *undeveloped* land and ran straight to the parkway. The distance was one-quarter mile.

Dirt and scrub. A few trees and low hills. This *undeveloped* stretch ran due north and south. The topography ran more problematic further up and down. *This* House and *This* Land plumb-lined perfect parkway egress.

Dudley vaulted the fence and went walking. The ground was all rough dirt and twigs. He walked straight to the parkway fence and straight back.

It might be city-county property. It might be Watanabe property. It might be property secretly purchased by the Exley-Patchett combine.

He grabbed a handful of soil and sniffed it. He caught a vague shrimp subscent. He quick-walked to the backyard fence and jumped it.

He got his car and hooked down to Figueroa. He donned a construction king's thinking cap.

The sin of undeveloped land. No parkway-flush commercial strips between downtown and Pasadena. A perfect spot, to the west.

Parkway-flush Highland Park. No meddlesome drainage creek. No high hills to block car traffic. Egress off the safety fence and the Watanabes' backyard.

He stopped at a pay phone and called Nort Layman. Nort was eager to chat. Shrimp residue and topsoil. Have you an opinion to share?

Yes. He's made studies. It's per the Watanabe case.

Shrimp oil solidifies urban dirt and contaminates it for crop planting. Shrimp oil could be used to undercoat topsoil. It might provide a baseline for poured cement.

Dudley thanked Nort. Dudley hung up. Dudley mind-screened a film vignette.

It stars the Watanabes. They're cinematically alive. They coat their feet with shrimp oil and trek through their backyard. They journey to the parkway fence. Someone bid them to do it. *Useless crop soil facilitates the pouring of cement.*

Dudley drove to City Hall. He popped two bennies. He screened visions of postwar L.A.

He'd seen that German movie *Metropolis.* It was dystopically shrill. He combined that vision with his vision.

Shop-and-dine terraces with grand parkway views. No jigaboos in sight. Spaceship cars skitting north and south.

He parked and went up to the Bureau. Mike Breuning lassoed him.

"I still don't believe it. I just jawed on the phone with Bette Davis. She said you should call her."

Dudley roared. He did a jigaboo two-step and cartwheeled up to his desk. He saw an envelope on the blotter.

A letter from Tommy Gilfoyle. That erratic block print. Blind Tommy never learned to type or write cursive.

Dudley slit the envelope. The letter ran two pages. He knew Tommy's print technique. Words devolved into alphabet stew.

"I know Beth wrote you about that 'horrible thing' last year, but she didn't tell you what it was."

Dudley got scalp bumps. Tommy's words broke up. Look—wet ink and dried tears.

Beth was raped, in Boston. It was November '40. Two thugs assaulted her. Boston PD ID'd them. Beth broke down at the show-up and blew her identification. The men were released.

She went to a doctor. He examined her and said she wasn't pregnant. He found benign cysts and told her she was barren. She would never be able to conceive.

Beth was devastated. She wanted children dearly. Tommy kept in touch with Boston PD. A cop told him that the rape-o's had joined the Marine Corps. They were stationed at Camp Pendleton, near San Diego.

PFC John Arcineaux, Private Robert Ettig.

"We'll be arriving in Los Angeles on Monday, December 22, and staying through Christmas. I wanted you to know this before we came, but please don't tell Beth that you know. I think she has spells where it doesn't weigh on her, and I want our Christmas with you to be one of them."

The pages turned wet. He didn't know why. He picked up a chair and started to hurl it. He sobbed and put the chair down.

The sob strangled him. He couldn't breathe. He opened his mouth and made animal sounds. *Werewolf, Werewolf.* He bit his arm to kill the sounds. He bit himself down to the skin.

77

LOS ANGELES | FRIDAY, DECEMBER 19, 1941

1:19 p.m.

Werewolf Shudo was *sin*-sational. He was a *Jap* werewolf. The radio harped on that.

Ashida tuned in the news. He worked the lab solo. KFI ran an all-Jap scroll.

A denuded synopsis of the Watanabe job. *"No Leads in Jap Phone*

Booth Slaying!" "No Leads on Jap Slain at Beach!" "Jap Jail Suiciders: Fifth Column All!"

He'd tuned in for word on the Anti-Axis raid. Mariko called and described what she saw. The Feds swooped down on the office. They grabbed a white girl in a red dress.

The Feds would grab the film. Claire and the others might name him. His Kay Lake kisses would be Fed-scrutinized.

It happened very fast. He had a chance to destroy the film. He went by the Lincoln Heights jail to do it. Kay scotched his chance. The film was out in the trailer. Kay was holed up there.

The radio hawked toothpaste. Back to Fuji Shudo and grid great Scotty Bennett. Hollywood High's hero blasts a tong thug last week! Last night, he storms The Wolfman's Den!

"You look apprehensive, lad. Given recent events, I can hardly blame you."

The door was open. He casts no shadow. He's the Real Werewolf.

Dudley locked the door and walked over. He killed the radio. He pulled out a revolver and popped the cylinder.

He held up the revolver. Six chambers, one bullet stuffed in.

He shut the cylinder and spun it. He put the barrel to Ashida's head and pulled the trigger twice. The hammer hit empty chambers.

Ashida opened his eyes. He didn't know he'd shut them. He wasn't dead. He was still at his desk.

Dudley lounged on the desk. Dudley tapped a legal pad.

"You are to swear out an affidavit in my presence. You will address it to District Attorney William McPherson, Chief of Police C. B. Horrall, Sheriff Eugene Biscailuz and Special Agent in Charge Richard Hood of the Los Angeles FBI. You will confess to all of your withholdings and suppressions of evidence in the Watanabe family homicides of December 6, 1941, both alone and in collusion with Captain William H. Parker. You will include your knowledge of Captain Parker's covert actions aimed at Miss Claire De Haven. You will sign and date it at the bottom of the final page. Dick Carlisle's wife is a notary public. She will affix the appropriate seals."

Ashida squared off the pad. His pen moved all by itself. He smelled iodine. Dudley had salved an arm wound.

Saturday, December 6th. Whalen's Drugstore. He pilfers bullet chunks and silencer threads.

Sunday, December 7th. The Watanabe house. He finds the

shortwave radio, tape rig and ledger. He steals them on Wednesday, December 10. He plays the radio and learns of the Goleta raid. Dudley confronts him outside the house. He lies about the tracts he stole. They fiercely attack the Los Angeles PD.

Dudley touches his arm. It rewards his candor.

Monday, December 8th. He visits Japanese farms in the Valley. Ryoshi Watanabe sold his farm—but who to? Wetbacks pick crops, Valley-wide. Mex Staties boss them. He sees Carlos Madrano behind it.

Dudley smiles. *Lad, you got there first.*

Monday, December 8th. He 459's the Deutsches Haus and steals their gun-silencer cache. He test-fires the guns. The ordnance used at the drugstore and house came from the Deutsches Haus batch.

Dudley winks. He knew that, somehow.

Thursday, December 11th. He views the sub-raid evidence. He sees a dead "Collaborationist." His body bears a starburst-style stab wound. It refracts a similar wound found on Ryoshi Watanabe. The soles of another dead man's feet reek of shrimp oil. That refracts the shrimp oil on the Watanabes' feet. He views cans of chopped shrimp among the collected debris.

Dudley slaps his knees. *Lad, you delight me.*

Friday, December 12th. He discovers odd tread marks in the Watanabes' driveway. The pattern looks familiar. He matches it to a Sheriff's bulletin, issued 12/7.

Hit-and-run. One fatality. James Larkin/British/age sixty-seven. He lives in Santa Monica Canyon. There's a vague description of the hit-and-run driver. He's a white man in a purple sweater. This refracts the white man seen outside the house, 12/6/41.

Dudley gawks. It's endearing.

Friday, December 12th. He takes the Larkin lead to Captain Bill Parker. They break into Larkin's bungalow.

They find a Japanese-language ledger. They find seventeen Lugers embossed with Nazi symbols and a fortune in Axis cash.

He translates the ledger. He believes that it details the house and farm buyouts. There is no conclusive proof.

They 459 the bungalow again. They see that Larkin possessed no telephone. They recall a Sheriff's bulletin. It lists "three pay-phone slugs" in Larkin's property. They steal the seventeen Lugers. He print-dusts them here at the lab. He gets a match to the unknown print at the house.

His collusive friendship with Bill Parker tanks. Parker's tirade at Kwan's Pagoda does it. He knows very little about the Kay Lake/Claire De Haven incursion. Kay Lake lured *him* in. *Her* motives? Specious and incomprehensible.

He omitted The Knife in Griffith Park. Bill Parker believed that Dudley and Ace Kwan killed those three men. He omitted the Wallace Hodaka interview. It provided no follow-up leads.

That's it. Sign it—Hideo Ashida, Ph.D.

Dudley made the hand-on-heart sign. "I am moved by you and honored to know you, Hideo. You bore up to the one-in-three prospect of instant death valiantly, and you are the only detective on God's grand earth who stands as my equal. I pledge my continued loyalty, as malign fate continues to plague your people. The next several months will surely be unkind, but I will do my best to provide you and yours with succor and devilish good fun."

Ashida swooned. It felt like a head-to-toe flush.

"My Irish brother."

"My yellow brother."

Rain drummed the window. Dudley smiled and lit a cigarette.

"Have you the skills to craft a preexisting document, lad? I was thinking of a letter from Fuji Shudo to Ryoshi Watanabe, vintage 1933."

Ashida smiled. "Yes, I can do it. I assume that you want it in kanji script."

Dudley said, "I do, yes. The text should detail a political disagreement pertaining to Asian geopolitics, and should foreshadow Fuji Shudo's ultimate psychic collapse. Can you apply convincing age spots to the paper and forge a postal cancellation?"

"Yes, and the letter should have been sent post office to post office. We can't be sure that the Watanabes had their house in '33. That official records backlog is still in effect."

Dudley said, "Bright child. I hadn't thought of that."

"I'll cut a stencil and write the characters within it. I'll get the closest approximation of Fuji's script that way."

Dudley smiled. "The cancellation mark?"

"Purple vegetable dye."

"The aged paper?"

"A chloral-phosphate spray and ultraviolet light."

Dudley blew smoke rings. "Have you a final perspective on the Parker-Lake matter?"

Ashida said, "They're both insane. They're in love with each other, but they're so crazy that they don't even know it."

78

KAY LAKE'S DIARY

LOS ANGELES | FRIDAY, DECEMBER 19, 1941

4:02 p.m.

I was back on the women's tier at Central Station. My first visit was eleven days ago. I'd improvised at the Paul Robeson concert, in an effort to force a meeting with Claire. She was in the adjoining cell now, withdrawing from her narcotics habit at a spiraling rate. Our male comrades were on the men's tier. Hideo Ashida was probably upstairs at the crime lab, or off subverting justice for Dudley Smith.

The women's tier was packed with Japanese women. They sat on their bunks just like their comrades did eleven days earlier. Pearl Harbor was *twelve* days ago. Did the world exist before it?

I watched Claire thrash. We had been here for nearly six hours; we'd been fingerprinted and forced to change into jail smocks. A Sheriff's matron named Dot Rothstein watched us undress. She was the largest butch I'd ever seen—Andrea Lesnick had told me about her. She wore Sheriff's greens, with beavertail saps stashed in the trouser-slit pockets. She chewed Beemans pepsin gum, vigorously.

My purse had been confiscated. Dot Rothstein saw Claire shivering, and snatched her overcoat. I knew of the impending raid, and assumed that the Feds had warned off Saul Lesnick. I burned my movie, and destroyed that evidence trail. I saved two film strips. They were tucked into a small rip in the lining of my purse.

Claire thrashed. I reached through the bars and stroked her

hair. We'd been booked for reckless endangerment and placed on a Federal hold. Ed Satterlee kept strolling down the tier. He told us that the real charges would be determined by a Federal grand jury. "You're looking at a gas-chamber bounce—so I'd advise you to cooperate."

I felt weightless. It was like the time I had measles and ran off during a blizzard. I was nine years old. My fever broke while I played in the snow. My father found me a few blocks from home, dressed in a nightgown. I wasn't shivering or sweating. My father believed me to be possessed from that moment on.

Claire burrowed into her pillow. Two women meet in a doctor's office nine days ago. A woman lights a woman's cigarette—and now we're here.

Claire slid down the mattress. Her smock was soaked through; it was dark wet from the hem to the neckline. I gripped the bunk ledge and sat there, facing the Japanese women. They all turned away from me.

My hands numbed on the ledge; I was grasping a sharp metal surface. A piece snapped off in my hands. I released my grip and snapped it back into place. I'd gouged my fingers near bloody.

I paced the cell. I counted out one hundred bar-to-wall trips. I thought of Bucky and Scotty.

Ed Satterlee walked up. He said, "Hello again, Katherine."

I walked to the bars and faced him. I said, "Call me 'Comrade.' "

Satterlee laughed. I said, "Get Miss De Haven a doctor."

"Any doctor we come up with would make her suffer through it. This isn't supposed to be easy. If she cops to a few Federal charges, though, I might find her some stuff that she'd like."

I said, "Habeus, you cocksucker. You have to let us make bail."

"Not for sixty-five hours and fourteen minutes, '*Comrade.*' We've got that much more time to make you feel antsy. You'll be snitching your dipshit granddad back in Sioux Falls by this time on Sunday."

I said, "You're a limp fuck, Ed. You've never been laid."

Satterlee smiled, oh so bored. "I've got a niece your age, back in Prairie du Chien, Wisconsin. She reminds me of you, without the pretense. Prairie du Chien was too small for her. She didn't know what to do, so she ran off with an eye-talian guy and got knocked up."

"Give me a cigarette. I'll be more inclined to talk if you do."

Satterlee shook his head. “I’m not in the mood to be nice. I think you were the one who torched the film in that trailer. Normally, I’d look to the men, but not with these guys. It’s bees where the women rule the roost, right? That’s why I’m looking to you and Claire, and she doesn’t seem like the firebug type right now.”

I said, “Habeus, Ed. Monday morning at 10:00.”

Satterlee shook his head. “You can’t bluff your way out of this one. You’re in superseding Federal custody, and you can’t flash some toy badge and say you’re a cop’s girlfriend.”

I flashed my right middle finger. Satterlee feigned amusement and walked off. I stretched out on my bunk and held an arm over my eyes. The ceiling lights threw down a red haze.

It felt like I was back in that blizzard. The red haze was just like Sioux Falls in the snow. I heard key-in-lock and sliding-metal sounds. I opened my eyes and saw Dot Rothstein sitting on the edge of the bunk.

She said, “Sweet dreams, cupcake?”

I said, “Call me ‘Comrade.’ ”

She said, “That’s a hard girl’s name. You’re not a hard girl. You’re a sweetie pie.”

She placed a hand on the mattress. She wore signet rings on three fingers. Her right knee brushed the bed rail. She carried a sap in that trouser-leg pocket. The handle sat flush on her calf.

I smelled Beemans pepsin chewing gum and Butch Wax. I watched her eyes, I watched her hand.

She said, “You’re a soft girl.”

She put her hand on my knee. She ran it slowly up my thigh. She leaned in and opened her mouth to kiss me. I opened my mouth and ran a hand up her leg, toward the sap. She shifted as she pressed down on me. I moved my hand to the bunk ledge and pulled that piece of loose metal free.

Her mouth was wide open. Chewing gum was stuck to her teeth. Our lips were in close. I gripped the mock shiv and brought my arm up.

I stabbed her in the arm. I stabbed her in the side. I stabbed her in the back. I held on to the shiv as she shrieked and punched straight down. My nose snapped—red, black, red. Blood blew into my eyes.

I rolled off the bunk. I stabbed her in the leg as my back hit the floor. She shrieked male falsetto. Her blood was all over the shiv. I gripped it that much harder. The mock blade cut my hand.

She rolled off the bunk and fell on top of me; she pinned me to the floor with her knees. She cocked her right fist and punched straight down.

I flailed. Her fist hit the floor. The blow carried her full weight.

Bones shattered. I *heard* it.

She shrieked. I stabbed her in the shoulder, I stabbed her in the back. She kept pressing down on me. I felt a rib snap. It's another kiss, her head's coming down, open your mouth.

She opened her mouth.

I opened my mouth.

I reached up and showed her my tongue.

She shut her eyes for the kiss.

I bit off her nose and spit it back in her face.

She *shrieked* and rolled off of me. She rubbed blood from her eyes and *shrieked.* I stood up and kicked her where her nose used to be; I stabbed her in the back, the arms, the legs. She *shrieked* and tried to pull herself under the bunk. I pulled the sap off her leg and smashed her hands on the ledge. She sobbed something like "Ruthie."

I blinked away blood. Men made male noises and ran down the tier. Dot sobbed for Ruthie and crawled away from me.

79

LOS ANGELES | FRIDAY, DECEMBER 19, 1941

8:22 p.m.

He touched her things.

She was locked up a block away. He parked at 1st and Hill, so he'd be close. He couldn't go home. Whose purse is that? *Helen Parker, meet Kay Lake.*

He filched the purse from the property room. He got in and out, unseen. Claire De Haven's slaves fomented. The Queen herself looked sedated. Miss Lake swapped jokes with the jailer. The man thought she was a sketch.

Joan Conville's picture sat on the dashboard. *Miss Conville, meet Miss Lake.*

Parker went through the purse. It was scotch-grained leather. Miss Lake owned a cheap lighter. It was a fight-night souvenir. Bleichert versus Saldivar, 4/12/39.

Lipstick-blotted tissues. A paisley scarf. A ticket stub for the Carthay Circle Theatre. She'd gone to the first L.A. showing of *Gone with the Wind.*

It wasn't supposed to end this way. They were supposed to work together all through the war. She was supposed to gain Claire De Haven's trust and slowly come to know her perfidy. They were supposed to work together as the Allies won the war and the Queen worked to further the Kremlin's agenda. They were supposed to build evidence and drink Russian vodka to toast the impaneled grand jury.

A cross on a chain. All too Protestant. A tortoiseshell comb and barrette.

It wasn't supposed to end this way. She was supposed to snap photographs at two dozen locations. They were supposed to dissect the subversive mind-set in a thousand late-night talks.

The cross was chipped at the four corners. She'd clutched it in girlish prayer or skeptic's frustration. Her hair brush matched the comb and barrette. Auburn strands were laced in.

A lipstick tube, a compact, a blue handkerchief.

He held the fabric up to his cheek. He recalled her scent that first Monday in the rain.

It wasn't supposed to end this way. They were out to create a decorous courtroom document. They were out to destroy a barbarous ideology. They were supposed to exchange letters and call each other Katherine and William in due time.

Parker emptied out the purse and put everything back in perfect order. He saw a rip in the lining. He felt something inside it.

He reached in. He touched a slick surface. He pulled out two film strips.

They were both two feet long. One was fully developed. One was a white-on-black negative.

He flicked on the dashboard light. He held the strips up, side by side. The developed strip showed images of two men talking. The negative strip showed a still figure.

Parker squinted at the white-on-black. He recognized the cut of her dress. It was her speech yesterday.

Blood libel.

"We are thus charged to the near-impossible task of enacting love that much more ruthlessly, and with a self-sacrifice that would have been unknowable had History not summoned us. At this moment, our options become do everything or do nothing."

Katherine, the valiant and foolish.

He ran his eyes down the strip. She barely moved. The picture run encompassed just seconds. He saw her in mute white on black. He heard her every word.

Blood libel. Moral duty and small-minded fear. Sioux Falls and Deadwood. Sodden Indians and nativist fiends.

He studied the developed strip. He recognized details and followed them, frame by frame.

1st and San Pedro. He knew that building. He knew that tall man, with that hat. It's Ed Satterlee. There's a small Chinaman. It's Ace Kwan's toady, Quon Chin.

Quon ran bag to Call-Me-Jack. Quon pimped Chinese girls to Brenda Allen. Quon laid bribes on the County Zoning Board.

Quon killed sixteen rival tong men. Quon purportedly beheaded four hundred Jap soldiers after the Rape of Nanking.

Parker studied the strip. Bravos to Kay Lake. She knew what she saw.

A bagman, a rogue Fed, a payoff. An evidential hole card—nailed on film.

He prayed off The Thirst. Sunday Mass would mark five days sober. He heard sirens running eastbound on 1st Street. It was ambulance pitch.

He saw cherry lights spin outside the station. Something said *NO*—

Christmas shoppers swarmed Hill Street. Buses blocked the north-south lanes. Some loudspeaker blared "Jingle Bells."

He ran. He left his prowl car unlocked. He ran and got winded inside two seconds. His holster flopped and almost flew off. He ran across Hill Street. He sideswiped a thin Santa Claus.

An ambulance was parked outside the station. Two men rolled a gurney up. A big woman was strapped in. She wore Sheriff's green. She was nothing but slash wounds and blood.

She *shrieked.* She *shrieked* for Ruthie and Huey. Parker sidestepped the gurney and ran up the steps.

He went through the door. The desk sergeant saw him. *Oh shit, Whiskey Bill, what's this here—*

Parker tumbled up to the desk. He got "Katherine Lake" out in one breath. The desk man got the heebie-jeebies. He double-clutched and slid a key across the desk.

He said, "The bin."

Parker grabbed the key. He wheeled and saw a dozen plainclothesmen, all huddled up. They cordoned off the hallway and looked straight at him. He looked straight back.

Those looks traveled. Those looks talked. Parker caught his breath and walked toward them. They looked at one another and passed signals. They stood aside and let him walk.

He walked. He walked to a bisecting hallway and turned right. The padded cell—it's that white door.

He jammed in the key and turned it. The door was dead-heavy. He shouldered it in.

She wore a straitjacket. Her arms were laced tight. Her face was blood-crust swollen. Her hair was patched black and matted red.

Parker went to her.

Her eyes told him to untie her.

Her eyes told him to brush that one crust off her cheek.

Her eyes said *Lift me. You can do it. I'll be light for you.*

He did all of it.

Her eyes said *Carry Me Now.*

80

LOS ANGELES | FRIDAY, DECEMBER 19, 1941

8:47 p.m.

Land grabs. War fever and cash schemes. Whores cut like movie stars.

Dudley inked a wall graph. Scotty Bennett and Dick Carlisle watched. The graph was a palliative. It subsumed Beth's "horrible thing."

He wallpapered his cubicle. The graph ran from floor to partition top. It was all shorthand-inked.

It detailed The Case and related cases. It detailed financial conspiracies and his Ace Kwan plans. Snoops would see it as gobbledygook.

Initials noted names. Proper nouns were initial-ID'd. Circles and rectangles blocked off business deals. He worked from his own memory and Hideo Ashida's confession. Buzz Meeks' spiel figured in.

The graph was a hospital chart. He caught the Watanabe case and contracted war fever. The graph was a prescription pad. He prescribed Benzedrine to keep himself going. He prescribed the graph to remember it all.

Dudley inked the graph. Bennies spiked his memory. The Parker-Lake fiasco was dead now. The Shudo case was big news. The graph was a crib sheet. The graph would expedite The Werewolf's greenroom trek.

Names, dates, leads. Opportunities highlighted. Cash trails sensed and tracked. War fever. His fevered twelve-day pace.

The phone rang. Carlisle took the call. Dudley worked. Scotty watched him work. The lad was damnably acute and retentive.

Dudley worked. His brain buzzed. Distractions came and went.

Ruth Mildred called and reported. Tojo Tom Chasco was still under guard. Some crazy girl shivved Dot. Her sweetie pie was now ensconced at Queen of Angels. He eschewed lectures. Dot called the tune and paid the piper. She'd been fondling jail cooze for years. Ruthie wondered if Terry Lux would plastic up Dot's kisser. He said he had a call in to Terry right now. Terry *would* stitch Dot's snout.

Collusive circles. Pierce Patchett planned to run cut whores. He had to know Terry Lux. Terry was *the* L.A. cut man.

Scotty said, "I think I get it. 'W.M.P.S.' means 'white man in purple sweater,' right? He's the guy who's really good for the snuffs."

Dudley said, "Hush, bright penny. We've got a Werewolf by the tail."

Carlisle dumped the phone. "The Doc's at Les Frères Taix. He'll meet you there in half an hour."

Dudley dropped his pen and grabbed his suit coat. Bette danced through his head. She was all vapors. He'd left her three messages. He got the "Miss Davis be out" brush-off.

He waltzed. Les Frères Taix was a frog joint in Echo Park. He popped two bennies and drove over. Terry was a gourmand. He kept a booth there.

Dudley joined him. Terry was immersed in truffled kidneys. His black bag was up on the table. He noshed and skimmed a medical chart.

A photo was clipped to the top page. Claire De Haven was wan. Her hairdo connoted Joan of Arc.

"I'll hazard a guess, Terry. The Feds have allowed Miss De Haven a phone call, which means a house call for you."

Terry waved his fork. "Jail call. The Feds think I can loosen Claire up to the point where she'll talk."

A waiter swished by. Dudley ordered a double scotch.

"I feel constellations aligning, Terry. I would guess that a man named Pierce Patchett has contacted you, and that it pertained to young women cut to resemble film stars."

The waiter brought Dudley's drink. Aesthete Terry sniffed his Bordeaux.

"He *commissioned* me, Dud. And I can cut his girls, because it's not high-volume jobs, like your Japs-into-Chinks play with Ace. I'm betting you'll slap me with too many patients and too little recovery time, and a lot of the high-tide Japs have had their assets confiscated, so it's not like they've got the scratch to pay you, Ace and me. There's that, and the fact that your deal plays nutty, beyond the whole admittedly seductive eugenic aspect."

Dudley sipped scotch. "Tell me about Patchett, Terry. I've heard he's quite the eclectic beast."

Terry said, "In spades, Irish. You know me, and you know that I'm in with the cognoscenti, and that I run a mean Dun & Bradstreet on my potential Collaborationists. Patchett comes to me, so my first task is to determine if this scheme he's proposing is on the come, or if he's got the gelt to pay me."

Dudley said, "Continue, please."

Terry swirled his wine. "Patchett's a race man, I'm a race man. We're gemütlich in that regard, so it facilitates our chat. Patchett is also a fucking name-dropper, so he tells me that he's hooked up with Preston Exley on some kind of furtive deal to grab Jap land in the Valley for chump change, but they're short on hard cash right now, and Exley's an ex-cop who wouldn't countenance his running whores. I take all this under advisement—tell Patchett that I want a percentage of his overall biz in exchange for my medical services, and Patchett agrees."

Dudley said, "Continue, please."

Terry said, "So, I think of my pals Ace and Dud then. They've got this smut-movie notion that I'm privy to, Ace has got his tunnels, movie-star prosties to smut films isn't too big a jump, and maybe there's a way to combine the two. I started thinking, If Dud's got a way to distribute the films, or leads on potential customers, this biz could fly, because we're at war now, and white folks have got a perv deal going with the Japs, and seeing them fucking and being humiliated could be enticing to the right brand of geek."

Dudley smiled. "Continue, please."

"You follow my drift, Irish. We need sales leads, camera equipment and some white on-camera talent to offset our all-Jap acting stable until I cut those girls to look like Myrna Loy, Joan Crawford and Bette Davis, et-fucking-al."

Dudley said, "I have mail-list leads and distribution, through a prominent hate merchant. I have leads on film equipment, and I'm raising money now."

Terry said, "Raise *more* money. I told Ace that, just a few hours ago. He said he's going to run another tile game at his place tomorrow night, to boost your revenues. I told him what I'll tell you, Dud. If we create a lucrative cash funnel now, we can finance our Jap deals and get in for a cut of Patchett and Exley's Jap deal at the gate, while they're cash-strapped."

The restaurant sparkled. The red banquettes *glowed.*

"The word *convergence* comes to mind, Terry. Miss De Haven has money and access to camera equipment, and she requires your services now. I would assume that she'll bail out soon, she has a flair for performing, and is also quite attractive. Her *bons frères* Loftis and Minear share her acting flair, and are handsome, if effeminate, men. Do you require a more explicit summation?"

Terry shook his head. Terry came on *très rapide.*

Très rapide—he snarfed good-bye truffles. *Très rapide*—they walked out to their cars. *Très rapide*—Dudley took the pole slot. *Très rapide*—they convoyed downtown.

Rain threatened. A werewolf's moon beamed.

Dudley bayed. The moon brought back Belfast, 1921. He blew up a railroad car and killed fourteen Black and Tans. He took lorry routes back to Dublin and had a piss break on the moors. A wolf sidled close to him. They shared their life stories in snarls. He prayed for the wolf every night. He pined for their heavenly reunion.

Rain threatened. Dudley bayed and urged it on. Terry swerved ahead of him. They made Central Station, *très rapide.*

Terry beat him there. Dudley parked in the DB lot and went in the jail door. It was late. The station was quiet. He heard female sobs and male coos.

Follow them. Down the hall, veer left. The white door is open. The padded walls are blood-slick.

Claire De Haven wore a jail smock. She rode the floor, cross-legged. She made a hand tourniquet and watched Terry feed her arm.

The spike went in. The plunger went down. The spike went back out. Dudley stood in the doorway. He saw Claire levitate.

Her back arched. She untangled her legs and stretched. She threw her arms over her head and floated.

She *levitated.* It was real or it wasn't. He didn't know and didn't care. He was back on the moors with his wolf.

She ignored them. She was somewhere else. He studied her. She was Joan of Arc.

Terry blathered. *You're a lovely woman, in a horrible jam. Your cooperation will vouch your safety and the safety of your comrades. You have equipment we require. I'll continue to service your medical needs. You're a born performer and a libertine. You might find the experience alluring.*

She stretched. *She levitated.* She spanned the full room.

Terry said, "You love dirty films, Claire. I've been to screenings at your home. Do you recall that Peruvian film in the style of Cocteau? You could duplicate the wedding-night sequence. I can already picture your gown."

Thunder cracked. The wolf brought them rain.

Terry blathered. It was fatuous. He preached to a she-wolf. *The films will be distributed covertly. You will shape their radical content. Submission is active seduction. I've heard you say it. There's quite the thrill in being coerced.*

Dudley stood in the doorway. Claire turned and faced him. Such metamorphosis. Red Queen, She-Wolf, Joan of Arc.

"I've seen you in church. You're friends with His Eminence. Monsignor Hayes told me that you've killed English soldiers. Belief is shaping this moment. It supersedes greed and perversion. Can you comprehend that?"

10:53 p.m.

She trumped them. He walked off, sans rejoinder. She knew who he was. She played to him. She nullified his coercive mission.

She *levitated.* A jail stint and an armful of hop left her blasé. He would not subject her to smut. A church girl and chum of Monsignor Joe Hayes? Proof that the wolf was out loose.

Dudley strolled through the station. Memo—send Dot Rothstein flowers. Memo—nail Fuji Shudo's formal confession and brace Tojo Tom.

The front desk buzzed. Four Japs escaped from T.I. They tore down a fence and ran to a getaway car. The crashout occurred at 7:00 p.m. The Japs were *loooooong* gone. They were all *biiiiiiig* fascist types.

Cops swamped the desk. The night sergeant blared his radio.

Massive San Pedro manhunt! Sheriff's dragnet out! All-points bulletins! Door-to-door canvass! Roadblocks, traffic stops!

Sheriff Gene hit the air. He sounded Friday-night blitzed. He announced a massive posse.

Calling all policemen! Special duty waivers provided! Twelve dollars in riot pay per day!

Cops rushed off. They ran upstairs and stormed the squadroom phones. The desk sergeant grabbed *his* phone. *Get the Japs! Get the Japs! Fuck incoming calls and L.A. Police business! Riot fun and twelve clams a day!*

Dudley walked outside. The rain felt delightful. He lit a cigarette. He heard radio squawk and squadroom phone jabber. He looked up at the third-floor windows.

They were open. He heard more squawk. He saw Hideo Ashida.

The lad worked late. *Calling all cops. Dragnet. Roadblocks.* Hideo smiled through the squawk.

Tweak. The Irish wolf cocks one ear. The Irish wolf gets a scent.

Hideo lived at Beverly and Loma. He knew the building. It was three-minutes close.

Dudley shagged his car and drove there. Belmont High stood close. It faced a walk-up building. Note the high playing-field views.

Dudley parked and walked into the foyer. He clocked the mailbox bank. H. Ashida, no. 219.

He walked up. The *JAP!* on the door signaled hatred. *The wolf cocks one ear. Why does Hideo let such blasphemy remain?*

He snapped the lock with his pocketknife. He invaded the apartment. He hit the living room lights.

The front room was spotless. He knew it would be. A Bunsen burner on a pedestal? A *très* Hideo touch.

Two gizmos on an end table. One looks old, one looks new. Note the flanges on the new one. Hideo improved his own prototype.

The trip-wire device. Hideo exonerates Fuji Shudo. He employs mechanical means, self-devised.

Dudley pulled a chair up. Dudley studied the new device. Levers, shutters, trip wires. Hidden film rolls. Car tires activate a lens and snap pictures. The pix appear under magnified glass.

He tripped a lever. He saw a car's rear license plate. A date mark appeared on the photo.

Snap—9:18 a.m., 12/6/41.

Dudley scrolled pictures. He tapped levers. He saw clock-marked images. Huey Cressmeyer showed. Stupid lad—such a shoddy heist.

Dudley scrolled through the day. Cars, cars, cars. Skewed sidewalk shots. Click/snap/click. 2:04, 2:17, 2:36 p.m. *Brilliant lad—what thou hath wrought.*

3:08 p.m., 3:18 p.m., 3:19 p.m. The Werewolf walks down Spring Street.

And he looks unkempt. And he might be lurching. And the square white folks around him *do* look perturbed.

But:

The square white folks walk *separately*. Fuji Shudo looks discomfiting. He does *not* look terrifying. *Why do the square white folks look identically perturbed?*

Tweak—the wolf cocks one ear. Tweak—something is wrong here.

Dudley studied the image. Dudley squinted at the image. Dudley moved his eyes around the frame.

There—the bottom-left corner. A square object. A white square, facing out.

Dudley squinted. He *thought* he saw it, he *almost* saw it, he *saw* it.

A sidewalk news rack. It faced the street. There's the headline—JAPANESE ATTACK PACIFIC FLEET!

So, *this*.

The device malfunctioned. It's not Saturday, December 6th. It's Sunday, December 7th.

The Watanabes are one-day dead. The Pearl Harbor news hits L.A. at 11:30. It's the rush-edition *Herald*. The square white folks are perturbed because we're at war. The outré Fuji Shudo? A radar blip of History.

Hideo Ashida fucked up. Hideo Ashida acted in self-destructive haste. Hideo Ashida tried to clear a fellow Jap and revealed his eugenic identity.

Dudley bayed. Dudley let his mind drift. Dudley fiddled with the old device.

He got the hang of it. He tripped levers and saw pix under glass.

Tiled surfaces. A shower enclosure. A lanky youth, naked. He's dark-haired, he's muscular, he's got big bucked teeth. A familiar lad. A local phenom. Dwight "Bucky" Bleichert.

Quite the light heavy. Soon to work the PD. He finked some Fifth Column Japs to get on.

Here's Bucky, naked. Here's Hideo's squalid toy, hidden from view.

Rain drummed the windows.

Dudley bayed.

Dudley thought *So, it's this.*

81

LOS ANGELES | FRIDAY, DECEMBER 19, 1941

11:52 p.m.

良治、貴殿はアメリカのファシズムの黄色い走狗だ。我ら一族は我らが母国、大日本帝国の影たる地にて何世紀も戦ってきたのである。いま我は、ここロサンジェルスにて、貴殿に宣戦を布告する。白人の抑圧者どもが我ら日本人のすべてを黄色い奴隷にせんとするこの土地で。

Ashida wrote inside precut stencils. He cut them himself. He wrote with a fountain pen and red ink. The color symbolized Fuji Shudo's psychosis. The Werewolf writes in simulated blood.

"You are the cowardly yellow dog of American fascism, Ryoshi. Our families have battled for centuries in the shadow land of our true nation—Imperial Japan. Now, I throw down the gauntlet to you here in Los Angeles, where the white oppressor seeks to make all Japanese his yellow slaves."

He age-spotted the paper and envelope. He used a 1933-vintage stamp. He drew the postal cancellation mark perfectly. He based the text on Dudley's interview with Fuji Shudo.

Shudo was out to fuck Nancy and kill Ryoshi. An argument at the Shotokan Baths blew out of hand. Shudo was delusional in 1933. The fraternal clubs were big then. His clan and the Watanabe clan had warred for centuries. Shudo wanted to impregnate Nancy and leave her to bear his wolf cubs. He communed with talking animals. This letter was his first formal statement of intent.

He impregnated Nancy on his nuthouse leave. His lunacy escalated during his loony-bin years. Nancy got an abortion and destroyed his wolf-cub litter. He left Atascadero and went on a terp run. His madness exploded on December 6.

Ashida worked in the lab. The station was a nuthouse. The Feds booked Claire and her coven. Four men escaped from Terminal Island. It put the PD in a siege state.

Phone buzz ran incessant. *Calling all cops. Sheriff's posse. Duty waivers and twelve scoots a day.*

Then this rumor spread. It spread up through the heat shaft. He heard it through the get-the-Japs roar. Lee Blanchard's girlfriend shanked Dot Rothstein.

Yeah, the Lake twist. Yeah, that big lez. What's Dot weigh—240? I heard the Lake twist bit her fucking nose off. Dot's getting transfusions at Queen of Angels right now.

He believed it. He didn't believe it. It was late. He was tired. He was *Jap*-overdosed.

Dead *Japs* in Highland Park. *Jap* werewolf Shudo. *Jap* jail suicides. The dead *Jap* in the phone booth. The dead *Jap* at the beach. Cops out to get escaped *Japs.*

He was tired. He locked his forgery kit in his briefcase. He walked down the back steps and ducked rain to his car.

He took 1st Street home. He dumped his car and walked upstairs. An envelope was taped to his door.

He opened it. He read the note inside.

You will testify for the Los Angeles County Grand Jury in the matter of the State of California versus Fujio Shudo. You will state under oath that you discovered the bloodstained fingerprint on the morning of December 7, 1941, and that you neglected to mention that fact in your initial reports.

Your new photographic device is faulty and perhaps obsolete. The picture of Fujio Shudo was taken on December 7 at 3:19 p.m., not December 6. The agitated pedestrians are reacting to news of the Pearl Harbor attack. A newspaper headline pertaining to the attack can be minimally glimpsed in the photo.

The note was unsigned. A big heart was sketched below.

Replete with an arrow. Replete with initials: *H.A. + B.B.*

Ashida screamed.

He thought he heard a wolf howl, somewhere close.

December 20, 1941

82

KAY LAKE'S DIARY

LOS ANGELES | SATURDAY, DECEMBER 20, 1941

12:09 a.m.

Gauze.

It was what I saw and what I was covered in. I knew I was in a hospital room and that I had been anesthetized. The walls were white, the bedding was white. I was in and out of a white-hazed consciousness. The gauze was just porous enough to let me glimpse the world. All my immediate memories were hazy white.

I recalled Bill Parker lifting me; the ambulance men wrapped me in white blankets and wore white coats. Parker told them to take me to Good Samaritan. A needle went in my arm. I came to on a white bed, dressed in gauze and floating in white.

My nose is broken—I heard a doctor say that. I know I'm wearing some sort of splint, like the ones Lee and Scotty wore after their fight. There's a tube in my arm, feeding me fortified water. The metallic taste in my mouth reminds me of the taste of Dot Rothstein's blood.

I fought as the Feds wrestled me out of the cell; it was the last thing I remember before the world turned white. The padded cell was white, my straitjacket was white. I spat blood in Ed Satterlee's face—I recall that.

I have a mild concussion; I heard a nurse say that. I'll be all right; I heard two doctors conferring. I'm not in the jail ward; I heard Bill Parker demand a private east-wing room. I'm a block away from the Pacific Dining Car and the world's best steak sandwich. I can taste it through the blood taste in my mouth.

I intended to kill her. I made up my mind the moment she

touched me. The decision did not shock me then; the decision does not shock me now. I was poised to kill her when the Feds stormed my cell.

She's going to survive. I heard two nurses talking. She's in surgery at Queen of Angels. A doctor is grafting her severed nose back onto her face.

Everything is white. All sensation is altered. Numbness subsumes pain, the floaty haze engulfs discomfort. Gauze is porous. Gauze allows me to pretend to sleep while I peek at the men who've come by to see me.

Lee came by, in his uniform. Scotty came by, in his brown wool suit and tartan bow tie. They came by separately; they sat on opposite sides of the bed and held my hands while they spoke to each other. They cracked jokes about their own broken noses. Scotty cried and wiped his face with my hazy white sheet. Lee said, "Holy shit, Bennett. She fucked up the Dotstress."

Bill Parker frosted out a mayhem beef—Lee told Scotty that. Parker called Gene Biscailuz and talked turkey. Dot's antics had been out of line for years now. Sheriff Gene kowtowed—no charges on Miss Lake.

Scotty said, "I wish I could have seen it." Lee said, "Yeah. It had to be a better dustup than you and me."

I started drifting off then. I recall talk of the Dining Car and "belt a few highballs."

Gauze and white haze. Familiar scents. Brenda and Elmer came by. I smelled Brenda's perfume and Elmer's cigar.

Gauze and white haze. A nurse says, "Telephone, Captain." William H. Parker says, "Thank you."

Gauze and haze. Then, "It's after midnight, Sergeant." A pause and "Yes, I know I proposed the meeting." Silence and "The rectory? Certainly, if His Eminence requests it."

Gauze and white haze. Scents. His cigarette smoke and a hint of the rainstorm I willed. The wet wool of his uniform.

Gauze and white haze. He's sitting beside the bed. *Tell me things, William. Tell me who the big redhead is. Tell me what you want from her.*

Gauze and white haze. He's praying. His eyes are shut. His elbows are up on his knees. His fingers are laced and pressed to his forehead.

Gauze and white haze. I'm in, I'm out. Chair scrapes and footsteps, departing. A glimpse through the haze—but he's gone.

I smelled the prairie. He left it here for me.

83

LOS ANGELES | SATURDAY, DECEMBER 20, 1941

1:53 a.m.

The Archbishop said, "I'm thrilled to receive you boys. I've had devilish insomnia since we entered this war, and brokering a truce between two uniquely brilliant Catholic laymen bodes as splendid good fun."

Cantwell's study aped the Wilshire Country Club taproom. The walls were golf trophy–festooned.

Dudley said, "I'm glad that I took the liberty of calling you, Your Eminence. Captain Parker suggested an intermediary, and I'm thrilled that you were available at this ungodly hour."

They sat in easy chairs. Rain tapped the windows. Cantwell sipped brandy. Dudley sipped scotch. Parker sipped ginger ale.

He had four days booze-free. His nerve endings *screeched.* The free world was up his ass. His blood pressure verged on 6,000.

He had Kay Lake's film strip. Dudley held a folder. Cantwell and Dud went back to Dublin. Cantwell was a papal up-and-comer. The Dudster was a kid assassin.

"Are we in the protected sphere of clerical confidence now, Your Eminence?"

"We are, Dud. You may both rest assured of my discretion. Consider this to be a grandly appointed confessional, and consider me to be your confessor."

Dudley passed the folder. "Hideo Ashida's notarized statement on the Watanabe case and what he knows and has surmised about your extracurricular operation."

Parker opened the folder and read the enclosed pages. Hideo Ashida—dear God.

Rampant suppression. The prim doctor goes rogue and goes snitch. He gives up all their rogue actions. The document was a torch. It would burn down his whole fucking life.

Parker passed the folder back. "I concede my predicament. I'm sure that you coerced Dr. Ashida with great verve."

Cantwell twinkled. Dudley winked. Parker passed him the film strip. Dudley rolled it out and studied it.

He scanned it, up and down. He scanned it six full times.

He said, "Yes, Captain. I concede."

Parker rubbed it in. "Your pal Ed Satterlee and Ace Kwan's pal Quon Chin. Let me extend the argument that this film so lucidly asserts. It's a payoff. You and Ace have plans to exploit the roundups and the forthcoming internment, and you're greasing a well-placed Fed in advance. If Ace is acting independent of you, I don't care. You and Ace cannot afford to have this film strip publicly viewed or logged as police evidence. You and Ace cannot afford to have the roundups in any way officially besmirched."

Dudley passed the strip back. "Your assumptions are soundly reasoned and entirely correct. I must ask Mr. Kwan why he is paying off Agent Satterlee. Knowing Mr. Kwan, I would guess that it pertains to business."

Cantwell twinkled. "It's all Greek to me, but I'm having a swell time anyway."

Parker said, "Describe your end of the agreement."

Dudley said, "I respectfully request your vow not to interfere in the legal processes attending the conviction of Fujio Shudo for the murders of Ryoshi, Aya, Johnny and Nancy Watanabe. Within that request, I offer this concession. You, with or without Dr. Ashida, may have a grand time searching for white men in purple sweaters, but you may not publicly or officially present evidence that anyone other than Mr. Shudo killed the Watanabe family. I also respectfully request your vow not to interfere in my endeavors with Ace Kwan in any way, shape, manner or form. I should add that I have vivid documentation of your near-fatal beating of your first wife, Francine Pomeroy."

Cantwell crossed himself. Parker willed his hand back from his gun.

"With God as my witness, you have my vow."

"Thank you, Captain. And on your end?"

Parker said, "I respectfully request your vow to make damn fucking sure that no Federal, state, or local charges are filed against Katherine Lake, Claire De Haven, the men in her cell and the film crew. There are to be no reprisals against Miss Lake for her justified assault on your friend Dot Rothstein. I respectfully request your vow to see to the timely release and the dropping of all charges for Miss Lake and the others. I respectfully request that you present my threat of public exposure to Richard Hood, the SAC of the FBI's Los Angeles Office, immediately. Within this request, I offer this concession. I will never again seek to entrap Fifth Columnists of any sort, with or without Miss Lake's participation."

Dudley tapped his belt wares. Stations of the cross. Knuckle dusters, sap, shiv.

"With God as my witness, you have my vow."

Parker stood up.

Dudley stood up.

They shook hands.

Cantwell stood and clapped. "White men, both of you. Good Catholic boys. Such dry wit, such decorum."

The walls compressed. The heat index climbed. Some unseen fireplace roared. Here come the jim-jams and quakes.

Dudley said something droll. Cantwell dished blarney. Parker made for the door.

He got outside. Rain hit him. He weaved down a walkway and puked into a hedge. The walls retracted. The heat index dropped. He lost his legs. He felt propelled. He made it to the sanctuary. The side door was unlocked.

He got to a pew. He got to his knees and faced the altar. He got squared away and got to it.

Holy Father, grant me reprieve. Take my fraudulent righteousness. Revoke the arrogance that blinds me to the plight of others and leads me to horrid error and misalliance. Temper my ambition with grace, Dear Lord. Forgive me for persecuting Claire De Haven. I am complicit in blood libel. Protect the innocent Japanese of this city as chaos attends them. Bring me Joan Conville and tell me what she portends. Grant Katherine Lake the will to self-rebuke, so that she might repent and forfeit her reckless urges. I will honor the vow that I just issued in Your Name. That oath of convenience makes me small in Your Eyes. I succumb to worldliness in this address. I speak to You in ghastly qualification. I cannot lose what I have fought so hard for and can only grasp and compromise when others seek to take it from me.

He stayed on his knees. He prayed. He got up to the edge and retreated. He knew the words and fought the words. He saw dawn through stained glass. The new vow lodged inside him and caused tremors.

He got up to it. He retreated. He said the words so he would not go insane.

Dear God, let this be my final compliance with evil. Dear God, I must never do this again.

84

LOS ANGELES | SATURDAY, DECEMBER 20, 1941

8:35 a.m.

Dick Hood said, "It's extortion. It's sheer blackmail."

Dudley said, "We have to comply. He'll levy the threat without hesitation."

"Tell me who 'He' is. I'll concede that it's a valid threat, and I'll get Mr. Hoover's okay. Just tell me who 'He' is."

They sat in Dudley's cubicle. Graph paper masked the walls. Arrows, boxes, initials. Baffling hieroglyphics. Hood kept glancing sidelong.

Dudley zipped his lips. Hood lit a cigarette.

"My money's on Thad Brown or Bill Parker. They're the front-runners for Chief when Jack the H. retires. Parker's a drunk and a religious nut, and Thad's subtle. *Shit.* Mr. Hoover's going to hit the roof."

Dudley rocked his chair. "You'll have to speak to the U.S. Attorney. You'll have to release Miss De Haven and the others, and disband that part of your investigation."

Hood made the jack-off sign. "I'll gird my fucking loins, make the fucking calls and take the fucking heat. And in case you haven't noticed, it's not really an 'investigation.' It's just round up the fucking Japs and make this a Jap-free city within sixty days."

Dudley said, "I spoke to Ace Kwan an hour ago. He explained the payoffs to me, and I would describe them as felicitous in intent. They were Ace's bequest to the agents who've been working so diligently to clean up this damnable mess. Ed Satterlee would have explained it to you by New Year's. Ace intends to throw a grand party for all of you, including the Hearst Rifle Team and some of our Alien Squad boys. You'll have a week at Cal Drake's Blue Lion Lodge, up in Victorville. There'll be bourbon, bird hunting and Cuban cigars. It's Ace's treat for you, once the Japs have been properly penned."

Hood grinned. "The goddamn war, the goddamn Japs. You've got escaped Japs, now. Gene Biscailuz is throwing his own party. Duty waivers and twelve scoots a day. He's got a lynch mob on his hands."

The Blue Lion tale was a dodge. Yes, he called Ace. Yes, Ace came clean. Ed Satterlee was hawking Jap-property leads. Ace had Quon Chin purchase some.

He called Ed. He told him about the film strip and its upscut. Ed came clean. He told him to comply with the Blue Lion dodge.

Hood said, "I like Ace. He's been feeding my boys on the cuff. Got a yen for egg rolls at 3:00 a.m.? See Ace the Chinaman."

Dudley said, "Ace is a thoughtful man. He knows that your niece Jane is getting married, and he's offered to cater the reception, free of charge."

Hood stood up. "Free of charge" echoed.

"Damn. The Blue Lion. Will you be joining us?"

"Regretfully, no. I'll be entering Army service at New Year's."

Hood stretched. "I'll go make those calls. Jesus, Mr. Hoover will piss blood."

Dudley tossed him his hat. They shook hands and sighed. *Ain't life a pisser?* Hood hit the road. Dudley coffee-chased two bennies. The graph summoned him.

He jotted notes. He updated the land grab. He detailed Dr. Terry's buy-in strategy. He drew a howling wolf.

He was keyed up. He barely dozed last night. He kept calling Bette. A coon maid kept stalling him. Beth and Tommy were due. He made calls and located the two rape-o Marines.

He spoke to Scotty. He rebuked him for the Lee Blanchard tiff. He requested a favor in recompense. Scotty said Sure.

He went by Carl Hull's house. Craven Carl spilled to Buzz Meeks. It mandated a severe beating.

Frau Carl diverted him. *Ensign* Carl had left for the Navy.

He was keyed-up. He needed investment gelt. He needed to plan the raid on Carlos Madrano's stash.

Dudley drew wolves and dollar signs. Money. Madrano's cash and dope. Money. Ace Kwan's tile game tomorrow.

Dudley studied his graph. Arrows, boxes, initials, contractions. Scotty walked up. Scotty studied the graph.

"It's interesting how the initials repeat. If you know the names, you can almost figure it out."

"Bright lad. I'm surrounded by acute young men these days."

Scotty smiled. "The Werewolf's in no. 2. Mr. Loew told me to get you."

Dudley grabbed his suit coat. "I'd like you to observe and follow my signals. There's that task, and a drive down to Oceanside later. It pertains to that amends I require. I'll explain it to you en route."

Scotty said, "Okay, Dud."

They walked down to 2. No gallery this time. No steno, no hallway speaker.

Ellis Loew sat with Fujio Shudo. Two extra chairs were pulled up.

Shudo was handcuffed. This interview was the stalker. The closer was later today.

Loew jiggled his Phi Beta key. Dudley and Scotty sat down. Shudo stood up.

He said, "I'm a whip-out man." He unzipped his trousers and whipped out his dick.

Dudley signaled Scotty.

Scotty improvised.

He grabbed Shudo by the neck and picked him up, one-handed. He lowered him and sat him back down in his chair.

Loew gawked. Shudo tucked his dick away and went *Ouch*.

Dudley said, "Good morning, Mr. Shudo. I've missed you. Have you missed me?"

Shudo said, "No."

Dudley smiled. "We left you on the avenues in Highland Park, around noon on Saturday, December 6th. You posed for a photograph with a little girl who thought you resembled a werewolf, which you most fetchingly do. You had been drinking terpin hydrate, you recall that day as being hazy, and you said that an 'instinct' drew you to Highland Park. You became upset when I brought up your visits to Japanese fraternal clubs in the early 1930s, your acrimonious relationship with a man named Ryoshi Watanabe, and your political arguments with him. Do you recall that, sir? It was only Thursday night that we had this discussion."

Shudo picked his nose. "I don't know. I told you I knew Ginzo Watanabe and Charlie Watanabe, but I don't remember no Ryoshi."

Dudley said, "You will in time, sir. We've come into possession of a letter that you wrote to him in 1933."

Loew gawked the letter. He was in on let's-get-him. He was clueless per the frame. He signaled Dudley: *My turn.*

"Mr. Shudo, do you carry sample knives on your cart? Sharp-bladed knives to show off the fine work you do?"

Shudo said, "Sure."

Dudley said, "We've reset the stage for you, sir. It's Saturday, December 6th, and you're in Highland Park on an 'instinct.' You've been drinking terpin hydrate, and things are hazy."

Shudo said, "I don't remember writing Ryoshi Watanabe no letter."

"But you *do* recall Ryoshi and your arguments with him at the fraternal clubs?"

Shudo shrugged. "Yeah, I guess so."

Clincher. Now, reverse the field.

"You were born in Yokohama, Japan, in 1903. Isn't that correct, Mr. Shudo? Your Atascadero file reports that you emigrated in 1908."

Shudo said, "That's right. I was born in the land of the rising sun. I'm not no Nisei Johnny-come-lately."

"Your father ran a fishing boat out of San Pedro, didn't he, Mr. Shudo?"

"That's right."

"Did he engage in political activities?"

"No, but he hated the Chinks, and he rumbled against the tongs."

"Did he educate you in the political ways of Imperial Japan?"

Shudo said, "No. He educated me with a croquet mallet."

"And when did this practice begin, sir?"

"When I was about eight years old. When he saw me whip it out on this Mex boy."

"And how long did this practice last?"

"Until I ran away. I think I was fourteen. The Beast told me to cut tracks, so I did."

"And who is 'The Beast,' Mr. Shudo?"

"The Beast is my dick."

"Do you view your dick as a separate being, sir? As something or someone attached to your body, but able to act and speak to you independently?"

"Yeah. The Beast is The Beast. Sometimes he gives me good advice, sometimes he leads me astray."

Loew gawked. Scotty gassed on Shudo. *This sure beats divinity school!*

Dudley said, "The Beast is your counselor and your confidant, is that correct, Mr. Shudo? He frequently guides your actions and advises you on what to do?"

Shudo said, "That's correct. The Beast is my baby boy. I'm a whip-out man. If I see something that I think The Beast will like, I show it to him. Your boy here is The Beast's type, so I gave him a peek."

Dudley said, "Are you referring to my colleague, Officer Robert S. Bennett?"

Shudo said, "That's right. The Beast likes husky boys."

Loew said, "Mr. Shudo, are you a homosexual?"

Shudo said, "No. I'm just the *ichiban* of The Beast."

Dudley said, "I'm curious about the advice that The Beast offers you, sir. Can you give me any examples of it?"

Shudo scratched his balls. "The Beast tells me to take the streetcar up to Hollywood, so I do it. The Beast tells me to break into houses and sniff jockstraps, so I do it. The Beast tells me to share my terp with him, so I do."

Dudley smiled. Shudo ogled Scotty.

"Mr. Shudo, a pair of women's panties were found in your hotel room. Were you aware of that?"

Shudo shrugged. Women's panties—so what?

"Sir, have you ever broken into a house for the express purpose of sniffing women's panties? Feel free to consult The Beast if you need to."

Shudo scrunched up his face. Shudo expressed deep thought. Shudo nodded yes.

"Yeah. I like to break into houses and sniff women's panties."

"Do you enjoy fucking the occasional girl, sir? Do you indulge the practice if there are no comely young men in sight?"

Shudo scrunched up. Shudo consulted The Beast. Shudo nodded yes.

"Yeah, boss. I go for gash if there's no cute brown eye around."

Loew cringed. Dudley tossed a curveball.

"Sir, did you fuck Nancy Watanabe during a work-furlough release from Atascadero, six months ago?"

Shudo scrunched up. Shudo consulted The Beast.

"Yeah, I fucked Nancy. I fucked her good."

Loew nudged Dudley. *He's in the house. We've got partial motive. We're halfway there.* Scotty chewed bubble gum. Shudo ogled him. Here comes curveball no. 2.

"You've been with Mr. Shudo a long time. Isn't that true, Beast?"

Shudo spoke basso profundo. "That's right. A *looooong* time."

"You've certainly taught him a few things, I'd venture to say."

Shudo, basso profundo. "I'll say. Fuji was a punk until I took him in."

"Why would you say something that harsh, Beast?"

The Beast said, "Because it's true. Fuji was the sissy until I made him the brunser. He gave out the brown at the San Pedro Y and up at Preston. I took him to the Murakami Nursery. They got bamboo shoots there. 'Bamboo Shoot' Shudo. Fuji owes that moniker to me."

Dudley said, "Would you say that Mr. Shudo owes his entire criminal career to you, Beast?"

The Beast said, "In spades, *ichiban.* I taught him the knife-sharpening trade and made him a knife man. I got him a job at a blood bank in Long Beach, so he could steal the cute sailors' blood. I took him to see *Dracula* at the Marcal Theatre. We kidnapped a sailor in the parking lot, so we could cut him and drink his blood. I showed him how to mix terp with blood, for a swell cocktail. I showed him how to cut himself when he couldn't find no cute brown eye to cut."

Loew leaned in. He ticked legal points, sotto voce.

"Get back to the 6th, and get to his weapons. Nort excluded the swords, but this isn't going all the way to a jury. The swords and his knife cart. Let's get back there."

Dudley nodded. Scotty blew a big bubble. Shudo giggled and squirmed in his seat.

"Beast, are you and Mr. Shudo familiar with the Japanese swords used in the practice of hara-kiri?"

The Beast said, "Yes."

"And were you and Mr. Shudo in possession of four such swords on Saturday, December 6th?"

The Beast said, "Yeah, boss."

Dudley said, "But you had lost the scabbards, hadn't you, Beast?"

The Beast said, "Right. We lost the scabbards."

"Do you know what scabbards *are*, Beast?"

"I'm not sure, boss."

"Beast, do you and Mr. Shudo keep an assortment of sample knives on your cart? Knives that you show to prospective customers to demonstrate the high quality of your work?"

The Beast said, "Yeah, we got some sample knives."

Dudley tossed a change-up. It's a for-real question. It's a head scratcher.

"Beast, we did not find the knife-sharpening cart in your room at the Kyoto Arms Hotel."

"Fuji sold it to a nigger, outside the Rosslyn Hotel."

"And when was that?"

The Beast said, "Sunday, December 7, 1941. A day that will live in glory for mighty Imperial Japan."

Loew leaned in. "What's with this letter Shudo wrote?"

Dudley leaned in. "Hideo Ashida found it at the house and transcribed it for me. It was posted in October '33. Fuji and Ryoshi had had some voluble disagreements at a Jap social club, and it's apparent that he was already quite smitten with Nancy, even though she was a scant eight years old, and female."

Loew said, "I don't get that part of it. This guy's a queer, and he keesters men with bamboo shoots."

Dudley sighed. "Sex is a devilishly complex phenomenon, Mr. Loew. There's that, and the considerable fact that Mr. Shudo is insane."

"Quit addressing his schlong, will you? It's giving me the willies."

Dudley smiled. Scotty blew bubbles. Shudo goo-goo-eyed him.

Loew leaned close. "Walk him up to it, Sergeant. He hates Ryoshi, he impregnated Nancy, but she got a scrape. We've got the letter and the print in Ryoshi's blood. We've got eyeball wits that place him in Highland Park that day. The knives versus the swords is problematic, but we know he's going to confess. Walk him up and walk him *through* when we go for the close this afternoon. Jack Horrall's bringing some Army brass in for the show. You'll have a full house."

Shudo said, "You're whispering and conspiring against me. The Beast told me so. I told him you're all right. The jailers get my grub at Kwan's Chinese Pagoda. I get peach duck for noon chow today."

Dudley grinned. "And two portions you shall have, sir."

Shudo went *Yum-yum.* "I've got no grudge on the Chinks. Eugenics is eugenics, boss. The Chinks got the better grub, but us Japs are the master race."

Dudley rode a brainstorm. "I agree with you, sir. The Japanese are quite the superior race. I'm wondering, sir. By and large, you prefer men over women—but you've sustained quite the lust for Nancy Watanabe over time."

"Yeah, Nancy. What a dish. Almost as good as brown eye."

"You were quite determined to impregnate her, weren't you, sir?"

"Yeah. Fuji and Nancy, and a little cub in the oven."

"Was propagating the Japanese master race your chief concern with Nancy, sir? Did it trump your sexual desire, given your longstanding and rather cruel lust for young men?"

"Yeah."

"And did Nancy's termination of her pregnancy consume you in waves of despair?"

"Yeah."

"And were those waves of despair in fact tidal waves, as you rolled your knife-sharpening cart down Avenue 45 in Highland Park in the early-afternoon hours of Saturday, December 6, 1941?"

"Yeah, boss."

"And were you in the hazy, dreamlike state common to those who habitually swill terpin hydrate?"

"Yeah, boss. Terp. Terp and blood-bank blood from a husky white boy."

"The Beast was leading you astray that day, wasn't he, Mr. Shudo? He had you teething on Nancy's abortion and all the indignities you had suffered during your contentious friendship with Ryoshi Watanabe."

"Yeah, boss. The Beast was talking to me. I remember that day. He said *Frankenstein* was playing at the Wiltern Theatre. That little girl said I looked like The Wolfman."

"The white residents of Highland Park viewed you with suspicion as you made your rounds that day, didn't they? They knew you to be a member of the master race, soon to go to war with our inferior white nation."

"That's right, boss. Pearl Harbor was coming up. *Banzai*, you white fuckers."

"You sensed the looming attack in the air, didn't you, Mr. Shudo? You knew it was coming. It moved you, thrilled you, and filled you with elation and a paradoxical rage. You were on that street, you were near that house, you had sharp weapons on your cart and at your disposal. You were enraged. You wanted to be poised on the deck of a Japanese aircraft carrier, headed for Pearl Harbor. You were surely a werewolf, but you wanted to be a werewolf of the sky, in the glorious service of Imperial Japan, and that disjuncture filled you with a maddening and murderous hunger. Nancy was in that house. She had slaughtered your eugenic contribution to the Japanese master race. Ryoshi was in that house. He had belittled you in numerous arguments, going back nearly a decade. You knew that Aya and Johnny were in that house, and you suddenly sensed, with all your being, that you were nearing your very own Pearl Harbor."

Shudo giggled. "That's right, *ichiban*. *Banzai*, you Jap fuckers."

Dudley tapped Loew. Scotty leaned close. Shoptalk, sotto voce.

"Call Kwan's in half an hour. Order peach duck, chop suey and pork fried rice. Tell Ace to throw in two vials of terpin hydrate."

85

LOS ANGELES | SATURDAY, DECEMBER 20, 1941

11:14 a.m.

The Reds walked. Newshounds scoped their jail exit. Ashida watched. He had a lab-window view.

Claire took the lead. Her slaves followed her. The film crew lagged behind.

Reporters and cameramen pounced. Sid Hudgens and Jack Webb led the pack. The Anti-Axis raid made the papers.

It got *some* ink. It should have gleaned *more*. The escaped Japs and The Werewolf gobbled print space.

Flashbulbs popped. Newsmen yelled. Claire magnetized them and breezed through. Two limos were parked curbside. Claire took the lead car. Her slaves piled in behind her.

Both sleds pulled out. The crew dispersed on the street. The newsmen ignored them. *Reds Lay Tracks in Looooooong Lincolns!* Photo men snapped the getaway.

The scene evaporated. *Poof!* It's over. Everyone walked away.

The Reds walked. Ashida sensed quixotic Bill Parker. He pulled Kay Lake from the bin last night. The station buzzed with the tale. Whiskey Bill's prom-night gesture.

Ashida stood at the window. The lab was Saturday dead. He had nowhere to go.

Dudley raided his apartment. Mariko's place was Fed-sieged. L.A. was a siege state. Blood libel. His myth of normalcy, dashed.

Ashida stood at the window. The squadroom phones blared. Detectives logged get-the-Japs scuttlebutt.

The Sidster and Jack Webb walked in. They glad-handed Ashida and lit cigarettes.

Jack said, "That Claire De Haven's a dish."

Sid said, "Yeah, if the dish is red borscht."

Jack said, "She can keep my tootsies warm in the Kremlin."

Sid said, "Hideo, what are we going to do with this kid? His tenuous wartime employment as a stooge for William Randolph Hearst is going to his head."

Ashida forced a laugh. *Sid, you're a sketch.*

Jack said, "The Dudster gave me a job for tomorrow night. Ace Kwan's throwing a big tile game, and he got a tip that some jigs are going to heist it. I'm supposed to observe the game and call him at a pay phone."

Sid winked. "Like I said, It's all going to his head. The Dudster and Mr. Hearst. What's the diff?"

Jack said, "Why mince words? This war's been good to me so far."

Sid winked. "Unlike some others. Unlike the bulk of the Japanese folks in *El Pueblo Grande* at this particular moment. Right, Hideo?"

Ashida flushed. Sid was a eugenic misfit. He was half cockroach, half maladroit dwarf.

"That's right, Sid."

"I'm thinking about doing a piece on you, Hideo. Dud got The Wolf, and you were a big part of the case. How about this? 'Hideo Ashida helped crack the baffling Watanabe job, and he's Japanese himself.' It's a good angle, given the way things are going for you folks."

Ashida said, "They couldn't go much worse."

Sid said, "Sure they could. Those escapee fools have got this town in a tizzy, and that posse is out for blood. All the jails are full, so there's talk of housing you folks in the horse paddocks at Santa Anita. You can dig that, right? You're eating broiled eel on 2nd and Alameda one minute, you're sharing a bale of tasty hay with Seabiscuit the next."

Jack yukked. Ashida gripped the window ledge. *Racial cur, cockroach, dwarf.*

Sid said, "And, to top it off, you've got Fletch Bowron, stinko at the Jonathan Club last night. Is he railing at the Japanese forces currently gutting the Philippines? No. He's ragging on a certain Nisei police chemist."

The window ledge cracked. Ashida said, "You *heard* him?"

Jack said, "Fletch the B. Elmer the J's got the goods on that boy."

Sid said, "I was there, and I heard him. He was talking up his plans to levy taxes on confiscated Japanese property, and he was hurling dirt on you and Whiskey Bill Parker. He was ragging Bill the P for that tapped-phone ploy that kept you on the PD, and he called you the 'yellow spot on his spotless political record.'"

Ashida gripped the window ledge. The whole thing snapped off.

86

KAY LAKE'S DIARY

LOS ANGELES | SATURDAY, DECEMBER 20, 1941

11:51 a.m.

The white haze and morphine were gone. The pain all over my body made me feel more like myself. I was going home in the late afternoon. My concussion was healing. The nose splint made me sneeze.

Lee and Scotty sat on opposite sides of the bed and held my hands. We all bore wounds from early-wartime altercations.

I pointed to my nose. "You should see the other girl."

Lee and Scotty laughed; Scotty plumped up my pillows. Lee said, "I tried to enlist. I wasn't going to mention it until I got in. Thad Brown got Jack Horrall's okay. I took the physical, but I'm 4-F. That punctured eardrum from my fight with Jimmy Bivens."

Scotty gave Lee a big stage look. Lee said, "Don't flatter yourself, Bennett. You don't hit that hard."

We all laughed. Scotty gave me a look. Lee caught it. He wiggled my feet and said, "I should go now."

Scotty said, "Wait downstairs for me, Blanchard. I'll drive you back to the Hall."

Lee blew me a kiss and walked out. Pain shot down my jaw. I sneezed and felt stitches tug loose.

Scotty handed me a tissue. I said, "You're going to tell me something."

He said, "That I'm breaking it off with you. Right's right and wrong's wrong, and we all know which one this is."

I squeezed his hand. "I would have said 'one more time when I'm feeling and looking better,' but you're right."

Scotty said, "Right's right."

I said, "You'll have to make do with Joan Crawford."

Scotty blushed. "Who told you?"

"Brenda Allen. She saw you with *La Grande Joan* at the Trocadero. She called it an astonishing moment. You were with Joan

Crawford, and Dudley Smith was with Bette Davis. It was when she knew that the war had changed everything."

Scotty shivered. I said, "You shouldn't be ashamed of being afraid of him. It's the proper response."

"He collects protégés and discards them. You've seen it. Lee Blanchard didn't cut the mustard, and now there's me."

I smiled. "You're learning."

"He's like a centipede. He's got his feelers spread out, but you can't see them. He's got this graph taped up in his cubicle. It's all about the Watanabe case and what you'd call 'related opportunities,' and it's in this special shorthand of his. I've been studying it when no one's around, and I've put some things together. You wouldn't believe what I've figured out."

"It's what you do with what you've learned."

Scotty shrugged. The good lad, the bad lad. The bright lad who cracked puzzles that stumped other kids. The troubled lad, always.

"I'm joining the Marines, right after New Year's. I just talked to Dud about it, and he already got Chief Horrall's okay. I can go fight the war and come back on the Department. That's the thing about Dudley that gets me. He's so damn generous."

I laced up our fingers. "Don't get killed, sweetie."

"Not this boy."

"I'm going to try to enlist again. Ward Littell told me that a lot of the Federal holds have been lifted."

Scotty touched my cheek. "That's you, Kay. You bite this big bull's nose off and go to war. It's like your speech. Your options are do everything or do nothing."

My eyes wetted up. Scotty handed me a tissue and went pensive. I said, "Tell me what you're thinking."

"I was thinking about Dud. He's got a job for me later today, and God knows how many more between now and New Year's. He knows that I'm inclined a certain way, so he uses me. I just want to get to some safe little island, so I can kill Japs with a clear conscience."

I said, "Tell me about this graph."

87

LOS ANGELES | SATURDAY, DECEMBER 20, 1941

12:21 p.m.

Parker burned graphs.

He torched his traffic graph and roundup graph. He torched *Watanabe Case/Details-Chronology* and *Lake/De Haven*. He found a jug under the kitchen sink and built a bourbon blaze.

He raised a stink. The flames blew high. He doused them with tap water.

The sink was a sludge mound. Parker scooped the mess into a bag and dumped it in a trash can. He washed his hands and aired out the kitchen. He walked back to the den. Call-Me-Jack stuck him with more shitwork.

It was punitive. He messed with Dudley's first go at The Wolf. He was back to the PD's "Auxiliary."

Call-Me-Jack got tight with the Hearst Rifle boys. They were his Auxiliary faves. They were out on Sheriff Gene's dragnet. Call-Me-Jack craved more men like that.

Parker read applicant files. A low tide rolled in. Bottom-feeders gleamed in the muck.

Klanned-up studio guards. A nudist preacher. A Negro janitor at Le Conte Junior High. Numerous stat-rape assertions.

Low tide. Denizens of the deep.

Parker flipped files. He hit four clipped-up sheets.

Boudreau, Costigan, Gutridge, Palwick. Ex–Nevada prison guards. All Spanish-fluent. All canned from their state jobs. All dumped for brutality.

Hard boys. Goon-squad types. A routing slip and photos clipped to the sheets.

A messenger picked them up. One-week paper loan-out. Four files, sent to:

Exley Construction. 6402 Wilshire Boulevard.

Hard boys. Ex–prison guards. All Spanish-fluent. It comes down to—

THIS:

The Valley. The Jap-owned farms. The wetback workers supplied by Carlos Madrano. Preston's law-enforcement ties. Preston's internment scheme.

Catch it now. It's a soft lob. You should have caught it before this.

Preston was behind the house and farm buyouts. Preston was linked to the Watanabe case.

88

LOS ANGELES | SATURDAY, DECEMBER 20, 1941

1:04 p.m.

The Werewolf read Hideo's letter. He was terp-primed. He moved his lips and read slow.

Dudley sat with Ellis Loew and a new steno. The hallway was packed. The wall speakers supplied crisp sound.

Call-Me-Jack hosted some Army pals. Said pals brought their children. The lads and lassies wore rubber werewolf masks. Shudo was quite the kiddie show.

Dudley said, "Do you recall that letter, sir?"

Shudo said, "Yeah. Sure. I guess so."

"With that in mind, sir, let us return to Saturday, December 6th."

"Okay, boss."

"You were in a state of both agitation and premeditation. You were, quite frankly, looped on terpin hydrate. By your own admission, sir, things were quite hazy for you."

Shudo said, "Terp, boss. It's like Wheaties. 'Breakfast of Champions.'"

Dudley said, "You had the deadly sharp knives on your cart. You had the Japanese ritual swords that you purchased in Little Tokyo, but you don't recall where, and you misplaced the four scabbards in your inebriated state. You had purchased four sachets of a rare Oriental poison from a chemist that you knew from your fraternal-club days, but you cannot recall his name—and, again, your consumption of terpin hydrate had rendered that patch of time hazy."

Shudo scratched his neck. "I think I remember that chemist guy. He was friends with The Beast way back when. I sold my cart to a coon outside the Rosslyn Hotel. I do remember that."

Dudley said, "We discussed it, sir. That stated, I should remind you. You sold the cart on Sunday, December 7th. It's still Saturday, December 6th, that we're discussing here."

Shudo said, "Right, boss. Saturday. This little girl says I look like The Wolfman, and her daddy takes a picture of me."

Dudley said, "That is correct, sir. And by our combined calculations, it was right before you knocked on Ryoshi Watanabe's door."

Shudo yawned. "Ryoshi was a wrong-o, boss. We went back to the clubs. I read that letter. We had this grudge going. I was full of no-good for him. It was bad, *ichiban.*"

"He was surprised to see you, wasn't he, sir?"

"Yeah, he was surprised. 'Hello there, Ryoshi. We go back, baby boy.' "

"You were shocked to see Nancy, weren't you, sir? She was the carrier of your wolf-cub litter, but she slaughtered the whelps in her womb."

"Yeah, Nancy. She was a wrong-o. The Beast hated her. She did me dirt."

Dudley lit a cigarette. The Wolf snatched the pack and lit up. Loew nudged Dudley. It meant *Close Him Now.*

Dudley said, "Aya and Johnny were there. You'd stashed your cart on the porch, out of sight from the street. The reunion with your hated foe and his family was uncomfortable at first, but you suggested a nice cup of tea, all around. The tea contained a slow-acting poison that induced euphoria before it induced death. The dope-addled Watanabes vomited on their clothing, but didn't seem to mind, because of their euphoric states. That display of sloth offended you and disrupted the fantasy that had been building ever so vividly within your mind. You made the four people change clothes. You spied on Nancy and Johnny and became aroused at their states of undress. You didn't want to be seen outside with their vomit-soaked clothing, so you dumped it in the washing machine. Your fantasy went into improvisation. It now entailed a period of waiting, postmortem. You would have to wait for the clothes to wash and hang them out on the line."

Shudo said, "Yeah, the fuckers puked. It made me real mad. What's that word? It 'disrupted' me."

Loew went *Wheeeeeeeew*. Dudley smiled.

"Ryoshi had been bragging. He told you that a Japanese attack on the Pacific Fleet was imminent, and his certainty infuriated you. You felt impotent, because your hated foe remained a vital and well-informed Fifth Columnist, while you moldered in an asylum on charges of bamboo-shoot rape. You improvised again. You capitalized on the euphoric states of your intended victims and had Ryoshi write a suicide note pertaining to the attack on his bedroom wall. The stage had been set, sir. Your victims had been lulled into a state of docile and euphoric compliance. 'Fuji, the Knife Man.' They had long underestimated you. You suggested a friendly game of charades and made them lie supine, four across, on the living room floor."

Shudo raised his hands. Shudo rattled his cuff chain. Shudo said, "Yeah, boss."

"And then you pulled a sharp knife from your waistband and gutted them in the manner of seppuku. Is that correct, sir?"

Shudo went *Heil Hitler!* Shudo said, "Yeah, boss."

"And then you removed the clothes from the washing machine and hung them on the clothesline. Is that correct, sir?"

Shudo went *Heil Hitler!* Shudo said, "Yeah, boss."

"And then you waited until nightfall, calmly gathered up your knife-sharpening cart and cautiously surveyed the outside world. You then wheeled your cart down to Figueroa Street and walked southbound, to your hotel. You were wonderfully elated, and consumed yet more terpin hydrate in celebration. You went up to your room and slept through to the following day. It is now Sunday, December 7th, sir. You went out in the world and learned that your misguided countrymen had, indeed, attacked the Pacific Fleet. You ventured southbound and sold your knife-sharpening cart to a Negro man outside the Rosslyn Hotel. You dropped the knife you used to kill the Watanabe family down a sewer grate. Is that correct, sir?"

Shudo said, "Yeah, *ichiban*. I did it all. Ryoshi got under my skin. Nancy killed my cubs, and Johnny said no to The Beast. Aya was mean to me, so she had to go. Pearl Harbor, boss. This caper ain't no gas-chamber bounce when my people win the war."

Ellis Loew sighed.

The steno sighed.

Dudley stood and bowed to the mirror. The door blew open wide.

The gallery ran in. They blitzkrieged Dudley and banzai'd The Wolf. Call-Me-Jack, Thad B., Fletch Bowron. Stray Feds, Army brass, little kids.

They pounded Dudley's back. Thad uncuffed The Wolf. The kids stormed him and hugged him. The Wolf mugged and ruffled their hair.

The kids wore Mummy masks and Werewolf masks. The Wolf hopped around. The kids poked him and squealed.

Dudley ducked out. More work loomed. Oceanside—eighty miles south.

He popped two bennies and hit the back stairs. Scotty was parked in his pastor dad's Dodge. Dudley loaded it this a.m.

One Navy seabag. Two .45's tucked in. Silencer-rigged. Loaded with Ace Kwan's dumdums. Eugenics. One slug killed whole dynasties.

Dudley jumped in the car. Scotty pulled out. Dudley dipped the seat and shut his eyes. *Don't talk to me.*

He'd talked to Ace. The tile game was Chink-only and high stakes. He called Harry Cohn and said stay away. He called Jack Webb and gave him a gig.

Watch the game for me. Chart the winners and losers. Call me, pay phone to pay phone. I fear a robbery.

The Smith-Kwan cartel needed money. Terry Lux was in with them now. Terry's business acumen juiced up their plans. Terry thought they could buy in with Exley and Patchett. It required big seed cash.

Scotty drove. Dudley rode a bennie surge and schemed the Mexican foray.

It was risky. It meant fucking Carlos Madrano. Carlos was Exley's and Patchett's tight pal. It meant a Mexican dope and cash raid. It meant planned obfuscation and convincing suspects killed in advance.

Scotty drove. Dudley opened his eyes. He saw the coast road. A sign read OCEANSIDE, 10 MILES.

Salt air. Late-afternoon mist. A rocky beach stretch.

Scotty passed him a note slip. "It's a phone message for you. Dick Carlisle gave it to me."

Dudley pocketed the slip. The topography grabbed him.

Scrub mounds on the land side. Roadhouses by the beach. Narrow parking strips. No cars tucked in. Storm clouds right at dusk.

"Two young Marines have grievously harmed a young woman who is quite dear to me. I've been told that they cast their lines at the same spot every Saturday. They're intrepid lads, undeterred by wind and cold air. We'll take them as they get into their car."

Scotty blinked. Dudley touched his wrist. Scotty's pulse skipped.

He saw their fishing spot. He saw their '40 Ford coupe. He pointed over. Long poles swooped toward the sunset.

Scotty pulled up by the Ford. He kicked off the ignition and set the brake.

Dudley reached back and unzipped the seabag. The silencers were screwed on tight.

Scotty said, "She's a good girl, right? It was bad what they did."

Dudley passed him his piece. "Am I a frivolous man, lad? Have you not sensed conscience and a fond regard for women beneath my raw streak?"

Scotty smiled—*So be it.*

Two men walked over the rocks. They wore Marine fatigue jackets. They carried surf poles and wicker baskets. Fish tails drooped out the top.

They walked to the Ford. One tall man, one stout man. The stout man checked out the Dodge.

The tall man popped the trunk. He loaded the baskets. The stout man dropped the poles in the backseat.

They got in the front. The stout man kicked the engine. The tall man lit a cigarette.

Cops, huh?

They knew it. They were cop-wise. They were too nonchalant.

Dudley stepped out. Scotty stepped out. They went in, flanking.

The rape-o's caught it. Intent, gun-barrel glint—*something.*

The tall man dropped his cigarette. The stout man fumbled at the wheel.

Dudley said, "For my beloved child, Beth Short."

He fired. Scotty fired. They aimed at their wide-open mouths. They blew up their faces and took all the windows out.

Ricochets took out the engine wall. The crankcase threw hot oil. The radiator threw steam.

The Ford rocked on its struts. Dudley and Scotty got back in the Dodge and pulled out.

The sun went down. The Ford sat on the blacktop. Dudley lit a cigarette and pulled out that note slip.

"Call Claire De Haven. CR-4424."

89

LOS ANGELES | SATURDAY, DECEMBER 20, 1941

5:49 p.m.

The Yellow Spot.

He treads cautiously.

He skulks by night.

It wasn't *quite* night. *Skulk* hyperbolized. City Hall was dead quiet and safe. He was two floors up from the Bureau. He almost blended in.

"The Yellow Spot." It went with "The Werewolf" and the monster-masked kids. He caught the backwash of Shudo's confession. Shudo signed autographs and posed with children. It was ghastly and hilarious.

The hallway was dead quiet. The mayor's office suite was a tomb. The watchman worked the Spring Street door. The Yellow Spot strikes—

Now.

A no. 3 pick got the door. His penlight drilled the waiting room. Chairs and the receptionist's desk. Fletch B.'s private office—right there.

A no. 2 pick popped the door. Ashida eased it shut and beamed his penlight. The office was all plaques and club chairs. There's Fletch Bowron's desk.

It was presidential. A tube-fed Dictaphone covered the right edge. A cord hooked the Dictaphone to the telephone. Fletch recorded his calls.

Ashida scanned the walls and floor. The Dictaphone and telephone shared one outlet.

Fletch recorded his calls. Fletch might have his calls transcribed. He might erase the tube scrolls. Pertinent talk was a long shot.

Ashida sat in Fletch B.'s chair and got situated. He held the penlight in his teeth and worked.

He studied the Dictaphone. He opened the tray and saw a tube pressed in. It was a live tube. The magnetic tape had recorded phone calls. The tube was still working. Used-up tubes ejected automatically.

Ashida checked his watch. It was 6:12 p.m., Saturday. The tube probably notched Friday's calls.

Ashida tweaked the volume knob. Ashida rewound the tube and hit the SPEAK switch. He heard line hiss and canned air. Fletch said, "It's Friday, December 19." That meant recorded calls.

Ashida kept the volume low. Ashida listened in. Ashida squelched through the boring calls.

Water and Power called. It was boring. Ashida squelched through. Four city councilmen called. We're at war now. Should we cancel the Rose Bowl?

Fletch called Ace Kwan. They discussed the mayor's Christmas stag-night menu. Fletch jawed with an Army one-star. The escaped Jap deal was one big snafu. Mrs. Fletch called and defamed their colored maid. Ace called back. He suggested a pig roast atop City Hall. Fletch said fuck that shit—it might rain.

Ashida listened in. Dead air and dead talk accumulated. Dead time eked by.

Sheriff Gene called. Hot update. The escaped Japs fled to the San Gabriel hills. The posse was up there. The Hearst boys went nuts and strafed a hobo jungle. Flesh wounds and no fatalities.

Line squelch. Dead air. Congrats on the Watanabe job. Did you see the *Herald* spread? Friday calls. Saturday-morning calls.

Time eked by. Ashida checked his watch. It was 10:41 p.m. Dead air, Ace Kwan again, Chief Jack Horrall on the line.

Squelch, hiss, crackle. Call-Me-Jack, bellicose.

". . . and if we cancel the Rose Parade, we'll look like chickenshits. It's a moneymaker, and it shores us up with Pasadena PD."

Bowron said, "Amen, brother."

Horrall said, "And while I'm griping, let me weigh in on Dick Hood, that pansy Hoover, and the Feds in general."

Bowron said, "I'm all ears on that one, Jack."

Horrall said, "Somebody pulled a squeeze play and got some Reds who were making some Red movie down in Japtown sprung from jail. The Dudster fielded the play, but he ain't talking, and Hoover's furious. That means he'll come down on us with that phone-tap probe that much harder. Bill Parker saved our bacon on that one, but Dick Hood thinks it was Parker who put the squeeze play on Dud."

Bowron said, "Parker. That meddling cocksucker. He fucks with Ace Kwan, he fucks with Dud's first go at The Werewolf. Parker and his Jap pal, Ashida. Those cocksuckers gore my goat."

Horrall said, "Ashida's ass'll be grass, come February. It's the tide of History, brother. Whiskey Bill and the Dudster can't save him on that one."

Bowron said, "Ashida gores my goat. He's the yellow spot on my spotless political record. He'll be out of my hair in February, but we'll still have Parker stirring up shit."

Horrall said, "I've got to say it, Fletch. I don't want that cocksucker to succeed me as Chief. He'll start defaming my regime the moment he takes the oath. That fucker lives to make regular men look small. It's like my man Elmer Jackson says, 'He talks to God and moves his lips while he does it.' "

Bowron said, "You bringing up Elmer the J reminds me. I've got to call Brenda. I want her to get me a girl for Monday night."

Horrall said, "I'm getting a boil on my ass about Parker. I do not want my legacy besmirched by some pious prig who sucks the giant imperial cock of papist Rome. You'll get fucked in the backwash of that, Fletch. He'll defame me, and slander your administration by implication. He won't stop at Chief, Fletch. He'll go for attorney general and the governor's chair."

Bowron said, "You're right, Jack. Let's derail that cocksucker while we've got time on our side. We'll build a derogatory profile on him. If he drops his drawers and makes even one false move, we'll know it and record it. When you step down, we show Bill the package. 'Sorry, Bill—but you fucked with the wrong guys and stepped on your dick too many times. It's Thad Brown's job, not yours.'"

Horrall said, "Amen, brother. We'll do it. Whiskey Bill's ass is grass, and we're the fucking lawn mower."

Bowron said, "You've got Parker, you've got Ashida. He's a conniving little cocksucker. Of all people, Dud Smith thinks the world of him."

Horrall said, "'Derogatory profile,' Fletch. We can't flag on that. We'll rue the day if we do."

Bowron said, "I'm in, Jack. But you've got to get out of my hair now. I've got to place my order with Brenda."

Horrall said, "Happy hunting, Mr. Mayor."

Bowron said, "Shoo, now. I've got to get down to the Bureau. Dud's going at The Werewolf again."

Horrall said, "I'll see you downstairs, sahib."

The call terminated. Ashida hit the OFF switch.

The Yellow Spot.

The Yellow Plague.

The Yellow Peril.

Dudley's valentine.

February '42—the Jap Diaspora.

Ashida put his feet up on the mayor's desk. Ashida ran a brain balance sheet.

90

KAY LAKE'S DIARY

LOS ANGELES | SATURDAY, DECEMBER 20, 1941

11:47 p.m.

Dudley Smith.

I couldn't think of anything else. I took a taxi home from the hospital and thought of Dudley Smith; I'm bearing wounds inflicted by

Dudley Smith's henchwoman, Dot Rothstein. Dudley Smith, Bette Davis' wartime-fling lover; Dudley Smith and his frame of the vilely pathetic Werewolf. Dudley Smith and his confluence of criminal cases, his collusive relationship with Ace Kwan, his land grabs and war-profiteering schemes, up to and including the distribution of "Anti-Axis" pornography, in league with his notorious namesake, Gerald L. K. Smith. Dudley Smith, the urbane. Dudley Smith, so given to casually expeditious murder. Dudley Smith and his corruption of young men. Dudley Smith and his stunningly democratic cultivation of family.

His "boys." His Catholic Archbishop, his lesbian doctor chum and her vicious paramour. More than anything else, his sincerely deep regard for Hideo Ashida.

I sat on my separate bedroom terrace and nursed a highball. Lee was off somewhere; I had the house to myself and was grateful for the spell of silent ponder. Dudley Liam Smith had severely underestimated the mental powers of Robert Sinclair Bennett, just as I had. I now knew everything that he had written on that astoundingly comprehensive and heedlessly conceived wall graph.

It was all police work and criminal business. Dudley Smith did not scheme or kill from petty rancor or from anything other than expeditiousness viewed as his sole option. He operated at an astoundingly complex level of deception. He adhered to family loyalty and did not name his minion who robbed Whalen's Drugstore and the Sheriff's van full of hijacked Japanese money. Scotty surmised that Dudley and Ace Kwan killed the three men in Griffith Park—but Dudley's partner in those killings was designated as "UA," for "unidentified accomplice." Those killings derived from his fatherly ethos and desire to avenge a ravaged young woman. Scotty ran through the graph three full times. He told me that Dudley had created this document so that he might be able to recall everything that he had done since the Whalen's robbery, the Watanabe homicides and the attack on Pearl Harbor. It was conceived as a study sheet and memory tool. It now burned within me, as a quintessentially bad and gifted man's confession. I had been teething on it for hours. I've come away thinking that Dudley has omitted something—perhaps horrifying, perhaps mundane, and surely revelatory—and that it derives from his relationship with Bette Davis.

And, I'm astonished that I don't hate this astonishingly bad man.

And that I am as beholden to him as I am beholden to Bill Parker. Their exchange of vows secured me my freedom. And Claire's freedom, and the freedom of all the others. Sergeant Smith and Captain Parker will honor their vows before God—I have no doubt of that. This shared vow feels grand to me. The vow—however expedient, corrupt and self-interested—acknowledges the power of the infinite to mediate worldly order. That such brutal men would accede to that power belittles my own recent machinations and renders me tiny in my soul.

Graph details keep unfurling. I'm stuck on Pierce Patchett and his plan to surgically re-create women as film stars. My nose is broken and splinted; I've achieved a partial re-creation myself. My fight with Dot Rothstein mirrors Dot's molesting of Claire. I learned of that act through a tract that Claire wrote. She wrote it for G. L. K. Smith—Dudley's graph said so.

The telephone rang. I walked inside and picked up the call.

"Hello?"

Hideo Ashida said, "Kay? I hope it's not too late to be calling." Dudley's lackey oozed deference.

"I'm always surprised to hear from you. And I'm always happy to talk, so the time doesn't really matter."

He said, "I overheard two phone calls. Mayor Bowron made them, but I can't tell you how I know."

Because you don't know what I know about you? Because you think I'll believe whatever you say?

I said, "Please tell me, anyway."

"I overheard Mayor Bowron and Chief Horrall talking. They're planning to create a 'derogatory profile' on Captain Parker, to prevent him from becoming Chief. There's that, and that Mayor Bowron ordered a girl from your friend Brenda, for Monday night."

So you called me. Because Captain Parker knows who you've thrown in with. So you called me. Because Captain Parker would refute this call. So you called me. Because you might need Captain Parker one day and this clumsy warning might somehow serve you.

I hung up. I thought about Pierce Patchett; I got an idea and picked the phone up again.

I called Brenda. She was still awake at midnight. She started to quiz me on my hospital stay. I cut her off, told her to round up Elmer and meet me at Dave's Blue Room, immediately.

Brenda blurted good-byes. I hung up, grabbed my coat and headed down to the Strip. The Blue Room was quiet; I found a booth in the back. The waiter gave my nose splint a double take. I ordered a highball and said, "You should see the other girl." He grinned and left me alone. I listened to a wall-radio newscast.

Japanese subs had been spotted near Monterey. Subs had fired on freighters above San Francisco. The reports brought me back to the graph and the Goleta Inlet attack.

My drink came. I pulled out my compact and examined myself in the mirror. I was badly bruised below my eyes; the cuts on my nose had congealed into scabs. I took a belt of my drink and pulled off my nose splint. It *hurt*—but there was no blood.

Brenda and Elmer walked over. Elmer said, "I liked you better in the gauze. It gave you panache beyond your years." Brenda said, "This better be worth it, Citizen."

I made room for them in the booth. I reported, with a rigorous degree of omission.

Jack Horrall and Fletch Bowron were colluding against Bill Parker. I'd come across valid information that might drastically undercut *their* biz. A police-protected businessman planned to run a string of girls cut to look like movie stars. Brenda whooped at that. Elmer fumbled his cigar.

Jack and Fletch were building a "derogatory profile" against Parker. Jack would surely sanction the businessman's operation. Parker would be a damn good ally for them. Parker might well become Chief. Fletch had ordered a Monday-night girl from them. Think shakedown. Think threat of misconduct exposed. Think "Put the skids to the cut-girl racket before it gets off the ground." Your options are do everything or do nothing.

Elmer said, "There's no guarantee that Parker makes Chief, which means we got no protection then."

I said, "That's a risk you take. In the meantime, you'll quash this racket, and we've made sure that Fletch doesn't tell Jack he's been squeezed. This is a future-safety gambit. If you squeeze Fletch now, he'll be able to lay the groundwork to say, 'Jack, I'm not so sure about this.' "

Brenda said, "Shake down the mayor of Los Angeles, *now*. Stall this rival *now*, and punt if your pal Bill don't get the job and worse comes to worse."

I said, "Yes. And this deal *is* going forward, and with all the right people to make it happen."

Elmer said, "If Parker's in it from the git, with a convincing handshake, I'd be inclined to say okay."

Brenda lit a cigarette. "I can't risk one of our girls for the bait. Miss Katherine Lake, fresh off the KO victory over the Dotstress, is feeling her oats—but she won't name names on this deal. I'm skeptical, Citizens."

I said, "There's names you'll recognize and names you'll respect. You'll want someone like Parker on your side. You'll want him because you don't trust him now, but you'll trust him if he gives you his word."

Elmer relit his cigar. "I'm inclined to say yes, then. Since this racket sounds like a big-name sure thing, we'd be stupid not to try something."

I lit a cigarette. "I'll be the bait. A little Helena Rubenstein no. 9, and Fletch won't know this girl's been in a tiff."

December 21, 1941

91

LOS ANGELES | SUNDAY, DECEMBER 21, 1941

12:52 a.m.

Parker cruised the Palisades. Shoreline blackout—night fifteen.

Ocean Avenue was fortified. Sub alert, sniper alert. Sub spotters lined the bluffs. Big searchlights swooped.

That fiend sniper lurked somewhere. Ocean Avenue was triple-manpowered. Thad Brown worked liaison with SaMo PD. The sniper packed a sawed-off carbine. Thad was running gun-sales checks.

Soldiers camped on the bluffs. Pup tents ran from Pico to Wilshire. Sub spotters perched every ten yards. Sub fear was weird juju. It connoted werewolves of the sea.

Wolf fear. Parker thought of Fujio Shudo. Sub fear. Parker thought of Hideo Ashida and the Goleta attack.

He cut east on Wilshire. There was zero traffic. Stop and go lights were cellophane-wrapped. The blackout ran to the L.A. city line. He cruised, aimless. His house was booby-trapped.

His wife nagged him. Phone calls plagued him. He couldn't sleep. That last call *Japped* him.

Hideo Ashida called. The truce rumor had spread. Ashida apologized for snitching him. He fawned and came on disingenuous.

He came on brusque. The Dudster had surpassed him as a patron. He told Ashida that. Ashida spieled two phone calls that he'd overheard.

Call-Me-Jack and Fletch Bowron talked. They hatched a "derogatory profile" to scotch his career. Fletch and Brenda Allen talked. Fletch ordered a girl.

Ashida was tizzied. He was playing angles. He threw in with Dudley. It canceled out his rogue actions. It would not cancel out his internment.

Sub fear. Derogatory profile. Parker cruised. Parker recalled Dudley Smith.

"You, with or without Dr. Ashida, may have a grand time searching for white men in purple sweaters, but you may not publicly present evidence that anyone other than Mr. Shudo killed the Watanabe family."

Parker turned north and parked. It was cold. He idled the engine and ran the heat.

He read Teletypes. Traffic deaths were up. The escaped Japs were Japped-in north of Monrovia. Cops swarmed the hillsides. The Hearst Rifle Team prowled.

Derogatory profile. Moral boomerang. His profile of Claire De Haven. God now indicts him.

Parker drove to SaMo Canyon. Larkin's bungalow was still there. The street was still still.

He grabbed his crowbar and a carton of fish food. He walked up and shouldered the door in.

He closed it behind him. He tapped the lights and got light. PG&E was swamped. Dead men got free utilities.

The living room koi stream sparkled. The koi darted to the surface and peered up at him. He sprinkled half the fish food on the water. The koi gobbled it.

Who is the white man in the purple sweater?

Parker walked into the bedroom. He tapped the lights and saw the koi pond outside. He opened the terrace door. The pond sparkled. The koi peered up at him.

He fed them. He emptied the container. The koi swarmed and chowed.

The toss was a long shot. Hidey-holes were rare. The Watanabes had a hidey-hole. Ashida's confession described it.

Who is the white man in the purple sweater?

Parker walked through the house.

He opened cabinets. He looked in drawers. He tapped the walls and listened for thunks.

He got angry. He got impatient. He told the koi that he'd build them a nice pond in his backyard. He'd keep them safe from dogs and cats.

All right, then.

He walked to the middle of the living room. He grabbed his crowbar and hurled it down at the floor.

He splintered the boards. It killed his arms. He saw nothing but dirt underneath.

He did it again.

He did it again.

He did it again.

He threw crowbar shots at the living room floor and the living room walls. He stopped at forty-three. He saw nothing but gypsum board and dirt. He worked his way back to the bedroom. He ran his body numb. He wheeled into the bedroom and destroyed it.

He threw crowbar shots at the bedroom floor and the bedroom walls. He saw nothing but gypsum board and dirt. He tore his hands bloody. He cracked the boards around the bed and put the bed down in the dirt.

He soaked himself black wet and ran his body numb. He smashed his way up to the terrace. He smashed the walls through to empty spaces and the floors through to wood chips and dust.

He saw dawn break. It meant shit-all-zero. He hit the floor, he smashed the floor, he fucking *Japped* the floor. He counted crowbar shots. He went to 286.

And there's a binder. It's flat in the dirt. It looks like that first binder. He was here with Ashida. They found it.

Parker picked it up and went through it. The writing was in Japanese.

92

LOS ANGELES | SUNDAY, DECEMBER 21, 1941

9:17 a.m.

He wore a chalk-stripe suit and brought flowers. He came straight from Mass. Whiskey Bill failed to show. The Archbishop was peeved.

Such a grand home. A plantation manse, sans darkies. A tall man mowed the neighboring lawn. It was Sergei Rachmaninoff.

Dudley rang the bell. Claire De Haven opened the door. Her hair was cut short. She wore a blue scarf over it.

He smelled church on her. She lit altar candles and covered her head before God.

She smiled and accepted the flowers. He took off his hat.

He said, "Miss De Haven."

She said, "Sergeant Smith."

He smelled her bath scent. Did she smell Bette? They made love all night. She left him for a studio breakfast. He left her for Mass.

Claire stood aside. Dudley walked in. Her habitat stunned.

Silk brocade, ebony, jade. Modernist paintings. The classical, the exquisite, the chic.

"Would I disapprove of the revelry that occurs here?"

Claire closed the door. "No, because you see through disapproval to bemusement. You might enjoy the spirit of the revelry, but you'd be enraged at the chat."

He passed her his hat. She sailed it across the room. It landed square on a hat rack.

Dudley whooped. Claire touched his arm and pointed to a red leather couch. She'd laid out tea. Service for two. She'd anticipated a guest.

Dudley sat to her right. Claire held his bouquet in her lap.

"I knew you'd appear in person, rather than call."

"I would have sent the flowers, if you hadn't called and left that message."

Claire tossed the bouquet. It sailed across the room. It landed square on a love seat.

Dudley said, "You're deft. You're an equestrienne of some note, a grand tennis player and a low-handicap golfer. Were you disappointed when those skills came to you so easily? You revel in the gilded as you despise it and plot against it. Were debauchery and revolution the only roads left to you?"

Claire said, "You're glib. You're an inquisitor and interlocutor of sterling gifts, and you fully understand that I do not accept compliments without reservations. You could have gleaned my sporting résumé from the *Los Angeles Blue Book*, or from Terry Lux, as I gleaned yours from Terry and Joe Hayes. You didn't, though. You went straight to well-reasoned surmise, and I am flattered and much impressed."

Her scarf matched her eyes. She saw him notice it. She untied the scarf and tossed it. Her Joan of Arc hair glowed.

"I've seen the Dreyer film a great many times. It created quite the stir in Dublin, my cousins tell me. Religious ecstasy and martyrdom, suffused with Marx. The Church apparatchiks didn't know whether to shit or go blind."

Claire said, "They did both. And Dreyer was a Protestant. They smelled Luther all over it."

"Has there ever been a greater tyrant than Luther?"

"Hitler comes to mind."

"And not Uncle Joe Stalin?"

"The current Russian-front war comes to mind. 'Uncle Joe' will bleed Hitler dry in the East, and facilitate the Western alliance in the ultimate division of European property. That must displease you, given your own revolutionary efforts levied against Great Britain."

"The Irish lit bonfires to create a flight path to London for Hitler's bombers. Gerald L. K. Smith reminded me of that recently. He also told me that you've purchased many of his left-wing tracts, and that you wrote one yourself."

Claire poured tea. "It very much rebutted the ways of your police department. I singled out a colleague of yours and portrayed him as emblematic. I won't tell you who he is, but I'm sure you know him. If you haven't read the tract, I'm sure you can extrapolate."

Dudley smiled. "I haven't read the tract, and I won't indulge guesses. Perhaps you'll string me along and tell me in good time."

Claire passed him his teacup and saucer. The herb scent braced him.

"I'll overconfide to you before you leave today, Sergeant. I'll be most curious to see what you don't ask."

Dudley said, "Pastor Smith and I discussed populism, utility and the blurred self-interest that supersedes and largely defines left and right. I would say that the two of us coexist within that orbit. I'm honored that you place my unruly actions in Ireland within a context of workers' revolt, but I must state that I'm as much of a czarist as Mr. Rachmaninoff next door."

Claire smiled. Her few harsh lines vanished.

"Have you heard the Opus 32 Prelude, number 10? It's very much a referendum on that."

Dudley sipped tea. "I play the piece on my phonograph, repeatedly. It's his treatise on exile. I play it when I begin to miss Ireland unduly. The maestro reminds me that I can never go back."

Claire opened an ebony box. Dudley removed two cigarettes. Claire produced a lighter. Dudley lit them up.

That grand pleasure. They'd been craving it. They laughed and blew smoke in the air.

Claire said, "Was Kay Lake a police informant?"

Dudley said, "Yes, but very much one entrapped."

"And who entrapped her?"

"The policeman you described as 'emblematic,' but judiciously declined to name."

"Do you think that my tract initiated his interest in me?"

"I doubt that he's read it. The man is powerfully given to provocative women and charts reckless courses through them."

Claire said, "And who secured my release?"

"That man and I sealed a pact, in the Archbishop's presence. Your release was part of it, at that man's instigation. He is given to effusive gestures in a way that I am not."

Claire crushed her cigarette. "I will contest the last part of your statement in time, and cite our meeting in that padded cell Friday night. What interests me now is why you acceded to the man's stipulation."

Dudley crushed his cigarette. "I do not consider you and your comrades 'seditious' or in any way traitorous. The current wartime hysteria and its related racial animus offends me. Since Monsignor Hayes has given you a primer on my early history, and I first viewed you in a moment of acute dissolution that you deftly transcended, I ascribed a meaning to the moment that I now know to be true. It was about 'belief.' You told me that, and you were right. I knew that the ever-opportunistic Terry Lux would describe my present endeavors with Ace Kwan, Preston Exley and Pierce Patchett to you, and that you would want to indulge significant risk and a clash of ideals and invest."

Claire touched her hair. Claire pointed to a lacquered box on the coffee table.

"Kay Lake unnerved me. I knew that she was fraudulent, but I was powerless to resist her. She reinstilled and served to revise a performer's sense within me. I've been taken with a desire to perform in perilous contexts that challenge my beliefs but allow me to retain my native integrity. Terry told me that you would be commissioned in Army Intelligence at New Year's. Whatever your conflicts of belief, you are going off to fight this war. I was hoping that my natural skills and scrutiny of Kay Lake might be put to good use in the Anti-Axis cause, and that we both might profit from it, personally and financially."

Dudley sipped tea. He was levitating. The cup and saucer shook.

"And what led you to this? Beyond your just-stated rationale?"

"I saw mercy in your eyes Friday night. I saw rebuke for Terry Lux in them, along with a desire not to hurt me."

The box was red and gold. Dragons and courtesans adorned it. Claire opened the top. Hundred-dollar bills were stacked in.

"It's fifty thousand. It's not that I approve of your schemes, it's just that I see the internment as inevitable. I will insist on safeguards to ensure that Messrs. Kwan and Exley don't bleed the fugitives from internment dry, and I trust that you'll treat them more humanely than the United States Government."

Dudley lowered his cup. The saucer rattled.

Claire said, "I smell a woman on you."

Dudley said, "There's a beast in me. I destroy those I cannot control. I must be certain that those close to me share my identical interests. I'm benevolent within that construction. I'm ghastly outside of it."

Claire said, "I know that."

"I'm hoping for a posting in Mexico. I'm Spanish-fluent, and there's considerable Fifth Column activity in Mexico City, as well as German rightist cells in the stunningly lovely Acapulco. Mexico is quite the place."

Claire smiled. "I'm Spanish- and German-fluent."

They looked away from each other. Dudley saw things.

The Kandinsky painting. A gold-framed piece of sheet music. It was Rachmaninoff's prelude of exile. He knew it.

They looked back at each other. He saw the flanking bumps on her nose. She wore glasses on occasion. His guess was tortoiseshell.

She said, "I think you'd be a good man to spend this war with."

He said, "Really, *you*?"

10:27 a.m.

Claire had freckles. It delighted him more than the rest.

The tour of the house. The things she said. The bedroom, saved for last.

Every furnishing and accoutrement stunned him. The aesthetic satirized her wealth and canonized her embrace of the Left. The effect was both seamless and discordant. Her library ran to the classics and Social Realist tomes. She owned the collected works of Saint Augustine. She had studied religious poetry and conceded that Marx was wrong about God. She'd read Stanislavski on acting and asserted that Kay Lake had, as well. Her phonograph records were alphabetized from Bach to Wieniawski. She loved Bruckner's symphonies as much as he did.

She rented a room to two of her slaves. It kept them close at hand. She disdained weak men and deployed them to facilitate her whims. She brought up Hideo Ashida and said that he undermined Kay Lake's verisimilitude. Dr. Ashida rang warning bells on Miss Lake. He was an unconvincing lover. She fell prey to *La Grande Kay*. She was *La Grande Joan* and given to a flawed egalitarianism. Kay Lake was South Dakota trash. She knew it going in. Kay was probably told to attend that Paul Robeson concert. She should never have lit the girl's cigarette.

Nao Hamano and *La Grande Joan* adorned Claire's bedroom. The suicide woman recalled Goro Shigeta. The recollection brought the echoes of gunshots and shattered glass.

There was no "G.S." on his graph. He was saving it for Bette. She said, "Kill a Jap for me." He'd tell her at an appropriate time. He wondered if Claire still smelled Bette.

She showed him the tract she wrote for Gerald L. K. Smith. It was convergence in the *spiritus mundi*. Her bête noire policeman was William H. Parker. His Catholicism sparked her leftist-humanist conversion. Her anti-Parker crusade was confined to this one tract. His anti-Claire crusade did not acknowledge the tract or the historical event that spawned it. Parker went looking for women to entrap and decided on Kay and Claire. It was serendipity or malign fate. Claire De Haven attended the same church as D. L. Smith and W. H. Parker. Sergeant Smith and Captain Parker did not notice Miss De Haven. Miss De Haven noticed them.

They shared an adversary. He decided not to tell her. It would encumber what might emerge between them. It might impinge upon his vow with the man.

He read the tract as Claire stood beside him. He marveled at her sharp précis of the jackbooted oppressor. The *spiritus mundi* coheres. Dot Rothstein fondles Claire in a Central Station cell. Kay Lake shivs Dot. Claire lies comatose, one cell away.

They walked out to the terrace. The view took in Beverly Hills and the Santa Monica Mountains. He described his moorside colloquy with the wolf. Claire described a spot of mischief, circa '24.

Her father took her to a gala at the Annandale Country Club. She was aghast that no Jews belonged. She sneaked out to the groundskeeper's shack and stole a sack of quicklime. She burned a six-point star into the ninth green.

It wasn't enough. She'd heard of a Silver Shirts rally up the Angeles Crest. She stole her father's car and drove there with arson in mind. A case of bootleg rye sat in the trunk. She found the Shirts' campground and uncorked the bottles in their equipment shed. She formed a cord with newspaper strips. One match torched dozens of hate screeds and nativist robes.

He laughed. She touched his arm. She said, "I have freckles." He said, "Show me, please."

2:17 p.m.

She did. He lost count at two hundred something. He kissed them in groups.

The terrace windows faced a high sun. The warmth off the glass became an early-dusk chill. They kept their eyes open and told each other why. We must not miss a first-time anything.

He showed her his scar from an Ulster jail riot. It came from a Black and Tan's cell key held over a flame. She took him back to Pershing Square in 1935. His blue comrades wore brownshirts that day. Horses bore down. A bridle bit gouged her shoulder. A stirrup flange cut her leg.

She was bigger and stronger than Bette. She kissed him harder. She refitted him to suit herself. She said his name more.

She flushed more than Bette. Her skin burned warmer. They kissed every moment they were locked together. She threw sweat like she threw sweat that time he saw her in the steam room. It turned her hair black and pooled on their lips.

He kissed her underarms. He brushed the stubble with his nose. He took her fingers in his mouth.

They passed a fever back and forth. She was grateful for him. She told him that. She said his name and *"I'm grateful."* He lost track of the times she said it. She held him close every time he said, *"You, Claire."*

10:27 p.m.

She fell asleep beside him. His name faded off in a whisper. He knew she was out then.

He dressed in the dark and walked downstairs. He replaced the lacquered box with Shakespeare. He folded the volume open. She'd see the page and go straight to the quote.

Othello. The mad Irishman as mad Moor. *"Perdition, catch my soul, / But I do love thee."*

He levitated out to the car. He drove straight to Chinatown.

Breuning and Carlisle were meeting him. That lot on Alameda was their rendezvous spot. Breuning and Carlisle would bring shotguns. Jack Webb would buzz the corner pay phone.

The tile game should go all night. Pesky Jack would report the cash ebb. The house cash didn't count. It was Kwan-Smith cash to begin with. They had to get the stake cash the marks brought with them.

They were tong Chinks out of Frisco. They were tile game–touring their way down to T.J. They had New Year's Eve plans. Let's ring in '42. We'll catch the midnite donkey show.

Ace predicted a sixty-grand cash stake. They might bring it all with them. They might leave a reserve in their car.

Dudley hit Chinatown. He caught a blockade at Alpine and Broadway. Four bluesuits stood around. Ray Pinker perused a deuce coupe. It featured chopped windows and flared fender skirts.

A bluesuit waved Dudley over. Dudley pulled up and badged him. The bluesuit snapped a salute.

"It's the Japs, sir. Four Japs dumped that jalopy and clouted a Chinked-up '36 Ford. Mr. Pinker's doing the forensic, and we got an eyeball wit. You want my take? They stole a Chinatown car to help themselves pass for Chink."

Japs. *The* Japs. Down from the San Gabriels.

Dudley saluted. The bluesuit slid a sawhorse back and waved him through. Dudley drove to the lot. Breuning and Carlisle stood by their K-car. Breuning walked over.

"Good night for it, boss."

Dudley said, "I think we'll be out until sunrise, but yes."

"Where's Scotty? This would be a sweet deal for him."

"He's running fraught, lad. He's seen a vexing amount of grief for a two-week rookie. I'm granting him the Marine Corps vacation he so richly deserves."

"We'll be reading about him. He'll storm some pissant island and eat the Japs whole."

"Or not, lad. He's a tortured boy, and he's only twenty years old."

Breuning lit a cigarette. "I cruised the game an hour age. Ace was taking a bath, there was a shitload of cash on the table, but I don't know about the tong guys' reserve."

Dudley pointed north. "Ray Pinker is working a heap at Alpine and Broadway. Those escaped Japs dumped it, or it's Chinks, off a bad eyeball wit. Go over, act unobtrusive and bag some trace evidence. The Japs are far better suspects than rampaging jigs."

Breuning winked and scrammed. Dudley checked his watch and popped three bennies. 10:58, 10:59—11:00 exactly.

The sidewalk phone rang. Like clockwork—Jack Webb.

Dudley walked over. He caught it four rings in.

"Hello, lad."

Jack was eager. He was a Hearst/PD lapdog. He lived to fetch.

"The Chinks are taking Ace to the cleaners. They're talking about playing all night, and I haven't seen those colored guys you told me about."

"Did you see the car the Chinks arrived in? I know you've got a grand eye for license plates."

Jack said, "It's a '39 Caddy sedan. Mint green, with whitewalls and some Chink flag on the antenna. California license BHO44."

Dudley said, "Grand work, lad. Go home, now. Create some mischief for Mr. Hearst, or get a good night's sleep."

Jack said, "Roger, boss."

Dudley hung up. Carlisle ambled over and went *What gives?*

"It's the morning, lad. The out-of-town fucks are winning, so I would assume that their reserve will be in the car. I predict a dozing Chinaman in the front seat, with a briefcase cuffed to his wrist."

"I figured that. We don't want loose cash, so I brought a hacksaw."

Dudley winked. Carlisle ambled back to the K-car and played dashboard solitaire. Dudley ambled to his prowler and tipped the seat full stretch.

Bette/Claire, Bette/Claire, Bette/Claire. He saw them naked. He smelled them. Claire said, *"I'm grateful."* Bette said, *"You inconvenienced me."*

He chain-smoked and orbed the headliner. New Year's, the Army. Comrade Claire and Acapulco. Mexican boys cliff-dive for pesos. Fetch, muchachos, fetch.

Time whizzed. Bennies did that. Breuning walked up. Note his paper bag.

"I got carpet fibers and dust. Pinker had his back turned, so I wedged three bullets behind the spare tire. They'll match our spent rounds."

"Have you been by Kwan's?"

"I checked the parking lot. The lookout's in the backseat. He's cuffed up to a big satchel, and he's got a belt piece."

Dudley said, "I'll take him. We'll get them all in the car. You and Dick take the other three."

Breuning whistled. Carlisle locked the K-car and lugged their wares over. Silencered Magnums. One shark-tooth hacksaw.

The lads piled in. They drove to Kwan's. It was 3:16 a.m. The Caddy was the sole sled tucked in the lot.

Dudley parked three slots over. Carlisle unplugged his flask. The lookout had to be supine. No yellow head showed.

They hunkered in. They bullshitted. It was all women and war.

Breuning was a native-born Kraut. He wanted to slay Krauts under George S. Patton. Carlisle craved flyboy action. He had an eight-year-old son. They built toy Jap Zeros and blew them up with cherry bombs.

Stray talk. Lee Blanchard's skirt shivved the Dotstress. Terry Lux stitched her Jew beak. Breuning harped on Bette. Holy shit—Bette Davis talked to me!

That New Year's Eve. That dance floor. "Perfidia." Claire says, *"I'm grateful."* Bette says, *"You inconvenienced me."*

They settled in. They bullshitted. Dick revealed his murky crush on Ellen Drew. He saw her in some oater—man, that's a dish!

Breuning dropped the wet blanket. She bunks at the Los Altos. She whores for Brenda Allen. Elmer J.'s poking her.

They *re*settled. They killed the flask. Breuning played sentry. Dudley rewired his bennie surge with Jim Beam.

The sun came up. The tong sled just sat there. All four windows were down. The lookout remained supine.

6:09, 6:21, 6:43.

They got ready. Carlisle passed out bandannas. Breuning loaded the Magnums. They covered their faces, snout-high.

Dudley palmed his Magnum and saw. 6:44, 6:45, 6:46. There—the rear kitchen door.

Three Chinamen walked out.

They beamed. They swerved and bumped one another. Ace served knockout mai tais.

They carried Kwan's take-out boxes. Yankee greenbacks bulged out. They carted two each.

The lookout stirred and sat up. One wrist was cuffed. The Chinks bumped to the car and got in.

Three doors slammed. Dudley said, "Now."

They wheeled out. Two strides got them there. Breuning took the driver. Carlisle took the passenger fuck.

It was head-to-muzzle tight. Dumdum blasts tore off faces and blew the steering column out. Dudley shot the lookout in the ear and the other fuck in the neck. Silencers went *kick-thud.*

There's the skull shrapnel. There's the eyelid flutter. Now they convulse.

Breuning and Carlisle scrambled. Get the doors, get the boxes, get the fuck out.

The lookout convulsed. Dudley opened the door and grabbed his wrist. Dudley sawed his hand off.

Breuning and Carlisle scrambled. They sprinkled trace evidence, they got the boxes, they looked back at the boss.

Dudley grabbed the satchel. It was cash heavy. A severed hand twitched on the grips.

December 22, 1941

93

LOS ANGELES | MONDAY, DECEMBER 22, 1941

6:49 a.m.

Sirens kicked on. It sounded all-points. Ashida pegged the distance. Call it close by, northeast.

Maybe Chinatown. Maybe Lincoln Heights.

He stood in the lab. He was the first Monday log-in. Ray Pinker spent the night at Alpine and Broadway.

It was Code 3 work. The escapees ditched a deuce coupe and stole a '36 Ford. "*Probable*" escapees—Pinker stressed that.

Squadroom jabber hit the vents. *Quadruple homicide outside Kwan's.* It's hot, hot, hot. Calling all cars, *now*.

Ashida sipped coffee. He had no real work. His real job was wait. He was the Yellow Spot, dispossessed.

A man weaved by the doorway. He was a stumblebum. He reeked of rotgut muscatel.

"If you're Dr. Ashida, I got a package. This great big kid gave me a buck and a jug to find you."

He slurred it. He wore a drunk-tank wristband. He waved a manila envelope.

Ashida snatched it. The bum did a double take. *Hey, you're a Jap.*

"Tell me about the kid."

"Well, the funny thing was he was a kid, but he was a cop. He was about six six, and he was wearing a gun. He had on a brown suit and a plaid bow tie."

Ashida slid the bum a dollar. The bum about-faced away. Ashida closed the door and leaned on it.

He slit the envelope. It contained four typed pages. Scotty used a Bureau typewriter. The stroke marks nailed that.

He skimmed the pages. He *got* it. Scotty deciphered Dudley's graph.

He'd seen the graph. It made no sense. Scotty B. decoded Dudley's mad hieroglyphs.

The Watanabe case. "Related opportunities." The land grab. The "two white stiffs" named. His own confession, recounted. Bill Parker, coindicted. Dudley and Ace Kwan's war-profit schemes.

Ashida read the pages. Ashida slid down the door and jammed it shut.

The war. Fifth Column overtones. Spycraft. Graphs, diaries, ledgers. Suicide notes, stenciled letters. Coerced confessions. Notarized statements. Doodles deciphered. Vows exchanged before priests.

Who is the white man in the purple sweater? We have ALL OF THIS. Why don't we know who he is?

Someone pushed against the door. Someone said, "Hey."

Ashida dug out a dime and tossed it. Scotty broke ranks. Tell someone. Don't think beyond the toss. Heads for Dudley, tails for Whiskey Bill.

He tossed the coin. It hit on heads. He stood up and got the door. The day-watch men filed in and fish-eyed him.

He walked.

He got downstairs and outside. He jaywalked across 1st. People glanced at him. They held up newspapers and moved at half his clip. They were off in the morning *Herald* and JAP SUBS PROWL COAST!

He ran. He made the Hall and took the freight lift. He hit the sixth floor. All-man rollout—*Four dead at Kwan's!*

Dudley was gone. His cubicle was empty. All-Bureau rollout. *Four dead at—*

There's the graph. It's genius. This brutish boy decoded it.

He studied the graph. He knew advanced mathematics. He knew cryptology. He read two full sheets and got nothing.

He walked to the washroom. He soaked his head and toweled off. He tossed his dime—heads, heads, tails. He blinked. Dudley kills people. *Who is the white man in the purple sweater?* Impotent Bill Parker kills no one.

He walked to Parker's office. The door was open. Parker sat at his desk. He stared at a binder. It matched the one from Jim Larkin's place.

The top page is kanji script. That's good. Parker can't read it.

Parker saw him. Ashida tossed Scotty's envelope on his desk.

Parker began reading. Ashida swiveled the binder and read standing up.

Parker read. Ashida read. They flipped pages in near sync. Parker finished first.

He got up and shut the door. He leaned against it. He watched Ashida read.

Ashida finished. Parker flipped the door lock.

"Who wrote this?"

"Scotty Bennett. He got Horrall's okay to enlist. I think he wanted to get square with all of this before he left."

Parker said, "Thad Brown told me about the graph. Dud told him it was his crib sheet."

Ashida nodded. Parker lit a cigarette.

"It's all there. So far as I know, the only facts missing are two things I've never revealed."

Ashida said, "Tell me."

Parker said, "I witnessed that shrimp-boat fracas down in Pedro. The men on the boat were Collaborationists. I saw them burn Axis currency with bookmaker's flash paper right before the suicides, and I got a lead on the warehouse where they off-loaded their shrimp. I broke in, but the place had been cleaned out and print-wiped. I saw discarded shrimp cans and smelled shrimp oil."

Ashida teethed on it. Parker pointed to the binder.

"I'm listening, Doctor. Don't make me coax you."

Ashida said, "Larkin wrote the diary, and we now know him to be Gerald L. K. Smith's Japanese-fluent author of those tracts that kept turning up in this aggregation of cases. He writes of his friendships with high-ranking officers of the Imperial Japanese Army and Navy, and states that he knew that the attack on the U.S. Fleet would occur on December 7, but that he'd become ambivalent about America's assured entry into the war. Larkin did not want to see a Japanese-American conflict, simply because he loved both peoples. He was stridently anti-Semitic, and did not want to see Japanese and American lives 'squandered' in what he viewed as 'a war to protect Jewish business interests.'"

Parker said, "Go on."

Ashida cleared his throat. "Larkin had a friend on the far-right flank. He doesn't name the man, but I can tell that he's white. The man was a rabid eugenicist, as Larkin was, and he owned a shortwave radio, as Larkin did. Like Larkin, the man was Japanese-fluent."

Parker said, "Go on."

"The man picked up early Japanese-language radio reports of the forthcoming Pearl Harbor attack, as I know the Watanabes did. The man wanted to see a U.S.-Japanese war and coerced Larkin into silence as the attack drew near. Larkin dumped his radio the day before the attack and wrote of his urgent desire to take the boys of the Santa Monica Cycleers someplace peaceful for the time that the news of attack would most likely occur. The rest of the entries are Larkin's views on eugenics. He repeatedly states that the science itself had been 'contaminated by the Jew left-wing intelligentsia,' who wanted to breed healthier human beings, rather than create a master race. Members of his 'cell' and their 'satellites' had engaged in a philosophical dialogue with various leftists, which infuriated Larkin. The concluding entries show Larkin succumbing to lunacy. The diary devolves into profane ramblings and a treatise on *Mein Kampf* as the lost book of the Holy Bible."

Parker checked the wall clock. He had that I've-got-to-go look.

"Larkin's shortwave pal is the purple-sweater man. He probably killed the Watanabes, and he sure as shit mowed down Larkin."

Ashida said, "Yes, that's what I'm thinking."

Parker scoped the clock. "We might get something off those pay-phone records. Pay phones are our one circumstantial Larkin-to-Watanabe link. The records are coming, but I'd guess that they're a good week away."

Ashida coughed. "And there's the print match. It probably wasn't Larkin, but someone touched one of Larkin's Lugers and left a print at the Watanabe house. The print establishes a relationship between that man, Larkin and the Watanabe family."

Parker said, "The purple-sweater man."

Ashida nodded. "The Watanabes had a shortwave radio and were tuned in to the same frequency. I would conclude that, like Larkin, they began to feel ambivalent about the Pearl Harbor attack, and threatened to rat it out. They were allied with Larkin and his shortwave-radio pal, and it went bad between the three of them."

Parker checked the wall clock. Parker checked his watch.

"And, there's this. No one working independently or in concert on this case has been able to link the Watanabes or Jim Larkin to

Preston Exley, Pierce Patchett and their buyout-internment prison scheme. And now Dudley and company are attempting to buy in with them."

Ashida shook his head. "We're not going to know. The Werewolf will burn, and we'll never get the pieces to click."

Parker shook his head. "Don't say 'we'll,' Doctor. I can't afford to indulge independent action on this, and neither can you. I don't judge you for naming me in your confession, because I know how persuasive Dudley Smith can be. I've taken some steps to protect you, but that's over. I won't break the law for you. Dudley Smith will. If your options are him or me, I think you'd be well advised to take the former route."

Ashida shook his head. "You're not *him*. You've never been *him* and you'll never *be* him. Does it gall you to know that he's more powerful than you, and that he'll always supersede you, however erratically hard that you try to put yourself on top?"

Parker said, "You're pouting, Doctor. You're simpering. I would advise you to examine what you're saying and to consider your effeminate tone."

94

KAY LAKE'S DIARY

LOS ANGELES | MONDAY, DECEMBER 22, 1941

9:41 a.m.

Parker was late. I'd left the message with his duty sergeant and got no return call. Citizen Brenda had spruced up her house and had laid out a breakfast buffet. Citizen Elmer talked a blue streak on the Chinatown killings.

"It was an all-Bureau callout, so I went. You got four dead Chinamen in one automobile, and an eyeball in some splattered chicken chow mein. Close-range fire, Citizens. They rob the Chinks, they kill them. One guy's got a money bag cuffed to his wrist, so they cut off his hand. Ray Pinker says it's them Japs who escaped from T.I. They drop a car and steal a car, right there in C-town. Ray found matching bullets in the trunk of the drop car and trace elements from the drop car in the Chink car. You had brains and shredded egg rolls all over the seats. There's roadblocks all the way up to the San Gabriel hills. The posse's up at four hundred men now. The Feds are passing out tommy guns. Ace Kwan's offered a twenty-five-thousand-dollar reward, and Mr. Hearst's matching it. Dud Smith and Thad Brown got the lead slots on the investigation. Ace told Call-Me-Jack that he'll pay a hundred grand for their heads in a sack. The Hearst Rifle Team boys bought some Jap shrunken heads from this loony Chink doctor, Lin Chung. Lin's the boss Chink eugenics man. He's been peddling shrunken Jap heads since the Rape of Nanking. The Hearst Rifle boys are wearing them around their necks."

Brenda said, "Citizen Elmer knows how to stir a girl's appetite. Citizen Bill's twenty-four minutes late, and the eggs are getting cold. I'm starting to think that Citizen Kay's been barking up the wrong tree with this deal of hers, and we should just go ahead and let Citizen Fletch get his ashes hauled."

Elmer said, "Fletch is a whip-out man. It's not like Kay has to go up to the doorway of being screwed, or anything close to it. Fletch just whips it out, and expects certain comments to follow. I'll be kind here. Fletch likes his girls to exaggerate."

I laughed and lit a cigarette. I'd spent the night swaddled in ice packs; my bruises had smoothed out and faded; a smattering of powder on and around my nose camouflaged the extent of my recent injuries. I could convincingly play a call-service girl for one night.

Elmer waved his cigar. "Lin Chung's got a stand set up outside Kwan's. He's peddling them shrunken heads for two clams apiece. I got one for my civilian car. I named it 'Tojo' and got it all dangled up on my rearview mirror. Lin's doing a land-office biz. Call-Me-Jack's on this whole shrunken head business like a rabid dog. He's issued chain saws and gunnysacks to them Hearst Rifle boys. Once the grand jury indicts our boy Shudo, Lin and Jack are going to start peddling twoskies. You get a shrunken head and a photo of yourself with The Werewolf in handcuffs. Five bucks a pop, three for ten. Christmas is Thursday, Citizens. See Doctor Chung and Chief C. B. Horrall for your wholesome shopping needs."

Brenda said, "I'm in the market for a wholesome, 10:00 a.m. eye-opener. I brought the maid in from browntown to doll the place up, but I don't see hide nor hair of Citizen Bill."

The bell rang. Elmer got up and opened the door. Bill Parker walked in. He wore a crisp uniform and new glasses.

Elmer said, "Morning, Cap." Parker looked over. He noted my appearance. He said, "Miss Allen, Miss Lake."

Elmer said, "We put on the dog for you, Cap." Parker registered the liquor on the buffet and reeled his eyes back.

I hadn't thanked him yet. I needed to thank him for myself, and for Claire. I needed time alone with him.

Parker tapped his watch. "I appreciate the trouble you went to, but I have a briefing back at the Hall."

Elmer said, "Okay, then." Brenda said, "Jack Horrall and Fletch Bowron are working up a 'derogatory profile' on you, Cap. I think—"

Parker cut her off. "I know. Hideo Ashida called and told me. If the three of you have concocted a countermeasure, I'd appreciate a summary."

Brenda said, "Citizen Kay has cooked something up. The floor's all hers."

I took the floor. I stressed Brenda and Elmer's self-interest. Pierce Patchett's cut-girl plan would deep-six their biz. I would portray a prostie tonight. A wall peek would be set up in Brenda's spot at the Roosevelt Hotel. We'd squeeze Fletch. No Patchett call-service sanction. No derogatory profile. *Parker's* sanction for Brenda and Elmer—should he become Chief.

Parker said, "Yes."

No hesitation. No qualms expressed.

Parker looked at me. "I'll be on the other side of the peek. Keep it to words, please. I don't want him to touch you."

95

LOS ANGELES | MONDAY, DECEMBER 22, 1941

11:09 a.m.

She waved from the door. Her smile was off-kilter. He liked her new bumpy nose.

Parker took Crescent Heights south. He was late for the briefing. The briefing was three-pronged. The coastal sub attacks, escaped Japs, the Kwan's slaughter.

He observed the callout alarm. He rerouted traffic by Kwan's. It was a hellish 187.

It oozed inside job. Some Hop Sing busboy got miffed at Uncle Ace. Tong tiff. The busboy fingered the tile game to Four Families. Four Families clued in some Collaborationist fucks. The fucks had a line on *The Japs.*

The job oozed hybrid. It was Fifth Column meets loot-and-slay. *The Japs* bolt their hillside hideout and hit C-town. Drop cars, getaway cars. Do they head back north or head south? The posse's all over the hills. The job oozed oddball and *skewed.*

Parker cut east on Beverly. *He* felt oddball-skewed. He had six days booze-free. He endorsed a sex shakedown. It revised his vow before God.

It did not abrogate it. It did not breach Dudley's stipulations. It gave him a loophole to crawl through.

He was splitting moral hairs. He knew why.

It was the war and his beloved *Pueblo Grande.* The war made everyday life *life in extremis.* Expedient gestures and moral stands stood a hairsbreadth apart. L.A. blazed with common cause in stark contradiction. L.A. would build up and out after the war. It would become unrecognizable. The war gave him L.A. ablaze with crazy purpose. The war let him love L.A. one last time as it was.

Parker hit City Hall. Posse men lounged on the steps. Kudos to Lin Chung. The boys wore shrunken heads on chains.

He parked in the basement. A Navy ensign ran the mayor's freight lift. They zoomed up to Fletch B.'s floor. The briefing spread out to the hallway.

Army brass schmoozed with reporters. Cops and politicos swarmed a doughnut tray. Parker stepped into the conference room. A Navy commander flanked a lectern and wall map.

Pins denoted coastal waters and recent sub attacks. The Navy man swept a pointer. Subs Jap U.S. freighters. Subs Jap U.S. tankers. Subs threaten the Mex coast. Our Mex Statie *amigos* are *scaaaaared.*

Remember the Goleta Inlet. These are *rogue* subs. L.A.'s shoreline waters could be next.

Ace Kwan and Lin Chung walked in. They wore shrunken heads. Call-Me-Jack and Sheriff Gene hugged them. The Navy man sat down. Mild applause trickled. Dudley Smith took the lectern.

The Merry Mick. Church pulpit–trained. He scanned the room. He let chitchat subside. He took the room, full brogue.

"Chaos attends our fair city. We rebuff invaders as havoc is cried and the dogs of war are let slip. 'The bay trees in our country are all withered, and meteors fright the fixed stars of heaven. The pale-faced moon looks bloody on the earth, and lean-looked prophets whisper fearful change.' "

The room *got* it. Big cop, big words. He ain't no American. It makes this shit okay.

"Would you have our city be less fair? Should we retract the nets of beauty that lure such a collage of splendid peoples and wolfen monsters here? December 7th is Genesis in the Unholy Bible. The normal phases of the moon have been canceled. Werewolves walk among us, sans lunar compass. They are lost. They know only that they must destroy the beauty that unites each one of us, the beauty that has brought each one of us here."

Dudley paused. He scanned the room. He saw Parker. He looked straight at him.

"I spoke to a wolf, twenty years ago. I commune with him in prayer and have enjoyed earthly visitations of late. The wolf told me that wolves are visible only to a scant few. My duty is to detect them and follow them to points where only one of us may survive. We carry weapons and wear heads that were once men around our necks. We carry the wolfen deeply within us. They are invisible as we become visible to destroy them. We love beauty in a way that they cannot. It subsumes our basest urges and sends us their way. 'I am but mad north-north-west. When the wind is southerly, I know a hawk from a handsaw.' The wolf told me that there is no Fifth

Column, because the Fifth Column is each one of us. We will track down the wolfen. We are mad with godly allegiance and now see the invisible plainly. We have drunk from the chalice of unholy blood and have become them that we might slay them."

Parker walked out to the hallway. Dudley sermonized and segued to cop talk.

There's laughter. He's cracking jokes now. He's issued his sermon. His sermon supplants his Satanic exchange of vows.

I am but mad north-north-west. I have exploited blood libel for profit. We are as one, William. You will let it all be.

96

LOS ANGELES | MONDAY, DECEMBER 22, 1941

1:29 p.m.

"DUD-LEY! DUD-LEY!"

Backslappers stormed the lectern. Grown men wolf-howled and waved shrunken heads.

Dudley scrammed for the freight lift. Fans blocked his path. They held up pens and Werewolf pix. He signed *D. L. Smith* twenty times.

The heads were de rigueur now. Call-Me-Jack wore one. Fletch B. wore *two.* Two-Gun Davis wore *three.*

Dudley made the lift and blew kisses. A woman slipped him her phone number. The doors slid shut.

He pushed B. The lift dropped. Ace had a limo waiting. The Pagoda—chop, chop.

Benzedrine and Shakespeare. 83 grand in the trunk. Ace retrieved his house stake, plus 41. He was mildly peeved and exuberant. *You should have warned me, Dudster. You shot up my parking lot.*

The doors slid open. The Lincoln idled close. Dudley ran over and got in the back. Ace was waiting. A partition sealed them off. The driver waved a shrunken head and pulled out.

Ace said, "My Irish brother never fails me. He gets the gelt, and he'll get the Japs."

What Japs? There were no Japs. He braced the eyeball wit on the car snatch. The man *thought* he saw Japs. He was war-fevered. Japs, Chinks—what's the diff? War fever served a purpose here. *We'll make it The Japs.*

Beth and Tommy were due. He sent a taxi to fetch them. Harry Cohn was meeting him. The Pagoda—chop, chop.

Dudley lit a cigarette. "How much does Harry owe you now, my brother?"

Ace stroked his shrunken head. "The Jew beast owes me one hundred and sixteen thou. He is the pus in the boil on my yellow ass."

"I will barter with Harry and secure us equipment in lieu of money. I have my friend Claire's donation, and I'll speak to my friend Bette tonight. We must accrue ready cash, in order to close Messrs. Exley and Patchett. Our friend Terry assures me that they are cash-strapped, and will be willing to let us partner in with them."

They hit the Pagoda. The lot was roped up. Bluesuits flanked the death car. Ray Pinker measured tread marks. Hideo Ashida vacuumed the backseat.

Mike B. and Dick C. played watchdog. Lin Chung peddled shrunken heads on the sidewalk. Harry Cohn bought a head and waddled in.

The limo swerved curbside and dropped them. Ace ran inside and tore for the kitchen. *Blood of the Infidel!* He always spit in Harry's soup.

Dudley strolled through the lot. Bluesuits saluted. He walked by the death sled. It reeked of solvents. Hideo Ashida glanced up.

They shared a look. Dudley winked. Hideo nodded back.

Dudley walked inside. Harry hogged a window booth. He wore his shrunken head and slurped wonton soup.

Dudley joined him. Harry scooped floating pork.

"I need an extension with Ace. And don't mention your *farkakte* smut racket, because my answer remains *nyet*, Comrade."

Dudley said, "Comrade, your new answer will have to be '*da.*' You will supply equipment upon command. You will let us employ the sets from your grand Frank Capra movies that extoll the human spirit, and you will provide beautiful gowns for our female performers, who will have been surgically cut to resemble your own brightest stars. You will do all of this, and much more, without complaint."

Harry waved his spoon. "Or what, *bubelah*? It's that, or you kill me? It's like I'm some *schvartzer* heist man you put the boots to to keep L.A. safe and clean?"

Dudley said, "No. But I'll release my sneak photographs of you cavorting with two fourteen-year-old girls in Hitler Youth outfits."

Harry went red. His arteries constricted. Dudley lit a cigarette and blew smoke in his face.

"Nod yes and enjoy your soup, Harry. Ace has embellished it, especially for you."

Harry coughed. Harry slurped soup. Harry lit a cigarette.

" 'Yes,' you mick cocksucker."

"You'll be in august company, Harry. Our pals Joe and Ben are investing, and I'm certain that Bette Davis will be, as well."

Harry waved his shrunken head. "A curse on you, you mick cocksucker. May giant circus elephants shit on your lawn. May bug-eyed gargoyles eat your young."

A taxi pulled up. There—a yellow smudge lights the window.

Dudley ran out. He buttoned his suit coat over his gun and squared his necktie. Fair Beth stepped up on the curb.

She was seventeen, now. She was taller. Her hair had gone to his shade.

Beth said, "Hello, Dad."

Dudley said, "My dear lass."

They embraced. Beth was overcoat warm. He kissed the top of her hat.

"What's going on out there? I'm blind, but I've got a nose for things."

Dudley laughed. Beth laughed. She stood on her tiptoes and kissed her dad's beak. They bundled into the cab and scrunched up beside Tommy.

He was a pudgy Irish boy. He worked for Packard Bell and built radios by touch.

Dudley pumped his hand. "It's good to see you, lad. You look delightfully fit for our grand L.A. adventure."

Tommy grinned. He wore dark glasses and a swell suit. Beth

groomed him. He missed shaving spots. Beth squared him away for the world.

"I can't see you, Uncle Dud. I can hear you, though. And you know you can't fool me. If you try to pass off a fake Bette Davis, Beth will see and I'll hear."

Dudley laughed. Beth laughed. Dudley winked at her and tapped the driver.

"Brentwood, please. Take Sunset out to Mandeville Canyon."

The driver U-turned. Beth leaned into Dudley. Tommy leaned into her. She looked out at L.A. She saw Chinatown choked with police cars. She said, "It's a dream."

The San Diego papers inked the oceanside snuffs. The Camp Pendleton cops caught the squawk. The early consensus was Baffler. It might be the Santa Monica sniper. It might be those escaped Japs.

Tommy rolled down his window. He wrinkled his nose and caught scents. Beth said, "There's a high cement retaining wall to your right. There's sycamore trees at the top."

Tommy said, "I can smell them. The limbs are full of oil. It's darker than eucalyptus."

Beth squeezed Dudley's hand. "It's dark, like my dad's Irish heart."

Dudley roared. Beth laughed and nuzzled into him. They passed a stretch of Mex eateries. Tommy said, "I smell fried pork."

The cab clocked westbound. Beth described Hollywood and the Sunset Strip. "There's a billboard for airplane flights to Palm Springs." "There's a man walking a spotted Great Dane." "There's the world-famous Mocambo. Maybe Miss Davis will take us there."

They hit Beverly Hills. Tommy said, "It's more green now. There's more oxygen in the air."

Dudley faked a cough and popped three bennies. Beth described Will Rogers Park. Dudley welled up. His fair child and fifty-foot palm trees. Such inexplicable love.

They passed the Bel-Air gates. Sunset went hairpin. The cab dipped and swerved. Beth and Tommy giggled. It was a fun-house ride for the blind lad. He took joy where he could.

Such gratitude. *"I'm grateful."* His sweet Claire said that.

Brentwood, Mandeville Canyon. There's a Tudor house. There's a Spanish house. There's a château. Dad, they're so *big*.

He saw the Airedale first. Bette stood on her lawn and tossed him a ball. The cab pulled into the driveway. Bette shouted something. Beth covered her mouth—*Oh my God.*

He got out. Bette skipped up to him. She wore gabardine slacks and a blue sweater. She went *Not in front of the neighbors* and embraced him. She ran a hand down his leg.

Beth helped Tommy out. She calmed herself. It was *très* decorous. It was more Smith than Short.

Bette went to them. It was hugs, two-hand greetings, skipped heartbeats. The Airedale jumped on Dudley. He stroked him head-to-tail and kissed his snout.

La Grande Bette. She's playing herself. She'll rebuff *Miss Davis this, Miss Davis that.*

She said, "Bette, please. I wouldn't dream of calling you Miss Short or Mr. Gilfoyle."

Beth and Tommy swooned. Bette pointed to a Rolls limo, curbside. She passed the cab man a wad and went *Shoo!*

The cab U-turned. Bette tucked the Airedale behind the gate and walked back over. She drew them in. She touched all three of them. She looked at Dudley, she looked at Beth.

She went *Mmmmmmmmmm.* She drew it out to nine thousand syllables. She said, "Yes, I see the resemblance."

Dudley roared. Beth doubled over. Tommy squealed and plucked at Bette's sleeve. She laced their fingers up.

"I know you can't *see* it, Tommy. But don't you think there's Ireland all over these two?"

Tommy leaned into Bette. "I don't know what Ireland looks like, but Uncle Dud and Beth both smell green."

Dudley welled up. Beth said, "Dad's more emotional than he lets on."

Bette jiggled Dudley's wrist. "Yes, and I can attest to that, in a rather intimate manner. So, before I lapse into the bawdy, I think we should go to the movies. I haven't seen *Citizen Kane,* and it's playing second-run in Hollywood. A Monday matinee shouldn't be too crowded, and I can observe Beth's narration technique."

Beth looked at Dudley. *Can we? Should we impose?*

Bette said, "How about it, Dad? The kids and I are in."

Dudley said, "Then I shall make it a quorum."

Bette stuck her fingers in her mouth and whistled. It was pure stagecraft.

The limo pulled up. Dudley got the door. Beth helped Tommy in. Dudley winked at Bette.

She said, "How many hearts have you broken with that one thing?"

He eased her inside. Tommy sniffed the air. The lad was a scent hound. Hold for his diagnosis.

"The prior inhabitant wore lime cologne and had a flask. He spilled brandy on the seat cushions."

The decree drew applause. Bette whistled. It was poor stagecraft. She whistled shrill. She was laying the hoi polloi on too thick.

The limo pulled out. They sat bundled and retraced Sunset, east. Beth *re*described the landscape.

Bette studied Beth. She would know Beth's every tic by suppertime. She would deftly mimic Beth by dessert.

He loved Beth more than his full-fledged daughters. She possessed the skewed will that they lacked. She affirmed his bent for the illicit. She did not plague him with the mundane.

They passed the Strip, eastbound. Beth described the Trocadero. Bette did not smile at him or touch him. He saw her there that first time. They made love upstairs. She said, "*Kill a Jap for me.*"

Claire was outwardly harsh. She was tall and patrician and used it to brusque effect. She fully succumbed to touch. Bette thought she did but did not.

Miss Davis remained Miss Davis, portraying raw appetite. It was about the future memory, recalled. Bette's passion was a recollective device.

They hit the Hawaii Theatre. Beth described the marquee. Starstudded *Citizen Kane*, late shows nitely. Palm-tree accents. REMEMBER PEARL HARBOR! signs by the ticket booth.

Bette donned dark glasses. It was a Miss Davis move. Dudley got out a five-dollar bill. Beth took charge of Tommy. It was a maneuver.

They stormed the booth and got their tickets. The blind man supplied a diversion. They got through the lobby. The place was near empty. The trailers had just ended. They steered Tommy out in front of them and got to their seats.

Bette went *Whew.* Tommy made a blind man's face. Dudley took the aisle seat and stretched his legs. Bette sat beside him. Beth sat next to her. Tommy took the end seat.

The lights redimmed. Dudley tucked close to Bette. She tucked away from him and tucked close to Beth.

The movie began. Beth tucked close to Tommy and whispered. She ran down the credits. She described a deathbed prologue. The film proper kicked in.

It was the late nineteenth century. Beth captured that. Deft girl, in soft sync.

Dudley ran his hand up Bette's leg. She smiled at him and turned back to Beth. The movie unfurled. Daylight scenes threw brightness. Beth whispered. She eyed the screen and squeezed Tommy's hands. The music got to him. Stringed crescendos made him cry.

Dudley watched them. Bette kept her head turned. He took his hand off Bette's leg. He thought she'd pull it back. She straightened the crease in her slacks.

The movie rankled. It was idiot muckraking and invasive technique. Beth caught the style and conveyed it, frame-to-frame. Dudley's mind raced. He drove to Mexico with Comrade Claire. He invaded Mexico with his boys.

This moronic motion picture. His Bette, dumbstruck. The chubby wunderkind, Orson Welles. Harry Cohn knew young Welles. Young Welles scrounged coon maids off Beverly Hills bus stops. He bamboozled them with maryjane and magic tricks. He plied them with his cricket dick and drove them home to coontown.

Dudley popped two bennies. He tapped his feet. He felt stretched. He got woman pangs. He panged Bette, Claire, Bette. He got daughter pangs. He panged for long talks with Beth.

The movie dragged on. It was Old Testament length.

Bette kept her back turned. Dark sequences hit. He couldn't see Bette, he couldn't see Beth. He was marooned on Mars.

It ended. The great Kane falls. His life was one hopped-up dance on a dunghill. It all pertained to a fucking child's sled.

His companions stood and clapped. Bette reprised her hoi polloi whistle. Dudley walked out to the lobby and lit a cigarette.

He was sweating. Benzedrine in a hot box. That tortuous movie. *Rubber-hose me—I'll confess.*

Bette and Beth walked Tommy out. They wore glazed culture looks. Bette cold-eyed him. Party pooper. *Don't you know how great that was?*

She suggested the Brown Derby. Beth and Tommy swooned. Dudley held an arm out. Bette linked up with him.

It felt perfunctory. She withheld her eyes. She gave them to Tommy and Beth.

Tommy kept going "Gee *whiz*, Uncle Dud." He heard Claire say "*I'm grateful.*" Beth took his free arm. He went instantly buoyant. They tumbled out to the limo, linked up.

The backseat was airless. Bette dropped his arm and threw chit-chat at Beth. Orson's a *genius*, you *must* meet him, he understands so *much*.

Dudley undid his necktie. Vine Street was just west. The ride traversed eons. Fat Orson, boy genius. No air in the fucking backseat.

They hit the Derby. Bette removed her dark glasses. She walked ahead of them. She led them. She came as Herself.

Hurricane Bette.

The homo maître d' fawns and shags them a booth. It's *the* Brown Derby. Beth steers Tommy and describes every inch. Tommy bumps a table. Bruce Cabot glares. He was the male ingénue in *King Kong*. Central Vice has a blue sheet on him. He enjoys underaged snatch.

Hurricane Bette.

She calls out to her filmland chums and blows kisses. She strides ahead of them. Heads turn: It's Bette! It's Bette! She walks ahead of the big man. He's the blind man's keeper. Who's that pretty girl in that cheap dress? My, what a procession! It's the Shanty Irish Dispossessed!

They made the booth. The homo seated them and swished off. Dudley squeezed in beside Bette.

He cupped her knee. She slid away and buttonholed Tommy. Her tone went arch. She had a foil and cued up deep compassion. Her voice went *TOO GODDAMN LOUD.*

Tell me, dear—how *does* one assemble radios without the gift of sight?

Tommy laid it out. His hands plucked at the tablecloth. He made blind man's faces. He glowed with Bette-Davis-is-being-nice-to-me love.

Beth was way across the booth. He couldn't touch her or tell her sweet things. She dabbed at Tommy's face and studied Bette. She'd wear Bette's hairdo tomorrow. She'd restitch her frocks for a more-Bette look.

Bette owned the room. People looked over. That's Gary Cooper. He's wearing a disabled vet's boutonniere.

A waiter came by. Dudley snagged him first. He ordered bonded bourbon, four shots. Menus appeared. Beth read Tommy's, aloud. Dudley inched closer to Bette. Bette inched closer to Tommy. *Tell me how you wire the antenna disks, dear.*

The drinks arrived. Beth had ginger ale. Tommy's Scotch Mist came with a straw. He slurped it. The sound echoed. Bette sipped a martini and scanned the room.

She trawled for recognition. She bestowed smiles and blew kisses. She doted on Tommy and one eye–cased the joint.

Dudley bolted his drink. He touched Bette's back. She reached around and patted his hand. The waiter reappeared. Dudley held four fingers up.

The waiter took orders. Bette ordered for Beth and Tommy—the New York steak, rare. Dudley ordered a well-done hamburger. Bette deadpanned the joke.

Dudley killed his drink. The refill appeared. He chugged half of it. The room resettled. His nerves smoothed out. He concocted small talk.

Be risqué for your brood. Orson Welles fucks nigger maids. Mr. Hearst will fuck *him*—and *soon*.

He cleared his throat.

Bette squeezed Tommy's hand and squeezed out of the booth.

Conquistadora.

She swirled, booth-to-booth. She snagged a waiter's pen and demanded war-bond pledges. Everybody coughed up. Bette wrote the names and amounts on her arm. Gary Cooper coughed up. Jean Arthur coughed up. An Army colonel wrote her a check. Bette curtsied and blew the ink dry.

Dudley killed his drink. It sent him gaga. He got a surge up his legs. He watched Bette swirl. He willed her to look his way and give him *something*.

She swirled. She fixed on her audience. She covered her arm in blue ink.

His tumbler vanished. A new one appeared. He slugged down two fingers and watched Bette swirl. John Wayne grabbed her wrist and kissed her arm above the ink line. Dudley pulled out his gun.

He felt something in his hand. He looked down and wondered how it got there. Beth saw it. Nobody else did. Bette had the room.

Beth looked at him. She made a little gesture. It meant *Dad, please.* He tucked his piece back in his holster. John Wayne released Bette's arm. Bette swirled away.

Dudley shut his eyes. Beth whispered something. Tommy's knees bumped the table. Dudley opened his eyes. Beth steered Tommy around a waiter.

His tumbler was back at four shots. He bolted half of it. The room blurred and cleared. He saw Bette, swirling his way.

She sat down. There's three of her, two of her, *one.* She smiled. She displayed her arm. Her sleeve was hiked up to her shoulder. Ink marks covered every inch.

She said, "For the war." "*Kill a Jap for me*" echoed.

He reached for her wrist. She jerked her arm back.

She said, "No, don't."

He killed his drink. There's three, two, *one* of her.

She said, "You're looking at a hundred thousand dollars for the war, from fifteen minutes of work."

Dudley gripped his tumbler. "I can make you five times that for a fifty-thousand-dollar investment that you won't even miss. It's smut movies, darling—of a level of artistry and perverted significance that will put that dithering piece of cinema we just witnessed to shame. Don't pretend that you don't love filth in the guise of art. Don't pretend that I don't understand that part of you. Don't pretend that you don't want me to fuck you tonight, and don't pretend that you won't write that check."

Bette slid close to him. Bette lowered her head. Lovers' tête-à-tête.

"How dare you inflict such vile presumption upon me at a time such as this? How dare you attribute your own basest urges to me? How dare you advance this obscene proposition with your daughter and her dear friend twenty feet away, on what is surely the most splendid night of their lives? How dare you think that you and I are anything more than a trivial and titillating footnote to this horrible moment in time, and that *you* can impose your brutal will upon *me* in such a cruel and casual manner?"

Dudley gripped the tumbler. His hand spasmed. The glass shattered.

Bourbon spilled. Shards crumbled. He held pure shrapnel and made a tight fist. Glass tore his hand. High-test booze scalded him.

Bette got up and walked out. Blood seeped through his fingers and drenched the tablecloth. People looked over. His suit coat was unbuttoned and wide open. His holster was out in plain view.

He stared at his hand. Blood covered it. The liquor burned, wicked bad. He saw three rooms, two rooms, *one*. He snatched up the table napkins. He wrapped his hand and watched the red seep through.

People looked at him. Movie stars gawked. Beth helped Tommy out of the washroom. Bette herded them toward the door.

Dudley Liam Smith. You took a spill. Take your leave, now.

He fished out two C-notes and dropped them on the table. He got up and squeezed out of the booth. His hand burned and throbbed. The pain gave him legs.

He trailed blood out to the sidewalk. He got in the limo. They all looked away from him.

The limo pulled away. The white napkins seeped to pure red. Beth and Tommy got out at the Roosevelt. Tommy fumbled at his hand. Beth whispered this astonishing thing.

She said, "I *know*, Dad."

They got out. Beth steered Tommy toward Grauman's Chinese. Dudley shut his eyes and went someplace. He knew he was moving. His hand throbbed. He smelled Bette's smoke.

The limo moved. A wheel hum settled him. *Dudley Liam Smith—you're someplace. That's Her smoke.*

Conquistadora.

Smoke, no smoke. She's there, she's gone.

The limo ran east on Sunset. His lap was blood-soaked. The seat cushions were slick.

He tapped the partition. He said, "Roxbury and Elevado, please."

It took five minutes. The house was lit up bright. He heard Fifth Column music. Atonal subversion. Dissonant dissidence.

He threw a C-note at the driver and weaved to the porch. He got the bell with his elbow. His hand leaked blood and throbbed.

She opened the door. The Red Empress. *Perdition, catch my soul.*

She smiled.

She said, "Really, *you*?"

97

LOS ANGELES | MONDAY, DECEMBER 22, 1941

8:11 p.m.

Yard work. Night work, by searchlight. Dudley's graph to Scotty's snitch sheet to Here.

Ashida carried a knapsack and lantern. It was confirmation work and last good-byes. He walked the ground between The House and the parkway. He'd bottled four soil samples so far.

Two stunk of shrimp oil. It confirmed the graph and snitch sheet.

Dudley trekked this path last Friday. Dudley spun theories.

Preston Exley and Pierce Patchett were land czars. Dudley's resultant surmise:

They buy land and destroy its crop-raising potential. They build parkway ramps and commercial structures right Here.

He'd been out all day. Confirmations, good-byes.

He drove to the Valley. He went by four wetback-staffed farms. Slave crews picked diseased-looking crops.

He bottled four soil samples. They all contained shrimp oil. He went by three *all*-Japanese farms. The crops there looked healthy. He bottled soil samples. There was no shrimp-oil scent.

It confirmed Dudley's theory. Destroy crops. Build internment centers. Usurp the all-Japanese farms. Build internment centers There.

He left the Valley and drove to Kwan's. He worked the death car and got *An Idea.* He clocked out and drove to the Bureau.

Dudley neglected a follow-up. It did not appear on his graph.

Check the reverse directories. The Watanabe house was one prospective ramp and land site. Dudley surmised other ramp and land sites. Dudley did not follow up.

Other houses had been bought. That was common case knowledge. Buzz Meeks tracked sales to Glassell Park and South Pasadena. South Pasadena was on the parkway. Glassell Park was close but not on. Glassell Park houses were valuable but not essential. Houses right by ramp sites were pure gelt.

He hit the Bureau. He shagged the Central Reverse Book. He worked the street-address and house owners' index. The Watanabes were the only Japanese in Highland Park. A *few* Japanese lived in South Pasadena.

He found three. Nagoya, Yoshimura, Kondo—all on the parkway.

Lincoln Heights ran parkway-parallel. It began just north of Chinatown and continued two miles up. A drainage creek nixed eastside-flush homes. Behind the creek and still close? Let's check right There.

He found three more. Takahama, Miyamo, Hatsuma. All close to the creek.

He drove by all six houses. All six were parkway-flush or creek-flush. He walked around the exteriors. All six houses had been cleaned out.

Dudley got most of it. He got the rest.

Who is the white man in the purple sweater? We both want to know.

Ashida walked up to the back door. He let himself in. He turned on the lights and strolled. Let's say farewell to The House.

It was still intact-furnished. The check-in log was still there.

He skimmed through. The entries ran from 12/7 to 12/19. He'd logged in fourteen times. Dudley checked in twelve times.

He checked the check boxes. Dust all touch surfaces—check. Dust all grab surfaces—check. Itemize the kitchen. Itemize the bedrooms. Itemize the living room.

Latent-print boxes. Inventory boxes. Empty the drain grates. Test all solvents. Print-dust all glassware. Carbon sheets by the work log. Everything in The House, itemized.

He went down the check boxes. He recognized his own check marks. Forty-two separate boxes checked, all the way to—

"*Master bedroom closet/victims' clothing (laundry marks, moneys, note slips, etc.).*"

Box no. 43—*un*-checked.

Oversight. It happened. Shitwork accumulated. Cases grew cold.

Box 43. Check it now. Formalize this farewell.

Ashida walked upstairs. Box 43 was the toss-the-pockets step. It was often overlooked. The victims' death garb *had* been checked.

He walked into the bedroom. He opened the closet. Aya left three smocks behind. There were no toss pockets sewn on or in. Ryoshi left two sports coats—blue serge, gray herringbone.

Four pairs of shoes. Neckties on a hook. Belts on a wall peg.

Ashida went through the blue serge and got zero. Ashida patted the herringbone breast pocket and felt a bulge.

He reached in and removed it. It was a pair of men's socks, turned inside out.

Tan, cable-knit, cashmere. Sized for a small-footed man. Maroon stains on the soles. Congealed matter—inside and out.

Men's hosiery. Expensive—and small. Ryoshi and Johnny Watanabe had large feet.

Ashida touched the stains. Ashida smelled them. They were dried blood.

The killer walked the house with his shoes off. The killer stepped in blood. The killer panicked and got rid of his socks.

No. That was wrong. That didn't fit. His killer would not do that.

Ashida thought it through. Ashida worked backward. The blood-dotted glass shards—12/7/41.

The Watanabes oil-doused their feet. They were soil contaminators. They sprinkled the shards on their feet. It aerated the ground. The Watanabes had *heavily callused feet.* Glass shards on *their* feet would not produce this much blood. These were men's socks. They wouldn't fit Ryoshi or Johnny. They might fit Aya and/or Nancy.

Ashida ran downstairs. Ashida read every carbon sheet. Every item of clothing in the house had been logged. There were no tan cashmere socks. There were no tan socks or cashmere socks—male/female, over and out.

He went out the front door. He got his car and drove to the morgue. He ran inside. An attendant buttonholed him. He said something about the crematorium.

Ashida quick-walked there. Nort was stoking an incinerator. Four sheet-covered stiffs were laid out on gurneys. The sheets were solvent-soaked and prepped to ignite.

"Jesus, you've got timing. Did you come to say good-bye?"

"How badly have they decomposed?"

Nort shook his head. "You've got something, son. Tell me what it is before they go."

Ashida tossed him the socks. "I found them at the house. They weren't itemized, and they're too small and too expensive for Ryoshi and Johnny. Look at those bloodstains. You can't attribute them to glass shards and shrimp oil on heavily callused feet."

Nort nodded. Ashida caught The Smell. They'd decomped past their use date. Their flesh was off the bone.

He pulled up all four sheets. Their feet were still intact. Nort held the socks up to them.

They were far too small for Ryoshi and Johnny. They were too small for Aya and Nancy. The Cashmere Sock Man had *tiny* feet.

A microscope was bolted to a workbench. A stack of files sat next to it. Nort ripped off a sock swatch and clamped it under the slide.

He dialed in. He looked down. He plucked a file and consulted an autopsy sheet. He looked back and forth six times. He wheeled and grinned.

"He stepped in visceral blood. It was Ryoshi's. He'd had a recent intestinal infection. There's leukocytes all through that stain."

Who is the white man in the—

Nort said, "Werewolves don't have small feet. Not that I didn't know it was a frame."

The incinerator kicked on. Ashida felt a big blast of heat.

He cranked up the gurneys and pushed them to the edge. He tipped the bodies into the flames.

Nort said, "*Sayonara*, folks. I wish we'd done better by you."

98

KAY LAKE'S DIARY

LOS ANGELES | MONDAY, DECEMBER 22, 1941

10:39 p.m.

I felt ridiculous.

I stood in front of the Roosevelt Hotel, across from the courtyard of Grauman's Chinese. I did not look like a whore. I looked like a prairie girl who'd misjudged the local climate.

My dress was winter-weight, pleated, and fell below the knee; the matching jacket fit loosely. The red silk blouse showed scant cleavage. My mink coat was too much for L.A. at Christmas. A mothball scent made me sneeze.

Elmer, Brenda and Bill Parker were up in suite 813. They were stationed behind a wall peek. A tripod-rigged camera pointed into the living room. The room was microphone-fitted. Elmer and Brenda knew Fletch B.'s "quirk" and assured me that this was strictly a living room deal.

Parker appeared to be off the sauce. He issued abrupt orders and comported himself with brusque civility. He agreed to the shakedown without a moment's pause. It astonished me.

I waited. Mayor Fletch was due momentarily. My broken nose was cosmetically masked and showed no sign of recent fracture. I chain-smoked; I watched rubes congregate outside Grauman's and slide their feet into movie stars' footprints. A pretty girl led a blind man through the courtyard and helped him compare his feet to Cary Grant's. It was heartbreakingly lovely.

A Lincoln sedan pulled to the curb, directly in front of me. The driver flashed his headlights twice—my signal. I leaned into the passenger window. Pinch me—it was Fletcher Bowron.

He looked over at me and leered. He wore Kiwanis, Moose, and Elks lodge pins, along with a Pearl Harbor mourning armband. I said, "Suite 813. Please give me a few minutes."

Fletch gave me the high sign. I walked into the hotel, took the elevator up and let myself into the suite.

It was Brenda's standing tryst spot. The living room and bedroom featured peeks built into wall-mounted mirrors. Camera stations stood in crawl spaces behind the walls; three people could crouch and covertly film assignations. Brenda, Elmer and Parker were behind the living room peek. I had been told to position myself sideways, eight feet from the wall. Elmer warned me that Fletch night be nervous and told me to have a stiff drink waiting.

I did a little soft-shoe and waved at the peek. Brenda yelled, "No mugging, Citizen. This ain't no high school play."

I laughed and walked to the bar. I poured Fletch a triple and siphoned in club soda. I smoothed my hair and heard the doorbell.

I carried the drink over and opened the door. Fletch snatched the glass and chugalugged it. I shut the door and threw the bolt.

He said, "You think I'm Fletcher Bowron, Esquire, but I'm not.

That guy's a pantywaist. The War Department's got me traveling incognito, and I'll admit I look a little bit like Fletch. Let me have it, sister. Tell me who you've got standing here."

Fletch always worked off a script. I had my part memorized.

I said, "You're Race Randall, the ace spy. You've been transporting secret documents from the Continent, and you're all tuckered out."

"That's right. I've been monitoring the progress of the eastern-front war, and I'm starting to think we should cut a deal with Hitler while we've still got the chance. Those Nazi boys have got oomph, and since I'm a man with lead in my pencil, I know oomph when I see it."

I walked to the bar and built another triple. I said, "Geopolitics fascinates me. Please tell me more."

Race snatched the glass. He chugalugged his drink and did a little cock-'o-the-walk strut.

"Russia's all right, if you like gruel and lezbo discus throwers, but Deutschland's got the goods. I was there with the L.A. Trade Commission in '38, and I say *der Führer*'s been getting a bum rap. The Abwehr tried to recruit me, but Race Randall's devoted to the good old U.S. of A. You know what they say about me, don't you, sister?"

I certainly did. "Everyone knows about *you*, Mr. Randall. You've got the biggest and the best."

Race reeled and sloshed his bourbon. "Marlene Dietrich will attest to that, sister. We were with some of the boys at a schnitzel palace on the Goetheplatz. You know the Horst Wessel song? '*Die Fahne hoch! Die Reihen dict geschlossen! SA marschiert mit ruhig festem Schritt.*'"

We were squarely in line with the wall peek. Race killed off his drink and began goose-stepping. He goose-stepped the length of the room, three times. I stood back and watched; I heard foot scuffs along the crawl space and observed the evening's climax before ace spy Race Randall did.

Citizens Brenda, Elmer and Bill were standing by the bedroom doorway. Race would see them the moment he turned and began goose-stepping back our way.

He goose-stepped.

He froze in mid-step.

He dropped his glass and screamed.

Brenda said, "We go back a coon's age, Fletch. But business is business."

Parker said, "No 'derogatory profile.' A closed-chambers, grand jury–sanctioned conference at 8:00 a.m. tomorrow. Immediate subpoenas for Preston Exley and a man named Pierce Morehouse Patchett. They may bring an attorney. I'll be the grand jury's ad hoc counsel."

I said, "Race, you've got the biggest and the best."

99

LOS ANGELES | MONDAY, DECEMBER 22, 1941

11:42 p.m.

Fletch started sobbing. Brenda mother-henned him.

We're still pals, sweetie. I'll still get you girls. Let's get some coffee in you. You'll be right as rain.

The pathos was unnerving. Parker ducked out. He elevatored downstairs. The lobby choir unnerved him. He ducked outside.

He'd parked his car off the boulevard. He brought his law texts and scrawl sheets. He jogged over and piled in.

He checked his watch. 2:00 a.m. would mark six days sober. He checked the 813 windows. Fletch boo-hoo'd. Miss Lake talked with her friends.

Parker got out his pencils and notepad. A girl walked a blind man in front of the car. He sent up a prayer for them.

Prayer gave him the idea. It densified the Bowron shakedown. Cease-and-desist was insufficient. The closed proceeding put Fletch at more risk. It upped the odds that he'd never break ranks and snitch.

The idea sidestepped The Vow. He plea-bargained God for just this one thing. Dudley's blithe sermon convinced him to try it.

It might convince Exley and Patchett to ditch their slave-camp plans. It might instill just *this much* doubt in them.

Parker worked. He studied statutes. He dog-eared pages. He

underlined legal points. He smoked himself hoarse. He swilled stale coffee and cogitated. He thought of Lieutenant Conville. He thought of Miss Lake.

He drove by Coulter's yesterday. He saw a tweed skirt in the window and thought of Miss Lake. That skirt and white stockings. Miss Lake in white gloves at church.

Lieutenant Conville was taller. She wore the winter uniform now. She'd go to the khaki in springtime. It would complement her red hair.

Parker worked all night. He wrote out a series of questions and phrased them loophole tight. He drove downtown at dawn.

He cadged a cot room nap. He slept between Thad Brown and Lee Blanchard. He got up at 7:40. He cleaned up and shaved in the washroom.

Crapshoot. The county grand jury room—546.

Parker walked down. Fletch delivered. The annex was set up.

One table, five chairs. A female stenographer. The participants, plus counsel.

Bill McPherson and Preston Exley. Pierce Patchett—tall and gaunt. *Counsel?* Ben Siegel's man, Sam Rummel.

The fit was tight. One small room and six people. Blasé Exley. Blasé Patchett. The DA—early-morning alert. A high-stakes shyster and early-a.m. subpoenas.

McPherson said, "We're all here. Let's not pretend that it's anything other than an inconvenience, and get to it."

The steno rigged her device. Rummel placed three sheets of paper on the table.

"The confidentiality forms. We'll need signatures from Mr. Exley, Mr. Patchett, and Captain Parker."

Pens came out. Exley signed. Patchett signed. Parker signed. Rummel cleared his throat.

"Are you here as a policeman, or as a specially deputized attorney and representative of the county grand jury, Captain Parker?"

"The latter, Mr. Rummel. I'll add that I'm legally prohibited from repeating testimony sworn here this morning to any outside agency, which includes the Los Angeles Police Department."

McPherson tapped his watch. "Let's get this thing going. Gentlemen, raise your right hands."

They complied. McPherson spieled the oath.

"Do the witnesses swear that their privately sworn testimony is fully true and free of all dissembling and evasion? Does counsel swear that his queries are proffered with full knowledge of California state and Federal law, and that this inquiry is undertaken to comport with the best interest of all citizens of and within Los Angeles County? Do all parties understand that upon completion of this interview, I will decide whether or not to pursue a full-scale inquiry, and that my decision will be final and conclusively binding?"

Exley said, "I so swear, and I do."

Patchett said, "I so swear, and I do."

Rummel said, "I so swear, and I do."

Parker said, "I so swear, and I do."

The steno typed it in. Rummel cleared his throat.

"Twelve questions, Captain Parker. If my clients decline to answer, please do not comment or badger them."

Exley and Patchett sat down. Parker sat facing them.

"All questions are directed to both Mr. Exley and Mr. Patchett. Either or both of them may answer, and they may elaborate if they wish."

Rummel shook his head. "They do not wish to, nor will they, 'elaborate.' "

McPherson straddled a chair. "Let's move this along. We've got three hotshot lawyers in the room. There won't be any hanky-panky."

Rummel sat down. Parker studied Patchett. Note his pinned eyes. Odds on drugstore hop.

"Here's my first question. Gentlemen, do you comprise a combine that has purchased, has attempted to purchase and is currently attempting to purchase Japanese-owned house properties in Highland Park, Glassell Park and South Pasadena, along with Japanese-owned farm property in the San Fernando Valley?"

Exley said, "Yes."

Parker said, "Is it your intention to raze those house properties in order to build ramps to the Arroyo Seco Parkway and shopping centers near the Arroyo Seco Parkway?"

Patchett said, "Yes."

Parker said, "Exley Construction has a proposal before the mayor's office and the City Council at this moment. The proposal theoretically supplants preexisting plans currently being implemented by the Federal government. Mr. Exley wishes to construct prison work camps to house Japanese subversives for the duration of the war, in the San Fernando Valley. Mr. Exley, have you purchased Japanese-owned farm property, and are you attempting to purchase Japanese-owned farm property in order to raze said properties to create prison work camp sites?"

Exley said, "Yes."

Parker said, "Are you employing illegal Mexican farm workers to pick your crops?"

Exley and Patchett leaned toward Rummel. Patchett's shirt cuffs slid up. Note his Asian-symbol tattoos.

Rummel said, "Point of order, Captain. Those workers have been granted temporary visas by Captain Carlos Madrano of the Mexican State Police."

Cluster fuck. *El Capitán* Carlos. *El Jefe, muy fascista.*

"I'll rephrase. Gentlemen, are your workers systematically destroying crop acreage by the application of shrimp oil upon topsoil, in an attempt to provide a baseline for the cement foundations of your prison work camp structures?"

Exley said, "Yes."

Parker said, "Have you created a dummy corporation and secretly recorded your purchases of the house and farm properties?"

Patchett said, "Yes."

"Will you present documentation of your purchases to the Los Angeles County grand jury?"

Rummel said, "Only in the event of a full-scale grand jury inquiry, and under official subpoena only."

Parker said, "Did you purchase the Highland Park home and the East Valley farm of Ryoshi Watanabe?"

Exley said, "Yes."

"Did you tell Mr. Watanabe and/or members of his family to walk the acreage behind the house with shrimp oil and/or glass shards applied to their feet, in order to aerate the acreage and provide a baseline for the pouring of cement?"

Patchett said, "Yes."

Parker said, "The property behind the houses you have purchased or have attempted to purchase is public land deeded to Los Angeles County, with first-purchase rights of refusal granted to Exley Construction, due to its proximity to the Arroyo Seco Parkway. Gentlemen, were you systematically attempting to reduce the value of those properties by your topsoil-destroying machinations, and had you realized that people *walking* the acreage would stand a better chance of going undetected than a mechanized application of shrimp oil would?"

Exley said, "Yes."

Parker said, "Did you murder Ryoshi, Aya, Johnny and Nancy Watanabe on December 6, 1941?"

Patchett said, "No."

"Do you know who killed them?"

Patchett said, "No."

"Do you have verifiable alibis for 2:00 to 5:00 p.m. on Saturday, December 6th? I would like both of you to answer, please."

Exley said, "Yes."

Patchett said, "Yes."

Parker said, "Will you present valid third-party proof of those alibis?"

Rummel cleared his throat. "In the event of a full-scale and official inquiry only, and only under direct subpoena."

Twelve questions. Added clarifications. Thirty-four minutes, door-to-door.

Parker looked at McPherson. "As your deputy, I call for a full-scale inquiry."

McPherson stood up. "Request denied. The Wolf's good for those homicides. Shrimp oil, farms and parkway ramps—who gives a shit?"

December 23, 1941

100

LOS ANGELES | TUESDAY, DECEMBER 23, 1941

8:53 a.m.

"BET-TE! BET-TE!"

They stormed the Miracle Mile. They commandeered parking lots and blitzed Christmas shoppers. Buy war bonds. Meet Miss Davis. She's Aunt Sam—and she wants *YOU!*

The late-shopping rush. Hollywood. War fever.

The big department stores ran down Wilshire. Desmond Silverwood's, Coulter's. The lots ran straight behind them. Platforms were set up by the exits. Bette stood above the crowds and worked off microphones.

She wowed the fans. Army color guards flanked her. Cops monitored the bond-purchase lines. Bette shook everyone's hand. Bette posed for photos. MPs handled the pledge slips and cash.

Beth and Tommy stuck close to Bette. Dudley stood not too close. Bette deadpanned him. Last night shrouded them.

His hand hurt wicked bad. Claire picked glass out of the cuts for two hours. She mummified his hand. He couldn't touch her with it. They made love awkwardly.

He put the onus on a cop's bash. He heard a grand joke and squeezed his glass too hard. The Red Empress seemed skeptical.

They discussed their Mexican plans. They talked blue streaks. She gave him a painkilling pill. They fell out, entwined.

He left her bed at 7:00. She inquired about his day. He said he'd been assigned to guard Bette Davis. Skeptic Claire roared.

"It was her I smelled on you Sunday. I met her once, at a premiere. I remember her perfume."

He laughed. Claire grabbed an atomizer and marked him with her scent.

"BET-TE! BET-TE! BET-TE!"

Dudley watched the crowd. Cops linked arms and held back the crowd. Silverwood's was Stop no. 2. Five hundred people showed up for Desmond's. Diehards slept in the lot overnight.

"BET-TE! BET-TE!"

The crowd shouted her name. A crowd shouted his name yesterday. Bette deadpanned him. *You inconvenienced me.*

"BET-TE! BET-TE!"

He worked the store cop's phone back at Desmond's. He called Huey. Huey reported. Huey said Tojo Tom was still tucked in tight. He talked to Tojo Tom. He quizzed him per Carlos Madrano's dope and cash stash. Tojo credibly reported and begged to be sprung. He said, "Merry Christmas, lad. You'll be released at New Year's."

He started *seeing* it. The raid itself. Let's utilize those Jap subs glimpsed in Baja.

Call-Me-Jack was sub-fixated. He feared attacks off the L.A. coast. Dudley called Call-Me-Jack and snow-jobbed him.

Chief, I fear sub raids. Let me liaise with the Staties. I'll take my boys down.

It all clicked his way then. Fate intervened.

Carlos Madrano was sub-fixated. *He'd* called Call-Me-Jack. Those Baja sub spottings spooked him. Call-Me-Jack played right in.

"Go down on the QT, Dud. Don't tell Carlos you're there. Chart scuttlebutt on the sub front. Ellis Loew presents to the grand jury today, and we'll get our indictment on Monday. You'll be commissioned at New Year's, and I know you want a Mexican posting. Lay the groundwork and poke some señoritas. Let me know what you hear."

Roger, Chief. I'll do just that.

"BET-TE! BET-TE! BET-TE!"

She deadpanned him. *You inconvenienced me.* She would not look his way.

Beth played to him. She kept glancing over. His hand throbbed. The crowd yelled for Bette.

Cops walked stiffs up to meet her.

She smiled at each and every one.

She posed for pictures and dispensed hugs.

She was an American. He was immigrant scum. She was native-born Protestant. He was papist rabble. It was her war—not his.

He thought of the Red Empress. He thought of Mexico and money. Schoolchildren stormed the platform. They waved American flags on sticks.

101

LOS ANGELES | TUESDAY, DECEMBER 23, 1941

11:04 a.m.

Ashida saw smoke. It billowed northeast. It might be a brush blaze. It might be morgue soot off the Watanabes.

Who is the white man in the purple sweater? He walked in Ryoshi's blood. He wears cashmere socks and has very small feet.

He sat outside Mariko's building. She was upstairs, asleep. Little Tokyo was peaceful. The Feds took a holiday breather. No street rousts, no bank raids.

A depleted population. Sidewalk Christmas trees.

Ashida read the morning *Herald.* It was his breather. He was due back at Kwan's after lunch.

They were disassembling the death car. It was make-do work. The escaped Japs had been preconvicted. Dudley would brutalize Hop Sing busboys and nail the finger man. It was all fait accompli.

He missed Dudley. He wanted to sit beside him. He wanted to see him wink.

The *Herald* was all Japs and Christmas. SHOPPERS SWARM MIRACLE MILE! BETTE DAVIS DUE AT COULTER'S! ARROW SHIRT SALE AT THE WILSHIRE MAY COMPANY!

Dudley and Bette. He'd love to see it. His camera, a wall peek.

Jap sub alerts in Baja. It's only a hundred miles. It *could* happen here.

The escaped Japs were spotted down in San Diego County. They skirted the dragnet. The posse was on its way.

Ashida tossed the paper. Hardy locals swept the street. The population was two-thirds dispersed. Padlocked buildings vouched that figure. February was coming. The papers euphemized "Concentration Camps."

A cab pulled up. Bucky Bleichert got out. He wore his Belmont jacket.

The cab U-turned. Bucky jiggled the coins in his pockets and looked over.

He was taller than Dudley. They both had small brown eyes. Bucky's arms were longer. Dudley's hands were twice his size.

Bucky walked up. He hemmed and hawed that Bucky way. He forked over an envelope. It felt like money.

"Is it a penance payment? You informed on my family, and you think this will erase that?"

Bucky shrugged. It was quintessential. His most dismissive poses evinced grace.

"It's my life savings. I think you'll be needing it."

"Complete the thought, Bucky. Why will I be needing it?"

Bucky said, "I was playing basketball at the Academy, and I heard these Feds talking. They were saying that you were involved in making some kind of Red-type movie, but their case against you and the Reds got blown somehow. They're looking for dogs to kick, so they're bypassing your pal Ward Littell and picking up you and your family after Christmas. They said all of you were Fifth Column from way back."

"Thanks, Bucky. You didn't have to tell me, but you did."

Bucky jiggled coins. "I always knew how you felt about me. I didn't care, until you got in my way."

Ashida said, "There's a woman looking for you. I'm sure she'll find you someday."

11:45 a.m.

He lunged. He blew off Bucky and the car job at Kwan's.

He drove to City Hall and lunged upstairs. Homicide was all Japs and Chinks. Mike Breuning and Dick Carlisle worked adjoining sweat rooms. Ashida scoped the hall mirrors.

Hop Sing boys were cuffed to drainpipes. The lads tossed phonebook shots.

Thad Brown worked the main briefing room. He traced routes on a wall map. He preached to forty hunting-garbed men.

The Japs dashed down to Dago. It's a border crashout. The Mex Staties are waiting. Spotter planes are up. They're camped in the boonies. They'll hit southbound roadways. We'll take them then.

Ashida counted shrunken heads. He got to twenty-three and stopped. Half the men carried hacksaws.

Enough.

Ashida walked to Bill Parker's office. The door was open. Parker wore Army fatigues.

He was posse-bound. Check his office. It's a loading zone.

Gas masks, grenades, Ithaca pumps. The spotter planes would gas hillsides. They'd flush out the Japs.

Ashida said, "Have you done anything? Is there anything more we can do?"

"I tried a play with Exley, Patchett and the grand jury. McPherson declined to pursue."

Cashmere socks. Bloody socks. Who is the white man in the—

"Is there anything more we can do?"

"We can wait for a callback on the pay-phone records."

Ashida scanned the room. He counted twenty Thompson submachine guns.

"The Feds are coming after my family."

Parker said, "I'm sorry."

"Is there anyone you can call?"

Parker checked the wall clock. "I've worn out my welcome with the Feds, Doctor. That shouldn't surprise you."

Two MPs rolled an ammo cart down the hallway. The metal wheels gouged the floor.

Ashida lunged. He cut down the hall. He made Homicide. He made the cubicle.

Dudley sat at his desk. His right hand was bandaged. He wore a tweed suit and brown brogues.

No man should be so deadly. No man should be so handsome. No man should be so adroit and so debonair.

Dudley smiled. Graph sheets enclosed him. Ink strokes covered all four sheets.

"WATANABE CASE CLEARED/12-7 TO 12/23/41."

Dudley said, "Hello, lad."

Ashida fluttered. "The FBI is coming after my family and me. I thought you could help."

Dudley said, "I'll take care of it immediately. In recompense, I will require your presence on a grand Mexican foray."

102

KAY LAKE'S DIARY

LOS ANGELES | TUESDAY, DECEMBER 23, 1941

12:39 p.m.

Nothing before this moment exists. The war is coming. I'm going to enlist.

I wrote those words in this same spot, seventeen days ago. I knew the war to be inevitable, and believed that I could control the onslaught with self-directed actions and statements of intent. Callow girl. Look at your face in the mirror and convincingly state that you believe it now.

Scotty Bennett has enlisted. I doubt that Pacific duty can match his two weeks as a wartime-hire policeman. I received a letter from Scotty a few hours ago; he wrote it en route to the Marine Corps recruit depot. There was no mention of Dudley Smith, the Watanabe murder case, the alleged killer he shot in Chinatown, his daring raid on The Werewolf's den or any other heinous errands he might have undertaken while under the Dudster's spell. He did not mention the graph summary that he sent to Hideo Ashida at great risk, or reveal that his flight to the war was a horrified repudiation of evil and his own compliance with it. He stated that he will seek to serve his country as a combat chaplain's assistant and thanked me for the love I gave him the month America entered the war and he became a policeman.

I wept then. I retrieved the Saint Christopher medal that I received at Trinity Lutheran Church in 1929. I know that I will never see Scotty Bennett again. I will wear the medal until I learn that he has returned safely or that he has died.

I did not know Scotty seventeen days ago. I did not know William H. Parker, Hideo Ashida or Claire De Haven. I had not enlisted in a political pogrom and had not maneuvered at a dozen levels of allegiance and betrayal. I had not perpetrated a shakedown on a noted public official, nor had I fought for my life with a jailhouse shiv. The war gave me this. It came to me in the form of a man who misread the war with his own self-directed actions and statements of intent. I am in no way comforted by the knowledge that Captain William H. Parker was every bit as reckless and foolish as I.

I've called Hideo's apartment repeatedly and gotten no answer. He betrayed me, he betrayed Claire, he betrayed a film venture that would have exposed the brutal blood libel of his people. I called him because we're at war and I've been imbued with a heightened understanding of instant allegiance and sudden betrayal. I've called Claire repeatedly and gotten no answer. I betrayed her. I betrayed my best ideals. I betrayed Claire's courage to confront injustice and her ability to surmount sophistry and acute dissipation.

I've called Saul Lesnick's office. I've left messages with his secretary, and gotten no calls back. I called Reynolds Loftis and talked to him. He told me that Claire came to believe that I was a police informant. Reynolds said, "Claire thought you possessed stunning artistry, but no character or conviction." He asked me if I *was* a police informant. I said, "Yes." He said, "You silly thing," and hung up.

I cannot cite the war to rebuff Claire's indictment. It's an accurate brief of my life to date.

The war. This storm. This storm that now indicts me.

Dudley Smith and his graph. Land grabs and the dead Watanabes. Lee Blanchard kills a gangland witness. Fletch Bowron's drunken goose step. A rumor Brenda shared with me. Dudley smokes opium in Ace Kwan's basement.

I miss Scotty. I miss Hideo. I miss Claire. *The Passion of Joan of Arc* is playing at the Filmarte Theatre. I'm going to see it and think of her.

I think of Dudley. He shadows me. I keep seeing him trading looks with Bette Davis. Lovers' glances across a dance floor.

The war. My own Japanese invasion. Hideo. The Goleta Inlet. Submarines, from Monterey to Mexico. The jail suicides. Goro Shigeta in the phone booth. I don't know where Lee is. I would guess that he's out with the posse. The men are wearing shrunken heads. Lee bought one for a car ornament.

I don't know where Hideo is. We share a love for a perfidious boxer with big buck teeth.

The war. Rash acts and injustice. I possess stunning artistry, but no character or conviction. I miss the people I've betrayed and who've betrayed me. I know only two things. America will win the war, and I'm alone with William H. Parker.

103

SAN DIEGO COUNTY | TUESDAY, DECEMBER 23, 1941

2:06 p.m.

Posse. Convoy. Pincer attack. Twenty vehicles and a crop-dusting biplane.

They moved south. Two hundred Jap hunters. The topography favored them.

They moved in two flanks. They held the high-vantage-point edge. Paved roads overlooked a north-to-south gulch. Thick foliage, scrub mounds, half-paved roadways. Tree cover and a shot to Mexico.

The Japs were down there somewhere. They were outnumbered and outflanked.

By jeeps and Army half-tracks. By black-and-whites rigged with off-road axles. By shotguns, tommy guns and grenades. By decapitation gear. By *baaaaad* shrunken-head voodoo.

The flanks pushed south. Pincers. Left-side/right-side canyon roads looked down on that gulch. The biplane flew low behind them. It sprayed yellow shit from a hundred feet up.

The shit flushed out bird flocks and wetbacks. It pushed all living things *south*. The shit burned and ate flesh. The shit dropped downward and stayed there. Get out, get to fresh air, get *south now*.

Parker rode *south*. He rode on the west flank. The ocean was off to the right. His black-and-white was radio-rigged. A Hearst Rifle man drove.

Parker sat up front. The backseat was stacked with tear-gas bombs and gas masks. They were somewhere near San Marcos. That yellow shit wafted below them. A breeze pushed it *south*.

The ride was bumpy and twisty. Parker craned his neck and looked *down*. Wetbacks ran out of the trees. They wiped their eyes. They pitched willy-nilly. They fled the yellow shit and ran *south*.

The Japs were somewhere back in the trees. The biplane spotted them and radioed a report.

Japs. They've got a brown car. They're down there. We need them out in the open. We need them to run SOUTH.

The roads down there ran *south*. They were one-lane wide and half dirt. They were escape routes. Local cops called the mass "Blood Alley." The alley ran straight into Mexico. It bypassed border crossings and stopped at a barbed-wire fence. A hundred fugitives had made the break. A hundred fugitives had died.

Posse. Convoy. Lynch mob. Kamikaze play.

Parker thought it through. He went back to Dudley's speech yesterday and pushed *out*. He might have read it wrong. He was Dudley-fixated and saw Dudley everywhere. It was Dudley Mania and Dudley Paranoia. Maybe he robbed and killed the Chinamen. Maybe he did not. Maybe he shot President Lincoln and bombed Pearl Harbor himself. He had the Dudley Juju *baaaaaaad*.

Still.

The breakout felt wrong. Why break for Mexico? The Japs had the tile-game money and could buy hideouts from fellow Japs. Why switch cars in Chinatown? Why clout cars so close to their intended heist? It felt like a Dudley Convergence and some Dudley Brainstorm.

Radio scoop crackled in. The San Gabriel posse flank issued a broadcast. They discovered the Japs' campground. It resembled the Griffith Park slaughter scene. They found rodents on sticks. They found a shortwave radio and charred-paper mounds. The radio was dead and could not receive or put out signals.

The Watanabes had shortwave gear. It clued Hideo Ashida in to the Goleta attack. Jap subs were prowling the Mexican coast *now*.

Confluence. Overlay. Frayed threads that read *Wrong*.

The convoy moved *south*. They ran above the yellow shit in the gulch.

The radio belched gibberish and squawked *LOUD*.

Jap alert. They're out of the bush. They're outrunning the yellow shit. *See the car, see the car*. It's coming up on a Statie roadblock. Cut left by them trees up ahead.

There's them trees—they're straight ahead.

Parker looked down. Parker looked *south*. Yellow shit, yellow shit, Blood Alley. There's the car. It's down there and southbound. It's out of the shit and in the clear.

The driver pulled hard left. The black-and-white brodied down a half-paved embankment. Parker saw the roadblock. It was six sawhorses wide. Mex Staties manned it. They wore Mussolini black shirts and jodhpurs. They held tommy guns, pointed straight *out*.

The black-and-white skidded and stopped. Parker and the driver got out. Parker looked across the gulch. Eight jeeps and half-tracks were parked on a matching embankment.

Men. Thirty-odd.

They've got tommy guns and rifles. They've got slug-loaded shotguns. They're crouched and aiming straight *down*.

Parker grabbed his binoculars. The driver aimed a scope-fitted Mauser. There's the car. It's coming at the roadblock. It's binocular-magnified, *right now*.

The guns exploded. *All* the guns exploded. *All* the guns exploded *down*.

Parker saw it, magnified. He *saw* metal hit metal. He *saw* metal pierce metal. He *saw* window glass blow. He *saw* the tires blow and the car swerve on bare rims.

He *saw* a bullet swarm. It was visibly *black*. He *saw* buckshot—one thick haze.

Parker looked left. His embankment was packed now. Sixty men fired straight *down*. The car fishtailed. The Staties opened up and fired straight at it. The car blew up red.

The Japs piled out and ran. Japs on fire, Japs batting at flames. Black swarms came down on them—bullets, buckshot, slugs. The Japs blew into pieces. He *saw* it, magnified.

They had heads. They had no heads. Their arms and legs disappeared. They vaporized.

Then a pause.

Then echoes and wind.

Then the pause extends.

Then the posse men run *down*.

Parker ran down with them. He stumbled off the embankment and tore for the roadblock. A hundred men converged and just stood there. The Japs were pulp in the dirt.

The Staties walked up. Parker looked at the car. It burned and whooshed black smoke. He noticed debris on the ground. He walked over and looked close.

Wood scraps. A radio tube. Three round metal objects. Pay-telephone slugs.

104

LOS ANGELES | TUESDAY, DECEMBER 23, 1941

2:48 p.m.

Summitry. The Smith-Kwan combine meets the Exley-Patchett boys.

He bagged Lyman's back room. A buffet was laid out. He'd represent the combine. Uncle Ace and Terry Lux would backstop him.

Exley and Patchett would represent themselves. They'd get down to brass tacks and handshakes. A Christmas tea would follow. Beth meets the Red Empress.

He had two lovers. Beth was illicitly bred. She was seventeen. Boston was provincial. She should observe the moral tone of a wartime hot spot.

She met Bette. It was nearly all bad. She remained starstruck nonetheless. Bette's bond gig drained him. His hand still throbbed and shot aches up his arm. He called Bette an hour ago. A coon maid rebuffed him.

He called Terry Lux and got no answer. He wanted Terry here. He was a key backer.

Terry found their cut-Japs play dicey. It was medically improbable and logistically unsound. The eugenics intrigued him. That was as far as it went.

Terry should be here. He said he'd be here. Ace made the arrangements this morning. Terry said he'd call and confirm.

Dudley popped three bennies. Dudley paced the room.

His pins were stacked tight. Mike and Dick were phone-booking Hop Sing boys right now. It sustained the "inside job" charade. The Oceanside snuffs would go unsolved. He just read a Teletype. The posse nailed the Japs outside San Diego. The assumed tile-game killers—*muertos*.

Dudley paced. Dudley chain-smoked. His hand throbbed wicked bad.

Ducks in order. Pins stacked tight. Nine days to New Year's. Let's tie up loose ends.

He talked with Hideo. They discussed Mexico. Hideo said he'd build a frame kit. He'd bring hair and tissue samples and semen slides. He'd bring a range of shell casings.

They'd create a thieves-fall-out scenario. Punks steal Carlos Madrano's cash and "H" and embark on a dope run themselves. Tempers flare. Psychopathy rages. Three deaths result.

Mike had a line on three hopheads. They're Tijuana scum. They boost the stash and hole up. The cash and dope vanish. They shoot barbiturates as a horse substitute. They overdose and die.

He conceived the plan with Hideo. They collaborated on every point. He called Dick Hood and pressed him. Dick agreed to postpone the Ashida family's detention. Dick pledged preferential treatment from that point on.

It was 3:00. The summit was set. Where's Terry Lux?

His hand throbbed. Benzedrine rushed blood to the wound. He poured a double scotch and nursed it. The booze ran the throb to a burn.

Uncle Ace walked in. Preston Exley trailed him. He saw Dudley's bad hand and bumped him. An *abrazo*—that friendly Mex gesture.

"Preston, it's grand to see you. You know Mr. Kwan, of course."

Exley bumped him. "How many free suppers have I bummed off of you, Ace? You've catered half the big events in my life."

Ace said, "Lobster à la Kwan and pork lo mein. That meant 'Inspector Exley is working late.' "

Dudley laughed. A tall man walked in. Pierce Patchett, doubtless. Check his all-black look.

Black suit, black shirt, black tie. *Muy fascista.* The Carlos Madrano look.

Patchett said, "Sergeant Smith, Mr. Kwan. This is some male preserve you've got here."

No handshake. No *abrazo*. Ace sniffed him. Ace Chink-eyed him. What gives with *you*?

Dudley said, "We have momentous plans to discuss, although our partner Terry Lux appears to be missing. I think we—"

Exley squeezed his arm. "We've got a colleague coming, Dud. I think we should wait for him."

Ace Chink-eyed Exley. Patchett built a scotch-rocks. Dudley's hand burned. He felt glass deep in the cuts.

Sammy Rummel walked in. *Some colleague?* Ben Siegel's backup counsel on the Greenie Greenberg snuff.

Rummel dropped his briefcase. Rummel oozed brusque.

Dudley said, "Hello, Sam. It's been too long."

Rummel said, "I'd shake your hand, but left-handed shakes are bad luck."

Ace said, "I know you, Sambo. My friend Lin Chung did your daughter's nose job."

Rummel said, "I know, and not much good came of it. She married a goy cook at Don the Beachcomber's. The food there is dreck, unlike the chow at your slop chute."

Laughs went around. They were forced. Dudley got hackle bumps.

"To briefly summarize, Mr. Kwan, the missing Dr. Lux and I form quite the tidy cartel. We are interested in merging with your tidy cartel, in an effort to expand wartime contingency plans that both factions have conceived independently, but would be well advised to implement as a unified partnership. Mr. Kwan has told you of our plans, and we learned of your plans in a rather roundabout and clandestine way. Forewarned is forearmed, gentlemen. We know about you, and now you've been told about us. We did not create this global conflict, nor have we ordered the mass imprisonment of the local Japanese. That stated, we would be remiss in not capitalizing on it."

Rummel said, "Well said, Dud, if a little flowery for my taste.

We've all come up with some bright ideas, although yours are more legally questionable than ours. I say 'ours,' because I'm a full partner with Mr. Patchett and Mr. Exley, as well as their attorney. Your ideas complement and embellish our ideas, and both factions bring savvy, gravitas, and sound notions to the table. There, that's the windup. The short version? If you want in, you've got in. The pitch? You have to bring in seed capital to make this partnership jell. We're taking ground-floor bids as an advance against potential profits, and the entry-floor bid is four hundred grand, cash, all due upon a handshake agreement. I negotiate for my boys, you bring in your own lawyer. Chop, chop, gentlemen. You're not the only girls on our dance card."

Boom. The ball drops. No backslaps, no winks, no hail-fellow farewells.

Exley walked out. Patchett walked out. Rummel herded them out.

Dudley blinked. The door flew open. The shits dispersed in the grill.

Boom. The ball drops. It's that prohibitive floor.

Ace said, "White cocksuckers. Some cocksucker came in with seed gelt and double-fucked us."

Dudley blinked. His hand throbbed. The grill proper buzzed. Beth and Claire stood at the bar. They found each other. Note their sisterly chat.

Ace waltzed. He seethed and walked off. He pulled out his shrunken head and caressed it. *Sayonara*, my Irish brother.

Dudley popped two bennies. His hand throbbed wicked bad. No deal. They got double-fucked. That double-dealing kike, Rummel. They had a preemptive bid.

Dudley teethed on it. He shut his eyes and talked to the wolf of the moors.

Beth and Claire walked in. They bumped him. It killed his hand and made him roar.

He gathered them close. They stood in his arms. Claire kicked the door shut.

Beth said, "I recognized Miss De Haven from your description and just started blabbing. It was so Boston and so shanty Irish of me."

Dudley smiled. Their blue eyes. Their trim suits. Freckled, both of them.

Claire said, "I've been giving your daughter a primer on men and women, and how the war has the phenomenon skewed. I hope I'm not turning her jaded before she reaches the age of consent."

Beth said, "It's putting you, Miss De Haven and Miss Davis in perspective."

Dudley laughed. "Tell me, dear. You'll be legal next July. Tell me while you're still possessed of some innocence."

Beth jiggled his good hand. "All right. The war's made everything crazy, so men and women are getting crisscrossed and trying to have a good time while their opportunities pan out."

Claire jiggled his good hand. "She's your daughter, love. She's a little moonstruck these days, but she'll be back in Boston with her sisters and schoolwork soon, and that's a perspective in itself."

Dudley touched her hair. "Have you seen Terry Lux, dear? He was due here a moment ago."

Claire said, "He's been weaning me, and he came to the house today. Lin Chung was with him. You know him, don't you? He's a plastic surgeon, and he's been to my parties."

Boom. The ball drops. Well, there it is.

Double cross. Go back to Tuesday, 12/9. Lin Chung cuts Jimmy Namura to look Chink. Terry lied to him. Terry called Jap-to-Chink cuts untenable. Race science. The Eugenic Brotherhood. Terry talked to Lin Chung. They got surgeon-to-surgeon tight. The cut jobs might or might not be feasible. Terry and Chung vowed to work around it and formed their own cartel. They were buying into the Exley cartel. Lin Chung was the floor bid. His own ideas convinced Terry to speed the buy-in process up.

Beth said, "Dad looks abstracted."

Claire said, "He's thinking."

Dudley touched her hair. He should see that Joan of Arc film again. It was playing in Hollywood.

Claire nuzzled his good hand. "Bette was in the *Herald* today. She always makes sure that her good deeds are publicized. She and her husband are hosting a group of soldiers for a late Christmas dinner. I don't think she'll invite you, but you and Beth can join me and a few left-wing friends."

105

LOS ANGELES | TUESDAY, DECEMBER 23, 1941

4:03 p.m.

Who is the white man in the purple sweater?

Ashida poached the USC Law Library. White students fish-eyed him. He worked with a notepad and textbooks. He worked with notes snatched from Bill Parker's desk.

Parker was down in San Diego. He left Dudley's cubicle and rifled Parker's drawers. Parker said he'd pulled a "grand jury play." Parker tried to nail Preston Exley and Pierce Patchett. He probably prepped before the implied proceeding. He might have left notes.

Parker *did* leave notes. Ashida found them and stole them. Parker might have missed something. That notion prompted his theft.

His assumption was pure hubris. He knew *he* missed something. Someone saw something/did something/said something. It would tell him something that would give him answers.

Who is the white man in the—

He missed something. It was like the missing scabbards at The Watanabe House. The Missing Something Gestalt kicked in this morning. Someone said something/did something/saw something. There's a puzzle piece. He can't quite snap it in.

Parker left notes. Parker noted the legal texts he'd studied and flagged them. Ashida studied the books Parker studied. The print was small. He got eyestrain. White kids skunk-eyed him. Who's this goddamn *Jap*?

Ashida ran through Parker's notes. Parker jotted "No. of questions permitted?" and "Question restraints?" That meant this: he couldn't ask all his questions.

Think from that perspective. What did Parker fail to ask Exley and Patchett?

Ashida studied Parker's notes. Ashida tracked the notes to texts. He worked off the notes and his read of Scotty B.'s snitch sheet. He layered in personal knowledge. He plumbed potential questions and got this:

Did Exley and Patchett have foreknowledge of the Pearl Harbor attack? Did it spawn their house/farm buyout and war-profit schemes?

Parker did not ask that question. Parker should have. Back to the Missing Something Gestalt.

Something was biting him. Someone did something. Someone saw something. *SOMEONE SAID SOMETHING.*

Pop.

Snap.

Click.

Gears mesh. Synapses crackle. *Said something* said it. It's a recent memory.

Thursday, December 11th. About 2:00 a.m., Beverly Hills. He's about to head up to Goleta. He sits in Linny's all-night deli with Kay Lake.

Kay said, "I saw Preston Exley, just yesterday. He was leaving an office four blocks from here."

Pop, snap, click. Now go to *this*:

Linny's was on Beverly Drive. Go to the following Monday. He spoke to Saul Lesnick at Claire De Haven's party. Lesnick said his office was at 416 Bedford. Bedford Drive was four blocks from Beverly Drive. Kay said she began her snitch gig with an office visit. Someone said something—yes. That's *two* someones so far. Now, don't forget this:

Someone Saw Something. Someone Did Something. Someone Wrote Something. Wait—there's a *pop, snap, click.*

Ashida went through Parker's notes. Yes—there it is.

Someone Wrote Something. *Parker* Wrote Something. Parker wrote this:

Business addresses. Exley: 6402 Wilshire Boulevard. Patchett: 416 Bedford Drive, Beverly Hills.

Click.

Click.

Click.

Ashida packed up and walked out. White kids eyeballed him. *Hey, Jap—where's your Jap Zero?*

It was 4:53. Storm clouds brewed low and brought dusk early. Ashida got his car and drove to Beverly Hills.

He pulled onto Bedford. He found a curbside slot and got out his tools. 416 was a white mock château.

Three floors. Innocuous. They'll lock the building at 6:00.

Ashida walked over. Early dusk covered him. He felt *un-Jap* invisible. He entered the lobby. He checked the directory.

Saul Lesnick—suite 216. Pierce Patchett—suite 217. *Pop, snap, click.* Confluence and convergence.

He walked up to the second floor and ducked into the men's room. He locked himself in a stall and perched on the toilet. He willed himself to sit tight.

He sat in a crouch. He heard doors slam. He heard footsteps in the men's room. He heard water run and urinals flush.

His legs held.

Someone stepped into the men's room. That someone killed the lights.

It was 6:11 p.m. More doors slammed. No doors slammed. It went quiet and thick dark.

6:21, 6:37, 6:49 p.m., 6:53, 6:58, 7:00.

Do it now.

Ashida stepped off the toilet. He stomped blood back in his legs. He got out his penlight and threw out a beam. Patchett, first. He's the Unknown Someone.

He breezed out of the men's room and walked down the hall. It was deep dark. The carpet hushed his footsteps.

There's 217. It's got a spring-keyhole door lock.

He jiggled a no. 4 pick and breezed in. He bit down on the penlight. He swiveled his head and aimed the beam. He locked himself into the waiting room. He put light on this:

A reception desk, two chairs, one couch. A wall print depicting Mount Fuji. Heedless Patchett. We're at war now. Mount Fuji is Japanese.

Phone records. Rolodex or address book. Financial books. Toss for those things.

The inner-office door stood ajar. Ashida walked in and penlight-strafed. Wall prints depicted geisha girls and snow monkeys. Heedless Patchett, redux.

Heedless Patchett had a large desk. A standing cabinet flanked it. The desk drawers were half-open. The cabinet door was unlocked and cracked a half inch.

Ashida walked back to the waiting room. He sat in the receptionist's chair and rifled the desk.

Nothing was locked. It felt unkosher. The office felt like a front. Pierce Patchett was a crooked "Entrepreneur." Pierce Patchett oozed incompetence.

Ashida beamed the top drawer. He saw pencils, pens, carbon sheets, paper clips, postage stamps, erasers. He shut the top drawer and beamed the middle drawer. He saw the August to December phone bills.

PC Bell envelopes. Note the postmarks. PC Bell sent out partial bills for December. He got *his* bill this morning. It covered his calls up to 12/21. It was a holiday-rush strategy.

He went through the envelopes. August, September, October, November, December. The bills tagged calls from 8/1 to now. He folded out the call lists. He arranged them by month. He started in August and scanned up to now.

He looked for familiar names first.

He saw innocuous names. He saw florists, haberdashers, drugstores and radio-supply stores. He got to the familiar names quick.

Familiar names. Confirming names. But to what end?

Patchett called *Preston Exley.* He called his home and office many times. The calls went back to 8/3/41.

Patchett called *Dr. Saul Lesnick.* He called his home many times. The calls went back to 8/4/41.

Patchett called *Dr. Terry Lux.* He called his home and dry-out farm many times. The calls went back three months only. They began 9/9/41.

Ashida read the bills. He went line by line. He held back the partial December bill and saved it for last. August, September, October, November. Innocuous calls. Calls to *Exley, Lesnick, Lux.* One number kept popping up. It was incongruous. No surnames or business names were logged beside it.

*GL*adstone-4782.

Think now.

It's familiar.

Think now.

Spark that brainstorm. Fuse that lightbulb.

Pop.

Snap.

Click.

Tick, tick, tick. That's no clock. That's your *craaaaaaazy* heartbeat.

*GL*adstone-4782.

There, there, yes—that's it.

The number denoted a pay phone. The booth was on Lincoln Boulevard. It was in Santa Monica. It was near Boeing, Lockheed and Douglas. The Watanabes called that pay phone. Jim Larkin lived near that pay phone. Jim Larkin might have/probably used it. Bill Parker requested records for that pay phone, plus two others. PC Bell was currently backlogged.

Ashida trembled. Sweat rolled into his eyes. His teeth chattered. The penlight dropped.

He picked it up. He wiped his face. He tore into the December bill. Where's *GL*-4782?

It's right there. There's nine calls—December 1, 2, 3. There's six calls December 4 and 5. There's no calls from 12/5 on.

We're up to *12/6/41. The Watanabes are murdered that day.*

Ashida scanned the bill. *Patchett's* calls to *Exley* decrease. *Patchett's* calls to *Lesnick* increase and stop at 12/6/41. *Patchett's* calls to *Lux* run sporadic. They stop at 12/19/41.

Then, we have *this:*

Patchett calls *Lux sixteen times*—December 19, 20, 21.

Confluence, convergence, coincidence. *Craaaaazy* chronology. No proof of anything.

Here's more convergence. It's December 19, 20, 21. Patchett calls Lin Chung, M.D.

Dr. Chung is a plastic surgeon. He met Dr. Chung at Claire De Haven's party. Dr. Chung sparred with Saul Lesnick. The argument pertained to eugenics.

Eugenics. Plastic surgery. Scotty's graph summary. Dudley's plan to cut Japanese to look Chinese. Lin Chung's botched cut on Jimmy Namura. Lin Chung, entrepreneur. A thriving shrunken-head merchant.

Convergence. Confounding, in its—

Ashida caught his breath.

He put the bills back in the envelopes. He put the envelopes back in the drawer. He rifled the other drawers. He saw more desk clutter. He walked to the inner office. He rifled the desk drawers there.

Fancy fountain pens. Stationery. Pornographic playing cards. A box of Sheik prophylactics. A letter opener with embossed swastikas.

A pervert trove. Some new *eeeeeeverything* confirmed. No hard evidence.

Ashida shut the drawers and faced the standing cabinet. The door was cracked. He popped it wide and beamed in.

Heedless Patchett—just like that.

A shortwave radio. A leather-bound ledger. It matched the Watanabes' ledger—*just like that.*

Ashida trembled. The penlight beam swerved. He hit the radio dials and tried to raise a signal. No sound issued. No bands lit up.

He followed the cord to a wall hitch. The radio was plugged in, the radio was dead.

He saw a clipped paper sheaf. It was just-like-that there on a shelf.

He grabbed it and skimmed it. It was a geologist's report.

It detailed soil components. It charted the East Valley, South Pasadena, Glassell Park and Highland Park. It confirmed the land grab. It echoed Parker's grand jury play.

Ashida put the pages back. Ashida picked up the ledger and leafed through it. All the pages were blank.

A folded sheet dropped out. He unfolded it and beamed his penlight. It was a mad child's map.

The West Coast, pencil-sketched. Sharks and submarines along the wave line. The sharks scream "Kill the Jews!" The speech balloons are twice their size.

Swastikas dot the waters. They're haphazardly scrawled. There's X marks along the coast. Submarines prowl. Note their rising suns.

The drawing is one-dimensional/stick-figure quality. Heedless Patchett. *Craaaazy* Patchett now.

There's inland L.A. County. There's jotted numbers and X marks. There's small subs up and down the coast. There's a giant shark swimming in Mexican waters.

He's screaming "Kill the Jews!" A submarine patrols beside him. The hull is scrawled with rising suns and dollar signs. It's headed for the Colonet Inlet.

Ashida caught something. Ashida went *Not so fast.*

Yes, it's madness. But I see something. It signifies design.

The numbers. They're megahertz and kilohertz listings. The X marks denote real locations. The small subs note coastal inlets.

That's the properly sketched and proportioned L.A. County. Now, look at *this:*

Northeast L.A. was mapped in detail. An X mark notes the Watanabe house. Santa Monica and Malibu are mapped in detail. There's an X mark near the Terry Lux nut farm.

There's an X mark by the Lincoln Boulevard pay phones. The little sub above Santa Barbara? It denotes the Goleta attack.

Ashida popped sweat. It dripped on the map. He wiped his eyes and pressed the map against the wall.

He beamed down for a close-up. He scanned north/south and east/west. He saw that sub drawn by the Colonet Inlet. The papers predicted Baja sub raids. *Confluence.* Call-Me-Jack told Dudley to scout the area. Dudley said he'd laughed. The scout run buttressed their "Mexican mission."

Here—double X mark. *Here*—the San Gabriel hills. *Here*—a possible *convergence.* The escapees hid *here*—and then broke for *Mexico.*

Ashida wiped his hands on his pant legs. He refolded the map. He tucked it back in the ledger and scanned the room.

He rechecked the room. He triple-checked the room. He walked into the waiting room and triple-checked it.

Intact? Yes.

He cracked the hallway door and looked out. *Safe? Yes.* All dark at 8:14.

He stepped out of Mad Patchett's office. He hugged the hallway wall. He toed the door shut and got out his no. 4 pick.

He wheeled and faced Doc Lesnick's door. He put light on the knob. Butterfingers—he dropped the pick.

He retrieved it. Butterfingers—he dropped it again. He retrieved it. He bit down on the penlight and cracked a tooth. He held the pick two-handed and stabbed the keyhole.

Eight stabs hit the slot. He wiped his hands and slid the tumblers. *Twelve* swipes popped the door.

Vertigo.

He stepped inside and shut the door. He caught some equilibrium. He swiveled his head and light-swept the room. *This* office looked professional. *This* office was well furnished. *This* office *did not* look like a pimp-fascist's front.

A sofa. A magazine rack. Bookshelves and filing cabinets. The receptionist's desk. The inner-office door—reinforced-steel locks.

He jiggled the cabinet doors. They were all locked. He jiggled the desk drawers. They were all locked. He checked the inner-office door. It was keyhole-locked tight.

Doc Lesnick was careful. His locks were pickproof. This office was tossproof.

Ashida sat on the couch. He caught his breath. He penlight-strafed the room. The shelf books were all Marx and Freud.

He saw four books on the desk. He got up and scanned the spines.

Medical books. *Nazi* medical books. Eugenics texts. He knew some German. He skimmed the books and got the gist.

Nazi surgical guides. Race science. "Reconstructive surgery." Cut Slavs to look Aryan.

A note, tucked below the books.

"Lynn—I know it's rather ghastly, but would you pls. messenger these to Dr. Chung? It's about a dialogue we've been having."

Pop.

Snap.

Click.

Ashida walked out of the office. He shut off his penlight and moved downstairs in the dark. The street door had a quaint snap-in-place lock. He walked out and click-snapped it shut.

It was 9:08. He walked to his car. The cool air burned his lungs and froze his sweat.

He drove through Beverly Hills and out Coldwater Canyon. He hit the Valley. He doubled back to Malibu. He had the map memorized. The X marks were surely shortwave-radio spots.

He had the perspectives memorized. He could calibrate the X's to near-exact spots.

He drove out to the coast road. He calibrated. Yes—Pacific Sanitarium is a shortwave-radio spot.

Convergence. Terry Lux and Pierce Patchett are shortwave-radio chums.

The coast road ran straight to Santa Monica. He should avoid it. Army spotters clogged the beachfront. He was an out-at-night Jap.

He doubled back inland and hit Lincoln Boulevard. He drove by the three pay phones. Yes—the booths matched X-marked shortwave-radio spots.

Someone close by had a shortwave radio. He was Pierce Patchett's radio chum.

Ashida U-turned and drove east. He made good time. He caught the Arroyo Seco above Chinatown. He drove two miles north. He hit the Watanabe house.

It matched the broadcast map. The certainty and fatality amazed him. *The Watanabes were Pierce Patchett's shortwave-radio chums.*

One X-marked spot remained. It was double-X-marked. It would confirm or refute his approximations.

He drove to a pay phone first. He checked the central directory. He found a home/office address for Lin Chung, M.D. The doctor lived at 282 Ord. It was four blocks from Kwan's Chinese Pagoda.

Ashida hooked back to the parkway. He got off and cut east through San Marino. The double X mark clocked the Monrovia hills. Thad Brown should still be there. The campsite was one big search scene.

He caught an access road to the foothills. He climbed straight up in low gear. He saw light way ahead. It had to be cop arc-light glow.

The glow went bright bright. He swooped over a hill and saw the campsite. There's Thad. There's cops bagging evidence.

Ashida parked and got out. Thad saw him and waved. Ashida waved back. Two cops boxed a busted-up radio.

Pierce Patchett was tied to the escaped Japanese. They were all shortwave-radio pals.

A hubbub drifted over. The posse got the Japs at Blood Alley! They were crashing out to Mexico!

Yes, they were. Here's why. They had a hot date with a submarine. Call it a saboteur's landing. See that X mark on that Nazi child's map? It denotes a cove in Baja, Mexico.

Thad doffed his hat and waved. Ashida waved back. Thad looked happy.

The posse got the Japs. It cleared the Kwan's job. The Werewolf cleared the Watanabe caper.

It was pushing midnight. Ashida drove to Chinatown. He cruised by Kwan's. The parking lot was cop-free. The search ropes were down. The death sled was gone.

Case cleared. The posse got the Japs at Blood Alley.

Ashida drove to 282 Ord. The front windows glowed. Lin Chung was a night owl. Ashida parked and ran a sit-tight stakeout.

Lin Chung lived medicine. His front room was wallpapered with anatomy charts. Maxillofacial charts. Occipital charts. Skin-flaps-pulled-all-the-way-back charts.

Ashida stared at the windows. Inside lights beamed. Lin Chung and Saul Lesnick appeared.

It did not surprise him. Nothing surprised him. The war is sixteen days old. The world is dark and flat. Cars are submarines.

Lin Chung and Saul Lesnick walked chart to chart. They argued and stabbed pointers. Lesnick paced the room. Ashida clocked his small feet. It did not surprise him. Nothing surprised him.

They strutted and argued all night. They pounded the charts and smoked ten million cigarettes. Ashida watched them. Contentious pals. The shrunken-head-peddling Chinaman and left-wing Jew.

Land grabs, plastic surgery, blood libel. Rogue cops, sub attacks, a lynch-mob massacre. Pay phones. A white man in a purple sweater. Secret radios and feigned seppuku. The haughty Left and the bellicose Right. A grand alliance of war profiteers.

He'll tell it all to Dudley Smith or to William H. Parker. He'll tell no one if it suits his needs. He has uncovered the real Fifth Column. It is not what anyone thinks.

December 24, 1941

106

KAY LAKE'S DIARY

LOS ANGELES | WEDNESDAY, DECEMBER 24, 1941

9:16 a.m.

I was bored. I "possessed stunning artistry, but no character or conviction." I was tired of looking at my new face. My leftist friends refused to talk to me. Hideo Ashida wasn't answering his telephone. There were no men I could sleep with out of early-wartime ennui. Elmer and Brenda were out in the vapors of police work and prostitution. Lee was back from "Blood Alley" and was working the overflow of Japanese prisoners at the Lincoln Heights jail. The first showing of *The Passion of Joan of Arc* was scheduled for 11:00 a.m. I kept hearing Claire's words and kept thinking of Dudley Smith. I kept hearing my own words: *do everything or do nothing*. I smoked and paced the house. I was coming out of my skin.

The house itself drove me crazy. Its perfection affirmed my shallow concerns. I thought of Scotty and reread his letter. I read the paper, three times. Wake Island fell to the Japs. The escaped Japs were mowed down in San Diego County. A Filipino man heard a song called "Johnny the Jap Killer" on the radio and took it as a sign from God. He promptly left his house, found a Japanese man and stabbed him to death. The man was really Chinese.

I was bored. Boredom is a common state for shallow folks like me. We become vexed and capitulate to antic notions. I looked up "Bleichert, Dwight W." in the central directory and called the number just to hear Bucky's voice. His "Hello?" was slightly harried and mid-range baritone. I hung up the phone, giggling. I felt ridiculous.

Christmas Eve was tonight. I had no plans and had received no invitations. There was no Christmas tree surrounded by wrapped gifts at the Blanchard-Lake home. My only plan was to spin the late Beethoven quartets and conjure the winter-locked prairie.

I went driving. I looked out at everything and engaged the act of memorization. I glimpsed odd people. Yes, I will remember him. Yes, I'll remember her. You don't know me and don't know that I have anointed you. I will feel less alone as I recall your face twenty years from now.

I drove east to Belmont High; I envisioned Bucky and Hideo on the playing field and Jack Webb scrounging votes for class president. A wino weaved by me on the sidewalk. I got out of the car and handed him five dollars. He did a gleeful dance step and embarrassed me. I got back in the car and drove to Hollywood.

The theater was just opening up; I bought my ticket and settled into a balcony seat. I saw a few people sitting below me: vagabond artistes with no place to go the day before Christmas.

The movie began. I slouched into my seat and slipped off my shoes. The film stock was grainy and flecked; the music ran out of line with the images. I watched Renée Falconetti as Joan of Arc and saw her concurrently as Claire Katherine De Haven. Claire as Joan spoke to me and castigated me for my inaction. I felt her fury. Devout Joan, plaintive Joan, Joan roused to quixotic rage. My options were do everything or do nothing. My stunning artistry trumped my weak character and lack of conviction.

I ran out of the theater. I dashed through the lobby, half-blind with tears. A tall man in a tweed suit brushed by me. I got a momentary sense that it was Dudley Smith, but discarded that delirious notion. It was raining. The weather gave me the option to run somewhere and hide in plain sight. I got my car and drove to Little Tokyo. It was just the right distance away. There was time to concentrate on the wet streets and compose myself.

The Friendly Moon Teahouse provided a destination. It was a venerable J-town spot, and had become a cop's hangout during the first two weeks of the roundups. That was arbitrary and grossly unfair—but the owner and all of his people had been spared incarceration. Why? The rice cakes were legendary, and the owner let the cops bring in jugs.

Little Tokyo was preholiday still; Lee told me that the Feds were on hiatus until the big roundup commenced after New Year's.

The PD's Alien Squad had been yanked and put on hold for 1/2/42 sweeps.

February '42 loomed as brutal. The "mass evacuation" and transport to the camps, the FBI's phone-tap probe on the PD. This storm. All the people I knew would be tossed through it.

I parked at the curb and ducked rain into the café; I hung my coat on the rack by the door and heard someone say "Miss Lake." I turned and saw Ward Littell, sitting at a window table. He had a pot of tea and a plate of rice cakes in front of him; he motioned toward an empty chair.

I walked over and sat down. Littell said, "I'm taking a break from Mariko Ashida."

I said, "I know she's difficult. Hideo's told me stories."

Littell poured me tea. "I'm an orphanage boy. I take family where I can get it."

"I've forgotten what my own family looks like."

"They probably look like you, before that new nose of yours."

I laughed and lit a cigarette. "You were very considerate to Claire and me at the booking. This is a good opportunity for me to thank you, so I will."

Littell said, "You and Dot Rothstein are the talk of the L.A. Office, along with Dudley Smith, Bill Parker and whatever sort of devil's deal they cut to get you and the others released."

He was fishing for gossip. I sidestepped him with a query.

"You'll be out of your cushy assignment soon. The Ashidas will be detained, and I'm wondering how that will sit with you."

"Not so soon for the Ashidas, I'm happy to say. Dudley Smith pulled strings and got them yanked from the arrest-and-detain list. They'll be escorted to a private train compartment at the last second."

I smiled. "Hideo's *valuable*. Powerful men are indebted to him."

Littell smiled. A decorous silence passed. I thought of Dudley Smith, ubiquitous. I pictured papal conclaves, 1514. It's the time of the Augsburg Confession. Luther is poised at Wittenberg and must be dealt with. The Dudster is dispatched on horseback. Agreements are sealed and heads secretly roll.

"What do you *know* about Dudley Smith, Mr. Littell?"

"Everything and nothing. He rigs evidence routinely, or only as a desperate last measure. He does favors for people. He kills people or doesn't kill people. The Watanabe case is either fishy or kosher, depending on who you talk to. It doesn't matter either way, because the grand jury just handed down a true bill."

I crushed my cigarette. "And that's all you know?"

Littell smiled and twirled his teacup. "There's the rumor that he's sleeping with Bette Davis. Which I choose not to believe, because I've always enjoyed Miss Davis' work."

I laughed. A woman at the counter called out. "Your office, Mr. Littell."

Littell got up and took the call; I sipped tea and ate the two remaining rice cakes. Littell came back, holding his raincoat and hat.

He said, "I should be going. I'm due in court."

I stood up and offered my hand. "Merry Christmas, Mr. Littell. And thank you. You were gracious beyond the occasion."

"Take care of yourself, Miss Lake. And try to be careful."

I smiled. Littell put on his coat and hat and walked into the rain. I sat at the table and watched the clouds break. I thought of Scotty and Christmas dinner at boot camp. I squeezed my Saint Chris medal.

The sun appeared. I walked outside and dawdled in front of the store next door. It was more than a curio shop and less than a gallery. Beautiful tapestries were displayed in the window, along with a shelf of painted Kabuki masks.

The faces were artfully rendered, paint on sculpted wood. The features were indistinguishable—except one.

I caught the resemblance immediately. It was a martyr's mask. It commemorated a ravaged lost soul. The mask derived from theatrical tradition. It purportedly summoned just vengeance and eased the ravaged-soul bearer to rest.

The painted features depicted Goro Shigeta. He was shot and killed in a phone booth, about ten days ago. I'd seen his picture in the papers. The case remained unsolved.

I walked in and bought the mask. It cost thirty-two dollars. The cash-register girl disapproved of the purchase. It was quite plain to me.

107

LOS ANGELES | WEDNESDAY, DECEMBER 24, 1941

12:14 p.m.

The line ran down to the sidewalk. The recruiters wore Santa Claus hats. Seventeen days since Pearl Harbor. A still-brisk enlistment trade.

The desks were stationed inside now. Regional offices smoothed out the Fed Building flow. The line crawled. Parker was two hours in.

He wore civilian clothes. He brought his birth certificate. He was playing a long shot. The war spawned paperwork chaos. Call-Me-Jack's enlistment holds might have been misplaced.

The line inched up. He still smelled Blood Alley. Wake Island couldn't be any worse.

A women's line flanked the men's line. It was one-tenth as long. He had a sideways view.

Kay Lake stood three from the end. She couldn't see him.

He was running. She was running. War enticed runners. A Filipino man stabbed a Chinese man last night. He had an alibi: "I thought he was a Jap."

Parker hit the desk. He flashed his badge and birth certificate. The recruiter checked his *P*-flagged papers.

He looked up at Parker. He shook his head.

"I'm sorry, sir. A hold's been filed on you. You've been declared 'civilian-essential.' "

Parker stepped out of line. He looked at the women's desk. Miss Lake stood there.

A recruiter said something. It was an easy read. The man said, "No, ma'am."

Katherine, the foolish huntress. Our purpose here eludes me.

108

LOS ANGELES | WEDNESDAY, DECEMBER 24, 1941

12:29 p.m.

Dudley cut through Mandeville Canyon. His hand throbbed and sent bolts up his arm. He wore the gray tweed with a Christmas boutonniere.

Bette through tonight. Mexico tomorrow. Rob and kill. Return for Christmas supper. Claire was serving braised goose.

Bette called impromptu and invited him over. She caught him leaving for the Joan of Arc film. He thought he saw Kay Lake in the lobby. It was eerie.

The movie was eerie. It was a crib sheet on Claire. He gleaned insight on her martyrdom. He vowed to teach her spontaneous joy.

Dudley drove one-handed. He chain-smoked to stifle the pain. His lads were meeting him outside Chez Bette, tomorrow. His trunk was ordnance-packed.

He pulled into the driveway and primped one-handed. Necktie, collar, starched cuffs pulled taut. He brought a white rose bouquet. I surrender, dear.

He ran across the lawn and rang the bell. The bolts hit his arm and his neck.

Bette opened the door. She wore riding breeches and boots. Dudley embraced her. She pulled back. One knee blocked the doorway.

His hand throbbed. She snatched the bouquet and threw it on the floor.

"We have to end this, Dudley. It's gotten away from us. I know it's Christmas, but—"

Bolts.

His hand throbbed, his arm throbbed, his knees throbbed the worst. He pitched forward. The sky fell. He saw Jesus Christ and Bette Davis, upside down.

1:12 p.m.

Upside down, right-side up. A bouncing Airedale and Ruth Mildred. A needle in his arm.

That warm-blanket rush. It wasn't opium and Kwan's basement. He was on the bed he fucked Bette on before she went cruel.

Ireland. That convent nun. Put your mouth here, boy. Another needle jab. A rocket-ship ride through the Bible. The Airedale lays down with the lion and the lamb.

A black box. A confessional. Monsignor Joe Hayes and cascades of his sin.

The rocket ship, in orbit. Ruth Mildred, with a stethoscope. Bette says, "The goddamn *inconvenience.*" Ruth Mildred says, "His fever's down. He's one tough mick."

Bette. Quite the fashion show. Succubus/equestrienne/nun. She whips him with a riding crop. Dominatrix, equestrienne.

Don't hit me.

Don't hit me.

A needle stab. Hush, now. You've sweated through the sheets. Ace and the tunnels. Race science and the bidding floor. Bette says, "*Kill a Jap for me.*"

Goro Shigeta's face blows up. Bette's holding a knife now. She's on leave from heaven or standing by the bed.

Ruth Mildred, with sponges. Bette, with her riding crop. "The goddamn *inconvenience.* I'd *invited* people. It's Christmas Eve."

I'm sorry.

Don't hit me.

I'm sorry.

Don't hit me.

Ruth Mildred says, "Hush, Dud. This ain't confession. Don't give up the world."

"Goddamn him, Ruthie. I had *plans.* The fucking *inconvenience.*"

Don't hit me. Don't hit me. Put your mouth here, son.

The rocket ship parked in the black box. The Airedale jumped on the bed. They discussed police work and cat hunting. The dog said he bit Bette's husband. It feels good to bite humans. You should try it.

The black box compressed. Joe Hayes said, "*Te absolvo.*" Claire said, "*It's not her, it's me.*"

8:00 a.m.

Bells rang. The rocket ship vanished. The black box dissolved to daylight.

The Airedale slept beside him. Bette pinned a note to the headboard.

"I went to a friend's. It's over. You inconvenienced me."

Ruth Mildred slept in two chairs pulled together. A bag and feeder tube were stuck to his arm. He pulled the needle out.

He was naked. His hand was freshly bandaged. The pain was gone.

Church bells. Christmas Day. *Dudley Liam Smith—you took a spill.*

He kissed the Airedale. He got up and stayed up. He was light-headed. He was hungry. He was swervy. He used chair backs as handholds and walked to the window. He looked out and down.

There's Mike and Dick. There's Hideo. They're standing by his car. They're Christmas fresh-scrubbed.

Ruth Mildred snored. She clutched a vial of anti-bug pills. He pried it loose and popped three. Ruthie snored on.

Dudley walked to the bathroom. He shaved and showered. He combed his hair and toweled off. He looked around the bedroom.

They'd laundered his clothes. His holster was hooked on a chair. He got dressed and felt his body cleave in strong.

He sent up a prayer for the Airedale. He snatched the pills and kissed Ruthie. The grand beast and lezzie snored on.

He walked downstairs and outside. The boys greeted him. Dick Carlisle was misty-eyed. Young Hideo lugged a briefcase. Mike Breuning was sprinkled with doughnut crumbs.

"Miss Davis fed us. She said you might be out for a while."

Dudley said, "She's good to common folk. They make her feel authentic. She covets their approval in small doses."

Carlisle got the back door. Dudley yawned and tossed Breuning the keys. Ashida got in the back. Dudley sat beside him.

Ashida said, "I've got a lead on that rogue sub in Baja. I think I know where it might be mooring. I'll explain later on."

Dudley winked. Hideo blushed. Breuning pulled out. Dudley yawned and shut his eyes.

He held his bad hand on his lap. He counted Claire's freckles and gave up at eighty. He walked through their rob-and-kill, Christmas '41.

The border crossings were cake. The Staties ran light Christmas shifts. Captain Carlos wouldn't know they were there.

He visited the clinic. Tojo Tom snitched the cache convincingly. They'd kill the guards at their mid-shift. It gave them six hours to snuff the patsies and plant the evidence. They couldn't clip them before they clipped the guards. They had to plant some bootjacked heroin at the death scene.

He was Spanish-fluent. He'd stiff a snitch call to the Statie HQ. *Hola, hombres*—big ruckus on Calle Calderón. The Staties would discover dead men and *some* stolen "H." It would coincide with the dead guards found at their end of shift.

An alarm would sound *muy explosivo*. Where's the *dinero*? Where's the rest of the "H"? The Staties would surmise a dope catastrophe or an obfuscated heist. They would not surmise American cops on a sub-spotting hunt.

Dudley shut his eyes. Dudley dozed. Dudley opened his eyes in T.J.

Feliz Navidad. Próspero año y felicidad.

Child beggars. Baby rodent swarms. They hawked religious medals and mugged for chump change. Rancid niteclubs. The Blue Fox, El Perro Blanco, El Gato Rojo.

Donkey-show fronts. Mex Statie–run. The proprietors Mickey Finn'd white swells and robbed them. Car-upholstery shops. Artisans fashioned seat covers and stuffed them with horseshit. Chancre-sored whores. On-leave sailors. He-shes in bullfighter garb.

Avenida Revolución. Street cops peddling nativity scenes. Prison inmates built them. They were made from matchbooks and ice-cream-bar sticks.

Dudley lit a cigarette and popped three anti-bug pills. Carlisle turned around. *¿Qué pasa, jefe?*

Dudley said, "Go right at the corner. Calle Calderón. Slow down by 229. Our patsies live there."

Carlisle looked at Ashida. *¿Es kosher, jefe?* Breuning shushed him. *Jefe* knows his shit.

They made the turn. Breuning slowed down. There's the address. It's a tin-roof shack up on crushed-beer-can stilts.

"We'll find them inside. Their PD file portrayed them as shut-ins. They make do with injected sedatives if there's no white horse to be had. I'm sure we'll find them in and conveniently docile."

Breuning said, "We weren't flagged at the border. Nobody knows we're here."

Carlisle said, "Call-Me-Jack knows. We're on that crazy sub hunt, remember? Jack's tight with Captain Carlos. He'll tell him, 'What a coincidence. The Dudster was down in Baja when your shit hit the fan.' "

Dudley shook his head. "Carlos won't tell Jack. He doesn't know that Carlos pushes white horse. Carlos won't reveal the thefts to him."

Breuning shook his head. "The forensic part of this worries me. The Staties send their evidence to a lab in Juárez. They've got all this up-to-date gear."

"Yes, lad. And we've got Dr. Hideo Ashida, which more than compensates."

There—Hideo swoons.

Breuning said, "I wish we'd prescouted this deal. Yeah, I did a good file scout on them, but it was a Statie loaner file, and who knows how up-to-date it was?"

Carlisle said, "They're hopheads. They never do anything but shoot hop and die. You didn't *requisition* the file, so nobody can trace you to it. Don't go fucking cuntish on Christmas Day."

Breuning flipped Carlisle off. They cut through T.J. They hit the coast road. Note the *baaaaaad* sub fear.

Mex Statie spotters. Sandbags and searchlights. Shoreline L.A., replicated. Blackshirts on beach patrol.

Dudley got out his map. He drew it from Tojo Tom's description. Tojo Tom ran him through it three times.

Pass Ensenada. Go inland at San Vicente. Go four miles. Take the bisecting road right. There's scrub brush for cover. Go one mile. There's an open cave.

There'll be three Staties. They work in twelve-hour shifts. There's two safes. One holds the *dinero*, one holds the "H."

The Staties know the combinations. They're *hombres muy feos.* They might not talk.

If so, kill them. If so, know this:

Carlos has four vials of nitro stashed. Pace off twelve yards, right. It's in a lead-lined strongbox, under a bush.

Dudley studied the map. Ashida hugged his briefcase. The boy was staunch in the manner of repressed Nipponese. He'd acquit himself bravely.

They passed Ensenada. Tile roofs and tin roofs. Abandoned-car settlements. Seaside docks and land-side *casitas*.

He saw it. Flanking movements and shotguns. Aim for their legs. They slip into shock and forfeit the combinations.

The sign. SAN VICENTE: 10 KI.

Breuning turned inland. Dudley brain-clocked the four miles. He flexed his good hand. He could shoot left-handed. Precise aim didn't count. The pellets dispersed.

Breuning turned right. He dropped into low gear. The throttle noise decreased.

They crawled. Breuning eyed the odometer. The dashboard numbers clicked. Breuning braked and stopped at .8.

Scrub mounds flanked the roadway. The road ran downhill and dipped left. The cave should be just beyond.

Dudley said, "Please wait here, Hideo."

Ashida nodded. Breuning and Carlisle got out and opened the trunk. Dudley joined them. A breeze blew their way. Loose scrub scraped the road.

It was too quiet. Something was *wrong*. They all caught it. Field hounds—both his lads.

Dudley said, "There should be voices. They can't all be sleeping."

Breuning said, "You can't get Mex cops to shut up."

Carlisle said, "Especially if they're bored and just standing around."

Dudley passed him the binoculars. Carlisle climbed on the hood of the car and looked downward left. Breuning got out the shotguns.

Carlisle climbed down. "No Staties. You've got the mouth of the cave and the two safes, right there. There's nobody around. I couldn't quite tell, but it looks like the safe doors are half-open."

Dudley pointed into the scrub. We come in diagonal. We draw blind fire or no fire.

They waded in. Dudley took the lead. The scrub dragged against them. They held their shotguns at port arms.

Dudley saw the cave and the safes. He saw footprints leading away. He triggered a round in the air.

It was loud. It drew no response. He counted ten seconds of *nada*.

He ran down. Breuning and Carlisle ran behind him. They pushed out of the scrub and into the cave.

The safe doors *were* half-open. There was *nothing* inside.

Dudley stepped outside and scanned all four directions. They were ambush-prone and wide open.

Breuning said, "Huey."

Carlisle said, "The Nazi fuck snitched us."

Dudley said, "I don't think so. I think he might have let Tojo Tom make a phone call, which would account for the cleaned-out safes."

Breuning said, "Then how come we're not dead? We're sitting ducks here."

Dudley said, "I'm too valuable to Carlos, lad. He wouldn't kill me. He'd call me in L.A. and politely tell me to call it off."

Breuning said, "Well, there's always Christmas in L.A."

Carlisle said, "And there's the nitro. My kid and I could sure have fun with that."

Dudley walked to the bush. It was exactly twelve paces. He saw the strongbox and grabbed it. It was lead-lined and a foot square. It was a tough one-hand scoop.

Breuning walked over and grabbed it. Carlisle jammed up. They lugged the box back to the car.

Ashida held the same pose. He hugged his briefcase and stared straight ahead.

They locked the shotguns and nitro in the trunk. Dudley got in the backseat. Ashida went *So?*

Dudley said, "The Staties were tipped. We'll need to determine if we were informed upon. We got a box full of nitroglycerin for our troubles."

Ashida said, "We should detonate it before we go back to L.A. It travels poorly. We shouldn't take the risk of a sudden explosion."

Dudley winked. Ashida blushed. Breuning and Carlisle piled in. They cut back to the coast road and hauled north.

Sub spotters lined the bluffs. They manned movie spotlights and scanned with binoculars. Breuning drove *rápidamente*. Dudley saw a cantina up ahead.

No name, tin roof, mismatched chairs out front. He tapped Breuning and pointed over. Breuning pulled up.

Dudley got out and walked in. It was a drunk tank. *Borrachos* slugged mescal from the bottle and fought over floating worms. The place connoted visions and night sweats.

Dudley braced the gent in the apron. He appeared lucid and in charge.

"Un teléfono y una oficina privada para llamar a Estados Unidos, por favor, señor. Pagaré sesenta dólares norteamericanos por este privilegio."

The man pointed to a door. Dudley greased him and ambled over. The office was ten by ten. The walls were lined with mescal jugs. Two hundred worms swirled in toxic sludge.

A desk, a chair, a telephone. When in Rome—

Dudley grabbed the phone and roused an operator. His brogue Spanish delighted her. He uncapped a jug and swirled brew. The worm floated up. He bit it in two and ate the top half.

"Los Ángeles, AX-catedral-2921, por favor. Y llamo a cobro revertido. Su nombre es Hubert Cressmeyer. Mi nombre es Dudley Smith."

The operator *sí, sí*'d him. The call crackled and went through. A nurse came on the line. Dudley did the collect-call shtick bilingual. The operator signed off.

The nurse seemed flustered. Dudley slugged mescal and nibbled the worm. *Get Huey now, darling. His Uncle Dud requires him.*

The nurse flustered off. The crackled line held. Dudley swigged mescal and noshed the worm whole. He felt volcano heat. The shit ran 180 proof.

Huey came on the line. He whined and whimpered. Dudley cut him off.

"You fucked up, lad. You let Tojo Tom call Mexico."

Huey simpered and whimpered. Huey stuttered and stammered. Huey was shit-your-pants scared.

"He didn't make no phone calls, Uncle Dud. This dorm lezzie snuck in and cut him loose this morning."

Dudley put the phone down. Huey long-distance boo-hoo'd.

They'll wait at the border. They'll put roadblocks up. You should have been warned off and escorted off by—

Blackshirts kicked the door in. They wore jackboots. They had little Hitler toothbrush—

1:49 p.m.

His hand throbbed. It woke him up. Steel ratchets cut into his wrists.

He was cuffed to a chair. The chair was floor-bolted. He made the room.

It was twelve by twelve. It was outré by all sweat-room standards. One table, two chairs. Wall outlets for ball-clamp electrodes. A cutlery rack. Bloodsucking scorpions, caged.

Carlos Madrano stood over him. He wore a Mussolini ensemble with an FDR cape.

Dudley said, "Tojo Tom called you."

Carlos waved his cigarette holder. It was pure FDR.

"Yes, he did. But his call would have only mandated a warning to you. 'My dear friend, please do not steal my money and heroin.' It was the other telephone call that troubled me."

Dudley flexed his arms. Carlos uncuffed him and fed him a cigarette.

"Tell me about that call. Was it Patchett or Exley? Were they concerned that I was attempting to buy into endeavors that tangentially concern you?"

Carlos tipped ash on the table. Mike Breuning screamed next door.

"Sam Rummel called. He said Bill Parker pulled something, and that he sensed you in the margins. It had to do with my farmworker endeavors and your Watanabe case. He said he had never seen Parker so fixated, and now I see that you've succumbed to quite the unprofessional lapse."

Dudley rubbed his wrists. His hands throbbed. His head throbbed. 180-proof booze and toxic worms.

"State the terms of my release and the release of my men."

"You will be released under any and all terms. You will see to it that your Army Intelligence posting is stamped 'Mexico,' and you will work with me to thwart Axis sabotage, despite our Axis sympathies. A large sum of money will secure the release of your men. You may not call Ace Kwan for a quick handout. I am determined to keep word of your mission contained."

The sweat room featured side windows. Dudley got up and peeped them. He saw Mike Breuning to the left, Hideo to the right.

Two spics worked over Mike. They rubber-hosed him and

electrode-clamped his ears. Hideo sat uncuffed. Scorpions crawled near his chair. Hideo sat prim-still.

He glanced up at the window. He saw Dudley. He smiled and drew a dollar sign in the air.

Dudley said, "Carlos, I would advise you to talk to Dr. Ashida. I think he may have something to tell you."

2:16 p.m.

He dozed in his chair. They left him his penicillin and fed him *arroz con pollo* and beer. His hand throbbed. His head throbbed. He was dead-man shot-to-shit.

He dozed and stirred. He counted the days since Pearl Harbor and the days to New Year's. He counted Claire's freckles. He dozed/stirred, dozed/stirred.

He checked Mike B.'s window. Mike was gone. He checked Hideo's window. Hideo was gone. The floor was smeared with scorpion pulp. The fuckers had been stomped to bug juice.

His hand quit throbbing. He pissed in a hole in the floor.

He dozed. He woke up and smoked cigarettes. He saw a note slip on the floor.

He got up and read it. He recognized Hideo's print.

"I tried something. It has to do with that sub I mentioned to you. Captain Madrano is in so far."

Dudley smiled. Dudley counted Claire's freckles. Dudley dozed in his bolted-down chair.

9:29 a.m.

The door lock clanged. Dudley went for his gun and got no gun. Hideo walked in. Insect pulp covered his shoes.

"I convinced Madrano to post a dozen men at the Colonet Inlet. It paid off. They snared a submarine."

"And how did you divine this mooring?"

"I saw a crazy map in Pierce Patchett's office. It was doodled with submarines covered in dollar signs. It reminded me of your graph."

Dudley smiled. He heard rain outside. Four *fascistas* stood behind Hideo.

"And your current assignment, lad?"

"We toss the sub. I interrogate the crew."

Dudley grabbed his suit coat. The Blackshirts hustled them outside. Two Caddy sedans idled by the barracks. They were tourist confiscations. Spic cops loved Jew canoes.

The sleds featured suicide doors and double backseats. The Blackshirts shoved them in. Breuning and Carlisle sat in the back.

They were sallow. They'd been tortured. Their necks were clamp-burned.

The sleds pulled out. Dudley made the slit-throat sign and mouthed "Madrano."

Mike and Dick grinned. The Caddy hit the coast road, north. The rain was bad. The Statie sleds crawled *slooooow*.

Black clouds hung low. The sun was off in deep nowhere. Dudley saw arc-light burn—up ahead/10:00 high.

A beach-bluff encampment. A search scene. Blackshirts and captured Japs. Pup tents to thwart the rain.

The sleds pulled onto a bluff. Ten arc lights were up. Twenty Staties loitered. They wore black slickers over their black shirts.

Dudley got out first. He pushed through the Staties and entered the near tent. Captain Carlos sat in a deck chair. Six Japs were shackle-chained, facedown in the dirt.

They wore water-soaked uniforms. They'd been manhandled and kicked to shit. Their mouths were taped shut.

Carlos said, "Dr. Ashida has promised me money. I hope he's right. His tips have proven credible so far."

10:51 a.m.

The sub was moored on hard sand up against rocks. Carlos ceded the toss to Dudley and Hideo. They boarded the fucking thing and ducked belowdecks. Five Staties stood outside the hatch.

It was toss and find or toss and die. It hedged on Patchett's nutty hieroglyphics.

They tossed. It was Hideo's show. The sub was all screw plates, gauge panels, wall instruments. Hideo knew everything mechanical. Hideo knew the needle-in-a-haystack and wild-goose concepts and the crazy-hieroglyphics gestalt.

They tossed. They went through the crewmen's quarters first. They tossed their lockers. They found L.A. tourist guidebooks and guidebooks per L.A. Chink culture. They found Chinese-language guides. Dudley teethed on it.

The deal oozed Fifth Column infiltration and sabotage. Hide in plain sight as Chink and deep-six L.A. from within.

They tossed. Hideo worked with socket wrenches and his bare hands. He unscrewed bolts and searched behind panels. He unwired instrument clusters and ran his hands over flush walls. He unscrewed the interior periscope mount and threw a flashlight beam on the gears.

They tossed. Carlos joined them. His kibitz spiel was all football and war. The Chicago Bears. Jew quarterback Sid Luckman. The Japs take Wake Island. Do you feel a racial tug, Dr. Ashida?

Carlos got loosey-goosey. Dudley hit him up for his car keys. His car was back on the bluff. He was out of cigarettes.

Carlos tossed him the keys. Dudley walked to his car, under guard escort. He grabbed his cigarettes. He palmed a vial of nitroglycerin.

He walked back to the sub. He winked at Hideo. Hideo winked back.

They tossed. Dudley lugged steel plates one-handed. His bad hand throbbed. He popped bennies and anti-bug pills. Carlos was no dumb beaner. He knew they might bolt. He kept one hand on his gun.

They tossed. The sub was a claustrophobe hot box. They sweated through their clothes. They sliced up their hands. Dudley ripped a fingernail half off.

They tossed systematically. They went from plated walls to plated catwalks. Everything was built narrow and Jap-size. Dudley kept banging his head.

They tossed. Hideo pulled up a floor plate and smiled.

Pierce Patchett. Crazy-kid hieroglyphics.

Five duffel bags stuffed in a hole. All bulging with Yankee C-notes.

Carlos was pleased. "Fate has decreed that you live. Now, Dr. Ashida must interrogate."

2:37 p.m.

The rain persisted. They worked in a pup tent. Blackshirts unhooked the Japs and rehooked them to chairs. Hideo pulled the tape off their mouths. Hitler mustaches tore free.

Dudley watched. Breuning and Carlisle watched. They had that fetching *Whew we don't die* look. Carlos supplied mescal. Everybody took pops. Hideo exhibited panache and ate the worm.

The Japs jabbered and rattled their cuff chains. They were Fuji Shudoesque. Hideo hectored them. It went on and on. It got boring and vexing. It required no translation. The Japs weren't giving up shit.

Hideo looked at Dudley.

Dudley looked at Carlos.

Carlos passed Hideo his gloves.

They were palm-weighted and fascist fetishistic. Hideo slipped them on.

The Japs rolled their eyes and giggled. *Punk, you ain't got the guts.*

Hideo hit them.

He windmilled lefts and rights. Their heads snapped at near-right angles. Teeth blew out. Severed scalps flew.

They dribbled teeth.

They coughed blood.

Their eyebrows flopped over their eyes.

They made garbled sounds and gave it all up.

It was six-man Jap-on-Jap jabber. Hideo crouched low and picked it all up.

The jabber overlapped and extended. Hideo took it all in.

"It's Terry Lux and Pierce Patchett, with Preston Exley off to the side. Patchett knows people in the office of Naval Intelligence. He's been fingering those sub attacks on freighters up the coastline, and he was in shortwave contact with the escaped Japanese. Lux took your plan with Ace Kwan and refined it into a sabotage front. The escaped men were on their way down here to rendezvous with the sub when the posse got them. Lux is going to work with Lin Chung and hide saboteurs in Chinatown. Chung has eugenic plans for them, which sounds draconian. At the very least, he's going to infiltrate them into the Chinese community and let them perpetrate their sabotage from there."

Dudley smiled. "Bright, bright penny. How gifted you are."

A fat Jap squirmed and spit blood at Hideo. He called up some English. He said, "You fairy."

Hideo grabbed Carlos Madrano's Luger and drew down on him. The other Japs froze. The whole tent froze.

Dudley watched his gears click. Yes/no, yes/no, yes/no.

Hideo lowered the gun.

Hideo said, "I'm an American."

5:18 p.m.

The cleanup extended. The Blackshirts loosened up. They let the gringos walk free.

Dudley loitered on the bluff. The rain covered him. He spotted Madrano's car. He wedged the nitro into the left-rear wheel well.

They hog-tied the Japs and dumped them in the sub. The Japs squirmed, squealed and begged. Breuning friction-taped their mouths. Hideo rigged a detonation kit beside them.

Hideo designed the kit. It featured nitroglycerin and shotgun shells.

Rip three pairs of trousers into strips and trail them out the hatch. Gasoline-soak them. Get the sub twenty yards out. Shotgun-blast the hull and manufacture combustion.

Hideo studied the sub's engine. He read a set of Jap-language guides and got the gist. Breuning and Carlisle ripped up the trousers and knotted the fuse. Dudley gas-soaked it and tucked the explosive end in with the nitro and shells.

They coated the fuse with sulfuric acid and rendered it waterproof. They packed the kit upside the Japs. The fuse tip draped over the hull.

Hideo stoked the engine and slammed the gears into reverse. The sub shimmied and lurched backward.

They jumped off. Rain drummed down and soaked them.

They stood with the Blackshirts and passed around the mescal. The sub caught water traction. The Blackshirts divvied up shotguns loaded with big-bore slugs.

It all felt ceremonial. It all went down in the rain and the dark.

The sub lurched twenty yards out. All right, now—

Uno, dos, tres—

Dudley did the count. They all fired on *cuatro*.

Twenty-four men fired. Twenty-four slugs pierced the hull. The sub blew to kingdom come.

7:08 p.m.

The sky burned red. Everybody yelled *adiós* and peeled to their cars. Carlos drove off with four Blackshirt pals.

Waves smothered the flames. Steam hissed off the water. Breuning burned tread. Carlisle waxed elegiac. Dudley and Hideo sat in the backseat.

It was over. The Watanabe case. The Smith-Kwan cartel. It ran twenty days, door-to-door.

Dudley touched Hideo's arm. "I won't begrudge you a last go at the Watanabe case. Do what you deem prudent, without mentioning my name. You'll be interned in late February. I'll break you out in early May."

Hideo smiled and winked at him. Dudley roared and slapped his knees.

The drive was a slog. The fucking rain. Fallen debris, abandoned cars, bobbing peons. Carlos lived two hours south of Ensenada. He might get halfway there.

Back to America. No border-crossing grief. A snail trail through San Diego. They rendezvoused at the Davis manse. They had to return and disperse there.

They stopped at the Friar Tuck Drive-In. The carhops wore rain slickers over wench garb. Hideo bounced for dinner. They gorged on cheeseburgers and mescal-spiked milk shakes.

Snail trail. They *craaaawled* up the coast road to Sunset. It was almost midnight. Dudley perked up. He'd get a last look at the house.

Sunset east. Mandeville Canyon north. Back to her street and her house. All her lights were on.

The gang said *adiós* on the sidewalk. The *abrazos* extended. The lads laid tracks home. Dudley walked up and peeped a front window. Tall trees shielded him from the rain.

Bette's "Late Christmas Dinner." The papers ballyhooed it.

She played to a group of soldiers. They were winter-uniform

spiffed. Bette's hubby sashayed. The Airedale hopped on Tommy Gilfoyle's lap.

Bette held court. The revelers drank eggnog. Beth danced into view. A handsome soldier twirled her. She wore her Irish green sweet sixteen dress.

She sailed by the window and disappeared. Dudley held back sobs.

Part Four

THE HUNTRESS

(December 27–December 29, 1941)

December 27, 1941

109

LOS ANGELES | SATURDAY, DECEMBER 27, 1941

12:04 a.m.

Dudley stood at the window. Ashida saw it. He made a green light and cut east. Dudley disappeared.

The rain subsided. He checked his rearview mirror every few seconds. His face still looked the same.

He toured Mexico with the Dudster. He thought he'd look different.

Kay Lake shivved a woman and looked different now. He thought he'd go the same route.

It was Christmas weekend. It was raining. There was no traffic. Dudley said, "Omit my name. Do whatever you deem prudent."

He knew most of it. He understood the Fifth Column text. Saul Lesnick had tiny feet. It was not binding proof. He could not name the white man in the purple sweater. Jack Webb described the man. He was "heavyset" and "middle-aged." Saul Lesnick was old and thin.

The USC Library was open-all-night. Law students were night owls. He was a night owl. He cooked up a scheme on the ride back.

He left 282 Ord at 8:00 a.m. Wednesday. Lin Chung and Saul Lesnick paced and argued on. He played a hunch and drove to the Hall of Records. The hunch played off Pierce Patchett's calls to Lin Chung.

Said calls—12/19, 12/20, 12/21. Patchett's only calls to Chung. Patchett calls Terry Lux *sixteen* times those three days.

The Hall was paperwork-swamped. He quick-skimmed a recent transaction list. Lin Chung owned twelve houses in the San Gabriel Valley. He had second-mortgaged *all* of them. The transactions *all* occurred on Monday, 12/22/41.

Patchett, Lux, Chung. Telephone lists. Hurried money scrounging. His theory was this:

Lux and Chung wanted in on the prison-camp deal. Patchett exhorted them to raise scratch. Convergent schemes were brewing. Come on—outbid Dudley and Ace Kwan.

He drove by all twelve houses then. He looked in the windows. He saw movie cameras on tripods and bedrooms that resembled smut-film sets. He saw rooms with mattress-covered floors.

Let's house Japs in plain sight. Great minds think alike. Dudley and Ace concocted the scheme. Let's usurp the scheme now.

Now he knew this:

The houses were smut-film sets. Only that explanation sufficed. The houses would also hide Japanese saboteurs.

Madness. Racial insanity.

Lin Chung was Chinese and anti-Japanese. He was a fascist-eugenicist and friend of left-wing Saul Lesnick. War profiteering superseded racial-political ties. Let's make money off innocent Japanese and assist the Jap enemy.

The rain let up. Ashida hit USC and parked outside the library. He ran inside. He knew the place now. He knew specific law books.

"Whatever you deem prudent."

Let's prevent more sabotage. Let's blitz the slave-camp deal. Exley, Patchett, Lux and Chung might desist. They could be legally dissuaded. They were not killers of the Smith-Kwan ilk.

Ashida read textbooks and jotted notes. They comprised a legal brief.

Memo to William H. Parker. Here's twelve questions for Terence Lux, M.D.

They all require "yes" or "no" answers. None of them touch Dudley. They circumscribe the Bedford Drive and Mexican revelations. They would reveal wisps to Parker. They would tell Lux this:

I know all about it. You and the others DESIST.

Ashida wrote it all out. Ashida folded his notes into a Christmas card and dropped them in an envelope.

He felt weightless. He smelled Dudley's wet tweeds on his skin.

The library was stuffy. Ashida walked outside and gulped cold air. He got his car and drove to Silver Lake. He parked outside Parker's house.

The living room light was on. He walked up and dropped the card in the mail slot. He checked the window.

Parker sat in an easy chair. He stared at a photograph. It was probably the big redhead.

110

KAY LAKE'S DIARY

LOS ANGELES | SATURDAY, DECEMBER 27, 1941

2:11 a.m.

Lee said, "It wasn't much of a Christmas."

I said, "No. But it's been a hell of a month."

We sat on my bedroom terrace and drank cask-aged scotch. It was a gift from Uncle Ace Kwan. All the posse men got a jug, a shrunken head and a free-meal chit for Kwan's Chinese Pagoda.

Lee said, "We should fill each other in on it one of these days. Scotty's gone off to the war, we both took some licks, and you got your face rearranged more than I did. I've been hiding out from you, but I know that there's some kind of story here."

Our chairs faced south. The clubs on the Strip had doused their lights a few minutes earlier. It was cool and clear; the late-traffic hum mesmerized me.

"Give me your version first. It's your college term paper, and the title is 'A Hell of a Month.' "

Lee said, "You're the college girl. You're the one who writes things down."

I smiled and sipped Ace Kwan's scotch. Uncle Ace and his best friend, the Dudster. All roads lead to Dudley Smith. All my thoughts circled back to him.

I said, "You're dodging me. I know when you've been holding back something you've been teething on. There's a perception here. We're going to sit here and enjoy Ace Kwan's largesse until you tell me."

Lee swirled his drink. "Call-Me-Jack got Count Basie for the Bureau New Year's bash. The Count clipped a black-and-white outside the Club Alabam, and the blues found reefers on him. It was our gig or six months in the clink."

I poked his arm. "You're dodging me. Give me the perception and we'll go back to small talk."

Lee put down his glass and prepared to make newspaper headlines. It was Leland C. Blanchard code—the way he ridiculed the big moments of his life before he buried them.

"Bivins Takes Blanchard in Tuff Tiff at Olympic!" "Hero Cop Rescues Gang Girl from Heist Mastermind!" "Southland's 'Great White Hope' Joins L.A. Police!"

I laughed. Those were some of his best.

Lee went bam-bam-bam and said, *"Epic Raw Deal for Local Japs! Ex–Heavyweight Contender Spills Beans! 'Most of These Fuckers Didn't Do Shit,' Officer L. C. Blanchard Says. 'It's All War Fever and Hopped-up woo-woo!' "*

I applauded the sentiment and the performance. Lee bowed and went back to his drink. He said, "This war's leaving me behind. Dud's going into the Army as a goddamn captain, while I herd Japs who didn't do shit into cattle cars and pop winos on skid row. You'll be entertaining the troops in the sack, and you'll probably write a book about it."

He stopped and made more headlines. *"Home-front Courtesan Tells All in Racy Memoir! Southland Holds Its Breath as She Names Names."*

I exploited the opening Lee gave me. I said, "Let's start with the name Dudley Smith."

Lee crashed. He simply gave out. He said, "Oh shit, babe."

I said, "You can do better than that."

He said, "Come on, Kay."

I made newspaper headlines—bam-bam-bam in the air.

"Irish Cop Beats Man to Death at Newton Station!" "Irish Cop Frames Werewolf! Gas-Chamber Bounce Looms!" "Irish Cop Suborns Young Cops into Rogue Cop Coven!" "Kid Cop Flees to Perilous War Duty! Fears Sergeant D. L. Smith More than Japs!"

Lee said, "Come on, Kay. Dudley's Dudley, and the world needs guys like him."

He was tired. He was beaten. The war, the roundups, his fight with Scotty. His trip to New York City, mid-November. He killed a man with the Dudster. He could have fought him or said no. There were options, but he was beaten, and he had me to come home to. And I possessed stunning artistry, but no character or conviction. And I was too possessed by his world of vile intrigue to exercise my own option to leave him.

Lee rolled his eyes. I was boring him. I was besieging him with schoolgirl idealism. He rolled his eyes; he checked his watch; he gave me this look. *Come on, Kay. Come on, Kay. Come on, Kay.*

I made headlines—bam-bam-bam.

"Ex-Boxer Cop Slays Gangland Witness! Canary Can Sing, But He Can't Fly!" "Slaying Facilitates Mobster's Jail Release!" "Ex-Boxer Cop Whimpers to Irish Cop: I'm Just a Boy Who Can't Say No."

Lee threw his glass over the terrace; it shattered down on the driveway. He kicked over his chair and looked at me. He wasn't outraged or hurt. He was just beaten. I knew what he'd say before he said it. He said, "Goddamn you, Kay."

It was all he had. He left me alone with it. He walked into the house and out of the house and slammed doors as he went. He got into his car and slammed the door and burned rubber down to the Strip.

He left me alone with Dudley Smith.

111

LOS ANGELES | SATURDAY, DECEMBER 27, 1941

3:08 a.m.

Night owl. Black coffee and the picture. Eleven days booze-free.

Lieutenant Joan Conville. The wayward farm girl makes rank. The picture was badly shredded. He should toss it soon.

Helen snored in the bedroom. She hated him now. He skipped Christmas for two car wrecks and a koi run.

Three Mexicans dug a big backyard pond and glazed it. He strung the fence around it himself. He drove to Jim Larkin's bungalow and brought the koi back in pails.

They all survived. They loved their new home. He fed them high-line fish food. The fence deterred cats and dogs and kept them safe.

Helen hated him. He deserted his marriage for pictures and colorful fish. He sat in the yard and looked at the koi. He sat in this chair and looked at the picture. He thought about Miss Lake.

Parker rubbed his eyes. The living room blurred. He glanced toward the door. He saw an envelope on the floor, under the mail slot.

He walked over and snatched it. He saw his name on the front. There was no postmark. It was probably a late Christmas card.

He opened it. The card depicted reindeer on Wilshire Boulevard. A note was folded in. Dr. Hideo Ashida sends Yule regards.

Ashida had tossed his office and found his grand jury notes. Ashida studied them and read those law texts himself. He made unexplained assertions per a shortwave radio mob. Patchett, Terry Lux, the Watanabes.

The Dudster went unnamed. He called Preston Exley a "non–Fifth Column colluder." The note further explicated Blood Alley. He implicated Pierce Patchett in the coastal sub attacks. He used mitigating language. He prepared a script. Brace Terry Lux—he might fold.

Elliptical. Damning by suggestion. Evidentially unverified and circumstantially sound.

Parker went punch-drunk. He bumped the doorside table. A stack of mail hit the floor.

He gathered it up. He snatched late Christmas cards in square envelopes. One long envelope stood out.

The return address juiced him. PC Bell/642 South Olive/"Official Query Reply."

They always *called*. They never *wrote*. He thought they'd *call*.

The postmark was 12/23. The Christmas rush stalled delivery.

Parker slit the envelope. Finally—the outgoing pay-phone list.

He skimmed the first page. The wall held him up.

One glance said *IT'S HIM*.

3:21 a.m.

Night owl. Night owls, plural. He'd be up. War insomnia ran epidemic.

It's raining again. The pavement's wet. You're punch-drunk. Keep your eyes on the road.

Parker drove to Santa Monica. He ran Sunset to Lincoln and south. Two pay phones stood a block away. *The* phone stood across the street.

He parked curbside. The plant was barb wire–enclosed. He walked to the gate and badged the guard. The man was ex-PD. He went *Yup, the boss is in.*

The boss had his own Quonset hut. Parker dodged camouflage nets and ducked over. He was punch-drunk. The rain carried him.

The door was open. Jim Davis was sprawled on a green leather couch. His office was slathered with shadowboxed guns and war flags.

Davis wore cross-draw .45's and picked his teeth with a knife. It was The Knife.

The rising sun flag was blood-streaked. The Chinese flag was bullet-ripped.

Davis said, "The pay phones?"

Parker nodded.

Davis said, "I locked my office keys up one night and got in a pinch. There was no gate guard on duty, so I used that pay phone to call home. Bill Parker on the job. I fuck up once and he nails it. I figured Dudley would get here first, and that he'd have his hand out."

Parker locked the door. Davis kicked a chair over. It slid on the floor and banged Parker's knees.

He sat down. He unholstered his belt gun. Davis unholstered. He placed his .45's on the floor and kicked them. They hit Parker's feet.

"It was my case, more than Dudley's. I should have jumped when the Larkin job came in. It was there in all the Watanabe reports, but nobody keyed on it. They called pay phones near Lockheed, Boeing and *Douglas.* You've run the force here since '38. You're as fascistic as Hitler. We went quail hunting once. You wore a purple sweater."

Davis said, "I've got three purple sweaters. And it's not your case, it's the Jap kid's. If I burn for this, I want a Jap to light the fuse."

"I can smell it on you, Jim. Everything about it is you."

The room reeked of liquor-soaked tobacco. Davis snatched a chaw cup off the floor.

"You were my trusty adjutant. I should tell you what we got here."

4:09 a.m.

You know me, Bill. I love the Oriental culture and the Oriental gash, but I kowtowed to eugenic pressure and married a white woman. I learned to speak Chink in a Chink whorehouse, which gave me a leg up on Chink culture when I worked Chinatown as a kid rookie. I got hooked on Jap culture when Hirohito started making noise, and I already gave my heart to Hitler back around the beer hall putsch. I met a nice old British guy named Jim Larkin in a bar a few blocks from here. He was some kind of Mickey Mouse code breaker back during the Great War, and he had a quite well-founded hatred for the Reds and quite an exhaustive knowledge of the Jew roots of the Russian Revolution. Jim was a big Jap-o-phile, and he creamed his jeans for a Japan-conquers-Russia revolt, to compensate for all the appeasement and stasis of the Sino-Russian War. Jim taught me to read and write Jap, which came easy to a Chink-fluent guy like me. The gang's forming now. You get that, Bill. I've met Jim, and I already know Preston Exley from my days on the PD. Now, Jim liked Jap twat, and he knew a budding Jap-o-phile pimp and alleged businessman named Pierce Morehouse Patchett.

Pierce was a chemist by legitimate trade, with a special interest in eugenics and Asian chemistry. Frankly, he was a dope fiend, and he had a sideline peddling Jap gash to the sailors and Marines down in Dago. If it's profitable and illicit, Pierce has done it or considered it, but I didn't trust him completely. He was too egalitarian for my taste. He was too populist and hooked on weird dialogues. He'd talk race science with all these Hindu health faddists and do-gooders, including this Red eugenics fiend with an office right next to his. That's Saul Lesnick, M.D. He wanted to build perfect human beings to fight the fascist beast. Since I am the fascist beast, I can't countenance old Saul, but Pierce the P dotes on him.

Preston wasn't political. It's 1937, and there's thunder on the Right—but Preston's nonplussed by all of it. He's on the sidelines, but Jim, Pierce and I are tub-thumping fascists. There's America First, the Shirts, the Bund, the Copperheads, the Thunderbolt Legion. I'm a public figure, so

I'm not as notably rabid as Jim and Pierce, who I've always found to be sloppy and impolitic, which is something, coming from a guy like me.

We're jungled up in Jap societies with names no white man this side of me can pronounce. That's how we meet Ryoshi Watanabe. At the time, Ryoshi was the A-number-one fascist ichiban *of the fucking western hemisphere. I still love the Chinks, but the Chinks hate the Japs. It's not that I'm confused or ambivalent, I'm just riding the zeitgeist for all it's worth. Ryoshi's an ex-Collaborationist, and his son Johnny is second-generation pro-Collaborationist, to Ryoshi's dismay. Ryoshi's got a knife scar that says it all, and our ex-Collaborationist pal Jim Larkin's got the same one. The Collaborationists had a ritual, Bill—and civilized white men like you will probably find it hard to believe. They'd fight each other with poison-dipped knives to see who survives, which Jim and Ryoshi did, some few times. The Collaborationists were vociferously pro-Jap and anti-Chink, despite their mixed-blood lineage. That's because they saw Jap fascism as the vanguard of the new Asian racial order. The Collaborationists were virulently antitong, because the tongs were virulently anti-Jap and represented a challenge to Japan's slant-eyed hegemony. You get it, right, Bill? The world is knee-deep in economic chaos, and some visionaries with rowdy tendencies and quaint rituals see a way out. The Collaborationists are staking their claim to usurp the tongs and take over their rackets, and terror tactics are their means. How's this for a ritual? Kill Chinks with poison-dipped knives, rape and kill the female kin of tong bosses, live outdoors in collaborative mixed-race harmony. Sound familiar, Bill? That Griffith Park multiple? I'm betting that Dud S. and Ace K. killed them boys that raped and killed Ace's niece.*

So—Jim, Pierce and I are jungled up with the Watanabes. We've got our kid's auxiliary: Johnny and Nancy W., and the Dudster's Nazi snitch, Huey Cressmeyer. Huey's the odd child out in all of this, and I made sure that Jim, Pierce and I steered clear of him, because he was close to Dud S. We're all one like-minded family. Pierce has got his property schemes and his Jap-twat stable, and he's peddling replica feudal knives to Collaborationists up and down the coast. I showed them how to acid-dip their fingerprints off to avoid identification, which they right-as-rain did. I'm the noted ex–*police chief who got crucified by the local Jew Grand Jury and castigated for poking some underaged snatch up in Ventura County, so I keep my head down as the boss here at Douglas. Larkin corrupts kids with his 'Santa Monica Cycleers' hobby and writes tracts from all perspectives, and in Kraut and Jap. There's money in it, but I don't invest. Here's where I'll concede a certain lack of foresight. Bill, I'll admit that I got carried away a bit. I know the war is inevitable, and I firmly believe that the Axis boys will win. I do some money hoarding and changing with Ryoshi, the Collaborationists and the Deutsches Haus kids. I've got a yen for yen and reichsmarks, because I know the war's coming and the right side will sure as shit win.*

But shit has this tendency to disperse, Bill—especially when money gets all fucked up with ideology. Because Preston knows a savvy Fed named Ed Satterlee. Ed says the Feds are building Fifth Column files on the local Japs, because the Feds are planning roundups when this inevitable war hits. Preston's a big land-development man and construction kingpin, and Pierce had made money turning over property. Pierce is a chemist and knows topsoil applications. Preston built the Arroyo Seco Parkway, and he's always had a yen to build more ramps to it, with shopping plazas adjacent, to take up the slack between L.A. proper and Pasadena. Now, this inevitable war and inevitable mass imprisonment jacks up his nonfascist but still-utilitarian thinking. He knows me, he knows Pierce, he's met Jim Larkin. He don't know the Watanabe family from the Jap man in the moon. But he comes up with a plan to buy Jap houses off the parkway and Jap farms in the East Valley, to goose his parkway plan and supplant it with a local Jap-internment plan, outside of the Federal government's schemes.

We're into '40 now, Bill. Everyone knows the war is coming. Preston's a straight-shooting guy, and he dispatches Jap-fluent Pierce and Jim to talk turkey to Japs who might want to prudently dump their property. The war's coming, you're fucked. You'll be imprisoned, your houses and farms will be seized. You can't win this one, Tojo. But we'll kick back gelt to you while you're in stir. Your options are to get royally fucked by Uncle Sam or to get prematurely exploited and covertly helped out by us. You and Dud have got most of this figured out, Bill. I'm sure of that. We get parkway Japs and farm Japs to sell out, but some refuse. We bring in Carlos Madrano and his wetback corps and start fucking up the land, so we can build parkway ramps and prison camps. Preston's nonfascist conscience is assuaged, which is fiscally imperative. He's the big construction fish in this pond of ours, and we want him happy. Sure, we love the Japs, but most of them aren't tub-thumping fascists like we are. A buck is a buck, and we're Americans first.

Ideology and money make for strange bedfellows. Did you hear the one about the Jap prostitute who went broke because no one had a yen for her? What Preston needs now is an angle to sell his prison-camp-within-prison-camp scheme to our local fathers and the Feds. The autonomous, build-the-local-economy angle is a cinch for Fletch Bowron—but Preston needs a clincher for J. Edgar Hoover. You know who gives it to him? Saul Lesnick, who's been off in eugenic dialogue with Pierce the P and a Chink doctor named Lin Chung.

The clincher is eugenics. Get it, Bill? We house the best Japs, the smartest Japs, the sturdiest Japs, and study them to determine what makes them different from us. Lesnick concocted it. Hoover loved it. Hoover hates the Jews and the Reds, Lesnick's a Jew Red and a Fed snitch, but populism ain't nothing but the big shared agenda. Will it get down to torture studies and rewiring Jap brains to the paws of rabid wombats? You tell me, Bill. We'll reconvene sometime in '43 and discuss it.

So, we all know the war's coming. We're all huddled up with our shortwave radios, except for Preston—who don't know shortwave shit from Shinola. But Jim Larkin's got his Jap-o-phile pal, Terry Lux, who's got a king-size shortwave setup and did a nose job on one of Jimbo's Jap girlfriends. Our plans are brewing. We're going to destroy crops and topsoil and sell canned shrimp oil and glass to Jap canners who want to kill white Americans. I know you witnessed that raid at the shrimp boat, Bill. Our Collaborationist pals and warehouse pals got that one by you. You're not really a detective, but I can tell you're following me.

It all came down to the radios, in the end. There's Pierce, Jim, Terry, me. Jim teaches Terry Jap. We all follow the buildup for the war in Japanese. Ryoshi came through there. He knew all the coded Jap Navy frequencies.

Our plans are percolating. Got a yen for glass-infused shrimp? You know who to see. Preston's in the shadows. Terry's glued to his radio and not much else, because he's busy sucking up to society dope fiends. Ed Satterlee's feeding us dope on the potential roundups. Pierce has got a plan to cut whores to look like movie stars, and Terry's adroitly considering it. Pierce and Terry are bankrolling Collaborationist villages. It violates Jap loyalty codes, but America's a democracy, as much as we don't like it. The villagers are laundering money and hawking that good glass-packed shrimp. Meanwhile, all we have to do is tune in our radios for the latest coded military news, straight from Jap Navy sources. We're still in 1940, Bill. And in walks a draconian character named Hikaru Tachibana.

I was fond of Tachi, but the cocksucker was a straight-up Jap spy. The

SaMo cops popped his yellow ass right outside of here, on Lincoln Boulevard. He had a little Minox spy camera on him, which served to get him slated for deportation. I bailed him out on the q.t. and made him my spy. I'd started to think that Ryoshi W. was a less than ardent fascist and was less than loyal to our little clique. He Jewed us up for more money than we wanted to pay for his house and farm, which sat poorly with us, because we'd eugenically elevated him to Sacred White Man Status and thought the world of him. I got Tachi a job on the Watanabe farm, sometime in mid-'40. He reported back and confirmed my suspicions that Ryoshi was indeed wishy-washy.

You had to take everything Tachi said with more than a grain of salt, Bill. He was temperamental and fanciful, and a bigger jailbait jumper than me. He ran street whores and sold maryjane to high school kids, which is highly immoral for one who ascribes to samurai codes of honor. That stated, I let things simmer for a good long while, because we were all enjoying the Jap military buildup, engagingly available on our radio sets. That, and I was fond of Tachi. Until the summer of '41, when we all figured out that he knocked up Nancy Watanabe.

Aya learned Nancy was pregnant, and told Ryoshi. Ryoshi spilled it to Pierce and me. We figured it had to be Johnny, because Johnny was perved on Nancy and told Pierce that he used to Mickey Finn her and fuck her with rubbers on, because he didn't want no mongoloid kids. Ryoshi beat on Johnny and determined that he wasn't the daddy, so our suspicions fell on Huey Cressmeyer. Ryoshi braced Huey. Huey said a Mex-Jap Collaborationist bragged that he knocked up Nancy. Terry Lux blood-tested Nancy and Huey and exonerated Huey. We got suspicious of Tachi and had Terry test him. Terry matched Tachi's blood type to Nancy's zygote. The wages of sin are death, Bill. Johnny and I snuffed Tachi. We stabbed him with poison-dipped knives and dumped his yellow ass down a well hole at the farm.

It was like this, Bill. I was in love with Nancy. Ryoshi had already sold her to me. She was pledged to be my concubine, but I hadn't poked her yet. We were going to live together in Tokyo or L.A., depending on who won the war. Don't look at me that way, Bill. I know she was sixteen, but I was going to wait, even though she was used goods already.

We're up to the fall of '41, now. Our enterprises are progressing, and we've all got our own little schemes. Pierce is sloppy. He's all over the shortwave frequencies, talking to his fascist chums, while I've got my own frequency here at the plant blocked by a dummy transistor. Pierce is coffee-

klatching with Doc Lesnick every chance he gets, because they're office mates. Eugenics, Bill. Lesnick's a Nazi do-gooder in his soul, Jew or no Jew. He wants to build more effective human beings, and he knows that it entails lab work. He's looking to build Übermenschen *with jumbo nigger-size dicks, Jew brains, Jap cunning, Russian resistance to disease and Nordic good looks. I'm not shitting you, Bill—Lesnick let Pierce eavesdrop on his psychiatric sessions, and old Saul is always laying race science on his patients.*

So, this fall progresses. We're glued to our radios, and we know the Japs are going to bomb Pearl Harbor. Pierce has got Office of Naval Intelligence and freight company connections, and he's relaying info on ordnance shipments to the Jap Navy and our Collaborationist pals. The Jap Navy and the Collaborationists hate each other, but we don't care—all we want is more destruction. Those sub attacks on those freighters up the coast? All over the papers? It's all off Pierce the P's intelligence. Those Japs who escaped from T.I.? Pierce supplied them with money, slugs for pay-phone drops, hideout leads, the megillah. He bankrolled their whole fucking escape, and those fuckers were headed down to hook up with a sub in Colonet, Mexico, when you cops took them out at Blood Alley.

We're reckless here, we're cautious there. I've got my frequency blocked, but Pierce and Terry are all over the airwaves. I'm on the air, Jim's on the air. He's got a shortwave set stashed in a garage out near Terry's farm in Malibu. Them pay phones are all working overtime, which was a security precaution I came up with myself. In the middle of all this prewar hoo-ha, I see that Ryoshi and Jimbo are getting cold feet about the war in general and Pearl in specific. I'm afraid that they're going to rat out the attack, and fuck up world history for all fucking time. I'm sanguine, Bill. I'm laissez-faire. We're going to war. If the Japs and Krauts win, great. Ditto the U.S.A. I'm spending time with Nancy. I want her to have the kid, so I can have a full-blood Jap son to bullshit, shoot guns and play catch with. Then she fucks me over and gets a scrape from some beaner quack down in T.J. I decide that the whole family has to go, and ditto that Brit fucker Jim Larkin. It's a two-tiered motive, Bill. There's revenge for the abortion and my allegiance to the Jap war effort.

I'm not sure when the Japs are going to hit Pearl, Bill. Frankly, I've spent this whole fall soused on sour mash and terpin hydrate. Saul Lesnick was peddling anesthetic dentists' cocaine to Pierce, who was letting me dip my beak as much as I liked. I told Pierce the Watanabes had to go, and he agreed with me. He cooked up some poison tea that would get them all loopy before I brought down the blade, and powdered it all up in little sachets. I set the date for December 6, and I bought the swords at a curio shop on Alameda. But I forget to buy scabbards to complete the package of obfuscation. I was fuzzy that fateful day, Bill. I'd set the date, and I picked up radio tips that the Japs were going to tap Pearl the next morning. Jimbo told me he was taking the Cycleers on a jaunt to San Berdoo come Sunday dawn, so I decided to clear up all my business, go home, sleep it off, and be bright-eyed and bushy-tailed by the time the big news hit.

So, I drive to Highland Park, but I get cold feet en route. I stop at a pay phone on Figueroa, call Pierce and get him to buck me up. 'Can you come over and watch, *pal? Just for the eugenics of it?' Pierce turned me down, because he had tickets for that Bruin-Trojan game at the Coliseum, but he told me to call Saul Lesnick, because the old Yid might gas on multiple seppuku. So I called Saul, and he said he'd try to make it, and I drove up to the fucking Watanabe house in more than a bit of a blur. Lucky for me, the family was all in and receptive to a nice bowl of "special" tea, supplied by their white* Kamerad, *Jungle Jim Davis. I was blurry, they* got *blurry. The tea induced nausea, and they puked all over their clothes. I made them change clothes, which they did in this giddy blur they were in. I told Ryoshi to write that "looming apocalypse" note in kanji on the wall, meaning this boding internment. Ryoshi does it, and then Saul Lesnick and Lin Chung show up at the back door, and I almost shit my britches, because I'd forgotten that I'd called Saul, and now he's brought his Chink pal with him, so they can watch ex–Los Angeles Police Chief James Edgar "Two-Gun" Davis commit multiple Murder One.*

But Saul and Lin were cagey, which I appreciated. They left their cars down on Figueroa and walked up by the parkway fence, so nobody saw them. They told me it took a while to get up their gumption for the show, so they stood by the fence, smoked some cigarettes and thought, Well, this is one we can't miss.

Ryoshi, Aya and the kids were so zorched that they hardly noticed Saul and Lin, who came to scientifically view this whole episode and catalogue it from their divergent perspectives. So I say "Excuse me," run out to the car and get the swords, all wrapped up in a blanket. Saul and Lin are watching real close, and they take their shoes off, because they've got some cockamamy notion about leaving shoe prints. The closer I get to it, the blurrier it gets. But I make them lay down on the living room floor, and I pull out my feudal knife and gut them, belly to sternum. They convulse and die, and there's blood everywhere, and Saul steps in it, gets his socks wet, takes them off, and runs upstairs in a tizzy. I wiped blood on the swords and laid them on the bodies, but I forgot the scabbards and all the Jap ritual shit that it takes to convincingly depict seppuku. Lin Chung held his mud, observed, and asked me questions about my mental state, which pissed me off, because he wasn't that Jew Red Sigmund Freud and I wasn't some neurasthenic woman. I told Lin and Saul to scoot and leave me alone, so they scrammed out the back door. I washed the puked-on clothes and hung them up to dry, and I tried to find Ryoshi's shortwave cache, but I fucking didn't find shit. I just stared at the bodies, talked to them, cleaned myself up and walked out the door under cover of nightfall. It's all real blurry, Bill. I take a snooze, wake up, drive out to that traffic call and schmooze with you, right there on Wilshire and Barrington. I go from a jaw with my old pal Bill Parker and drive out to Valley Boulevard, where I mow down my old pal Jim Larkin. Then I go home to sleep it all off, and my wife wakes me up and says, "Jim, the Japs bombed Pearl Harbor."

So, the PD gets the case. Dudley Smith's the lead, and he's the single smartest white man on earth—he's right up there with you. I'm holding my breath now. Then Dud gets wise to the land grab, then Pierce and Terry's movie-star-cut-job scheme takes flight with them, then Dud and Ace Kwan cook up their own bunch of like-minded schemes, which Lin Chung rats out to Pierce. Then Dud spills the schemes to Terry, and Terry extrapolates and goes wild with them and gets on his radio to the Jap Navy—we can move Japs in to work the old Fifth Column and all of white L.A. will think that they're Chink. Before you know it, Dud and Ace are in a bidding war with Lin Chung, and you're knocking on my door, because I was drunk and lazy and called my home phone from one of our own tub-thumping fascist pay phones.

Davis stopped. He was pale. He verged on green.

Ten million pins dropped. Parker unloaded the guns on the floor.

Davis said, "I've got congestive heart disease, Bill. I won't live to Armistice Day, whoever wins the war. I wouldn't make it through the legal proceedings and up to the gas chamber in my own lifetime."

Parker said, "Are you lucid, Jim? Do you see things that aren't there? Do you talk to people who aren't in the room with you?"

Davis said, "That's *you*, Bill. That's not *me*. And nix on the loony bin. I'm not The Werewolf, and I won't go that route. There's only two ways we can play this. The first is Captain William H. Parker, the former adjutant and lackey of widely defamed former L.A. Police Chief Jim Davis, walks ex-Chief Davis out of here in handcuffs and hands him over to the DA. It's the first month of a staggering world conflict, and ex-Chief Davis is justly accused of hideously butchering four Japs, two of them women. It's the most sensational news story of the century, whatever prestige the L.A. Police Department has accrued since ex-Chief Davis was ousted is now squandered, and ex-Chief Davis' tenure as Chief is microscopically scrutinized. This fact is widely publicized. Ex-Chief Davis' hatchet man was a liquored-up papist prig named Bill Parker, a ruthless man of overweening ambition who sacrifices his fatuous ideals at the slightest hint of personal or professional advancement. Bill Parker is the largest subsidiary casualty of Jim Davis' Murder One indictments. While on trial, the flamboyant Davis indicts the Los Angeles Police Department with the breathtaking clarity of a man who has seen and done it all, and with men who still serve on that police department. You will go first, Bill. I have an affidavit that your brutalized ex-wife signed. Jack Horrall goes next. I have a wire recording of Brenda Allen giving him a blow job. I had the private room of Mike Lyman's wired all the time I was Chief. You go, Thad Brown goes. There'll be a nigger Chief from the Belgian Congo by the time I'm through. It comes down to this, Bill. If you take me in, I'll fuck you and the L.A. Police Department up the ass so hard that they'll hear the screams in Tokyo and Berlin. Here's your second option, Bill. You walk out of here, now. You say a few prayers to your evil, cocksucking God of papal Rome, then you jerk off while you look at yourself in the mirror and lust for a few college girls that you don't have the nuts to move on. Do you read me, papa-san? I killed four Japs the day before Pearl Harbor, and burning me for it costs more than it's worth. I'm sitting here fat and sassy, because I've got history on my side."

Parker stood up.

Davis said, "Shoo, Bill."

Parker walked out into the rain.

112

LOS ANGELES | SATURDAY, DECEMBER 27, 1941

9:32 a.m.

Teatime. Service for three.

Ace Kwan catered the do. They relaxed in Dudley's cubicle. His tea was bennie-laced. Beth's and Tommy's was not. Tommy read the Braille-version *Herald*. GRAND JURY INDICTS WEREWOLF! wowed him.

Beth ate almond cookies. Dudley smoked and bennie-twirled. They perused catalogues. Phelps-Terkel offered custom-made uniforms. Bullock's Wilshire hawked their women's line.

Beth said, "Blue is Claire's color, but it's not a winter shade. Mexico won't be too cold, so she should favor dresses over suits."

He couldn't shake Mexico. His losses felt victorious. Hideo was revelatory.

Tommy said, "Can I get a picture with The Werewolf, Uncle Dud? I won't be able to see it, but my pals at work will think it's swell."

Such goodness. Such gratitude.

Dudley said, "Of course, lad. I'll arrange it immediately."

Call-Me-Jack walked up. He was pale. He verged on green.

"Carlos Madrano's *muerto*. His car blew up on the coast road south of Ensenada. I just saw the Teletype. There's some kind of Jap angle on it."

Dudley said, "I'll miss him. He was quite the grand fascist."

113

LOS ANGELES | SATURDAY, DECEMBER 27, 1941

9:35 a.m.

Littell said, "We don't know where you'll be sent, but it won't be until late February. In the meantime, Dudley Smith's arranged some sweet digs for you and your family. He got you a three-bedroom suite at the Biltmore, all on the cuff. Mike Breuning's brothers will work your farm until you get out. You'll keep drawing a paycheck and get your old job back. Dudley squared it with Jack Horrall."

They stood on the fire escape. Ashida scanned the living room. Akira packed boxes. Mariko dozed on the couch.

Somebody whistled, due east. Ashida tracked it. Elmer Jackson prowled a neighboring rooftop. He waved his shotgun.

He yelled, "Hey, Hideo!"

Ashida yelled, "Hey, Elmer!"

Ashida thought, *I'M AN AMERICAN.*

114

KAY LAKE'S DIARY

LOS ANGELES | SATURDAY, DECEMBER 27, 1941

9:42 a.m.

Brenda supplied the address, but stopped short of an introduction. It would have been embarrassing. The husband ordered boys from a "Tomcat" service run by one of Brenda's friends. It was L.A. Everyone knew someone big—and primarily within illicit context. I had one name to drop. She'd take the bait or she wouldn't. I walked up to the door and rang the bell.

The approaching footsteps were *Her.* Stacked heels on hardwood. What *is* this unsolicited interruption?

Bette Davis opened the door. She wore a plaid shirt over dungarees and riding boots. Her look was *unkind.* No amenity would work here. I said, "Dudley Smith."

It brought her up short. Her look went from unkind to *Oh shit.* She said, "Who are you, and what do you hope to gain by mentioning that name to me?"

I said, "My name is Kay Lake, and I'm not looking to gain anything. I'm hoping that we both might benefit, or at least achieve a measure of relief, from a discussion."

She held the door open. She said, "I can give you a few minutes," and stood aside to let me in. She pointed to two thronelike chairs. It was *Sit, you.*

I followed her lead and obeyed. *There, now.* She walked off toward the back of the house.

Which was unwelcoming and overly conceived. Large beams and too-large furniture. Too much dark wood. The home of a British baroness—and an unruly Airedale bounding my way.

I embraced him and held him off; he ignored my entreaties to *sit.* He wanted all my attention and seemed to know how beguiling he was. I gave in and gushed over him.

Miss Davis returned and resumed her performance. She was brusque—but now amenable. She balanced a pewter tray like a drive-in carhop and swooped over to me. She placed the tray on a table by our thrones. The baroness, her petitioner. The pewter pitcher and mugs. The props covered her skittishness. She was dying to hear what I had to say.

She filled the mugs with rum punch. She opened a pewter box and pointed to a pewter lighter. I lit a cigarette and reclined in my throne; Miss Davis did the same. The Airedale hopped on an ottoman and went to sleep.

"Dudley was besotted by the dog. There's a way that certain men behave with animals. They regress in a certain way. Dudley *kissed* the dog, which I found discomfiting."

I sipped grog. "I live in a policeman's world. In a sense, I've been seduced by it. It's my résumé for any discussion of Dudley Smith."

Miss Davis tucked her legs up on the throne. She placed a pewter ashtray on the ledge between us.

"I know from seduction, as you might have guessed. I thought I recognized him, and then convinced myself that I knew him and could restrict him within the boundaries that I impose upon my men. I erred there, and I will never see him again. Which does not mean that he will fail to haunt me."

I said, "You haven't asked me to explain my résumé, or asked me if there's a specific purpose for my visit."

"Why should I? You're an artful inconvenience, and I'm momentarily taken with your approach. It's a cool Saturday morning, and we're having a chat. We're going to get shit-faced and become overfamiliar, because the war has sanctioned such indecorous behavior. Your introduction was entirely sufficient."

I sipped punch. Dark rum, Pernod, fruit juice. Pinch me—am I really here?

"Tell me about you and Dudley Smith, please."

Miss Davis said, "He fell ill here Wednesday afternoon. He became delirious and muttered things in his sleep."

10:26 a.m.

There was no quick revelation. I knew why, instantly. Miss Davis was at loose ends. She was lonely and needed an audience; she knew that she could hold me enthralled, in my front-row seat. She would bid me to speak, in time. She would ignore telephone calls and intrusions, such as her husband and any lovers she might have on a string. I expected autobiography, and got it.

Miss Davis, Broadway ingénue. She runs afoul of her family and makes her way to the Big Town. The '20s. Prohibition. Jewish intellectuals, eager to fuck her. George Gershwin succeeds. Poor George. He may or may not have been queer. She's there for the Carnegie Hall debut of Concerto in F. She smokes hashish with Scott Fitzgerald and finds herself weeping at the Cathedral of Saint John the Divine. She witnesses a May Day parade that leaves three dead. She's outside the prison when Sacco and Vanzetti fry. I sat silent and steady-eyed. I made no attempt to intrude on the woman's one great theme of Herself.

The stories went on. The day passed in one long monologue. We moved room to room. Miss Davis tossed flapjacks and deep-fried them into egg-stuffed enchiladas. Every movement was graceful and calculated to appear nonchalant. She was teaching me how to act in the world. The baroness and her protégée. She knew that I was studying her and believed that I would mimic her for the rest of my life. Miss Davis failed at insight and excelled at technique. This put her at odds with Claire De Haven. Claire embraced drama and employed it as but one approach to her fierce assignment of task.

We sipped grog, smoked cigarettes and stayed short of pie-eyed. Miss Davis had her one story. This shortcoming outlived its novelty and taxed me over time. I resisted her story, in all its accomplished seduction. I saw how deeply she fell prey to Glamour and how willfully she reconstructed it as Life's Big Romance. Her Forced March to Hollywood. Her Conquests of Famous Men, all weaker than she. Her Tiffs with Studio Chieftains and Directors.

It went on through the night and two bottles of red wine with coq au vin. The Airedale reappeared at fetching intervals. He brought the baroness a fresh-killed squirrel at one point. I dutifully cleaned up the mess as Dudley Smith loomed in ellipsis. The dog reminded her of him. Miss Davis was all artifice, save for her fear and rage. It was fear of nothingness and rage at the prospect fulfilled. It was her appetite for men at war with her need to orchestrate her every life's moment. Dudley Smith terrified her. He was the brutal blank page of her unconscious and had hurled her beyond her ken. They had breached each other's façades.

Miss Davis goes to Hollywood. Miss Lake goes to Hollywood. The film star, the round-heeled carhop. She was there at the premiere of *Gone with the Wind*—and was almost cast and should have been cast as Scarlett O'Hara. I attended the first public showing and still kept the ticket stub in my purse.

My visit ran through the wee small hours and up through dawn. I realized that she'd done this many times. She got lonely and became bored with all the people in her life. She needed a new audience. Someone might offer her a perfect new reflection. It would cut her loose to be someone less furious and less arch.

She gave me my opening. It was her critique of Victor McLaglen in *The Informer*. I told her that Dudley Smith brought to mind McLaglen, writ suave.

So she told me. She phrased it as a Bette Davis Story. Miss Davis and her Demon Lover. His infected hand, his delirium, the studio abortionist she brought in. She invited him here to screw him one last time and then banish him. She changed her mind at the door. He collapsed and said things in his sleep.

What things, Miss Davis? Please tell me. I can tell that they disturbed you.

She said she heard Dudley confess. He blathered in Catholic Latin and English. His utterings shocked her.

Extortion and robbery. Murder. The killing that took her past Her Ken—*Because She Caused It.*

"There was a party for Ben Siegel, a little over two weeks ago. It was at the Trocadero. I keep a room there, over the club."

Yes, Miss Davis. And then?

"I spent the night there with Dudley, and I made a harmless wisecrack as I fell asleep. I said, 'Kill a Jap for me.' I read the newspaper the next day, and there was a horrible account of that Japanese man shot in the phone booth. Dudley confessed to the murder in his sleep."

Miss Davis wept then. It was the crescendo of her performance. She wanted to be held, so I held her. I thought of my Kabuki mask and heard Japanese music. I held Bette Davis and let her sob into me.

December 28, 1941

115

LOS ANGELES | SUNDAY, DECEMBER 28, 1941

7:53 a.m.

Church. A High Mass for the Pearl Harbor dead.

The Archbishop sermonized. He extolled goodness in a world gone mad. He cited statistics—lives lost and battleships sunk.

Parker sat in the fourth row. Dudley sat two rows up. The Archbishop assailed the madness of nations and men.

Parker smelled bourbon-doused tobacco. Parker saw Pierce Patchett at his shortwave radio. Parker heard civilian freighters explode.

He went by The House at dawn. He walked to the parkway and saw those cigarette butts. Saul Lesnick and Lin Chung killed time there.

The Archbishop sermonized. He preached to a full house. The Mass drew nonbelievers who showed up just for show. Fletch Bowron showed. Bill McPherson showed. Call-Me-Jack showed. Brenda Allen's lipstick showed on his neck.

War. The will to atrocity. Invisible subversion. Detectable and eradicable. The duty of God-driven men.

Parker stared at Dudley. The Archbishop segued to patter. There's a war-bond rally. Hollywood, tomorrow night. It's star-studded and free. Here's the cutie: a Catholic setter and Protestant spaniel fall in love at the pound.

The celebrants roared. Dudley roared—*Your Eminence, that's rich!*

The Archbishop announced the "Gloria Patria." The celebrants stood. Hideo Ashida entered the church.

He's putting out rays. *Jap, Jap, Jap.* There's the looks and whispers. He's sliding down the second row. The Archbishop is miffed.

Ashida walked straight to the Dudster. Dudley draped an arm around him.

Now the gasps. Now the shudders. Now the big *NO*.

The Archbishop put the skids to it. The Archbishop closed the show.

Glory be to the Father, and to the Son, and to the Holy Ghost. As it was in the beginn—

Parker walked. He tripped out of the pew. He stumbled to the aisle and made the side door. An usher gulped and looked away.

He made the parking lot and his black-and-white. He kicked an empty pop bottle and shattered it. A flock of nuns crossed themselves.

Parker gunned it and took Wilshire west. The Miracle Mile and Beverly Hills were Sunday quiet. He cut north and ditched the car at Bedford and Dayton. He reached under the seat.

There—weighted sap gloves. The nightwatch man kept them stashed close.

The front door stood open. Parker walked through the lobby and took the hallway stairs. The second floor was quiet. Saul Lesnick's door was shut. The 216 door stood open. Parker walked right in.

Patchett was sorting mail. He wore tennis garb. The shorts and cable sweater. The polo shirt.

"It's the cop-lawyer. What's with the gloves? They look too sexy for a guy like—"

Parker ran up and hit him. A tight uppercut snapped his chin and rocked him back. Parker came in behind glove weight. He stepped close and saw Patchett *get fear*.

He put his hands out. *Don't hit me—we can talk about this.* Parker stepped in close and went for his face.

He hit him. Bones cracked. He had stitched lead in both fists. Patchett stumbled and crashed into the doorway. Parker pinned him there.

Parker hit him. He swung left-rights. He broke his nose. He broke his jaw. He sheared off one nostril and his lower lip.

There was all this blood. Bone showed white under it. Patchett screamed. Parker screamed over him. No Sabotage, No Prisons, No Parkway, No Eugenics.

Patchett's eyes rolled back. Parker smelled his piss and sprayed shit.

He hit him. He got his nose. He hit him. He got his mouth. He hit him. He cracked his teeth gum-deep. There, one ear's dangling. There, his scalp's gone. There, he's got no eyebrows. There, you've soaked your arms red.

There, he's half-dead.

There, he's eradicated.

There, you're God-driven now.

116

LOS ANGELES | SUNDAY, DECEMBER 28, 1941

9:02 a.m.

Opium.

The pallet, the tar, the pipe. Kick off those shoes, spark that flame.

The smoke hit his blood. It was immediate. The body was all conduit. Monsignor Meehan taught biology and smuggled arms by night. Dublin, 1918. Machine Gun Meehan knew from blood.

Opium. Three match strikes. The pallet drifts.

Stopover, L.A. Airplanes arrive and depart. The Airedale stares out a passenger window, agog.

He drove Beth and Tommy to the airport. It was sweet wartime *l'adieux.* He takes his oath of service tomorrow. Joe Kennedy will fly in.

He invited Hideo. Claire would appreciate that.

Stopover, Acapulco. Cliff divers and lobster salad. Claire in frocks from ritzy catalogues and Claire walking naked through steam.

Dudley smoked opium. He drifted through his own body and swam in red arteries.

He heard something. It was not of this drift on this pallet. It was a *click*. It was a *creak*.

He heard something. It was a footfall. It was a *creak*.

IT brushed the pallet.

He opened his eyes.

IT had a knife.

IT was Goro Shigeta, resurrected. He returned with a lacquered-wood face.

He covered his own face. He had no voice to say *Please don't hit me.*

A knife came down. This thing stabbed him. This thing raked his arms and his neck. He hid his face. This thing stabbed him. He had no voice. This thing cut him—his back, his legs, his feet.

He heard Chink voices. They were far, they were close. This thing vanished. The pallet dropped through a hole in the world. His blood was ice on his lips.

117

LOS ANGELES | SUNDAY, DECEMBER 28, 1941

9:43 a.m.

The Werewolf sleeps.

He had his own cell row. It accommodated his fans. Jailers sold photos. The Werewolf snarls. He bites your neck for five bucks.

Ashida watched him sleep. The urge to see him hit out of nowhere. It took his mind off Mexico.

The Werewolf sleeps. He's curled around his pillows. He's unshaven and knocked out behind terp.

Ashida stood in the catwalk. The adjoining tiers ran all-Japanese. He lived at the Biltmore Hotel now. His suite overlooked Pershing Square.

Ray Pinker walked up. "I don't know what this means, so you tell me. Dudley Smith was attacked, over at Kwan's. Your name was on a card in his wallet. You know, 'in case of emergency.' "

9:51 a.m.

His car was boxed in. He kicked the gas and plowed a row of trash cans. He popped the clutch and fishtailed east. He blew a red light and made Main.

A logjam held him back. Temple Street was blocked. Flag wavers and drum beaters stalled traffic dead. It was some ragtag parade. *Remember Pearl Harbor! Lest we forget!*

Ashida nudged the gas. He grazed the car in front of him. The driver looked back and saw *Jap*. He shot Ashida the finger—*Lest we forget!*

The logjam broke. Ashida swerved around the finger man and blew two reds.

He fishtailed across Temple and hooked to Broadway. He saw grief outside Kwan's.

Mike Breuning and Dick Carlisle ditched a K-car. Lin Chung pushed a gurney. Fluid bags swung on a pole.

He swerved up and parked on the curb. A crowd pushed into Kwan's. Nort Layman and a tall woman ran in.

The car blew hot oil and steam. Ashida tripped out and fought leg cramps. He half walked, half ran over. He caught an antiseptic stink. He pushed his way in.

Tables were shoved aside. Floor space was cleared. Dudley was stretched out on a bloody tablecloth.

Lin Chung fed him fluids. Ace Kwan waved a shrunken head. He thought he saw/he saw Claire De Haven. She was the tall woman. She was squeezing prayer beads.

All eyes on Dudley. All prayers for Dudley. He's stripped to his shorts. He's been gored and ripped.

Nort Layman made napkin tourniquets. Lin Chung swabbed Dudley's neck and plunged a syringe. A thin woman rigged fluid bags. Mike Breuning called her "Ruthie."

Dick Carlisle said, "It's good you were close."

Ruthie said, "Dud's been in the shit lately."

Ashida pressed close. Dudley bled out, ruddy to pale. Claire stood close. Her feet touched the tablecloth. Blood seeped into her shoes.

Busboys talked pidgin. *Four Families attack Dudster. Blue kerchief boy. Very small. Bandanna on face. Run through office. Escape out alley.*

Nort swabbed Dudley's arms. Lin Chung rolled Dudley on his

back and swabbed posterior wounds. Nort said, "The neck cut's superficial." Chung said, "Back cuts, too."

Ruthie hung a plasma bag. Nort counted wounds. Ace ran up with a bottle of vodka. Ruthie wiped Dudley's back with high-test Smirnoff. Nort said, "We're good so far. He missed the arteries."

The tourniquets stanched blood. Ruthie dug in a doctor's bag. She pulled out stitches and bandage clamps. Breuning yelled. Carlisle yelled. It was all *no hospital/no cops*.

Ruthie threaded stitch needles. Chung held up Dudley's arms. Nort pumped his veins and passed out fluid bags. Busboys stood on their tiptoes and hooked them to ceiling beams.

The vodka went around. Nort and Ruthie chugged. Dudley stirred and coughed. He raised his hands and made fists.

The whole room cheered. Ruthie winked at Claire. It was a great faux-Dudley wink.

Ashida walked back to the alley. His legs gave out. He sat on a stack of bald tires and sobbed.

They cheered inside the restaurant. Nort warbled that Irish song "Kilgary Mountain." Ace announced free pupu platters and drinks.

Ashida wiped his face and kicked rocks across the alley. His lab smock was tear-drenched.

"Were you really Kay's lover?"

Ashida looked over. Claire sat on her own stack of tires. Her dress was soaked red. Her cheeks were bloody. She'd knelt to kiss him.

"No. I wasn't."

"I found her miraculous and disturbing. She taught me things."

Ashida nodded. Claire dabbed her cheeks.

"It's very powerful to love someone that you shouldn't."

Ashida said, "Yes. I know what you mean."

118

KAY LAKE'S DIARY

LOS ANGELES | SUNDAY, DECEMBER 28, 1941

1:28 p.m.

I burned the evidence in my backyard incinerator. The bloody clothing, the blue kerchief, the mask. I wadded up newspaper and covered all of it. A single match made it all flame.

I intended to kill him, and may or may not have succeeded. Radio bulletins will confirm the murder. No news will ascribe a clandestine convalescence and prepare me for a fateful knock on the door. In either case, I'll be ready.

I might waltz altogether. I might be sent to the green room at San Quentin Prison. I'll walk that last mile with Bette Davis defiance or in the spirit of Claire De Haven as Joan of Arc. I will exhibit stunning artistry in any and all cases. Character and conviction? Maybe, maybe not. I'm only twenty-one, and this war is but three weeks old. These past days affirm my appetite for heedless adventure. Opportunity may or may not find me. In the meantime, I will sit perfectly still.

Approaching footsteps forced me to flee. Busboys saw me escape down the alley, disguised as a small Chinese man. I removed my male clothing in a gas station men's room and walked out as a woman in blouse and slacks. I was not seen entering or leaving the men's room and had stashed a handbag under some rocks near the corner of Temple and Main. The bloody clothes and mask went in them; the bloody knife went down a sewer grate. I blended into a passing parade and chanted "*Lest we forget!*"

The clothes and mask burned. I watched the smoke rise over Wetherly Drive and drift down to the Strip. I sat at the backyard table and wrote Scotty a letter.

Dear boy, I will wear my Saint Christopher medal until you safely return. What are you thinking now? Will full-scale war seem prosaic after what you saw here? I wish I could run off to Scotland with you. We would make love in a cottage on the moors and frolic with a rambunctious dog I just met. We had only a few weeks together, and I never saw you in kilts.

I left the letter outside for the postman and went in to the piano. I was badly out of practice, but gained momentum as I played. Lee failed to appear. The phone failed to ring. No one knocked on the door. The Chopin was for Claire, the Grieg was for Scotty, the dank Rachmaninoff étude was for Hideo. I sent magisterial Beethoven out for the only one who had earned it.

I learned to play in the dark. I seemed to acquire the skill instantaneously. I strung together variations on already-learned harmonies and phrased them as one long sonata *reminiscenza.* I stayed up all night and all through the following day; I improvised contrasting themes and built them from the raw stuff of fresh war and raw men and women. I banged low chords to announce the conflicts of the man I had come to love dearly.

War. Blood libel. Twenty-three days, this storm, *reminiscenza.* It was for all of them and him most of all. It was a transcendental *mémoire.* Here we were in Los Angeles. We were at odds with one another and afire with crazed duty. We were as one and bound by a terrible allegiance in the time of Pearl Harbor.

December 29, 1941

119

LOS ANGELES | MONDAY, DECEMBER 29, 1941

6:17 p.m.

Dudley swore allegiance.

It was a bedside ceremony. An Army major read the oath. Joe Kennedy and Hideo Ashida stood witness. Uncle Ace supplied a room above the Pagoda. He made love to Bette Davis on this self-same bed.

He repeated the major's words. His voice fluttered and held. Claire pinned captain's bars to his smock. Ace wheeled in egg rolls and mai tais.

Captain D. L. Smith, United States Army. *Dudley Liam Smith—a ghost attacked you.*

He survived. Ruth Mildred credited Big "O." It prevented shock and provided baseline anesthesia. It stalled the rush of spilled blood.

The lads proposed a tong sweep. Find the boy and skin his hide. He nixed it.

"The creature wasn't human, and I summoned him myself. I've been rowdy of late, and brought on retribution. The best of us err and sin, and I'm only grateful that my Creator chose to spare me."

They thought he was nuts. They were empiricist hardheads. He was a mystic. Wolves spoke to him.

Claire stayed by his side. She'd knelt in his blood. *Steadfast girl, who are you? Did I conjure you or did you conjure me?*

Ace dished out snacks and drinks. The gang dished out toasts.

The major said, "Congratulations, Captain."

Joe said, "You're one lucky mick."

Hideo said, "I'm honored to be here."

Ace said, "Which makes you honorary Chinese."

Claire laughed and plumped his pillow. Dudley kissed her hand and winked.

120

LOS ANGELES | MONDAY, DECEMBER 29, 1941

6:29 p.m.

Mob scene. Hollywood Boulevard at Las Palmas Avenue.

The crowd ran two thousand. The cop crew ran two hundred. Note the double barricades and loudspeakers on streetlamps.

Movie spotlights swooping. A twenty-foot-high bandstand with curb-to-curb span. Geek citizens stretched out a half mile.

Cross streets blocked off. Cars diverted and rerouted. Bottlenecks south to Melrose and north to the Hollywood Bowl.

The rally started at 7:00. Ann Sheridan and Ellen Drew. Ronald Reagan and Joan Crawford. Two half-gassed Ritz Brothers.

L.A. was a cluster fuck. Miss Sheridan was a Narco snitch. Elmer Jackson was screwing Miss Drew.

Parker paced a stretch of sidewalk. Crowd noise slammed him. Ditto a hot rumor. A tong punk sliced the Dudster at Kwan's yesterday.

Dudley survived. He was now Army-commissioned and Mexico-bound.

The celebs were ensconced at Musso & Frank's. A "U.S.A. Buffet" was set up. The Ritz Brothers were grab-assing Miss Sheridan and Miss Drew.

His nerves were shot to shit. He was thirteen days sober. This was all shit that he didn't need.

He ducked into Musso's. The crowd noise abated. The bartender saw him and held up a telephone.

He walked over. The celebs had lacquered photos pinned to their coats. The pix honored Our Boys in Service. Cluster fuck. Miss Crawford's pic noted Scotty Bennett, USMC.

The bartender passed the phone. Parker cupped his free ear.

"Yes?"

"It's Preston Exley, Bill. I'm calling to tell you that we're folding our tent. That means on all of it. You convinced us that it's not worth the trouble. For what it's worth, you won."

Parker said, "Thank you."

Exley said something else. The restaurant started broiling. Parker hung up and walked outside.

He stood on the sidewalk. He felt shot-to-shit numb. That big noise washed over him.

He smoked and watched the crowd. The spotlights swept low. They illuminated odd people.

He stared at the crowd. That big noise escalated. The celebs climbed the bandstand. The spotlights lit up geeks standing close in.

He caught half a glimpse. The light swerved away. He'd caught her tall sway and red hair. The light swerved back. He caught her face. He saw the gold braid on her uniform.

He ran toward her. He jumped off the curb and made the street at a sprint. People saw *Cop* and stepped back. People caught a blur and stood still. He saw her, he lost her, he saw her. He thought he saw her blow smoke.

He hit the crowd. He lost her. He elbowed through the crowd. People moved away and tripped away from him. He stumbled and lost his hat. He saw her, he lost her.

He elbowed people. He pushed people back. He saw her, he lost her. He shoved people. They shoved him back. He staggered and stayed upright. He saw her close, he lost her, he saw her farther back.

He tried to turn toward her. People blocked his path. He shoved them. They shoved him. He shoved harder. They shoved harder. He saw her gold uniform braid.

He caught an elbow. He caught rabbit punches. Someone coffee-doused him. Someone stuck a foot out and tripped him. He hit the pavement and heard people laugh.

He stumbled up and tried to run. He got tripped again. He got up, he fell down, he got up. He thought he saw her. He tripped and lost her. People laughed at him and kicked him. He crouched low and ran. He knocked down a fat man and made the south curb.

His trousers were ripped. His hat was gone. He stumbled to a streetlamp and pulled himself up on a ledge. He looked above the crowd and down at the crowd and tried to catch her red hair.

He lost his grip. He slid off the pole and hit the curb. People laughed at him. Patriotic music blasted. Two thousand fools screeched.

He steadied himself and walked off the boulevard. He saw a COCKTAILS sign down Las Palmas.

He beelined. The door was propped open. The bottle row above the bar was backlit.

The barman saw him and quick-read him. He laid down a napkin. Parker pointed to the Old Crow and held two fingers up.

The barman poured him a double. He downed it. The barman refilled him. He downed it. The barman refilled him. He downed it and dropped a twenty on the bartop.

The booze quick-scorched him. He walked outside with the flush. Stray spotlights hit him. He saw a cab.

He got in the back. The cabbie went *Where to?* He went *It's off the Strip.*

The cabbie U-turned. Parker steered him around the bottlenecks and got him away from the shit. They caught a lull. They made all greens to the Strip. He pointed him up the hill.

The porch light was on. Blanchard's car was gone. Her car was there.

He paid the cabbie and walked up. The living room was dark. The door was halfway cracked. There was just fireplace glow.

She was there. She was tucked asleep on the couch.

He stepped inside. He grabbed a stray chair and carried it over. He sat facing her. One arm was draped toward him. He saw the fresh knife nicks. Dear lord, she did it.

He pulled his chair closer. His legs bumped the couch. Her eyes fluttered. She said, "William," and went back to sleep.

A breeze stirred the fire and lit her hair red. He smelled the prairie. He touched her face and said, "Katherine, love."

DRAMATIS PERSONAE

Perfidia is the first volume of the Second L.A. Quartet. The L.A. Quartet—*The Black Dahlia, The Big Nowhere, L.A. Confidential* and *White Jazz*—covers the years 1946 to 1958 in Los Angeles. The Underworld U.S.A. Trilogy—*American Tabloid, The Cold Six Thousand* and *Blood's A Rover*—covers 1958 to 1972, on a national scale.

The Second L.A. Quartet places real-life and fictional characters from the first two bodies of work in Los Angeles during World War II, as significantly younger people. These three series span thirty-one years and will stand as one novelistic history. The following list notes the previous appearances of characters in *Perfidia.*

BRENDA ALLEN. The real-life Allen appears in *The Big Nowhere.*

AKIRA ASHIDA. The brother of police chemist Hideo Ashida.

HIDEO ASHIDA. This character is referenced in *The Black Dahlia.*

MARIKO ASHIDA. The mother of Hideo and Akira Ashida.

OFFICER SCOTTY BENNETT, Los Angeles Police Department. Bennett appears in *Blood's A Rover.*

LEONARD BERNSTEIN. The real-life pianist, conductor and composer.

EUGENE BISCAILUZ. The real-life sheriff of Los Angeles County.

OFFICER LEE BLANCHARD, Los Angeles Police Department. Blanchard appears in *The Black Dahlia.*

BUCKY BLEICHERT. This character appears in *The Black Dahlia.*

FLETCHER BOWRON. The real-life mayor of Los Angeles.

SERGEANT MIKE BREUNING, Los Angeles Police Department.

Breuning appears in *The Big Nowhere, L.A. Confidential* and *White Jazz.*

LIEUTENANT THAD BROWN, Los Angeles Police Department. A noted real-life policeman.

ARCHBISHOP J. J. CANTWELL. The real-life head of the L.A. Archdiocese.

SERGEANT DICK CARLISLE, Los Angeles Police Department. Carlisle appears in *The Big Nowhere, L.A. Confidential* and *White Jazz.*

"TOJO TOM" CHASCO. A Japanese-Mexican criminal and Fifth Columnist.

DR. LIN CHUNG. A plastic surgeon and proponent of eugenics.

MICKEY COHEN. The real-life Cohen appears in *The Big Nowhere, L.A. Confidential* and *White Jazz.*

HARRY COHN. The real-life boss of Columbia Pictures.

LIEUTENANT JOAN CONVILLE, USNR. A Navy nurse adrift in Los Angeles.

JOAN CRAWFORD. The real-life film actress.

HUEY CRESSMEYER. This character appears in *American Tabloid.*

DR. RUTH MILDRED CRESSMEYER. Dr. Cressmeyer appears in *American Tabloid.*

BETTE DAVIS. The real-life film actress.

JAMES EDGAR "TWO-GUN" DAVIS. The real-life former chief of the Los Angeles Police Department.

CLAIRE DE HAVEN. Miss De Haven appears in *The Big Nowhere.*

ELLEN DREW. A real-life "B" movie actress.

PRESTON EXLEY. This character appears in *L.A. Confidential.*

ARTHUR FARNSWORTH. The real-life second husband of Bette Davis.

TOMMY GILFOYLE. This character appears in *The Black Dahlia.*

MRS. NAO HAMANO. A real-life Japanese housewife.

MONSIGNOR JOE HAYES. A Catholic priest and the confessor of Captain William H. Parker.

THE HEARST RIFLE TEAM. Real-life sharpshooters employed by tycoon William Randolph Hearst.

DR. FRED HILTZ. This character appears in *Blood's A Rover.*

WALLACE HODAKA. A suspected Japanese Fifth Columnist.

RICHARD HOOD, FBI. The real-life head man at the FBI's Los Angeles Office.

J. EDGAR HOOVER, FBI. The real-life Hoover appears in *American Tabloid, The Cold Six Thousand* and *Blood's A Rover.*

BOB HOPE. The real-life film and radio comedian.

CLEMENCE B. "CALL-ME-JACK" HORRALL. The real-life chief of the Los Angeles Police Department.

SID HUDGENS. This character appears in *L.A. Confidential.*

LAURA HUGHES. The illegitimate daughter of Joseph P. Kennedy, Sr., and Gloria Swanson.

LIEUTENANT CARL HULL, Los Angeles Police Department. Friend and ideological consort of Captain William H. Parker.

SERGEANT ELMER JACKSON, Los Angeles Police Department. A notorious real-life policeman.

ENSIGN JACK KENNEDY. The real-life Kennedy appears in *American Tabloid.*

JOSEPH P. KENNEDY. The real-life Kennedy *père* appears in *American Tabloid.*

SERGEANT BILL KOENIG, Los Angeles Police Department. Koenig appears in *The Black Dahlia.*

ROSE EILEEN KWAN. The niece of Uncle Ace Kwan.

UNCLE ACE KWAN. This character appears in *L.A. Confidential.*

FIORELLO LA GUARDIA. The real-life mayor of New York City and director of the U.S. Office of War Preparedness.

KAY LAKE. Miss Lake appears in *The Black Dahlia.*

JIM LARKIN. A real-life British spy, retired in Los Angeles.

DR. NORT LAYMAN. Dr. Layman appears in *The Big Nowhere* and *L.A. Confidential.*

ANDREA LESNICK. Miss Lesnick appears in *The Big Nowhere.*

DR. SAUL LESNICK. Dr. Lesnick appears in *The Big Nowhere.*

WARD LITTELL, FBI. Littell appears in *American Tabloid* and *The Cold Six Thousand.*

ELLIS LOEW. This character appears in *The Black Dahlia*, *The Big Nowhere* and *L.A. Confidential.*

REYNOLDS LOFTIS. This character appears in *The Big Nowhere.*

DR. TERRY LUX. Dr. Lux appears in *The Big Nowhere.*

CAPTAIN CARLOS MADRANO, Mexican State Police. A Nazi sympathizer and alleged Fifth Columnist.

DISTRICT ATTORNEY BILL McPHERSON. This character appears in *L.A. Confidential.*

SERGEANT TURNER "BUZZ" MEEKS, Los Angeles Police Department. Meeks appears in *The Big Nowhere* and *L.A. Confidential.*

CHAZ MINEAR. This character appears in *The Big Nowhere.*

"JIMMY THE JAP" NAMURA. A Japanese Fifth Columnist.

ROBERT NOBLE. A real-life Nazi sympathizer.

CAPTAIN WILLIAM H. PARKER, Los Angeles Police Department. The real-life Parker appears in *L.A. Confidential* and *White Jazz.*

PIERCE PATCHETT. This character appears in *L.A. Confidential.*

JEROME JOSEPH PAVLIK. A rapist at large in Los Angeles.

RAY PINKER, Los Angeles Police Department. The real-life Pinker appears in *L.A. Confidential* and *White Jazz.*

SERGEI RACHMANINOFF. The real-life pianist and composer.

PAUL ROBESON. The real-life actor, singer and political lightning rod.

ELEANOR ROOSEVELT. The real-life First Lady.

HOOKY ROTHMAN. A real-life minor hoodlum.

DOT ROTHSTEIN. Miss Rothstein appears in *L.A. Confidential.*

SAM RUMMEL. A real-life criminal lawyer.

ED SATTERLEE, FBI. Satterlee appears in *The Big Nowhere.*

GORO SHIGETA. A Japanese businessman and murder victim.

ELIZABETH SHORT. Miss Short appears in *The Black Dahlia.*

FUJIO "BAMBOO" SHUDO. A Japanese psychopath.

BENJAMIN "BUGSY" SIEGEL. The real-life Siegel appears in *The Big Nowhere* and *L.A. Confidential.*

SERGEANT DUDLEY SMITH, Los Angeles Police Department. Smith appears in *The Big Nowhere, L.A. Confidential* and *White Jazz.*

GERALD L. K. SMITH. The real-life native fascist.

GLORIA SWANSON. The real-life film actress.

SERGEANT FRITZ VOGEL, Los Angeles Police Department. Vogel appears in *The Black Dahlia.*

DEPUTY DOUGLAS WALDNER, Los Angeles County Sheriff's Office. A Klanned-up local cop.

AYA WATANABE. The matriarch of a traitorous Japanese family.

JOHNNY WATANABE. The son of Aya and Ryoshi Watanabe.

NANCY WATANABE. The daughter of Aya and Ryoshi Watanabe.

RYOSHI WATANABE. The patriarch of a traitorous Japanese family.

A NOTE ON THE TYPE

This book was set in Janson, a typeface long thought to have been made by the Dutchman Anton Janson, who was a practicing typefounder in Leipzig during the years 1668–1687. However, it has been conclusively demonstrated that these types are actually the work of Nicholas Kis (1650–1702), a Hungarian, who most probably learned his trade from the master Dutch typefounder Dirk Voskens. The type is an excellent example of the influential and sturdy Dutch types that prevailed in England up to the time William Caslon (1692–1766) developed his own incomparable designs from them.